FORGE OF FAITH

OTHER TITLES BY TYRANNOSAURUS PRESS

Boundary's Fall (by Bret Funk)
Book One: Path of Glory
Book Two: Sword of Honor
Book Three: Jewel of Truth
Book Four: Forge of Faith

The Heart of the Sisters (by A. Christopher Drown)
Book One: A Mage of None Magic

Anthologies of Speculative Fiction
Beacons of Tomorrow, Volume One
Beacons of Tomorrow, Volume Two

FORGE OF FAITH
BOOK FOUR OF BOUNDARY'S FALL

by BRET FUNK

TYRANNOSAURUS PRESS LLC
ZACHARY, LA
WWW.TYRANNOSAURUSPRESS.COM

Tyrannosaurus Press
Zachary, LA
www.TyrannosaurusPress.com
Info@TyrannosaurusPress.com

To my wife
For her unwavering friendship, love and support

I hope for little
And have faith in only what I can see
But I can see our future
So I know I have nothing to fear

ACKNOWLEDGEMENTS

My most sincere gratitude to the following people for their contributions to this book, and to the Boundary's Fall series:
Doug Roper, Allison Martinez, Terry Crotinger,
Roxanne Reiken, Stephanie Frederic, Jeffrey Frederic,
Maree Jeanne Funk, Jordan Black, Danielle Parker

And special thanks to everyone who participated in the pre-release error-finding contest. Without your eyes, a few rather significant mistakes would have slipped into the final product.

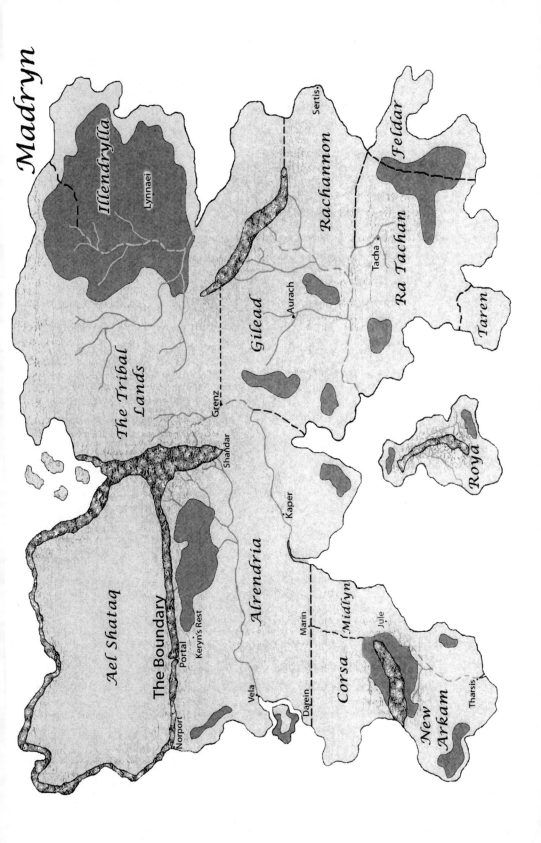

Madryn

REMEMBRANCE

"Mage Lorthas, you have the floor."

Lorthas stepped to the center of the dais. Aemon and a score of the Assembly's most renowned Magi sat behind a long table at the base of the platform. The reactions to his presence were mixed: some eyed him askance; a few acknowledged him with open smiles. Most, however, affected the clinical disinterest so common among Magi.

The remainder of the hall stood empty, the rows of seats and jutting balconies barren. Lorthas bowed, hiding his frown behind a display of deference. "I had hoped to address the full Assembly."

Treal pursed his lips, drawing ebony skin taut over already sharp features. "Your ideas have caused considerable disturbance in the past, Lorthas," he said in a gravelly voice. Aside from Aemon, Treal was the oldest Mage in the Assembly, one of only a few remaining who had fought beside the High Wizard against the Darklords. "You may share your thoughts with us. If we find merit in them, we will allow you to address the Assembly."

"I submit to the will of the Council," Lorthas said, inclining his head. He shot a glance at Aemon, who shrugged and offered a reassuring smile. *He has only to snap, and the Council jumps to do his bidding. Why does he let them dictate his actions?*

The silence stretched, earning Lorthas the disfavor of Breanne Dujon. Once heir to the throne of Alrendria, manifestation of the Gift had forced Breanne to set aside her political aims. "Do you have something to say, Lorthas? My apprentices are waiting." Her waspish tone and sense of self-importance made the average Mage seem modest in comparison.

Lorthas cleared his throat. "As you know, I've spent much of the last fourseason in Kaper, advising King Carstellian. The King is worried; he fears for the sanctity of Alrendria. There is unrest in the northern Houses, and the Arkamians test the southern border. The Gileans have withdrawn from Western Grenz, closing themselves to trade. *Ael Shende Ruhl* grows quiet; the Elves and Garun'ah have returned to their warring ways and no longer send trade caravans as once they did.

"The people look to the Magi for encouragement, but we have abandoned them. The Assembly authorized the closing of the Academy in Merriadoc, and I hear whispers among my brethren that the Academy in Vela may also be forsaken. The councilors we once sent out by the hundreds have been recalled, and now only the most influential Houses receive an advisor.

"Alrendria is dying—it has been dying since the time of Peitr Arkam!—and bold action must be taken if we are to restore this land to its former glory. We Magi have a responsibility to guide the Commons, to lead them—by the hand if necessary!—to the future they deserve."

Lorthas drew a breath to calm himself. His enthusiasm had earned him the Council's disfavor in the past, and he struggled to affect the casual indifference the

Magi prided themselves on while he gauged their reactions. Aemon wore a broad smile and nodded his approval, but the others were harder to read. Only Pholis, a distant ancestor of King Carstellian and one of Lorthas's old instructors, showed outward support. The others wore masks of perfect objectivity.

"Can we presume you already have a solution to our problems?" Breanne asked. "Or did you summon us simply to warn us of society's imminent collapse and scold us for our role in it?"

"King Carstellian has conceived of a bold plan, one that will galvanize the Houses and provide Alrendria with the momentum it needs to shrug off the shroud of decay it wears. He has ordered the Guard to Kaper and asked the Houses to raise additional troops for a grand campaign. Winters ago, the Arkamians shattered the unity of this great land, taking from us—"

"We are not impressed by grandstanding and theatrics, Lorthas." Jiulan leaned forward and drummed his fingers on the table. His hatred of Lorthas stretched back decades, but for no cause that Lorthas had ever been able to discern. "Make your case, or wake me when you're about to."

Beneath his cold smile, Lorthas seethed. "I am no apprentice, fresh to the Academy, Mage Jiulan. My life is measured in centuries, as is yours."

"Then no doubt you've learned to evaluate proposals dispassionately. Pleading to emotions is a tactic often used by Commons, especially when they know reason alone will be insufficient. As a Mage, you should be beyond using such manipulations." He fixed a disapproving gaze on Lorthas. "As a Mage, you should be immune to them."

"Your advice is—" Lorthas caught Aemon's minute head shake and sought to soften his reply. "Your advice is acknowledged, Mage Jiulan. I will not insult you again by treating you like a human… I'm sorry, like a Common."

Lorthas paced the dais. He had prepared for days; without his speech, he felt unprotected, especially from himself. His quick temper and frustration with the Assembly's complacency had led him to trouble before. He did not fear for himself, but one misstep today could cost Alrendria its future.

"Civilization is crumbling around us. Ambition and greed broke Alrendria; pride and adherence to archaic tradition threatens to shatter it." Lorthas stopped walking and turned back to the council. "*Our* pride and *our* adherence."

He opened himself to magic, savoring the feel of power rushing into him. The flows of energy emboldened him. "We vowed to guide the Commons, to lead them to the enlightenment we have achieved by virtue of our longevity. But the Assembly has turned its back on that promise, forsaking Alrendria when it needs us most. You sit idly while fear and suspicion poison our reputation. You watch unconcerned as those in power strive to make us an underclass, deny us the right to govern or even the right to fraternize with those who govern." Breanne grunted at the last, but the others remained impassive.

"The Assembly should denounce these laws and strive to prove to the Commons that we are no threat, that despite our Gift, we are no different than they. But as usual, the Assembly chooses inaction. Worse, it's chosen to withdraw from the world, to accede to the demands of a boisterous few, to lend strength to the assertions that we have something to hide, and that if given power we will certainly abuse it.

"How can a land of freedom exist when a minority of its populace is denied the rights guaranteed to all? How can we Magi uphold our promises if we isolate ourselves from the world? You can't stop fear from growing by allowing it to take root. The Imperium taught us that, if it taught us anything."

"You spout rhetoric, Lorthas," Jiulan said, impatience showing through his mask. "And though you have a poetic flair, I can't see how any of this is relevant to—"

"Of course you can't!" Lorthas whirled to face the Mage. "If any one of you could see as far as the nose on your face you wouldn't need me here today! Now is not the time to hide from our responsibilities. Now is the time to take the steps required to make Alrendria, to *really* make Alrendria, a land of freedom and equality.

"King Carstellian has conceived of a plan capable of achieving that goal. Centuries ago, Peitr Arkam carved his Imperium from the heart of this land and turned it into a mockery of Alrendrian ideals. The King wishes to right that travesty, to heal the wound caused by The Secession. Even now his forces prepare to march on the Arkam Imperium, to bring those lands back under Alrendrian control. Envoys have been sent to the Elves… the Garun'ah… even to the Orog! With the right guidance—the guidance of the Mage Assembly—this campaign can achieve our greatest goal: the unification of the Four Races and the creation of a truly egalitarian Alrendria."

An excited mumble went up among the Council. Even Aemon seemed taken by surprise, his mouth agape and his cheeks slightly flushed. When he had outlined the plan to the High Wizard, Lorthas had purposefully kept his description vague. Too often the Assembly had attributed his successes to Aemon. This time, they would have no choice but to acknowledge him.

Phyleis, newly raised to the Council and entrenched in Jiulan's outdated philosophy, spoke first. "You can't believe the Elves and Garun'ah will set aside their differences to join a Human war? And the Orog resist confrontation as if—"

"History has proven that the Four Races can work together," Lorthas interrupted. "In Aemon's Revolt and many times since, the races have worked to achieve a common goal. The Tribes need little excuse to fight, but the Arkamian practice of slavery will provide more than enough motivation if it's required. The Elves I have already approached. Emperor Alwellyn has reservations but has agreed to throw in his support if the Assembly approves. And the Orog…? Aemon has but to beckon and they will come."

"Your goals are laudable, Lorthas," Breanne said, "but do we really want to mire ourselves in another conflict? We desire peace. The Assembly should not be seen as supporting any war, let alone one that is not necessary."

"Not necessary?" White-hot anger clawed at Lorthas's innards, but he contained it. "The bonds fostered in Aemon's Revolt have fractured. Soon they'll disappear completely. If nothing is changed, Alrendria will descend into anarchy, and the fear the Commons have for us now will seem pale in comparison.

"Complacency breeds apathy. For our dream of true peace to be realized, the Commons must be reminded why Alrendria was founded, why Aemon led his revolt against the Darklords, and why setting aside personal ambitions for the greater good is necessary. The Imperium is the perfect target, as near to a Darklord in ideology and action as one can be without being a Mage. For us, they are a blight, the source of the apprehension toward magic spreading through Alrendria like a plague. By removing them, we remove our single greatest threat in this world."

"What you propose is not a matter to be taken lightly," Treal said. "I like what is happening to the Gifted no more than you, Mage Lorthas, but I wonder if this is really the method we should use to attain our goals."

"Your current methods have had such splendid success, I can see why you'd be hesitant to try a new approach," Lorthas mumbled, but not quietly enough. Most of the eyes in the room narrowed, and a few supporting smiles turned to frowns.

He sought to repair the damage his mouth had wrought. "I know that what I propose carries risks, but this is not a Mage-created war; King Carstellian requests an alliance. When I informed him that the Assembly would support his campaign—"

"You promised him the aid of the Assembly without consulting us! Once again, you show no regard for our ways!" Jiulan's chair clattered to the floor as he stood. The veins at his temple throbbed, and he opened himself to magic. Lorthas half expected the older Mage to attack him on the spot, and he readied a defense and fought the urge to strike first.

"I misspoke, Mage Jiulan," Lorthas said, offering the Mage a humble bow. "I'm well versed in our laws and would never be so bold as to guarantee aid without the firm support of the Assembly." A smug smile crept across Lorthas's face. "But I also know the prevailing attitude among the Magi. I know how they will vote on my proposal."

"Thank you, Lorthas," Aemon said, standing. He gestured toward the door, and it swung open of its own accord. "The Council will discuss this matter, and I will inform you of the decision. You may go."

It was an abrupt dismissal, and an unexpected one, but the outwardly cold demeanor did not faze Lorthas; Aemon often showed reserve in the presence of other Magi. He kowtowed too often to their foolish love of propriety. Lorthas bowed again and strode from the Hall, his head held high.

He walked the corridors of the Academy, ignoring the eyes that followed him. A few younger Magi cheered as he passed, held out a hand, or in some other way showed their support. Apprentices by the score gaped at him, and one young boy shouted, "Hooray for Lorthas, the next High Wizard of the Assembly!" Two stoop-shouldered Magi inclined their heads, and their simple display of support moved Lorthas more than the cheering of a thousand apprentices.

Lorthas made no comment. Most of the Assembly knew the basics of his proposal—he had made sure that word of his work in Kaper had leaked to the right people—but he would do nothing to jeopardize his standing with the Council. Their adherence to canon was absolute, and if he were to formally announce his plan without their consent, they would never support it.

The Assembly is ready for a change; it needs a change. Lorthas felt the hum of dissatisfaction building. The younger Magi in particular, those raised to Mage within the last two centuries, did not agree with the Assembly's hands-off approach to guiding Alrendria. They, like Lorthas, felt the time had come to take a more active role.

He pushed open the door to a small library and slipped inside. Cherub-faced Yassik hunched over a tome, scribbling notes with fervor. He looked up and dipped his head in acknowledgement before his eyes sank back to the page. His free hand absently tapped a narrow, leather-bound volume.

Kalsbad leapt from his seat at Lorthas's entry. "You were magnificent, Sir! I didn't think anyone had the guts to talk to the Council like that."

Lorthas chuckled. His apprentice would have praised him had he jumped on the table and tickled Breanne. "Like as not, all I did today was goad them. I should have kept a better rein on my temper. *They* should have let me recite my speech."

"My speech, you mean," Yassik grunted, his eyes never rising.

"The ideas were mine, Yassik. You merely adjusted the wording to better suit the climate."

This time, Yassik set his pen down and met Lorthas's burning gaze. "Ideas mean nothing if you don't have the ability to express them well. Propose your plan to the Assembly the way you proposed it to me, and they'll think you mad."

Lorthas strove to control his anger, but his face remained a mask of composure. "Mad? Is it mad to want to take the steps necessary to ensure our right to exist? Is it mad to guide the Commons to see that we are one people, and that together we can accomplish much more than we can apart? The Assembly has counseled patience, yet in a thousand winters things have only gotten worse. I—"

"You don't have to lecture me, Lorthas," Yassik yelled. "I agreed with you, remember? Stop treating me like a fool just because I don't moon over you like an apprentice—"

Resentment poured from Kalsbad's face like water from a well, and he rounded on Yassik, but Lorthas waved him back. "There's no need to insult my students. If you have an issue with me, have the courage to direct your affronts at me."

"Fine!" Yassik pushed back from the table and stood. His ruddy cheeks flared an even brighter shade as he clamped his hands down on the table edge. "You strut around as if you devised this scheme alone, but there are others—myself, Alwen, Virgyl, even Kalsbad there—who have worked just as hard."

"Is that what this is about, Yassik? Is having your name plastered across every library and Academy in Madryn not enough? Do you want to make sure you get proper acknowledgment for your role here too?"

"It's not about recognition; it's about respect. From you!" Yassik slammed his hand down on the table, spilling ink across the exposed page. "To the Nothing with the Assembly! I don't care if they know the names of everyone we've worked with or if they think Balan approached you in a dream and told you what to do over tea. But I'll tell you this; if this grand design of yours *was* divinely inspired, the Gods did a *da'frakt* job of explaining the details."

"No doubt you'll next claim that you're the architect of our entire enterprise. I did conceive of the idea when reading your essay, *On The Unification Of The Four Races In Response To the Threat Posed By The Darklords.*"

"You're not paying attention to what I'm saying. I—"

"Want to be remembered as the most brilliant Mage of all time," Lorthas finished for him. "I know, Yassik. Rest assured, I have no such ambition, and I'll give you credit for—"

"Enough of this nonsense!" Alwen stormed through the door, her golden blonde hair falling in waves to her waist. Her lips were pursed, her expression determined, and she interposed herself between the two combatants. "Yassik, Lorthas hasn't forgotten about all the work you've done. Lorthas, stop goading the few people willing to consider your idea as anything other than radical nonsense. If we can't present a unified front to the Assembly, they'll never accept our proposal."

A broad smile split Yassik's face, and his deportment underwent a dramatic shift. "As usual, Alwen, you're the voice of reason." He grabbed a rag and daubed at the ink blotch on his ruined page. "I lost my temper, that's all."

Alwen sniffed, and she wrapped her arms around Lorthas. He planted a light kiss on her forehead but kept one eye on Yassik and the besotted way he studied Alwen's back. Lips pressed together so tightly they hurt, Lorthas fought the urge to seize magic. *She's mine, Yassik. Forever.*

"Did you listen in?" Lorthas asked, breaking the embrace.

"Did you have to provoke Jiulan? Convince him, and you'll have the Council wrapped around your finger. But instead of exercising some discretion, you insult him. What good will that accomplish? For 'the next High Wizard' or whatever other nonsense they're calling you in the halls, you're exceptionally obtuse. I've—"

Lorthas put a finger to Alwen's lips. "I'll take that as a yes. Forgiving me my lack of decorum, what else—?"

The door to the library opened again, and Aemon entered. He walked as if pulling a heavy weight, his eyes roving the room with the weariness of ages. "I hate to intrude, but I must speak to Lorthas."

"H... Hi... High Wizard Aemon," Kalsbad stammered, bowing low, as one would bow to a king. He was still not accustomed to seeing Aemon face to face and refused to believe the man did not appreciate formality.

The others held no such illusions. "It's never an intrusion, Aemon," Alwen said with a smile. "You know you're always welcome here."

"It's good to see you, Alwen," Aemon replied. "Yassik, I read your treatise on relations between Elves and Garun'ah when I was in Lynnaei. The book is causing quite a stir."

"Yes, well, anything that implies the Tribesmen aren't simply savages in need of a leash causes a stir among Elves," Yassik laughed. "Especially when it's written by a Human. According to the Elves, we generally need help telling one season from the next."

Aemon smiled, but it did not reach his eyes, and an uncomfortable silence fell on the room. "I must speak with Lorthas," he repeated. With a shuffling of chairs, the others started for the door.

"They are as much a part of this as I," Lorthas said, fixing Yassik with a mocking gaze. "I will keep no secrets from them."

"Then tell them after I've gone," Aemon replied, "but I'd like to speak to you alone."

After a moment, Lorthas nodded, and the others went for the door. Yassik handed him the narrow leather-bound volume as he passed. "Read this. There are some ideas in there I think you'll appreciate." Lorthas accepted the book with a nod and Yassik followed Alwen and Kalsbad from the room.

Lorthas turned to face Aemon. "The Council has decided? When do I address the Assembly?"

Aemon turned away and leaned against a bookshelf. "You don't."

"They ruled against me!" Anger resurfaced, and Lorthas barely had the strength to control it. The Council rarely denied a Mage the right to speak; they prided themselves on their willingness to listen to all opinions before acceding to the wishes of the majority. Of those they did refuse, most were rogue Magi captured and condemned to death. To be rebuked in such a way meant they feared his ideas more than he had imagined. "What was the vote?"

Aemon drew a slow breath. He refused to meet Lorthas's eyes. "The Council was split."

"But if the Council was split, then..." Disbelief fueled Lorthas's confusion, and cold indignation gave way to white-hot fury. "*You* voted against me?"

It took a supreme effort of will, but Aemon turned to face Lorthas. "I had no choice. What you're proposing is too radical a shift for the Assembly, and a dangerous path to tread. One wrong step and we could slip back into the role of Darklords, ruling Madryn with an iron fist, using our magic to maintain dominance, slowly turning against each other until—"

"We are not Darklords! And I'm not recommending that we supplant the leaders of the Human nations. My deal with Carstellian is a simple one: We declare war on the Imperium and aid him in returning those lands to Alrendrian control, and he will abolish the laws prohibiting Magi from governing. There are no pitfalls, here. We remove an old enemy and set ourselves back on equal footing with the ungifted."

"You want to involve the Magi in a war!" Aemon raged like an exasperated father dealing with a willful child. "Worse, you want it to be known that you instigated this war. That's a precipice with a crumbling edge, Lorthas! If the Commons think for even a moment that we Magi will take matters into our own hands without waiting for an expressed request for help, their fear will only worsen. It's our reluctance to enter into conflicts that's kept them from hating us."

"It's our refusal to deal with the crises of the day that makes them think we want no part of the world!"

"Listen to reason, Lorthas. Let Carstellian start his war. Once entrenched, he can request our aid, and we will help him. You have my word."

"If we aren't seen as equal partners in this attempt to reunite Alrendria, then we'll never convince the Commons that we deserve a place in their society."

"I will not allow the Assembly to become a band of mercenaries available to whoever offers the sweetest deal. Equality and tolerance cannot be bought; they must be given."

"I'm not suggesting that this will solve our problems overnight. I—"

"I have never before instigated a war. I will not start—"

"Never instigated a war? You have one named after you!" Lorthas gripped the thin volume so hard his knuckles turned white. "And I've watched you manipulate people for centuries, starting and stopping wars at a whim. The only difference now is that instead of skulking in the shadows, I want to proclaim to all of Madryn where our allegiance lies."

Aemon puffed out his chest and fixed Lorthas with a gaze that had brought kings to their knees. "I have guided people in the past, and I have tweaked and prodded events when necessary, but I have never embarked upon such a reckless course as you have proposed. I had hoped that, by now, you—"

"Do you really think us that simple-minded?" Lorthas moved so he stood only a hand away from Aemon. He felt magic pulsing around him, knew that his eyes beat in time with the energy. "We've seen your hand in this from the beginning. *You* asked me to go to Kaper to advise King Carstellian. *You* advised Yassik to write his essay on the Darklords and made sure I was one of the five Magi who reviewed it. *You* all but begged me to take Kalsbad as an apprentice. And I doubt Emperor Alwellyn would have let me finish my *brandei* if you hadn't asked him to do what he could to help me. You're subtle, old man, but this entire affair reeks of your manipulation."

They faced each other for a long time, ice blue eyes and fire red. Lorthas had known Aemon almost all his life. He knew the man as well as he knew himself. Aemon never made a move without a reason, but he never turned away from a course once he had committed himself. "What's changed? Why set this up only to let it fail? What are you hiding?"

Aemon said nothing. "Is it another Divining?" Lorthas asked. Exasperation heated his voice. "Have you had another ominous prediction?"

"Yes," Aemon whispered. "It was a Divining."

Lorthas heaved a heavy sigh. "I swear, old man, that talent of yours is nothing but trouble. Every vision is direr than the last. It's enough to make me wonder what would happen if you ignored the 'warnings'. Did you ever try?"

"Once." This whisper was quiet, barely audible.

Lorthas had heard the tone before, though not often. Getting Aemon to speak more about the matter would be impossible. "Just explain why. Tell me what you saw. Tell me why I wasted the last four seasons and why I now have to explain to Carstellian that the aid I promised will never appear. Explain to me why the Assembly will be forced to follow the narrow-minded doctrine of the Council, when you agree that a time of change is upon us. Make me understand, Aemon, and I will let the matter drop."

Aemon ran a trembling hand through his beard. "I don't need to explain myself to you. It should be enough that the Council has ruled against you. It should be enough that I am High Wizard and have told you it is not to be. I don't care whether you play the humbled servant or the castigated martyr when you walk out that door. Choose whichever suits your temperament better. Nor do I care what you tell Carstellian, except that I expect you to tell him the Assembly will not declare war on the Imperium."

Never before in their time together had Aemon spoken so harshly, nor used his position in the Assembly to command obedience. Lorthas did not know how to respond; he drew the leather-bound volume to his chest and stared at his one-time teacher with undisguised disappointment. And fury.

"You can prevent me from addressing the Assembly," Lorthas said, "but you can't deny my right to speak. The ways of the Assembly are obsolete. Change is required if the Magi are to survive. The others know this even if they won't admit it. Once my intentions are known, they'll join me."

"Everything I've done my entire life has been for the good of Madryn," Aemon said, his voice strained. "I will do everything in my power to make sure my vision—the vision we shared—comes to be."

"So will I, Aemon. So will I." His jaw aching from the effort of not screaming, Lorthas stormed toward the door, slamming it open with enough force to knock books from the shelves. "If either of us has lost sight of our goal, it's you."

Even numbed with rage, Lorthas did not fail to notice the tear tracing a path down Aemon's cheek, nor the stubborn set of his jaw that spoke of a decision made, a course determined.

CHAPTER 1

The wind howled over the Boundary, whipping through the mountains, blowing snow in blinding sheets that could bury a man in an instant. The sun made a feeble effort, teasing the land with a hint of warmth before retreating behind slate grey clouds and allowing winter to unleash its full fury on Dranakohr, blasting the castle, sending rock and ice skittering down the sides of the mountain. A moment later, the sun reappeared, only to be swallowed again.

Jeran sat at his desk, reviewing reports and rifling through a box recovered from one of Tylor's many storerooms. Trinkets, mostly, odds and ends the Bull had chosen not to display in his Trophy Room. A dozen similar crates lined the walls waiting for his inspection.

Katya stood at the balcony, cold and impassive. Her coppery curls danced in the gusts, whipping and slapping at her face, but she paid them little mind. Since the Battle of Dranakohr she had never been far from Jeran's side, but whether it was for his protection or hers, Jeran had never been able to decide. Those who remained had little love for Salos's daughter, and more than a few would have killed her if not for Jeran's order preventing it. Even with it he had been forced to stop several attempts on her life.

He removed a dagger from a box and gave it a cursory examination before dropping it into a crate beside his chair. He thumbed through a report on weapon stocks from Dralin, then studied the latest maps of the tunnel system beneath the Boundary, where dozens of teams worked to map chambers and find additional passages to *Ael Shataq*. Jeran worried about them—several had died in cave-ins or by losing their way in the dark caverns—but it was necessary work. All passages to Lorthas's realm had to be sealed. *And if one can be discovered that he doesn't know about...*

A small painting, a jewelry box, and a glove followed the dagger into the crate, but a crystal globe with a rose blossom preserved in its center went to a smaller pile on Jeran's desk. His hand glided over the surface of the globe, and he opened himself to it briefly, basking in its history.

"What are you doing?" Katya asked, turning away from the balcony long enough to cast a confused look at Jeran.

"Learning what I can." Jeran released the globe and pushed back from his desk, crossing the distance to the balcony in several slow steps. He looked at the lush grass and ordered squares of farmland filling the valley below and watched as the falling snow melted into rain and then rose again as wisps of steam.

"That's no answer." Katya's eyes fastened on the squads practicing in the shadow of the wall. On one side of the battlement, trainees sparred shirtless and sweat-soaked; on the other, men bound in thick white cloaks learned how to survive in the harsh environment of the Boundary. "I still can't believe it."

Jeran did not have to ask what she was talking about. "Tylor's use of magic was short-sighted; it can be more than just a weapon. We don't have a steady stream of supplies from *Ael Shataq* to sustain us through the winter, and the grain we received from Alrendria will not last long. I am forced to develop alternatives."

Indistinct figures worked the fields, some former slaves who had agreed to stay in Dranakohr, but most were ShadowMagi, bound and controlled by the collars they once forced on their prisoners. Now they labored for Jeran, though more than a few, deprived of magic and fearing they would never feel its power again, had tossed themselves from cliffs or made foolish attempts to flee into the mountains. Jeran regretted the losses to his work force, but he thanked those ShadowMagi for helping him solve one of his greatest dilemmas. Killing men in cold blood did not sit well with him, but few of the Gifted trained by Salos the Scorpion could be redeemed.

Apprentices wandered the valley, using the Gift to hold winter at bay. A great undertaking that had been, to melt the snows and thaw the fields around Dranakohr, but far easier to maintain than to produce. What had initially taken the combined effort of all his Gifted—and Yassik, Oto, and himself besides—could be sustained by a handful of bright-eyed youths. As a result, fresh produce grew in the fields and small pastures of livestock grazed on sweet summer grass. *Food might be scarce now, but by next winter Dranakohr will feed itself.*

A handful of guards patrolled the top of the wall, though Jeran had told them it was no longer necessary. Until the spring thaw, the only way in to and out of Dranakohr was by Gate. No one inside the wall was foolish enough to risk the wrath of winter, and no one outside could survive it. By spring he hoped to have enough trained apprentices to keep the road to Alrendria clear, though hope alone would be no match for Alwen.

Most of the Assembly's apprentices and dozens of young Magi eager to help but untrained in the use of magic had defied the Assembly and flocked to Jeran's call. He had ordered Oto, Alwen, and Yassik to share in the task of creating an Academy and supervising the training, but Alwen had placed herself in a position of authority, doling out tasks to the other Magi as readily as to the apprentices. Jeran she all but ignored, seeking him out only when he demanded it. Though he stressed the need for haste, Alwen refused to press the students, insisting that the risks of an apprentice losing control of magic outweighed the handful of days they stood to save by overexertion.

I need trained Magi now, and she promises me some in a decade! Without Gifted ready to fight beside him he stood no chance against Salos's ShadowMagi, let alone what would happen if the Boundary collapsed and Lorthas was free to unleash the full might of *Ael Shataq* against Madryn, or if the Mage Assembly named him a criminal and ordered his capture.

A solution to the problem existed, or soon would, but implementing it would mean another argument with Alwen. And probably one with Yassik as well. In the end, it did not matter; Jeran would endure a thousand of Alwen's tirades if it gave him just a dozen trained Magi.

"No one understands why I let you live." Jeran let his gaze wander up into the mountains. Come spring, men and Orog would explore the crags and valleys of the Boundary, mapping the terrain and seeking passes into the Darklord's domain. They worked well together, Human and Orog, and Jeran wondered if the unity fostered in Dranakohr would prove universal, or if it were merely a result of their shared enslavement.

"I don't understand either," Katya replied. "It would have been easier for everyone if you had let Dahr kill me."

"He wouldn't have killed you. He wanted to, but he couldn't."

"With the Blood Rage on him, do you think he'd remember his promise to you? Or care about it?"

"No, but that only proves my promise wasn't what held his sword." Jeran drew a deep breath. He wondered how Dahr was, and if his friend would answer the summons he had sent. Dahr walked a dangerous precipice, and if he fell, there might be no redemption for him, but that did not mean Jeran could give him the solitude he desired.

Jeran felt a twinge in the back of his mind, a spike of distant fear. He tried to ignore it. "They think we're lovers, you know."

Rich laughter echoed through the chamber. "Such a rumor will have my uncle turning in his grave." Katya looked at Jeran, allowed her eyes to move up and down his body, a body hardened by seasons of labor in the mines below. "I could do worse."

A smile touched Jeran's lips. "You just want Dahr to kill us both." Images of rock and darkness and pain flashed through his head, and the sense of fear intensified until Jeran could not ignore it. "There's been another cave-in."

"You told me about it already."

"Not that one. Another, just now. At least one person's buried and two dead."

"How can you...? Are you alright?"

For Katya to show such outward concern, Jeran knew his attempt to hide the pain had failed. "I'm fine. It'll pass in a moment. It's a... It has something to do with magic." Usually that was enough to make Katya drop the subject.

Not this time. "I don't see any of the other Magi looking as if they have one foot in the grave. Maybe you should talk about it with one of them."

"They have more important things to do than—" A frantic knock cut him off, and the door flew open before Jeran could say, "Enter!"

A young man wearing a black uniform with the Odaran Wolf stitched on the chest stepped inside, nearly tripping over his own feet in the process. Jeran had not seen the uniform before, though Ehvan had talked of little else in recent days. Binding together the diverse peoples kidnapped from across Madryn was essential if they were to prove an effective force in the fight to come, and Ehvan believed the uniform gave the soldiers the identity they desired. Jeran had thought Guardsmen's uniforms more than sufficient, but the rebel leader disagreed. "Half of these people aren't from Alrendria," Ehvan had told him, "and most have no faith in the Guard. They do have faith in you, though."

What his soldiers wore did not matter, as long as they did what was asked of them, so Jeran had not fought Ehvan on the issue. He wondered, though, how Martyn would react. "What is it, soldier?"

"Lord Odara, I was sent to warn you. A Mage is coming. She arrived moments ago, demanding to see you, and when no one jumped to show her the way, she threatened to tear Dranakohr apart with her own hands." He gasped for air as if he had run halfway across Dranakohr in his haste to warn Jeran, and perhaps he had. His people expected the Magi—whether Salos's or the Assembly's, Jeran was not sure—to descend on them at any moment.

"One Mage can't cause much damage in Dranakohr." Lying did not bother Jeran if it served a purpose, but he avoided it as much as possible. This time, he spoke almost the truth; only a select few Magi had the skill to utilize magic with any confidence here. A slight smile tugged at his lips. "Besides, this one is expected." The young soldier nodded but did not leave. "Is there something else?"

"My Lord, is it true the Darklord has an army a hundred thousand strong?"

"The army at Portal is easily half that large, and I suspect it's only a fraction of what Lorthas can muster. The Tachan lands teem with men who bear a grudge against Alrendria, and *Ael Shataq* has been untouched by war for almost a thousand winters. The Magi did us no favors when they sealed Lorthas in his prison."

The boy's face paled, and he looked ready to vomit. For a moment Jeran wondered if he should have lied again. He dismissed the thought. Those who joined him should know what they were up against. They offered him their lives; the least he could offer in return was the truth.

"I won't hold you here," he said. "Come spring, you're free to seek your own path. A war to rival the MageWar is coming, and what we've witnessed so far is just the opening volley. But there's time yet—maybe seasons, maybe decades—and I'd prefer to see you follow your own heart than cling to an oath given hastily."

The boy straightened and smoothed out the wrinkles on his uniform. He breathed easier, too. "If it's all the same to you, Lord Odara, I'll stay. Ehvan says you have only a fraction of the men you need. You've given us so much; I'd hate to let you down."

The warmth of loyalty drove the pain and fear from Jeran's head. "Then back to your post, man! We've a war to fight." Jeran feigned a stern expression that could not quite hide the smile that faded as soon as the boy hurried off.

"Talk like that too often, and you'll find yourself alone in Dranakohr," Katya said.

"I won't lie to them. If they don't want to be here, they're no good to me. I won't demand they die for a cause they don't believe in." Katya cocked her head to the side, and Jeran felt her eyes digging into him. "But I can sense how the wind is blowing," he admitted. "If I thought my words would have driven him away, I'd have found a different way to tell him the truth."

Katya chuckled, but any response she intended cut off when the door flew open again. "How dare you!" Jes said, storming into the chamber. She wore a gown of white, modest but not quite loose enough to hide her figure. Black curls framed a perfect face, but her lips narrowed in a frown.

"Jes," Jeran said as if her greeting had been a friendly one. He waved to a chair on the far side of his desk, indicating that she should sit. "I'm so glad you could find the time to visit." He sat as well, locking his impassive gaze on her fiery blue eyes.

"A visit? Your messenger all but kidnapped me." Jeran waved for her to sit again, but Jes ignored him. "I am First Seat of House Velan and a respected Mage in the Assembly. I do not take well to threats, and I certainly don't—"

"That's one of the things I wanted to discuss with you," Jeran said, "but in a moment. First I should apologize for Astore. My apprentices are overzealous at times. My message was to inform you of my need to speak to you, and to convince you to arrange a visit to Dranakohr, not to force you here against your will."

"*Your* apprentices? You—"

"My apprentices," Jeran agreed, cutting her off. He uncorked a bottle of wine, and Jes jumped at the pop. For a moment Jeran's hand lingered on the bottle, and he opened himself to the images flickering from its past. "But Astore is just a child; I'm sure he couldn't force you here against your will. Though I, for one, am pleased to see you." He poured a glass half full and slid it across the desk. His own glass he left empty.

"I couldn't risk a confrontation, you know that. Not where people could see." Jes took the wine, but she did not drink. Her eyes roved the room. No doubt she sensed the Boundary—it was too distant from this chamber to have any serious effect on magic, but few knew that—and the icy tickle between her shoulders apparently did not sit well with her. "What do you want? I have a House to run."

"Straight to the point. No pleasantries or frivolities. That's one of the things I've always liked about you." Jeran paced the distance between his desk and the wall. "Katya, the door please. Jes and I have a few things to discuss, and I don't think she'll want anyone to overhear."

As Katya started toward the door, her hand reached for the blade sheathed at her side. "He's bound to anger you, Mage. When he does, don't use your Gift. If you do and the Boundary doesn't kill you, I will. Or if not me, the Orog." She strode from the room and slammed the door.

"A pleasant girl," Jes said, a wry expression pinching her face. "A bit domineering for your tastes, isn't she?"

"Do you think?" Jeran drummed his fingers on the desk. "And I thought my tastes ran toward overbearing women."

Jes's grin faded, and she shifted uncomfortably from foot to foot before sitting and sipping from her glass. "I have no time for friendly chats. Why have you summoned me here?"

"There's a war brewing, Jes, and I need to know what side you stand on."

Jes's brow furrowed. "You forced me here to secure a promise to help stop Lorthas? I—"

"That fight is brewing too," Jeran said, "or maybe it's about to boil over, but that is not the war I'm talking about. I defied the Mage Assembly. Worse, I've caused a rift within their ranks. Those long-winded fools may debate for a century before taking action, but I have a feeling I know what they'll decide.

"I need to know where you stand. I hope it's with me. The fate of Alrendria— the fate of all Madryn—rests on how we Gifted choose to face the world. I want your help. I'll need it in the seasons to come, but I need to hear from you which side you're on. When the time comes to choose, will you side with me or go to them?"

"Magi still appear in Vela all the time," Jes said, turning away from Jeran's piercing gaze. "If you're patient, the Assembly will decide to—"

"That the Assembly refuses to stop those who announce their intention to leave shows how they cling to the memories of the ideals they've abandoned. That so many slip away under cover of darkness proves how tenuous their grip on those ideals is."

"You can't possibly—"

"They *will* decide," Jeran interrupted, and Jes flushed at having her words cut off again. "I *will* be named their enemy. How they choose to oppose me depends solely on who wrests control of the Assembly from High Wizard Iosa. But whether it is harsh words in a public forum or pitched battle here at Dranakohr, I need to be ready for them. I need to know who my allies are. I need to know who I can trust."

"Aemon will talk to them. He'll make them see. The Assembly won't abandon Alrendria."

"Humor me, then!" Jeran slapped his hand against the desk. Distant pain flared through his mind, and then a wave of sadness. *Not my pain. Not my sadness.* He pushed it away. "If the Assembly chooses to oppose me, which side will you take? Answer honestly. You've been a Mage a long time. I won't hold it against you if you feel their way is better."

Jes sipped her wine, studying Jeran, or perhaps examining herself under the guise of studying him. Jeran pulled a brooch from the box on his desk and turned it over in his hand. The tingle of a Reading ran through his arm, and he opened himself to it, losing himself in the object's history. Sometimes the Readings were the only things capable of driving off the emotions flitting through his head. Other people's emotions.

"The Assembly has done great things," Jes said, her voice flat, "even during my lifetime. They've been my family ever since Aemon took me to them, and I owe them more than just my life." Jeran placed the brooch in the small box atop his desk and leaned forward to listen to her. "But since Shandar they've grown timid in their role as guardians. Perhaps they *have* lost their way."

Tears glistened in Jes's eyes, but they did not fall. "If they stand against you, you have my support. Lorthas must be stopped, even if it means breaking the Assembly to do it. But I have faith in them, Jeran. They'll do what's best for Madryn." Her conviction rang through the room; for a moment, it restored Jeran's confidence in the Magi.

Only for a moment, though. "What they think is best for Madryn, and what I think is best will likely never be the same. That's why the Assembly will never let me live outside their control. Majority rule is a noble idea, but if a thousand voices agree that the sun rises in the west, it makes them no less wrong. I refuse to let Alrendria descend into the Nothing just because the Assembly agrees it's the best thing to do."

Jes opened her mouth, but Jeran raised a hand for silence. "Sargan? I need to know."

The shadows in the corner sprang to life, and an Orog stepped into the light. He wore simple clothes, not much different from what the Orog had worn as slaves, but the tassels naming him *choupik* hung from his shoulders. He carried a short staff, capped at one end with a curved blade. Though none had so much as held the *va'dasheran* before Dranakohr was liberated, the *choupik* had resumed their place as warriors with a fervor to rival that of the most devout Guardsmen. Jeran often watched them sparring in the fields, and he did not envy the man who picked a fight with his Orog.

"She speaks the truth, friend Jeran," Sargan said, his voice a low rumble. "She believes."

The Gift made Jes's eyes flare, and for a moment, Jeran thought she intended to use magic, but then her eyes flicked north toward the Boundary and she shuddered. "My word carries no weight? You require a second opinion?"

"Truthsense is a weapon denied our enemies. It would be foolish of me not to use it. I don't doubt your intentions, Jes, but the Orog can see beyond intention. They hear what your heart believes. I have enemies aplenty and spies lurking in every shadow; I can't risk a traitor who doesn't realize her own treachery until too late."

For a moment, Jes said nothing. Then she sighed. "I would call you a fool if you didn't do that to another. I'll try not to fault you for doing it to me." She stood, but the way she stared did not make Jeran feel as if all had been forgiven. "Am I free to go? Or was there something else you wished to discuss?"

"There is," Jeran said, walking around the desk, "but I see no need for haste. You've come all this way; why not a tour before journeying back to Vela? Our progress hasn't been what I hoped for, but Alwen assures me it's more than I should expect."

He offered Jes his arm, and after a brief hesitation, she took it, and Jeran led her from the room. Katya cocked an eyebrow at their appearance. "The way she was looking at you," she said, falling into place behind Jeran, "I expected you armless when she left, not arm-in-arm."

Sargan walked beside Katya, the butt of his *va'dasheran* clacking on the stone with every other step. He showed neither disgust nor suspicion at the presence of a Durange, and he deferred to her when their path took them through narrow doorways. The Humans still feared Tylor's niece, who once had ruled over Dranakohr, but the Orog accepted her. *They can see where her loyalties lie, even if she can't.*

Jeran led Jes through Dranakohr, down long curving tunnels cut through the rock, smoothed and etched with magic to give the appearance of man-made corridors. Sconces hung at regular intervals, though none held torches. Instead, dozens of spheres hovered beneath the ceiling, casting warm illumination through the halls. Most held a steady light, though a number still flickered, or their glow had weakened until the passage dimmed and Jeran was forced to seize magic long enough to renew their glow. Under the ShadowMagi, the halls had glowed bright as day, the lights dimming or brightening as needed to maintain a constant illumination. In time, his apprentices would grow as skilled, but few had training enough—or courage enough—to use magic so close to the Boundary.

Before the battle, gilded paintings, finely-woven tapestries, and displays of treasures fine enough to rival the palace in Kaper had filled the corridors of Dranakohr; statues of the Bull and his ancestors had guarded every intersection. Jeran had toppled the statues, reusing their stone to better purpose; the few surviving tapestries and paintings he gave to anyone who requested them, as he had done with the treasures in Tylor's collections. Jeran intended to bring color and life back to Dranakohr's stark halls, but the adornments he used would be earned or given freely.

Scorch marks blackened many walls, and several had collapsed, spewing rubble through the corridors. The fighting had been fierce, and Salos's ShadowMagi showed little regard for their home. Workers carted the debris outside day and night, and the apprentices were learning how to coax the rock to repair the damage, but it was a monumental task and other matters—like securing ample provisions for the winter—required more immediate attention of his Gifted.

"This place is cold," Jes said, shivering. "Something lingers in the air. A... specter."

"Dranakohr is an open wound," Jeran said, allowing his mind to skim across the Readings permeating the corridor. There was hardly a chamber in the labyrinthine fortress that did not hold a dark memory. "Forged in the blood and tears of the people who lived here. I will heal that wound, Jes." She looked at him and cocked an eyebrow. "If this can be made a happy place, then there's hope for the rest of the world."

Jes studied him for a time, her eyes boring into him, until a young soldier turned the corner and nearly crashed into her. He danced backward, bowing with an awkwardness that made him appear even younger. "Lord Odara, I was sent to tell you about a cave-in Farside. Commander Wardel believes the Darklord is weakening the tunnels to catch our scouts."

Farside. Across the Boundary. "Tell Commander Wardel to be more careful," Jeran replied, "but the explorations must continue. All passages to *Ael Shataq* must be secured. If Lorthas wants to collapse them on our heads, it just saves us the effort. Have the dead cremated, and see if a Healer can be found to tend to the survivor. She's terrified of the tunnels now, so quarter her in one of the higher chambers, one with a view of the valley."

"Yes, my Lord! I—" He cut off and fixed Jeran with an awed expression. Stammering assurances, he took his leave.

Once he was gone, Katya choked back a laugh. "Do you enjoy frightening people so?" Jes's gaze had returned to Jeran, but now she studied him like a jeweler appraising a gemstone, admiring the cut but with a keen eye for flaws.

"I forget, sometimes," Jeran said, his expression growing sour. "But he's not frightened. He's impressed. I'd not convince him to leave Dranakohr even if I had a mind to."

A heavy sigh escaped Jeran's lips before he resumed the tour. An urgency pulled at him, but he made no effort to increase his pace. If anything he slowed, stopping to discuss the purpose of certain chambers or highlight architectural oddities that normally escaped his notice. Something told him that the delays frustrated Jes, but his anecdotes also fascinated her, and he took every chance to impress her with Dranakohr's eccentricities.

Their path took them farther from the Boundary, until Jeran knew he could use magic without any risk of perversion. Opening a door, he stepped inside a broad cavern open to the valley. Swirling snows danced fifty hands above the grass, but the dome held in place by the apprentices turned it into a fine rain. Other than one stray gust of chill air, nothing of winter penetrated the fires of the forges spread about the room. Muscled men sweated over anvils, repairing damaged tools and weapons or melting down broken items to reforge into new. The rhythmic clanging pounded in Jeran's ears, but the sound provided him with an odd sort of solace.

Jeran sought Dralin, Master of Smiths, but the burly man was nowhere to be seen. The smith's absence did not surprise him. Though this room held Drana-kohr's most talented craftsmen, the fortress had a score of chambers like this one, and several smithies remained deep underground, awaiting the discovery of more suitable accommodations at the surface. Dralin's army of blacksmiths and armor-ers churned out wares faster than they ever had under Tylor's control, and the smith made constant inspections to ensure the quality of those implements. At their present output, Jeran's forces would be fully outfitted by late summer, and he could shift his focus to supplying arms and armor to the Alrendrian Guard.

He had hoped for Jes to hear a report directly from Dralin, but with the Master Smith missing he had no choice but to tell her himself as he led her toward the valley. The other smiths stopped working as Jeran passed, and a few raised hammers over their heads and cheered him.

One forge stood nestled in the corner of the vast chamber, far from the others. A young man worked the iron, leaning over his anvil and pounding with fervor. Sweat soaked his light brown hair, and each swing of the hammer sent droplets hissing into the flames. Three apprentices crowded around him. One held a second band of iron over the fire; the other two watched with fascination. Two more children hunched over a broad table pressed against the cavern wall, fidgeting with works of their own.

Hearing Jeran's name, the smith's hammer fell twice more and then stopped. Azure eyes blazing with the power of the Gift rose to greet him, but they lingered for a moment on Jes. With a smile, Albion adjusted his grip on the tongs and shoved the piece into the bucket at his side, which belched a cloud of white steam and issued a hiss loud enough to be heard over the racket of the smithy.

Setting down his hammer, Albion started toward him, and Jeran adjusted his own course to meet the MageSmith. Like a ghost, Sargan slipped past Jes and interposed himself between Jeran and Albion. Two more Orog detached themselves from the wall and followed a step behind the MageSmith.

"Bring it, Mahx," Albion called, looking over his shoulder. He seemed not to notice the Orog guards. Jes, however, grew suspicious, though whether of the Orog or Albion, Jeran could only guess. One of the apprentices at the table set down the piece he was working on and grabbed something from the shelf behind him. "Bring yours too," Albion laughed. "Lord Odara will want to see them both."

Excitement brightened the youth's features, and he reclaimed his own work before running over to meet them. "Master Albion," Jeran said, inclining his head, "this is Lady Jessandra Vela, First of House Velan. Jes, this is Master Albion Kale."

"An honor, Lady Jessandra," Albion said, bowing his head. "My shadows are Pak and Khorga"—he gestured at the Orog—"and the young man beside me is Mahx. He's showing great promise at the craft."

"Master Albion," Jes said, running her eyes over him in the cold, appraising manner she had. "You are the MageSmith? Your name has caused quite a stir at the Assembly. There are some who would very much like to meet you."

"Begging your pardon, Lady, but I have little desire to meet them." A bead of sweat formed above Albion's lip, but he held himself steady despite the fear Jeran felt pulsing through him. *If I can sense his fear, does that mean what I think it means? I wish I understood what was happening to me!* "Mage Yassik has made it quite clear how the Assembly deals with Gifted who serve a Darklord."

Jes's warm laughter brought an unbidden smile to Jeran's face. "They would bend their rules for you, Master Albion. The thought of having a MageSmith again would force them to forgive you for serving a dozen Darklords, willingly or no. Word of your creations has reached Vela, and I'm sure they've reached Atol Domiar. Jeran was wise to grant you clemency."

"Lord Odara spared me because he, too, needs my craft. I hope I have shown him I am a man of my word. A man to be trusted."

Jeran believed it, but he was careful to school his features so it did not show. "What do you have for me today, Albion?"

A toothy smile spread across the MageSmith's face. "Something you've been asking after for quite some time." He nodded to Mahx, and the young man handed Jeran the narrow band. Holding it up to the light, Jeran examined it. Two pieces of metal woven together and hinged so they opened and closed with ease. He fastened the band around his wrist, and as soon as the clasp snapped, a dullness suffused him. Panic surged, but he suppressed it. With a simple squeeze, the band came undone and the feeling fled.

"It works as expected?" he asked the MageSmith.

"Its range is somewhat greater, but I didn't think that would trouble you." Jeran shook his head and looked at the bracelet one more time before placing it in his pocket. "What I find most odd," Albion said, "is how differently the flows had to be added to create the same effect. The band itself is not so different in design or composition. I fear there's much I don't understand about the craft, Lord Odara."

"Then we wade through the same ocean, Albion, and the only island that could offer solace is full of hostiles." He patted his pocket. "I thank you for this, and I'll need as many as you can make as fast as you can make them. All other pursuits can be ignored for the time being."

"I understand," Albion said, but when Jeran turned to leave, the MageSmith grabbed his shoulder to stop him. In an instant, three sets of Orog hands were on him. The moment they grabbed Albion, Jeran felt his connection to magic severed. It did not return until Sargan pried the MageSmith's fingers from his shoulder.

"It's alright," Jeran said, and the Orog released Albion.

"My student has something he'd like to show you, Lord Odara."

"Of course." Jeran looked at the boy, no more than fourteen winters, and remembered for a moment his own youth on his uncle's farm. He wondered if this boy missed the life he had known, or if the opportunities that had presented themselves offset his suffering enough to bring him joy. Sometimes, Jeran wondered that about himself, too. "What do you have for me, young man?"

Mahx held out his hand, and Jeran took the object from it, a circle of wood with the letter 'N' inscribed along one edge, capped with glass and filled with water. A thin strip of metal floated in the fluid. Jeran studied it for a moment, and then offered it back. "It's very nice."

"You don't understand," Albion said. "Turn until the metal bar lines up with the letter." Jeran spun slowly, watching the needle spin within the vessel until it pointed toward the inscribed letter. When he looked up, he stared toward *Ael Shataq.*

"It detects the Boundary?" Jeran asked, awed.

"I thought so at first, too," Albion replied, "but in fact, the needle points north. With that device, no matter how lost you become in the tunnels or how cloudy the skies above, you can track your direction with confidence."

"A great discovery!" Jeran exclaimed, and he sensed pride burst forth from Mahx. "You puzzled out the magic for this device yourself?"

"No, my Lord."

"Ah," Jeran said, turning to Albion, "You aided him, then?"

"Not as such, Lord Odara," the MageSmith replied. "I suggested the glass cover to better contain the water, but the device is Mahx's."

"But—?"

"The device you hold employs no magic, my Lord," Albion explained. "It's purely of nature, and perhaps the greatest invention of our time."

The implications of such a device were not lost on Jeran, nor were the conveniences it would offer the likes of ship captains and merchants. "Can you make more of these, Mahx?"

"I believe so, my Lord."

"Then do so. With my blessing." The boy ducked his head and returned to the bench, bidding Jeran keep the device as a gift. After he left, Jeran looked at Albion. "Nurture that one. I sense greatness in him."

"If his knack with magic rivals his gift with machinery," Albion confided, "he'll prove a formidable resource to you. I'll do what I can to encourage him."

Jeran patted his pocket. "Make more of these, Albion. With all haste."

"As you command, Lord Odara."

Leading Jes toward the sunlight, Jeran did his best to ignore the inquisitive glances she shot at him. She said nothing, but he felt her eyes boring into his breast pocket, trying to discern the nature of his bracelet. *She'll find out soon enough. And like as not it will disgust her.*

They stepped from the cavern into the blazing light of day. No sun was visible, but the skies above were blinding white except to the north, where stark grey clouds promised heavier weather to come. Snow swirled above them, but instead of frigid gusts and stinging snow, a cool breeze and the smells of spring greeted them. Tiny drops of water flitted down from above, leaving dew-like beads on the growth. To the west, ordered rows of crops pushed up from the dark soil. Those fields would not be ready to harvest for some time yet, but once they were, Dranakohr would have no more need of the outside world. *Self-sufficiency will give me the leverage I need to do what must be done.*

"The apprentices maintain the dome," Jeran told Jes, gesturing up. "It serves to strengthen their Gift while serving Dranakohr's greatest need. Without them, snows as tall as a man would already choke this valley, with no end in sight for seasons to come."

"Your approach to training differs greatly from that of the Assembly," Jes said, and when Jeran whirled to face her, she raised a hand. "I don't mean to suggest that your way is worse or better. Just different. If Alwen approves of the tactic, then I trust no harm has come to your students. She wears a stern countenance, but Alwen has always had great concern for the well being of apprentices."

"She would not take well to the implication that she harbors a kind heart," Jeran said, turning Jes onto a path that paralleled the sheer wall of Dranakohr. "But our next stop will be her Academy, so if you'd like to commend her work, you'll have opportunity. I—"

"Friend Jeran?" The voice was different, yet unmistakable. Jeran turned, eager to see. Afraid to see.

"Grendor?"

CHAPTER 2

"You have turned Dranakohr into a garden, friend Jeran," Grendor said, spinning slowly, face upturned to catch the raindrops. The smile he wore stretched from ear to ear, and the laugh that issued from his chest when he saw the budding farmland brought a warmth to Jeran's heart even as he fought back tears.

White scars streaked what had once been unblemished grey skin, a mass of melted flesh replaced Grendor's right ear, and a patch covered his ruined eye. Orog men had little hair, but the bristly tufts now grew only down the left side of his face, and the beginnings of a beard cut off just beyond his chin. He limped toward Jeran on a staff, exposing matching scars on his arms. Two fingers of his right hand ended at the first knuckle; the remainder of the flesh was as white as new snow. When he looked at Jeran, the smile did not leave his face, but Jeran felt sadness roll off the stalwart Orog. Not sadness for his plight, though, but sadness that his condition caused Jeran so much pain.

Even him? How can I know what he's *feeling? That shouldn't be possible.*

"You should not grieve for me, friend Jeran. To free my people, I offered myself to Shael. In Her wisdom, the Goddess saw fit only to take half. I consider it a bargain well made." A troop of *choupik* ran past, *va'dasheran* held on their shoulders, and Grendor's expression became one of awe. "I only regret that my injuries denied me the chance to watch Dranakohr's transformation."

"The work is far from done, my friend," Jeran said. He reached out to embrace the Orog but hesitated. With a gentle touch, Grendor took Jeran's hand and placed it on his burned arm. The skin felt smooth, not rough like true Orog skin, and Jeran gasped when their contact tore the Gift from him.

"It no longer pains me, friend Jeran, except in my dreams," Grendor said, mistaking the reason for Jeran's gasp. "As the Elders say, 'The bear remembered is larger than the bear that was, his claws a thousand times as sharp."

"The 'Scorpion that was' is nightmare enough," Dahr said, stepping forward to join them. Dark rings circled almond-shaped eyes, and the misting rain soaked his hair, pressing the twisting curls flat against his head. Standing beside Dahr, the Orog looked like children, and Jeran had to crane his neck back to meet Dahr's gaze.

He greeted Jeran and Jes warmly—as warmly as Dahr greeted anyone these days—and offered Sargan a measured bow. He refused to look at Katya, and she obliged him by not acknowledging his presence, but she did not make a move to leave. Shyrock perched on his shoulder, and Fang sniffed the grass several hands behind him.

"I'm glad you returned," Jeran said, grasping Dahr's arm. Pain and anger rolled over Dahr, enough to make Jeran's gut clench at the feel of it, but it was muted in a way he had never expected, and that worried him. "And I thank you for saving Grendor."

Dahr snorted, and he glanced at the Orog. "I did little enough. The Healers could not help him, and the apothecaries could not restore him. He—"

"Would have died if you had not carried me to Vela," Grendor finished. "None here had the skills to treat my burns, and none here had Sheriza's winters of knowledge. Her magic may not have been able to touch me, but she saved my life as sure as rivers run to the sea. You promised to try to accept my condition, friend Dahr, and not to blame yourself for it."

"Trying and doing are not the same," Dahr replied. "But I am trying."

"Not so well that you believe it. Deceive me as you will, but deceive yourself and you risk your soul."

Dahr frowned, and an awkward silence descended. Jes cleared her throat. "Perhaps we could continue the tour? And perhaps your Orog friend would grant me an audience before I return to Vela? I would welcome his insight."

"If Grendor wishes it," Jeran answered, resuming his measured pace down the stone-lined path. "There is someone else who wants to see him, but that reunion can wait a while longer."

They walked along the base of the ridge, past fields of grain and newly-planted orchards, past cattle grazing in fenced-off pastures. A handful of apprentices dressed in blue so dark it could easily be mistaken for black patrolled the fields, each accompanied by at least one Orog and one Human soldier, and all avoiding the laborers hunched among the growing plants. Dark iron bands circled the throats of the prisoners, but one need not see the collars to name them ShadowMagi; the acid glares and scornful derision they cast about spoke volumes. Dozens of *choupik* and a few of the Magi who had left the Assembly guarded them; even with the collars they feared the ShadowMagi, and Jeran did not try to dissuade them of it. All too often when fear faded, pity for the collared replaced it.

They passed dozens of caves into Dranakohr, more than Jeran had ever imagined existed. His explorers mapped the caverns relentlessly, and Jeran encouraged their work. New passages were found daily, and some as-yet-undiscovered could pose a threat to Dranakohr. *If a tunnel exists that bypasses all of our fortifications...*

Tylor had made Dranakohr impregnable to conventional assault, but the Bull had failed to look beyond the ordinary. Jeran intended to understand every corner, every stone in his new home. He planned to make it truly unassailable, for only as a haven from assaults of all types could it provide the security he needed.

A tremendous structure appeared before them, cut stone merged perfectly with the mountain beyond. The walls ended in jagged rows at the fourth story, and teams of workers labored to place the next row of stones. A few Magi circled the base of the building, and Jeran saw their auras flare with magic. Using complex weaves of energy, they fused the rocks, binding them to their neighbors.

"I haven't seen construction of this magnitude since Shandar," Jes said, and her voice carried a note of wistful memory.

"Alwen wanted something smaller," Jeran said, "but Oto suggested that building for our current needs might not send the right message. He conceived of the design, and somehow even managed to supply our architects with a model." Dahr and Grendor gaped at the thought of the blind Mage constructing a model, but Jes merely nodded, a knowing smile quirking her lips.

Jeran led them around the Academy and in through the unfinished front entrance—arched double doors fifty hands high with two embossed plates bound to the edges. When they closed, the plates formed a wolf's head as broad as a man with an eagle above, wings unfolded protectively over the entrance.

Vast windows of clear quartz lined the front of the building to let in natural light, and interspersed between those were smaller windows of glass that opened and closed on tracks. Narrow balconies—or the starts of them—surrounded the higher floors, matching the style of Dranakohr, but flowering vines already grew along the lowest, and the workers had to fight them as much as the gusting winds to achieve their tasks.

Six broad stairs led up to the archway and into the Academy's main hall. Even unfinished, it impressed; a vast vault six hundred hands across and two hundred high with a domed ceiling that seemed impossible because one knew the mountain continued on above. Marble staircases started on either side of the entrance and wrapped around the chamber, and arched doors led to brightly-lit halls. Magi on the far end of the room used the Gift to work the rock of an amphitheatre, smoothing the stone so that sound would carry to the farthest reaches of the chamber.

"To the right will be rooms for the younger apprentices," Jeran said, making a sweeping gesture, "and to the left are halls for training and instruction. The floors above will be devoted to those Magi wishing to pursue their own studies, and the highest floor will hold a library."

"Once construction of the main Academy is complete," Oto added, feeling his way through the door and shambling across the chamber, "we will construct an adjunct Academy for the ungifted. Those seeking instruction in the disciplines of science, mathematics, and philosophy—or even in the theories of magic!—may come to Dranakohr and learn beside the Gifted. The students will be housed together and will learn side by side as their courses of study permit. The commonality of their purpose will bind them together, and to us."

"A far grander plan than you ever proposed to the Assembly, Otello," Jes said, her face lighting up when she saw the rotund Mage. Oto turned his sightless eyes on her, and they delved into her soul, but if Jes felt uncomfortable under the scrutiny, she showed no sign of it.

"I can't claim responsibility," Oto said, a broad grin splitting his face. "The concept of this Academy is Jeran's. It has Alwen in a tizzy, as you might guess, but Yassik and I think it's a grand idea."

"Oto will govern the students," Jeran explained, "and offer them guidance. He could calm a rabid lion with words alone; I suspect the vagaries of our students will not prove a difficult challenge."

Oto's rich laughter filled the hall. "I have already accepted the position, Jeran. You need not flatter me." As he moved closer, he traced a hand through the air, back and forth, and when it contacted the stone wall, he nodded. "As Jeran said, I will govern the students, make sure they do not lag in their studies, and maintain a dialogue with their instructors."

"Instructors?" Jes sounded perplexed.

"Yes! It's a marvelous idea. Instead of assigning an apprentice to one Mage, Jeran proposes having a panel of Magi teach our students. Since the actual application of the Gift varies on an individual level, Jeran thinks exposure to a variety of different styles will shorten the time required to complete the training." Something akin to regret ghosted across Oto's face. "It's a concept so pure that it's embarrassing the Assembly never thought of it before."

"Tradition clouds reason and stifles ingenuity," Jeran said. "That's true whether you speak of man or Mage, and the Mage Assembly is as ancient an order as there is, older even than Alrendria." Jeran sighed, and his eyes rose to the vaulted ceiling. "If Dranakohr survives the war, it too will eventually become enslaved to its traditions."

Jes cast a dark, inquisitive look at Jeran, but her words were for Oto. "The reason the Assembly trains apprentices in the manner it does is not purely out of tradition," she said. "Apprentices develop a bond with their master, and subsequent teachers have far less influence in guiding an apprentice's flows."

"But how much of that is because no other Magi have access to an apprentice for winters once they're assigned a master?" Oto asked. "Fear not, my dear. This Academy does not do away with the old in favor of the new. We strive to merge the best of both ways, and we hope to keep our minds open for even better ideas down the road.

"I will guide those too young for lessons or in their first days of training, but at the conclusion of their first four-season, the students will sit with their instructors and together choose who will oversee their training. Gone will be the days when Magi steal promising apprentices from more deserving teachers and force them down paths they had no interest in." Determination filled Oto's voice, and the satisfaction of a battle long fought and finally won.

"What's to keep the instructors from contradicting each other, or from allowing personal rivalries to hinder the training of their colleagues' students?" Skepticism poured from Jes with every question, but her curiosity was piqued.

"We hope to eliminate the belief that an apprentice 'belongs' to any one Mage," Oto replied. "But the rivalries you speak of are no small worry. Yassik has been tasked with administering the instructors. He will determine the curriculum, monitor the coursework, and ensure that whatever rivalries do exist are confined to the academic. He will also maintain the library and has already talked of making it the most complete collection in all of Madryn."

"Maintaining a library and telling other Magi how best to teach?" A wry grin brightened Jes's features. "I bet you had to twist Yassik's arm to get him to accept such an onerous duty."

"I did," Jeran said, "once he learned that Alwen would supervise the running of the Academy! She'll be the one to dole out punishments when they're necessary and rewards when they're deserved. She's also the one Oto and Yassik have to report to." Oto and Jeran shared a laugh, and then a look of intense concentration spread across Oto's face.

"Forgive me," he said, his eyes moving from side to side as if to take in the entire room. "I know there are others here, and I've been neglectful. The sight I used so freely in the wide world comes with a price here. In time I'll master magic near the Boundary, but for now I prefer the darkness to the headaches. If you'll indulge me a moment while I..."

Oto's head snapped around so he faced Dahr. "A pleasure to see you again, Hunter." Dahr shifted from foot to foot and seemed surprised that Oto had picked him out so easily. "The hurt you feel radiates from you like a fire, my friend, and your desire to quench that pain pulses through the world around you. That's why I see you so clearly."

Oto stepped closer, and his hands floated through the air around Dahr's head. "Confusion, too, I see. But maybe there I can help. During the MageWar I knew a Tribesman named Narouk, a *Tier'sorahn* of the Sahna Tribe. Perhaps, later, you would honor me with a visit and I can share my stories of him with you."

Dahr started to shake his head, but Fang nudged him and Shyrock flapped his wings in irritation. "Very well," Dahr muttered, and then louder, "Once I've settled in?"

"Wonderful!" Oto said, clapping his hands. He turned to Grendor, and his smile faded. "I cannot see you, friend Grendor, so I know you're there. There's another of your kind present as well, but somehow your absence is... unmistakable. Does that sound as strange to you as it does to me? I hope your injuries don't burden you much."

"Friend Oto," Grendor lowered his eyes in deference to the Mage. "My wounds bother others more than me. To my eyes, they were justly earned and will be proudly worn."

"And to mine, they affect your beauty not at all," Oto chuckled. "The nobility of your people is legend among humanity. I administered to the surviving Orog after the Raising, and in my youth had the honor of studying under the Elder Inouk, who taught me of the Mother and her wisdom. Perhaps you would come with the Tribesman, and I can share my knowledge with you as well?"

"The man who refuses to sip from the fount of knowledge dies of thirst without knowing it." Grendor's slitted eyes grew wide with wonder. "Inouk," he murmured. "I will gladly share stories with you, friend Otello."

"Excellent! I shall await the evening with anticipation. Commander. Friend Orog"—he nodded to each in turn—"I wonder what brings you all to this unfinished…" Oto cut off in midsentence and turned to Jeran. In an instant, his entire demeanor changed; his shoulders collapsed under a weight, and the excitement faded from his eyes. "He finished it, didn't he? That's why you're here. She won't like it."

"That's why I told you what I had planned," Jeran said, irritation flashing across his face. "You were supposed to prepare her."

"I'd have sooner prepared myself for slaughter. If Alwen thinks I've supported you in this—"

"If I think you supported him in what?"

All heads turned toward the sound. Across the hall, a door opened of its own volition and Alwen strode in with Yassik at her side. Gone were the faded hides and frazzled appearance she had favored in Keryn's Rest. Sparkles flowed down her iridescent grey dress in a cascade of light and flashed off jewels on wrists and fingers. Her hair she wore up in a bun, except for a single lock down the center that fanned out across her back. She moved toward them, gliding across the chamber, but her eyes prowled, pouncing from one person to the next as if trying to discern the nature of the visit.

Yassik, burdened by the weight of a half dozen volumes, hurried to keep up. He stumbled twice, and heaved a sigh when he reached the wall and set the books on a bench. The scathing glare he directed at Alwen had no effect, and Yassik gulped for air as he massaged his arms.

"How does the training progress, Alwen?" Jeran asked. Oto harrumphed and daubed at his brow with a kerchief. Yassik winced as if he had just been dealt a heavy blow.

Alwen caught the confidence in Jeran's voice, and suspicion followed her frown. "The same as yesterday. And the same as the day before that. As well as can be expected." After nodding to Jes, who returned the gesture with a slight bow of her own, Alwen fastened her gaze on Dahr and Grendor. "If you think to frighten me into rash action with that giant and his scarred companion, you've spent too much time inside the mountain. Dahr has friends I'd like as not ever see again, but him I do not fear."

Dahr bristled at the accusation; he raised himself to full height, and Shyrock shared his frustration, spreading his wings and shrieking in defiance. Jeran raised a hand. "Don't take her bait, Dahr. She attempts to distract me and knows your temper is an easy target."

A crooked smile twitched the edges of Alwen's lips, and she ducked her head as if conceding a point. "We've had this discussion before, and often enough that you should be as tired of it as I. Learning to control the flows of magic is a dangerous thing, and not something to be done lightly or with undue haste. I recognize our need for trained Magi, and I acknowledge the pressures we are under to train them quickly. But do you really want to risk the lives of these children? Will having a score of Magi make you happy if two score die in the process?"

Impatience surged up within Jeran, but he let it go. "No... No, that wouldn't be worth it." Just as Alwen let her smile show through the stern façade she wore, Jeran stopped. "But if there were a way to train them faster, without harming them, you would do it?"

"Of course," Alwen said, moving to Jeran's side. Jeran felt a jolt of sympathy and sadness as she took his arm. "Do you think I do this just to frustrate you?"

"Then I have a surprise for you." He reached into his shirt and withdrew the bracelet, placing the ornament on Alwen's wrist and squeezing until the snap of the hinge echoed across the room.

When the bracelet locked, Alwen gave a start, and confusion flashed across her face. "Jeran," Yassik asked, "what is—?"

Alwen's scream cut off the rest of Yassik's question. "A collar?" she yelled, hurling herself at Jeran. He held her off without effort but made no move to comfort her. If anything, he looked smug. "After all I've done, this is how you repay me?"

In an instant, Yassik was there, hauling Alwen away and interposing himself between Jeran and his wife. "What's come over you, boy? Didn't you wear one of those abominations long enough to remember what it's like?" He clutched Alwen to him, and when Jeran saw her pale flesh and trembling manner, guilt suffused him. He started to apologize, but before he could speak, Yassik filled himself with magic. His aura flared to life, and colors danced around him. Jeran opened himself to his Gift as well and prepared to defend himself.

"Enough!" Oto's yell reverberated throughout the hall, more so because hearing anger in his kindly voice was a rare phenomenon. "Release your Gift, Yassik. If you don't have enough trust to give Jeran a chance to explain himself, then perhaps Dranakohr isn't the best place for you." Yassik drew a deep breath, but he released his hold on magic.

"And you," Oto snapped, turning toward Jeran, magic flashing across his blank eyes. "If you intended this as a joke, it was poorly thought out. If you did not, then Yassik has every right for his anger. In either case, you're not making a good case for yourself."

"You're right," Jeran said, crossing the distance to stand beside Yassik and Alwen. "I had no right to do that without explaining myself first, and what little pleasure I had hoped to gain by the surprise was lost in your reaction. As you're so fond of pointing out, Alwen, I'm young and foolish. Perhaps you'll find it in your heart to forgive a fool."

Alwen looked at Jeran for a moment, then shoved Yassik away and smoothed her dress. "A fool you are. But I've known bigger fools. Explain why you collared me, and then I'll decide whether you'll leave this Academy alive."

Jeran laughed aloud, and the fierce determination and indignation he felt from Alwen only served to heighten his mirth. "First of all, it's not a collar; it's a bracelet, though the magic is similar. While wearing one, the Gifted can seize magic and manipulate the flows, but any attempt to use those flows—intended or accidental—dissolves. With these, our students can learn to manipulate magic without risk of it running wild; they can take chances that even I in my haste would have deemed hazardous.

"With the collar I wore and Yassik's training, I learned in a four-season what it takes the Assembly winters to teach. You claim it takes a decade to train a Mage?

With these bracelets and the three of you, I expect to see a force of Magi to rival the Assembly in half that time."

Yassik snatched Alwen's arm and held it up to the light, examining the bracelet. "Whether you call it a collar, a bracelet, or a fairy's kiss, this device deprives the Gifted of their ability to use magic. How can you justify forcing them on those who haven't misused their powers?"

"Simple," Jeran said. He took Alwen's wrist and squeezed the bracelet at the hinge. It opened with a snap, and Jeran caught it before it hit the floor. "Unlike a collar, these can be removed at will. Worn for training exercises, off otherwise." Seriousness replaced Jeran's smile, and he lowered himself to one knee. "I was wrong to put this on you without warning, but don't punish our cause for my imprudence. You must see that this is what we've been waiting for?"

For a time, Alwen stared at Jeran. "The next time I have my cane..."

"I'll bend over so you can reach my head easier."

"You won't have time to see it coming."

Jeran chuckled. "You'll use them, then?"

"I'll try them," Alwen replied. "And I'll keep this one to practice with on my own. If I think for even an instant that these things might harm the children, having another collar fastened around your throat will be the least of your worries, Odara."

"That's the rousing praise I was hoping for," Jeran said, standing. "Yassik, I'm—"

"It's a touchy subject for me," the old man replied. "Under any other circumstances, I'd love to see someone get the upper hand on her. I don't like these things, though, and we're going to have a long talk about why this is the first I've heard of it, but we worked wonders with you, didn't we? It took me far longer than a decade to do half of what you've done. If we can..."

Yassik's words faded, and his features took on the vacant look they often did when he lost himself in thought. "These are tumultuous times for the Magi, aren't they?"

"Not all change is bad," Alwen said. In an unusual display, she wrapped an arm around Yassik and leaned her head against his arm. "Maybe this is the opportunity we've waited for. The chance we've always wanted to make things better." They looked at each other, and volumes of meaning passed between their tender glance.

Jes cleared her throat. "I appreciate the entertainment, Jeran, but I really do have a lot of work to do. Perhaps you could find me a room where I could refresh myself, and then I'd like to meet with your Orog friend before returning to Vela."

"That's something I wanted to talk to you about, Jes," Jeran said. "I need you to stay."

Pursing her lips, Jes's eyes drifted upward. "I suppose I could arrange a short visit. A day or two? I could send word that I'm visiting the countryside to inspect the damage wrought by Tylor's army. I—"

"No," Jeran interrupted. "I need you to stay and resume my training."

Jes froze and shook her head, seeking words. "No... No, I... I can't do that. I have a House to run, and I am no good as a teacher."

"Nevertheless, you began my training, and we worked together long enough that Yassik and Oto both noticed similarities in our styles. You said it yourself: apprentices develop a bond with their teachers. Like it or not, you were my teacher."

Hand trembling, Jes pointed at Alwen, Yassik, and Oto. "They can teach you far better than I. Aemon, too. He'd relish the opportunity! I can have him here in less than a day. You—"

"They can teach me what I need to know," Jeran admitted. "Any Mage could. But I need to learn as fast as possible, and the way to do that is with you guiding my training. I have no choice, Jes, and neither do you. You told me your allegiance was to me and what we're trying to accomplish here. This is how you're needed."

"No," Jes said, and then with more conviction, "No! I have a House to run."

"There are others who can run the House. Step down or appoint a steward. You are needed here."

"My people need me! Especially now. I will not forsake them to become your nursemaid."

Drawing a deep breath, Jeran reached into his coat. "I had hoped it wouldn't come to this," he said, handing Jes a sealed letter. "This is not the way I wanted to renew our relationship."

"What's this?" Jes turned the letter over in her hand.

"It's a copy of a dispatch my apprentices will distribute across House Velan if you return to the city without my permission." Jes tore open the letter and read; the surprise struggling to widen her eyes fought with the anger attempting to narrow them. "It provides evidence to the fact that you're a Mage."

Alwen hissed in a breath, and Oto muttered something about strongarm tactics not always being the best, but Yassik simply nodded as if he had seen this move coming. Anger defeated surprise, and Jes turned a caustic glare on Jeran. "Why?"

"I thought it only fair to warn you. If you had returned to Vela without my mentioning—"

"No! Why are you doing this?"

"Because I need you. Salos is free, Lorthas wants to be, and as soon as the Assembly realizes that they have a better chance of defeating me now rather than after I attain mastery of the Gift, they'll be coming for me too."

"But if it becomes known that I'm a Mage…"

"The people will riot. They'll tear Vela down in their haste to free themselves from the domination of the Magi. They'll hunt you down to prosecute you for your crime, and the suspicions many harbor about the deceitful and treacherous Magi will be proven true."

The silence that filled the Academy was total. The light rain falling outside was the loudest sound. "You're bluffing," Jes said at last.

"Why would you think so?"

"You're in the same position as I. If you condemn me, you condemn yourself."

"You're wrong, Jes. For one, the law says that no Mage of the Assembly can aspire to rule Alrendria. Before you argue, I had Martyn find the decree. The language is very exact. I'm not a Mage of the Assembly. In fact, I defied them openly. You, however, are, so even if the law might apply to me, it definitely applies to you.

"You also forget that I'm not yet First of House Odara. If people choose to obey me as if I am, that's not my concern. But perhaps most important is the fact that I've made no secret of my Gift. Those who follow me do so despite my magic. Can you boast the same?"

Jes's cheeks flushed with anger, and she looked to be on the verge of seizing magic. Alwen did too, for that matter. "Call my bluff at your own risk," Jeran said, taking her arm, "but before you do, consider whether ruling House Odara will mean much to me if Alrendria is overrun by the Tachans, or if Lorthas breaks free of *Ael Shataq*. Personally, I'd prefer the training necessary to defeat our foes over assurances that I'll be able to take my rightful place as head of House Odara when this war is over."

Jes tried to withdraw, but Jeran kept his grip firm, refusing to let her turn away. "I don't presume to believe I'm the lynchpin upon which our success depends," he said, "but this place and the things we're doing here just may be, and for the time being *I* am the reason Dranakohr exists. If keeping the Assembly's secret was the best way to protect my people, I'd take it to the grave. But it's not; learning as much as I can about magic is the only way I'll be able to defeat the enemies arrayed against us.

"This isn't how I wanted things to be. I need a teacher who trusts me, perhaps even one who can stand my company, but a teacher who despises me is still better than none at all. The choice is yours. Find a reason to leave Vela and preserve your secret, or return and deal with the consequences. Eventually, you'll be forced to flee, and the only refuges will be here or Atol Domiar. I think you already know where you'll end up."

Rising up to full height, Jes seized magic. She faced Jeran with the full measure of her power and winters of living as a ruler of men. "You," she said in a voice that rasped like sand dragged across paper, "are worse than Aemon. At least he has the decency to make you believe you're doing something of your own volition."

"Funny," Jeran mused. "I was just thinking that, of all his faults, at least Lorthas has the decency to tell you outright why he's forcing you to do something you don't want to do."

"With your permission"—Jes spat the word—"I'll return to Vela and name a steward to watch over the House in my absence. I'll tell them I'm needed in the north, aiding Lord Odara in setting right the shambles of his House." Jeran's smirk and approving nod infuriated her. "You'll have your teacher, but you'll regret your decision by the time I'm done with you."

Jeran's laughter drove Jes from the Academy. "When do I not, Jes? When do I not?"

CHAPTER 3

"This is the fourth time this ten-day, Dorias!" Frustration pulsed through Jeran, beating in time with the pounding of his heart, but he kept a rein on his anger. "I begin to suspect that you're *letting* the ShadowMagi slip away."

Dorias flinched as if struck, but he straightened his back and fixed small dark eyes on Jeran. "You believe I'm trying to set them free?" One of only a few fully-trained Magi to have split with the Assembly to join Jeran, Dorias acted as if his decision guaranteed him a place of prominence in Dranakohr. Jeran wished the man had left his pride and ego in Atol Domiar along with his belongings.

"No, I think you want them to die. You know the only path they can take is north, you know they can't cross the Boundary, and you know the weather will kill a man in days."

"The Orog—"

"Are not prison guards! Because of their abilities, I've asked the *choupik* for assistance, but I've left the punishment—and the responsibility—for the ShadowMagi to the Gifted. If the task is too difficult for you, I *will* ask the *choupik* to do it, but if controlling collared Magi is beyond your abilities, I'm not sure what you think you can contribute to Dranakohr."

Furious at being singled out—Jeran could not sense it, but he did not need his strange new gift to see the Mage's anger—Dorias struck an imperious pose. "My apologies, Lord Odara. There will be no more escapes."

"I should think not." Jeran let his eyes rove among the others assembled in his office, and his hand flitted across the objects arrayed on his desk: a silver hairbrush, a jewelry box, a battered child's doll, two daggers, a scrivener's quill, and a few other odds and ends. Readings flared from each, and Jeran opened himself to them one after the other.

Ehvan, with the tassels of command dangling from the shoulder of his new uniform, ran a hand through the beard he wore to hide his youth and surveyed the chamber with dispassionate eyes, eyes that had seen far too much suffering. Commander of Dranakohr. Jeran feared the post would heap too much responsibility on Ehvan's shoulders, but he had had no choice; Ehvan was the only person trusted by all of Dranakohr's disparate groups. The young man had risen to the challenge, though, and for Jeran's faith, Ehvan rewarded him with fervent loyalty.

Wardel sat across the desk from Ehvan. He wore a Guardsman's uniform again—where he had found one, Jeran had no idea—but he stole glances at Ehvan's Odaran black when he thought no one was looking. *Maybe a new uniform wasn't such a good idea after all.*

In addition to overseeing the explorations Farside, Wardel had taken on the responsibility of training the Human soldiers. He worked closely with Drogon, who commanded the *choupik*, and together they sought a way to merge the fighting styles of both Races into an effective weapon.

"Iyrene," Jeran said, turning to the sandy-haired woman opposite him, "you've done a marvelous job. Gustav tells me we'll be self-sufficient by spring."

Spots of color bloomed on the woman's cheeks. "I've done little, Lord Odara. It's the Magi—"

"Nonsense. The Gifted keep the weather warm, but they don't make the fields grow or care for the herds. I lived as a farmer, remember? I know the difficulty of breaking new land. The results you've shown are little less than miraculous." Iyrene straightened, and her surge of confidence brought a smile to Jeran's lips. He knew these meetings made her uncomfortable—she felt the others served him in far more important ways—and Jeran missed no chance to comment upon the woman's contributions.

"Lord Odara?" Suan wiped smudges from her face. "I found two more tunnels Farside. One shows promise. There's no evidence that it's been traveled before."

"You think it will lead into *Ael Shataq*?"

"It's heading in the right direction, but the only way to know for sure is to follow it to the end. I plan to do so after we're done here, but if the tunnel's long I may miss the next—"

"Do you think it's wise to explore the tunnels in your condition?" Jeran asked.

Suan perked up her head. "My Lord?"

"Aren't the tunnels dangerous for the child? I'm not sure crawling through the black, risking the Darklord's traps is the best thing for you. Other duties can be found, for the time being at least."

Suan's hand went to her belly, and she fixed a wide-eyed stare on Jeran. "How do you—? I was only certain myself this morning!"

"A… A lucky guess. You have a light in your eyes I never noticed before." Jeran felt Katya's eyes on his back, boring into him, demanding an answer to the things she had witnessed. *Damn my Gifts! What I wouldn't give to be normal again. Why can't I sense what Dorias feels?*

Jeran placed his hand on the hairbrush and opened himself to the Reading. What had once stolen long stretches of his day now lasted only an instant, but right now it was not the mysteries of the past Jeran sought to unravel; the visions drove away the strange feelings, what he was certain were other people's emotions, fears and desires. The Readings were the only thing capable of clearing his head and muting the aching pain haunting the recesses of his mind.

"I should be fine for a few more ten-days at least, my Lord," Suan replied amidst congratulations from Wardel, Ehvan, and Iyrene. "I'd prefer to continue my work, unless you insist."

A frown tugged at Jeran's face, but he fought it. *I don't want more innocent lives laid at my feet!* "I wouldn't deprive you of something I know brings you so much joy. Just be mindful of the child, and when she starts to show, keep yourself from the tunnels."

"Friend Jeran, I wonder if there is not something to be done about the Rachannen?" Squat but nearly as broad as Dahr, with arms as thick as tree trunks and a scar running from the top of his bald head to the tip of his chin, Junden was the closest thing to an irritable Orog Jeran had met. He wore the new uniform, though Jeran had seen few Orog in the Black.

"Are they causing trouble, Junden?"

"They are a nuisance. They entice my *choupik* to drink and gamble, and they taunt the prisoners at every opportunity. Three were found casting stones at a ShadowMage, and the others—"

"I thought those three were dealt with."

"The first time, Lord Grondellan bound the men to a wall and had the rest of his soldiers throw stones at them. One would think such a punishment sufficient to teach, but it was not. They blame the ShadowMage for their bruises and seek him out at every opportunity. They no longer hit him, but I have twice caught them throwing stones at the man, laughing as he dances and dodges."

Fury rose through Jeran like a tide, and the power of the Gift made his eyes shine with blue fire. "Have Lord Grondellan sent to me so we can discuss the conduct of his men. Inform the Rachannen that the next one who annoys me will find himself across the wall, digging his way back to Alrendria." He stood, and the glare he let roam over his lieutenants made all but the Orog cringe. "I won't tolerate this! The Rachannen are the worst, but I see mistrust and prejudice in the eyes of all. I may not be able to coerce friendship or compel tolerance, but I demand my people treat others with respect. If they can't, there's no place for them in Dranakohr."

Silence dominated the room until Jeran realized he still held the hairbrush in a white-knuckled grip. As he set the brush down, he drew a deep breath and waved them away. "Enough. We'll meet again in two days time. I have—"

The door to Jeran's office opened after a light knock. "Friend Jeran, did you send for me?" Grendor stepped inside, limping on his staff. The mere sight of him lightened Jeran's heart. Wardel jumped to his feet and greeted the Orog with a fond embrace. The other Humans said nothing, but the two *choupik* stood and bowed their heads, pressing fingers to their lips and then extending their hands toward Grendor, whose cheeks flushed dark grey.

"Welcome home, Grendor," Drogon said in his booming voice. He crossed the distance between them in three quick steps and clapped a hand on Grendor's unscarred shoulder. "The *choupik* have risen to your call; we learn what has been lost and will resume the struggle against those who would cast chains upon the soul. We await only the word of Lord Odara and the return of our *Avilidar*."

"It is good to see you, my friend." Grendor gripped the Orog's shoulders. "*Avilidar*? I am sorry I missed the vote. Who have the *choupik* chosen to lead them?"

Drogon looked from Grendor to Jeran and back again, a cautious expression plastered on his broad face. "You, Grendor. You are *Avilidar*."

Slitted eyes widened to the size of teacups. "Me?" Grendor laughed. "Do the *choupik* search for the sunrise in the west? What do I know of war? What do I know of leading soldiers?"

"What do any of us know, friend Grendor, except that the time has come for us to rejoin the world. We know the future is a black void into which only the Gods can see, but we trust that the Mother has you firmly in her grip and will lead you into the light of tomorrow."

"Hmm," Katya snorted. "All hail the Orog King."

Drogon took Grendor's silence for agreement, and he dipped his head to the others. "I must go. I lead the afternoon's field exercises." Wardel escorted the remaining lieutenants from the room, leaving Grendor alone with Jeran—and with Katya, who hovered in the shadows by the balcony.

It took some time before Grendor found his voice again. "I... I do not want to lead the *choupik*, friend Jeran," he whispered. "I do not want the deaths of so many on my conscience."

Jeran's thoughts flashed to the emotions he had felt coming off his people for the last few days. Eagerness, anger, and sadness were common, but fear overshadowed all else. Fear of the future. Fear of living in a world ruled by Lorthas or Salos. Fear of death most of all. "Who does? It's a grave responsibility they've saddled you with." As soon as the words left his mouth, he felt Grendor's anxiety take root, and he wished he had conveyed more excitement.

They grant him a great honor, and I make it sound like they've condemned him to death!

"But," Jeran added, forcing a smile, "your concern for others will make you a great *Avilidar*. We will get through this, my friend. Together we'll teach each other what we need to survive."

"The orphan farmer and the Orog cripple," Katya said under her breath. "Surely a story to rival Roya and Makan!"

Grendor's lips compressed into a line, and he flashed a look at Katya, but his fear had lessened. "You sent for me?" he asked Jeran.

"There's someone who wants to see you," Jeran told him, leading Grendor toward the door. Katya fell in step behind them, a silent guardian shadowing them through Dranakohr. The scowl darkening her features sent all but the bravest souls scurrying down side tunnels to avoid passing too close. Her temper had worsened since Dahr's return, and Jeran wondered if she feared his wrath. *I sense no fear, only disappointment. Does she still want to die? Does she still think he'll kill her?*

"The things I have seen and heard, friend Jeran!" Grendor said, breaking the silence and drawing Jeran out of his musings. "To see *choupik* practicing with *va'dasheran*, just like in the stories... And your Academy... A beautiful sight! Do you really intend to let anyone attend your Mage Academy, even Orog? Dahr and I have been spending time with Oto, and he's been telling us about the great things you are doing. He's also been telling me about his life. Did you know he studied under Inouk, perhaps the wisest Elder of all? I—"

Grendor's enthusiasm made Jeran feel good about what he was trying to create in Dranakohr, but Katya's scowl deepened into a glower. "He needn't worry about sending men to their death in battle," she said. "He'll talk his enemies into the grave long before they cross blades."

In mid-stride Grendor froze, and he turned so abruptly that Jeran had no time to dodge. The Orog's staff caught him in the shin, and he sucked in a sharp breath. "All creatures of the Gods feel pain," Grendor said, studying Katya with his remaining eye, "but only those gifted with intellect try to share their pain. You and he are more alike than either will admit, but at least Dahr never *intends* to spread his suffering to those around him. At least he feels remorse when he realizes his actions have hurt."

Katya's jaw clenched until her face seemed carved from stone, and her eyes bored into Grendor with a show of fierce anger. Jeran knew the truth, though; embarrassment echoed in her mind, all but drowning out a distant but persistent tremble of fear. "I will not stand here and be insulted by a—"

"You will listen to me!" Grendor said, and Jeran marveled at the change that had overtaken his friend. "Dahr stands on the brink of oblivion, staring into the blackness of the Nothing, and you are the only light that can bring him back. Much like you, he refuses to see the honor of his actions. Much like you, he dwells on the evils he has done and thinks himself a monster because of them. He seeks death as a release, but knows only love can free him. He does not have your courage, Katya Durange. You must set aside your fears and make... Friend Jeran, are you crying?"

Jeran brushed a hand across his cheek and it came away wet. The aching sadness in the back of his mind swelled, with spikes of fear waxing and waning like the tide. The pain was distant, but sharp. "It's nothing. You have a way with words, that's all." *What's happening?* A spike of pain made colors flash through his vision and left him fighting to maintain balance. "We should go."

Jeran stormed off, doing his best to keep the others at his back, hoping they could not see the pain tightening his eyes and making the veins at his temples throb. Grendor pressed for details of their destination, which Jeran refused to divulge, but Katya's earlier ire had disappeared. The expression she wore still frightened off those they passed, but Jeran noted that she was quick to avert her eyes whenever Grendor looked in her direction.

Deep into Dranakohr they marched, skirting the Barrows and descending into the *ghrat*. In a small *lientou* tucked in the corner of a broad passage, Yassik hovered over a pallet, daubing water on the head of Craj, the Eldest. When they entered, the Mage looked up, and seeing Jeran, he offered a slight shake of his head.

"Grendor," wheezed Craj, "is that you, my child?" The color had leached from the ancient Orog's skin; his flesh hung from the bones in deep furrows, mimicking the crags and valleys of the landscape outside. A dark film covered the old man's sightless eyes, but he turned his head toward the new arrivals and stretched out a trembling hand.

"I am here, Eldest," Grendor said, ignoring his own injuries and hastening to Craj's side. "Jeran said someone wished to see me, but he did not say it was you, nor did he tell me you were ill."

"I am not ill, my friend. The Mother is calling me home."

Grief contorted Grendor's features, but he did not let anguish enter his voice. "Then the Mother is as wise as they claim, to bring one such as you to her side."

A rasping chuckle came from the pallet. "The honeyed tongue catches more flies than the salted fist, but you waste your time flattering one such as me. Let me see you…" Craj's hand glided over Grendor's face, hovering over his scars and the dark patch covering his eye, then slid down his arm, stopping on the remains of Grendor's burned hand.

"You wear the scars of our people's suffering, young one, but you wear them well. I suspected for a long time that you were to be the vessel through which the Mother set us free." The ancient Orog chuckled again. "It is good to know I was right one last time."

Fear flickered in Grendor's eyes, more fear than when he had faced a charge of Tylor's soldiers, or when he lay dying on Dranakohr's stone floor. "What are we to do without your guidance, Eldest?"

A weak, rasping cough delayed Craj's response. "The Elders have discussed my replacement at great length. Few have the capacity to lead our people through the times to come, but Najim has shown an adaptability I never expected. The vote has not been made, but I suspect she will take my place."

"We trust in the wisdom of the Elders," Grendor replied, almost by rote. Then he smiled. "I have faith in your choice. But—"

"L… Lord Odara?"

Jeran turned at the tremulous sound to find a young woman, no more than sixteen winters, in an apprentice's uniform. The girl's face was ashen, her eyes wide, her lips trembling. She tried to speak but could not find her voice. Seeing her broke the blocks Jeran had wound around the emotions in his head, and fear and pain surged forth, nearly knocking him to his knees in a tornado of frenetic agony. With no small amount of effort he steadied himself. "Yes?"

"He was there," she said, and tears streamed from her eyes. "I was on watch, and he came!" Jeran closed the distance between them and put his arms on her shoulders. For the first time he noticed that she clutched something in her hand. "His eyes! How can you stand to look into his eyes?"

"Shhh." Jeran stroked a hand through the apprentice's hair, and she collapsed into him, sobbing. A quick glance showed Katya studying him from the shadows, and Yassik stared at him too, a deep frown pulling at his features. He started toward them, but Jeran waved him back. "Did the Orog—"

"No!" the apprentice said with a vehemence Jeran had not expected. "When the Darklord appeared, they moved to attack, but he said something in Ourok, and they stopped. They still obey him!"

"I'm sure they had their reasons. I will learn the truth of it." Inside, Jeran fumed. *They were to kill him if he returned here! Why did they disobey me? When I find out who ignored my orders...* "Did he hurt you? Has the alarm been sounded? How many others were with him? Why—?"

"He... He was alone. He said he had a message to deliver, and a gift. I tried to run, to sound the alarm, but his eyes... They held me as if by magic, but I *know* his magic can't pass through the Boundary. Can it?"

Her terror had returned in full force; Jeran felt it as well as saw it painted across her face. "No, not even Lorthas's magic can cross the Boundary. He... Did you say a gift? For me?"

Trembling, she held out the timeworn volume. A spider web of cracks covered the binding, and a few dark spots marred the yellowed pages. "He said any man opposing the Assembly should read this first, that the secrets held within its pages would open your eyes to frightening new possibilities. He said he underestimated you, and that he wishes you better success than he enjoyed. He..." Her lips tightened down, and the set of her jaw said that she fought the urge to give voice to the rest of Lorthas's words.

"What else did he say?" Jeran asked, and when she did not speak, a hard edge entered his voice. "Tell me!"

She struggled with herself but finally relented. "He said, 'The Assembly makes Darklords of those they fear. I wore the title proudly—I thought at the time for the greater good—but only after they nailed it to my chest. Don't make my mistake. If you wear a crown long enough, you begin to think yourself a king.' "

The words resonated in Jeran's ears. The apprentice held out the book, and Jeran took it from her. As soon as he touched it a Reading flared, filling his head with a myriad of confusing images. In an instant Jeran had the vision controlled, but he stared at the leather bound volume as if it might attack. *What events has this book witnessed that it tries to force them upon the world so?*

"What is that?" Yassik asked. Jeran had not heard him approach.

He waved the older Mage back. "What's your name, apprentice?"

"Elisan."

"Return to the Academy. Tell Oto that you're to be spared sentry duty for a ten-day. Devote yourself to your studies and do your best to forget what you saw. And remember, the Boundary protects us."

She bowed her head. "May it protect us forever." She left at a stately pace, but as soon as she thought she could not be seen, Elisan sprinted down the tunnel.

Jeran held the volume up to the light, turning it over in his hands. The tingling of the Readings danced around him, and Jeran felt them surge against him several more times, but now that he was ready for it, they proved no threat. Gold letters, faded until they could barely be read were stamped across the front. *The Forge of Faith.*

"What is that?" Yassik asked again, stepping in close. With exaggerated calm, he reached for the book. "Let me see it!"

Jeran snatched the volume away. "You forget yourself. I'm not one of your students. You don't command me." Realizing he had revealed something with his overt interest in the book, Yassik turned away.

"Do you know what this is?" Jeran asked.

"It's a book."

"Are you playing games with me?"

"How am I supposed to know any more if you won't let me see it?"

"Just once, I'd like a straight answer from—"

"No!" Grendor's strangled cry cut Jeran off, and he whirled to face his friend. Grendor still crouched by the Eldest's side, flinging tears from his cheeks with the violence of his head shaking. Craj held Grendor's arm in a tight grip. "It's too much! Too much!"

"When Najim becomes Eldest, someone will have to take her place," Craj said. His words carried the sound of weary repetition. "There are none better suited than you."

"There are many with more experience," Grendor answered. His skin had flushed dark grey, and panic danced in his eye. "Many with more winters to their lives."

"Far more than age goes into choosing an Elder," Craj explained. "A true Elder must have wisdom and experience, honor and compassion. All know of life in the *ghrat*, but our future no longer lies in the tunnels. We are free to travel the world, and you are the only one who knows of the world.

"There are others"—Craj's trembling arm swept the cavern in a gesture that took in all of Dranakohr—"who covet the position of Elder, and a few who could serve adequately. But they still see the world as it was. They don't understand the meaning of freedom, or the value of it. The Orog need a new vision to match our new lives. You, Grendor, see that vision clearest. We have waited for one such as you for a long time."

Jeran approached, and the old Orog grabbed his sleeve. "We have waited for you both. You have my gratitude. And my sorrow."

Confusion plastered itself on Grendor's face. "Sorrow, Eldest?"

"You walk a dangerous path through troubled times, my child. The Mother has shown me that our people will endure, but with all that we have yet to face, I wonder how many will survive to see the future."

"To reach the peak of serenity," Grendor said, his voice low, "one must cross the valley of despair and brave the crags of uncertainty."

"You see," Craj chuckled, the breath hissing through thin lips. "You speak like an Elder already."

"You should go now," Yassik said, stepping up beside them. "The Eldest needs rest."

"Rest I will have plenty of, soon enough," Craj replied, but a fit of coughing stole his words. After he regained his breath, he looked on the verge of exhaustion. "Though perhaps a short slumber would do me well. We will speak soon, Grendor. I have much to tell you, if the Goddess grants me the time."

Jeran bowed to the Eldest and started from the chamber. Yassik moved in on his left. "About that book…"

The pain and fear in the back of Jeran's mind exploded outward without warning, crashing over him like a wave upon the shore. Agony twisted his muscles, and he stumbled, fighting the urge to retch. The cries of thousands echoed in his ears, begging for help, pleading for mercy, praying for salvation. He heard them, heard them all, and he felt their terror as if it were his own. One by one those voices silenced, but new ones rose to take their place. Throughout it all, the pain and fear lingered, amplified, until it pressed upon Jeran with a weight greater than that of the mountain beneath which he stood.

He lurched toward Katya, and as his knees buckled, she caught him and lowered him to the *leintou*'s floor. "What's happening?" she demanded, and Jeran saw concern in her emerald eyes.

He shoved the ancient text into her hands. "Don't let Yassik touch this," he commanded before the next wave crashed over him, sending him reeling into a world of darkness.

CHAPTER 4

Jeran hovered over a sea of infinite darkness broken by a myriad of flashing lights. Spheres of varying size and color twinkled beneath, flirting and dancing through the expansive emptiness. No sounds permeated the otherworldly night; no bitter winds battered his face with the fury of the Boundary.

With consciousness came the realization that he was alone. Blissfully and completely alone. Gone were the flitting thoughts and random insights, gone the constant sensation of others' pain, and the only emotions in his head were his own. That fear remained the dominant one brought no comfort, and he drew in a slow breath, relishing the quiet, calming his nerves.

He had been in this place many times, and for reasons most would consider foolhardy at best. Below him drifted the souls of Madryn, each unique, each remarkably similar. The dimmer lights belonged to those awake, the brighter to the dreamers. With time and patience, Jeran could find anyone he knew among that pool of stars, but only one soul did he know by appearance alone, and even as he sought it out a knot of dread tightened in his gut.

Lorthas's presence was unmistakable; streaks of red, gold and black pulsed through a sphere of blinding white, far brighter than any of its neighbors, and as Jeran drifted toward the orb he matched the beat of his heart to its pulsing. With his mind, he reached out to it, and upon contact the world blurred.

Jeran stood in a chamber reminiscent of the Assembly Hall on Atol Domiar. A domed ceiling stretched to impossible heights above, with narrow staircases wrapped around the circular hall leading to dozens of latticed balconies. On the floor, row upon row of benches on a gentle slope faced a raised platform. Few seats remained empty, and the clamor of thousands drowned out rational sound.

Lorthas entered through the main doorway and strode toward the center of the platform, and the hall erupted in a harmony of cheers and angry shouts. Immaculate white robes matched the pristine purity of his shoulder-length curls, and blood red eyes burned with the power of the Gift, but Lorthas's gaze held no malice and only a fraction of the self-righteousness Jeran had come to associate with the Darklord. At the center of the dais, Lorthas raised his hand, and the hall fell silent.

"Alrendria's war with the Arkam Imperium is over." The cheers overpowered Lorthas, and he had to wait for the hall to quiet again. "What King Carstellian's vaunted Guard could not do in ten winters, I and the brave Magi who fought with me have done in one. The peace High Wizard Aemon—with his millennia of experience!—failed to negotiate, I have made a reality. I—"

"You act the hero, Lorthas," one Mage said from the floor, "but this war was your creation. If not for you—"

"If not for me, Jiulan, the Arkamians would be outside this hall, and the Assembly would still be debating whether or not they posed a threat. No matter what rumors flit around the Academies, I did not design this war, and I did not start it. But I did end it, and the world will remember that the Magi—not me, but the Magi!—saved them from themselves."

"Yet you failed to destroy the Arkam Imperium!" shouted a voice from the balconies. "You failed to bring those lands back into Alrendria. Isn't that what you wanted? Isn't that what you claim is needed?"

"The Assembly authorized me to end the war, and I had neither permission nor authority to do more. Yes, I believe the Imperium represents the single greatest threat to Alrendria. Yes, I feel such a threat is the force needed to unify the Four Races and bring about an era of peace. And yes, I would like to see nothing more than the blight of the Imperium stripped off the face of Madryn. But I am a Mage of this Assembly, and bound by its decisions. There—"

"Your claim of obedience to this Assembly is quite convenient," Jiulan said, folding his arms across his chest and facing the Darklord with an imperious stare. "Your devotion to our decisions did not prevent you from destroying dozens of Arkamian villages, even though you were expressly ordered not to take the battle into the Imperium."

"I was asked to put an end to the Arkamian invasion of Alrendria." Anger danced in Lorthas's eyes, but not a shred of it entered his voice. "Pushing their armies back to the border would not have been sufficient. We had to eliminate their ability to stage another attack. Furthermore, the Assembly's instructions were never violated. My people never left Alrendria."

"Semantics! Using the Gift to flatten villages from across the border is not what the Assembly intended when they authorized you to intercede on behalf of Alrendria. If you had obeyed my orders as they were intended instead of—"

"Then the Arkamians would have resumed their assault as soon as my Magi were gone, and you'd be berating me in front of the Assembly for my failure in such a simple matter." The Gift flared in Lorthas's eyes, making them glow like smoldering embers, and his affected smile slipped. The scowl that replaced it darkened his features and made the very air of the chamber crackle with threat.

"Was that your plan from the start, Jiulan? To discredit me before the Assembly? In that, you have failed, and you've lost whatever remained of my respect for—You! What are you doing here?"

Lorthas's eyes settled on Jeran, and the rage he had directed at the Mage Jiulan transferred easily to Jeran. The Assembly Hall wavered and buckled, the ceiling descended, and the walls raced toward Jeran with enough speed to make his stomach flutter. The Magi faded from sight or were consumed by the collapsing chamber, but Lorthas stood unaffected, moving with the room without taking a step, and when the dais sank into the floor, Jeran found himself standing face to face with the Darklord in a simple chamber of unadorned stone. A single window showed snow blanketing rolling lands, and a wind to rival the gales of Dranakohr howled outside.

"After all your talk of respecting other's privacy, you force your way into *my* dreams?"

The passion had left the Darklord's voice, but the slight smile he wore terrified Jeran far more than any amount of anger. He knew enough of the Twilight World to know he was safe from Lorthas—as long as he believed himself safe—but the Darklord's grin hinted at an unexpected victory, and Jeran wondered which of his actions had made Lorthas feel triumphant.

Jeran raised his hand, and an image of the leather bound volume appeared. "Why did you risk your life to bring this to Dranakohr?"

"I was in no danger, though your concern is touching." A gesture of his own made two chairs appear, and Lorthas motioned for Jeran to sit. When he did not, the Darklord sighed and the chairs vanished. "Orog are such noble creatures. Convince them you've come on a matter of honor, and they'll almost always let you live. I find it amusing that the Races' strengths often prove to be their weaknesses, don't you?"

"Whatever you hoped to gain by bringing this to me, you've failed." No emotion tempered Jeran's words, though his insides roiled with fear. To win the upper hand on Lorthas, you had to convince him you were in better control of the situation than he was. Jeran did not know what game Lorthas played, or what was at stake, but he had no intention of losing.

"You read it?" Lorthas asked, searching Jeran's eyes for the answer. "No. You don't trust me enough, and I suppose with some justification. The book is no ploy on my part. It's intended neither as a distraction nor a ruse. I'm not trying to subvert you or bring about your fall. If anything, I'm envious! And I want to help however I can. That book has some ideas you'll find enlightening."

The sincerity of the Darklord's words staggered Jeran. "Envious?" he repeated, stilling the trembling of his hand. All moisture had left his mouth, and he fought to speak without rasping the words, fought to hide the confusion from his eyes. "Help me? Why?"

"With little training and barely enough winters—even by Common standards!—to call yourself a man, you defied the Assembly and split the Magi. It took me a millennium to find the courage to attempt the same feat, and with barely better success. Worse, in a handful of seasons you've come closer than I ever did to creating a truly egalitarian society in the heart of Alrendria.

"I should hate you for making my life's work seem like so much wasted time, but you'll have enemies enough without me, and any efforts I made to thwart you would only be out of hubris and counter to my goals. We're fighting for the same things, Jeran, though ironically we're fighting each other, too. The MageWar has three factions now: one trying to preserve the systems that led Madryn to its current state, and two struggling to create a better world. We're allies of a sort, and I'm glad to know the odds are in our favor."

"We are not allies, and we are not alike!" The lock Jeran held on his emotions snapped, and his own bottled up rage surged forth, given extra force by the revulsion he felt at the part of him that agreed with Lorthas. "You rule through fear. You care nothing for the lives you crush in your attempts to seize power. You use the likes of Tylor and Salos to further your goals, and even allied with the same Arkam Imperium you've accused of being the greatest evil Madryn had ever seen."

"Don't confuse indifference to suffering with acceptance that suffering is necessary. Knowing that my actions ended so many innocent lives hangs on my conscience, but the choices I made were essential, the sacrifice required. The Assembly vilifies me for the destruction wrought upon Madryn, but it was they who brought Madryn into our fight, not I."

Lorthas's grin grew wider. To him, Jeran's loss of control signaled a victory. "As for fear, it's a tool like any other, and harnessed properly it can be a powerful one. But it's not universal. Inside *Ael Shataq* I'm loved as much as loathed. As the legend surrounding your name grows, you'll find fear growing as well. Even now, I wonder how many of your followers are suspicious of your Gift, how many wonder what your true objectives are."

Fear thrived in most of his people, but in those whose emotions he could sense, Jeran knew that fear was not of him. *What of the thousands I can't sense? I've seen some avert their eyes when I near, or turn and run.* "Be that as it may, it doesn't explain how you can ally with the likes of the Durange or the Imperium."

Lorthas's sigh carried a weariness that transcended time. "To accomplish any goal, one must use the tools on hand. Unifying the Four Races and ridding Alrendria of intolerance was always my ambition. Using the Imperium to further my goals was not a light decision, and there are still days when I doubt the wisdom of my decision, but I knew that once the Assembly had been replaced, my Magi and I could deal with the Imperium.

"As for the Durange... To prepare Madryn for the Boundary's fall, I needed tools with access to your world. Salos is a heartless monster, but he knows his place, and Tylor's ambitions for a time coincided with my own. In the end, Tylor proved unstable, but I wanted—indeed, I tried!—to replace him long before his demise. Had you been more cooperative, his reign would have been far shorter, and once you had mastered your Gift, we could have dealt with Salos as well."

"You think you can placate me so easily? If I've learned anything about you, it's how good you are at taking bits of truth and weaving them into a tapestry of deception. You can't hide behind the actions of others, Lorthas. The evils committed by those under your command are your evils, regardless of whether you'd do the same thing in their place. I—"

"Such naivety," Lorthas chuckled. "I sometimes forget how young you are. Talk to me of right and wrong after you've lived a few hundred winters. Tell me how you feel responsible for every misdeed committed by every individual in your service after you've finished this war. Once you've been knocked off that pedestal you're preening on, we might be able to discuss such matters with some degree of intelligence."

Jeran scowled, and he broke his connection to the Twilight World. As the world faded to black, he heard Lorthas say, "Read the book. I look forward to your next visit."

His eyes snapped open, and Jeran sat up, but he nearly toppled over again when a wave of nausea hit him. His head pounded, and spots of color danced in front of his eyes. He ignored it all and struggled to regain control of his body as he steadied himself.

He was in his chambers, on a cot by the fire. Katya sat in the corner, absently sharpening a dagger. Across from her stood Dahr, arms crossed and Shyrock perched on one shoulder. Neither so much as flinched when Jeran moved. The tension between them had the solidity of a wall, and the silence carried all the foreboding of a waking volcano.

Between the two stone-faced statues, Yassik lounged in a cushioned chair. When Jeran threw off his blankets, the Mage sat forward. "We need to talk. I have—"

Jeran cut him off with a gesture. "Why are you here?" he asked, turning to Katya.

"You have enemies everywhere," she said, her eyes never leaving his. Her hands slid the sharpening stone across the blade in a blur. "I would not have you attacked while unable to defend yourself."

A frown pulled at Jeran's lips, and his gaze snapped to the other side of the room. "And you?"

"She refused to leave," Dahr said, using his chin to point at Katya. "I won't allow a Durange to guard your sleep unattended."

Yassik cleared his throat. "Jeran, what I—"

"Quiet, Yassik!" Jeran snapped. The fear and pain roiled through the back of his mind, distant and foreboding, but they translated to anger when he spoke. The Mage stiffened, but he settled back in his seat without another word. Jeran ignored his sulking; he would have time for Yassik shortly.

"Was I out long?"

"It's nearly morning," Katya and Dahr said simultaneously. Then they glared at each other as if each had been insulted.

This must end. They can fight it out or come to terms with what happened, but I need them focused. "Stop mooning over each other like lovesick children! There are serious matters that require our attention." Katya stiffened as if struck, and a stark anger clouded Dahr's eyes. *Good, he will need that anger in the days to come.*

"Dahr, Harol Grondellan is stationed in the outer wall. Tell him to assemble his men in the main courtyard by sunrise. Then go into the *ghrat* and find Grendor. I need him and two dozen of the *choupik*. The best of them. Katya, do you remember an apprentice named Kile? Sandy hair, dark eyes. Can't look at you without stammering and blushing? Find him and send him here. Then tell Ehvan and Alwen to meet us in the courtyard."

"Why don't you let her find the Orog and the… Rachannan?" Dahr suggested. "I'll find this boy—"

"Because I need him found quickly, and she knows where to look. We have discussed this before. I have reasons for what I do, and I don't need you questioning my every decision. If there's some reason you feel incapable of finding Lord Grondellan or Grendor, tell me. If not, then do as you're ordered. If I can't count on you for a simple request like this, how can I count on you for anything?"

Shyrock screeched, and Dahr's hands clenched into fists. "Where are we going?" he asked through clenched teeth.

Reasons for all your decisions? What reason do you have to goad him like this? "We're going to war. Bring Fang and Jardelle. We won't be back for a while."

Anticipation replaced anger, and a grin spread across Dahr's face as he started toward the door. Katya moved to follow him out, but Jeran stopped her. "Where's the book?"

Katya glanced at Yassik, then her eyes slid to the pillow upon which Jeran had slept. "There," she said. "He asked for it twice since getting here. Just to take a look." Her eyes slid back to the Mage, distrust radiating from her gaze. A word from Jeran sent her into the hall.

Jeran reached beneath his pillow and withdrew the volume. He let his hand trace the cover, careful to keep his eyes on Yassik. The Mage's earlier surprise had faded—the mere sight of the book could no longer distract him—and his features remained a mask of perfect composure. "Jeran, we need to talk about—"

"I don't have time for one of your lectures, Yassik. I have to leave for…" The words trailed off when Jeran opened the cover and read the inscription.

Lorthas
We have our differences, you and I, but we want the same things for the Assembly. The world is a forge, and the events we must suffer through will test our mettle. I know you look only to the future, but read this, and in the wisdom of the past you'll find what you need to endure.
—Yassik

A whirlwind of thought spun through Jeran's mind. "You… were friends with Lorthas before the MageWar? Why—"

Yassik heaved a sigh. "I would hardly call us friends. He—"

"Allies, then. You worked together."

"For a time, we shared a common purpose. Alwen and I—"

"Alwen too?" Inside, Jeran seethed, but he kept a tight rein on his temper. "I should have known. What other secrets have you been keeping from me?"

"Every Mage who lived before the MageWar knew Lorthas," Yassik snapped, rising to his feet. Jeran had never seen the old Mage so angry. He strode forward with a commanding presence, the fire of the Gift burning in his eyes despite their proximity to the Boundary. "He was once a great Mage, with high ideals and a noble purpose, certain to be Aemon's successor. Condemning us casts a darker light on you than it does on Alwen or I. At least we worked with Lorthas *before* he was named Darklord!"

Without thinking, Jeran opened himself to magic. Energy poured into him, and he wove the multi-hued strands into a tapestry. An instant before he unleashed his Gift, he realized what he was about to do and severed his connection. Cutting himself off took a great deal of effort, and the Boundary fought him every step of the way, but as the last glimmer of power faded, he heard the anger and fear clamoring in the back of his mind, seeking an escape.

"Good," Yassik said, taking his seat. His too pale face and quick breathing contrasted his calm façade. "You're not too far gone, then."

"What... What are you talking about?" Readings danced off the book in Jeran's hand, but he ignored them. Something in Yassik's bearing, something more than the terror hidden in the recesses of his eyes, worried him.

"How much do you know of the BattleMagi?"

Jeran fell back onto his bed, pondering the question. "As much as anyone not a Mage, I guess. They were warrior-Magi, men who held themselves to the strictest code. Why?"

"Do you know any by name?"

"Tyre," Jeran answered. "I've seen him in several Readings. He—"

"Any others?" Yassik asked, and when Jeran shook his head he muttered, "It figures. Dozens of BattleMagi, and he only knows the exception." Yassik turned his gaze to the window, his eyes distant and calculating, and Jeran watched the wind whip up swirls of snow on the craggy slopes.

"I'll give you some names," Yassik said after a time, "and you tell me what you know of them. Salizar. Jolam Strongarm. Mariska Mazihara. Viritas. Paladian. Isa—"

"They were commanders during the MageWar," Jeran answered. "Revered for their skill in battle, feared for their cruel and ruthless treatment of the enemy. I know more of Jolam Strongarm than..." Understanding dawned, and Jeran could not hide his shock. "You're saying *they* were BattleMagi?"

"Each and every one," Yassik replied. "And quite a few besides. What made them unique was—"

"I really don't have time for this," Jeran said, crossing the room and stuffing clothes into a small travel pack. "There's something—"

"Make time! Pack if you must, but you have to listen to what I'm telling you."

The concern in Yassik's plea won Jeran over. "Very well," he said, stuffing another outfit into the pack and reaching for his *dolchek*. After buckling the sheath to his belt, he took the curved blade and ran a sharpening stone down its length.

"I've told you before that the Gift demands balance from those who use it." Yassik paced the chamber, his hands clasped behind his back. "For those who seek a deeper understanding of one aspect of magic, a price must be paid. Healers can all but bring back the dead, but any harm they cause to others is revisited upon them tenfold. Learning to work magic into objects robs a MageSmith of his life; for some reason, MageSmiths do not Slow as much as—"

"You've told me all this before! I—"

"Do you know what trade a BattleMage makes?"

"I... No... I thought a BattleMage was just a Mage who used his Gift in combat."

"And that's your biggest weakness, Jeran. You think you understand every-thing about the world. That you understand more than most only feeds your delu-sion." Chagrinned, Jeran resolved to hold his tongue until Yassik finished.

"Any Mage can use magic in battle," Yassik continued, "but most of us don't fight with blade or bow. The Gift is our weapon, and the proper use of it can make a single Mage more dangerous than a thousand swordsmen. However, the very thing that makes us a threat in the field is also our greatest weakness. When focus-ing magic, a Mage is vulnerable. The effort required to weave the flows makes it all but impossible to defend ourselves."

"I know what you mean," Jeran said. "In the battle for Dranakohr, there were several times when I nearly lost control of the Gift because I was forced to defend myself."

"That you did not die the first time—and take half this mountain with you—only confirms what I'm about to tell you." Yassik waved off Jeran's questions. "A BattleMage has training in arms, but more than that, a BattleMage develops the ability to use magic and steel simultaneously, seamlessly flowing from one to the other as the situation requires."

"That doesn't sound like a bad trade," Jeran said.

"You are a terrible student," Yassik told him. "It's customary to wait until the end of a lecture before making comments. A BattleMage also forms a bond with those dependent upon them. Once a person pledges themselves to a BattleMage, they draw strength from him. Through the bond, their loyalty is amplified until they'll follow any order without question; their resolve is strengthened so they'll face any foe no matter the odds. So long as the BattleMage lives, they draw on his strength.

"The bond works both ways, though, and in return for sharing his strength, the BattleMage feels the pain of his people. When they hunger, his gut clenches; when they're injured, the BattleMage feels an echo of the pain. He senses their emotions: fear or anger, happiness or grief. When one of the bonded dies, the Bat-tleMage shares that death, and the memories of the pain he causes his people stays with him throughout his life.

"The people I named… Jolam Strongarm, Paladian and the other BattleMa-gi, they cultivated their reputations. The men and women under their command worshipped them, and they returned that love, but they wanted—maybe even needed!—to be feared by the rest of Alrendria. To be assaulted by the fears and failings of so many…

"Tyre was the only exception, loved by all, respected by even his staunchest foes. I have never witnessed such a transformation in all my life. In his youth, Tyre's voice rang with laughter, and the smile he wore brightened a room. By the time of his death in Shandar, despair dogged his every step, and grief over the deaths he had caused—not his enemies', but the deaths of those who served him—haunted him."

"This is all very fascinating," Jeran said, driving his *dolchek* into its sheath. He stood and strapped on his sword, then went to the door. "But I don't see how any of this…" He opened the door, revealing a young, sandy-haired man poised on the verge of knocking. The apprentice, startled by Jeran's appearance, stepped back. From the way he puffed air, it seemed as if he had run all the way from the Academy.

"You needed me?" Kile asked.

"A moment," Jeran said, turning back to Yassik. "You think *I'm* a BattleMage?"

"I don't think it, boy, I know it. If the ever-present sense I have of your well being isn't proof enough, then the strange insights Katya tells me you've been having of late is, or the way you just happened to know the boy was here. Like it or not, Jeran, you're on the road to becoming a BattleMage. You need to continue your training before the emotions whirling through your mind drive you mad."

"And who can teach me?" Jeran asked. "You? Tyre was the last BattleMage, and he died decades ago. Besides, I never devoted myself to any aspect of the Gift, much less—"

"Not consciously, perhaps. But something about you, or about the way you approach magic, is turning you into a BattleMage. And no, that's not something I can help you with, exactly, but there are those who can help you find the path, even if they don't walk it themselves. They're waiting for you—"

"I know where they are; I received their cryptic messages. And I'll go to them. But another event demands my attention first." Yassik frowned—from his stance he had expected an argument—but he said nothing as Jeran turned back to the doorway.

"Come in, Kile." He stepped aside to allow the apprentice entry. "Oto tells me you're progressing very rapidly with your training. Have you learned how to make a Gate yet?"

"Yes, Lord Odara."

"How many men can you transport?"

"I moved seven to Vela the other day, but any more and I start to get sick."

"Seven? That's pretty good," Jeran said. "But how many do you think you can Gate without killing yourself?"

CHAPTER 5

Kile collapsed on the grass of Dranakohr and his Gate wavered, folding in upon itself. Two Orog women rushed to help the unconscious apprentice, and when the Orog touched him, the Gate disappeared with a loud pop.

He transported twelve men, Jeran thought. *I shouldn't have asked him to move more than eight, but what choice did I have? He knows this place well.*

When the Gate closed, Kile's incapacitating nausea changed from a sharp stab to a gentle quiver in the back of Jeran's mind, like the notes plucked on a harp. That he could still differentiate the apprentice's presence from all the others in his head despite the leagues separating them concerned Jeran, but the knowledge that the boy survived brought a measure of joy. Kile had learned to create a Gate quickly, and that he had the strength to transport so many made Jeran confident the changes he was making in Dranakohr were working. *They'll be ready by the time I need them. They have to be!*

Smoke hung in the air, casting a murky shadow and filling the crisp air with an acrid stench. Of the handful of buildings visible, only two were untouched; the others lay in various states of collapse. Snow and ash mixed until it was impossible to tell how much of the ground's thick blanket belonged to each. The crackle of fire came from all around, and several distant structures blazed like giant torches, beacons calling from the gloom. Against the corner of one crumbled building hunched a body, the hilt of a sword clutched in its frozen hand. The remains of the blade, twisted and half melted, lay several hands away on the edge of a dark pool.

Somewhere far off a scream pierced the darkness and phantom pain sliced across Jeran's chest, but it hurt no more than a scrape and disappeared when the shriek cut off. Katya's blade slipped free of its sheath, not because of the scream but because of the eerie silence that followed. Grendor and the *choupik* tensed, *va'dasheran* spinning into defensive positions. Ehvan and the soldiers he insisted on bringing formed a knot around Jeran, but of them all, only Ehvan did not radiate terror. The five Magi looked calm, but the flare of light around them showed that each had seized the Gift.

Only Dahr and the Rachannen seemed unfazed. Through the muted bond they shared, Jeran sensed anticipation from Dahr, and the way his fingers flexed and unflexed around the hilt of his greatsword confirmed that feeling. Harol Grondellan yawned and pulled an axe from its hook over his shoulder. The other Rachannen studied their surroundings, but few so much as reached for their blades.

"Where are we?" Harol asked. With a sound like a roaring monster, a building collapsed, sending stone and wood flying and adding more dust to the darkening sky. "It looks like you've brought us halfway to the Nothing."

"May the Mother have mercy on us!" Grendor said, his eye wide enough to rival the patch he wore. "I know this place. This is—"

"Portal," Jeran told them. "It was attacked last night. Before you ask, I don't know by whom or how many, nor do I know if the keep is intact or if the path to *Ael Shataq* is secure." Readings danced around him, several with a resonance different than the others, a freshness. Jeran opened himself to those. "Tachans. And ShadowMagi." The image of Keldon Durange, Tylor's favorite son, danced in Jeran's eyes even after he severed his connection to the Reading.

He focused on the fear, pain, and hopelessness coursing through his consciousness, trying to separate the closer souls from those farther away. "There are pockets of resistance throughout the city, and a larger concentration of allies to the north, either in Portal Keep or the wall beyond."

At Jeran's command, Ehvan produced a map of Portal from the pack he wore. "Dahr, I can guess where our allies are hiding, but I can't sense our enemies. I'm going to need your friends."

Dahr looked at Shyrock, and the golden eagle cocked its head to one side. After a moment, he launched into the air, disappearing into the smoke. "He won't be able to see much through this," Dahr admitted, "but the fires will have scared away most of the local beasts. I'll do my best, but trained animals—"

"Just do what you can." Jeran sensed several people, but only one group large enough to matter. He pointed to a fortified structure marked on the map. "Some of our people are to the south. My guess is that they're here. We'll go there first and bolster our numbers, then make our way toward the keep."

Another scream cut through the haze, and the wind howled down from the Boundary, swirling the smoke and lifting it up. For a moment the view cleared, and they saw Portal aflame. Fires raged in every quarter of the city, billowing dark smoke and ash like miniature volcanoes. Even the towers of the keep smoldered, and before the dark gray swirls closed in again, a ball of fire slammed into the wall of the castle with a bone-grinding crash.

"The enemy is among us," Jeran said, "and we don't know their numbers. But they don't know we're here. Move quietly, follow orders, and I'll see you out of here alive." *Most of you.* "Grendor, have the *choupik* spread out. If we spot ShadowMagi, Yassik and the others will distract them, but the quickest way to eliminate them is with your touch. In this haze, they won't be able to see you coming until it's too late.

"Ehvan. Wardel. Guard the Magi. They must leave here alive." The words he did not speak—*You and the other Commons aren't as important*—galled him, and knowing it was true did not make him feel better about it.

"Harol?" Lord Grondellan, a bear of a man with a bushy, graying beard and an eager smile stepped forward. "Your men have more experience in combat, especially in these conditions. I don't want you to think—"

"If you wanted to rid yourself of these poor excuses for soldiers," Harol laughed, flicking his fingers toward the Rachannen, "you could do it with a wave of your hand. If you need some fools to lead a charge against an unknown enemy in conditions worse than a blizzard on Mount Kalan, then you've asked the right fools." A hearty laugh roared up from his gut, and he clapped Dahr on the shoulder. "By the Gods, we could leave the rest behind and take on this army alone, eh, Hunter?"

Dahr grinned, but then he remembered who had spoken and a hint of grimace entered the expression. "There are a handful of men north and west of here, moving away," he said. "A large concentration in the plaza outside the castle, and a smaller one south of us. There are other groups moving around the city, but friend or foe...?"

"It's good enough," Jeran said, turning south. "We'll gather more men and work our way toward the keep. If you learn anything more, just tell me."

He chose his path carefully, stepping around loose debris, and the others picked up on his mood, falling silent. Everyone, even the Rachannen, wore the new Odaran uniform, and ghosting through the smoke-filled streets they looked like *shini-kami*, the death angels from Aelvin lore, hunting for souls in the Twilight World.

Shadows played and danced off the ruined buildings, and Ehvan's men jumped at every unexpected movement. The Rachannen chuckled at their timidity, but even they made no comment about the Orog. The *choupik* darted from building to building like statues come alive, and when motionless they blended into the gray rock and dark shadows. Gone were the jovial smiles; the Orog stalked the streets of Portal like predators.

A mound of rubble blocked the road ahead, and Jeran signaled for silence as he neared it. He seized magic, allowing a trickle of energy to flow into him, and extended his perceptions. He signaled for Dahr and Harol to join him and crawled to a better vantage point.

Three score men stood outside the only fully standing building on the block. Scars and pits marred the gray stone fortification, and a crack ran from the foundation to the apex of the main turret, but a half dozen archers manned the walls, taking careful aim at the attackers below.

Under cover of shields, the Tachans rushed the door with a battering ram fashioned from an inn's ceiling joist. Their first blow hammered the door with little effect, and the rain of arrows from the battlements took out two, but the Tachans pulled back and rammed again. This time, the door shuddered. Only a handful of arrows fell, and none hit their marks. The Tachans returned a full volley that sent the Guardsmen scurrying for cover.

"No ShadowMagi here," Harol said, his dark eyes surveying the field. "Else this building would be rubble like the others."

"It's only a matter of time," Jeran replied. "Like as not they've already sent for reinforcements. I just don't understand why they didn't wait for—"

"There are more men coming." Dahr's hand shot out to the west. "A dozen soldiers and at least two ShadowMagi."

Jeran crept down the pile and back to the party. "Grendor, lead the *choupik* around the plaza and see if you can sneak up behind the ShadowMagi. Falkon, go with them." The Mage nodded, and he and his guards ran north behind the Orog. "Yassik, take the other Gifted into those buildings and see if you can find a place to support our attack without being seen."

Ehvan looked stricken. "Lord Odara—!"

"There will be blood and danger aplenty, Ehvan. Guard the Magi for this skirmish, and be ready to race to my rescue if the battle goes sour. Harol, have your men follow me and Dahr. Katya—"

"I go with you."

Jeran started to argue, then thought better of it. "Fine. Stay close to Dahr. When he's communicating with his friends, he doesn't always see what's going on around him. His safety is in your hands." The glare Dahr fixed on him could have flayed the hide from a bull, but Jeran ignored it. Dahr, Katya, and the Rachannen fell into step behind him as he circled south around the fortification.

As he neared the building, the ram slammed against the door with a thunderous crash, splintering it. A cheer went up from the Tachans as they drew back for another assault. Intent on their target, they ignored Jeran's charge until it was too late.

Opening himself to magic, Jeran reveled in the feeling of power that swept through him. The rush of energy heightened his senses and muted the growing well of pain and fear in his head. Paradoxically, he felt the connection to his people strengthen even as their emotions faded; some of the men inside the building he could call by name, and with his eyes closed he could tell in which building Ehvan waited.

He ran into the fray, carving a path through the soldiers he encountered. Dahr shot past him, vaulting over the battering ram and crashing into a cluster of enemy. The Rachannan berserkers trailed behind, screaming in their fervor for blood, weapons swinging with an anticipation to rival a starving man at a midwinter feast. The Tachans faltered, and their disorganization cost them whatever chance they had to withstand the attack.

The ram fell and the Tachans fled, their leaders shouting for them to regroup. Their path took them toward Ehvan, and a hail of arrows fell. Screams echoed through the air, but instead of sending chills down Jeran's spine, these screams brought a morbid sense of satisfaction.

"Stop them here!" Jeran shouted as he brought his sword up to fend off an attack.

To his left, the ground erupted in a shower of rock and flame, and several Rachannen arced overhead, falling back to the ground in smoldering heaps. To the north, two black-robed figures rained magic down upon the Alrendrians. A dozen archers surrounded the Gifted, firing arrows as fast as they could notch them, heedless of the Tachans still fighting their way out of the courtyard.

A second explosion rocked the plaza, then a third. Jeran drove his Aelvin blade forward, and the magic-wrought sword slid through his opponent's armor. As the man fell, gurgling and mewling, Jeran opened himself to magic and prepared to meet the ShadowMagi's next attack.

Before he could unleash his Gift, a whirlwind of grey and black descended upon the enemy. The *choupik* burst from the shadows, slicing through the archers before the ShadowMagi could react. Drogon dove through the gap, his *va'dasheran* piercing one black-robed Mage's heart even as he collided with the other. Blade discarded, he wrestled the other man and held him fast while the other *choupik* made short work of the archers. Throughout it all, only the screams of the enemy reached across the courtyard.

With the ShadowMagi gone, Jeran's men surged forward, and Ehvan led his troops from concealment. Trapped between three forces, the Tachans put up little resistance, falling back until Jeran, Ehvan, and Grendor met at the center of the plaza.

Losses were lighter than Jeran expected, but worse than he had hoped. An emptiness echoed throughout his gut, and without looking he could point to the bodies of at least a half dozen of his soldiers. *How many others are dead who weren't bonded to me? Too many. There's still a city to recapture!*

A spatter of bright blood added color to the grey of Grendor's face, and the gaze he leveled on the battlefield held a sadness even deeper than Jeran's. "We caught them unawares, friend Jeran," the Orog said. "But Naris and Josep have gone to meet the Mother."

"The Magi are safe," Ehvan told Jeran. He had seen little of this battle, but his expression held none of the frustration he once would have worn at being kept from the fighting. *Maybe the battle for Dranakohr had a greater effect on him than I thought.*

Dahr prowled the plaza, sword in hand, scanning the bodies for signs of survivors. Jeran wondered what he would do if he found one, then decided he had better not dwell on such things. When Lord Grondellan approached, Dahr stalked away, but if the Rachannan noble realized he was the cause of Dahr's anger, he gave no sign. He followed Dahr through the rubble, poking bodies with his boot and tallying his dead.

"Form a perimeter around this plaza," Jeran ordered. "Have the Magi use their Gift to search for enemy troops, and tell Dahr that if his friends see anything else, he should come to me immediately. I'll be inside."

A terrible crash filled the night, the thunder of crumbling stone as a distant building collapsed, its upper stories engulfed in swirling flames that disappeared in a growing ball of smoke. Jeran walked forward alone, but he carried with him a sense of his men, felt them gathering their courage and hastening to carry out the orders barked by Ehvan, Grendor, and Lord Grondellan. He had a sense of the men inside the broad structure too—some of them—but courage was not high among the emotions they felt. Not yet.

A couple arrows lofted at him from above, but Jeran used his Gift to flick them aside. He did not bother to announce himself or call for the archers to hold; no one who did not already know he was coming was likely to obey. A wave of his hand pushed the battering ram aside, and another thought unhinged the massive timber locking the door and pulled it open amidst the creaking of bent hinges.

The effort of using magic drained Jeran more than he expected, but the sight that confronted him as he crossed the threshold tore at his soul, even though he strove to hide his feelings from those around him.

Wounded, dying, and dead soldiers lay everywhere. Their plaintive cries formed a roll of thunder accentuated by spikes of agonized screaming. Blood slicked a floor littered with debris, discarded weapons, and bodies. A few score men in tattered uniforms clung to the shadows, weapons drawn, eyes wild like cornered beasts. A few tended the wounded, those who had a chance of survival. No one approached him, but Jeran felt their eyes on him.

"I am Jeran Odara," he announced, surprising himself with the steadiness of his voice. "Who commands here?"

"This way, Lord Odara," someone called from the gloom, and Jeran turned toward the sound. A shadow-cloaked form, one of the handful Jeran felt a connection with, crouched beside a body. Jeran moved toward the pair, listening to the thuds of his footfalls, wishing they were loud enough to drown out the cries of his people. *Is Yassik right? Am I becoming a BattleMage? Is this the price I have to pay for a chance at victory?*

Pain lanced his side, burned across his throat, pierced his chest and legs. The pain was an echo though, not his, and Jeran had begun to understand the difference, begun to differentiate the two. *Why didn't I bring my Healers?* A darker thought followed, one that made Jeran hate himself. *I couldn't risk them. I'll need them later.*

Two figures emerged from the darkness: Tourin Talbot kneeling beside the prone form of his brother, Alic. Blood caked Tourin's face and seeped from a bandage wrapped around his arm, but through their bond Jeran knew he faced no danger. Alic did not fare as well. An arrow pierced his chest, a deep gash ran across his gut, and other wounds crisscrossed his flesh.

"He held them back while the men retreated into the guardpost," Tourin said, his voice strained with grief. Jeran felt the man's sadness pouring into him, and wondered what Talbot's son could possibly gain from him. His heart felt as empty as a well in the Feldarian Desert. "I tried to help him, but he ordered me inside. Told me that someone had to save the Portal."

"Lord… Odara?" Alic's eyes fluttered open. Jeran felt nothing from him, but the pain lurking in the man's gaze hurt more than enough. *How can I tell Lord Talbot that I killed his son?* "Lord Odara, is it really you?"

"I'm here, Alic."

Alic chuckled, and blood pooled on his lips. "I hope you brought an army." He winced, and his eyes clouded over. "Tourin… said you were coming."

Jeran looked at Tourin. "I know."

"I didn't believe him." A grimace contorted Alic's face. "I didn't believe in you."

Pain shot through Jeran's arm, just beneath the left shoulder, and his eyes immediately sought the arrow embedded in Alic's chest. A second fire spread across his gut, radiating outward in waves that masked the other injuries he shared. He knelt across from Tourin and put a hand on Alic's brow, wiping away the sweat and grime. "I know."

Alic's hand shot up and grasped Jeran's arm at the shoulder. "I believe now, my Lord. I believe."

Fear faded, replaced by peaceful composure. Life followed, but in those last moments Jeran felt a swell of pride, an eagerness to race into the unknown. "I should have come sooner."

"How could you have known?" Touring asked. "How *did* you know? I—" Tourin cut himself off with a wave of his hand. "You want to atone for something not your fault, then win back this city from the Durange. I can think of no more fitting a memorial for my brother."

Jeran surveyed the room. He had hoped for hundreds, but only a few score men remained able to fight, and terror paralyzed most of those he could sense. Not knowing what else to do, he opened himself to their fear, to the pain of those around him. It hit like a hammer blow, and had he not already been kneeling it would have floored him. But even that simple gesture affected the men, stirring some to step from the shadows. More surprising, the rush of fear, pain, and loss woke something in Jeran, a grim and burning desire to punish those who had caused his people pain.

"Today, the Gods tested Portal," he said, rising to his feet, his words booming across the building, aided by his Gift. "They tested you. I saw the carnage wrought upon this once great city and know what you must think: that you failed that test. You're wrong, my friends. That Portal burns is no sign of failure. That so many lie dead or dying is no sign of weakness.

"Against odds heavy enough to crush the strongest soul, you stood firm. Without so much as a single Gifted among you, you faced the powers of ShadowMagi and did so without flinching. Cornered and outmatched, you kept your oath to Alrendria while your commander planned a counterattack to drive the enemy from your home.

"You think you've failed? Portal Keep still stands. The gateway to *Ael Shataq* remains closed. You've proven yourselves Guardsmen of the first order, and Alrendria should demand nothing more from you save a long and happy life!"

His words roused the men, and a murmur sprang up among them. More emerged from the shadows, and Jeran felt resolve and hope building, pride in what they had accomplished. Terror and pain still dominated, but it was a start.

"I should ask no more of you," he added, "but I must, for now the Gods are testing me. I have men and Magi outside, but not enough to secure the city. I need your help. I need you to raise your swords and follow me into the nightmare. With your aid, we'll retake Portal and send those who dared violate it to the Nothing!"

One soldier hefted his sword above his head, shouting that he would follow Jeran. A few mimicked him, but too many held back. Jeran placed a hand on Alic's chest. "For eight hundred winters, the Wardens of Portal have been buried in the Wall, where they guard the passage into *Ael Shataq* for eternity. Alic was not Warden in name, but his spirit matched those of Portal's greatest leaders. I ask you to help me. Help me win back this city so we can place him where he belongs, with the men who devoted their lives to keeping Alrendria safe. Come with me, and we'll show the Gods that no amount of horror can break the spirit of Alrendrian Guardsmen!"

The soldier cheered again, and this time his cry brought forth a burst of primal emotion from his companions. The chamber vibrated with the force of their shouting, and dozens of new links burst into being. More shadow pain followed, but loyalty, devotion and confidence dulled it to the point that Jeran barely noticed. He drew strength from the men, and the men drew strength from him in a synergistic loop.

Aelvin steel sang as it came free of its scabbard, and Jeran stalked toward the doorway, leading an army three times as large as the one he arrived with.

Dahr paced the edge of the plaza, eager to be on the hunt. The scent of death filled his nostrils, sickening him, exciting him. Out there, somewhere, the enemy waited like unsuspecting game, frolicking through a macabre forest. He hungered for the thrill of the chase, the ferocity of battle, the sweet taste of blood and victory. Anger surged in him like a tide. He had held it in check too long; it yearned to be free.

"You'll wear a hole in the stone, you keep that up," Lord Grondellan said. The Rachannan leaned against the remains of a statue, wiping blood from his axe with a rag torn from a dead soldier. "He won't be long."

"He's been too long already." The voices in Dahr's head clamored and shrieked. There were few, too few for even a city of man, and fear made most of them incoherent. He had tried to calm them at first, tried to tell them help had arrived, but domesticated animals did not hear him as clearly as those in the wild, and the few minds he managed to touch recoiled.

Shyrock and Fang remained anchors in that sea of chaos. Their thoughts came to him like beacons from the darkness, though the foul air and thick smoke made both ineffective at finding prey. A few others had reached out to him as well, rats and carrion birds reaping the rewards of battle. Dahr had called upon them, asked them to be his eyes, promised a feast of corpses for their aid.

A roar reverberated from the building, and a moment later Jeran appeared, leading a host of soot-covered Guardsmen with the fire of fervor in their eyes. Above, the sun strove to push through the gloom, an eerie, barely-visible circle that only added to the strangeness of the day.

Jeran stopped to confer with Ehvan and Tourin, and Dahr's patience reached an end. "Where you goin', lad?" Lord Grondellan asked, hefting his axe onto his shoulder.

"To scout. Jeran will need to know where the enemy is."

"Friend Dahr, do you think that wise?" Grendor stepped from the shadows, appearing as if from nowhere. Startled, Dahr had his *dolchek* half drawn before he realized who had spoken.

"Jeran will need to know where the enemy is." He said nothing else, but Grendor's eye followed him, and Dahr wondered if an Orog's Truthsense could tell when a person spoke only part of the truth.

"You are right, friend Dahr, but you should not go alone. Master Grondellan, will you accompany us?"

A broad grin split Lord Grondellan's face. "I thought you'd never ask. Should I round up my boys?"

"The four of us should be adequate for a scouting party," Katya said. Dahr had almost forgotten her, standing stone-still in the shadow of the alleyway. Her voice sent a grating chill down his spine, even as the sight of her reawakened feelings he had thought long dead, murdered the day she had betrayed him. "It's not like Dahr really intends to hunt down every Tachan himself."

A low growl rose in Dahr's chest, and he fought the urge to charge, to exact payment for what he had lost, for what *she* had cost him. Katya tormented him with the constant reminder of the happiness he might have had, of the man he might have been. He had promised Jeran he would let her live, and that friendship was one of the few things that still mattered to him, even if Jeran's ascendancy was driving a wedge between them. But not killing Katya sometimes took great effort.

Only a monster would attack; a man would honor his friend's wishes. Only a monster would attack; a man would not. Only a monster… The litany drove off the Blood Rage, or suppressed it enough to save Katya's life.

"Will Jeran not worry if we are gone?" Grendor asked.

Katya's musical laughter made Dahr's gut clench. He wanted to be reviled by it, yet something in the sound still drew him. "Jeran will know where we are even if we try to hide from him. You and me, at least."

"A strange ability that," Lord Grondellan said, "to sense where your friends are. But useful, especially when Dahr can see our enemies through walls." His leather mail creaked as he started for the cobbled street. "Let's be about it. We've Durange to kill and a city to retake. No insult intended, lass."

They maneuvered through the narrow alleys and smaller streets, careful to avoid the major thoroughfares and open spaces. Dahr sent out a constant call, asking the Lesser Voices to direct him to his enemy, but the first patrol they stumbled across without warning.

Five enemy soldiers lounged against the shell of a smithy, drinking from soot-covered flasks. Dahr dove at them from his place of concealment, greatsword humming with its thirst for blood. By the time the enemy reacted, Dahr had killed one of them. Katya and Lord Grondellan accounted for two more, and Grendor took the fourth, wielding his *va'dasheran* with a skill Dahr found surprising given the extent of the Orog's injuries.

The fifth man ran, and Dahr chased him. His footfalls pounded the street, and his long strides put distance between him and his companions. On the verge of overtaking the soldier, Fang burst from the shadows and bore the man to the ground. Jaws clamped down, and the Tachan issued a final hiss before lying still.

"That was my kill," Dahr said, and Fang growled.

By the time the others reached him, Shyrock had brought news of another patrol not far from where they stood. The second ambush went better, and the third not much worse, except that one soldier managed to disarm Dahr, forcing him to kill the man with his bare hands.

Then Dahr heard a new voice, an aging hound whose master had been tortured and killed by the Tachans. The hound was too frail to exact revenge but had tracked the murderers. Dahr promised help, and he followed the hound's directions to the Tachan host.

"There's too many, lad," Lord Grondellan said, grabbing Dahr's shoulder and pulling him back. The touch made Dahr's skin crawl, but not killing his former Master was another of Jeran's requests. That the man proved to be so likeable only added to his frustration.

Dahr scanned the intersection again. "I only count twelve."

"And at least one ShadowMage," Katya said, pointing to a shrouded figure standing apart from the others. "He alone makes this attack unwise."

"You don't have to come," Dahr snarled. "But I made a promise."

"To whom?" Lord Grondellan laughed. "The Gods will forgive you if you leave a few alive."

"I make no demands of the Gods and expect the same courtesy from them. These men deserve to die, and I promised a friend they would."

"There will be no talking him out of it," Grendor said. "Ask a stone to float and you will have better luck." The Orog eyed the layout of the intersection, then moved toward a side alley. "Count to fifty, friend Dahr, and the Mage will pose you no threat."

Dahr did the count in his head, fighting the urge to speed the numbers. Days of pent up rage bubbled to the surface, demanding to be acknowledged. The sips of blood had whetted his appetite; the desire to kill consumed him. The stench of burning flesh burned his nose, and a woman's shriek broke the last shred of his control. At a count of thirty-three, Dahr launched himself from concealment, his defiant cry drawing the eyes of the enemy.

These were not sloppy scouts or overconfident fools; these soldiers had their weapons ready in an instant. The ShadowMage raised a hand, and the ground before Dahr erupted, sending him somersaulting. He landed on his hands and knees, greatsword skittering out of reach. He ignored the pain blossoming across his limbs and dove for his blade.

The ShadowMage raised a hand again, but Grendor leapt out of the shadows and grabbed him, severing his connection to the Gift, leaving the Mage screaming and struggling to free himself.

Dahr lost sight of Grendor and concentrated on his own battle. Dodging one man's swing, he drove his sword through the chainmail vest of a second. His empty hand grabbed a third by the throat, and he felt the soldier's windpipe snap before he tossed the man into his companions, knocking several more off balance.

Katya joined him then, her blade a blur of silvered steel, and Lord Grondellan hacked and chopped to his right, axe swinging like a woodsman carving a path through thick brush. The Rachannan held a long dagger in his other hand, and it darted and slashed at anything that slipped around the broad half-moon of his axe blade.

It ended too quickly for Dahr, and as he stood heaving for breath, blood splattered across his face, he silently wished for more. As if in answer, a dozen voices sprang to life, asking for protection, to avenge a loved one, or just to supply him with the information he wanted: the location and number of his enemies.

For the first time in a long while, Dahr felt at peace, and he smiled. He wanted to share his elation, his exhilaration. He looked at Grendor, who stood with one foot on the ShadowMage's back, trying to wrench his *va'dasheran* free. Their eyes met, and the sadness Dahr saw in the Orog's gaze stole some of his joy.

But only some. And only for a moment.

"You're sure this is the place?"

Jeran stared at the gutted building, its stone walls scorched and pitted, its tile roof cracked. The Guardsman nodded with a nervous ferocity. "There's a trapdoor, my Lord, I swear it!" Jeran felt nothing from the man—or from the building—but neither of those things meant the Guardsman was a liar.

"Wait here." Jeran went inside the husk, sword in hand, Gift focused and ready to use. He sent his perceptions ahead, flitting through the rooms in search of danger, but kept aware of his surroundings as well. Twice now he had been caught off guard while scouting the city with his mind. Twice was far too many times to make such a grave mistake in battle.

Tourin had known scores of safe houses where the Guard was to hide in times of emergency, and Jeran had split his burgeoning army into small groups to search them, hoping not only to swell his numbers but also to flush out any remaining pockets of enemy soldiers. They were to rendezvous at midday to begin the final assault, and a quick glance through the paneless window frame told Jeran his time was running out. He quickened his pace, using his Gift to clear a path through the still-smoking rubble.

The trapdoor was in the kitchen behind a butcher's chopping block. Jeran slid the block aside and tugged the door open. He peered into the darkness, then sent his perceptions down. "Hello?" Silence answered his call, and even with his magic-enhanced vision he could not see through total darkness.

He turned away, and an arrow thudded into the wall behind him, missing his shoulder by a finger's width. "Hold!" Jeran cried, throwing himself to the side and using his Gift to ignite a globe of pure white light in the basement. He intended only a modest light, but prompted by the suddenness of the attack his control on magic slipped. White brighter than the midday sun flooded the basement, and a strangled cry echoed up the stairs followed an instant later by the sound of steel rasping against leather.

"I mean you no harm," Jeran said, adjusting the grip on his sword. "I am Jeran Odara, First of House Odara. I've come to defend Portal."

"Lord... Lord Odara?" A tremulous voice climbed the stairs, and Jeran regained control of magic, dimming the light while he encouraged the speaker to join him. A Guardsman—a woman, flesh turned black with ash and soot, face caked with dry blood—emerged from concealment. Two children followed her: a boy of six winters and a girl not much older.

The Guardsman had her shortsword pointed at Jeran's chest. "It is you," she said, shoulders slumping. She looked to be on the verge of crying.

"Are there others?" he asked, peering into the basement.

"None who'll be climbing out again," the Guardsman replied. Her eyes acquired a frantic urgency. "Down the street, my Lord! My squad commander found a warehouse spared the worst of the initial onslaught, and we were using it to hide those pulled from the rubble. Able-bodied men—and most women who had no children to tend to—were given weapons and told to fight, but mothers and children we hid in the warehouse. My last trip back, with these two and a few others, the Tachans ambushed us. I escaped, but the rest of my squad... We need to get to that warehouse, my Lord!"

Cold dread knotted Jeran's gut, and the aching loss he had kept bottled up since arriving in Portal burst free, threatening to drown him. For a moment the dead occupied his mind, accusing, forlorn, demanding to know why their lives had been sacrificed while his was spared. In the face of that despair, drawing strength from Tourin and the others' growing resolve became difficult, but their needs did not diminish. Out of balance, the link threatened to crush him, to overwhelm him with unyielding viciousness.

"My Lord?"

"Is it far?" Jeran managed, his voice straining. Time was running out, both for him and Portal. He needed to stop the assault on Portal Keep soon. *But there's time to save a few more children! Children!*

"No, my Lord. Just down the street." Jeran nodded, and the woman preceded him from the building. One of the men outside approached with a flask, which the Guardswoman sipped and then offered to the girl, but Jeran urged her on without waiting for the children to drink.

At the end of the intersection, Jeran saw a broad building engulfed in flames, the heat so intense he felt it from several hundred hands distant. The woman's face fell when she saw the building. "Oh, Gods!" she said, lurching forward. Jeran chased after her, drawing on his Gift, trying to remember how to make rain.

Someone grabbed him, slamming him into the wall. Panic filled Jeran, and he fought against his attacker and his magic both. The sudden threat weakened his control of the flows, and his Gift threatened to break free again. Another touch sent a chill across his body, severing his connection to magic. "It is us, friend Jeran," Grendor said. "Be at peace."

Jeran ceased his struggles, and he silently thanked Grendor despite the thunderous pounding the Orog's touch set off inside his head. *A loss of control here, holding as much magic as I was holding…* The thought frightened Jeran more than a thousand Tachan soldiers.

Katya and Lord Grondellan tried to grab the woman, but she dodged them and sprinted into the open. Before she made it a dozen steps, arrows riddled her body, and she fell to the stones, body twitching and spasming.

"They've fortified a building across the way," Lord Grondellan said, turning away from the fallen Guardsman. He pulled a dagger from one of the sheathes hanging crosswise on a strap over his shoulder and used it to pick something from beneath a nail. "Our best guess is half a hundred to a hundred men."

"The Guard's been using that warehouse to hide refugees," Jeran said. "We need to find a way to get them out." Dahr shook his head, but before he could speak, Jeran grabbed him by the shoulders. "I don't care if lives mean nothing to you anymore, Dahr! These are my people. Our people! I won't leave them to die just to satiate your need for blood."

Anger and affront surged through Dahr—Jeran felt it through their bond more clearly than he felt his own emotions—and Dahr shoved him. "There's nothing to be done," he growled. "Anyone the Tachans left breathing was consumed by the flames long ago. Try to save them, and you risk your life needlessly."

For a moment, they stood staring at each other, silent and brooding. Prompted by guilt, Jeran started to apologize, but when Dahr turned away he made no move to follow. The screams of the dead filled his mind, tormenting him. He heard their cries, not just from the warehouse but from all over Portal; he heard their harsh accusations. Rage powered him, blinded him, consumed him. He felt anger pour forth, fueling his people, causing some to rush into danger, inspiring others to feats of bravery they would otherwise never have committed.

Jeran surrendered himself to magic, let it into him in a way he had only allowed a handful of times before, and he stepped out from the protection of the building. Katya tried to stop him, but she hit a wall of air more solid than stone.

Dahr, guessing Jeran's intentions, raced forward too, not to save him but to join him. When he hit the invisible barrier, he beat on it with his fists and howled like a caged beast. When he sought a way around and found himself penned in, he screamed. Jeran ignored him.

Arrows flew from a building across the street, but they landed as splinters at Jeran's feet, and the plinking of arrowheads raining down on the paving stones played a gentle tune. For a time, Jeran did nothing but watch, letting the Tachans waste their shafts and wonder what he planned. The heat from the warehouse fire burned his face, and flaming rubble spread across the intersection. Jeran ignored it too, except to offer a silent apology to the souls inside.

They killed my people. Innocent people! Unable to help himself, he wove the flows of magic, twisting them into a pattern he had never seen before. The weave settled over the building like a net, and Jeran held out his hand, palm open. He tensed his fingers, and the structure groaned. With deliberate slowness, he made a fist.

The groaning increased, and the ground shook, subtly at first but in a crescendo, until violent tremors ripped through the building and the few intact windows shattered. Screams came from inside, terrified cries that should have made Jeran think of mercy but only served to intensify his determination. The roof collapsed; wood and tile fell with a clamor loud enough to stir the dead. Fists beat at the doors, and some tried to jump from open windows only to find themselves trapped as surely as Dahr.

With a roar like a thousand lions, the building fell, but the debris, contained by Jeran's magic, piled up upon the Tachans. Their screams grew more frantic at first, then subsided. After a moment more, the rumbling faded too, and the only sound left was the crackling of fire.

Jeran opened his hand. Drained, he let go his hold on magic and struggled to hide the effort it took to stay standing. Free to move, Dahr raced toward him with the desperation of the mad, grabbed him by the shoulders, and pinned him to the ground. Guardsmen moved to stop him, but Jeran signaled for them to hold.

"You've denied me much," Dahr said, his eyes locked on the remains of the building. "Do not deny me battle."

The apology froze halfway to Jeran's mouth. "It's not being caged that bothers you?" Jeran removed Dahr's hands and sat up. He made no effort to hide his disappointment. "I won't stop you again, even if a charge means certain death. You have my word."

"Don't..." Dahr's jaw clenched, but he backed away from Jeran's icy eyes. "Don't pity me!"

"Pity?" Jeran stood and brushed the dust from his clothing. "What's there to pity? You've chosen your path. It may not be the path I'd have chosen for you, but you can still be of use to me. Before we're done, Madryn will be drenched in blood."

"Of use? Is that all I am, a tool? Is that all any of us are to you?" Dahr spit on the ground. "You sound like Lorthas. Better watch yourself, Jeran; you're in danger of losing your humanity."

"At least I still have it to lose."

Jeran turned away, depriving Dahr of the chance to respond. He ordered the Guard forward, and ordered runners to gather Tourin and the others. They could wait no longer, enemy at their heels or not. Portal had to be reclaimed; he had other places to be.

The satisfaction he felt at the self doubt radiating from Dahr shamed him as much as it pleased him.

"There must be two thousand men out there," Tourin said, peeking out from the safety of concealment.

"Less than that, lad." Lord Grondellan scanned the broad plaza leading up to Portal Keep. "Not by much."

"We've a fraction of that number!"

"They've only a handful of ShadowMagi, and we've the element of surprise." The Rachannan grunted when a catapult released with a loud crack, and a hands-wide rock flew toward the castle. Before impact, it burst to life with an unnatural green flame that clung to the walls, eating away at the fortification. "Then again, a handful might be more than enough."

"Harol's right," Jeran said, with a nod toward Lord Grondellan. "There are far fewer Magi here than were used to raze the city, and our patrols claim that resistance throughout Portal is almost gone." His Readings confirmed the former, and Dahr's unique abilities the latter. "If we can rout this group, we'll control the city."

The buildings ended with a striking suddenness, giving way to tiled squares and once finely-tended gardens. Portal's three main roads all led here, funneled by the mountains to a sharp promontory where Portal Keep stood in isolation. Sheer cliffs marked the northern boundary, protecting the keep on two sides, and the Portal Wall guarded its rear, but its front approach was ill protected.

The gardens were gone now, the trees burnt to cinders, the flowers trampled, and soldiers clustered in the plazas where children once played. A turtled ram battered the main gate and the Magi unleashed their Gift on the walls with withering effect. Had Portal Keep not been strengthened by the Gifted who helped build it, it would have long since fallen.

"*If*, he says," Tourin groaned. "They outman us four to one, match us Mage for Mage, and use seasoned troops while half our men are conscripted farmers. What tool, exactly, do you plan to use to even the odds?"

Jeran fixed Talbot's son with a cold blue gaze. "Fear," he said, a slight smile playing across his face. "Harol, lead your men to the eastern road. On my signal, march—march, I say, not that reckless charging your men are so fond of!—toward the castle. Tourin, take your men to the western road. Ehvan will lead our men up the center."

"Just walk up to them?" Tourin said. "You think those Magi will let us get close enough for an honest fight?" Confidence gleaned through their bond warred with the doubt he had good reason to feel.

"We won't give them the option," Jeran said. "Yassik, you and the others remain hidden here. Concentrate your Gift on protecting our men. Exhaust yourselves if you have to, but let nothing touch them until battle is joined."

"You're risking a lot," Yassik said. "If we have nothing left for the battle—"

"Once our men are mingled, I'm trusting that the ShadowMagi will be less inclined to blatant destruction. They might have no regard for their soldiers' lives, but those swords offer them as much protection as their magic. If they must choose their targets with care, we've a far greater chance at victory, even against their magic."

Jeran dismissed his men with a wave. "Go! When you see me enter the field, begin your march." Lord Grondellan slipped away to the east, and Tourin, after a final wistful look at the keep, led his men west. Ehvan and Grendor mobilized several blocks back so as to remain unseen by the army attacking the keep.

"Are you sure we've taken out all their scouts?" Jeran asked. Extending his perceptions, he ghosted up and down Portal's alleys and through its buildings, checking the most likely hiding spots. He found nothing.

Dahr's eyes unfocused, and for a time he said nothing. "I'm as sure as I can be," he said at last. "My friends say most of the humans left Portal sometime before midday. I already killed the sentries they found for us."

"You didn't need to do that alone," Jeran told him. "You could have reported their positions to me."

"Alone?" Dahr scowled. "With that Rachannan glued to my hip and your shadow following me everywhere I go? I don't remember what it feels like to be alone."

"I can't tell Harol where to go, though I regret that he's taken such a liking to you. As for Katya, I send her with you to—"

"Torment me?"

"No... To remind you. Of who you once were. Of who I'd like you to be again."

"I don't need your reminders."

"That's where you're wrong. You don't *want* my reminders." The bond between them wavered, and for a moment, Jeran felt nothing from his friend. It returned, but tenuous and with a hazy, wavering feel to it. "Will your friends do as I want?"

"They expect to die. But they'll do it. For me." He spat the last, and Jeran did not need the bond to know why. Dahr hated responsibility, hated to know that people—even beasts—suffered because of his commands. *He had best get used to it. There's no denying what he is. Not anymore.*

They watched the field in silence, watched as the walls of the keep cracked and blistered, as the turrets crumbled, sending showers of dark stone raining down upon the enemy. A few bolts, poorly aimed or turned aside by the ShadowMagi, flew from the battlements, but Portal Keep was not designed to take an assault from the south.

After a time, Jeran sent his perceptions east and west again. "Everyone's ready," he announced. "Dahr, Grendor…" Jeran eased his blades into their sheaths. The Aelvin sword felt cold at his hip, but the *dolchek* hummed with anticipation. He swept the dust from his uniform but made no effort to wipe the dried blood from his face and hands, then stepped from concealment. Dahr and Grendor followed a step behind.

At his signal, Ehvan sounded a fanfare, and Yassik amplified the sound, blasting the notes across the plaza. The attack faltered, and the enemy turned to survey the new threat. A full volley from the castle took the Tachans by surprise, and a number of men fell to the sudden attack before the ShadowMagi protected them.

Jeran marched out, weapons undrawn, as if unconcerned by the numbers he faced. Dahr held his greatsword easily in one hand, and Grendor limped with the aid of his *va'dasheran*. Tachan archers fired at them, but Jeran turned the shafts aside. His hand caressed the hilt of his sword. *What happens once battle is joined? Can I trust my Gift while fighting?*

As one, his units appeared from all three roads, marching in near unison. The Rachannen berserkers had their weapons drawn, and they bellowed and taunted with every step; the Guardsmen marched in precise and silent formation, but only drew their blades when ordered to by their commanders.

The Tachans rallied to the new threat, trusting the ShadowMagi to protect them from the archers behind. Jeran moved well ahead of his troops. "What terms do you plan to offer?" Grendor asked.

"There will be no terms," Jeran said. "Salos sought to teach me a lesson today, but I have one to teach as well."

The ShadowMagi gathered in a cluster, then faced the Alrendrians. Jeran saw their auras flare, and the ground between the two forces erupted in flame and exploding dirt. Lightning fell from the sky in a blinding torrent, and a strong wind whipped up the tendrils of smoke, sending them swirling in tornadic spirals.

The Alrendrians continued on despite their fear, and Jeran felt a surge of pride for his men. When the explosions could not reach them and the lightning failed to hit the ground, their confidence returned. Ehvan started to chant, "Odara! Odara! Odara!" and the others took up the cry. Their words thundered across the field.

"You," Jeran said, aiming his blade at a trembling young Tachan, "will leave here untouched." The man's sword flew from his hand and he slid forward. Scrabbling on hands and knees, the boy struggled against Jeran's magic but could do nothing as he was whisked through the Alrendrian lines and dumped into a wicker cage at an abandoned hawker's stall. "Take this message to your master: You sought to poison me, but you forgot that when a scorpion stings a wolf, it risks getting bitten. I will not rest until you've joined your brother in the Nothing."

Another Tachan soldier rushed forward in a suicidal charge. Grendor pivoted, knocked the man off balance with the butt of his *va'dasheran*, then sliced him across the midriff with his blade. In the ensuing confusion, a ShadowMage reached for magic. Jeran opened himself to the flows, pulling them away from the Mage, and with a fluid motion, drew his *dolchek*. The blade sailed impossibly far, impossibly fast, and took the Mage in the throat, blasting through the weak shield he was able to raise at the last instant. He fell to the ground gurgling, and the other ShadowMagi redoubled their efforts, but Yassik and the others had them countered for the time being.

"Now, Dahr," Jeran said.

Rats exploded from the buildings, racing around and between the Alrendrians' legs, teeth gnashing as they charged the Tachans. Vultures and raptors darkened the sky, wheeling in circles above the enemy but leaving the air about Jeran and his allies untouched. A swarm of wasps ten hands across shot past a finger's width from Jeran's head. Startled, he craned his head around but said nothing when he saw his shock mirrored on Dahr's face.

The Tachans screamed; their rigid formations broke before the rats reached them. Jeran held his sword aloft, allowing it to catch the light of the ShadowMagi's lightning. The battle seemed to halt, time itself stretched and slowed, and Jeran felt the Gift pour into him. The anxieties and injuries of his men took on a new dimension. He felt each keenly, as if they were his own, and the mélange of emotions threatened to overwhelm his consciousness. At the same time, everything felt more distant, and Jeran surveyed it all dispassionately. He knew which men were near paralyzed with fear; he knew which would fight on unto death. When he saw a weakness in the Tachan lines and a way to exploit it, he knew those he bonded had heard his orders without him speaking them.

He marched, and his men followed, their pace unhurried. The Tachans backed away until pressed against Portal Keep, and then cornered, they made a stand. *Had I left them an escape, they'd have taken it. Pity that none deserve to live.*

Trapped, the Tachans charged, and Jeran met their assault. He held the enemy back with his sword, but he lost sight of Dahr and Grendor within the first few moments of battle. He held magic but used it sparingly; he knew full well the risks if he lost his hold on the flows.

The enemy broke before him, fleeing the justice wrought by his Aelvin blade. Those who engaged him he cut down without remorse, wishing their souls a quick passage to the Twilight World.

Pain sliced across his shoulder, and almost simultaneously he felt something stab into his gut. Confused, he looked down and saw no injury, but another blow pounded the back of his skull, and fire raced across his left hamstring. Injury after injury assaulted him, the pain fading as quickly as it came, replaced with a growing howl of torment and terror.

Not my injuries, Jeran thought, but the realization did little to quell the agony. Nor did it make holding magic any easier, and Jeran felt his control slip away. He sought an outlet, and caught a glimpse of the ShadowMagi in the distance. He focused on the Mage, directing the torrent of magic at him.

A blinding explosion rocked the square, knocking Jeran to the ground. Dirt and rock rained down upon the plaza, and in the clearing dust he saw a gaping hole where the ShadowMagi had stood.

He severed his connection to magic and almost wept when the barrage of injuries he had been forced to sustain lessened in intensity. They still plagued him, lingering longer before fading, but without magic, they felt more like scratches and bee stings than mortal wounds.

Jeran regained his feet and saw most everyone around him doing likewise. The enemy was routed but not defeated. Terror fueled them; they knew their death was near, and that knowledge lent them strength. For a moment, Jeran considered offering quarter.

If they want mercy, they should have offered some.

Dahr's blade sliced through the armor of another Tachan, and he turned from the spray of blood that spattered his face. He had lost track of his kills, but they numbered in the dozens. *Surely this is enough to quench my thirst.* Had he faith in the Gods, he would have prayed for it to be enough.

The plaza was chaos; a thousand tiny battles raged across the open field. Groups of men and Orog in Odaran black fought side by side with Rachannen berserkers and armored Guardsmen, driving the Tachans toward the keep. The only area spared fighting was the crater where the ShadowMagi had once stood. By unspoken agreement the combatants stayed a healthy distance from the gaping hole with its tendrils of dark smoke swirling toward the sky.

Rats were everywhere, thousands of them, more than Dahr had ever imagined existed, running between the soldiers' legs, harassing the Tachans, keeping them from regrouping. Grateful that he only heard a handful of voices and not one for every beast with whom he shared the battlefield, Dahr again told them they could go, that they had served their purpose, and served it well. They ignored him, intentionally or because of the bloodlust radiating from them, the righteous retribution for centuries of ill-treatment at the hands of man.

A shrill note drew Dahr's eyes to the castle, where Guardsmen poured forth from the opening gates. Lord Talbot led the charge atop a black stallion, dark eyes glaring out from beneath his helmet. His horsemen drove into the Tachan flank, breaking what little resolve the enemy still had. Tightening his grip on his greatsword, Dahr ran forward, bellowing a challenge.

At the sight of a giant bearing down on them, lips drawn back in a hungry snarl, two soldiers dropped their weapons and ran. "Cowards!" Dahr howled, bringing his blade down upon the third, a nervous child with no right to a weapon.

The boy parried, but the force of Dahr's strike knocked him to his knees. He twisted in an attempt at an answering attack, but Dahr kicked and heard the crunch of bone. The soldier flopped on his back, frothy blood bubbling from his lips. Pain haunted his gaze until Dahr ended his suffering with a single thrust of his greatsword.

A wild cry pulled him around, but he only had time to tense before a dozen Tachans driven by the charge of Alrendrian horsemen plowed into him. His greatsword fell from his hand, and he grappled with the enemy, clawing at them, biting. A dagger sliced his side, and Dahr wrenched it from a soldier's hand and threw it, then drove his fist into the man's face with such force that his knuckles ached.

Two more soldiers jumped on his back; one wrapped an arm around his windpipe with crushing force. More men piled atop him, pounding with their fists. A flash of fear ran through Dahr, but excitement eclipsed it. He tossed himself backward, pinning the men behind him to the ground, kicking and flailing at those atop.

He heard a scream, and then felt the fur of a rat slide across his arm. More screams followed, and then a gauntleted hand ripped one of the men off him and pulled him to his feet.

"Gods, lad," Lord Talbot said, handing Dahr his sword. He stared at the blood and ash painting Dahr's body, at the welts that would soon darken to bruises. "You're a wretched sight. But I've never been happier to see you."

Dahr smiled, but said nothing as he turned back to the fray. Talbot's hand restrained him. "This battle's done. Let the boys mop up the remnants. We need to find Jeran and my sons."

They gathered in the keep's main yard under a tattered Odaran flag. Hundreds of commoners crowded the keep and castle, and as many more had been given sanctuary in the vast catacombs of Portal Wall, but the devastation to both the city and the morale of its people tortured Jeran. The hundreds of new presences that filled his mind only added to his guilt and the growing nausea he fought to control.

He divided the Guardsmen into small parties and sent them to scour the city, proclaiming the Tachans defeated, gathering any survivors and dispatching any remaining pockets of resistance. Ehvan and Lord Grondellan sent their men out as well; at the moment, Jeran had no better use for them.

Lord and Lady Talbot stood with Dahr, Grendor, and Lord Grondellan in the shadow of the gate. Jeran went to join them, noting the tears freely falling down Grendor's face. The muted sadness he felt from Dahr—a sadness that did not touch his eyes or stone-hard face—encouraged him, made him think there might still be a chance to save his friend.

"Gideon," Jeran said, "Lady Talbot. I wish... I wish I had known to come sooner."

Lord Talbot clapped him on the shoulder. "That you came at all was a miracle, Jeran. How you knew... Well, as to that, I can only guess, but I'll thank the Gods for it every day of my life."

"About your son... I'm sorry."

Lord Talbot looked stricken, and Aleesa turned away, weeping. Grendor put a comforting arm around her shoulder and whispered something in her ear. "You know about Kristaf then?" Talbot asked. "A good boy. We were all of us watching the Portal, but he was in the city. He saw the Tachans breach the wall, and he sounded the alarm. If not for him... If he hadn't..."

Jeran hated himself, he hated fate, or the Gods, or whatever had transpired to put him in this place at this time. Kristaf's death burned into him like a brand, and he wondered which of the holes in his soul belonged to the boy. "Gideon, I'm so sorry. I didn't know about Kristaf."

He recounted what he knew of Alic's death and of his valiant attempt to rally the men against the enemy. Talbot slumped, his shoulders bent under the strain, and Dahr moved to lend him an arm. Aleesa wailed, clutching Grendor to her as if they were lifelong friends, and the Orog continued his whispered words. Jeran wondered what magic Grendor controlled, because in a very short time Aleesa's sobbing stopped, and her eyes held a glimmer of hope.

"Father!" Tourin called, bursting through the guards. He gripped Lord Talbot in a bear hug, then went to his mother, who parted from Grendor long enough to embrace her son. She held him as if he were crystal, afraid that he might break.

"At least we stopped them," Talbot said. "At least we kept them from opening the Portal." Tourin looked at Jeran, but said nothing when Jeran shook his head. Talbot noticed, though. "What? For the Gods' sakes, Tourin, tell me what you know!"

"Most of their soldiers—and all but a handful of Magi—abandoned the city before they took the keep. The troops they left were expendable, boys and old men. The city was theirs for the taking, but they abandoned it."

"Salos wanted to teach me a lesson, and punish me for Tylor's death," Jeran said.

Tourin did not look convinced. "I wonder if his actions here tell us something more important."

"More important?" Dahr demanded, sweeping his hand out to encompass the smoking wreckage of Portal. "Is this message not important enough for you?"

"Open the Portal, and the might of *Ael Shataq* is at his disposal," Tourin said. "Madryn is not ready for that. By not casting open the gates, Salos reveals something."

"We'd be foolish to think that Dranakohr is the only passage Lorthas carved," Jeran said. "No doubt similar tunnels exist. Portal is no longer necessary to Lorthas's plans. This was meant as a warning that any attempt to interfere would carry consequences."

"Your reports claim that traversing the tunnels carries great risk," Tourin replied. "We must assume the other passages harbor similar dangers. Portal may no longer be required, but if one wanted to ferry thousands of out *Ael Shataq*, Portal would make the task far easier."

"This debate is pointless," Dahr growled. "Portal was not conquered. The path to *Ael Shataq* remains closed. I—"

"His argument has merit," Jeran said, cutting Dahr off. "Where are you leading, Tourin?"

"By withdrawing the bulk of his forces from the city, Salos makes it clear that he had no intention of casting open the Portal. Why, I wonder, would he not want to, since an army of his allies camps on the other side? With Portal under their control, Lorthas could ferry men and supplies south in great numbers, and with virtually no opposition between here and Kaper, most of Alrendria could be his before King Mathis had a chance to regroup."

Lord Talbot jerked upright. "Gods, boy, you don't think...? Could it be true?"

Jeran saw the destination now, and he wondered how close to the mark Tourin's arrow had fallen. "If what you say is true, this could prove the best tidings we've heard in seasons."

"The best tidings?" Dahr fumed. "How has the destruction of Portal and the slaughter of thousands gone from a tragedy to a victory?"

"Peace, friend Dahr," Grendor said, stepping away from Aleesa. "Now is not the time for anger. If we ask, I am sure our friends will share their knowledge with us."

"What reason would Salos have of not opening the gate to his allies?" Jeran asked. "Only one: Those who stand across the Boundary are not his allies."

"But then why attack at all?"

"Because he was ordered to," Tourin said.

"If Salos is not allied with Lorthas..."

"The Scorpion has strings on both sides of the Boundary, and he makes us all dance like marionettes. He attacks to keep Lorthas happy, and he loses to keep him bottled up. By withdrawing the bulk of his troops and Magi as soon as Jeran arrives, he all but guarantees defeat; by leaving the inexperienced, the old, and I presume those devoutly loyal to Lorthas, he can demand more resources from *Ael Shataq*, yet keep the reins of this conflict firmly in his hands."

"So the Scorpion plays his own game?" Talbot asked.

Jeran hoped it was so, but was not yet convinced. "Does he? Or is this an even more elaborate scheme of Lorthas's, designed to divide our attention?" He frowned, his mind whirling in a thousand different directions. New possibilities abounded, but so did new risks.

"I must think on this," he said, "but other matters demand our attention first. We must secure the city, rebuild its defenses, and make sure neither Lorthas nor Salos ever takes the Portal." Jeran waved, and a Mage stepped forward. "Gideon, this is Kostas. He'll keep you connected to my people in Dranakohr. Within a tenday you'll have two thousand men and Orog here, and a handful more Magi as well. Hundreds more can be brought in an instant if another attack occurs, but these men are yours. I should have sent them long ago. Use them to let your men grieve their losses and recover from the nightmare you've lived, then focus on refortifying the city. Patrols should be sent out as soon as you're able. The villagers must be assured that we're here to protect them, and they must be warned about the bands of Tachans that may yet roam the countryside."

"You're not staying then?" Talbot asked, his voice carrying a bone-numbing weariness. "You're returning to Dranakohr?"

"No, to both your questions." Even now, with the battle well over, Jeran feared using magic. His head pounded, and he remembered how close he had come to obliterating himself and those he cared about. "There are things I must learn, and I can't learn them in Dranakohr."

He called Ehvan over and ordered him to return to Dranakohr and assume command. The rest of his soldiers he put under Tourin's charge, and the younger Talbot accepted the command with solemn grace. "Should they not go to my father?"

"Your father guards the Portal," Jeran said, gripping the young man's arm in parting. "You, I ask to guard House Odara. If you need me, Kostas will know how to find me."

Grendor, Dahr, and Katya joined him in the center of the courtyard, and Jeran bade Yassik join them as well. "Lord Grondellan," he called, and the Rachannan turned at his name. "I must go. Your aid this past season has been invaluable. My Magi will return you to Dranakohr, or to Rachannon. Tell them where you wish to go, and they'll take you there."

"My men should return to Vela and rejoin their brothers," Harol called back. At his signal, his steward Yurs joined him. "With your permission, Yurs and I would like to stay with you."

"Your service is no longer needed, and the reports we have from Rachannon—"

"There's nothing to be done about Rachannon. Vestlin sealed his fate when he defied the Durange, though I advised him to do it. The only way to save my home is to win this war. My men have orders to return to the Corsan front and aid Commander Jasova. I would go with you."

Dahr stood rigid as a statue, and Jeran sensed frustration at his inability to be free of his former master. But he thought he detected something else too, something buried so deep he could scarcely feel it through their bond. He thought he sensed joy.

"Why would—?"

"Why?" Harol laughed. "I'm not getting younger, my friend. This may be my last chance to recapture the wildness of youth, and you draw adventure like honey draws flies." Something more serious entered his expression. "I know which side of the war I want to win, lad, and I'll stick with it till the end. Tell me you need me elsewhere, and I'll go gladly."

"How can I refuse after hearing such words?" Jeran asked, a broad smile conquering his face. "Yassik, can you take us all?"

The request surprised Yassik, but he nodded, and a Gate opened on the courtyard. Jeran bid a final farewell to Lord and Lady Talbot, and expressed his deepest sympathy for their loss before turning toward the Gate.

A snow-covered field spread out before them, and in the background an obsidian tower capped with a golden eagle. Nine figures wrapped in dark cloaks stood before the obelisk, watching the Gate. Watching Jeran.

"Where are we going?" Dahr asked, stopping Jeran before he stepped through.

"To Aemon's Tomb," Jeran said. "To Shandar."

CHAPTER 6

Snow clung to the ground, but an early wind blew up from the south, bringing the unwelcome smells of spring. Water dripped from the icicles along the eaves like the sands in an hourglass, carving channels through Kaper's armor. Each drop sounded like the steady beat of an executioner's drum to Martyn; he knew too well that every day Kaper drew nearer to siege and suffering.

In Makan's Market, the city seemed not to notice. Wagons laden with goods crowded the main avenue; hawkers paced and shouted before their stalls; shop boys dodged between horses, carrying packages or relaying messages between merchants. Even the usually subdued Aelvin quarter, the shops and stalls appropriated for the Aelvin craftsmen who had come to Kaper as part of the agreement with Emperor Alwellyn, bustled with life.

Martyn prided himself on his people's confidence in the face of adversity. Outside the market squares, squads of militia patrolled the streets, marching in a semblance of precision. No Guardsmen could be seen. Most had been sent east or west, where heavy fighting demanded their presence, and the rest held key locations in and about the city. Volunteers had arrived in a steady stream since the victory in Vela, but Guardsmen Bystral and Lisandaer kept the newly-raised Guardsmen high in Old Kaper, where they were less inclined to succumb to the temptations of the city. *Not that they'd have much energy for debauchery. Bystral trains them with a devilish fervor.* Kaper had too few trained soldiers protecting it, and the unreliable conscripts and green soldiers worried the garrison commander.

"This early thaw doesn't bode well for us, Martyn," Brell Morrena said from his saddle. Martyn looked at the man from the corner of his eyes. Short and slim, with an oiled, pointed beard and dark eyes, Brell still made Martyn's skin crawl, but his recent acts of loyalty had earned him a level of popularity Martyn never would have believed if he had not witnessed it.

Martyn remembered well that day—and eternity ago, at the start of winter—when he brought news of an approaching army. His father went to prepare Kaper for siege, and in a rare moment of distraction granted Martyn permission to join the scouting party.

Martyn had wasted no time leaving the city, but he made the approach with a caution learned along the Corsan border. With only two squads of fast horsemen and no idea of what he faced, he had no intention of engaging the enemy, only in surveying them. But when he saw Brell astride a horse, cloak torn and smeared with mud, leading a thousand battered Guardsmen and an army of weary commoners, Martyn had nearly fallen from his horse. Disregarding his own orders he approached, shouting for Brell to lay down his arms.

Brell had complied, and the tale he told of treachery and murder still curdled Martyn's blood. Jysin, First of Morrena, had cast his lot with the Darklord. Guardsmen loyal to Alrendria had been killed by the hundreds, and an army swelled with cutthroats sworn to Jysin had swept over House Morrena. With King Murdir of Corsa, he had pushed Commander Jasova's lines back almost to the outpost of Darein, though a fortified garrison still held the city of Ulanoc and the road between. In the face of this treachery, Brell had rallied the loyalists in his House and brought as many as he could to Kaper.

With Brell's reputation as an opportunist, the numerous schemes he had hatched to increase his House's power, and the well-known enmity between him and King Mathis, Martyn had asked why.

"I love my House, Prince Martyn," Brell had replied, "and I loved my Family, but I am Alrendrian. I swore an oath, and I would keep that oath even if it were my father or son across the field of battle, and not that Gods-cursed Jysin."

Though he still harbored suspicions about the man, with allies stretched far and wide, Martyn had no choice but to accept the statement as truth. Moreover, Brell's heroism had roused the imaginations of the citizenry, and comparisons were already being made to Roya and Makan. A smile ghosted across Martyn's face as he remembered the first time he heard his father and Brell spoken of as lifelong friends who had hidden behind a façade of animosity to draw out their enemies. He wondered which of them it rankled more.

"We can hope the cold returns," Martyn said. "A quick thaw and freeze would slow the approach even more than snow." He wiped his brow; he had expected colder weather, or perhaps he had dressed for it as a hint to the Gods. Now he regretted his subtlety. "Though I suspect spring is here to stay, and our fortunes have run out."

"Kaper has never fallen," Brell told him. "The Gods willing, we can say that again next winter."

A cry of alarm went up to their right, and Martyn turned to see an urchin running with an armful of withered fruit. A shopkeeper cried 'thief', and a dozen or so militiamen chased the boy down an alley. Pained screams echoed from it, and Martyn turned his horse, but Brell grabbed his shoulder. "They won't kill the boy. They'll rough him up a bit, and if he's old enough, he'll find himself in a practice ring by morning. You shouldn't involve yourself."

Martyn ripped his arm away, but he knew Brell was right. He had business to attend to more important than following militiamen into alleys after thieves. "I regret their use of such brutal tactics."

Brell barked a laugh. "Brutal tactics are sometimes the most effective. Especially in a city under as much stress as Kaper."

Though not yet as crowded as Vela before Tylor's attack, Kaper had nearly doubled in population. Farmers and craftsmen from the north had trickled in throughout the winter, dragging half-frozen families behind them. With Jysin's betrayal, an army followed Brell out of House Morrena, pushing refugees east until the dead of winter forced them to halt and secure their holdings or risk losing more men to cold and hunger than to battle. With the early thaw, they had resumed their advance and would reach Kaper in less than a ten-day.

Word of a second army, brought by terrified peasants fleeing the soldiers, reached the castle just yesterday. At first, Martyn thought Jeran was sending reinforcements, either from his stronghold in Dranakohr or from Portal, where Lord Talbot had fallen strangely silent. Talbot's regular couriers—begging the King for additional troops and supplies—had stopped arriving in midwinter, and they had heard nothing from House Odara since.

But Jeran would not march under the banner of Tylor the Bull, nor would he put his own lands to the torch. The first few reports Martyn dismissed as hysteria brought on by the difficult journey. After a few dozen similar tales, he was forced to admit that the Durange were sending a second army against Kaper.

The Celaan provided them their best protection. Both armies would have to cross it to attack Kaper, and the broad waters and swift currents made passage difficult except on the sturdiest of vessels. With the King's Rakers in firm control of the river, Martyn knew his men would be able to hold the Great Bridge against all but the most determined assault.

Unbidden, the sight of the windstorm before Vela that had stripped buildings from their foundations and cleared a way for Tylor's advance filled Martyn's mind. With neither Jeran's renegades nor the Mage Assembly clamoring to aid in the defense of Kaper, Salos's ShadowMagi could prove the city's undoing.

The Great Bridge dominated the northern end of Makan's Market, cutting a graceful arc over the river. Scores of Guardsmen patrolled the southern shore, and even more led men and materials over the expanse, guiding and guarding the evacuation of Nuren. Still others—Guardsmen and militia—constructed fortifications along the bank on the Celaan, securing the docks and the approaches into the city. No fewer than a dozen Rakers lay anchored in the river, out of bowshot from the far bank. At the apex of the bridge, a barricade thirty hands high with a swinging gate just wide enough for a single wagon had been erected, and a full squad of Guardsmen defended it at all times.

"How sad," Treloran said. The Aelvin Prince had been silent for much of the journey from the castle. "The approach to Kaper had such majesty. Now it is just another Human fortification."

"Majesty doesn't protect you from arrows, Elf," Brell muttered. Then, remembering how well Elves could hear, he added, "It's a sign of your gentle nature, Prince Treloran, that you find the necessity of such things as this regrettable."

The Aelvin Prince opened his mouth, but Martyn made a gesture, and Treloran held his tongue. For once, Brell had meant no insult, but *Ael Chatorra* like Treloran were as touchy about their demeanor as any Guardsman, and far more likely to take offense.

Martyn nodded to the Guardsman commanding the unit at the foot of the bridge, and the soldier saluted, making way for the prince and his companions. The contingent of soldiers who had shadowed his steps since leaving the castle waited while he, Brell, and Treloran made the long trip to the top of the Great Bridge.

At the peak, Martyn ordered the gate opened, and when the subcommander hesitated, he smiled. "There's no invisible army out there, and I'll not be straying far." At the squad commander's signal, Guardsmen drew the bolts back and pushed open the gate. Martyn led his horse through a few dozen paces, then dismounted and walked to the edge of the bridge.

Nuren already looked like a battlefield dominated by gutted buildings and debris. King Mathis had ordered the city evacuated as soon as word of the approaching armies had been confirmed, but Martyn never expected the job to be so complete or so quickly done. Yet fear motivated, and the citizens of Nuren neither wanted to be waiting when the Durange arrived nor did they want to abandon their hard-earned belongings to the enemy.

Martyn stared at Nuren for some time, at the empty streets and slate-topped buildings, at the empty fields beyond, fallow and unplanted. No farms for fifty leagues north of Kaper would be planted this spring, and those to the south had orders only to plant fast-growing crops.

"You must give the order, Martyn," Brell said.

The man's sudden familiarity infuriated Martyn, but not so much as the casual, chiding reminder. He glared at Brell, and dense as he was, the nobleman was smart enough to step away. Martyn turned toward the barricade. "Burn it."

One Guardsman raised a torch and waved it; another soldier played a series of notes on a horn. Below, a half dozen fires flared to life, spreading from building to building with alarming rapidity. Soldiers raced ahead of the flames, driving the last few holdouts of Nuren before them. Those fires would be left to rage, and once they died, the Guardsmen would return and burn whatever remained.

"Was this necessary?" Treloran asked.

"Spring may have come early, but the nights will still be cold," Brell answered. "If you can't rout your enemy, you make him as uncomfortable as possible."

Treloran shivered. "It's barbaric. Even the Garun'ah do not engage in destruction of this magnitude, not against their own Race, and certainly not upon their own holdings."

"War is barbaric no matter how much structure you give it," Martyn said. The fires burned within him, darkening his mood with their sour smoke. "You pride yourself on how your people never fight each other, but the *Kohrnodra* are Elves the same as you, and their tactics make ours seem chivalrous.

"And when you criticize us for our casual disregard for life, you always fail to consider the atrocities your people have committed against the Garun'ah. *Ael Alluya* justifies the slaughter by making the Tribesmen into mindless, brutal savages. You know they're far more than that, but by turning them into beasts you've veiled your eyes and protected your consciences. Kill a man and you are condemned; kill a monster and you're revered."

The roar and crackle of the flames added emphasis to Martyn's words, and Treloran, lips drawn down in a vinegary pout, said nothing more. Martyn watched the fire until he could no longer stomach it. "We have business at the palace."

He descended the bridge in silence and observed the city with a fresh perspective. Though the market squares buzzed with life, Martyn now realized that anxiety fueled his people, not confidence. Away from the shops and watchful eyes, Kaper seemed a place already under siege. Shutters remained drawn despite the sunshine, and few besides patrolling soldiers traveled the streets. Those who did traveled in groups and kept away from the narrower alleys.

At the base of the bridge, a courier raced toward him. "Prince Martyn, when I heard you were on the bridge I waited to bring you this dispatch. It's from Commander Batai, in Aurach." The man held out a letter sealed with Joam's sigil.

Martyn took it and tore the seal. His face paled as he read, and the churning in his gut intensified until the discomfort he had felt atop the bridge seemed a pleasant memory.

"Rachannon is no more," Martyn said, his voice lifeless. "Vestlin is dead, his army scattered. Ryan Durange has reclaimed all of the Tachan Empire."

"Ryan Durange!" Brell spit the name. "That whelp doesn't even know how to hold a sword. It's that commander of theirs, the one-eyed scoundrel who destroys most of what he conquers."

"Not this time," Martyn replied. "Rachannon was won by treachery. Vestlin's son Balkias murdered him and declared for the Durange. Joam says Rachannon is wracked with civil war, but Balkias holds the capital and all ports and major fortifications. Half the army—those who didn't join Balkias—is running amok through Rachannon, killing rebels and loyalists alike; the other half has regrouped inside Gilead. Joam has their commanders' support for the moment, but he doubts he can keep it indefinitely, and without the Rachannen..."

"Gilead and the bulk of our army will be surrounded and outnumbered," Brell finished. He cursed and kicked at a beggar boy who approached his horse, making the child scamper backward. "We should advise your father to withdraw the army from Gilead. Kohr damn us! We should advise the Gileans to withdraw as well. If we abandon Gilead and fortify the border, we can regroup and strike at the Durange later."

"Withdrawing our troops from Gilead will not sit well with my betrothed," Martyn said. "Nor is it likely to win the support of the Gilean people. We've lost one ally today, Brell. I think it wise not to intentionally lose another."

"It may not matter," Treloran said. "If the Tachan army no longer needs to worry about attack from Rachannon, then their commander has likely shifted his forces west, trapping Commander Batai and the Gilean army. Were I he, I would not risk assaulting such a well fortified force when penning them up serves as great a purpose. With his flank secure, he could overrun enough of the border crossings to open a path to Kaper."

"That would be a bold plan," Brell said, "leaving an army at his rear. The Tachan commander isn't so foolish."

"The strategy is sound," Treloran said, looking down his nose at the nobleman. "So long as he keeps a strong garrison watching Aurach and Commander Batai's fortifications in the foothills, he need not worry. If our forces attack, he will hold the better ground; if they don't, it leaves Kaper open to attack from the east with whatever men and material can be spared. It is a tactic my uncle used successfully against the Tribesmen on many campaigns."

"Let's hope the Tachans don't think your plan so flawless," Martyn said. "Right now we have the river to protect us, but an army from the east would put more pressure on our defenses than I'd like."

An alarm sounded ahead of them, the clanging of a bell followed by the cries of a woman. Martyn started toward the sound, but Brell restrained him. "Do you think that wise, Martyn?"

"I have a squad of Guardsmen behind me, and half the garrison within sight," Martyn snapped, pulling away from Brell's grip and urging his horse forward. "I will see what this is about."

They met a group of militiamen outside a small shop, its windows decorated with Aelvin Runes. Through the open windows, baked delicacies Martyn had not seen since leaving Lynnaei created a scent that made his mouth water. An Aelvin woman, face concealed behind a veil, wept on the stoop, and two militiamen prodded at a body just inside the door. Dirt smeared their uniforms; the weapons they wore were dull. They looked more like street thugs than soldiers.

"What's this?" Martyn demanded, shouldering his way through the door and shoving the men aside. An Aelvin man lay on the floor, throat slit ear to ear and blood pooling on the wooden floor. A midnight blossom lay in the corpse's hand.

Martyn picked up the flower and examined it. Six such blooms had been found since the delegation arrived from Illendrylla, each beside the body of an Elf. Martyn suspected the Elf murdered in the castle would have held a similar flower if Mika had not stumbled upon the crime.

"Did you see who did this?" he asked, kneeling beside the grieving woman.

"No, my Lord," she replied, careful to keep her eyes fixed no higher than his chest. One of a thousand odd Aelvin customs. "He was hooded against the cold. He and Telivias were debating the cost for a hundred *lienteva* cakes when I went into the back. When I returned…"

Seven! And all Elves. How long before the murders are connected? How long before the Elves demand to leave. We can't afford to lose what little bond we have with them.

"May the Blessing of the Goddess be on you," Martyn said, and the woman bowed her head. Her quiet weeping dug at him like barbs.

"Did anyone see anything?" he asked the militiamen. Both shrugged, and Martyn knew they had not even bothered to ask. "Somebody must hang for this," he snapped. "If the murderer can't be found, I know of two who might suffice in his place." The men blanched and raced out the door, shouting for order among the crowd outside.

Treloran looked aghast—*As if I really meant to kill them!*—but Brell wore a smile of approval. The latter bothered Martyn far more, but he ignored them both for now and waved to the commander of his bodyguard. "Post a guard—Guardsmen, not militia!—outside this woman's door for a ten-day. And have Commander Lisandaer increase patrols through the... through the merchants' districts. I will not abide murder in Kaper, especially not in broad daylight!"

The Guardsman saluted and barked orders to his men. Martyn started toward his horse, but Treloran intercepted him. "This troubles me."

"This troubles me too," Martyn answered. "A merchant, killed in his own shop, and in—"

"That is not what I mean," Treloran interrupted. He kept his voice low, but Martyn heard the urgency in it. "This is not the first Elf murdered, and the pace of the killing has increased. My people did not expect love from Humans, but they also did not expect to be slaughtered as cattle."

"This is the work of one man," Martyn whispered. "Surely you don't think all Humans, or even most—"

"No, Martyn, but what I think is irrelevant. My people expect—they deserve!—to feel safe in their own homes and shops. Whether it is one man or one hundred, if you can't stop these murders, my people will demand to return to the Great Forest. Jaenaryn will demand it, and as he is the Emperor's chosen ambassador, I will not be able to overrule him."

The journey back to the palace was a silent one. Dark thoughts plagued Martyn, and he saw his own doubts mirrored in the weary faces of every man they passed. Even the Guardsmen, always before beacons of power and confidence, walked with resignation, shoulders stooped by unseen weights and eyes fastened firmly on their destinations.

The palace had metamorphosed over the winter. Gone were the sprawling gardens and ornate courtyards, shrubs and flowerbeds had been cleared, the land plowed and fertilized for planting. Architects and masons worked ceaselessly to improve the fortifications, utilizing the swelling population to supplement the work force. Behind the castle, the armory and smithies had been expanded, adding room for more stores and weapon-makers.

How much difference will it make? If our enemies breach the Wall separating Old Kaper from New, what challenge will these fortifications present to them? His father thought the measures prudent, though, and so long as the King continued to prepare the defenses around Old Kaper as well, Martyn saw no need to gainsay him.

The courtyards within the sprawling buildings of the palace had been converted to practice yards, and Martyn saw Commander Bystral working with a group of young recruits in one. Though untried and barely old enough to enlist, each and every one showed more promise than the miltiamen patrolling the city. Commanders Lisandaer and Bystral worked closely to enhance Kaper's garrison, with the former sending any conscripts who showed skill with a blade or the ability to follow orders to the castle for Bystral—the more persuasive of the two—to convince to join the Guard.

Mika, the boy Jeran had freed from the Slavers, and now the King's self-appointed shadow, sat to one side, his hawkish eyes riveted to the duels. Though not much younger—and somewhat more skilled—than the men he watched, he was not yet old enough to join the Guard. To see him out here, and not following on his father's heels surprised Martyn, though it likely meant the King had closeted himself in his chambers to catch up on reports. Guards watched the King's chambers constantly, and even Mika did not suspect a murderer to be hidden inside. Not after he had searched the rooms, in any case.

That the boy had taken Martyn's request to protect his father so seriously had come as no shock to the prince. The boy strove to mimic Jeran as much as possible and had succeeded in far more than his stoic manner and strict interpretation of honor. What shocked Martyn was his father's willing acceptance of the boy. Their easy manner and what could only be termed friendship confounded him, as did the pangs of envy that sometimes accompanied seeing the two of them together, laughing at some joke or sharing a private conversation.

Within the castle proper, Martyn left Brell and Treloran to inform Jaenaryn of the murder, and went in search of Miriam, to tell her of the developments in Rachannon and the threat it posed to Gilead. When he turned a corner and saw Kaeille, his heart raced. He yearned to go to her, to tell her what had happened in the city and take comfort in her wise counsel and soothing touch, but he ducked out of sight and waited until she was gone before continuing on. *Miriam won't want Kaeille there when I tell her about Joam's letter. Neither likes to show the other weakness.*

"Prince Martyn," a quiet voice called from within a nearby room, "if I could have a moment of your time."

Martyn tensed, and his hand went to the dagger he wore concealed. "Step out here! Show yourself."

"If I meant you harm, don't you think I'd have waited until you passed and then attacked without announcing myself? I understand your concern, but I must beg your indulgence. Secrecy is somewhat of importance."

Wary, Martyn approached the chamber, but when he threw the door open, it took all of his willpower not to drop to his knees. "Great One! Why didn't you announce yourself?"

When confronted by Aemon during the siege of Vela, Martyn had been awestruck and speechless most of the time they were together. Though proud that he had somehow managed to keep his voice now, he nevertheless worried that he was not showing the legendary Mage appropriate deference.

"Announce myself?" Aemon laughed, closing the door behind the prince. "It's hard to maintain secrecy when you go about trumpeting your presence, my boy."

A cloaked woman hovered in the corner of the chamber, hood drawn over her head and eyes locked on the floor. Martyn eyed the stranger for a moment, then returned his attention to Aemon. "I don't know what I can do to help you, Great One, but if it's within my power…"

"You can start by calling me Aemon. That's within your power, isn't it?"

The harsh undertones worried Martyn. "I meant no disrespect. I only—"

"I know. But if I were half as great as the stories claim, then I wouldn't be sneaking about through your castle, now would I? I could just snap my fingers and all Madryn's problems would go away."

Aemon beckoned, and the cloaked figure approached. "I need a favor of you, Prince Martyn. My friend and a few of her allies need sanctuary in Kaper. I must ask you to find a place for them, and to keep their presence secret from everyone, including your father."

"Of course, Great— Aemon. But why shouldn't we tell my father?"

"He'll be dealing with parties interested in finding these people, and it would be best if he actually believed they weren't hiding under his nose." Martyn started to speak, but Aemon interrupted him. "Before you argue, this isn't a one-sided proposition. I think you'll get something quite useful out of the arrangement."

"I had no intention of refusing you, Aemon," Martyn said, "But who could be so important that—" The words died on his lips as the figure threw back her cowl. "High Wizard Iosa?"

The woman frowned so severely that Martyn stepped away. "You can call her Lelani now," Aemon laughed, and the woman's scowl deepened. "Oh, come now, Lelani. You're old enough to take a joke. Titles are meaningless. To my eyes, you're a far better person today than yesterday."

Martyn's eyes shifted from Aemon to Lelani and back again. "I don't understand."

"Valkov," Lelani said through clenched teeth. "He cast me out of the Assembly."

"There's no need to dramatize," Aemon said. "Valkov called a vote, and the Assembly voted in his favor."

"He accused me of abusing my position and conspiring to draw the Magi into war!"

"And he was correct, at least in the second accusation. It's been your intent from the start to bring the Magi to Alrendria's defense. There's no point in denying it. I wouldn't have supported your candidacy as High Wizard if I thought you'd turn your back on Alrendria when it needed you."

"Then why didn't you stand up for me yesterday in the Assembly Hall?"

Aemon eyed her askance. "Alwen's right. You have no concept of politics, do you? I have no more power in the Assembly than you anymore, my dear. In fact, only my reputation kept Valkov from ordering my arrest as well. Most of the Magi who would side with me against Valkov left when Jeran did, either to follow him or to withdraw from this conflict altogether. Those who remain are loyal to the Isolationist party or too timid to make a stand."

"You almost sound as if you're glad this happened!" Lelani said, her anger now directed in full against Aemon. "You sound as if you wanted the Assembly to split."

"A thousand winters ago I did what I had to do to preserve the Assembly," Aemon replied, the Gift adding power to his voice and giving his sky blue eyes an otherworldly light. "It cost me far more than you know, and with little gain. Instead of dying outright, the Assembly withered slowly, until only the husk that 'cast you out' remains."

"Don't lie to me, old man!" Lelani snarled. "You turned on Lorthas the moment he declared war on the Assembly. I was there! If Jeran weren't your blood, you'd have rallied the Assembly against him the moment he started training his own Magi."

"Don't dare presume to have the slightest insight into my actions, past or future," Aemon said, his voice rumbling like distant thunder. His presence filled the chamber, and Lelani shrank away until she huddled once more in the corner, trembling. Of all emotions, Martyn had least expected to see terror on the unflappable woman's face. "You were a child when Lorthas split from the Assembly and know nothing of the man he was, or what he did before naming himself Darklord. And Jeran... If I believed he posed a threat to Alrendria or the Magi, then our shared blood would save him no more than the centuries I shared with Lorthas saved him."

He glared at Lelani a moment more, then turned to Martyn and resumed his normal size. "As I was saying, Lelani and her supporters have run into a bit of trouble with the new controlling faction of the Mage Assembly. I was hoping you might be able to find a place for her here until Valkov's blood has had a chance to cool. In return, Lelani would be more than willing to use her considerable talents to help defend this city."

Magi sworn to defend the city as I command! A miracle if ever I've seen one. Martyn thanked all Five Gods, and asked each for their continued favor. He did his best not to smile, lest Lelani mistake the reason of his joy. "I'd be honored to help you in any way I can, Aemon. Mage Iosa will be shown every courtesy, and her aid will be greatly appreciated."

A grin split Aemon's face. "I suspected you'd be amenable to my proposition. Lelani and I will bring the others to a tavern in the Old City. She'll seek you out tomorrow, and the two of you can decide where best to hide them. It might be best to keep their presence a closely guarded secret. No doubt Valkov will be sending an emissary to meet with your father; he won't take it kindly if he discovers you're hiding his enemies."

"I understand," Martyn said. Aemon drew a deep breath, and a Gate opened. Martyn marveled at the swirling spiral of silver sparks, but after Aemon and Lelani stepped through he said, "Wait! Have you any word of Jeran or Dahr?"

"No," Aemon replied, "Though I hear rumors that Jeran's making radical changes in Dranakohr. I hope to see them soon, and I'll be happy to take a message."

"Tell them..." Martyn frowned. "Tell them to hurry. I fear I'll need both before summer's end."

Aemon nodded, but said nothing more as he and Lelani disappeared. The Gate closed behind them, and Martyn stared for a time at the small pile of snow that had accumulated on the floor, then he slipped from the chamber and hurried to Miriam's quarters.

The princess sat behind a desk, going through a mountain of dispatches. "There you are!" she exclaimed, frustration radiating from her voice. She waved at the piles of paper before her. "I expected you back long ago. You promised to help me sort through these!"

"I was delayed," Martyn replied, drawing Joam's letter from his pocket. He had intended to tell Miriam about the Magi, but at the last instant decided it best to keep the knowledge to himself. The fewer people who knew about them, the less chance someone would say something by accident.

He handed the letter to Miriam. As she read it, her hand began to tremble, and Martyn went to her. She felt frail in his arms, on the verge of breaking, and he resolved to do everything in his power to keep her safe.

"This is terrible news," she said, sniffing away tears. "My father will be worried sick about us."

"About us?" Martyn replied. "He's the one surrounded."

"A wise commander would never attack Aurach, not with my father and your uncle defending it. It would be far simpler to trap them there and strike at us in Kaper. We already face two armies; a third could spell our doom."

"Treloran said the same, but the city has never fallen—"

"The state of our defenses is no well kept secret. Kaper's fortifications are among the best in Madryn, but we have a pittance to guard it. The new city will fall in the first successful attack; after that it will only be a matter of time before we starve or they break through the old city's fortifications. With spies and sympathizers running rampant within the walls, it may not even take an attack."

She set the letter down and bit at her knuckle. "This is too much, Martyn. Too much, too fast. What should we do?"

Martyn forced a smile. "We should marry."

Miriam jerked upright. "What?"

"Our marriage will tighten the bonds between our lands and increase morale among our soldiers. With a child or two on the way, we can show that the succession is secure. By the time the Tachans can spare troops to send toward Kaper, we'll have roused the people against them. They'll not be able to march through a single village or town without the peasants pelting them with rocks or showering them with arrows."

"You're being ridiculous," Miriam said, but the smile Martyn loved played across her lips. "Besides, you wanted to wait until your friends could attend."

"And you wanted to wait for your father. But we must make sacrifices for our people."

"This is preposterous. Our marriage won't really change anything."

"It will make me happy, at the very least," Martyn said, affecting a sour grimace. "You don't think a prince who looks like this capable of defeating an overwhelming enemy, do you?"

Miriam laughed, and brushed his lips with a kiss. "I need to find Kaeille," she said. "We've thousands of details to arrange!"

Thousands? All we need is my father to pronounce us wed. Martyn wondered about that while Miriam dashed from the room. He considered following his princess to learn what details he had not considered, then reached for the topmost dispatch. *Some chores are far less onerous than others.*

CHAPTER 7

Jeran walked the snow-covered path toward the cloaked figures, and Dahr followed a few steps behind. He opened his mind to the Lesser Voices—to the thoughts of the creatures who inhabited Shandar's meticulous park—hoping to determine how much of a threat waited for them around the obelisk. The animals remained strangely quiet; though Dahr sensed their presence in the trees and bushes, they offered no insights.

The chaotic swirl in the back of his mind stilled. Dahr would have relished the peace at any other time, but this silence frustrated him. *Why are they only silent when I want something of them?* Of the dozen or so creatures he could differentiate amidst the tumult, the only two he felt clear thoughts from were Fang and Shyrock. The hound loped forward to walk beside Jeran, telling Dahr that *he* had nothing to fear here, and Shyrock launched from his shoulder and circled. Dahr studied the city through the eagle's eyes, admiring its beauty and mapping an escape route should one prove necessary.

In the depth of winter, Shandar was a different place than Dahr remembered, more foreboding. The chill air clamped around his heart like a skeletal claw, quenching his anger and awakening regret. Jeran did well to call this place a tomb. It belonged to the dead, and Dahr wondered what could have drawn Jeran here, what could have made him choose this place above all.

The nine cloaked forms watched them approach, their faces hidden under hoods. But hoods were for protection as much as concealment, and the biting wind driving chunks of ice against his flesh made Dahr wish for a stout cloak too. If danger were to come, he did not think it would come from ahead.

Far worse than the threat of death was the sound of pleasant conversation behind him. Katya's warm voice melded with Lord Grondellan's booming bass, a gentle buzz Dahr could not quite discern as words. He wanted to hate them for the things they had done—Katya more than his former Master—but he owed both debts as well. He wanted to punish them for their crimes, but his promise to Jeran denied him even that. *A fitting punishment for my own transgressions. Condemned to wander the world saddled with the two people I despise most, forced to pretend they are not my enemies.*

Eyes burned in his back, and Dahr craned his neck to see which of his two shadows stared at him. Neither did; it was Yurs, Lord Grondellan's castellan, whose gaze bored into him down a beaked nose. Dahr turned away, unwilling to look at the man for too long. Yurs had an unyielding memory. He managed Lord Grondellan's vast estates and numerous possessions without ledgers or logs. Dahr avoided him as much as possible.

"You didn't have to wait for me out here," Jeran announced, stopping in front of the strangers. "You didn't have to disguise yourselves like the Dryids of ancient lore, either. Those of your ilk carry enough prestige without theatrics."

"You may not have noticed, my boy," Aemon said, throwing back his hood, "but it's cold out here. The elderly don't fare as well in the weather as the young." Rings circled Aemon's eyes, and new wrinkles had sprouted from the corners of them like raven's claws. He smiled, but it lacked the power Dahr remembered; everything about him seemed diminished. *Old. I never thought of him as old before.*

"Who else did you bring?" Jeran asked, his eyes flicking down the line, over the still-hooded figures. "This was your plan from the start, wasn't it? This is where your vision was leading? Me trained to use the Gift faster than ever thought possible, and the Assembly split the way you split it before?"

"Me?" Aemon sputtered. "I never—"

"You may think me more malleable than Lorthas," Jeran interrupted, "more enamored of you because you're my grandfather and I lack the winters to know better. You may think to steer events with me as your puppet. If you do, you're mistaken. For what he did during the MageWar, Lorthas deserves the punishment he endures, but there are others no less guilty who walk free, with only their consciences to condemn them."

"He has changed so much," a voice from the other end of the line said. A thin, delicate hand reached for a hood.

"That is the way of the young," a similar voice replied. The hoods fell back to reveal matching Aelvin faces, lined but still hinting at vitality. "Especially when they suffer as this one has."

"Still, he should trust."

"I think he does. He just doesn't trust *us.*"

"Ah, he sees webs and schemes when he looks at the Gifted."

"As did we, before we started casting webs of our own."

Nahrona and Nahrima, the Aelvin Magi. Jeran had told Dahr about them, but seeing the twins side by side defied the mental image he had created. These Elves seemed patient and wise, far from the obscure riddle-makers Jeran had described. Dahr caught the scent of vigor on them, and a long-suppressed eagerness to fight. These thin, wan creatures were warriors.

"You think this pup is a BattleMage?" A hard-eyed Human with a scar slashed across his scalp threw back his hood and shook his head. He spoke with an accent Dahr could not place, but he, too, carried himself as a warrior. "He doesn't have the heart for it. I'm surprised he's not weeping now from the pain."

Jeran looked at the stranger but said nothing. He turned when another familiar face lowered his hood and said, "That one is a sour one, my friend, but he can teach you some things no one else alive can. That is why he is here."

"Jakal!" Dahr stepped forward, surprised to see the *Tsha'ma* standing in the snow, surprised by his own excitement. "How's Yarchik? How are the Channa?"

"The *Kranor* is well," Jakal said. "He sends you a message, but I am not to deliver it yet."

"A message? What—" Dahr caught Jeran's eyes on him and fell silent.

"And what are you here to teach me, Jakal?" Jeran asked.

At a signal from Jakal, two more Garun'ah dropped their hoods, a giant with yellow eyes and a woman shorter than Jeran and nearly as broad as Dahr, yet curved in such a way that she did not look oddly-sized. "Aemon tells us that you defy all Human knowledge and surrender to magic instead of taking it under your control. For many winters my people have known of such a thing, a special Gift handed to a chosen few."

Aemon frowned and looked at the Tribesman with a suspicion bordering on jealousy. Jakal laughed. "Have the Magi shared all of their tricks and secrets with us? You cannot condemn us for not telling you what you refuse to believe possible. Those who sought the knowledge learned of it easy enough."

"BattleMagi," Jeran said. "You taught the BattleMagi."

"Tyre sought the *Tsha'ma* when his studies led him down a path no Human had ever walked. We showed him our ways, and he melded the knowledge with his own, becoming something more, something new. *Tsha'koranadahr*. BattleMage."

"Tyre's curiosity cost him dearly," Oto said, lowering his hood. Jeran scowled, sending shadows cascading down the creases of his face, but the plump Mage beamed at him. "I won't be gone from Dranakohr long. Aemon asked me to come, to help you, and I—"

"Aemon?" Anger darkened Jeran's features. "You abandon our trainees at his whim?"

"Aemon remains my friend, and the children will survive a day without me. As I was about to say, Aemon asked me to help you, and I couldn't refuse. I remember Tyre's suffering well, and I hope to spare you a measure of it."

"Spare me? How?"

"By convincing you it's not your fault, of course," Oto replied. "The echoes of pain and suffering you feel. All who live endure pain; even if those bonded to you suffer terribly, they've *chosen* to do so. They follow through their own free will and can choose at any time to turn away. I must make you understand that."

"But the students, they—"

"You see, you have proven my point. You want me to go, and I refuse. That makes me no less devoted to your cause, but it demonstrates how I retain the right to make decisions for myself. Don't worry, Jeran. I'll be in Shandar transiently, coming for your lessons and returning to Dranakohr to see to my charges. You've devised a splendid system; I suspect they won't even realize I'm gone."

"Very well," Jeran said, though he seemed not to like being disobeyed. He turned to the final cloaked figure. "And who is the last of my teachers?" he asked, directing his question at Aemon. "I suspected Jes, but that one is too tall for her."

"I had no need to ask Jes," Aemon said, studying Jeran as a grizzled wolfhound might study a young rival. "You had already done so. She won't speak of it, and refused to come down to meet you. She waits in the Assembly Hall."

Withered hands rose and drew back the hood with deliberate slowness, not for show, Dahr guessed, but to keep them from trembling. "Grandfather," Jeran whispered, bowing his head. A confused murmur rose from Katya and Lord Grondellan, who looked from the ancient Elf to Jeran, back and forth, but Grendor raced forward and prostrated himself in the snow.

"Eternal One," Grendor breathed. "May the Mother's blessing be on You."

"Rise, my child," Emperor Alwellyn said. "These frail bones do not deserve such humility, especially from one whose people I helped send into exile." The Emperor stooped, and even that small effort took its toll. He took Grendor by the arm and pulled the Orog to his feet. "Seeing one of your Race after all this time is more than honor enough."

The Emperor stepped past Grendor. His robes barely fluttered when he walked, so that he appeared to glide across the snow-packed ground toward Jeran. One age-spotted hand grasped Jeran's chin, twisting it from side to side. Dahr expected an outburst from Jeran, a flare of the temper that churned beneath the surface, but Jeran accepted the Elf's ministrations without complaint. It disappointed Dahr; he took great satisfaction in seeing others, especially Jeran, succumb to their hidden rages.

"My poor boy," the Emperor whispered.

"You did what you had to do," Jeran said, stepping back.

"I did what I thought I had to," the Emperor replied. "There is a great difference."

"Enough talk," Jeran said. "You've presented yourselves as my instructors, and I accept. My time is short, and there are many things I need to learn. We should begin immediately."

"We'll begin tomorrow," Aemon said. "There—"

"We will begin now," Jeran interrupted, the Gift making his eyes flare.

Aemon drew a slow breath. "Jeran, now's not the time—"

"If I may," Yassik said, inserting himself between Jeran and Aemon. "You've had something of an exhausting day. The kind of training you plan to subject yourself to will make you feel as if you've hauled boulders from one end of Dranakohr to the other and back again. Don't overextend yourself. If you do, you risk not only your own life, but the lives of those who have agreed to train you."

Jeran put a hand to his jacket, as if feeling something inside. He studied Yassik for some time. "We will begin tomorrow," he said after a long pause.

"There's food waiting at the Hall," Oto said, "and a warm fire. I suggest we hurry. The sun is already sinking, and Shandar grows frigid in the shadow of Aemon's Shame."

Oto led them into the streets of Shandar, heading toward the great plaza at the foot of the mountain, the giant carved staircase leading up to massive doors in the side of a rock face. Not for the first time, Dahr wondered at the irony of following a blind man, but Oto's steps never faltered. He walked with a confidence Dahr had not seen since Atol Domiar. Oto had returned to familiar territory.

So had Dahr, but his days in Shandar were distant, hard-to-see things, vague memories he had to fight to hold on to. He longed for that time, before the world had turned cruel and he had seen the monster within, when he had believed himself Human and Jeran his long lost brother. Even hunted by the Durange, certain that every day would prove his last, he had been happier.

I should go back to the Darkwood, or up into the mountains. Jeran doesn't need me anymore. He pities me, but he doesn't need me. I cause him more pain than anything, and I owe him more than pain.

But alone he would find few outlets for his anger, few opportunities to let the beast roam free. With Jeran enemies abounded, and Dahr took satisfaction in unleashing his hunger on those he knew to be evil. Without Jeran's direction, he wondered how long it would take for him to lose all sense of himself, until it was the monster who unleashed him from time to time.

The snow had been cleared from the center of the plaza before the Hall. A mountain of red debris lay off to one side, remnants of the building Jeran had destroyed to save Jes from the Durange. Dahr looked at the rubble and wondered how he could have been so foolish, how he could not have realized Jeran's Gift at the time. He saw Jeran staring at the pile as well, his expression blank, and figured similar thoughts ran through his head.

Jes sat in the center of the clearing, stirring a spoon through a cauldron of stew. The sight brought Dahr's memories back in full force, and he savored the aroma of cooking meat almost as much as the image of him, Jeran, and Aemon playing Seeker through the buildings while they waited for Jes to recover from Tylor's attack.

"This place is a graveyard," Lord Grondellan said, joining Dahr on a makeshift bench beside the fire. "Why would Jeran choose to come here?"

"Shandar is haunted by the shadows of the Magi slaughtered here," Dahr said, "and by the imaginations of those who did not come to help until it was too late. If Jeran needs solitude, this is one place where he'll find it."

Lord Grondellan's nearness made the monster stir, but Dahr tightened the reins. "I don't like this place," the Rachannan nobleman said. "I hear whispers everywhere, and see shades dancing in the shadows. The cold numbs me."

"It's colder in Dranakohr," Dahr said. "Even the slopes of Mount Kalan are worse than this."

"You've been to Rachannon, lad?" Grondellan asked, straightening. "You didn't tell me that! My holdings aren't far from Kalan. When were you there, before joining the Odaras or after?"

"Long ago," Dahr said, a terseness to the words he hoped Grondellan would understand. "I was there long ago."

"Ah." Lord Grondellan clapped a hand to Dahr's shoulder. "There are places in this world I'd rather forget too." They were silent for a time, and Dahr sought a reason to leave his perch by the fire, but no good ones came to mind.

"Let's hunt tomorrow," Lord Grondellan said. "Jeran won't need us, and these hills must teem with game. No words, Hunter. We can bury ourselves in our wretched thoughts and unleash our anger on the prey."

Leave me be! I want nothing to do with you! But the monster stirred at the mention of prey, and Dahr, too, thought a day on the hunt would offer a much-needed diversion. "Tomorrow," he whispered.

"Hah! I knew you couldn't refuse. Excuse me, lad. I need to find Yurs. He and I have things to discuss."

Lord Grondellan left him staring into the fire. Dahr let his mind wander, dancing around the chaotic knot at the periphery of this thoughts. The Lesser Voices chattered, but Dahr had no interest in what they said. He yearned for solitude, for a life with no demands or responsibilities, a life with no pain. Alrendria thought him a hero, the Garun'ah some kind of demigod. He had asked to be neither, wanted neither.

"Terrible evening," Oto said, shuffling forward to join Dahr by the fire. "There's something in the air about Shandar, something that makes the cold drive into your bones. I wonder how you can sit here so placidly in such flimsy clothes."

Dahr looked at his bare arms and felt a chill along his legs where the fire had melted the snow picked up during the walk in Shandar's park. "I don't feel the cold as other men."

"No doubt," Oto replied. "I've known Tribesmen to run half-naked through drifts waist deep and laugh off the chill as if they'd just taken a pleasant dip in a summer stream. But you... There's something else about you. It's as if... As if you've tamped down your inner fire until there's nothing left to warm your soul. You shouldn't fear your passions, Dahr. You can't rid yourself of them, and confining them only strengthens them."

"You can't begin to know what lurks inside me," Dahr snapped. "You Magi pretend to have all the answers, but you—"

Oto's blank stared pierced him to the core, forcing him to silence. "Let me give you an example. I feel a fire. Is there a kettle upon it?" Dahr glanced to the side and saw an iron kettle, steam pouring from its spout. "Yes, I see it now," Oto continued in his even, soothing voice, his eyes never leaving Dahr. "Your emotions are boiling water. Properly harnessed, they can serve you in a number of ways. But if you bottle them up..."

Oto gestured, and the river of steam stopped. An instant later, the kettle began to shake and tremble. "I worry about you, my friend. I've known other Garun'ah to run from their soul's fire, and the results have never been pleasant. If you weren't *Tier'sorahn*—"

"What does that have to do with anything," Dahr mumbled. The voices in his head clamored for attention, but he ignored them. He had more important things to do than deal with than the complaints of owls and squirrels, or listen to the greetings of beasts whose ancestors had walked with men before him.

"The Lesser Voices keep you balanced," Oto said. Over the fire, the kettle jumped and bounced, and droplets of water escaped the Mage's seal, hissing as they fell into the flames. "They help you as you help them. No *Tier'sorahn* in the history of Madryn—none that I have heard of, in any case—has ever lost his path completely. Garun speaks to his chosen ones, to you, through the animals, and the voices of the multitude cannot be ignored.

"I had a bit of a temper myself, when I was young," Oto laughed, "and I was ashamed of it. I did everything I could to suppress the emotions churning inside me, to display a logical and dispassionate façade the way I thought all Magi were supposed to. The effort nearly killed me, and it did kill others. It was only when I was forced to see how—"

With a bang that shook the plaza, the kettle exploded, showering Dahr and Oto with scalding droplets and sending the iron pot off its hook and into the fire. The lid clattered and bounced on the stone far out of sight, and people came running at the sound. Oto waved them back. "You see," he said, ignoring the speckled pink burns on his cheek, "That's what happens when emotion is trapped too long. It needs a release, and it will find one."

"I don't need lectures from you," Dahr snarled.

"Then I recommend conversations," Oto laughed, "but they require you to take a part."

"Why do you care?"

"I care about all the Gods' creatures! No? Too trite? Then let me tell you this: the way I view the world gives me some small insight into the souls of men. In you, I see a battle waging that I've not seen since the time of the MageWar. I've watched too many good men fall because they thought they were something worse than what they were. I don't want to ever see it again."

"Leave me be!" Dahr launched himself from the bench and stomped into the night. Fang started to follow, but Dahr sent her back. He needed time alone, time to contain the anger. The Mage seemed genuinely concerned. Even if Dahr wanted no part of his pity, Oto did not deserve to face the full might of his wrath.

The Lesser Voices did not afford him any peace. They surged and danced in his head, demanding attention. Dahr clamped down on the knot, forcing it to the farthest recesses of his mind. He knew little of his powers, but he knew how to block out the voices. For a while, at least, he could block them out, and at the reasonable cost of a numbing headache.

His path wound through the empty streets of Shandar, past buildings long abandoned and left as a shrine to those who had died here. *They wanted a place of true equality. A place where all men could live together without fear or ridicule. Tylor disabused them of their vision. The hearts of men have little room for kindness and compassion.*

"I thought I could live here once," Dahr told the empty buildings, "back when I was young... and happy. Shandar suits me far better now."

A shadow broke from one building and stepped into the dying light playing across the avenue. A Tribesman in simple hides blocked the path, arms and legs bare to the cold, with streaks of red paint outlining his high cheekbones and beads woven through his raven black hair. The Garun'ah stared at Dahr with a disgust he had come to expect whenever a Hunter first saw him dressed in Human clothes.

"If you're looking for Jakal," Dahr said, pointing toward the mountain, "he's back at the Assembly Hall. If you don't speak *Huma*, I can't—" The Lesser Voices broke through his control, and their piercing message shrieked through his head even as he sensed another shadow breaking from the walls behind him.

Danger.

Dahr reached over his shoulder, but his greatsword lay back at the campsite, left behind in his haste to be free of Oto. He cursed himself for his imprudence, raising his hand to show he meant no harm. When the Tribesman reached for the *dolchek* at his hip, Dahr charged.

He sprinted toward the Garun'ah warrior and grasped the man's hand at the wrist, trapping the tip of the serrated blade in its sheath. He stepped past, locking his other hand on the man's shoulder, and pivoted, lifting the Tribesman from his feet. With all his might, Dahr threw, and the Tribesman hit the wall of the nearest building with the flat of his back. The building shook, and debris rained down upon the Tribesman as he sank to the ground, stunned.

Dahr spun to find another Hunter closing the distance between them. This one had his *dolchek* drawn, and the evening light glinted off the honed blade. The Lesser Voices told him of other forms slinking through the shadows of Shandar.

Fear grasped his heart, but so did exhilaration. When he felt the Lesser Voices rallying to him, he ordered them away. *Not me. Protect the men in the shadow of the mountain.* Most even listened.

The Tribesman dove toward him, and Dahr felt the *dolchek* slice him above the elbow. Pain lanced up his arm, but the wound served to ignite the fire in his blood, and he lashed out as the Garun'ah ran past, slamming the heel of his hand under the man's jaw. The Tribesman, knocked several hands in the air by the blow, hit the ground with a thud, and Dahr dropped atop him. His knees dug into the Tribesman's gut, forcing the air from his lungs. Dahr wrenched the *dolchek* free of the man's spasming grip and drove it into his throat.

Dahr heard footfalls on the street behind him and dove to the side. A blade came slashing down through where his back had been, driving into the corpse. Rolling to his feet, Dahr hefted the *dolchek* taken from his last opponent. The short blade felt odd in his hand, but it would serve him well enough.

The first Tribesman had regained his feet, and he leaned heavily on the wall, gasping for air. Dahr rushed toward him, blade drawn back to strike, dodging a wild swing from the other Tribesman as he passed. His prey saw him coming, but could not move enough to escape Dahr's fatal thrust. He took the blade in the gut, and the blow drove him back into the stone.

Dahr thought the Hunter finished, but the Tribesman's arms snaked out and encircled him, drawing Dahr forward and using his momentum to ram him against the wall. Pain flared in Dahr's shoulder, and he gasped for air, but the Tribesman's grip around his throat crushed like a vice, keeping air from his lungs. They struggled, and Dahr tried to draw the *dolchek* free for another stab, but the Tribesman kept their bodies pinned.

Loss of blood made the Tribesman's grip slacken, and Dahr shoved the Garun'ah warrior away, sucking in a mouthful of much needed air. The Tribesman staggered but refused to fall; he clutched a hand over his wound and limped forward, murder in his eyes. The other Tribesman joined him, and together they advanced.

Backed against the wall, Dahr had no escape. He tightened his grip on the *dolchek* and prepared to attack. When Fang came darting out of the shadows, teeth bared and a growl reverberating through the evening chill, Dahr shouted a warning, but it came too late.

Fang launched herself at the enemy, but the Garun'ah were ready. The hound's target barely staggered, and when Fang's jaws clamped down on his arm, little more than a grimace touched his lips. With his free hand, he pried Fang off his arm, tearing bits of his own flesh in the process. He cuffed Fang, stunning her, and as his hands tightened around her throat, the wounded Tribesman drew a hunting knife from his belt and moved to finish her.

Blood Rage consumed Dahr, and he bellowed a challenge as he dove toward his assailants. His vision narrowed until he only saw his enemy; his blood pounded in tune with theirs. The *dolchek* was no longer in his hand, and it took him a moment to realize that the blade lay buried in the throat of the wounded Tribesman. The other Garun'ah dropped Fang, but Dahr was on him before he raised his knife. They crashed to the ground, and Dahr punched and scratched, clawing at his enemy like a beast.

He pounded until blood covered his body like a blanket and the thing below him no longer resembled a man. Exhausted, he rolled off the body and toward Fang, relieved to see the hound's chest rising and falling. She whimpered when he neared, and Dahr touched a hand to her head, offering comfort.

"An impressive display," whispered a quiet voice. Dahr grabbed for a *dolchek* and rolled to confront his newest foe. Seeing an Elf froze him in place. Tall and lithe, with slanted green eyes and slightly-pointed ears, the Aelvin warrior prodded the body of one Garun'ah with his toe. His sword remained down, but he carried the blade with purpose and Dahr suspected he knew its use well. "I have seen these three bring down a bear with naught but their hands. I will consider it an honor to kill you, Dahr Odara, savior of the Garun'ah."

CHAPTER 8

"Who are you?" Dahr asked, crawling backward. He sought his feet, but his knees felt like water, his arms burned with fatigue. The sight of an Elf here, in the company of Tribesmen and all of them out to kill him, drove the anger from him, leaving him without the advantages of unbridled emotion. The *dolchek* he held looked insignificant next to the Elf's finely-wrought blade; his own size and greater reach paled beside the Elf's supreme confidence.

"My name is unimportant. I am that one who will deliver you to Kohr, and I will earn a place of honor at the Father's table because of it." The Elf advanced, his blade rising to a ready position. Part of Dahr wanted to turn and flee, trusting his legs to keep him from death; the rest of him knew that flight was impossible, that his stubborn pride and thirst for battle would never allow it.

The Elf leapt forward, blade a blur, the sword sailing a finger's width over Dahr's ducked head. As it passed, Dahr lunged, hoping to catch his opponent off guard and wrestle the blade free, but the Elf moved like a gazelle, and he struck again, bringing the hilt of his sword down against Dahr's skull.

Spots of color danced in Dahr's vision, and he staggered. He saw the sword whistling toward him again and threw himself down, rolling across the debris-strewn paving stones and back to his feet. The Elf glided toward him, blade darting out like a serpent's tongue. The point dug into his thigh, just deep enough to draw blood, then again into his gut. A third stab hit his shoulder, but Dahr jumped away, and instead of scoring a light touch, the Elf's attack tore through Dahr's shirt, exposing his shoulder to the biting cold.

Moving only as pursuit required and attacking with deliberate precision, the Elf watched Dahr's worry turn to panic. Every attack Dahr attempted ended in him nursing a new wound; the Elf's every movement made him flinch like a foundling doe. His enemy taunted him, telling him where to step to avoid the next attack, telling him when to move and how fast, rewarding him with a smile when he listened, and punishing him when he did not.

"Sit!" The Elf barked the word like a command, lunging forward, and in Dahr's haste to dodge he stumbled over one of the dead Tribesmen and crashed to the street.

"And they said one could never train a Wildman," the Elf chuckled. "You are more tractable than a housecat."

Dahr felt the fire of rage flare in him again, but it came too late. The Elf had him on the ground, and his *dolchek*, lost in the fall, lay out of reach. Fang lay unmoving, and none of the other Lesser Voices were near enough to help. Blood oozed from a dozen small wounds, freezing on his flesh in red rivulets. "Kill me, and be done with it," he growled. "I'd rather see the Twilight World than suffer another moment of your company. The disciples of Kohr are a blight upon the Balance. You are a traitor to your people and to nature itself. Spare me your mocking; neither impresses me."

"Defiant to the end," the Elf said, pulling back his sword. "I should make you howl for your insolence, but those chosen by the Gods—even a God as dim-witted at Garun—deserve respect. I will send you—"

A blade erupted from the Elf's chest, and his final words cut off in a gurgle. Blood ran from his lips and dribbled down his too-pale face. As he slid to the ground, Katya's lithe form appeared behind him. "That one prattles on worse than Prince Martyn," she said, wiping her blade on the Elf's cloak.

"You…" *Another debt. I owe her my life again!*

"Owe me nothing," Katya replied, and Dahr wondered if he had spoken the last aloud or if Katya had guessed his thoughts. "You saved me at *Cha'kuhn*, and you didn't kill me in Dranakohr, though we both wanted you to." For an instant before she turned away, Dahr thought he saw moisture in her eyes. *Not her. Not tears.*

When she faced him again, her eyes were dry, but something haunted them. "You saved more than my life. If not for you, I'd have never seen Jeran as anything but an enemy. You made me see him as you do, and you cast into doubt everything I was raised to believe. Hate me if you must, Dahr, but never think you owe me anything." She offered him a hand.

Her words flayed his heart, as did the pain she wore. Part of him yearned to comfort her, to reach out to her, but a bitter voice stayed his hand. *She betrayed you. She lied to you. She used you. She betrayed you…*

"Why are you here?" He brushed aside her outstretched hand and climbed to his feet.

"Grendor," Katya answered. "When Fang bolted from the camp, the Orog begged me to follow her. He was convinced you were in danger."

"Why not come himself?"

"He thinks himself inept." Katya's laugh made Dahr smile. He schooled his features, cursing himself for his weakness. "His wounds may handicap him, but not as much as he believes. He models himself after you, the great warrior."

Dahr ignored her attempt at humor and cast out his mind to the Lesser Voices, asking them to be his eyes. They showed him other shadowy forms slinking through the streets of Shandar, their criss-crossing paths taking them ever nearer the Assembly Hall.

"We must hurry," Dahr said, putting a hand on Fang. She whimpered and stood, favoring a leg. Dahr told her to wait until the fighting was done, then started toward the Hall at a slow jog. The cold had frozen his wounds, and every step pulled at the icy scabs, sending shocks of pain through his body. Katya trotted beside him, sword ready, eyes on the shadows, so he made an effort to hide his pain, fixing upon his face a mask of grim determination.

They encountered no one until they reached the Hall, though Dahr felt eyes on his back the whole way. The others stood around the fire, the Magi facing in varying directions, their eyes distant—or sometimes closed—and Grendor pacing before them, the butt of his *va'dasheran* clacking on the stones. Yurs and Lord Grondellan stood off to one side, the Rachannan nobleman watching the shadows like a hawk, his eyes darting back and forth at every assumed movement; his steward stared at Dahr and Katya, watching their approach.

"We are surrounded," Dahr said, retrieving his greatsword from its place near the fire. He caressed the shining steel and promised himself that he would never go weaponless again. "I was attacked by—"

"Tribesmen," Aemon interrupted. "We know, my boy. Grendor warned us of the danger. There are dozens out there, closing in on the camp."

"Fools," said the grim-faced Human Mage. He had a sword drawn and a small shield buckled halfway up his left forearm. The air around him hummed with power. "Attacking a camp full of Magi. Even if they'd caught us by surprise—"

"The servants of Kohr are not known for wisdom," Jakal said. He carried no weapon, nor did the stout Garun'ah woman, but the scarred giant held a strange weapon, half axe and half hammer, on a haft nearly as tall as Dahr. "They serve with blind devotion. If they have been asked to attack this camp, they will do so until the last of their numbers has fallen."

A howl rose from the deepening twilight, the chorus of a hundred voices raised in challenge. Dahr saw figures darting through the shadows, jockeying for position, studying the field. "What are they waiting for?" Lord Grondellan demanded, a nervousness in his voice Dahr had never before heard. "They're here. We're here. If it's battle they want, let's get on with it!"

"Maybe they're waiting for the Elves," Katya said.

The Magi looked at her as if she had spoken gibberish. "Blood no work with *Aelva*," said the *Tsha'ma* woman. "Too long feud."

"She's right, my child," Nahrona said. "Our Races would not work together."

"We have been fighting for many winters," Nahrima added. "Such grievances do not give way lightly,"

"The last time we worked toward the same goal was during the MageWar."

"And even then relations were… strained."

"*You're* working together now," Katya countered, anger flushing her cheeks. Watching her stand up to the Gifted—hands on her hips, green eyes defiant— something stirred within Dahr, a feeling beyond lust. A feeling he thought long dead.

"Katya's right," Jeran said. "It's not just *Tsha'ma* and *Ael Maulle* who can set aside their differences. We must assume our enemies can encourage cooperation among the Races at least as well as we can."

"This is no assumption," Dahr said, stepping into the light to display his criss-crossing wounds. "These were caused by Tribesmen and an Elf. If they weren't exactly working together, they were at least working toward the same goal!"

"It's not that I don't believe you, my boy," Aemon said, but his voice hinted at exasperation, "but if there were Elves here, we'd be able to see—"

A shape whirred through the night, and the giant *Tsha'ma* fell. He regained his feet in an instant, but the barbed head of an arrow stuck out from his back, and the feathered end jutted from his chest below the shoulder. Other arrows followed from all directions, clattering upon the paving stones like iron rain.

Aemon's brows drew down in concentration, and the other Gifted took up defensive postures. The air around them hardened, deflecting most of the missiles, but a few passed through the magical shields, missing their targets by the narrowest of margins.

The howl of the Garun'ah grew louder, and Dahr readied for battle, gripping the hilt of his sword and fighting the urge to plunge into the darkness in search of prey.

"Do you see anything?" Aemon asked the scarred Human Mage.

"Nothing," the Mage spat. "If they're out there, they're invisible."

Aemon spun in a staccato pivot, fixing his eyes on the surrounding buildings one at a time. Each arrow brought a curse to his lips, and he studied their paths, trying to trace them back to their origins. "Jakal? Oto?"

"*Si'aelvakesh* have one foot in the Twilight World," the *Tsha'ma* said. "Finding them is like finding spirits."

"Oto!" Aemon shouted. "We're no good at seeing what's not there."

"I'm looking, Aemon," Oto replied, his voice a bastion of serenity. "We're still capable of independent thought. We don't need you to tell us when to breathe." The air crackled with tension; the Magi had lost their pretense of control. "There!" Oto said, his finger jutting to a distant building. "Two in there. I'll—"

"This is taking too long!" Aemon shouted, watching an arrow glance off the air in front of him.

"I'm not exactly taking my time." Frustration tinged Oto's voice.

"Enough bickering!" Jeran said. "Dahr, the Magi are incapable of finding the Elves. Can you do it?"

Dahr opened himself to the Lesser Voices, asked them to search Shandar for Elves and report their locations to him. He begged them not to involve themselves in the fighting, even though he knew few would heed his request. "Two to the southeast. One in that building. Two more—"

"Good. You, Lord Grondellan, and the *Tsha'ma* will hunt them down. Grandfather?"

"Yes?" said Aemon.

"Yes?" said the Emperor, rousing himself. The ancient Elf had not moved since Dahr had returned to camp.

"I'd prefer you to seek shelter," Jeran said, approaching the Emperor, "but I know you won't. Our enemies thrive on darkness. Can you take away the source of their power?"

A grin split the Elf's face, though Dahr thought even that simple gesture took effort, pulling the Emperor's flesh tight across his skeletal frame. "Yes, child, I believe I can." He closed his eyes, and the air stilled. A moment later, a sphere of light appeared above the campfire, growing in size and brilliance. Dahr turned away from it, shielding his eyes, and watched as the plaza brightened from late twilight to near midday.

The howling of the Garun'ah stopped, and Shandar grew silent as a tomb. Jes broke from her place on the far side of the camp and took Jeran by the shoulder. "What are you planning? What have you brought to Shandar?"

"You've lived with Aemon too long," Jeran said, a sad smile touching his lips. He drew his sword; the Aelvin blade hummed as it left its sheath. "You see plots and strategies in every action. I planned nothing for Shandar aside from my training, and Shandar was not my choice, but Aemon's. Our enemies brought the battle to me. I did not expect them, but I won't deny them."

He turned to Yassik. "Are there Gifted out there?"

"If there are, they're going to great lengths to conceal themselves."

"You and Grendor are responsible for dealing with any we find. I—"

Whatever else Jeran planned drowned under the renewed roar of the enemy. Dozens of Tribesmen burst from Shandar's streets and alleys, filling the plaza with feral cries. They charged, ignoring the hum of power that emanated from the Gifted and made the flesh of Dahr's arms prickle.

"Let's cut a path through these mongrels and go Elf hunting," Lord Grondellan said, hefting his axe. Beyond him, Dahr watched Katya ease the blade in her hand and prepare to meet the charge.

The thrill of battle electrified Dahr, and an eager smile forced its way onto his lips. "I did promise you a hunt."

They sprinted forward side by side, and Dahr howled his own war cry. To his surprise, Lord Grondellan mimicked the sound, baring his teeth in a snarl. The burly Rachannan knocked the *dolchek* of his first opponent aside and lowered his shoulder, plowing the Tribesman to the ground. He pivoted, almost casually, and let his axe fall, then tore the blade free of the dying Garun'ah and rammed the butt of the haft into another Tribesman.

A Garun'ah Hunter, face painted in red and blue stripes and standing head and shoulders taller than Dahr, broke from the pack and ran toward him. The Hunter carried a hatchet, but its reach was no match for Dahr's greatsword. He sliced the Tribesman across the middle and dodged the awkward attack that followed. The Tribesmen, holding his guts closed with one hand, turned to renew his attack, but Dahr raced ahead, ignoring the accented cries of 'coward' that followed.

He had nearly reached the first building when a black arrow flashed past his shoulder. An instant later, three Tribesmen flew from the shadows. Dahr impaled one on his sword, but the Garun'ah's weight dragged the blade down. Dahr struggled to free his weapon as the other two closed in.

One Hunter lunged, and Dahr twisted, but he felt a new fire ignite along his arm and saw bright blood mixing with the darker stains of his earlier wounds. He wrenched his sword free and stumbled back, barely dodging another attack. Then Lord Grondellan appeared, hacking at one Tribesman. The giant *Tsha'ma*, arrow still imbedded in his chest, fought at the Rachannan's side, wielding a *dolchek* as long as a shortsword.

A fourth Tribesmen ran toward them, bellowing, "*Kadath uva Kohr!*" The *Tsha'ma* glanced at the newcomer, and the Hunter launched backward, hitting the wall with so much force the stone cracked. He toppled to the street, blood dripping from his mouth and debris raining down upon him.

In the moment of shock that followed, the *Tsha'ma* sliced his opponent's throat, and Lord Grondellan cleaved the arm from his own foe, then followed up with a blow that silenced the Tribesman's scream.

Dahr walked toward the *Tsha'ma*, wiping blood from his blade. "Who are you?" he asked, annoyed by the awe he heard in his voice.

"I Goshen Shadowkiller, of Sahna." He grunted something in Garu, and his eyes consumed Dahr. Golden yellow but streaked with bands of red, those eyes terrified him. It was an effort not to turn away.

"I honor fight with *Cho Korahn Garun*," Goshen said, clapping Dahr on the shoulder. Dahr winced at the pain that slid down his arm. "Come. We hunt *Aelva*."

The *Tsha'ma* strode down the alley, out of the light of the Emperor's sun. "I'd hate to be across the battlefield from that one," Lord Grondellan said, earning a nod of mute agreement from Dahr. After a moment, the Rachannan asked, "Where are we going, lad? I'm not going to be able to see anything out there."

Dahr opened himself to the Lesser Voices, asking them to lead him to the Elves. "There," he said, pointing toward a five-story stone structure at the end of the block. "There are two on the roof."

Goshen waited for them at the entrance. "Good, you smell Aelva too. You have these. I kill those." He pointed to a building at the other end of the block.

"Down there? There aren't any Elves…" Dahr cut off when Shyrock showed him four more archers, concealed on the third story of the far building and taking careful aim at the plaza.

Four kills, the monster within thought, struggling to break free. *He wants to steal four kills from me!* "Wouldn't it be better if we worked together?" Dahr asked, thinking he might be able to beat the *Tsha'ma* to the next target.

Goshen turned his eerie gaze on Dahr again. "You need help?"

"No! I just—"

"My find," Goshen said, loping into the darkness. "My kill."

"Come along, lad," Lord Grondellan said, laying a hand on Dahr's shoulder. "I've a feeling that one can take care of himself."

Dahr wrenched away from the Rachannan and pushed inside. He took the stairs at a run—the Lesser Voices assured him the building was clear save for the Elves on the roof—and Lord Grondellan followed, puffing with the effort of keeping up. He opened the door with care, crouched low in case the archers saw him, but their attention remained rooted on the plaza below.

They crept forward, and Grondellan drew a throwing knife from one of the sheathes strapped across his chest. At Dahr's nod, he threw, and the blade took one Elf in the back. Dahr crossed the remaining distance before the other could trade bow for blade, and his greatsword sliced from face to thigh, leaving a trail of red down the Elf's body.

Dahr's opponent fell, but Lord Grondellan's jerked and jumped, flailing his arms about in an effort to grip the dagger jutting from his back. The Rachannan ripped out the blade and shoved the Elf over the edge. They heard no scream from either enemy; the first sound was the thud of their bodies hitting the street.

"Should we help Goshen?" Dahr asked as the Lesser Voices showed him two more sets of Elves laying an ambush across the plaza. Below, Jeran and Katya fought back to back, spinning through the rush of Tribesmen, their blades working with a synchronicity that astounded Dahr. Aemon and the other Magi—except the scarred Human Mage, who ran counter to Jeran and Katya, carving his own path through the Garun'ah—remained in the center of the camp, holding the enemy at bay with magic. The Aelvin twins danced around the Emperor, the staffs they had used to support their weight now whirled around their bodies in a blur. Fire and wind battered the Tribesmen, but with deliberate precision, not the wholesale destruction Dahr had seen used in previous battles. *Are they so concerned about Shandar*, Dahr wondered, *or is this Jeran's first lesson in control?*

Flames exploded from the building at the other end of the block, and a charred form fell from a third story window. Another body was shoved through the window and held aloft by the muscular arm of a Tribesman. The Elf fought to maintain a grip on his attacker, but when the *Tsha'ma* released him with a casual flick of the wrist, he followed his companion to the street.

His Elf screamed, Dahr thought, listening to the panicked cry that preceded the Elf's death. *But not because of the fall. He screamed until Goshen let him go.*

"I think that one can take care of himself," Lord Grondellan repeated, his expression somber.

A hunger built within Dahr, and his lips drew down in a snarl. "Then let's get back to our hunt."

They searched dozens of buildings on the word of the Lesser Voices, though in more than half he found the Elves already dead. Each empty building made the Blood Rage worse, and he urged Lord Grondellan for speed, sprinting through the streets and buildings with no regard for stealth. All that mattered was beating the *Tsha'ma* to his prey, to give the monster a chance to run wild, so that tomorrow, when among friends, it could slumber.

The Elves he encountered stood no chance; he set upon them like a rabid dog, using his bare hands as often as his sword. The wounds he earned in the process barely registered; they were scratches compared to the beating he had taken earlier. Lord Grondellan, gasping for breath and always a step behind, constantly urged caution, but Dahr ignored him. That the man saved his life several times earned him neither Dahr's respect nor gratitude. If anything, he resented that Grondellan's intervention was required, and that his own foolishness put him deeper in the man's debt. But the monster wanted blood, and tonight Dahr saw no reason to deny it.

When the Emperor's sun faded, Dahr knew the battle was over, but he asked the Lesser Voices to continue their search. When they finally refused, insisting that none but his friends remained alive in Shandar, Dahr stifled the monster and led Lord Grondellan back to the plaza in the shadow of Aemon's Shame.

He limped in, clothes torn and tattered by a hundred cuts, blood covering his body. He no longer knew how much of the blood was his and how much his enemies', but the burning agony of his wounds dulled to an ache, and with the pain went his concern about them. Bodies of Tribesmen—burned, broken, or bloodied, sometimes all three—lay about the plaza. Oto, Aemon, and the other Human Magi gathered them together, inspecting each before piling them into a heap at one corner of the plaza. Jakal and Grendor worked in silent concert, building a pyre separate from that of their enemies. The melody of Jakal's somber dirge drifted to Dahr on the chill night wind.

The Gifted had not survived unscathed. Aemon nursed a leg, and Goshen sported two broad slashes in addition to the arrow piercing his flesh. Jes tended to the *Tsha'ma*, though she, herself, clutched an arm to her side, and a dark stain at the shoulder ruined the color of her blue traveling dress. The female Tribesman lay dead, her body feathered with arrows.

Jeran stood before the Elves, watching the twins fuss over a blood-crusted scratch on the Emperor's arm. The Emperor remained silent, eyes transfixed on the night sky, and Dahr saw a familiar regret in the Elf's eyes. He understood the Emperor's pain; he, too, had once yearned for death in battle.

"*Noedra Synissti?*" Jeran asked. "The Elves we fought were *Noedra Synissti?*"

"Not all," Nahrona replied, wiping the blood from the Emperor's now-healed wound. "One or two, at most. The Brotherhood's skills come at too high a cost to risk so many on one battle."

"No wise commander would risk *Noedra Synissti* in open battle."

"Their skills lend themselves to more subtle use."

"These Elves used the tools of the Brotherhood, though," Nahrima added.

Jeran turned, a calculating curiosity in his eyes. "What do you mean?"

"The Gifted represent a powerful weapon," Nahrona said, drawing the Emperor's cloak tight about the ancient Elf's shoulders.

Nahrima offered the Emperor a flask of minted water, which he ignored. "Finding ways to kill the Gifted undetected became an area of great study during the MageWar."

"The Orog, untouched by magic and invisible to our descrying, made excellent assassins."

"But few Orog sided with Lorthas. He had to be more creative."

"He had his MageSmiths fashion amulets that mimicked the Orog's invisibility, hiding them from our perceptions."

"They were given to the Darklord's finest assassins."

"By the time we saw them coming, it was often too late."

"And what of her?" Jeran asked, pointing to the body of the *Tsha'ma*. "She had a shield around her. Another secret you've kept from me?"

"A harsh accusation, that." Nahrona shook his head as if disappointed.

"It's only a secret if the knowledge is withheld deliberately."

"Since you've never asked about such matters, it hardly constitutes obscuration."

"Wipe that look off your face, Jeran," the Emperor said, clearing his throat. "These two have weathered far more scathing glares from me without flinching. The arrows have been infused with magic as well. They cannot penetrate all magical shields, but they are better able to slip through the gaps in the shells of air we weave."

"Why didn't someone tell me about this, Grandfather? What other tidbits of unrevealed knowledge might make a difference in this war?"

"I have more than six thousand winters of life, child. Would you like me to start from the beginning? You'll be ready to fight the Darklord by the end of your first millennium. You cannot expect foreknowledge of everything. I, myself, did not even remember Lorthas's assassins or their tools until they attacked."

Jeran drew a deep breath, and Dahr watched the war for control raging within him. That Jeran had the strength to win the war infuriated him. "We need to collect as many of the amulets and arrowheads as possible. And any other 'tools' these assassins might use. I want them sent to Albion for study."

"Is that wise?" Yassik asked, joining them in the light of the fire. "It's likely that Albion is the one who fashioned the items in the first place."

"If so," Jeran countered, "he'll be able to explain their use and make more, should we require it. If not, he's the only one capable of understanding their construction and designing countermeasures. I—"

Yassik's face flushed, a color made more acute contrasted to the bone white of his beard and the pale faces of the Elves. "You conveniently forget that Albion served the Darklord. You trust him far more than is wise."

"If I suspected everyone with a bond to our enemies," Jeran said, his face impassive, "I'd have no one left to trust, myself included. Albion never served willingly."

Yassik's lips compressed into a narrow line. He looked as if he wanted to say more, but something held his tongue. He stormed off into the night.

Jeran watched the Mage go, then turned back to the Emperor. "I don't need a daily accounting of your lives, Grandfather, but knowing about any other omissions that may leap from the shadows to kill us could prove important."

"Yes, child, you're right. The twins and I will delve our memories. We will hold nothing back, you have my word. Now, as to your performance tonight, I had a few observations I wanted to share."

"Yes!" Nahrona and Nahrima said in unison, crowding toward Jeran. "That was a fascinating weave you used to create a gust of wind," Nahrona added. "Yet I've never seen such complexity required to perform so simple a task. Do you..."

Dahr stopped listening when a hand touched his arm and gently pulled him around. Exhaustion rimmed Jes's eyes, wisps of hair stood out at odd angles, and splotches of dirt and soot marred her dress. The sight of the prim and proper Mage so disheveled almost made Dahr laugh, but he held it in check. Enough of his mirth must have made it to his eyes, though, for Jes's expression hardened when she looked upon him.

"You're a sight," she said, glancing at the blood-crusted wounds criss-crossing his body. She drew a deep breath and commanded him to sit.

"I don't want Healing," Dahr said.

"Sit," Jes snapped, hitting the butt of her hand against his midriff in such a way that she drove the breath from his lungs. Gasping, he staggered back and collapsed onto a bench before the fire. Anger returned, white hot and desperate to be released, but Jes caught a glimpse of it and sniffed.

"Save your theatrics for someone who's frightened by them," she said, pulling his shirt aside to examine his wounds with more care. "I'm tired, but not so tired I can't bind you until I've finished my work."

"I don't want Healing," Dahr repeated.

"I didn't want to be blackmailed into coming here," Jes snapped, and Dahr saw an anger hot enough to rival his own burning beneath her unruffled surface. "If we're attacked again, we'll need you fresh, and you won't be if you've leaked your life's blood all over the camp. Now sit still."

Jes grasped his head and unleashed her magic upon him. When she let go, Dahr felt lethargic, drained of energy, but the sharp stab of his wounds faded to a dull ache. Jes nearly collapsed from the effort though, and without thinking Dahr steadied her until she regained her balance and pulled away.

"We've not had much luck in Shandar, have we?" Dahr asked.

Jes studied him for a moment. "This place has always appeared safer than it is. I thought he'd learned that last time."

Oto, Yassik, Aemon, and Jakal joined the Elves by the fire. Jeran paced in front of them, stopping now and again to ask a question and holding his ground until he received a satisfactory answer. Dahr watched their exchange for a moment. "Gods, he's arrogant! Look at him. He even treats Aemon and the Emperor as his subjects, demanding and coercing."

"He is what they made him," Jes said, her voice resonating with a haunting regret. "What *we* made him. But you're right; he's grown audacious to the point of foolishness."

"Why do they let him get away with it?"

"Why do you?" Jes asked. Dahr fought the urge to turn away from her probing blue gaze. "He pulls your strings with more skill than anyone's. Why do you let him if you despise it so much?"

"He... He's my friend. I owe him. But them?"—His gesture took in the assembled Magi—"What is he to them but an upstart child?"

"He's their last hope. This is the twilight of their lives, and everything they've worked to build is crumbling around them. They've invested much in Jeran; they've entrusted him with the completion of their dream. Now they have to believe in him, or it means they've wasted their lives."

"Why Jeran?" Dahr asked. "Why do they follow him? Why do we all follow him?"

"He accepts what the Gods force on him. He doesn't run from his fears or responsibilities. He's not afraid to look at old problems and propose solutions that oppose tradition and convention. We follow him because we see the promise of his vision, and we sense he'll lead us to something better even if we refuse to help. We follow because, in some ways, we have no choice. Change is inevitable, and I'd take Jeran's changes over Lorthas's any day."

Dahr saw something as she turned her gaze on Jeran, something nebulous and ephemeral, but powerful. It fled as quickly as it arrived, and the tender smile that touched Jes's lips left with it, replaced by her customary dispassion. "People would follow you too, I think, if you stopped trying to side-step your fate long enough to let them."

Dahr's expression soured. "My life is more than I wish responsibility for. I have no need for Gods or destinies."

"The Orog have a saying," Jes told him, straightening her dress. "Serve the Gods and be burdened; deny them and be cursed. But ignore them at your peril, for none can shout louder than the divine."

She watched him a moment more, and this time, he did turn away. "If you'll excuse me," Jes said, turning to look at Goshen, "I have to convince that infuriating Garun'ah... the other infuriating Garun'ah... to let me remove the arrow from his chest. He wants to keep it as a trophy!"

She left him to his thoughts, and Dahr shivered in her absence, but not from the cold. He felt eyes on him, watching, waiting. "What do you want from me?" he growled, casting his eyes skyward. Only then did he notice the figure standing in the shadow of a building, eyes fastened on his shoulder where the cloth had torn away to reveal the condor brand, the sigil of House Grondellan, burned into his flesh.

Yurs. Dahr's eyes narrowed to slits as he watched Lord Grondellan's castellan slip into the shadows.

CHAPTER 9

Dahr sat beneath a torn awning in an abandoned corner of Shandar. A stiff breeze blew the flaps of canvas, playing shadows across the ground. He watched the swirl of light and darkness, thinking back to the morning spent in the forested hills above the city hunting deer with Lord Grondellan. He had resisted the Ra-channan nobleman for as long as he could, but the hunt had called to him, as had the desire to get out from under the eyes of the Gifted. They were not here for him, he knew, but whenever duty drew Jeran away, the eyes of the Gifted sought him, probing and assessing. He wearied of the attention, of feeling like a showpiece in a collection of oddities. *At least Lord Grondellan treats me as a man. Even if he knew me as his slave, that would be better than what the Gifted see.*

That the Magi could be watching him even now was never far from Dahr's thoughts, but somehow he knew they were not. Obsessed with Jeran's training, the Gifted had gathered in the park, where they could lecture and practice without worrying about laying waste to more of Shandar. Even without the guidance of the Lesser Voices, Dahr could point to them, to Jeran, whose presence filled another spot at the back of his mind, separate from the Lesser Voices but just as nagging in its permanence. He could not block it out in the same way as the animals, but some days, like today, it was less distinct.

Statue still and unblinking, he watched the street before him. Fang and Shy-rock were gone; for reasons Dahr could not fathom, they refused to take part in what he planned. Their small betrayal annoyed him, but he granted them the free-dom of choice. He did not need their help.

"You crouch in the shadows like a *tigran*," Jakal said, announcing his presence. Dahr choked down the fear that gripped his heart and released the hold he had taken on his sword. "I thought you had returned from your hunt."

"The hunt is never finished," Dahr replied. "Only the hunters and hunted change. The Balance demands no less."

"Spoken like a Voice of Garun," Jakal chuckled. The *Tsha'ma* crouched beside Dahr, tracing a finger through the layer of dirt accumulated on the paving stones. "I am to give you Yarchik's message now."

"Why? What's changed?"

"When the children of the Storm King shed the cloak of hatred and descend upon the frozen city, then shall the Korahn be warned. The precipice nears; the maw of the Nothing beckons. With His coming shall the Blood be broken, crashed against the stones of man like a wave of death. Dread the Korahn's return, but dread more his absence. Without His guidance shall the Blood be lost forever, and the Balance wholly destroyed."

Dahr's frown deepened with every word, until his jaw ached with the effort. "I am not your chosen one," he said. "I am *Tier'sorahn*; I can't deny that. But why would Garun choose me as his prophet? I know nothing of the Blood. I know nothing of the Balance. Yarchik interprets the *Prah'phetia* as he wishes. Have you ever considered that he's wrong?"

"I have," Jakal replied, "but not for many moons. One can call the truth a lie only so many times. Yarchik's understanding of Garun's warning is singular among our people. Woe to the Blood if he is wrong this time, for if you are not the Korahn then it must be he, and we have squandered our time with Garun's Chosen One."

Dahr faced the *Tsha'ma*, looked into his eyes seeking deception. He saw none. "I won't go. The Tribes deserve someone better."

"Now you challenge the wisdom of a God? You have the courage of a thousand *tigrans*." Jakal studied Dahr as Dahr studied him, but whatever the *Tsha'ma* sought, he must have found, for a broad smile split his face.

"Cast out by the Redeemer," Jakal intoned, "the Korahn will march toward a blood-soaked horizon to cast judgment on Garun's Children. Two and two shall they come, Great Bear, warden of His body; Black Cat, guardian of His heart; Stone Lion, steward of His soul. Together shall they serve Him. Together shall they bind Him. Together shall they betray Him, and in their betrayal shall the Blood be delivered or destroyed."

"I will not go," Dahr repeated through clenched teeth. "I have no interest in the Gods or their plans for me, and I have no right to judge your people. The crimes you seek atonement for are centuries old. You do not need my forgiveness."

"It is not forgiveness we seek," Jakal said. "It is guidance. The Blood have lost their way. They work to achieve a false Balance, though opposite in design to that of the *Aelva*."

"I won't go. I can't do what you think I can."

"Yarchik thought the words of a God might not be enough," Jakal said, "so he sent his own. 'I stand with one foot in the Twilight World. If Dahr will not come at Garun's request, ask him to come at mine. Tell him I wish to lay eyes on my friend one last time.'"

Dahr thought about the aging Tribesman and the many conversations they had shared. Yarchik had a unique perspective, but the *Kranor* of the Channa saw *Cho Korahn Garun* when he looked at Dahr. He saw something that did not exist. *He befriended a myth, not me. He doesn't deserve to see what's become of his savior.*

"Tell him I can't go," Dahr said. "I have a duty to Jeran and Alrendria."

"I must remain in Shandar as well. Jeran requires knowledge only a few can give him." The *Tsha'ma* ran fingers over his lips, across the patchy blonde stubble that heralded the Human blood in his veins. "I wonder what you are here to teach him."

The *Tsha'ma* departed, and Dahr snatched the flask from the ground, downing a deep draught of fiery *brandei*. The drink burned his throat, but it dulled the edge of his fury and fortified his resolve. *I have to do it. There's no other way.*

Crouching in the shadows, drinking *brandei*, Dahr's thoughts drifted to Katya. Her presence tormented him. He reviled her for her betrayal and her bloodline, but the mere sight of her resurrected feelings he thought long dead. Jeran's friendship with her confounded him; that she had earned a place of trust equal or beyond his own stoked the fire of his hatred. *I want her to pay for what she did. So why do I envision her as I thought she was, and not as I know she is?*

By the time he heard movement in the distance, the *brandei* bottle lay upended on the ground, and Dahr had to steady himself on the low stone wall. Yurs appeared, two buckets dripping water slung across his shoulders on a pole. He approached unsuspecting, unconcerned, but Dahr waited until only a few hands separated them before he pounced.

Yurs spotted him, and the buckets fell from his shoulders as one hand slipped toward the opposite sleeve. Dahr had studied his prey and knew his tricks; he grabbed Yurs by the wrists and shook the concealed blades free, then slammed the man against the wall with enough force to drive the breath from his lungs. One hand pinned Yurs's favored hand behind his back, the other clamped around the man's throat. "You know who I am," he growled, fighting the urge to break the man's neck.

Yurs regarded Dahr with probing grey eyes, eyes that, to Dahr's dismay, showed not a hint of fear. "I've suspected for a while, ever since I saw the trinket your woman wears. But necklaces can be found or duplicated; the brand was the proof I needed."

My woman? I want nothing to do with her! Dahr's hand clenched, and Yurs's faced turned red, but he made no move to fight. "I should kill you for what you've done," Dahr snarled.

"Perhaps. I've done a lot of things. But nothing to you."

"You made me a slave!"

"You were a slave when I found you, and an ill-treated one at that. You had no family, no home, and no idea what you were. Some might say I did you a favor when I suggested that Lord Grondellan buy you from that disgusting man."

The man's unflappable calm drove Dahr mad, and his fingers tightened until Yurs's words came out hoarse. The monster raged to be freed, to exact vengeance. *No! I'll kill him, but in my own time. I will not let you savage him just to appease your bloodlust.*

Dahr leaned in close, stooping so his nose almost touched Yurs's hooked beak and their eyes were of a level. "You branded me. You made me property."

"Is that why I deserve to die? Will my murder chasten all who in live in a land where slavery is condoned? Was your life so terrible under our yoke of oppression?" Baring his teeth, Dahr imagined crushing the man's throat, watching the smug superiority fade from his face along with life. "You, among all of Lord Grondellan's slaves, have little right for complaint. You were given every advantage, treated better than he treats his own daughters. He denied you nothing."

"He denied me freedom!"

"What life would you have had, wandering Rachannon as a beggar child? Where would you have gone? You had no family. You didn't even know you were Garun'ah. Few Humans would have taken you, and the Tribes would have seen a creature tainted by man. Freedom would have cost you far more than you imagine."

"Is that what you think?" Dahr trembled with the effort required to keep Yurs alive. "It's easy to espouse the virtues of slavery when you own your freedom."

Yurs's knee jerked up, slamming into Dahr's gut. He staggered backward, gasping for air, and prepared to give chase. To his surprise, Yurs did not run. Instead, the man turned and pulled at his collar, revealing the condor brand on his shoulder. "Lord Grondellan saved me from a horrible death," Yurs hissed. "I offered myself to him because I know what my life is worth, and I know I have lived well with what the Gods gave me."

Dahr felt his greatsword heavy on his back. He considered reaching for the blade, ending this quickly. "You disgust me," he said, heaving in gulps of air. "You traded your freedom for comfort, sold your soul to add a few winters to your life."

"I have seen more—done more!—as Lord Grondellan's slave than I would have in ten lifetimes as a freeman. Before Lord Grondellan saved me, I toiled in a grinding mill under intolerable conditions. A free man, in a way, but harnessed to a yoke no less tightly than a slave, and beaten with a ferocity I doubt you've ever witnessed. Freedom is a word like any other, experienced in degrees and subject to interpretation."

Dahr's head pounded from the drink and Yurs's ongoing defiance. *Why isn't he afraid of me!* "Shut up. Shut up, or I'll kill you now!"

"You won't kill me, Dahr Odara. You're too weak."

Weak! He advanced again, forgoing the sword. This was a kill he wanted to feel. "I've killed before."

"But not without reason." Yurs stood his ground, but he shifted his stance and raised his arms to a ready position. Dahr had seen the man fight; he knew how deadly the man's hands could be. "I see into men's minds like you see into beasts', Dahr Odara. You are a creature of passion, but that passion is contained by a knot of integrity too strong to break. You are a killer, but a killer who requires justification, and in your heart, you know I've done you no wrong severe enough to warrant death."

Dahr hesitated. The monster raged and clawed at his innards, but Yurs's words held him. "The irony of it all," Yurs said, "is that the foundation of your virtuous nature was laid during your servitude to Lord Grondellan. You are who you are because of his kindnesses. You cannot kill me; he taught you too well for that."

Something in Dahr snapped, and he flew toward Yurs. The castellan dodged, but Dahr expected the move, and his first blow caught the man in the temple, staggering him. His second took Yurs in the gut, knocking him back into the building, and his third felled him. With his opponent prostrate and gasping for air, Dahr ran forward and planted a solid kick in his ribs, then crouched over the curled up figure and sneered. "Do you fear me yet, Rachannan?"

Yurs groaned as he lifted his head, but Dahr saw only triumph in his calculating gaze. "I'm not dead, am I?" Yurs tried to stand, but the effort proved too great. "You need to tell him who you are."

"So he can demand I return to his service? Or order me killed outright? He's lucky that my promises to Jeran prevent me from killing him."

"He needs to know. He thinks—"

"He will never know!" Dahr crouched over Yurs, hands clenched into fists. "If I think you've even hinted—"

"My telling him would do no good. He should know the truth, but that truth should come from you."

"What have we here?" called a gruff voice. "It looks like the Rachannan has taken a spill, and the domesticated Tribesman is lending a kind hand." Dahr whirled around to see the scarred Human Mage walking toward them. He wore a sword on one hip and a serrated dagger across from it, but even with the weapons sheathed he moved like a creature on the prowl.

Dahr drew himself to full height and glowered at the man. "This doesn't concern you. Leave us!"

"You know, I once had a friend from among the Tribes. Temper like a summer storm on the Sea of Aln Adale. Slave to that temper, really. Let it chew him up from the insides until he couldn't fight it anymore. I watched him do things... In any case, you remind me a lot of him."

"I said, get out of here!"

The Mage continued to approach, his eyes never leaving Dahr yet showing not the slightest hint of concern. "Emotion can be a powerful tool, but it must be controlled to work effectively. Let it rule you, and you do things you regret. My friend regretted a great many things, but by the time he came to his senses, it was always too late." The Mage chuckled then, and a nostalgic smile flitted across his face. "I guess I'm not guiltless in that area, myself."

"I don't need lectures from—"

"I don't lecture, boy, I teach." Affronted, Dahr reached for his sword, but when he gripped the hilt, he froze. The Mage wore an expression of such overwhelming disappointment that Dahr could not draw the blade.

"You truly are a terrifying sight," the Mage told him, never slowing his advance, "but you'd do well to remember that I can kill you with a thought." He pushed Dahr aside and knelt beside Yurs. After inspecting him for a moment, the Mage offered a hand and pulled Yurs to his feet.

"Don't Heal him," Dahr snarled. Foolish or not, he was ready to attack if the Mage erased Yurs's injuries.

"I'm no Healer," the Mage said. "Besides, I believe the Gods do things for a reason, and it's not a particularly powerful lesson if I go around fixing every little bruise They hand out." He waved for Yurs to go, and after the briefest of hesitations, the Rachannan hefted the buckets back onto his shoulders and hobbled off in the direction he had come.

The Mage studied Dahr as if he were a painting, and not one that pleased him. "I also believe that anyone who threatens a man half his size and twice his age deserves whatever punishment the Gods have in store." He glanced around, then cast his eyes skyward. "Where are your friends today? Did they think this was a bad idea too?"

Dahr turned to stalk away. "What they do is their concern, not mine. I have no intention of discussing my gifts with any more Magi, certainly not an old man who fashions himself a BattleMage."

An invisible hand seized Dahr's throat, and against his will he pivoted to face the Mage. Anger bloomed in the man's eyes, an anger colder than the winds that howled down from the Anvil in the dead of night. "To call me a BattleMage insults every man and woman who earned the title. A BattleMage shows compassion even in the face of his enemy; a BattleMage will fight when all the world is against him. The bond demands no less."

The Mage poked Dahr's chest, and he nearly fell. He fought against the magic binding him, against the indignity of being held in thrall, but to no avail. "Remember that we're all allies here," the Mage said, jabbing a finger into the center of Dahr's chest. Even with that light touch, it took all Dahr's effort to remain standing. "After all, if I can control myself enough to keep from killing you, you should be able to show the same courtesy to others."

Dahr tried to growl a response but found his mouth frozen as surely as his arms and legs. The Mage turned and walked away, leaving Dahr standing statue still in the middle of the street. He thrashed against the magic, praying that no one stumbled across him helpless. By the time the flows dissolved, the Blood Rage had consumed him. He raced down the street, sword drawn, demanding that the Lesser Voices lead him to the Mage.

The animals were strangely silent, which fueled Dahr's anger. He raced through the narrow alleys and cut-throughs, trusting to his instincts, and when a voice rose up and told him where he needed to go, he blessed the animal and followed blindly.

The voice directed him down an alley and around a corner, but when Dahr turned he ran into a wall of brick. The sudden stop staggered him, and his vision swam from the impact. Dazed, he turned to find a razor-backed mountain cat staring at him from the second story ledge of a house. *Why?*

Instead of answering, the cat pounced, slamming Dahr into the wall. The second impact drove consciousness away, and the last thing Dahr saw were the razor-back's yellow eyes descending toward him.

He woke in a field devoid of features. No hills or mountains graced the horizon; no trees broke the monotony of the plains. The sky above hinted at sunshine, but the light was diffuse, coming from everywhere and nowhere. *Such a barren place. Even emptier than my heart.*

The cry of a great beast reverberated over the plains, though Dahr saw nothing aside from the rustling of far distant grass. The sound terrified him in a way he thought impossible, seeping into his bones, leaving him barely able to draw breath. He reached for his sword with a trembling hand, and only when he realized it was not there did he sense his nakedness, his complete lack of protection at whatever monster pursued him.

The shriek came again, this time closer, and Dahr ran. The monster followed, sensing fear, and Dahr knew he could never outrun the creature. More bestial cries, each closer than the last, echoed in Dahr's ears. Certain of death, Dahr considered facing his end with a semblance of bravery, but he could not will himself to obey. Not long ago he would have welcomed death, yet now he fled it as surely as he fled his feelings for Katya.

A shadow darkened the grass around him, the great heaving silhouette of the beast. Dahr kept his eyes fixed ahead, breaking a path through the tall grass. Hot breath beat upon his neck, and the ground trembled with the creature's every step. It neared until it blotted out all light, and Dahr felt its jaws snapping at the base of his neck.

With hope all but gone, a door appeared ahead of him. "This way, little brother," Lorthas said, beckoning. "I can't see you, but I feel your need."

Dahr felt claws rake his back, and the fetid breath of the monster at his throat, but when he dove for the doorway and grasped Lorthas's hand, everything changed. The creature vanished, and with it a strange sense of disappointment that had hounded Dahr through the plains. The landscape changed too, metamorphosing from bland grasslands to the more familiar setting of Lorthas's chambers.

Dahr sought to hide his nakedness, realizing only after a frantic search that he once again wore his clothes and felt the comforting weight of his greatsword on his shoulder. Lorthas watched him from across the room, red eyes blazing with the power of the Gift. "You haven't had troubled sleep in some time," Lorthas said. "Have your nightmares returned?"

The Darklord offered wine, and Dahr snatched the bottle, downing its contents and feeling the warmth spread through him in a blissful wave, dulling the edge of his fear. Lorthas watched, amused, and when Dahr set the bottle down, a simple gesture from the Darklord filled it again. In the Twilight World, Lorthas had even greater powers than in the waking world.

"What happens in my dreams is none of your concern," Dahr snapped. He eyed the wine bottle, but left it sitting on the table.

"Such anger," Lorthas said. "The haste with which you ran to greet me made me think you eager for our meeting."

"Why would I want to meet with someone who sent assassins to kill me?"

The Darklord sat back in his chair and tapped a finger on his lips. "Assassins? And you're certain I sent them?"

"I tire of your games, Lorthas! Who else would send Elves and Tribesmen into Shandar to kill me and Jeran? Who else could have so quickly discovered where Jeran had taken us after Portal?"

Lorthas sighed, a heavy breath that carried the sound of eternal weariness. "I'll admit that as suspects go, I can see why you might place me atop your list, but I have no more qualms regarding Jeran. He and I strive toward the same goals: the reorganization of the Magi and the formation of a unified, unstratified society."

"You and Jeran are nothing alike."

"We have our differences, but we are more alike than you might care to admit. As are you and I, little brother. Regardless, if Jeran's enemies are mine, what purpose would killing him serve, when his living divides their attention." Lorthas's eyes roved up and down, taking in Dahr's healed but still prominent scars. "You seem to have accounted for yourself well."

"I killed enough of them."

"Do you really think so? The look in your eyes says you hunger for more blood. Such raw passion, unbridled by reason. I worry about you, little brother."

"And I should be grateful? For the concern of the Darklord?"

"You should be worried, for if the most dire villain in the history of Madryn is concerned about you, then what must your kind and noble friends think?"

"I do everything I'm asked. Jeran need not doubt my loyalty."

"True enough, I suppose, but a tool—don't glower like that, Dahr; each of us is a tool in the machinations of others—is only effective when you're certain it won't break. How often would you use an axe whose head slips from the shaft? You'd fix that tool or discard it before you'd trust it to any important task, wouldn't you?"

"Now you think me broken?"

"I think you unreliable, and thus of little value. Your passion, combined with the gifts the Gods bestowed upon you, could make you a formidable figure in the power struggle going on around us. But instead of harnessing your emotions, you let them dictate your actions, eschewing strategy, reason, and everything else that might temper your more... audacious... decisions."

Dahr laughed. He settled into the chair opposite Lorthas and raised the wine bottle to his lips, hoping his show of confidence convinced Lorthas. "The Darklord thinks me a useless tool. Oh, the tragedy of it all."

"You try my patience, little brother!" A hint of frustration broke through the Darklord's mask but was quickly concealed. "I'm not the one you should wonder about. Does Jeran trust you? Does he send you out to conquer foes or recruit allies, or are you kept on a tight leash, where he can prevent you from running wild? You are a raging fire, a powerful force that with one change in the winds will cause more damage among your friends than your enemies."

Lorthas knew just where to strike, the perfect combination of words and tone to drive home Dahr's hidden fears. Emptiness gnawed at his gut, and he fought to hold onto the false bravado he had prided himself on a moment ago. "Why do you care?"

"Without you as an ally, I suspect that Jeran will be unable to win his war against the Mage Assembly."

"Now you expect me to believe you want Jeran to win. And—Wait! Jeran's not at war with the Magi. He fights Salos the Scorpion, your agent on this side of the Boundary."

Standing, Lorthas paced the room. His gaze never wavered from Dahr; those fire red eyes carried a sad wisdom. "I have no grudge against Jeran. Or you, little brother. How could I? We're separated by leagues and centuries. My war was against the hypocrites of the Assembly, those who espoused a world where Magi were not feared, a world where all men and all Races were equal, but then turned against me when I offered them precisely what they demanded I provide. My war was against the institutions and nations who saw difference as evil, who sought to impose rigid social hierarchies based on gifts, Race, or wealth.

"Jeran's fighting the same things. To oppose him is to oppose myself. The Assembly knows this as well as I, which is why they will attack him if he doesn't attack them first. That they haven't done so already is a testament to the impression Jeran made at Atol Domiar, and to the fact that he's won several prominent figures to his cause, a feat I was unable to accomplish in my day."

"None of this has to do with me, so why torture me with your speeches?" Dahr stood and faced the Darklord. "I care nothing of politics or Magi. I'm here to help my friend, that's all. As soon as this war is over, as soon as Salos joins his brother in the Nothing, I'm done with it. I'm done with Madryn, with Alrendria, with everything!"

Lorthas wrung his hands as he walked and occasionally looked at Dahr. He pursed his lips, as if searching for the right words. "I had an apprentice once, long ago, named Kalsbad. Brilliant young man, but impetuous and prone to bouts of temper. He was one of the first to side with me against the Assembly, one of the first who left the Hall determined to form a new body of Gifted. He was a dear friend, almost as dear to me as you are to Jeran."

The Darklord stopped, and Dahr saw regret plastered on his bone-white features. "He was also one of the first to die, and his execution triggered an… excessive response on my part. A great deal of what happened afterward, a great deal of the MageWar, might have been averted if I had made an effort to mitigate his temper."

Dahr heard a crunch. Wine splashed against his foot, and the remnants of the bottle dug into his hand, leaving speckles of blood. "This has nothing to do with me."

"We are enslaved in a way to our friends, little brother. Obligated to them. You stay with Jeran because you feel you owe him something. He keeps you with him for the same reason, even though each day makes you a greater liability. You are an… extraordinary individual, but you are spiraling out of control. A dangerous crossroads approaches; choose your path with care, or I may one day see Jeran in a prison like mine, lamenting the decisions he made in haste out of friendship."

The sun-hot fury that burned beneath Dahr's flesh flared, and he could do nothing to contain it. The anger emboldened him, though, and he stormed toward the Darklord, who glided away without seeming to move. "You speak as if your words should mean something. You tried to kill me!"

"If Salos was responsible for the attack on Shandar, I will learn of it, and he'll be punished. Jeran is not my enemy. And neither are you." Lorthas showed no fear at Dahr's approach, and only mild amusement when he drew his blade. He made a tsking sound. "I thought you beyond such displays. At least here." He snapped his fingers.

Light burned Dahr's eyes, and he found himself back in Shandar, staring up at the midday sun. The razorback cat was gone, but Dahr's head pounded from his contact with the wall, and he had a claw mark running the length of his shirt as a vivid reminder of the attack.

His anger did not leave with the Darklord; it built and pushed against his bonds, turning his flesh red and making his heart pound with the thunder of a thousand hooves. His bestial howl echoed through the streets, a tormented sound that scared birds to flight.

Dahr grabbed a barrel, undisturbed since Shandar's abandonment, and smashed it into the wall. Relishing the sweet release of emotion, he pounded a crate to splinters with his hands, howling with a mixture of joy and pain as splinters dug into his flesh. For a time he let the monster roam free.

The days that followed drifted by in a haze. Dahr experienced them but did not live them. He strove to distance himself from the others, though he kept a wary eye on Yurs, who continued on as if nothing had happened and explained his injuries as an 'unfortunate misstep'.

For the most part, the others ignored him as assiduously as he ignored them. Aemon and Jes argued over Jeran. The Elves and Tribesmen argued over which Race's ideology should be central to Jeran's training. Yassik and Oto—when both were present—argued over what things Jeran needed to learn, and in what order he should learn those things. Even Katya and Grendor argued about Jeran, though Dahr only caught snippets of their conversations and both tended to fall silent whenever he approached. The world, it seemed, revolved around Jeran, and Dahr preferred it that way. With the attention off him, he could return to the periphery and focus his energies on caging the beast within.

Jeran stood in a tiled market several blocks from the Assembly Hall. He faced the scarred human Mage whose name Dahr had never heard, a grim and foreboding man whose cold, inhuman eyes saw through the mask of humanity he wore, and whose piercing gaze churned Dahr's guts as if he stared instead at an entire army. Dahr could barely stand to be in the man's presence, but with the Mage's attention riveted on Jeran, he hovered around the edge of the market and watched.

The Aelvin twins stood some ways behind Jeran, one to either side. Each had a sphere of colored light hovering around him, and from time to time the colors shifted. When they did, Jeran was to call out the change, though his gaze was to remain firmly on the Human Mage the whole time.

"Red," Jeran called out when Nahrona's sphere changed.

"Good," the Elf said, "Though I'd call it more of an amaranth, myself."

"Violet."

"You were late," Nahrima told him. "It changed some time ago. It's not enough to shift your perception back and forth, like you're watching us with your eyes."

"No matter how good you get," Nahrona added, "you'll never be able to see both at once that way."

"You're allowing your physical senses to limit your magical one," Nahrima told him. "Forget what you know of your eyes and ears. With your Gift you can sense everything at once, as far as your magic will allow you to extend."

"Blue." Sweat beaded Jeran's brow, and his forehead wrinkled with the effort of concentration. "Green."

"Better, but still not fast enough," Nahrona said. "And you're doing nothing but watching. For this to be an effective defense, you must be able to use magic and extend your perceptions."

"It's too much," Jeran said, gasping for breath.

"Nonsense," the Elves said at the same time. They looked at each other, then Nahrona continued. "We can do it, and your potential far exceeds ours."

"It will get easier with time."

"I've extended my perceptions before, and it hasn't hurt like this." The Human Mage rolled his eyes but said nothing. He did lean in closer, though, until his nose and Jeran's were only a finger's width apart.

"The narrower your focus, the easier it is," Nahrima said. "The more magic used, the greater the exertion. Which is easier, to walk or run?"

"To juggle two balls," Nahrona asked, "or five?"

"Brown." Jeran gasped. "Blue."

"Try something simple, but make sure you don't lose sight of us."

A small ball of fire ignited beside Jeran, though it flickered and wavered as if about to die. The Human Mage stepped back, his eyes narrowing. A grin spread across his face.

"Very good," Nahrona said. "But you missed it when I changed the ball back to yellow."

The Elves continued to lecture, praising Jeran when he succeeded and chastising him when he failed. Between color changes, they told him of the doctrine set down by *Ael Maulle* over the centuries, particularly the teaching methods they thought would work especially well at Jeran's Academy. The spheres changed color with increasing frequency, until Jeran could barely pause for breath.

"Red. Blue. Green. Green. Brown. Yellow. Violet."

Springing into motion, the Human Mage drew back his fist and punched Jeran in the jaw, knocking him from his feet. Jeran landed with a thud, blood pooling on his lip, and stared at the man aghast. "Why...?"

"Doesn't do you any good to watch everywhere but in front of you," the Mage said. "Split your attention in as many directions as you can, but make sure one of those directions is always forward."

Jeran rubbed at his jaw. "You could have just told me that."

"You'll learn better this way. It's more fun, too. Now get up and try it again."

As Jeran climbed to his feet, Dahr saw movement out of the corner of his eye. He turned to see a Gate open on the road before the Assembly Hall. Three men stepped through, one of them Wardel, and Dahr hopped down from the garden wall on which he sat and walked over to welcome the Guardsman.

The Mage stayed at the Gate, but Wardel and the other man—the one Jeran had left in charge at Dranakohr—saw him and approached. Both wore the black uniform popular among the soldiers in Dranakohr, but on Wardel it looked especially odd. *I wonder what Martyn will have to say about that?*

"Dahr, it's good to see you," Wardel said, clapping him on the shoulder. "You remember Commander Myaklos?"

Dahr gripped Wardel's arm at the elbow and dipped his head in acknowledgement of the other. "What brings you to this cemetery, Wardel?"

"Dispatches and reports, mostly," the Guardsman replied. "And transporting a few odds and ends for Jeran." He jerked his chin back toward the Gate, where pairs of men hauled heavy crates toward the Assembly Hall. The Mage winced with every new arrival, and after the fifth passed him by, he raised a hand. The Gate collapsed, and a moment later, so did the Mage. He sat on the ground, heaving for air.

"Is that Jeran over there?" Ehvan asked, attempting to shoulder past Dahr.

"He's in the middle of a lesson," Dahr said, blocking the man. "He doesn't like to be disturbed. He'll be finished soon."

Ehvan frowned but acquiesced, and Dahr pointed to where he had been sitting. "You can wait with me, if you want. I chilled a cask of ale."

"Sounds good," Wardel told him. "Come on, Ehvan! Jeran won't begrudge you a cup of ale."

"What news is so important it brings both of Jeran's top commanders to Shandar?" Dahr asked as he escorted the pair to his table at the edge of the market.

"Word came from Kaper," Ehvan said, "demanding all available soldiers be sent to the defense of the city."

"A similar dispatch arrived in Portal," Wardel admitted. "The Tachans control the border of Gilead, the remnants of Tylor's army is marching south, and a third army is approaching out of Corsa, bolstered by the traitors of House Morrena."

"Gods!" Dahr thought of Kaper, as much his home as anywhere, besieged by two or more armies, cut off from reinforcements, and left to Salos's cruel mercy. "How many men are you sending?"

"None," Ehvan said. Dahr turned an incredulous gaze on Wardel, who nodded.

"None! You're just going to leave them to their fate? What of Portal?"

Wardel looked Dahr in the eyes and saw something that made him back a half step away. "Talbot told the troops that anyone who wanted to defend Kaper had his blessing, but that he'd order no one to leave."

"Only a handful went," Ehvan said, and the pride in his voice angered Dahr far more than the statement. "Most everyone in Portal, Talbot included, wears the Black now."

"You're just going to let them destroy Kaper, kill Prince Martyn and the King?" He spoke to both, but his eyes fastened to Wardel. "What of your Guardsman's oath?"

"I have my orders," Wardel muttered.

"Orders? From Jeran? He's not a commander in the Guard, not even really First Seat of House Odara yet! Yet orders from him supersede those from your King?"

"Sacrificing men to a foolish order helps no one," Ehvan snapped. "Lord Odara will see us through this war."

"Kaper has never fallen," Wardel said, though Dahr saw guilt and doubt playing across his face. "It can hold until Jeran's ready."

"You have a lot of faith in Jeran," Dahr growled.

"He has a lot of faith in us," Ehvan replied.

"The cask's over there. I've lost my thirst." Dahr threw himself down on the low wall ringing the market, brooding over Martyn's fate, and that of Kaper. *Maybe I should go. I could be of some help, and at least there'd be prey enough to satisfy me for a time.*

Ehvan and Wardel sat a few dozen hands away, filled two mugs with frothy ale from the cask Dahr had set out, and settled back to watch the end of Jeran's lesson. Blindfolded, Jeran stood in the center of a ring of orbiting fireballs. From time to time, one of the fireballs darted toward him, and Jeran either dodged or extinguished the flames with magic. The one time he missed, his scream echoed through the market and a walnut sized scorch mark appeared on his shirt.

"That reminds me," Ehvan said to Wardel. "We need to ask Jeran if he wants to stop the branding."

"Branding?" Dahr turned his head at that, and the condor on his shoulder ached.

"Some of the guards worried that they'd forget which of the prisoners were soldiers, which were thieves, and which were ShadowMagi—"

"Seems easy enough there," Wardel chuckled. "The ones in the big iron collars are ShadowMagi."

Ehvan shot the Guardsman a dirty look. "Anyway, they started branding the prisoners so they could tell them apart. Nasty business, but it does have its uses. You can keep the thieves away from sensitive areas, and the soldiers make far better laborers than—"

Dahr leapt from his seat, crossed the plaza in a handful of loping steps, and dragged Ehvan to the ground. "Those are men you're talking about," he snarled, reveling in the feel of flesh yielding to his fists. He heard Wardel's shouts only distantly. "Men, not cattle! You can't brand them and put them to work in the fields. You—"

A vise squeezed around him, forcing the air from his lungs. Something pulled him away from Ehvan, lifting him off the ground as easily as he could lift a puppy. He felt a rush of wind as he sailed forward, saw a building looming before him, and hit the wall with enough force to drive the breath from his lungs again and leave him fighting for consciousness.

"No more!" Jeran's voice thundered in his head. "I can take no more, Dahr! I trusted you to keep a rein on your temper, but you continue to show that you can't distinguish between friend and foe."

"Me?" The urge to fight battled common sense, but Dahr could do little more than suck in a hurried breath. The very air pressed him to the wall, holding him captive. "Martyn sent a dispatch demanding help. Your *commander* here sent him back to Kaper alone. Kaper is in danger, and you accuse me of not knowing who my friends are?"

"It was my decision," Jeran replied, stepping up beside him. Imperious and confident, even sweat-soaked and covered in bruises, Dahr saw a fury in Jeran's eyes he had never thought to see directed at him. "My students are not ready. My soldiers are not ready. To send them to Kaper now is to send them to the Nothing. Martyn will have to fend for himself until they can do him some good."

"And the prisoners, was that your decision too? Branding them... enslaving them? Do you have them beaten, too, if they disobey?"

"My prisoners are murderers, traitors, Tachan soldiers and ShadowMagi. Enslavement is far better than they deserve and far better treatment than they gave their captives. But no, it was not my idea, and the branding—if this is not another concoction of your mind—will stop. And when the war is over, a place will be found for my prisoners. Until then, they will continue to serve as I see fit."

"Release me. I'll apologize and never—"

"No. This was your last chance. I was willing to overlook the beating you gave Yurs; I won't overlook this. You will always be my friend, Dahr, but I can't afford to be saddled with any more burdens."

"What... What are you saying?"

"You're leaving Shandar. Before nightfall. The twins are gathering your belongings."

Alone. He's sending me off alone. Not again! Memories of the Darkwood returned, disjointed images of the days and nights spent prowling the forest like a beast, killing any Tachans who dared cross his path. Panic gave Dahr the strength he needed to pull a finger's width away from the wall. When the bonds holding him in place evaporated, he tumbled forward, crashing to the ground.

"Friend Jeran." Grendor approached, a light pack slung over one shoulder and his *va'dasheran* in hand. "To abandon Dahr completely is too cruel a penalty. Take light from the blind and you deprive him of nothing; take light from the lost and you deprive him of all. I will follow where the winds take him."

Jeran pursed his lips, considering the request. "You will be missed, my friend, but maybe you can do more good with him than with me."

"I hope I'll be missed almost as much," Lord Grondellan laughed. He led two horses laden with gear. "The *Tsha'ma* told me Dahr was leaving today. I didn't think it was gonna be like this, but we take what the Gods give us. No offense, Jeran, but I'm on my last adventure, and I think danger seeks Dahr, or he it. From you, it runs."

"If only that were true," Jeran said. "I thank you for your counsel, Harol. Dranakohr would not be near what it is without your advice."

"Any time, lad. Any time."

A shadow appeared behind Jeran, and Katya leaned in to whisper in Jeran's ear. "You too?" he asked, and she nodded. He hesitated only a moment before whispering something back.

The Aelvin twins returned leading Jardelle. Fang walked at the horse's side, and Shyrock perched on the saddle. Dahr stood and brushed the dirt from his clothes. He mounted and started east without a word of parting. The others followed behind, talking amongst themselves but leaving him to his thoughts.

At the edge of the market, he found Jakal waiting, arms folded at his chest and a wry grin on his face. "Don't look so smug," Dahr said. "Your *Prah'phetia* said I'd go with three, but Yurs travels everywhere with Lord Grondellan."

"I don't want to disappoint you, lad," Lord Grondellan said, "but Yurs left for my holdings in Rachannon this morning. There's civil war afoot, and someone has to keep the men in line."

Jakal laughed, and Dahr spurred his horse to escape the *Tsha'ma*. Galloping through the streets, he refused to slow until this path took him through a stone archway marking the edge of the city. There, he brought Jardelle to a jarring stop, and the stallion twisted and stomped at the rough treatment. Dahr ignored his horse's protests and stared at the sky in disbelief.

On the horizon, a full moon stared at him from a sky of crimson.

CHAPTER 10

As Martyn's party crossed beneath the castle wall, two thirds of his body-guard broke off and rode in the direction of the stables. The prince drew a deep breath, relishing the illusion of freedom as the remaining ten Guardsmen redeployed around him. They kept some distance back and made no move to stop anyone from approaching. *Why should they? The grounds used to be open to all; now my people need permission to haul away the refuse.*

The precautions made sense; Martyn could not deny that, but the harsh measures taken to ensure the safety of Kaper grated on his nerves. The war with the Durange had cost so much already, and now it threatened the freedoms so integral to Alrendrian society.

Curfews. Impressment. Confiscation of property. Where do I draw the line? At what point have we compromised so much that we lose the very thing we're fighting for?

"You look troubled, Prince Martyn. Was it worse than we expected?" Aryn Odara stood in the shadow of the castle wall. His fusain darted with furious precision across the broad parchment secured to a cedar board before him. Aryn wore a Guardsman's uniform, the tassels of command hanging from his shoulder, a sword at his hip. The blade looked at ease there, and Aryn looked at ease with it.

The King had restored Aryn's rank and given him overall command of Kaper's defenses despite Martyn's privately-mentioned concerns over the man's state of mind. When Martyn stressed Aryn's bouts of melancholy and periods of insanity, his father dismissed the tales as exaggeration. When Martyn changed tactics and spoke of the slight to Guardsmen Bystral and Lisandaer, his father had dismissed that too.

For their part, neither Guardsman had helped. Each seemed eager to relinquish responsibility to Aryn, though Bystral remained in command of the castle and Lisandaer, the city garrison. Aryn, too, had done his part to make Martyn look the fool. Since taking command, the prince had not witnessed a single episode from the man.

"Right now we face only the remnants of the army defeated at Vela and whatever reinforcements the Durange have added since," Martyn said, sidling around to get a glimpse at Aryn's work, a detailed map of the immediate area with numerous annotations. A half dozen completed sketches lay at the man's feet, and a score more unrolled parchments rested in a container slung over his shoulder. "It's daunting, but nothing the Guard can't stop. It's the Corsans and traitors from House Morrena I'm worried about. From all reports their army dwarfs the Durange."

"As long as we keep them across the Celaan, we need not fear," Aryn said. He studied his map for a moment, then started drawing light rectangles in ordered rows. He surveyed the layout, then erased half the charcoal shapes and started again. "A handful of trained soldiers could defend the bridge."

"And what happens when the Durange in the east turn their attention on us?"

"A problem for another time. Today, we need only worry about the army across the Celaan. It does a commander no good to fret over what might happen. You shouldn't worry too much about the future."

"Sage advice from the madman," Martyn muttered. He wondered about Aryn Odara. The man's reputation gave him great authority, and the troops rallied to him in a way Martyn had never seen before, but the prince wondered how far he could trust a man who had lived as Tylor's plaything for so many winters.

Or one who spends half his waking hours thinking he's living in the past. If only he would do it now, where someone else could see him! Martyn jerked his head at the sketch. "What are you doing there?"

"Trying to figure out the best way to lay the tents."

"Tents?"

"For garrisoning our militia. And for the refugees sure to follow. There's empty space in the palace, but I'd prefer to station the Guardsmen and the Elves inside the castle and billet as many commoners as possible out here. It'll be too easy for the Durange to slip an assassin in among them."

"Just a moment ago you acted as if the Celaan were an impassable barrier. Now you're making plans to house the entire city on the castle grounds."

"I said a handful of men could hold the bridge against an army. I never said the Durange wouldn't get across the river. I fully expect to lose New Kaper. The real question is: will we be able to hold on to the old city?"

Martyn wanted to scream. "I thought you said a good commander doesn't fret over the future."

"I didn't say he ignored it completely."

Hands clenched, Martyn continued toward the castle. Aryn called after him. "Commanders Bystral, Lisandaer, and I are meeting this evening to discuss the situation. Will you be able to join us, Prince Martyn?"

Martyn froze. "Are you inviting me to a war council? Joam would be doing everything in his power to convince me my proper place was here, safely ensconced in the castle."

"Joam's main concern was protecting the succession. Mine is protecting Kaper and Alrendria. You have experience fighting both the Durange and the Corsans; that gives you and the handful of men you brought from Vela an advantage over everyone here besides me. I'd be a poor Guard Commander indeed if I didn't utilize that to our advantage."

Suspicion warred with pride. "I'll be there, Commander. In your offices?"

Aryn nodded. "At sunset." He returned to his drawing.

As Martyn walked toward the castle through once vibrant flower gardens now sown with ordered rows of vegetables, he revised his estimation of Jeran's uncle. That the man was insane remained unquestioned in his mind, but at least Martyn believed Aryn would let nothing, not even his prince's well being, compromise his duty to Alrendria.

The castle itself proved eerily silent compared to the bustle on the grounds outside. Servants moved in groups, silent or speaking in hushed tones, and when they saw Martyn, they pressed themselves against the walls. Guards stood posted at every major intersection, and even those who dwelled in the castle since before Martyn's birth could not escape their scrutiny.

Rounding a corner, Martyn found himself facing a tall man with slicked black hair, narrow eyes, and a hooked nose that gave him a hawkish appearance. The man wore all black, and though he carried no weapon, he regarded the Guardsmen behind Martyn as one might regard a group of unruly children. When one soldier stepped around the prince to confront the stranger, the man gestured and all ten Guardsmen moved to the walls, where they stood as if held back by a great weight.

A Mage! Heart pounding, Martyn stepped back, but a stern voice held him in place.

"Do stand still, Prince Martyn. If I wanted you dead, you'd no longer be breathing."

Martyn drew a steadying breath. "Why should I trust you?" He glanced around, looking for something to use to his advantage, hoping for someone to appear in the distance so he could shout for help.

"Because you have no choice," the man said, walking toward him. "I am Valkov, High Wizard of the Mage Assembly. I had hoped to speak with your father, but my time is short, and you are acceptable. I bring terms from the Assembly."

"Terms?" Martyn furrowed his brow. "Do you seek my surrender, Mage Valkov?"

"Very droll, your Highness. Terms for alliance, not surrender."

"Well, in that case, perhaps we should find a more suitable location for negotiations. I could have food and wine brought to—"

"Matters require my attention elsewhere. I regret I have no time for niceties and politics."

"I see." Martyn took a moment to compose himself, hoping to slow his racing pulse and present at least the illusion of composure. "Perhaps you could release my Guardsmen, at least. As a sign of good faith?"

The soldiers fell from the wall and scrambled to unsheathe their weapons. Martyn waved them back. "What are the Assembly's conditions, High Wizard?"

"You must issue a proclamation throughout Alrendria protecting the Gifted from molestation and persecution. Any Common found guilty of harassing a Mage will be arrested and sent to us for trial."

"We may be able to find a wording for such a proclamation suitable to all," Martyn said, his mind whirling around the possibility of adding scores of Magi to the ranks of his army. "I presume that is not your only condition?"

Valkov sniffed and stared down his hooked nose at Martyn. "You will aid us in identifying all Alrendrians born with the Gift and encourage them to come to us for training."

"As long as encourage is not a polite way of saying force, I believe that can be arranged."

"All Magi sent to aid you will be allowed to use magic at their discretion. They will not be ordered about by you or your Guard commanders. They will not use their Gift in any way they deem inappropriate."

"My field commanders may have specific uses for your Magi. If they can't—"

Valkov sighed. "Your commanders may make suggestions. If my Magi have no objections, they will do as they are asked."

Martyn opened his mouth, but Valkov waved him to silence. "A number of Magi have gone missing in recent months. I will provide you a list of names. Should you or your agents learn the whereabouts of any Mage on the list, you will share that information with me."

Does he already know about Lelani and the others? "A reasonable request... We wouldn't want any misplaced Magi wandering about out there all alone, would we?" The silence between them grew strained. "Is that all?"

"Almost, your Highness. The bonds between Alrendria and the Assembly go back millennia, but recent times have seen those bonds strained. To risk our lives in your defense, we must feel confident that you harbor no allegiance to our enemies. Alliances with rogue Magi will not be tolerated."

He does know! Martyn swallowed and took several slow breaths, hoping to hide his nervousness. "If you think we would consider negotiation with Salos—"

"Playing the fool does not suit you, Prince Martyn. You must denounce Jeran Odara and those who follow him. If it is within your power, you must deliver him to the Assembly. Only then—"

"Jeran is a loyal subject of Alrendria. I will not hand him over for you to murder."

"You have my word that he will not be executed. We wish only to contain him. The Assembly cannot allow him to incite dissent among the Gifted. Denounce him, and you'll have a hundred Magi at your immediate disposal. Bring him to me, and the full might of the Assembly will be at your command for as long as you need it."

A cold anger seethed within Martyn, but he held it in check. "I must discuss this with my father. I cannot—"

"Of course. Take your time. Konasi will remain here as my agent. When you're ready to meet my demands, he'll bring word to me. In the meantime... I wish you well in defending the city."

Valkov waved his hand, and a door appeared in the wall beside him, opening without a touch. "And Prince Martyn," he said as he stepped through the Gate, "are you so certain of Odara's loyalty? My agents report that he's training an army, and that as many men have cast aside their Guardsmen uniforms as have left the Assembly."

"Jeran's no traitor."

"Have you heard word from Portal? Jeran and an army were spotted there too, and now the city has fallen silent."

"He would never attack his own House."

"You are in a difficult situation here, but I haven't seen him answer your call for help. Do you even know where he is? He's not in Dranakohr. Some claim he already wearies of politics and intrigue."

"Jeran will come. He won't abandon Alrendria."

"If he does come," Valkov said, "he'll come with conditions of his own. He's young and brash, and confident to a fault. His demands will rock the very foundation of our world, and if you give in to them, you'll be the King under whom Alrendria was destroyed." The Gate faded to gray stone again, leaving Martyn and his guards alone in the corridor.

I must discuss this with Miriam. And with Lelani.

Martyn hurried through the halls, into a more crowded section of the palace. His arrival evoked some excitement, but he ignored the petitioners who tried to slow him. Common or noble, he brushed them aside, rarely taking time to offer excuse, and left his guards laboring to keep up and keep the pressing throng away.

He burst into the rooms he shared with Miriam and cast his eyes about for her. Few decorations remained on the walls; detailed maps of Madryn and its nations had replaced woven tapestries and fine paintings. Two desks piled high with letters sat side by side along one wall, and a broad table dominated the center of the main chamber. Books and piles of dispatches covered it as well, though with far more order than upon the desks.

Miriam was not there, but Zarin Mahl sat at the table, studying a dispatch. A man of small stature and humble demeanor, Zarin had proved himself an invaluable resource. The man controlled an elaborate network of agents across the length and breadth of Madryn, from all parts of Kaper to the farthest reaches of the Tachan Empire. He even claimed to have men among Jeran's followers, though Martyn doubted reliable agents could have been acquired in the single season since Jeran took over Dranakohr.

Regardless, Zarin knew the truth of events long before the King's own agents brought news. His only real failure had been Jysin's betrayal and House Morrena's defection to the Darklord. Zarin had not forgiven himself for the oversight, and had since made efforts to bolster the number and quality of his spies within the Great Houses. "Prince Martyn," he said, looking up from his letter, "you look as if you've seen a ghost."

"Worse, a Mage. Is Miriam here?"

"She's indisposed at the moment." Zarin glanced to the door to the washroom. "I expect her back presently. Will you be staying long? I could have the servants bring food."

Martyn looked at his desk, at the pile of papers that had grown another two hands high since he had last been here. Sighing, he grabbed a stack and sat across from Zarin. He read the first two—complaints from minor nobles about Guardsmen demanding food stocks and supplies. *Fools. Do they think the Guardsmen are taking it for themselves? We're preparing for a siege!*

After a half dozen such trivialities, Martyn's patience wore thin. "Is Jeran raising his own army?"

Zarin blinked and looked at Martyn. He carefully folded the letter he was reading and set it upon the desk. "You gave the Firsts permission to train their own militias outside the auspices of the Guard. Legally, I don't think—"

"Is Jeran training his own army? Is he subverting the Guard?"

"Subverting may be too harsh a term. I don't believe Lord Odara is encouraging defection. However, I have received reports recently of Guardsmen deserting to join his militia. 'Putting on the Black' they call it."

Martyn glowered. "If he hasn't stopped it, then he's encouraging it."

"Not necessarily. My agents claim that he has closeted himself inside Dranakohr, and that only his most trusted advisors have access to him. His commanders welcome any trained soldier to their cause; he may not even be aware that he has Guardsmen among his militia."

"You're usually far more suspicious, Zarin. You must have a great deal of trust in Jeran."

"Trust is something I never give and that few earn from me, Prince Martyn. However, I don't believe Jeran Odara would forsake his duty to you or Alrendria. You must have faith."

Martyn leafed through the next handful of letters, discarding most as trivial and not deserving his attention. A report from Jasova on the Corsan front he set aside for detailed study, and a scout's report of Tachan movements in the east he read immediately.

"I believe I know who's killing the Elves."

Zarin's comment stunned Martyn; the report fell from his limp hand. "And you thought this an insignificant matter, one to mention only as an afterthought?" He had learned something of Zarin Mahl in the seasons they had worked together; the man liked his games, and he liked to surprise people with the extent of his knowledge.

"Perhaps I exaggerated," Zarin admitted. "I don't have a name for you, but I believe we can narrow down the suspects by applying what we know of the assassin."

Intrigued, Martyn set aside the pile of papers. "Go on."

"The assassin is well trained and very good at what he does. Perhaps he underestimated us during his first murder, but since then he hasn't been seen again, even though the quantity and severity of his crimes have increased."

Martyn nodded, waving for Zarin to continue. "He targets only Elves, presumably to undermine our burgeoning relationship with them. Since the Elves relocated to the city, no more attacks have occurred here, despite the still significant Aelvin population surrounding Jaenaryn and Treloran."

"If you intend to recite things we already know," Martyn snapped, reaching for the next dispatch, "I have more important things to do."

Zarin shook his head. "Your wife has a far better head for this type of work, Prince Martyn. Patience and thorough analysis are what solves puzzles like this, not rash action and flaring emotions."

Sucking in a breath, Martyn muttered, "Keep it up, and I'll show you rash action and flaring emotions." He forced a smile, and Zarin returned it with one of his own.

"All of the murders in the city have occurred in Aelvin districts. By their nature, Elves are suspicious, particularly in regards to other Races. They expect the worst from us already."

"And someone is proving their suspicious right! They came here in good faith, and someone is killing them. Murdering them beneath the noses of our own soldiers! I—"

"Murder?" Miriam said as she stepped into the room. She wore a simple white dress, unadorned, and it billowed as she walked toward the table. She had tied her blonde locks back with a lace ribbon to keep them away from her too-pale face. She moved slowly to hide her discomfort, but the gliding stride only added to her ghostly appearance. "Are you telling Martyn that the assassin is an Elf?"

Martyn rushed to Miriam's side and escorted her to a chair. Not many tendays after their wedding, Miriam had taken ill and despite all efforts had yet to recover. Martyn worried about her, though she claimed the malady was not worsening. "Are you still unwell, Miriam? Have you eaten today? I could send for some... Did you say an Elf?"

"I'm fine, Martyn," Miriam said, shaking off his arm. "And I can't keep food down, so having some brought would just be cruel."

Martyn looked from Miriam to Zarin and back again. "An Elf?"

"It makes sense," Zarin said. "There are elements among the Elves as hateful of Humans as they claim we are of them. They have separatist factions and groups allied with the Darklord, just as we do. More importantly, an Elf is more likely to trust another Elf, to welcome one into his home or business, to turn a blind eye for a moment. Eliminating them as suspects makes no sense."

"An Elf murdering Elves." Martyn took a moment to wrap his mind around the idea. He chastised himself for not seeing the simple truth of it. "The Emperor was so careful in choosing his delegates. If this—"

"Oh, Martyn," Miriam laughed. The sound brightened the prince's smile, until he realized it was directed at him. "You can be so delightfully naïve sometimes. You're acting as if Humans don't murder each other every day, or as if Alrendria has had no spies among its numbers. Didn't you tell me Salos's own daughter insinuated—"

"That's not what I meant!" Martyn interrupted, his smile gone. An image of Katya Durange came unbidden to his mind. Her betrayal would never be forgotten, never forgiven. *How can Jeran keep her at his side, knowing what she is? How can he trust her? How can he torture Dahr like that?* For the moment, Katya remained safe, but if she ever strayed too far from Jeran's protection, Martyn planned to make her accountable for her crimes against Alrendria.

Miriam pursed her lips in an expression Martyn had become all too familiar with. "I will thank you to remember that I'm your wife, and not some common scullion for you to snap at whenever your mood sours. It's not my fault a Durange worked her way into your circle of friends, or that you allow her to live, or that she has convinced Odara to raise an army."

"Jeran's not raising an army!"

"Well, they do call it the Army of the Boundary," Zarin said, handing Martyn the stack of papers he had been reading, "but as I said before, it seems to be no more an army than the militias being raised by the other Great Houses. Commoners and retired Guardsmen are flocking to join, but that's to be expected. A number of garrison commanders in the north have reported desertions, but we can't prove the deserters have gone to Dranakohr. Portal and Norport have fallen silent, but again, that is not proof that Lord Odara has done anything wrong."

"It's proof enough, if you ask me," Miriam said.

"It's nothing but rumor and hearsay, Princess," Zarin said. "There are no official statements from Dranakohr supporting the formation of a standing army outside the Guard."

"There aren't any statements denouncing it either!" Miriam shot back.

"Without more concrete evidence, I think it unwise to make accusations."

"If he's not up to something, then why hasn't he answered the King's summons?"

"Jeran's not even at Dranakohr!" Martyn said.

Miriam rolled her eyes. "Oh, please, Martyn. How could you possibly know that?"

"I… I…" Telling Miriam the news had come from Valkov, a Mage who wanted to drive a wedge between Kaper and Dranakohr, would lead little credence to the statement. That Martyn somehow knew the man spoke truth meant nothing, not without some form of evidence. "I have agents of my own."

"Oh," Miriam sniffed. "Of course you do. I'm sorry we've wasted so much of your time, Master Mahl. I sometimes forget the extent of my husband's imaginary spy network."

Zarin said nothing. His eyes remained focused on the paper in his hands, his lips pressed together in a thin line.

Martyn seethed inside, and the hot flush of embarrassment on his cheeks served to fuel his anger. "I don't need to be belittled every time I come to this room, Miriam."

"At least you're allowed to leave. I thought marriage might loosen the chains you've fastened to me, but I can barely step outside the castle without someone ushering me back in."

"You can barely make it from these rooms to our chambers without falling over or running to the privy. The city is not safe, and with the number of workers wandering the castle grounds, my father worries that—"

"That doesn't stop you from leaving whenever it suits your mood."

"We don't have time to discuss this now," Martyn said, sweeping his hand in a gesture that encompassed the room, the stacks of unread reports and letters, the notes on troop movements and unit strengths, the tallies of goods and supplies.

"Excuse me," Zarin said.

"Perhaps we'd be better able to keep up if you spent more than a fraction of each day here with us! And stop yelling at me!" Miriam's voice rose two octaves, and Martyn glanced around to make sure nothing more dangerous than a book lay within her reach.

Zarin cleared his throat. "Your Highnesses?"

"Other things require my attention, Miriam," Martyn said, certain he had hardly so much as raised his voice. "I can't always be here."

A loud thump shocked them both to silence. Zarin held a thick volume over the floor; a similarly-sized one lay at his feet. "My apologies," he said. "I must have dropped that book. I have more news."

"What?" Martyn and Miriam said in unison, then shot each other a scathing glare.

"Another mystery is solved. We know where the Black Fleet is."

"Where?" This time, Martyn almost laughed when he and Miriam both spoke, but Miriam seemed to find nothing amusing in it.

"They've blockaded Roya and the mouth of the Alren. All trade from the sea has stopped, and we will see no reinforcements from the island."

Miriam blew out an exasperated breath, and Martyn pounded the table with his fist. "Have we done something to offend the Gods? Can we get word to Vela, have Captain Corrine organize the fleet and break the blockade?"

"I can have a dispatch on its way by nightfall," Zarin said, "but might I remind you that our fleet has no Magi among the crew. Asking them to break the blockade is akin to asking them to throw themselves into the sea."

"They broke it before," Martyn said, but he regretted the statement as soon as he uttered it. He knew too well why the Alrendrian fleet had succeeded, and now he knew he would have to listen to Miriam explain to him why he was an idiot.

"They didn't break the blockade before, they ran it. If not for Lord Odara—"

The door to the chamber opened to admit Sheriza. Two guards flanked the Healer, resuming their posts only after Martyn waved for them to go. "Prince Martyn, they said I would find you here. I've brought news from Vela. You should know that..." Sheriza gasped, and she all but ran to Miriam's side. "Oh, you poor dear. Why didn't anyone tell me?"

Martyn leapt to his feet. "What do you—?"

"You," Sheriza pointed to Zarin. Her hands danced above Miriam's flesh. "Go find Mage Tevanica, and tell her to attend me. She arrived with my party in the main courtyard just a few moments ago. Well? Go!" Zarin jumped to his feet, made a hasty bow, and darted from the room.

"You haven't been eating," Sheriza said. "We must get some broth into you, or things could get a lot worse."

"Worse?" Worry dispelled Martyn's anger. "Is it serious?"

"I should say so," Sheriza replied, directing a wry look at the prince. "She's carrying *your* child."

CHAPTER 11

The summer sun beat with unrelenting fervor upon the grassy plains of the Tribal Lands. Dahr rode ahead of the others, listening to snippets of their conversation and watching the world through the eyes of the animals around him. Shyrock soared the skies, and Dahr caught glimpses of sweeping landscapes and sunparched grasslands, but no Tribesmen. Fang trotted at his side, and Dahr inhaled a mixture of scents old and new, but no Tribesmen. Even the creatures native to these lands could provide no direction. The chittering squirrels insisted that Garun'ah had walked these plains within a ten-day, but the other beasts remained unhelpful, even uncommunicative. *Some gift. Now they won't talk to me when I want them to.*

"...ridiculous! You're telling me you harbor no grudge against my uncle?" Skepticism poisoned Katya's tone, and she fixed a probing gaze on Grendor. The Orog faced her with a confidence gained over the past few seasons. The fiery glare from her emerald eyes would once have driven the shy man into apologetic stammering, but now Grendor stood firm.

"Your uncle did what he thought he had to do to protect his family, friend Katya. His methods were less than exemplary, and if he yet lived I would do what I could to stop him. But the Gods have already exacted punishment on Tylor Durange. The matter is settled, and it serves no purpose to harbor ill will against him."

Lord Grondellan's laughter rumbled through the air. "You're a kinder man than me, Orog! I haven't seen the Bull since he was a boy, let alone languished as his prisoner, and I still hate the man, dead or not."

Dahr opened his mouth, but snapped it shut again, choosing to hold his tongue. Silently, he asked Fang to drop back beside his companions so he could see them. She obeyed, and he watched their conversation through her eyes.

Katya pursed her lips. "So, you hate no one, Orog?"

"I strive to follow the Mother's teachings, friend Katya. She tells us that hate is a tool of Kohr the Destroyer, used to bring the Races to ruination and win his wager with the other Gods. Hate serves little purpose when directed at the living; it serves none when focused on the dead. As the Elders say, 'The rabid dog bites himself when he bites his master.' "

Nodding as if she had expected the answer, Katya asked, "And you believe everyone redeemable?"

Grendor frowned, pulling taut the burned flesh on the side of his face and forming deep creases around the patch covering his eye. Dahr found it an odd expression on a face so often lit up with smiles, and it gave the Orog such an air of sternness that Dahr almost laughed aloud. *Such an imposing figure, yet he blanches if he accidentally crushes a butterfly.*

"Every soul is worth saving," Grendor said. "No one should be abandoned to the Nothing."

"So you would forgive my father?" Katya asked, masking a triumphant smile. "You would help Salos find the path to the Gods?"

Grendor touched his face, tracing a finger along the scarred flesh. "Were I true to the teachings of the Mother, then yes. But I am a child compared to the other Elders, so I must be forgiven if I fall short of Her ideals."

Lord Grondellan laughed again. "Besides, the Scorpion still lives, so by your own words there is *some* purpose in hating him. Me, I'd rather not spoil the afterlife, so unless we're sure he's going to the Nothing, I'd rather keep Salos alive."

"We should stop here," Dahr said, stepping down from Jardelle where a small stream snaked between two broad hills. He dropped to his knees at the bank, splashing water on his face and arms, and glimpsed at his reflection, noting the hard eyes and grim scowl. It took some effort not to recoil from it. *This is not what I wanted to be.*

"Already?" Lord Grondellan cast his eyes toward the sky. "The sun's high yet, Hunter, and we've still no sign of the Tribesmen."

Dahr's reflex was to shout, but he quieted his voice to a snarl. "This stream is the last water for leagues, and the horses are tiring. There's a stretch of forest not far off where we might find game. And I'm in no hurry to find the Garun'ah. If you want more reasons, you'll not get them from me, but if you'd rather continue on till nightfall, you're welcome to go on alone."

Lord Grondellan looked at him, then whispered something to Katya, who laughed. The sound sent chills down Dahr's spine, and he opened his mind to the beasts of the plains, striving to spare himself from the lyrical torture of her happiness.

"Here's as good a place as any, lad." Lord Grondellan jumped down from his horse. He groaned when he landed and rubbed at his knees, then set to work unstrapping his mount's saddle.

Dahr tied the horses to a post he pounded into the ground while his companions unpacked their gear. Once they set their tent posts, Dahr carried his packs a hundred hands downstream. The others watched without comment while he pitched his tent; they had stopped asking him to camp near them long ago, when the repeated requests made his temper flare.

Why do they follow me? I just want to be alone.

Dahr took out his greatsword and examined the blade. The edge gleamed in the sunlight, and he found no reason to sharpen it again, so he polished it with an oiled cloth and returned it to its sheath. Dark thoughts plagued him, thoughts of Jeran and why he had sent him away.

Even Lorthas can see what's happening, and it troubles him. The Darklord *fears what I've become; so how can I expect Jeran to keep me around?*

Because he's your friend. The thought was his, yet not. It rumbled up from deep within, and it carried such a current of anger than it startled Dahr, who had long since grown accustomed to rage. *He's your brother! You're supposed to take care of each other first, and then the rest of the world.*

Once Dahr had shared a bond with Jeran. Not long past he could sense Jeran's moods as easily as his own, find him even in the labyrinth of Kaper's palace, draw strength from his friend and share his own when needed. That bond had been strained since the Darkwood, and after leaving Shandar, the part of him that could turn and point and *know* in which direction Jeran stood had abandoned him.

His hands clenched until his knuckles ached, and the need to hunt consumed him. He shoved his *dolchek* into a belt loop and strung his bow, then stalked from the camp. He did not need to look—not even through Fang's eyes—to see Lord Grondellan following. The Rachannan never let him hunt alone, just as Katya never let him scout without her, and Grendor joined Dahr at his tent for every evening meal. *They conspire against me, to deprive me of the solitude I crave!*

Thick forest ran the length of a hilltop to the west, and Dahr loped toward it, taking some small delight in the quick pace which kept the Rachannan panting to keep up. He waited within the treeline—not so Lord Grondellan could catch his breath, he told himself, but to give him a chance to hide himself from the Lesser Voices. With the beasts of the forest able to hear his thoughts, hunting sometimes lost its thrill. Far too many times, the animals had known of his presence and fled, or in a few cases ambled up to him as a sacrifice. The chase excited Dahr far more than the kill, so he had learned to hide from the consciousnesses in his head. For a time, at least, he could hide from them.

"Gods, lad, I'm starting to think you want me dead," Lord Grondellan said, leaning against a tree and heaving in great gasps of air. Dahr's gut clenched, and Lord Grondellan laughed when he saw the expression. "I've not run so much in decades."

"It does us good to use our legs," Dahr replied. He drew his bow and fitted an arrow to the string. "I sensed boar and deer in this forest. Which should we hunt?"

"If you want boar, I suggest you put away that toy and help me make some spears. Unless you put one through its eye, no single arrow's going to stop a charge."

To kill with my hands... Memories of past hunts filled his mind, and battles where he fought with hand and foot. Taking a life in such a manner drained his bloodlust and made him feel—afterwards, at least—more human. But the price was too high. The monster within clawed closer to the surface with every kill. Best to keep the beast leashed. "Deer, then."

Dahr crept down a narrow game path. Lord Grondellan followed, moving far more quietly than Dahr would have expected, but the great bear of a man had always been a nimble hunter. Memories surfaced of a time long gone, when Dahr had shared a hunt with the Rachannan nobleman. A day's tracking had brought them within a stone's throw of a white stag, a prized trophy for any collection. On the verge of making the kill, Lord Grondellan slipped on a wet stone, plunging into a river dotted with the final remnants of winter ice. The stag bolted at the splash, and their shared laughter scared off every other creature in the woods.

"What are you chuckling about, lad?" Lord Grondellan asked. The Rachannan's hand squeezed his shoulder, restraining him.

"I was just remembering when you—" Dahr caught himself, and his smile vanished. He pulled free of Lord Grondellan's grasp. "It was nothing. Just something you said once."

"Well, keep it down. We're out of meat, and I can't stomach another night of the Orog's cooking."

Grimacing, Dahr stalked forward. He paid no heed to the thorned vines digging at his arms, nor to the mounds of spoor and criss-crossing tracks on the trail. His hand twitched on the notched arrow, tensing and relaxing, and he dared not look back at Lord Grondellan's face, into the Rachannan's proud eyes and good-humored grin.

An errant gust of wind brought a fresh scent to Dahr's nose, and he drew up short. His sudden stop caught Lord Grondellan by surprise, and the larger man nearly fell in his effort to avoid crashing into Dahr.

Dahr raised his bow, arrow half drawn, and signaled for Lord Grondellan to circle left. The nobleman anticipated his order, though, and disappeared into the trees before Dahr's hand finished its motion. His speed belied his girth; he slipped through the dense branches without causing so much as a rustle of leaves.

Crouched low, Dahr crept toward the curved jut of rock marking the apex of the forested hill. Easing around the stone, he caught sight of a stag foraging in the center of a clearing some distance below. Other deer hesitated in the shadows around the clearing, testing the wind and jumping at every sound.

Dahr took aim. He focused on the stag, let his breathing slow. His heart pounded in his chest at first, then the rhythm changed, slowed, matched the heartbeat of his prey. His *dolchek* pressed into his leg, enticing him with its presence, but even the thought of running the stag down made the monster stir. He let loose the bowstring, more to remove the temptation than because he desired the kill.

The arrow struck the stag, piercing its chest and knocking it to the ground. Its terrified scream sent the rest of the herd into panicked flight, but Lord Grondellan felled a doe before the eerie silence of a disturbed forest descended upon them.

Dahr hurried down the hill, dropping to his knees beside the stag. Blood pooled on the ground, but the creature had not yet died. It struggled to rise with ever weakening effort, crying out like an injured fawn. The loss of dignity sickened Dahr, and he clamped a hand around the stag's throat, whispering soothing words while the life faded from its eyes.

"You barely gave me time to get set," Lord Grondellan complained, gasping for breath as he burst from the trees. Grabbing the doe with one hand, he dragged it to a flat rock and drew one of the knives sheathed across his chest. Dahr watched as the Rachannan made the first cut, then turned away.

"What's wrong, lad? You look like you've never seen an animal gutted before. I've seen you laugh off gorier wounds than this on the battlefield."

"It's not that." Dahr struggled to find the words, to understand himself. *I've been on hundreds of hunts before. Why does this one feel ignoble?* "I didn't want to kill him. He deserved better than to stand proxy for the people I really want to kill."

Lord Grondellan remained silent for so long Dahr wondered if the Rachannan were still there. "You'll get your chance, Hunter. When Jeran's ready to face the Durange, he'll call you back."

Not them, though they deserve it. You... Her... Me... Grendor's hands are clean, his soul pure, but if he stays with us, how long before he deserves death too?

A shift in the wind brought a strange scent to Dahr's nose, earthy sweat mixed with terror. He released his grip on the stag's throat and wiped the blood from his hands, wishing the rest of the herd a safe flight from the forest. The arrow he wrenched free of the deer's hide and inspected it for damage before wiping it clean and returning it to his quiver.

Drawing his dagger, he grabbed the stag by the antlers and dragged it toward the flat rock where the doe lay. The distant crack of a stick caused him no alarm, but Lord Grondellan glanced up from his work, and the smile he wore washed off as his eyes drifted toward the trees.

"Dahr, behind you!" Shapes exploded from the trees behind the Rachannan, grabbing him and pulling him into the shadows. The butt of a spear drove into the back of Dahr's skull, making the world blur and swirl. He struggled to turn, to raise his *dolchek*, to open his mind to the Lesser Voices, but another blow to his temple sent him crashing to the ground.

Dahr woke to silence. Thick vines bound him to a tree at the periphery of the clearing. Of his attackers he saw no sign, but the stag and deer were gone, as were his weapons. He opened his mind but sensed nothing, neither the familiar presences of Fang and Shyrock nor the irritating babble of other creatures.

His head pounded, and the vines dug into his flesh, pulling his shoulders taut against the rough bark of the tree. He strained his ears but heard nothing. Gritting his teeth, he pulled at his bonds but succeeded only in turning the ache in his shoulders to agony.

Something rustled the trees, and an unexpected spike of fear drove up Dahr's spine. "Grondellan?" he called out, but it earned him no response. When the rustling returned, close enough that Dahr saw branches shaking in accompaniment, terror consumed him. "Harol!"

The roar that answered Dahr's cry turned his guts to jelly and brought forth images from his darkest nightmares. He struggled against his bonds until the vines slicked with blood and the tree groaned in protest. The rustling stopped, and Dahr imagined the great beast testing the air, its maw moving back and forth as it tried to pinpoint his location. He renewed his efforts with care, working the vines with deliberate movements and increased stealth.

Another roar filled the forest, and a tree at the edge of Dahr's vision fell in a swirl of branches and dust. Desperate, he opened his mind to the beast, willing it away, begging it to heed his call.

Let me loose, the monster within him cried. *I can stop the pain. I can set us free!*

"No!" Dahr shouted the denial, and the forest fell silent. Only for an instant, though, and then the beast raced toward him. The trees bent out of its path, and the air howled past in its haste to flee the creature. Desperate, Dahr called out to the only being he knew could help him in this place.

"Lorthas! Lorthas, please! If you can hear me—"

Dahr sensed more than felt movement beside him. A Tribesman stepped from the trees. Hands taller than the *Tsha'ma* Goshen, with a physique bronzed by the sun and hardened by a warrior's life, the Hunter glanced at Dahr before drawing a javelin from a knotted leather cord looped over one shoulder. He hurled the javelin into the trees, and the creature howled. A second javelin followed, then a third, and the beast roared with every throw. Before the fourth shaft left the Tribesman's hand, the creature fled into the forest.

The Garun'ah stood poised until the thunder of the creature's passage faded, then he slipped the javelin back into its holder. "You have my thanks, Tribesman," Dahr said, working moisture into his throat. "I thought that thing had me this time."

Lips drawn down in a dark frown, the Garun'ah looked sidelong at Dahr. "You shrieked like a child in the claws of a *tigran*. Is this how Balan's children train their Hunters? Did you seek to cripple your foe with noise?"

The embers of anger flared in his chest, and Dahr struggled to control them. "I was bound and bloodied. What choice did I have?"

The Tribesman's sharp exhale spoke of frustration. "Choices… They have poisoned you with His teachings. What does a Child of Garun need with choices? The Hunter has shown the Blood its path, and you he has given guides aplenty."

"What would you have me do," Dahr asked, leaning forward until the pull of his bindings strained the muscles of his shoulders, "gnash my teeth and growl at it?"

With a single, fluid motion the Tribesman drew his *dolchek*, spun, and threw it so the blade sliced the vines and Dahr tumbled face-first to the forest floor. "I would have you use the gifts the Gods gave you to defend yourself. I would have you own who you are instead of running like a jackrabbit from the shadow of your own soul. I would have you call your Blood for help instead of the Fallen One."

Spitting dirt and leaves, Dahr tried to rise, but the Tribesman planted a knee in his back and drove him to the earth. The hot breath of a predator blew across the base of his neck. "You are *Cho Korahn Garun*. Your wanderings were to make you stand above the Blood, to take the strength of the warrior and temper it with Balan's wisdom."

The pressure vanished from Dahr's back. "Woe to you, Dahr Odara, for you have failed two Gods today."

Dahr leapt to his feet and whirled around, but the Garun'ah was gone. He scoured the clearing, but not so much as a footprint remained to give proof to the Tribesman's presence. "Coward! Why won't you face me now, on my feet?"

Self-loathing warred with rage. Unable to trust his legs, he leaned against the tree that had held him captive. Deafening quiet filled his head, and Dahr yearned for even a single presence, but one over all.

Dahr woke to silence. Thick vines bound him to a tree on the periphery of the clearing. His head felt as if a blacksmith pounded upon it; spikes of pain shot from his temple, radiating across his eyes and jaw. When he opened his mouth to ease the stiffness in his jaw, something ripped along his scalp and a trickle of hot blood ran down his cheek.

Lord Grondellan lay not far off, on his stomach with wrists and ankles tied together behind his back. The Rachannan nobleman shifted, but the movement pulled one arm tight, and he grunted in such a way that even Dahr pitied him. He leaned the other way to relieve the pressure and succeeded in drawing one leg back to a perilous angle. Each movement loosened one limb and strained another beyond endurance, bringing a fresh moan to the man's lips.

On the flat rock in the center of the clearing, two young Tribesmen worked the flesh of the fallen deer, stripping the skin and slicing the meat into long strips. An old woman tended a fire built beneath a makeshift lean-to. A row of cords hung across the interior of the lean-to, and once the children finished preparing the meat, the three set to hanging the strips above the fire. A handful of green wood, leaves, and herbs dumped atop the flames created a thick smoke.

Dahr shut his eyes and feigned unconsciousness when the Tribesmen covered the front of the structure with a flap of canvas and turned toward him. He watched through slitted eyes as the children rummaged through the gear taken from him and Lord Grondellan. The boy child hefted Dahr's greatsword, the blade nearly twice as long as he stood tall, and danced back and forth from leg to leg, uttering something in *Garu* and laughing. Dahr winced when the weight of the sword pulled the boy off balance and the blade slipped within a few fingers of his companion.

Sharp words from the old woman cracked across the clearing like a whip, and the boy dropped the greatsword, embarrassment reddening his features. She hobbled toward them, waving a gnarled stick in a way that reminded Dahr of Alwen. The children fled to the trees, and the old woman followed, her tirade continuing even after the two younglings disappeared into the thick foliage.

"Are you alive, Dahr?" Lord Grondellan asked. Dahr opened his eyes and saw the Rachannan staring at him, lips drawn back in a rictus.

"If this is the Twilight World," Dahr replied, "then I think I'd prefer the Nothing."

Lord Grondellan chuckled, but the sound cut off in a groan of pain. "Don't do that, Hunter. I can barely breathe as is. How many are there?"

"I've seen only two children and an old woman. There must be more out there."

"Our pride demands no less than six, all men in their prime. Can you free yourself?"

Dahr tested his bonds. They gave a little, but not enough for him to maneuver. "Not without help." He opened his mind to the Lesser Voices, but they were distant, distracted. His call for help received no overt response, and those he trusted the most were too far away for him to sense. "It'll take time."

"I don't know how much of that we have, lad. I think—"

"*Chorka! Trela! Habdahr weckt!*"

Dahr turned toward the speaker, a boy barely out of childhood but dressed in the garb of a Hunter, with feathers laced through his hair and a circle of glass beads around his throat. His hair was unkempt, and dirt smeared his cheeks and arms. He clutched a short spear, holding the point toward Dahr in a manner both threatening and comical.

Two younger boys burst from the trees a moment later. One held a bow and the other a *dolchek* honed and polished till it gleamed in the stray rays of sunlight filtering through the trees. They formed a semi-circle around Dahr, though the smallest turned his attention on Lord Grondellan. They stared at him without speaking, and when Dahr tried to start a conversation, all three shoved their weapons at him until he quieted.

The old woman and young children returned and took up places near the smoke house. The children held rocks in each hand, and stood behind the old Tribeswoman, who shielded them with her body and cane. They, too, stared at Dahr.

"I mean you no harm," Dahr said, wincing when the spear point edged closer to his throat. "I am looking for Yarchik, *Kranor* of the Channa."

The boys shared a glance and stepped back a ways. Their mumbled conversation drifted to Dahr, but he understood no part of it. When they laughed, he grew confused. "What are they saying?" he wondered aloud.

"Something about a Human in Hunter's clothing," Lord Grondellan whispered. "You speak Garu?"

"Enough to get by. I had enough encounters with the Afelda to warrant it. The Tribesmen are fun to fight, but times are when a man prefers talk to tactics."

"*Stahl!*" shrieked the boy with the spear, jabbing it against Lord Grondellan's side. The Rachannan took the hint and fell silent.

"Don't hurt him," Dahr warned, but a part of him urged the boy to do what he, himself, had proved incapable of doing. "He's done you no wrong."

"Everyone wronged Drekka." A new figure emerged from the forest, a woman of a height with Dahr, skin bronzed and muscles toned. She walked with the bearing of a warrior but bore no weapons and wore a simple hide dress looped across one shoulder and exposing a fair amount of flesh. Hair the color of deepest night but smeared with mud and accented with bits of twigs and leaves hung past her shoulders. Almond-shaped eyes matched her hair in coloring, twin pools of darkness conveying untold suffering and sorrow. "Drekka wronged everyone."

"We mean you no harm," Dahr said again. He pointed toward the smokehouse with his chin. "Take the deer. You have more need of it than we do. Let us return to our people, and we can set this behind us." The monster inside argued that the affront was too great, that pride demanded revenge for this treatment.

"We you people now." The woman looked at her companions, the two toddlers clutching the old woman's clothes, the three boys pretending to be men. "We seek peace. You come us. You take Channa. You give home."

"Release me and my friend. We will take you to the Channa. The *Kranor* is a friend."

"No let go. You run. You take Channa. You…" She looked at her companions, confusion plastered across her face. She said something to the old woman, who grunted a word back. "You *tsallos*."

Dahr frowned, and he looked at Lord Grondellan. The Rachannan stared back. "Slave. She says we're her slaves."

Chapter 12

The sun beat down with merciless fury, turning the grass brown and leaving cracks in the parched earth. The air itself blurred in the heat, wavering and dancing. A handful of wispy clouds clung to the sky, the thin tendrils offering no hope of rain.

The cords binding Dahr's wrists dug against his flesh, and sweat poured from beneath the harness straps across his chest. He shuffled forward, teeth bared, struggling to ignore the pain. Sunburnt flesh and blistered feet made the task difficult, as did the Garun'ah children who dogged his steps and jabbed him with spears whenever he slowed too much. Walking itself became an agony, and Dahr yearned to escape his torment, to cast himself to the scorched earth and demand to be freed or killed.

But he could not. In the final reckoning, he had been proven a coward. Part of him clung to life, refused to lay down and die, forced him to take one humiliating step after another.

It's not fear of death. It's pride. I will not give up before Grondellan!

Lord Grondellan labored beside him, panting and gasping, all but doubled over from exertion. Sweat drenched the man, soaking his clothes and caking the dust to his flesh. His eyes rarely lifted from the ground, but when Dahr stumbled, the Rachannan's hand shot out to steady him.

"Careful, lad. I can't pull this load without you."

The wagon they hauled was loaded down with odds and ends scavenged from a thousand places. Half-spoiled food, trinkets from abandoned campsites, the detritus of long-ago fought battles, these Tribesmen kept anything they found, and everything found its way into the wagon.

"Are you sure you know where we're going?" Lord Grondellan asked. "I'd like to reach the Channa before I die of exhaustion."

"Thirst will kill us long before exhaustion," Dahr said. He had not intended it as a joke, but the Rachannan nobleman laughed. *How can he keep his humor at a time like this?*

"That's it, Hunter. Help me keep my perspective. What of the Channa?"

"I don't know." Dahr opened his mind, but once again found the Lesser Voices missing. He ground his teeth together. *I know you're out there! Why won't you talk to me?*

The animals had not spoken to him since his capture. He longed for the familiar voices of Fang, Shyrock, or Jardelle, but even the rasp of a snake or the twittering of a songbird would have been a welcome sound. Without the babble of wildlife or the calming certainty of Jeran's presence, Dahr was alone in his mind. For a time, he had welcomed the silence, but now the emptiness tormented him.

"Hai!" Dahr grimaced as the butt of a spear drove into his back, just above the kidney. He nearly lost his footing at the second blow, then one of the young

Garun'ah stepped forward far enough for him to see. "Hai!" he said again, shoving the spear point toward the horizon.

"Kohr's Blood!" Lord Grondellan grasped his side, where a spot of red showed on his ragged clothes. "Use the flat end, you fool, unless you want a dead slave pulling your wagon. The flat end! *Da na Kolb!*"

The child jumped at the Rachannan's howl, but a grim expression fell upon his face. He grasped the haft of his spear and lunged in for another stab. Dahr dove to the side, ignoring the way the harness straps dug into his shoulder and throat. The sudden movement pulled Lord Grondellan and the wagon half a step to the side and just out of the boy's reach. The Tribesman shadowing Dahr leapt toward his companion, shouting something in *Garu* that Dahr could only hope was reproachment.

"I owe you for that, too," Lord Grondellan mumbled once they resumed their plodding gait.

"You owe me nothing. I don't want to haul this thing by myself either."

Through the day they trundled north, urged on by the spears of their youthful shadows, over hills steep enough they felt like mountains to Dahr's aching muscles. No respite from the heat presented itself. Their path meandered between patches of desiccated shrubs, their few remaining leaves limp with thirst, the only water a shallow pool bubbling up from the ground. When Dahr knelt to drink, the young Tribesman kicked him.

Bound as he was, Dahr toppled, and his head hit a stone with enough force to dizzy him. He started to rise, to roll toward his captor, to find some way to repay the boy for his insult and degradation, but his eyes fell on the corpse of a cow, its head fingers from the pool. Then he noticed other dead animals, too many to be coincidence, arrayed around the pond. He climbed to his feet and resumed walking, but he could not bring himself to thank the Tribesman.

Each hilltop brought a brief thrill of relief. The weight of the wagon disappeared, and off in the distance—always at the periphery—stands of thick trees beckoned with shade and sustenance. Then, with a few more steps, the wagon began its descent and relief turned to regret. Stopping it from rolling over them on the way down took far more effort than hauling it up the hills.

When the sun stood low in the west, they stopped along the banks of a stream, its once broad span reduced to a single hand's width. As usual, the Garun'ah tossed them some dried fruit and a single skin of water and left them bound to the wagon for the night.

"Two ten-days of this treatment!" Lord Grondellan snarled as he raised the skin to his lips. He took a small sip, then held it out. Dahr nodded, and Lord Grondellan placed it against his mouth, tilting it up until the water poured from the spout. Dahr gagged when the first touch of wetness hit his tongue, but he was careful not to waste a drop. Coolness spread down his throat, quenching the fire in his gut.

"I'll tell you one thing," Grondellan said. He set aside the skin and started sorting through the fruit. "Men can't be treated in this manner. Men like us were meant to walk free, not live bound to a wagon like oxen."

Dahr snorted. "Odd words from a man with an entire wing of his manor dedicated to housing slaves."

Lord Grondellan bristled. "I never treated the worst of my slaves the way these Tribesmen have treated us! My people want for neither food nor shelter. They can learn a trade and contribute to the welfare of the entire house, and the more they earn, the better they are treated. I allow them to marry, and I make sure families are never separated. Most are better off as my slaves than as the Gods originally intended."

"A gilded cage is still a cage," Dahr replied. "You drape the trappings of freedom around your prison and deceive men, even clever men like Yurs, into loving you for their incarceration. Freedom is the essence of the soul, and you have stolen it from so many. You hold a knife to their hearts, and your whim can see them dead. You perpetuate the evil regardless of whether or not you, yourself, are evil."

"I have taken offense at others for far less insult, pup," Lord Grondellan said, climbing to his feet. He threw a dried plum at Dahr, and chuckled when the fruit stuck to Dahr's cheek. "Your King's whim can make far more men dead than mine. Jeran's too."

"Jeran commands men. You control them."

"I have done nothing wrong!" Lord Grondellan grabbed Dahr by the shoulders and shoved him against the wagon. A twenty hand leash held the Rachannan, but ropes bound Dahr hand and foot, and he could do nothing to defend himself. "There are three types of people in Rachannon: those who own slaves, those who sell slaves, and those who are slaves. I know which of those groups I want to be in."

"And I know which of those groups you belong to now," Dahr said. He relished the pain shooting through the back of his head, the chance to goad the Rachannan nobleman. His promises to Jeran meant he could not lay a hand on the man, but one did not need weapons to wound. "Perhaps the Gods brought us here as part of your penance."

Grondellan's backhand sent a jolt down Dahr's spine, but he turned back to face the man laughing, despite the blood pooling on his lip. "Watch yourself, Hunter," Lord Grondellan growled.

"Is this the fine treatment your slaves can expect?" Dahr asked. He knew it was not; Harol Grondellan never laid a hand on a slave in all the time Dahr had lived on the estate. The worst punishment he ever doled out was an extended stint in the fields.

Grondellan's face turned red as an apple, and his eyes narrowed to slits. He struck again, and Dahr accepted the blow, silently wishing for more. He knew that once the anger had fled, remorse would plague the Rachannan. *Savor the small victories*, Dahr thought as his head made contact with the wagon and he struggled to maintain consciousness.

Suddenly, Lord Grondellan was gone, and Dahr opened his eyes. The Rachannan lay on the ground breathing hard. The Tribeswoman stood over him, a spear held against his throat. She wore a grim scowl, but hesitation danced across her eyes. After a moment, her hands tightened on the haft.

"*Stahl*," Dahr shouted, and the Tribeswoman jumped. Dahr watched relief flash across both her face and Lord Grondellan's. "Do not kill him."

"He... kill you." The woman's brow furrowed as she sought the right words. "You make us home. You die... we die."

"He wouldn't kill me. It was... I goaded him to it. He won't kill me. Please, let him go."

Uncertainty danced across her eyes, but the Tribeswoman stepped back and lowered the spear. Dahr drew a calming breath. "What is your name, *Dahrina*?"

Her haunting eyes pierced into Dahr's soul. "Meila *uvan* Conesta, *pristari* Drekka."

Dahr glanced at Lord Grondellan. "A holy woman," the Rachannan said, gasping for air, "but not a Mage."

"Meila, there's no need to bind us." Dahr tugged the cords around his wrists. "Free us, and I will take you to the Channa. I will find you a new home."

The Tribeswoman stared at him for a time, her eyes weighing him. "Chains crush Blood. Even Half-man like you. Sorrow, but you last chance. Take to Channa, then free."

"My friends among the Channa won't like to see me enslaved."

"You make understand." She walked away, but Dahr noticed a heaviness to her steps he had not seen before.

Lord Grondellan sat beside him, leaning back against the wagon. "Sorry about that, Hunter, I—"

"I brought it upon myself," Dahr said. His eyes swept the camp. The old woman and children huddled around the small, smokeless cookfire in the center of the valley, upon which roasted three rabbits. A mound of earth had been piled onto a square of canvas, ready to dump on the flames in a moment's notice. Only the smallest of the children went weaponless; most carried a *dolchek*, or at the very least a hunting knife.

The older boys took up positions on the hills. Crouched low, they crept back and forth like stalking lions. Their heads rarely lifted above the tall grass, but Dahr recognized a sentry patrol when he saw it.

"They're expecting an attack," he said.

"They'd better be. Katya and Grendor—"

"No, our companions are not near enough, and they're patrolling the northern hills. It's Tribesmen they're worried about."

"These are Drekka. There isn't a tribe of Garun'ah out there who wouldn't go out of its way to harass Drekka."

"But Garun'ah don't attack children, and women only if they are *dahrina*."

"If not Tribesmen, then who? No one else lives on these plains."

"I don't know, but we had best be ready."

"Ready for what? A transfer of ownership? We're not likely to be much help in a fight." Grondellan raised his hands to show off the cords harnessing him to the wagon.

"I haven't forgotten," Dahr said. "But chaos brings opportunity. We may be able to use our captors' misfortune to our advantage."

A scowl pulled at Grondellan's lips. "I can't say I like wishing harm on babes and women."

"Bondage poisons the souls of men; it destroys those of the Blood. Those who take freedom deserve the punishment meted out by the Gods, no matter their age or gender."

"As cold-hearted a thought as I have ever heard," Lord Grondellan replied. "And as narrow-minded." Dahr clenched his teeth but said nothing. "We may be prisoners, but you can't tell me you think this Meila woman wanted to make us slaves. You can see remorse every time she looks at us. She's afraid, Dahr, even you must realize that, and she thinks that somehow you are the key to her salvation. To the salvation of her people."

"It's no excuse. There's no excuse for this."

The strained silence that fell between them echoed in Dahr's mind. *What's happening to me? What am I becoming?* His eyes drifted southwest, drawn there against his will. *Is that you, Jeran? Why have you abandoned me?*

"You know, I owned one once," Grondellan said, his voice somber. "A Tribesman." Dahr's head whipped around. He expected accusation or recognition, not the sadness he saw painted on the Rachannan's features.

"It's not what you think. He was a foundling like you, not a true Tribesman, a cub raised by some old soldier on the slopes of Mount Kalan. The slaver I bought him from—I swear, no crueler a creature ever existed—had slaughtered the boy's father and left his mother for dead. I'd have bought that slaver's whole caravan if I could have, but the little Tribesman... There was something between him and slaver, a festering hatred. I couldn't leave the boy in the hands of that monster."

Dahr fought to keep his voice calm, his tone even. "How kind of you... to add another slave to your manor... for the child's sake."

Again Grondellan surprised him, this time with laughter. "So much naivety in one who's suffered so much. No doubt you'd have had me set him free?"

"Better free than a slave."

"He was four winters old, if that! A babe with no family, no friends, no chance on his own. Most foundlings aren't as lucky as you were... Odaras don't live around every corner. I sent messengers to the Afelda, but they said they had lost no cubs, and that none of the Blood would take a child tainted by the Soul-Stealers. A child like that was already dead.

"So the Tribes didn't want him, and most Humans would have feared him, and feared him more the older he grew, especially in Rachannon, where skirmishes with Tribesmen are not uncommon. Even my own people mocked him against my wishes, tormented him at every opportunity. They called him *Kranor*, but they called him other things, too. Things far less flattering."

Lord Grondellan broke off, and he pressed his lips together hard. "Not me. I called him *Nai'segare*. Have you heard that word before?"

Dahr had heard it many times, but he shook his head. "Not many have," Grondellan told him. "It's an old Aelvin word I came across. It means 'son', but more than that, a secret son. A child you love as your own but dare not recognize."

The exuberance with which Grondellan faced life faded, and for a moment, Dahr saw a man past his prime, a man tormented. "I have no sons, you know. And Rachannan law leaves nothing to daughters. I had dreams... I loved him, Hunter. My *Nai'segare*. How could keeping him have been worse than letting him die?"

Lord Grondellan's pain tugged at a part of Dahr he thought long dead, but the monster within reared its head as well, demanding to know what right this man had to pity. "What happened to your pet Tribesman?" Dahr asked, unable to keep the venom from his tongue.

The Rachannan turned away. "I killed him."

The callous tone stunned Dahr, but the loathing in Lord Grondellan's eyes was directed inward. "You..." Dahr worked some moisture into his mouth. "You killed him?"

"Aye. I took the boy hunting with me. I tell you, we had some adventures. But one time, when an early snow fell, we caught sight of a snow tiger, the largest of its kind I had ever seen. I insisted on tracking it, and it led us far from the rest of our party."

Lord Grondellan shook his head as if to banish the memories plaguing him, but he was ultimately unsuccessful. "The beast was as clever as it was beautiful. It pulled us into an ambush, then launched at me from concealment. I was unhorsed, knocked unconscious, and I was certain I'd wake to find myself in the Twilight World. The last thing I remember was *Nai'segare* standing over me, holding a stick like a sword."

More laughter rang out from the Rachannan, but this one carried an edge. "Can you even imagine that, Hunter? A child defending me, his *master*, from a creature twice his size? The Tribesmen hold foundlings in low regard, but I tell you the heart of the Hunter beats in them as strongly as in any Garun'ah."

Overcome with emotion, Lord Grondellan turned his head away to compose himself. Dahr fought the urge to reach out, a struggle aided by his bonds. He managed to murmur, "I'm sure he's in a better place," but the irony of the statement did not amuse him.

"A better place than this, no doubt." Grondellan's words carried bitterness, and a hurt Dahr never expected to hear from his one-time master. "When I woke there was blood everywhere, and tiger tracks leading north. I followed them until the next snowfall obscured the trail. I hunted that creature for winters, desperate to wreak my revenge, but the beast eluded me. A ghost it was, and a ghost it remains, haunting me until the end of my days."

The monster raged, but Dahr shoved it down. "What could you have done? You—"

One of the boys approached, sprinting toward them on silent feet. "*Stahl!*" he hissed, desperation cracking his voice. He covered his mouth, then pointed to the hilltop.

"Someone's coming," Dahr whispered, and he worked himself to his feet, scanning the ridgeline.

To the northeast, one of the children raised an alarm, but before he lifted his weapon, the grass around him exploded and a Tribesman enveloped the boy in a tight grip. The other took up the cry, drawing weapons and running toward their companions' aid, but other Hunters jumped from concealment. The fight was fierce but brief; soon all of Dahr's captors were herded to the center of the valley.

With her followers crowded around her, Meila stood defiant, even when the leader of the Tribesman, a scarred and grim-visaged Hunter wearing a cracked leather vest the color of dried blood approached. Red dripped from the blade of his *dolchek*, and Dahr saw the young man who had saved him from drinking the poisoned water clutching an arm.

Meila and the newcomer exchanged words, but even Lord Grondellan could not decipher what was said. After a few moments, their speech grew heated, and the Tribesman grew enraged. With lightning-fast movements his hand lashed out, striking Meila to the ground. The *pristari* regained her feet, wiping blood from her lips, and when the Tribesman leaned in and laughed, she spit on him.

The fury in his eyes made his anger of a moment ago seem the caress of a gentle breeze. He struck again, and when Meila did not fall, he curled his hand into a fist and swung with the brunt of his strength. She hit the ground with a thud and lay unmoving, but the Tribesman was not finished. He advanced on her, murder in his eyes.

One of the boys screamed, a cry of fear and anger, and wrestled away from his captor's grasp. He sprinted forward, grabbing a brand from the edge of the firepit, and attacked with a wild swing the Tribesman easily dodged. The Tribesman drew his *dolchek*, but the boy proved a nimble foe, ducking around the swipe of the blade and scoring a light touch with the glowing end of the stick.

The Tribesman shrieked, and fueled by pain, his next blow caught the child in the side. The boy fell, but the Tribesman pounced upon him like a predator, stabbing until his prey lay still. Then he stalked toward Meila, and his blade drew back again.

"Stop!" Dahr yelled, snapping the Tribesman out of his frenzy.

The man turned toward him as if surprised he had spoken, and studied him for some time before approaching. Dahr straightened his shoulders and stood firm, his gaze locked on the Tribesman, wondering what had prompted him to cry out.

The point of the *dolchek* touched Dahr's chin, moving his head back and forth. "What say?" the Tribesman asked.

"These people are under my protection. I will not allow you to harm them."

The Tribesman chuckled, and his eyes flicked toward the ropes at Dahr's wrist and ankles, and at the stouter cord holding him to the wagon. "You bound, Half-man."

"Nevertheless, you harm them at your own peril. Lower your weapons and leave, and I will let you live."

"Lad," Grondellan whispered out the side of his mouth, "I like a good fight as much as the next man, but I'm not in favor of the odds you've chosen."

"Who you?" the Tribesman demanded. With his *dolchek*, he inspected Dahr's clothes, as if curious but loathe to touch him.

"Who I am is not important. It is what I am you should concern yourself with."

Amusement curled the Tribesman's lip. "What you?"

"I am *Cho Korahn Garun*. These are my people. I will not let you hurt them."

Harsh laughter and fetid breath hit Dahr's face. The Tribesman turned and said something to his companions in Garu, and they laughed as well. "You Korahn?" the Tribesman asked. "Garun's chosen? Captured by *pristari* and fangless cubs?"

"I am where I am out of design." The words issued from Dahr's mouth without thought. Even as he said them, he doubted them, but he kept the uncertainty from entering his eyes. "Thwart your God's will at your own risk."

"My God?" The Tribesman laughed. "I not serve God whose prophet slave to children. I serve Kohr, Father of Storms, one true God. We see Drekka restored and those cast us out sent to Nothing."

"You not Drekka!" Meila shrieked. She launched herself toward the Tribesman, but one of his companions intercepted her. "You betray Drekka when you cast aside Hunter's teachings and offer self to Kraltir and his Human master."

"*Kohr'adjin* see us restored," the Tribesman said. "*Kohr'adjin* offer freedom. I no more hide in frost cave, wait for Hunter's forgiveness. I make own future."

He turned toward Dahr, cruelty and hunger dancing in his eyes. "I leave you for last, Korahn. You see how weak the Hunter's people when confronted by the Father's."

"My patience wears thin," Dahr said. "I will give you no other warning."

The Tribesman kicked Dahr in the gut, sending him crashing back into the wagon. Pain jarred through his head, and he fell, spots of color dancing before his eyes. He pulled at his bonds, but the cords remained as strong as ever.

Isn't this what you wanted? Dahr screamed inside his head. *Are you just going to watch while your people are slaughtered? I can't do this alone!*

Awareness poured into him, and he heard his plea answered by a hundred voices. *We are coming, brother.*

CHAPTER 13

While the *Kohr'adjin* dragged the struggling children and women toward the center of the valley, their leader toyed with his *dolchek*, eyeing Lord Grondellan the way one might eye a cow ripe for the slaughter. He turned away from the Rachannan and planted another kick in Dahr's gut before strutting toward his companions.

Dahr grunted with the force of the blow, but he rolled with it so that his hands were hidden from view and beneath the wagon. The first of his allies waited for him there, several large rodents with teeth designed for gnawing. One chewed at the bonds around his wrist while another worked his ankles; the third struggled to free Lord Grondellan.

"I hope this creature is here because of you," Grondellan whispered, casting nervous glances over his shoulder.

"If it wanted to eat you," Dahr replied, "it wouldn't waste time with the ropes. Be ready."

"Lad, I've been ready for the last twenty days."

Dahr opened his mind, and he felt the presence of a number of animals, most unfamiliar to him. He welcomed their company, and told them how they could best serve him. One consciousness stood out among the bunch, and Dahr smiled. "Our friends are coming. They finally know where to look for us."

"Then we should just hold tight and wait for them. I'll like the odds better then."

"We don't have time. Those *Kohr'adjin* are going to kill Meila."

"A moment ago, you were ready to kill her yourself."

"There's a difference between killing one's captors and watching captives slaughtered. Meila's people are no different than us now."

Grondellan's mouth worked, but it took some time before he could speak. "You are a strange man, Hunter."

Dahr chose not to reply. Across the clearing, the Tribesmen arranged Meila's followers in a line, oldest to youngest. The boys were restrained, and several bled from gashes earned in the fight. To their credit, none gave up; all struggled against their captives, snarling and gnashing their teeth like wild animals. Meila carried out a heated debate with the *Kohr'adjin* leader, but despite the plea in her eyes, her words carried only contempt.

The cord binding Dahr's legs separated, as did the one holding him to the wagon. The ones on his wrist he left secure, but frayed enough that he could break them with ease. He stood and warned the animals who had answered his call to be ready. When the Tribesman signaled his men to begin the slaughter, Dahr shouted. "Release them now, and you may leave here alive."

The Tribesman's glare dripped with venom. "I Garun'ah. Not take orders from soulless pet of Human." He shoved Meila back and stalked toward Dahr.

Dahr readied himself to meet an attack. "I am Dahr Odara, *Tier'sorahn* and *Cho Korahn Garun*. You have strayed from the teachings of your God. He demands obedience or blood, but he leaves the choice to you."

Narrow eyes darted to Lord Grondellan and then back to Dahr. "That thing animal," the Tribesman said, spitting at the Rachannan, "but it follow you not make you *Tier'sorahn*." He barked a string of orders, and the *Kohr'adjin* not restraining Meila's people fanned out around the wagon.

We are ready, brother. Dahr bared a vicious smile. "I had hoped you'd choose blood, though I suspect I'd find a better fight with one of the cubs behind you."

The Tribesman launched himself at Dahr, who sidestepped and met the Tribesman's attack by catching the *dolchek* between his hands and twisting. The blade wrapped around his frayed ropes, parting the last strands and ripping away from the Tribesman's grasp. It clattered to the ground not far from Lord Grondellan, who scooped it up and stood. The Rachannan jockeyed for position, spinning to keep the other Tribesmen in view while Dahr fought their leader.

Finally free, Dahr stretched his arms wide and howled, and the hilltop burst into motion. Lions launched from the dry grass, bearing Tribesmen to the ground and mauling them with fang and claw. The ground began to tremble, and an armored beast with a horn the length of Dahr's forearm thundered into the valley, scattering the *Kohr'adjin* and trampling any who fell before it.

Dahr dove at the man who had attacked him, and they tumbled through the grass exchanging blows. He caught the Tribesman off guard, but the Garun'ah was far from unskilled in combat, and the long days hauling the wagon had exhausted Dahr. Before long he found himself on the defensive, blocking punch after punch and looking for a way to disentangle himself from his opponent.

An elbow slammed his jaw, numbing him, and then Dahr felt hands at his throat. The Tribesman gloated over him, eyes wild, teeth bared in a snarl, slavering like a rabid dog on the verge of a kill.

Dahr gripped the Tribesman's wrists and fought for air. He was stronger than his opponent, but the *Kohr'adjin* had the advantage of leverage. Pinned beneath his attacker's weight, Dahr could do nothing save flail about and hope.

The low note of a bone horn pierced the air, reverberating over the shouts and screams of battle. The Tribesman glanced up, and the momentary slackening of his grip was all Dahr needed. He released his hold on the attacker's wrists and drove his hands upward. One caught the *Kohr'adjin* leader in the throat, the other in the sternum.

As the Tribesman choked and sputtered, Dahr kicked his legs, throwing his opponent into the grass. They both rolled to their feet and squared off, but now Dahr felt he held the advantage. *You hate, but your hatred is not so well honed as mine. You seek something, but you know not what. I seek only release.*

The Tribesman hurled a curse at him, but Dahr laughed it off. He stalked forward, eyes intent on his prey. The beast within surged forth, and Dahr gave it free rein. When the Tribesman launched his next attack, Dahr was ready. His training in Kaper remembered, Dahr used his opponent's momentum against him, slipping past his charge.

Pivot and twist. The Tribesman's arm snapped, and he screamed, but to his credit, the *Kohr'adjin* neither fled nor surrendered. He resumed his attack with one arm hanging useless at his side, and even managed to press Dahr back with a series of frenzied attacks.

Dahr let his opponent exhaust himself, then moved in for the kill. A blow to the gut staggered the Tribesman, another to the kidney left him dazed and gasping for air. Offering no respite, Dahr slipped behind his opponent and wrapped an arm around his neck. He tensed, felt the man's throat press into his bicep, and squeezed until the Tribesman's struggles ceased. He laid the corpse on the ground with a bit more reverence than it deserved.

The lions circled the remaining *Kohr'adjin*, though only a handful of the Tribesmen still breathed. A second ring of animals, mostly prairie dogs and foxes, kept watch on Meila and her followers. Lord Grondellan sat astride the horned beast, which trundled about the valley in slow, meandering circles.

The Rachannan laughed when he saw Dahr. "Life with you is always an adventure, Hunter. When else could a man ride a creature like this and live to tell the tale?"

A golden eagle soared overhead, shrieking out greetings. *Shyrock! You've been this close the whole time? I wish I could say I was glad to see you, but I'm furious.* The eagle shrieked again, wheeled about and flew out of sight. "I was joking," Dahr muttered.

More Tribesmen appeared on the hilltop, but interspersed with them were familiar faces. "Vyrina?" Dahr called out to the Guardswoman, and she raised a hand in greeting.

"It's good to see you, Dahr," Vyrina said, jogging toward him. Tribal hides and a *dolchek* had replaced her Guardsman's uniform, but she still carried an Alrendrian bow over her shoulder. She looked happy, happier than Dahr remembered from her days in Kaper. A stab of envy dug at his gut.

"You remember Frodel?" she asked, indicating the Tribesman at her side.

"Yes." Dahr ducked his head. Lean and tall, Frodel walked like a caged tiger and studied Dahr with a wary eye. He returned the greeting with a slight bow of his own, but he kept his distance, and his hand never strayed far from the blade looped at his hip. Dahr knew little of the Tribesman, save that he had devoted himself to Vyrina and protected the woman like a guard dog.

"What are you doing here?" Dahr asked.

"Looking for you," replied Vyrina. "We'd been tracking the *Kohr'adjin* for almost a ten-day when we met Katya and her companion. She said you'd been captured and that they'd been unable to find you." Vyrina looked at the chaos of the camp and the bodies of the Tribesmen. "For a prisoner, you managed to cause a lot of trouble."

"It's even worse than that," Lord Grondellan laughed, hopping off his strange mount as it passed by. He hooked a thumb toward Meila. "Those are the ones that put us in chains. Dahr was protecting them from the *Kohr'adjin*."

Vyrina's eyes widened as she looked at Meila and the children surrounding her, but Frodel's expression hardened. A young Hunter hovering behind the pair surged forward. "You protect Drekka? Why you protect ones as they?"

"Ah, lad," Lord Grondellan said, shaking his head. "That's not a good idea."

Dahr drew a deep breath and vowed to control his temper. "They are children, and don't—"

"They Drekka! Have you not drop of Garun's Blood? You captured by cubs and protect Lost Tribe. Better to let *Kohr'adjin* send them to Nothing."

Dahr's hand shot out and grasped the Tribesman by the throat. He lifted him off his feet and slammed him to the ground. His knee pressed into the young man's gut, and with his other hand he tore the Hunter's blade away.

"Harm them at your own risk," Dahr said, tightening his grip on the Tribesman's throat. "Drekka they may have been, but they seek their way back to the world of men, and I will show them the path. They are under my protection now."

He released the Tribesman. Gasping for air, the young Hunter asked, "Who you to command Blood?"

"I am *Cho Korahn Garun*. I will be the Blood's salvation. And it's destruction. Heed my words, or I know which of the two paths I will send you down."

Aghast, the Tribesman scrabbled to his feet and glanced at Frodel for confirmation. The older Tribesman nodded almost imperceptibly, but it had a dramatic effect on the younger man.

"Dahr?"

The sound of her voice sent a chill down his spine, and his heart quickened at the sound of it. He turned to face Katya, watched her ride toward him, holding Jardelle's reins in one hand. The powerful warhorse followed docilely, but Dahr sensed frustration from the noble beast. Framed in the afternoon light, Katya was a vision, as beautiful as in the memories that haunted his dreams.

He fought the grin that tried to blossom at the sight of her. "Where's Grendor?"

"Yarchik wouldn't let him go. There's some prophecy about grey men returning before the Blood's reckoning, or something like that." She laughed, and the music of her laughter lightened Dahr's heart even as it sickened him. "I bet Grendor will be wishing for the inquisition of the Magi before that old man gets through with him."

She looked Dahr up and down, frowning at the bruises on his arms and the blood pooling beneath a scratch on his cheek. "Are you alright?"

"I'm fine," he grunted, dismissing her with a wave. "It's—"

"We go." Frodel grunted. "*Kohr'adjin* not travel in such small groups."

Dahr whirled toward the Tribesman, annoyed at being interrupted. "He's right," Vyrina agreed. "This was a small band. Odds are there are more around. We should get back to the camp."

"What are you going to do with them?" Dahr asked, pointing at Meila.

Vyrina looked at Frodel and said something in Garu. His reply was short, and it touched off what sounded like an argument.

"He wants nothing to do with them," the Guardswoman told Dahr. "He says too many already live in the tents. But they are your prisoners, and therefore your responsibility. So the question is: what are you going to do with them?"

Dahr grimaced. Part of him wanted to leave the Drekka to their fate, part of him wanted to save them. A third part, a part he desperately tried to ignore, wanted to finish what the *Kohr'adjin* had started. He signaled for the others to wait and walked over to the prisoners, stopping to retrieve his gear and sheath his greatsword over his shoulder.

Meila studied him as he approached, not looking at all like a prisoner. Pride dominated her features, and her probing, measuring gaze bored into Dahr.

"You really what you claim?" she asked. "You *Cho Korahn Garun?*"

Dahr snorted. "They think I am."

"But you not sure. *Korahn* must have faith. In Blood. In Garun. In self."

"I'm not here to discuss religion," Dahr snapped. "I need an oath from you and your followers that you will cause no harm to the Channa, that you will follow my instructions."

Meila pursed her lips. "You not put us in chains?"

"I have no love of chains. Words bind better, when a person has a good soul. I think you have a good soul."

"Even though I Drekka?"

"Garun's blood flows in my veins, but I am not of the Blood. I do not share their prejudices. To me, you're just another Tribeswoman, one who deserves freedom as much as any other. The sins of your ancestors should not reflect upon your own honor."

The sins of your ancestors should not reflect upon your own honor. The words echoed in his mind, and he found his gaze drawn to Katya.

Silence reigned for a time, but eventually Meila nodded. "You have oath. And oath of others." Dahr turned away, dismissing the creatures standing guard around the prisoners with a thought, and sending them his thanks.

"Doubts cloud mind," Meila said, freezing Dahr in his tracks, "but Garun smiles on you. If you not *Korahn*, you at least favored by the Hunter. Fortunate for me that he delivered you to us."

"Yes," Dahr mumbled. "It really shows how much he favors me."

Dahr walked north, ignoring calls from Lord Grondellan and Vyrina. "They're coming with us," he grunted to Frodel as he stomped past. "I will seek refuge for them with the Channa."

Frodel looked displeased, but he said nothing, and Dahr moved north out of the camp, followed by Fang. The hound said nothing, for which Dahr was grateful, and he drew strength from her presence. Jardelle jerked free of Katya's grip and trotted over to Dahr as well. He rubbed the great warhorse's neck and fastened his gear, then climbed into the saddle. From there, he watched the Garun'ah dismantle Meila's camp and usher the captured Drekka out of the valley.

CHAPTER 14

The Channa's camp lay not two days ride to the northeast, but the journey there seemed longer than the ten-days spent a captive. Left alone to brood, Dahr caught snippets of warm conversation from his companions, endured the harmony of Katya's light laugh merge with Grondellan's booming bass. He yearned to be part of their joy, but he sought to distance himself from it, until he no longer seemed a member of the troupe traveling toward Channa territory, but a solitary figure dogged by Tribesmen through the wilderness.

Dahr caught the scent of trouble before he heard the distant screams, the clang of clashing weaponry. A glance over his shoulder showed Frodel forming a band of Hunters. He did not wait for them, but raced toward the fray, calling for Shyrock to scout the scene and bidding Fang to stay close. The eagle sent him images of a great battle, with three sets of Tribesmen fighting before a collection of tents. *But which are friend, and which foe?* Dahr unsheathed his sword, confident that when the time came he would know who to kill.

Topping a hill, he pulled Jardelle to a stop and assessed the field with his own eyes. The plains below had been churned, the grasses trampled; great clouds of dust rose, save where the pooling blood turned the ground to mud. The flank of the attacking host stood before him, with the tents of the Channa arrayed beyond. A third group stood off to the side, remaining curiously out of the fray.

After a brief deliberation, Dahr spurred Jardelle toward the center of the attacker's line. A battlecry surged up within him, but he bit his tongue. Surprise would serve him better than reckless abandon.

This is suicide. Wait for the others.

Dahr did not know if the thought was his or Fang's, but he ignored it. He did not open his mind to the Lesser Voices either. Enough had fought for him, had died for him, already. He did not want to sacrifice them every time he sought battle.

The Tribesmen heard his approach, but too late to prepare for it. One whirled around in time to be trampled by Jardelle; another noticed Dahr when his greatsword sliced a line of red down the Hunter's side. Dahr cursed—he had grown unused to combat from horseback and had intended the cut to be instantly mortal—but he left the Tribesman to a slow death and urged Jardelle forward.

The warhorse kicked and stomped through the warring Hunters, and Dahr marveled at the restraint of his foe. The Garun'ah he fought in the past displayed incredible martial skills, but they fought alone, or at best in small groups, more like hunting packs than organized units. These Tribesmen showed far more control, fighting in formation and reacting in concert to a series of horn blasts, shifting from attack to defense at a moment's notice, responding with a discipline that rivaled the Alrendrian Guard.

The Garun'ah defending the camp could not stop the relentless press. Many threw themselves forward in pointless assaults, either out of desperation or caught in the throes of Blood Rage. Others held back, uncertain how to proceed, knowing that individual efforts would fail but not certain how to work together effectively. The third group of Tribesmen—which Dahr labeled allies only because they faced the *Kohr'adjin* and not the Channa—watched with keen interest, but only roused themselves when one of the other groups drew too near.

Find the horn blower. Dahr sent the thought to Fang and Shyrock. *Kill him first.* He wanted to tell them to be careful, but feared the insult such a thing would cause.

He carved a path through the *Kohr'adjin*, emerging in the thick of the melee. Dead men lay all around, but more Tribesmen poured into the fray, fighting around or on top of fallen comrades. The clang of steel and the screams of the dying filled his ears, warring for attention.

A gap opened around him, and Dahr spun Jardelle. Every moment saw the *Kohr'adjin* push the Channa Hunters farther back, bringing them closer to the tents where women and older children clutched weapons, ready to defend the young ones should the warriors fail. Determination and terror warred on their faces, but Dahr knew that if the situation demanded it, determination would win and they would fight to the last.

"To me!" Dahr shouted, surprised by the sound of his own voice ringing out over the cacophony of battle. "Channa! To me! We must meet them on their own terms if we hope to turn them back. Listen to me, you fools, or you'll be watching your families slaughtered from the Twilight World tonight!"

He leapt from Jardelle's saddle, and the warhorse whinnied and stomped, waving his hooves in the air. Turning toward the *Kohr'adjin*, Dahr found two Hunters descending upon him. He sidestepped, bringing his sword up beneath the swing of one assailant and feeling the satisfying crunch as the blade ground against bone.

The other Tribesman lunged forward, swinging a double-bladed axe over his head. Dahr dodged but nearly took the back end of the axe head in the gut when the Hunter reversed his swing. The blade tore his shirt and left a narrow trail of blood across his chest.

Dahr wasted no time in exploiting his enemy's defenseless stance. He brought his sword over and down, cleaving the Tribesman's arm above the elbow, then catching him with a reverse thrust just above the hip. The man fell atop his companion, leaving Dahr gasping for breath and wondering if any of the Channa would heed his call.

He grabbed the nearest, a boy barely old enough to have earned the right to fight away from the tents. The child took a blind swing at him, but Dahr caught his hand. "I am Dahr Odara. Do you know that name?"

The young Hunter grunted an answer. Dahr took it as affirmation.

"Tell your companions to rally to this spot. If we fight the *Kohr'adjin* as individuals, all is lost. We must fight together. Do you understand me? We must fight together." He made dramatic hand gestures as he spoke, praying that the Tribesman would understand.

The young man pulled away, but he started shouting in Garu, and several Channa turned toward him. After a moment, they took up the cry and worked their way toward Dahr.

A new series of trumpet blasts echoed across the battlefield, but the last note cut off abruptly. The *Kohr'adjin* forces hesitated, but it took their commanders only a moment to restore discipline and resume the advance.

When twenty Channa had joined him, Dahr shouted a string of commands, and a grizzled old Tribesman—the only one with even a hint of gray or a scar from a previous battle—repeated his words in Garu. The Channa formed a wedge with

Dahr in the lead and charged the tallest hill. They hit the enemy, plowing a deep rent in their formation. The *Kohr'adjin* line buckled at the sudden assault, and Dahr pressed his advantage, hacking left and right, seeking the weakest of his foes, hoping to cause as much carnage and sow as much doubt as possible with this one wild charge.

Confronted with an organized foe, the *Kohr'adjin* advance slowed, the solid formation broke. As his small troupe pressed deeper into the enemy line, Dahr spotted a commander, his hides differentiated from the regular troops by strips of dyed cloth. The man stayed a few steps back from the thick of battle, though the effort of it seemed to grate against his warrior nature, and he shouted orders that Dahr could not understand but which he was almost certain he could guess.

Dahr ordered the Hunters at his side to open a path for him, and they lunged forward with renewed vigor. Confidence restored, they snarled like a pack of wolves, driving all before them until Dahr stood within a dozen hands of the enemy commander. Their eyes locked, and the *Kohr'adjin* commander saw in Dahr the reason his men had lost their advantage.

Relief flooded his face as he drew a *dolchek* and dove to the attack, slipping past Dahr's greatsword before he could bring the massive blade to bear. Dahr discarded the weapon and grappled with his assailant, stopping the man's thrust a finger's width from his throat. He watched the tip of the *dolchek* quiver in the air below his chin, the light glinting off the polished surface.

When the Tribesman tried to force the blade forward, Dahr fell back and twisted, using his opponent's momentum to his advantage, and then rolled to his feet again, his hand dipping down to draw his own dagger. His opponent landed more roughly, and the moment of stunned gasping was all Dahr needed to drive the blade home.

He pulled the *dolchek* free and wiped it on the Tribesman's shirt, then grabbed for his greatsword.

Shyrock! Dahr sent the thought screaming into the void, and the golden eagle shrieked a reply. He formed an image in his mind, and Shyrock swooped overhead, flying in the direction of the Channa camp.

His followers took up defensive positions around the summit of the hill, and their rousing shouts drew the eyes of the Channa. More Tribesmen poured into the breach, widening the gap in the *Kohr'adjin* lines and flooding Dahr's position with fresh troops. Dahr told his men to hold the hill—he had to grab a few of the more eager warriors and throw them to the ground to prevent a wild charge into the enemy throng—and scoured the field for one of the *Kohr'adjin*'s long, barbed spears.

He found one just as Shyrock returned with a triumphant shriek. A saddlebag landed at his side, the straps shredded by talons, and Dahr tore at the fastenings. He unrolled the standard, a gift from King Mathis given long ago and nearly forgotten, and attached it to the haft of the spear. Standing, he drove the point of the weapon into the ground and watched as the breeze caught the cloth. A razor-backed cat stalked out of the rising sun, predatory eyes fixed on the horizon.

"*Ko na Korahn! Korahn kehr ruhk!*" shouted one of Dahr's men, and others took up the cry. "*Ko na Korahn! Ko na Korahn!*"

Dahr spotted Frodel and his companions in the distance, driving into the *Kohr'adjin* rear and opening another gap in their lines. Lord Grondellan fought beside them, lumbering beside the Tribesmen, puffing for breath with every swing of his axe. But he never slowed, and when they reached the thick of the fray, his bellow drowned out the battlecries of the Tribesmen.

Katya danced beside the Rachannan, her blade weaving among the weapons of her enemies. She moved with a grace that defied the grim expression plastered to her face, driving her sword into one Tribesman while ducking the attack of another, then slipping behind her wounded foe to attack the other man on his flank. Her movements throughout remained precise and always beautiful.

From the direction of the tents another force joined the battle, a short grey form at the forefront. Despite his grievous scars, Grendor kept pace with the Hunters, his *va'dasheran* acting as cane and weapon, catching his weight with one step and flicking out to stab at an enemy with the next. The long reach of the weapon kept most at bay, as did the shock at seeing an Orog among the Channa. Oblivious to the stares, Grendor fought doggedly, his features pinched into a grimace of distaste. Dahr chuckled at the thought of the Orog fighting back tears for the men he had to kill.

His allies fought their way up the hill, as Dahr fought the urge to lead his men down into the fray. Watching others fight while he pranced about a hilltop curdled his gut, but he knew that to win this battle, they must not let the *Kohr'adjin* reform their lines. He moved from side to side, encouraging the men who followed him, sending new arrivals where they were most needed, and doing his best to keep the headstrong Garun'ah from losing themselves to bloodlust and throwing themselves into the arms of the enemy.

"We need to keep these men in order," he shouted to Vyrina when the Guardswoman cleared the perimeter. "They're worse than first winter recruits!"

Vyrina laughed. "They're Garun'ah, Dahr! They want to race to battle, not wait for it to come to them." She yelled to Frodel, and the Tribesman replied, but his words were lost in the din. "Just tell us what you need. He'll make them do it."

"Secure the hilltop. Then you and Frodel take the western slope. Slow advance to there, where that stand of trees meets the rock. Wait for my signal." Vyrina saluted and turned, but Dahr called her back. "I need someone to lead in the east. Will the Tribesmen follow Katya?"

The Guardswoman pursed her lips. "She is unknown to them, except that she was the daughter of our enemy. Blood carries much weight with the Garun'ah, even when actions deny it. She could earn their trust, but she does not have it yet."

Dahr cursed. *I need a third commander. Who? That boy who came to my call? The old man who speaks Human?*

"They would probably follow the Orog," Vyrina said.

"Grendor?"

"The Orog have a mystical quality in Garun'ah lore. They are revered for their humility and for their sacrifice in the MageWar. Yes, I think they'd follow the Orog." Vyrina nodded as if confirming her words, then joined Frodel to begin the advance.

Grendor and Katya joined forces on the southern slope, where they helped two young Tribesmen dislodge a boulder. It tumbled down the hillside, crashing into the *Kohr'adjin* ranks, sending dozens diving for cover and leaving a mass of screaming, mangled bodies in its wake. Dahr hurried to join them, but when he told Grendor what he needed, the Orog blanched.

"I am no Commander, friend Dahr. I cannot lead these men."

"You have no choice. I need someone I can trust, someone calm enough to lead the advance without the Tribesmen succumbing to the Blood Rage. The Tribesmen won't follow Katya."

"Come along, Commander One-Eye," Katya laughed. "I'll hold your hand if you want."

Grendor's smile seemed out of place amidst the clash of weapons and screams of wounded men. "It is not the jackal who laughs loudest, friend Katya," he said as they moved east, where another group of Tribesmen rallied for a charge, "but the jackal who laughs last that matters most. The Gods reward those such as you for the *kindnesses* you show your friends. I look forward to the day you earn your reward."

Dahr watched as Grendor calmed the young Hunters, and he almost laughed aloud when he saw the awe with which most stared at him. The Orog hated command, and adoring eyes drove him mad with humility.

Why do you enjoy torturing him?

An angrier voice rose up within him. *He wants me to be something I am not.*

He wants you to see yourself as a man. He wants you to accept yourself, flaws and all. You want to make him into a monster, to crush what remains of his innocence.

He tortures me with his very presence!

You torture yourself. You can't understand how he can remain so pure after all he has suffered, and what you don't understand, you destroy.

I— Dahr cut off, looking around, wondering which of the voices inside his head he had been speaking with. But his mind stood empty again; none of the Lesser Voices were in attendance.

"Watch it, lad. Behind you." Dahr had not seen Lord Grondellan walk up, nor had he heard the Tribesman approaching. The Hunter walked cautiously, eyes darting back and forth as if he expected an attack at any moment. He had his weapons sheathed, though, and when he saw Dahr, he hurried forward.

"*Dra'kalath!*" Someone behind Dahr shouted, and three Hunters whirled around, throwing themselves at the newcomer.

"Hold!" Dahr yelled, rushing forward. "*Stahl!*"

With Grondellan's aid, Dahr kept the Channa from killing the newcomer. The Hunter watched without making a move for his weapon, and if he feared his brush with death, it did not touch his face.

"Who are you?" Dahr demanded.

"Tarouk *uvan* Natihm."

One of the Tribesmen lunged forward again. Dahr had to twist the man's arm almost to breaking to stop him. "He Drekka, *Korahn!*" the young man said. It sounded like a plea, all the justification Dahr should need to let the Channa kill the man.

Tarouk frowned. "I Vahr Drekka."

Dahr mouthed the word and glanced at Lord Grondellan. "True," the Rachannan said. "He says he's a true Drekka."

Dahr studied the Tribesman. "Why are you here, Tarouk?"

The Tribesman gestured to the northeast, where the third army of Tribesmen had been watching the battle. "*Tsha'ma* say *Cho Korahn Garun* come. They say time of exile over. All Vahr Drekka must return Tribal Lands. Many refuse. Many join *Kohr'adjin*. I lead Vahr Drekka to *Korahn*."

"Why haven't you joined the fight against the *Kohr'adjin*?" Dahr asked.

"Channa not ask. Channa not want." The Channa Tribesmen grunted their affirmation.

"Do you need the Channa's invitation, or mine?"

Tarouk grinned. "I here fight for *Korahn*, not Channa."

Dahr opened his mind to the Lesser Voices. A moment later, Shyrock and Fang appeared. "They will grant you safe passage. Hurry to your Hunters. Tell them to attack on my signal."

"What signal is?" Tarouk asked.

"You'll know it," Dahr said, and the Drekka loped off with Fang and Shyrock at his side.

Dahr watched until Tarouk disappeared, then turned to the three Channa staring at him with a mixture of disbelief and disgust. "Find me a *Tsha'ma*." he snapped. They left without speaking, but their eyes carried harsh accusation.

Waiting nearly drove Dahr mad. Each moment allowed the enemy time to recover from his surprise attack and deprived him of the battle he desperately craved. Yet it also swelled his own ranks; hundreds of Channa poured into the breach he had created, until the hilltop turned into a sea of axes, spears, and bows. The remainder of the Channa line held more or less tenuously. The *Kohr'adjin*, recognizing their greatest threat lay in Dahr and his organized resistance, turned their attention toward him.

When a young Hunter appeared, followed by a stoop-shouldered man with feathers laced through his hair, Dahr leapt toward them, nearly knocking them down in his haste to explain what he needed. The *Tsha'ma* agreed to help, though the way the man studied him made Dahr feel like hot pokers hovered a finger's width from his body, and he shifted uncomfortably under the intense scrutiny.

He looked west, and Vyrina gave him a ready signal. On the eastern slope, Katya and Grendor had steadied their line, but they faced stiffer resistance from the *Kohr'adjin*. As if sensing his eyes on her, she turned and signaled that they, too, were ready. He reached out to Shyrock, but could not sense the eagle's mind amidst the tumult.

"Now," he said, and the *Tsha'ma* closed his eyes. After a moment, he nodded, and a column of light appeared around Dahr. His standard rose in the center of that column, spinning slowly and flapping as if caught in a stiff breeze, and it appeared to expand in size until it could be seen from every corner of the battlefield.

"I have returned," Dahr said, and his voice boomed across the field. A Tribesman repeated the words in Garu, and those words thundered forth as well. "Too many among the Blood have turned from Garun, and the God grows restive. I am Garun's Chosen. I bring salvation and death, and I will drive the followers of Kohr back to the abyss from which they sprang."

Silence followed, an absolute, unbroken stillness out of place on a battlefield, and Dahr felt thousands of eyes upon him. He hated the attention, but he ignored his discomfort, for his ploy succeeded far beyond his expectations. The *Kohr'adjin* assault faltered, and a palpable wave of uncertainty rose from the army amassed below.

"For Garun's honor!" Dahr shouted, sprinting toward the southern slope. Lord Grondellan followed him, axe over his shoulder and bellowing like a mad bull. Scores of Tribesmen trailed the Rachannan. Frodel and Grendor led similar charges down the eastern and western slopes, driving the *Kohr'adjin* back and filling the air with their shouting.

Dahr lost sight of the others and focused on the nearest enemy. He batted the man's *dolchek* aside with a leisurely swing, and drove an elbow into his jaw. The Tribesman crumpled, but Dahr left him on the ground for those behind him to dispatch. He barreled past two more men, narrowly missing a spear thrust from one while driving his blade into the thigh of the other.

That man fell too, and Dahr pressed on, hacking and swinging at any *Kohr'adjin* fool enough to step into his range. He reached the bottom of the hill and started to climb again. A Tribesman sprung out from behind a narrow gully carved in the hillside, and the club he wielded made a solid connection on Dahr's left shoulder. Pain exploded down his arm, but Dahr laughed it off. His answering blow drove deep into the warrior's gut. The effort of dislodging the blade slowed his momentum, and he stopped to assess the field.

He had put some distance between him and his men; in fact, he had nearly passed the farthest line of *Kohr'adjin*. *Had you run much farther*, he chided himself, *you'd have run yourself right out of the battle.*

Dahr opened his mind, aware that a handful of *Kohr'adjin* had spotted him and were approaching. This time, Shyrock answered, and he saw that all along the line, the Channa resolve had strengthened. Though Grendor and Katya had made little headway, Frodel and Vyrina had nearly reached the bottom of the hill. The general retreat slowed, then stopped altogether, but it was only when the children and women guarding the tents launched their own assault, charging past the Hunters with cries of *"Ko na Korahn!"* that the *Kohr'adjin* advance reversed.

Shyrock shrieked a warning, and Dahr threw himself to the side. The axe head whistled through the air where he had been standing, and the man who wielded it looked shocked by Dahr's sudden movement. Dahr stabbed, but the Tribesman dodged, and they traded blows until a second *Kohr'adjin* joined the fray, followed by a third. Dahr found himself on the defensive, lucky to keep the blades at bay, and he howled with the need to kill. One *dolchek* slipped through his guard, leaving a shallow gash along his midriff; another dug into the flesh of his shoulder. Frustration built within him even as the breath burned in his lungs, and he tightened his grip on the greatsword, readying for a suicidal charge.

Suddenly, his enemies were washed away in a tide of Tribesmen. The Channa poured around him, driving the *Kohr'adjin* back, though more than a few slowed to catch his eye and offer a nod of respect before loping south after the enemy. Dahr hated the assistance, hated that he needed it, but he bottled his anger, saving it for his enemies. He tried to resume the lead in the assault, and then simply to follow, but he could no longer match the Channa's energy or enthusiasm. The beast within roared at the dishonor, but a small part of him savored the idea of giving up the hunt.

He made his way back up the hillside, tending to the wounded as he found them, treating his allies' injuries and offering his enemies a simpler mercy. Those he helped said nothing, but most stared at him in a way that made him wish for the dancing blades of the enemy Hunters. He preferred derision to devotion.

On the hilltop he surveyed the battle and called for runners to carry orders to his commanders. Frodel's Hunters had driven the *Kohr'adjin* back, but they were thinning themselves too much in their eagerness to chase the enemy. Dahr sent word to consolidate their gains before giving full chase. On the western slope Grendor continued to face the most disciplined of the enemy, yet before Dahr could seek reinforcements, Tarouk drove the Vahr Drekka into the *Kohr'adjin's* rear. In moments, the *Kohr'adjin* fled south across the plains with a howling horde of Drekka in pursuit.

"I wondered when you would come," a gravelly voice called out. Dahr turned to see four young warriors carrying a palanquin, an aged Tribesman reclining on the thin, straw-filled cushion. Time had sucked the strength from Yarchik's withered legs, but his eyes held depths of knowledge. "I thought it your Prince who liked dramatic rescues and grandiose theatrics."

"Yarchik," Dahr said, a smile coming unbidden to his lips. He hurried to the palanquin, bowing his head in respect. "A wise man once told me the smart warrior uses whatever tools he has, and in doing so, will save himself much effort over the strong warrior."

Yarchik snorted a laugh. "I never said the smart warrior had to wait until the last possible moment!" The chiding tone did not match the smile on the *Kranor's* face as he took Dahr's hand in his own. "It is good to see you, *Korahn*. Ah! Do not look at me in that way. You wear the title by your own choice; it is not a thing to be donned and discarded at your convenience."

"I think tomorrow he will wish to have never uttered the words he spoke on this hill." Arik, *Kranor* of the Tacha, strode toward them. Hands taller than Dahr and even broader across the shoulder, Arik wore the pelt of a giant bear over his shoulders with the head drawn over his own like a cowl. When he stopped moving, he looked to be a bear himself, though a bear wearing pants and wielding a wickedly-curved axe.

"*Kranor,*" Dahr said, turning his gaze on Arik and offering the proper respect. "It has been many days since I last saw your son, but I left him well and well-respected among the soldiers he serves with."

The hint of a smile touched Arik's lips, but he said nothing. Dahr looked toward the tents. "I did not expect to find the Tacha here. Will there be another *Cha'kuhn?*"

"The *Kohr'adjin* and Drekka control the north," Arik said, his voice a feral snarl. "*Cha'kuhn* is lost to us, as are much of the ancestral lands. The Tacha and Channa have banded together to survive, and we have offered refuge to any tribe willing to join us."

"We fight for our lives, *Korahn.* For our very existence." Yarchik studied Dahr, and Dahr wondered what the old man sought in him. "The ways of the Blood are in danger. You could not have picked a better time to return."

"The Drekka?" Dahr's eyes went west. "I thought the Drekka were here. I invited them to the battle." Arik spat on the ground at that, and for a moment Dahr thought the *Kranor* intended to attack him.

"Those here are not Drekka, exactly," Yarchik said, "nor are the Drekka in the north true Drekka." He laughed at that, or at Dahr's confusion, but the sound brought a ray of warmth to Dahr's soul. "That is, those who are here, the Vahr Drekka, seek to rejoin the Blood. They claim to follow the teachings of Garun. Those in the north are Drekka as we know them, except that they are not. They are little different than *Kohr'adjin,* and they swell the ranks of the Father's army. It is their combined might which has driven the Blood to the brink. Both are Drekka, both are not."

"Vahr Drekka," Arik spat again. "There are no true Drekka. They are blind to the ways of Garun."

Dahr steeled himself, and his hand drifted toward the hilt of his sword. "I have promised the Vahr Drekka a place in the tents in exchange for their aid in the battle."

Arik tensed, but Yarchik's hand shot out, demanding peace even as he requested it. "No matter their true hearts, they aided us today. I would not toss them into the night to face the wrath of our enemies. The Channa open their tents to the Vahr Drekka." He glanced at Arik, who after a moment's grim impassivity, ducked his head in acceptance.

Yarchik gestured, and a young man ran up to him. He spoke a quick string of orders in Garu, then the boy darted off toward the tents. At Dahr's questioning look, the *Kranor* said, "He is to tell the Blood that *Cho Korahn Garun* has delivered us this day, and that he demands the tents be opened to the Vahr Drekka, so that we may lead them back to Garun's path."

"That's not exactly what I said," Dahr mumbled, but he made no louder protest. He knew the Garun'ah would heed Yarchik's words, even if the old man pretended they came from Dahr.

Dahr cast out his mind to the Lesser Voices, searching for his companions. *Bring them to me.* He walked to his standard, conscious of the eyes following his every moment. He inspected the sigil, noting the twin tears beneath the razorback's legs, and carefully folded the banner, tying it with a cord pulled from the clothes of a dead Tribesman.

Before long, Fang loped up the hill, followed by Frodel and Vyrina. The Tribesman bled from a shallow gash across his chest, and the Guardswoman limped, leaning heavily on a makeshift staff. Grendor appeared on the opposite slope, with Katya not far behind. Neither appeared the worse for the battle, though the Orog's eye carried a deep sadness, the kind he only wore after killing.

Dahr listened to their reports, then took them to the two *Kranora*. "You remember Katya, daughter of Salos Durange."

"I remember Katya," Yarchik replied, "*bahlova* of Dahr Odara. Among our people the family one chooses precedes the family one is given. I am glad the Gods have returned you to us."

Dahr frowned, and turned to Grendor. "I believe you have already met Grendor, *choupik* and Elder of the Vassta."

Grendor stepped forward, his scarred visage warring with the smile that spread across his face. "I have spoken much with Yarchik, and heard much of Arik, *Kranor* of the Tacha. I am pleased that the meager aid I could lend today leaves allies such as you to fight with us tomorrow."

Arik clasped Grendor's hand in greeting, and though the Tribesman towered over the Orog, there was an air of equality shared in their gazes. Dahr had not noticed before, but something had changed in Grendor over the last few seasons. Confidence and command were replacing innocence and shyness. *I wonder how much of that I am responsible for.*

You flatter yourself.

Dahr glared at Fang, but Yarchik's sudden words forestalled any retort. "When the Grey Men spring forth from the bowels of darkness, then will the reckoning begin. With the Hammer of Kohr will the Redeemer build a new world, even as he sunders the old. When the demons of chaos cast their shadow over the Blood, then will the *Korahn* proclaim himself returned. And with a blade will he bind the Blood together, and with a smile will he lead them unto the slaughter."

Into the stunned silence that followed, Yarchik laughed. "This is a time for celebration," he said, banging on the side of his palanquin. "Rouse the tents. Tell all to prepare for a feast. We—"

Dahr turned to follow the *Kranor*'s eyes. Lord Grondellan, bleeding from a half dozen minor wounds and leaning heavily on Jardelle, preceded Tarouk to the gathering. The Drekka stopped a handful of steps back and opened his arms, palms out, to the *Kranora*.

Arik's jaw clenched. "I must see to my people," he said, stomping down the hill toward the tents.

Yarchik beckoned, and Tarouk approached. The old Tribesman's eyes roved the Drekka from top to bottom, and there seemed a hint of recognition in them as they did. "You are *Kranor* of the Drekka?"

"I speak for Vahr Drekka. No *Kranor*."

This time, Yarchik's words carried no question. "To join the Blood gathered to fight the *Kohr'adjin*, you must be a Tribe. To be a Tribe, you must have a *Kranor*. Tell your people to choose a *Kranor*."

Tarouk bowed again. Though he said nothing, a proud smile flitted across his face, though it could not subdue the slight tremble in his hands whenever he gazed up into the knowing eyes of the Channa leader.

"Gather your people," Yarchik told him. "We hold a feast at sundown to honor our victory and the arrival of new allies." He tapped on the side of the palanquin, and his litter bearers started the march back to the tents.

The afternoon was a blur of activity. Dahr collected Meila and returned her to the Drekka, where she proclaimed him the *Korahn* and ordered Tarouk to pledge himself to follow him. A quick escape proved impossible; everywhere he turned, women and children followed him, asking for his blessing or simply wishing to touch his clothes. Tarouk and his most experienced Hunters delayed him as well, asking for advice on dealing with the *Kranora* of the other Tribes and seeking to share with him all of their knowledge of the *Kohr'adjin* and their battle tactics.

When he did manage to slip out of the Drekka camp, he found himself way-laid by other Tribesmen, mostly young Hunters who wanted to congratulate him on his victory. A few *Tsha'ma* approached to ask him about his ability to converse with the Lesser Voices, but those he could quickly distract by mentioning Grendor and the return of the Orog. Lord Grondellan and Katya wanted to know among which tents they should pitch their camp. Vyrina wanted news from home. The *Kranora* desired knowledge of the war, particularly how the Tachan armies fared in the south. His movement through the camp was a tedious and laborious process.

By the time the sun set and the feasting began, exhaustion enveloped Dahr like a cloak. After a brief circuit among the fires, just long enough to satisfy Garun'ah etiquette, he lowered himself to a set of straw-filled cushions beside Yarchik. The ailing Tribesman watched the celebration with smiling eyes, but when he turned his gaze on Dahr, a measure of sadness entered them. Sadness and pity.

"Why do you look at me so?" Dahr asked, trying to affect a casual air and quelling the rumble of annoyance that flashed in his gut.

"When last I saw you, there was much joy in you. Now you are as an empty vessel, and I worry over what is filling that vessel."

Dahr snorted. "What have I to be happy about?"

Yarchik did not answer right away. Instead, he leaned forward and removed a kettle from a small fire burning beside him. Into a wooden cup he poured the steaming water and a mixture of pungent herbs. "You must forgive her," the *Kranor* told him. "She holds your heart. Without it, you are not complete."

Jaw clenched, Dahr snarled, "She betrayed me."

"In omission, yes. In intention, perhaps. But in deed? What did that dear child actually do to earn such derision?" Yarchik leaned over the cup, whispering words in Garu and wafting the steam toward his face with slow, circular gestures. He drew a deep breath, inhaling the aroma.

"She... She..." Dahr turned away. "It is not something I wish to discuss."

"Then we shall not discuss it. But think on what I have said." Yarchik drew another breath over his tea, then cast his eyes skyward and whispered another prayer. "You were a sight to behold today. I have never seen the Blood rallied so quickly, or made to fight in the manner of Humans with so little effort. You have a gift, Dahr."

Dahr felt eyes upon him. Across the camp, he caught several Tribesmen star-ing at him. Even when he met their gaze, they refused to turn away. "Your people would have won the day without me. I did nothing but show them where to strike. A child could have done as much."

"Most Hunters have no eye for strategy. They care only for the kill, and lose themselves in the glory of the fight." Yarchik clasped the cup in two hands and lifted it high, then brought it to his lips and drank. "It is a rare man who can har-ness the might of the Blood, to bend them to his will and use them to a greater purpose. You are such a person. Our people would be wise to follow you."

More were watching him now. Dozens. Hundreds. Dahr loathed the attention. He wanted nothing more than to fade into the darkness beyond the fires. *At least they're all keeping their distance. At least none of them are close enough to hear.*

"Maybe you're right about the first," Dahr admitted, "but none should follow me. I know not where my path leads, but I journey through darkness. Misery and suffering wait for anyone foolish enough to call me their leader."

Yarchik handed Dahr the cup and bid him drink. "All lives are measured in tragedies and triumphs. You have suffered much, but enduring that suffering has made you stronger. It has made you what we need you to be."

Dahr hesitated; the strong smell from the tea turned his stomach. "There is no love in me anymore, Yarchik. I see the whole world in shades of hate. I respect little, and trust less. Even Jeran. I see schemes behind all his actions; he, who is as a brother to me."

The *Kranor's* chuckle echoed in the night. "For one so young, that boy weaves webs to make the silkspinner proud. But I have seen him in my dreams. His methods may not always be to your liking, but his motives are pure." A measure of sadness entered Yarchik's eyes, as of a man who has labored to bring his fields to fruit only to see a drought coming. "His will be a life even you will pity ere it ends, I think."

"At least Jeran has a destination. His path may be bloody, but he knows where he wants it to take him."

"He will need your strength to survive. As does the Blood." Yarchik gestured to the cup. "Drink, my friend. The tea will soothe you."

Dahr raised the cup to his lips. The liquid burned down his throat, and the aroma brought a different fire to his nose. He gasped for air and was amazed when it tasted sweet and cool, soothing like a mountain spring. "Jeran sent me away. You would be wise to do so as well."

"Enough!" Anger from the old Hunter was something Dahr had rarely seen, and to hear it now surprised him. It took a moment for the fire in Yarchik's eyes to dim, but his tone still carried a dagger's edge. "Pitying your misfortunes solves nothing. We each of us have demons in our souls, failings to overcome. You are neither unique nor overburdened in that regard. You deceive yourself if you believe otherwise."

Yarchik leaned over and sprinkled more herbs in the cup. He touched his hands to his lips and then to the cup. "You are a good man, Dahr Odara. You are an honorable man. Garun would not select one destined to fail as his messenger."

Dahr expected anger at the *Kranor's* words, but something else burst from within, something that shocked him with its very presence. Hope. "How can you be sure?"

A smile spread across Yarchik's face. "I see you, Dahr. I see who you really are." He gestured at the cup.

Dahr drank deeply. This time, he welcomed the fire of the drink, the clarity that followed. "It's of no matter," he laughed. "I led today, but my part is done. I do not want to lead men to their deaths. That's why I left Alrendria."

The sadness returned to Yarchik's gaze. "Then I am sorry, my friend."

"For what?" Dahr glanced up to find the camp silent, the eyes of the Garun'ah fixed upon him.

Yarchik reached out and grasped Dahr's hands around the cup, raising them above his head. "*Beauhtz Dahr odra Odara, Kranach na Tacha!*"

Kranach. The word reverberated like the peal of a bell. Within, Dahr heard the monster laughing.

CHAPTER 15

"Another murder?" Martyn looked at the dispatch in his hand, more to collect his thoughts than to reread the report on grain stores and projected needs. A dozen stacks of such dispatches awaited his inspection, and it seemed that for every one he finished, five took its place. With his child wreaking havoc on Miriam's innards, the task of keeping abreast of events in and around Kaper had proven overwhelming.

"Two, actually, in less than a ten-day." Treloran sat when Martyn gestured, but the Aelvin Prince took little comfort in the cushioned chair. "There is whispering among my people. They begin to fear. They want assurances that your Guardsmen will protect them."

Martyn snorted a laugh. "Protect them? From a ghost? Over a score of murders these last few seasons, and our only witness is a boy, our only evidence the flowers our assassin so politely leaves for us." Martyn set aside the dispatch and drummed his fingers on the table. "Have you given thought to what I suggested?"

"That the murderer is an Elf?" Green eyes regarded him coolly. "I resisted it at first, but with all the rumors circulating around the Aelvin District, my people are now… cautious whenever Humans are near. That our murderer remains undetected adds some measure of credence to your idea."

That was as close to an apology as Martyn was likely to get for the tirade his suggestion had prompted. He looked pointedly at Treloran. "I don't suppose… no."

"What?"

"It's of no matter. Forget I spoke."

The Aelvin Prince's sigh was for show. "Just tell me, Martyn."

"I don't suppose you'd be willing to spread the news among your people. Coming from me, it would look as if I hope to divert blame. But if you were to propose that the assassin were an Elf, your people would be more likely to believe."

"It will not quell their fear, or their desire for protection."

"Perhaps not, but it will make them stop glaring at every Human in sight, and perhaps remind them that we are not their enemies." Martyn drew a deep breath and selected another dispatch from the pile. "I will increase patrols inside the Aelvin District and take whatever other precautions you deem necessary. Just name your terms. For the sake of our alliance, I will agree."

Treloran studied the map of Kaper on the wall. "For the sake of our alliance, I will do it." Martyn worked to keep his expression schooled. The Elves had a keen memory for obligation; if Treloran knew how much Martyn needed his assistance in this matter, it would be a millstone around his neck.

"Where in the old city do you plan to house my people?" Treloran asked suddenly.

"In the old city?"

"It's a poorly kept secret that you believe we will lose the new city to the Durange. One need only look at the construction in Old Kaper and on the palace grounds. I wonder where my people will be moved to."

"If it comes to that," Martyn said, "we have reserved the Tiravian and Barati estates on the north side of Old Kaper for their use."

"One expects tensions to be high if the Durange push into the city. Relations between our peoples are already strained. They would feel safer on the palace grounds."

"Of course you and Jaenaryn, and all of your retainers, will remain in the palace as my guests."

"I was thinking about this section of the palace," Treloran said, indicating a long unused section stretching out like fingers toward the southern side of the map. "It's peaceful back there, and from the layer of dust, not even your servants walk those halls often."

"You want me to move all of the Elves into the palace? Do you know how many hundreds arrived in the seasons following Jaenaryn?"

"Several thousand, one would imagine. It will be a tight fit, but they will feel safer here."

"But what of my people? What will they think when I turn them out into the city but house thousands of Elves within the walls of the palace?"

"Perhaps they will think you are concerned for the well being of your guests. Guests who already have to contend with a murderer hunting them down in the streets."

Martyn scanned the dispatch he had taken, a report that more weapons—daggers, short swords, and bows, along with a handful of helmets—had gone missing. He had received similar reports in days past, despite the increased guards he had posted around the armories. *Perhaps I should use one of the Magi, if one can be found who can use his Gift discreetly.*

"Your request is reasonable," Martyn said, though he knew his acquiescence sounded forced. "If the new city is taken, your people will take refuge within the palace."

"That takes a great burden off their shoulders, Prince Martyn." Treloran looked at the table full of dispatches. He reached toward one, arching an eyebrow. "I do not mean to overstep my bounds, but you look as if you—"

"Read!" Martyn exclaimed. "If the Darklord popped in and offered to help me wade through this mess, I'd be hard pressed not to accept. The greatest secret I've yet discovered was the ledger from the kitchens. Did you know that butter consumption has tripled in the last season?"

Treloran chuckled. "It must be those rich meals your wife has been requesting of late." Miriam's appetite had undergone a dramatic shift in recent days. She had been demanding traditional Gilean fare, forcing the heavy sauces and battered meats on the court of Kaper.

Martyn made no comment, and he looked at another dispatch. "The Black Fleet holds its blockade of Roya and the Celaan. We will see no more grain ships."

"The Guard broke up three fights on the palace grounds in the last ten-day," Treloran announced. "All servant boys eight to twelve winters old. In two of the instances, other boys stood in attendance. The Guardsman filing the report believes they were sparring."

"You see what I mean?" Martyn puffed out a frustrated breath. "They waste paper on trivialities like that and expect me to give each equal attention! If someone wrote up a report for every scuffle I was in as a child, they'd fill a room twice this size."

Martyn grabbed another dispatch. "Here's something… The traitors across the river led an assault on the bridge yesterday. They were repulsed with ease. No casualties among our people." No doubt he would learn more details at his council with Aryn tomorrow, but it would be nice to enter the room with at least some idea of the situation at the bridge.

"The blacksmiths are running out of ore," Treloran said. "Production of new weapons and wares will stop in about a ten-day."

Martyn muttered a curse at that, but there was nothing to be done. The army across the river blocked the land routes to his mines, and the Black Fleet controlled the seas. *Perhaps if I can get word to Lord Peitr in Grenz, he can send barges down the river.* Cursing again, Martyn leafed through another set of dispatches. "Troop rosters… Troop rosters… A list of newly-raised Guardsmen… Here's a bit of good news. Jasova has reclaimed some of the lands along the border. Jysin and Murdir have moved so many men east, we've been able to take advantage of it… A request for more barracks in the—"

"Portal has fallen."

Martyn's eyes jerked up, and he saw in the paleness of Treloran's face that the Elf made no jest. "The Durange control the gateway to *Ael Shataq*?"

"No. Jeran arrived and saved the castle. His troops control the Portal, but the city is destroyed. Thousands are dead, and—. Here, this is better seen by your eyes."

Martyn took the letter from Treloran's hand and examined the seal. "Now we know why Lord Talbot's been quiet for so long. I was wondering what had happened to that old…" As his eyes slid down the page, Martyn's quip faded, and anger flushed his cheeks crimson.

He stood abruptly and bid Treloran follow. "We must show this to my father."

Martyn threw open the door to the hall and was met by a glowering Sheriza. "Prince Martyn, I have just found out—"

"Mage Sheriza, I do not have time. There is a matter of great import I must bring to my father's attention." He tried to brush past the Healer, but the small woman proved unmovable.

"Is your matter more important than the abduction of the First of a Great House?"

"Abducted? Who?"

"Lady Jessandra Vela. She—"

"When? By whom?"

"Prince Martyn! Kindly keep quiet, and I will answer those questions."

Chagrinned, Martyn held his tongue, wondering which of the Darklord's minions had the ability to spirit away a First—and a Mage—from her very own city. *Salos, no doubt, and if Lady Jessandra can be abducted, then we all need fear. We should increase the guards around the King. And Miriam! Even, I suppose, around myself.*

"The date of the abduction is uncertain, but she appointed a steward at the start of winter and went north, presumably to help Lord Odara put his House in order. For a time, no one suspected anything out of the ordinary, but repeated dispatches to her have returned unanswered. When I went to Dranakohr to seek her out, I was informed that she was not in attendance. When I asked where she was, and when she would be returning, I was given no answer. When I asked when she would be returning to Vela, I was laughed at."

Martyn pursed his lips, confused. "If she is with Jeran, then why do you think she's been—"

"Odara is the one who's abducted her, you fool! I don't know his reasons, and I don't know his whereabouts, but I do know that Jes would not abandon her people at this crucial time. She is needed in Vela, not traipsing around the wilderness with that upstart friend of yours."

Could it be true? "I don't know why Jeran would want to hold hostage another First."

"Do even you forget that he is not yet First of House Odara?" Sheriza asked. "That boy has no oaths binding him, and his ambition knows no end. The why of it is a mystery; it's not like him to play a hand so unwisely. But I tell you, she would not be gone this long without coercion, and she would never refuse to answer my letters."

"I will look into the matter, Mage Sheriza."

"Is that all I get? A half-hearted promise to 'look into matters'?"

"What would you have me do?" Martyn retorted. The Healer had proven herself a valuable ally, but she still infuriated him with her brash tone and condescension. "Declare war on House Odara? You may not have noticed, but I have enemies aplenty at the moment. As I said, I will look into the matter."

Sheriza's lips pressed into a narrow line. "Very well, Your Highness."

Martyn slipped past her, but he made it only a handful of steps before stopping. "Sheriza?"

"Yes, Prince Martyn?"

"In regards to the Mage Assembly, where do your loyalties lie?"

"Excuse me?"

"You appear to have little love for Jeran, but you do not strike me as one who would be fond of a Mage such as Valkov. I wonder, should the conflict escalate between them, on which side would you land."

"I endeavor to keep my people out of such quarrels. We Healers are ill-disposed in such situations."

"Let us say, for argument's sake, that neutrality is not an option. Who do you follow?"

Sheriza remained silent for a time, though whether weighing her answer or deciding if she should share it with him, Martyn could not tell. "I do not know. If Lelani had struck a more defiant stance, I would have followed her lead. But she fled, and following her is no longer an option. With a few hundred winters of experience to cool his temperament, your friend might make a formidable High Wizard, but he is not ready now. And Valkov... I do not know where I would lend my support, Prince Martyn, and I hope I need not make that decision. For now, my Healers are at your disposal, regardless of who runs the Assembly."

"Thank you, Mage Sheriza." Martyn offered her a respectful bow, then resumed his hurried passage through the halls. He waved off those who requested a moment of his time. He even denied Kaeille, whom he had barely seen in recent days. The Aelvin woman closeted herself with Miriam day and night, watching the princess when she slept and hovering over her when she was awake. The only time they were not together was when Martyn was with the princess, or when Miriam was attended by her cousin Jaem. Kaeille could not stand the Gilean nobleman, and made sure to attend to other business whenever he came around.

He burst into the King's audience chamber to find his father meeting with a group of lesser nobility, discussing the confiscation of their estates in the old city and the uses that would be applied to those lands. Mika, stone-still and glowering, stood behind the King, his eyes flitting around the room at every slight movement. The boy had changed much since Martyn had first met him. Next winter he would be of age, a man, and able to join the Guard, but for now he still appeared somewhat comical in his cobbled-together arms and armor.

"Father, I must speak with you. My Lords, I must beg your indulgence, but a matter of some urgency has arisen."

He waited for the noblemen to make their way toward the door, then turned to Mika. "I must ask you to leave too. This is a matter for my father's ears only."

Mika's gaze slid over Martyn's shoulder. "And the Aelvin Prince?"

"Prince Treloran brought the matter to my attention, so having him leave serves no purpose." Explaining himself to a child rankled Martyn, but the boy meant well, and rationalization had proved more effective than ranting in the past.

"Very well. King Mathis, I will wait for you in the hall. I request that you not try to leave without proper escort."

"Of course. Your service is appreciated." Mathis tried to hide his smile until Mika closed the door, then he turned to Martyn. "An amusing boy. Possibly the best bodyguard I've had in my entire life. In terms of dedication to duty, at least."

"Jeran is raising an army."

Mathis pursed his lips. "Of course he is. We commanded all the Firsts to strengthen their militias. Jeran's situation in Dranakohr requires—"

"Jeran has not confined his recruiting to commoners. The garrisons in Portal and Norport have forsworn their oaths to Alrendria. Guardposts across House Odara—and even a few in House Velan!—are declaring for him and 'putting on the Black,' as they call it. Lord Talbot himself writes to ask you to release him from his oath, as he has released those of his men who wish to follow Jeran. The few who remain loyal, he ordered to join Jasova since he saw no way to fulfill our command to get them to Kaper."

Mathis took the letter Martyn offered and studied it. After a moment, his face contorted in anger. That it was directed at him shocked Martyn. "You did not think to tell me that the Durange sacked Portal? That thousands of my people were slaughtered? That Talbot lost two sons? None of that struck you as important?"

"I believe the more important issue is that Jeran is overstepping his bounds." Martyn struggled to keep his tone even, his wording neutral. "Many have reported Jeran's disregard for tradition and law. He uses what he can and ignores what he wants. He is my friend, but his excesses and ambitions grow by the ten-day. I wonder if he needs to be reminded whom he serves."

With great deliberation, King Mathis schooled his features. "What would you have me do?" When Martyn struck a defensive posture, the King waved him to silence. "Seriously, Martyn, what can we do? Would a stern letter suffice, or should I ask the army across the river if they wouldn't mind ravaging the Odaran countryside for a while, so that a headstrong youth could be put in his place?"

Mathis gestured for the two princes to sit, and when neither made a move to, he sighed. "I realize how difficult coming here must have been, putting duty ahead of friendship. Don't think I don't appreciate that. But step back and look at things from Jeran's perspective—"

"From Jeran's perspective? He refuses your summons, as well as your demands for reinforcements. He keeps his own counsel and refuses to divulge details of his plans for Dranakohr, despite regular requests for information from his prince and king. He raises an army, and weakens the Guard in the process. And Sheriza believes he has abducted Lady Jessandra for some unknown purpose. He—"

"Abducted Jessandra Vela?" Mathis laughed at that. At hearing himself spout Sheriza's fears, fears he had but a few moments earlier heartily dismissed, laughter bubbled up from within Martyn too. By the time it subsided, the tension had eased, and when his father again bid him sit, Martyn did.

"We let the Durange scourge House Odara for seasons, because we had more important things to deal with," Mathis said while Martyn and Treloran refreshed themselves with wine and bread. "We ignored Portal's requests for resources despite the army arrayed against them across the Boundary. We did all of this willingly, because we had a better understanding of the greater situation.

"Now, we're trapped in a box, and our enemies close the lid tighter every day. We get news in fits and starts, with no idea how much of what we receive is reliable or current. Our allies grow cautious, our enemies bold. We are, for the moment, at the mercy of the Gods.

"I see only three possibilities with regards to Jeran. He now commands a better view of the situation, and his defiance is an odd form of loyalty; his situation is worse than we believe, and he has no resources to send; or he is a traitor. If it is either of the former, we must trust that he'll send aid before we are lost. If it is the latter, there is nothing we can do at the moment. But Alic and Aryn Odara are like brothers to me, as Jeran is to you; no matter how I try, I cannot see a Jysin Morrena in him."

"Even if Jeran Odara proves a slave to his ambitions," Treloran said, "he will have to fight through the army across the Celaan to get to Kaper."

"A good point," Mathis chuckled. "Until he does that much, he remains our ally no matter his intentions."

"I wonder if we might be well advised to get a liaison to Dranakohr," Martyn said, drumming his fingers on the tabletop. "Someone through which we might relay reliable intelligence."

"I presume you mean a Mage," Mathis said. "We have few enough to spare. Your Healers and Konasi. Neither would be agreeable to staying in Dranakohr, I think."

"I may have an alternative… I won't bore you with details until I am sure, Father."

"Yes," Mathis replied, "I'm well aware of your flair for intrigue. How go the city defenses?"

"Aryn works tirelessly; one would think the man afraid to sleep." Like as not, he was. Something haunted Jeran's uncle, and in the rare moments of respite he received, Martyn still saw darkness lurking within Aryn's gaze. But focusing on the coming battle kept his wits sharp. For the time being. "He organized a work force of able-bodied men to shore up defenses in the new city. Even still, he does not expect us to hold New Kaper for more than a few ten-days once the Durange take the Bridge."

"A few ten-days? Aryn remains an optimist. He plans an organized withdrawal, then?"

"Yes, Guardsmen and militia will hold key lines while the populace relocates to Old Kaper. Once everyone is inside the Wall, he will torch as much of Kaper as he can and bring the Guard inside the old city. The docks will be destroyed the moment the first Durange sets foot in Makan's Market."

"Destroy Kaper to save it…" Mathis ran a hand through his graying beard. "It is not a plan I relish. I just hope some remain to rebuild it when this is done."

With a suddenness that startled Martyn, his father jumped from his seat and moved to the door, calling for servants to bring food. "Enough of this moping. Dine with me tonight, Martyn. You, too, Prince Treloran. It's been too long since we've shared a meal, and I'd like to hear more of the city's defenses. And about Miriam and my grandchild! I've been locked inside this palace since winter's end, and—"

When Mathis flung open the door, they saw Mika facing off with a young soldier, arguing that the King was not to be disturbed. "What goes on here?" Mathis demanded.

Mika puffed out his cheeks. "Go on, then. Give him your message. You've already disturbed them."

The soldier saluted awkwardly. "My... My King. There is rioting in New Kaper. Fires have broken out in the city. At least one of the armories has been overrun. I am to convey this message from Commander Anatole: the city will be secured by dawn, but we should expect the traitors to make a push for the Bridge."

"Gods!" Mathis pounded his fist against the wall, but in a moment's time his expression resumed its usual calm. "Inform Commander Odara, if he doesn't already know. I expect regular and detailed reports. Go!" The recruit sprinted down the hall, and Mathis turned back to the table.

"We might as well eat," he said, but the mirth had left his eyes. "Not much any of us can do out there until the fighting's settled. Don't look at me like that, Martyn. What would you prefer to do: lead a fire brigade, or force your own people into submission at sword point? It's best if we leave this fight to the Guard."

Martyn considered arguing, but thought better of it. "Might I suggest something a bit stronger than wine, then? Perhaps some *brandei*? I have a feeling this will be a long night."

Mathis frowned. "We have longer coming."

CHAPTER 16

Sweat poured from Jeran, stinging his eyes. It ran down his body in slick streams but offered no respite from the clingy, humid air. The summer sun beat against him, burning a back tanned dark from days of hard training. Tiny sprite flies danced around his face, but he ignored them. Soft birdsong drifted to his ears in the dead air, but it sounded distant, hollow. Neither presented a threat, and therefore were of no importance.

Stout leather cords bound his hands, the knots chafing against the flesh of his wrists. That, too, he ignored. His gaze remained on Goshen, the mountain of a Garun'ah who stood before him. The giant held a spiked hammer half his height in one hand, handling the massive weight as if it were a toy. He stalked toward him, pacing around Jeran in a semicircle, a feral smile on his face.

Magic poured into Jeran; thin filaments of colored light swirled around him in a vortex. He could not see his own aura, but he could feel the power thrumming through his body, knew that he shone like a beacon to any who could harness their own Gift. Exhaustion hovered in the distance, but the energy he held filled him with vitality even as it fought for release.

With effortless quickness, Goshen whirled, and the hammer flew toward Jeran. He dodged, feeling the blow's cool breath as the weapon slid past a finger's breadth from his body. The Tribesman pivoted, continuing the swing, and this time Jeran leapt over the attack.

"That is good." He heard Jakal's voice plainly, even though the *Tsha'ma* sat across the clearing from them. "I no longer see the flows so much as twinge when you concentrate on defending yourself. But the true test will be how the magic reacts while you are actually using it. Juggle for me."

Jeran drew a deep breath and closed his eyes to focus. Goshen lunged at just that instant, the spiked head of the hammer aimed at Jeran's chest. But Jeran no longer needed eyes to see, not within his immediate vicinity, and he twisted to avoid the blow. Hands clasped in a double fist, he struck Goshen a solid blow on the back as he passed.

The Tribesman laughed. "That good. But you use magic now, not body. Do again, and I bind arms as well as hands. Ankles too."

Jeran said nothing. Instead, he allowed a trickle of magic to flow through him, weaving the flows in such a way that three small balls of light appeared. They began to move in a double circle. He added a fourth, and then a fifth, feeling a twinge with each new addition.

Goshen resumed his circling, testing Jeran with feints and quick jabs that came nowhere near their mark. Even still, each attack strained Jeran's hold on magic. Once, when the Tribesman altered a swing unexpectedly and Jeran had to lunge aside to avoid it, the spheres wavered and slowed. But they did not die.

"Better," Jakal said. "But you still handle magic as if it is a separate thing. It is a part of you, as much so as your flesh. Do your legs freeze when you swing your sword? Do your eyes grow dark when you listen to my words? The magic must be as natural as breathing. Only then will you not need to fear it."

Jeran slowed his breaths, focused on the flows. He fell in tune with Goshen's predatory dance and felt his hold on magic strengthen. The balls of light stabilized in size and brilliance, and they began to dance around the Tribesman in an intricate pattern. Even the presences inside his head, the awareness of the thousands who had pledged themselves to him, fell into a surprising harmony. Their pain and fear became a distant thing, barely felt, and a feeling of tranquility Jeran had never thought to experience again took hold of him.

Goshen's attacks grew faster, more frequent, and closer. Twice Jeran could not dodge in time and had to use magic to deflect the attack. He expected criticism from his teachers, but instead saw a wicked grin on Goshen's face, and outright approval on Jakal's.

It's because the spheres didn't waver. I split my magic without losing control.

He no longer saw as with his eyes when he used magic to extend his perceptions, unless he chose to view the world that way or if he needed to maximize the range of his awareness. He sensed a light breeze stirring the grass, making the blades quiver with the hope of relief. When that same breeze played across his flesh a moment later, it offered no respite, but the foreknowledge of it was reward enough.

Jakal stood, and though Jeran no longer faced the *Tsha'ma*, he knew the man was edging closer, slipping around to get a better view. Far outside the park, Jeran intuited snippets of an argument between Oto and Yassik, a debate about procedure at the Academy, with Alwen no doubt the instigator of Yassik's frustration. A myriad of sights, sounds, and smells presented themselves, and Jeran sifted and sorted them, discarding the irrelevant.

His perceptions warned him of the sword striking toward his back, though not until the blade was less than a few hands away. He yelled, diving toward the ground and rolling, wrenching his magic toward a new purpose.

The bonds on his wrist disintegrated in a flash of blue flame, as did the juggling balls circling Goshen. Jeran took more flows as those faded and wove them together, grasping the sword blade and binding it in hardened air. It slowed to a crawl, then stopped about a hand away from his gut. The effort exhausted him, though; simply holding onto the magic made him feel as if his heart were about to explode from his chest.

The scarred Human Mage nodded with something approaching satisfaction. It was the closest to approval Jeran had yet to see on the man's face. "Saw it coming? Good. And you didn't scorch half the practice yard this time. Woulda preferred it if you hadn't lost control of those baubles you like to play with, but you didn't get cut, and I guess that's a bit more important."

"He look like boulder sits on chest," Goshen said, leaning against the handle of his hammer. "I one do hard work. He just stand there."

The two warriors laughed at that, but Jakal's expression carried more concern. "Perhaps it would be best if you released your hold on magic, Jeran. I doubt our friend intends to continue his attack."

With little reluctance, Jeran let go of magic. Its departure loosened his lungs, and he gasped in a desperate breath, but the exhaustion that danced at the periphery of his consciousness a moment ago fell upon him with vengeance. His vision wavered, and his first attempt to stand proved an embarrassing failure.

He brushed off Jakal's outstretched hands and stood, ignoring the protests of his body and determined to hide the extent of his fatigue. When he saw Jes approaching, beautiful despite the worn travelling dress she wore, he straightened his back and made a show of stretching the kinks from his shoulders and wrists.

"You've had enough for today," she said, her tone flat.

Jeran feigned a smile. "You don't think I intended to try that again, do you?"

"I expect you intended to move on to some other exercise," Jes snorted. "I tell you, you are done for the day. And if you pretend that the way you are holding yourself soldier stiff is not a sign of near collapse, I'll—"

"Fear not, my most honored instructor," Jeran said. "I would never think of disobeying you. I will retire to my house and confine myself to more mundane matters for the remainder of the day."

Jes bristled at his tone, but she did not let her emotions touch her face. "You have shown some improvement. Before your lessons tomorrow, we will discuss several adjustments to your technique which may improve the ease of weaving the flows."

"I will welcome any suggestions that improve my mastery of magic. As always, your attention to detail and concern for my well being are most appreciated."

Lips narrowed to a thin line, Jes whirled around and marched from the park, her passage accompanied by a breeze that could almost be called icy in the stifling heat of summer.

"Why do you goad her so?" Jakal asked. "It is not in your nature." The *Tsha'ma* looked more curious than concerned; his probing gaze sought to find some great truth.

Jeran sought out Jes from the collection of presences in his mind. His bond with her remained weak, but that he sensed it at all proved he had done the right thing in Dranakohr. Restrained fury burned through her, but Jeran also sensed spikes of pride and satisfaction—and even a few of amusement.

"I do it because she desires it," he told Jakal. "She feels forced into her position as my teacher and seeks justification for her anger. By providing her with that justification, I allow her the freedom she requires and the outlet she needs."

"Bind her to you by making her think she hates you," Jakal mused. "The ways of the BattleMagi are complicated."

"That pup is as much a BattleMage as this blade of grass is a tree," the scarred Human said. "I fought with BattleMagi."

"So you have said," Jeran mused. "Which ones? Were you bonded to any? Do you understand the nature of the bond? How to control it? I would welcome your insight into such matters."

The Mage's posture did not change, but his mood altered so dramatically that even Goshen took a wary step back. "I have no *insights* into BattleMagi that you would find helpful. Becoming one is a fool's mistake, and twice the fool who welcomes it. To encourage the bond... Only one other was so foolish as that, and in the end, even cold-hearted Kohr wept for the man."

With a scowl that could make mountains tremble, the Mage left, moving silently through the dry grasses of the park. "That is one whose past I would like to know," Jakal said.

"His past is blood," Goshen said, hefting his hammer onto his shoulder and starting toward the camp. "Blood and pain."

"He was a BattleMage," Jeran said, though his words lacked the Sahna Tribesman's poetry. "Or trained to be one. I suspect he broke his bond, or failed those bonded to him."

"Can you see into his heart, as you see into the hearts of others?" Jakal voiced the question, but he did not look as if he believed it to be true.

Jeran shook his head. "No. He is as much a mystery to me as he is to you, but I can think of no other thing that would scar a man in such a manner. His pain runs so deep that his very passage makes the earth mourn."

"We fight tomorrow," Goshen said as he walked from the practice field. "Real fight. Need to stretch muscles."

"I'd welcome the exercise," Jeran told him. "I have a session with the twins in the morning, and a delegate from Dranakohr arrives at midday. Will evening suffice?" Goshen grunted an affirmative over his shoulder.

"Will you walk with me?" Jakal asked Jeran, as he started back toward the city. "I'll be along in a moment."

Jeran sat in the trampled grass and drew a slow breath, opening his mind to the presences knotted in the back of his mind. That so many had bonded to him amazed him, as did the knowledge that he could distinguish many of them from one another. Most were too distant for any direct insights beyond vague impressions of emotion. Fear dominated, followed closely by uncertainty, but a growing core of confidence had infused itself in his people.

A handful stood out like beacons in the darkness. In Dranakohr, Ehvan and Wardel felt pride at what they had accomplished, and both felt a growing responsibility for the people under their command. Most surprising to Jeran, though, was the small knot of envy each man felt for the other, despite their strong friendship.

In Portal, exhaustion heralded the presences of Lord Talbot and Tourin, but beneath the bone-numbing fatigue lay a growing calm and order. Far to the south, a fiery presence Jeran believed must be Mika fretted over the well-being of the King and worried about the skills of his soldiers, wondering if they would be ready before they were needed. And in the northeast, Grendor's pureness called to him like the sweet tones of a lyre. Katya and Lord Grondellan were nearby, but they were washed out by the power of the Orog's soul.

Some were noticeably absent. Dahr, so long a fixture in Jeran's mind, even before he knew or understood what he was, was missing. His friend occasionally flickered in his consciousness, gone almost before Jeran had time to register his appearance. In those brief moments of insight, Jeran sensed pain, doubt, and indecision. That worried him, but whatever Dahr was suffering through, it was something he needed. Without it, his unfocused anger would devour him.

Jes was missing too, though not because her connection to Jeran was broken. She had found a way to hide herself from him, appearing and disappearing seemingly at will, though he suspected that the ability was something random, or at least something she had no direct control over. If it had been cultivated, she would have been more careful in its use.

And, of course, Martyn's mind was closed to him. It was not the way of kings to devote themselves to another. But it would be helpful to have access to the prince. A useful tool for assaying conditions in Kaper. As things stood he could only sense Mika, whose youth clouded his perception, and his Uncle Aryn, whose mind was a tumult of emotion hidden behind a veneer of sanity. He could glean little of use from either of them.

That will have to change soon. The situation in Kaper is deteriorating. But who can I trust?

Jeran stood, brushed the grass from his clothes, and made his way to a collection of small, two-story houses circling a fountained plaza in the shadow of the old Assembly Hall. He had refused Aemon's suggestion of staying within the Hall itself; that place belonged too much to the Assembly for Jeran's liking. More Readings flickered in and around the Hall as well, when compared to the rest of Shandar, and the city held few enough pleasant memories for Jeran to quarter himself where they were more prevalent.

The house he chose had never been lived in, nor had it suffered any damage during Tylor's attack. Echoes of the battle sometimes reached him, but for the most part it was a silent place, a sanctuary of sorts. Built of smooth stone cut from the mountains of the Anvil, it had an open balcony that faced the plaza outside and a handful of simple, unadorned rooms.

A black uniformed guard stood at the door. He saluted as Jeran passed, and Jeran stopped for a moment to greet the man before stepping inside. After learning of the attack, Ehvan had insisted on stationing a contingent of soldiers in Shandar for Jeran's protection. After much debate, Jeran relented to the presence of a small detachment, which he housed in the building next to his. The guards were rotated every ten-day, and consisted of equal numbers of Humans and Orog. At Jeran's command, no Magi or apprentices were ever to be among those sent to protect him.

The house was sparsely furnished, the walls devoid of ornamentation. A small table with three chairs and a broad writing desk sat on opposite sides of the hearth. The table stood empty save for a pitcher of water, but piles of dispatches and letters from Dranakohr all but obscured the top of the desk. A few of the items scavenged from Tylor's horde sat out, not on display but because Jeran had not finished studying them, and a chest of similar items lay pressed into one corner. The room beyond the main chamber held more boxes and crates brought from Dranakohr.

Upstairs was even more spartan. One of the three bedchambers held a mattress and wash basin; the others stood empty. Jeran could not even remember when he had last used the bed. More nights than not he curled up on the floor by the hearth or simply slept at the desk.

He sat and poured himself some water, then ran his hands across a hairpin pulled from Tylor's trophy room. A Reading played across the simple trinket, and Jeran opened himself to it. He did that for a time, moving from one object to the next, pausing occasionally to jot down some notes before resuming his inspections.

The last item he picked up was *The Forge of Faith*, the gift bestowed upon him by Lorthas. Touching it made the Readings it held swirl in his mind, but this time Jeran fought them off. He opened to his mark and read, jotting down frequent notes on scraps of blank paper he kept within easy reach.

A knock on the door signaled a changing of the guard, and Jeran closed the book when the *choupik* Pelagin entered bearing a bowl of steaming stew and some fresh vegetables on a tray. The Orog set the tray on the table and left without speaking.

As Jeran ate, he wondered about events across Madryn, and sought to find the purpose to Salos's schemes. That the Scorpion played his own game he no longer doubted; Salos was no mere tool of the Darklord's, though Lorthas refused to believe it. But empire was likely a means to Salos's goal, not the goal itself. *The Scorpion is not one to give much attention to politics or wealth, though pursuit of power could drive his actions.*

As the shadows of evening spilled across the room, Jeran turned his attention from Salos to his own burgeoning Gift. After setting aside his bowl, he moved back from the table and opened himself to magic. A hum of energy suffused him, and he welcomed the vibrancy of life that accompanied use of magic.

He allowed his perceptions to flow from his body, careful to keep sight of the room around him even as his senses expanded upward and through his house. He explored every corner, every crevasse, sometimes seeking to 'see' with his mind's eye and other times contenting himself with simple awareness, knowledge detached from any specific sensation.

Outside the building, Pelagin had taken over guard duty, and the Human soldier had returned to the barracks. Another soldier guarded the rear entrance to Jeran's house, and two more stood watch on the roof, where they could monitor all routes approaching the plaza.

Across from Jeran's main entrance, Nahrona and Nahrima engaged in animated debate. Jeran focused on the Elves' conversation, though he endeavored to keep his presence unknown by minimizing the magical energies he focused around them.

"This is too taxing an endeavor for him," Nahrona said, concern weighing his words. "He should spend more time in the Vale."

"I agree, brother," Nahrima replied, "but he is determined. Would you like to be the one to tell the Emperor how he must behave?"

"I would do so, except..."

"...you know it would be a futile endeavor?"

"And incurring his wrath for no gain seems unwise."

"That just shows how much you have learned over the winters," Nahrima laughed. "You used to incur his wrath all the time, and for far less reason than this."

Nahrona smiled, but the gesture held far less mirth than Nahrima's laughter. "The reasons always seemed justified at the time. But..."

"But you know it doesn't really matter anymore?"

"He senses the end approaching, and he wants..."

"...to matter again."

Nahrona sighed. "I will miss him when he is gone."

"The whole world will." Nahrima's eyes focused on Jeran's house. "That was very good, Jeran. A little more subtlety in your approach, and you might have gone unnoticed entirely."

"I am particularly impressed in how you resisted the urge to tighten your awareness around us," Nahrona added. "It is that narrowing of focus that almost always gives away the Gifted when they spy on each other."

At being called out, Jeran recoiled, his perceptions whipping away from the Elves in an instant. After the initial shock wore off, he chuckled. *Spying? They might consider this spying, but they are the ones who instructed me in this matter and demanded that I practice whenever opportunity allowed.*

He spread his mind out again, weaving through the other buildings of the plaza, even extending some distance into the city. Jakal and Goshen shunned the city's houses, preferring to sleep on the edge of the park, on pallets under the stars except when storms drove them into their tents. They sat around a fire, eating venison caught on a recent hunt. The Human Mage was with them, grim and silent, staring into the flames. A haunting sadness radiated from him, but it never reached his eyes. Only anger lived there, anger and grim determination.

The flash of another aura, emerald green, pulsating and powerful, called to him, and Jeran moved the web of his outcast perceptions toward it. The Emperor's aura in no way matched his frail and failing form, and in it Jeran saw the vitality that had dominated the man's life and understood his frustration at the futility of his current existence. He lived more as a trophy now than as a man, kept and tended by his people as a living legend, an item of such exquisite uniqueness that it must not be so much as breathed upon lest it break.

The Emperor approached Jes, who sat at a table in the house she had claimed for herself, going through a stack of dispatches as high as the one on Jeran's desk. She had seemed surprised when Jeran suggested that she have one of his apprentices ferry reports back and forth for her, so that she could direct her House from exile. Though she had not thanked him—Jes would never thank him for giving back a fraction of what he had stolen—her attitude had nevertheless improved once she was allowed to strum the strings of her own web again.

"What troubles you, child?" the Emperor asked. "You once had a far more lovely light in your eyes."

A fond smile touched Jes's lips. "These are not lovely times, Grandfather."

"True. But one must find what joy one can. I have lived through far darker times than these."

"You are not a prisoner here."

"No," the Emperor gave a wheezing laugh. "I escaped centuries of captivity to come to this place for a few seasons of adventure. You will forgive me if I do not take your *incarceration* seriously, will you not? As beautiful as the Vale is, one does yearn to see the outside world from time to time."

"Of all people, I would expect you to sympathize with me."

"What truly holds you here, child? Maybe Jeran would call you out if you left, strip you of your House and title, turn you into a fugitive Mage, but I suspect it is a bluff. Having you here to guide his training may serve his purposes, but having you in control of Velan serves them too, far more than forcing you into hiding or driving you back to the Assembly."

"He is neither so innocent nor as kind as you and Aemon believe."

"Perhaps not, but he is just, and I am certain he would do nothing to hurt one devoted to his cause. You, in particular. If you told him you wanted to leave, I believe he would let you go. So I ask again, what holds you here, child? Is it the same thing that makes you so sad?"

Jes looked at the Emperor, a war of doubt and guilt on her face. Seeing her pain unmasked, Jeran recoiled. He wondered if he should let her leave immediately, though he knew he could not. "It's not right," she whispered. "He needs my help, but this bond between us... It is not right."

"Time is a strange thing, child. I have lived longer than any being on Madryn, yet I wonder how much I have learned beyond what I knew at the end of my first century. Oh, there are facts aplenty from the intervening winters, and refinements to skills acquired, but how many new skills? How much have my attitudes changed? Much of who we are is determined in those first few magical winters. The intervening seasons seem to do little but petrify the convictions we held in youth."

"It's not just that, Grandfather. We have saddled him with such a terrible duty. If he fails, the Assembly will cast him down as a rebel and possibly another Darklord. If he succeeds in what he intends... Madryn might be made better for it, but I wonder what we have condemned him to in the process."

"We may have nudged him onto a trail, but Jeran has the reins now. We go where he leads, and the best an old man like me can do is hold on."

The anguish Jes felt made her aura pulsate with exquisite color, and Jeran yearned to comfort her, to tell her that she was not to blame for his situation or its outcome. But he could not. Confronting her on the issue would strengthen the barriers she had erected between them. He needed her focused on his training, not on hiding her emotions from him.

The Emperor took Jes's hand. "Do you remember my third wife, Baetrean? She was before your time, I think. As beautiful a creature as ever walked this world. Stubborn as a mule, though, and confident to a fault. Our marriage started as one of political convenience, and I maneuvered her in such a way as to solve several problems for me. She never resolved matters in the way I intended, though, and her... solutions... often frustrated me with their lack of tact and subtlety.

"I thought youth made her rash and impulsive—she was many winters my junior, as are all beings in this world—but she lived to a ripe old age and died no more patient than she had lived, no more prone to thoughtful contemplation or circumspect methods. As the Orog say, 'Ask a rock to be a rock, and you will be well satisfied; ask it to be a cloud, and you will be disheartened.' "

Jes shook her head. "He is barely a man, even by Common standards."

"You do him an injustice, child," the Emperor chuckled. "Jeran earned his manhood by Alrendrian standards many winters ago, and he has proven it in trial in the seasons since. But you would be surprised, I think, to learn how much life he has lived. Ask him how many winters he has seen."

"To what end? I know how old he is. Aemon talked of little else after his birth."

"Ask him, my dear. Ask him how many winters he has seen. I think—"

"You're spying again."

The words jolted Jeran back to his body. He had grown so focused on the Emperor's conversation that he had forgotten to watch the room he sat in. He expected chastisement from Yassik, who stood inside the door with a sheaf of papers, but the old Mage made no criticism. "Growing good at it too, else I'd expect you'd have an irate Mage or two outside your door. The Gifted do not like having their conversations listened to by magical means, even when they employ similar tactics on a regular basis."

Yassik stepped forward and handed Jeran another stack of papers. "From Dranakohr." When Jeran took the dispatches and added them to the piles on his desk, the Mage turned to leave.

"Wait," Jeran called, and when Yassik craned his neck around, Jeran gestured for him to sit. For a time, they stared at each other in silence.

Eventually, Jeran lifted the time-worn volume from his desk and turned it over in his hand. *The Forge of Faith* glimmered in embossed letters on the cover. Yassik frowned when he saw the volume, but said nothing. He merely watched as Jeran studied it, opened it to the handwritten inscription, and let his mind skim over the Readings that played across the book like waves on the ocean.

"Why did you follow him?" Jeran asked at last. "I need to understand."

"It was a long time ago, Jeran." Yassik's mouth drew down in a tight frown. "I'm not—"

"This has nothing to do with trusting you. If I did not, you wouldn't be allowed in Dranakohr, let alone entrusted with responsibility at the Academy. I need to understand him. I need to understand what happened, so that I can avoid starting another MageWar."

For a time, Yassik said nothing. He cast his eyes around the chamber, latching on to a wine bottle set atop the mantle. When Jeran offered a glass, he refused. "At first, I followed him because we believed we were doing the right thing. In the wake of Peitr's Revolt, the Assembly grew stale and cautious, so afraid of damaging its standing among the Houses that it refused all but the most dire requests for aid. And as fear of magic spread through Alrendria, the Assembly grew even more withdrawn.

"I knew something had to be done. I wrote a number of papers about the Assembly's glorious past. I tried to reinvigorate the Magi, remind them that they could do little good if they isolated themselves, that their very isolation contributed to the fear and hatred among the Commons, the very things driving them to abandon Alrendria in the first place.

"Few would listen, but Lorthas did. He was arrogant even then, and patronizing to those he thought abused their Gift or failed to use it properly, but he was popular, especially among the younger Magi. He became the mouthpiece through which my ideas were spread, the figurehead for change we rallied behind."

"Are you saying *you* were the architect of the MageWar?" Such a revelation should have surprised Jeran, but for some reason it did not.

"I don't like to think of it in those terms, but in a way, yes. I determined that Alrendria needed a rallying point, that some unifying factor was required to prove to the Commons that we Magi were not all evil, and to prove to the Magi that our presence in the world was required. In the end, my plan worked, but not in any way I ever imagined."

Jeran leaned forward, resting his chin on his folded hands. "What went wrong?"

"The leadership of the Magi arranged an elaborate scheme to discredit Lorthas, and when it failed, he left, splitting the Assembly much as you have. A greater part of the Gifted actually followed him, but most were young and inexperienced.

"None of us wanted war. Not even Lorthas. Maybe especially not Lorthas. His goal had always been to destroy the Arkam Imperium and restore Alrendria; disunion among the Assembly delayed the realization of that goal. So he sent his apprentice, Kalsbad, to negotiate with the Assembly with the hope of gaining a voice for our people.

"I never found out what happened exactly, but during the negotiations, Kalsbad was executed by the Assembly. Lorthas flew into a rage upon hearing the news, and planned a surprise attack on the Assembly at Tyrmalin. He hoped to take the Magi by surprise, eliminate the upper levels of the hierarchy, and rebuild the Assembly in our image.

"In truth, it was a good plan, but Aemon called for a full assembly of Magi to discuss their options, and few Magi were in Tyrmalin when we attacked. The Assembly's response was less aggressive, but equally cruel. They proclaimed Lorthas a Darklord and sought to undermine his standing with the nations of man."

"If you were such an integral part of the movement," Jeran asked, "what made you change your allegiance? That's what I don't understand."

Yassik sat stone still for a moment, then went to the mantle and grabbed the wine bottle, pouring himself a glass and taking a long draught. "At first, I stayed because I believed in what we were doing. As the winters dragged on and Lorthas's methods grew more extreme, I began to doubt. When he formed a union with the Imperium, I knew I could no longer work with him. But..."

"You stayed?"

Yassik nodded. "For Alwen. I couldn't leave without her. For seasons I tried to convince her to go, but she was more dedicated to changing the Assembly than either Lorthas or I. That's one of the reasons she's such a staunch supporter of yours."

Jeran spit out a laugh. "Alwen? A supporter of mine?"

"Well," Yassik chuckled, "maybe not to your face. But to any Mage of the Assembly, she'll say that you're the only chance the Gifted have for survival."

Doubt played across Jeran's face, but he let the matter go. "How did you convince her to leave?"

Yassik's cheeks blossomed red. "As to that, I convinced her by knocking her unconscious and dragging her bodily back to the Assembly, where Aemon and I held her captive until we could make her see the truth of things."

Again Jeran could barely restrain laughter. "I bet that went over well."

"She was not pleased," Yassik said, and the words had the ring of understatement in them. "Don't you worry, though. She punished me for it in the end. She married me."

"There's one more thing I want to—" A hard knock on the door cut Jeran off. "Enter."

Pelagin opened the door. "My apologies, friend Jeran, but a Mage named Kostas arrived from Dranakohr and demanded to see you. He claims that Salos Durange sent a ShadowMage to open talks with you. He believes he speaks the truth, but I could not get the other to confirm his story."

Jeran stood abruptly, his chair grating against the floorboards. "He brought the ShadowMage here?" Anger flashed across his features. "Where are they?"

"Both men are being held in the building across the plaza. Lady Jessandra and Lord Aemon are already questioning them." Pelagin hesitated, and Jeran signaled for him to speak. "Mage Kostas grew impatient when we would not bring him to you directly. When he grew belligerent, some of my *choupik* took it upon themselves to hobble him. He promises retribution once he is freed."

Hobble him. Jeran almost smiled at the term the Orog had adopted to describe their ability to rob a Mage of his Gift. "When I am through with him," he said, starting toward the door, "punishing your soldiers will be the furthest thing from his mind."

CHAPTER 17

Jeran searched the Twilight World with frantic urgency, laughing at his desperation to find the Darklord. He never looked forward to meeting with Lorthas, but it often provided insight into the conflict he no longer appeared able to avoid. Enemies surrounded him, and they saw his people as the weakest faction, the easiest to eliminate. Of all those arrayed against him, he was safe only from Lorthas, who did not see himself as a separate player in this game, and who, in any case, stood trapped behind the Boundary.

His efforts were fruitless; the twinkling lights of the dreamers did not include Lorthas's unmistakable presence. He would have to wait, or try again another night and hope to catch the Darklord sleeping. But the news he had was urgent, and though it might prove more helpful to Lorthas than to him, he needed confirmation. He would wait.

He concentrated, and felt his body form around his consciousness. A lush pasture, not unlike those of northern Alrendria where he had been raised, replaced the depthless night with innumerable stars. A stream babbled through the center of the field, and a tree reached out long arms on the bank, offering respite from the summer sun.

Jeran sat beneath the tree and listened to the silence. The connections to his people were muted here, present but distant, and Jeran took a moment to savor the quiet, the solitude he no longer enjoyed in the waking world. *I could sleep for days,* he thought, then wondered if one could sleep in a world where one already slept, and wondered what would happen if he did.

A tortured howl ruined the serenity, and Jeran leapt to his feet. Across the pasture he saw Dahr, wide-eyed and panic-stricken, fall to the ground and scuttle backward on hands and feet. A looming shadow fell over him, obscuring his features. "What do you want of me?" he screamed.

Jeran started forward to help, but a hand grabbed his shoulder. "It would be wise of you to leave him be. He will not be harmed."

"You!" Jeran whirled around to face the man who called himself a guide, a man who refused to divulge much about himself but who had no trouble sharing with Jeran things no one else had the right—or should have had the ability—to know about the inner workings of Jeran's own thoughts. "Do you dog my steps in the Twilight World? Hover in the shadows until I dream and then follow me?"

The Guide smiled his knowing, infuriating smile. "I have nowhere else to be, and you are always on the verge of doing something foolish. There!" He pointed, and Jeran watched Dahr fade from view. "Your friend awakens. He is safe for another day."

"And what of me?" Jeran asked. "From where he sat, did Dahr see us engaged in pleasant conversation, or does my face reflect the mask of terror he wore?"

"If you do not welcome my advice, you need not listen to it. The Twilight World is a big place. Our paths may cross from time to time, but you are free to move on if you find my company distasteful."

Jeran drew a deep breath. "My frustrations are at the world at large, not at you, but you pose an easier target. Your counsel has not yet led me astray. I'd be foolish not to listen to it."

The man clapped Jeran on the shoulder. "You've learned a lot in the last few seasons. Grown a lot. You might almost be ready to walk the path you've chosen." He sat, leaning back against the tree and cupping his hands behind his head. "And save your apologies. I remember the frustrations of the waking world, though it's more like a memory of a memory."

Jeran sat too, and he wondered how far he could trust this man. *Should I share with him the news I was to share with Lorthas? Could he help me figure out how best to proceed?*

"I don't know what to do," he said at last, testing the Guide with a vague question.

"You seek to make friends of enemies, but fear such an action might make enemies of some friends." The man frowned. "It is a slippery slope you tread, but one with great potential. The real question is: can you afford not to do it? There is little need to debate your course if the alternative sends you crashing into the shoals."

"How do you know—" Jeran broke off his question. The Guide would not answer, and nothing the man knew really surprised him anymore. "Salos sent an ambassador to Dranakohr. The Scorpion seeks a truce. He guarantees my people freedom in the west if I make no move against him."

"And you are entertaining this proposal?"

"Not for an instant!" Jeran said, affronted. *Maybe he doesn't know everything after all.* A cryptic grin spread across the Guide's face, and Jeran wondered what it signified.

"Salos needs time to consolidate his hold on the Tachan Lands and to finish his war against Alrendria. Then he will move against the Assembly, and if he can find a way, against Lorthas. He promises me freedom because my Gifted pose the least threat to him at the moment. The Assembly will debate until he is at their doorstep, and Lorthas still believes the Scorpion his pawn, not to mention the Boundary divides them. Salos would be wise to dispatch well-trained foes who think him no more than a nuisance rather than dispense with an untrained foe who thinks him a dire threat."

"So if you seek no concord with Salos, with whom would you ally?" the Guide asked, his tone measuring.

"I would prefer the Assembly," Jeran admitted, "but I believe they've already cast their lot against me."

"So you seek a deal with Lorthas? What have you to offer?"

"I don't intend to hand him Madryn, if that's what you're implying!"

"It's a legitimate question. I meant to cast no aspersion."

"I don't intend to trade one evil for another, but Lorthas represents a far lesser danger than Salos."

"And the Boundary holds him."

"Yes, though not as much as one might like. And only for a time. We both know it will fall eventually…" Jeran paused, and he eyed the Guide askance. "And even now, it can be circumvented."

"I was wondering if you had realized," the Guide laughed, then his expression grew grim again. "And you think Lorthas can be trusted?"

"Trusted...? I think that if he makes a promise, he will keep it. At least the letter of it, if not the spirit. And at heart, Lorthas strives toward a noble goal; his methods are what I question, and what tarnish his results. But Salos... The Scorpion wants only power, and the ability to destroy."

"He has become a true servant of Kohr," the Guide said. For a time, he sat in silence, his eyes watching the clouds drifting past. "It sounds as if you have made your decision."

"Nothing is done yet," Jeran said. "It would be nice to know that someone else thinks this a prudent move."

"Lorthas never sought dominion for dominion's sake, but he has spent centuries reviled by Madryn, hated by the people he sought to save. If he ever did escape the Boundary, the methods he might use to subdue resistance would make his tactics during the MageWar seem restrained. You are powerful, and you have much potential, but you could never control him, just as he could never control you."

"Not control," Jeran admitted. "But perhaps constrain? Direct?"

The Guide laughed again. "As I said before, you tread a slippery path. But you are right in one thing: you cannot win surrounded by enemies. Removing the threat to the north allows you to direct your focus elsewhere, and may provide you with a useful tool if ever you need to use it."

The Guide stood suddenly and studied Jeran. "But you know all of this. Why do you seek my approval so desperately?"

Jeran hesitated. He had held suspicions for some time, but he had no proof, did not know how to fashion proof, and was not sure he believed anyway. "Are you my God?"

This time, the Guide's laughter echoed across the plain. "Who a man chooses to worship is a personal thing, and a question only he can answer."

Frustration flared through Jeran. "Are you Balan the Scholar?"

The Guide affected a domineering stance. "That is not a tone one should adopt when addressing any God, let alone one's own." A smirk broke through the stoic facade.

"I am nothing more than what I have claimed to be," he told Jeran. "I am your friend, and if you are willing to listen, a guide. Gods have plans for their followers, and for the universe. Gods also have obligations. I have none of those."

"But if I have questions?" Jeran asked. "If I need to talk."

The man spread his arms wide. "Then you know where to find me."

The Twilight World blurred, and Jeran woke to find himself at his desk, his hand clutching the cover of *The Forge of Faith*. Jes stood inside the door, but the concern Jeran felt so clearly through their bond fled from her face the moment Jeran opened his eyes.

"You did not come to our morning lesson," Jes said, her face a mask of impassivity.

The sun had not yet crested the horizon, but warm bands of yellow and red graced the eastern sky. "I did not sleep well last night."

"Perhaps your recent preference for chairs and floorboards is to blame. A bed might deepen your slumber."

Jeran went to the hearth and poured a small amount of water into a porcelain bowl salvaged from the ruins of Shandar. He splashed the water against his face and ran some through his hair, wiping away the last vestiges of sleep and invigorating himself with the cold shock. He considered excusing himself to change clothes, but his morning exercises would only require that he do so again, so he decided against it. "Seeking my bed would be far easier if those in Dranakohr could harvest the crop or change the linens without seeking my approval first."

"Ah, the joys of leadership," Jes said. Though her plain white dress was somewhat worn at the fringes, the material remained pristine in color and devoid of wrinkles. It flowed along the length of her body. Jeran wiped thoughts of her from his mind; the bond did not carry his emotions out as readily as it carried others' to him, but enough of his thoughts could reach her—especially when they stood so close—that he wanted to take no chances.

"It will get better," she told him. "Marginally. For now, they're unsure how far they can take matters on their own, and would rather frustrate you with minutiae than anger you by overstepping their authority. Once your House is established, things will run more smoothly, and you will find yourself wishing your people sought your counsel more often."

"I look forward to that day," Jeran said, preceding Jes from his house. They walked side by side through Shandar to a secluded garden some distance from their houses, where a series of benches circled an elliptical fountain. Jeran waited for Jes to sit, then took a place opposite her.

"What do you have in store for me today?" he asked.

"I watched you working with the twins yesterday. You are still struggling too much with what should be simple matters. I think some minor modification to the flows you use will ease your burden. Seize magic."

Jeran opened himself to his Gift. He wove the strands of energy to the verge of creation, to the instant before they snapped together and magic manifested, and held them. Then, at Jes's instruction, he shifted the flows. This one to the left. These two encircling a third. Preventing the flows from releasing their magic brought a sheen of sweat to his skin; the effort of adjusting them to Jes's exacting standards tortured him. His muscles quaked as if he held aloft a great weight; his heart thundered in his chest as one long into the chase.

In the end, though, Jes's recommendations proved effective. When the flows met her approval, they fell into place with graceful ease, not with the jarring snap that usually accompanied Jeran's natural use of magic. And as they dissipated, Jeran felt far less of his own reserves drained. Though he still had much to learn, improvements to his technique had already substantially lessened the burden he felt from using magic.

The others taught him what to do, but Jes taught him how to do it properly. Her training allowed him to handle far more magic before exhaustion overwhelmed him. Her training taught him nuance and subtlety; where before he had used magic as a hammer, he could now use it as a tailor's needle when circumstances required it. His mastery of the Gift progressed remarkably fast, and he had Jes alone to thank for it.

By the end of their session, Jeran felt as if he could sleep for a ten-day, but the sun still stood low in the east, and he had more work to do. He met with a courier from Dranakohr, exchanging dispatches and listening to a status report on conditions. Midsummer had finally seen the pass to Alrendria clear, and many of those who had waited for their chance to leave had done so. Jeran smiled at that: he could have had his Magi clear the pass a season ago, or he could have used Gates to transport those people out, but he had needed the laborers. They had served their purpose, helping prepare Dranakohr for those who wanted to stay. He wished them well, and hoped they found peace in the winters ahead.

As it turned out, a fair number of those who intended to go had changed their minds, and the ranks of Dranakohr had been further swelled by a group of refugees seeking entrance through the pass. Word of Jeran's citadel had spread through House Odara, as had news of the destruction of Portal and the carnage caused by the passage of the Tachan army as it made its way south. Most of those who survived the Tachan advance descended on Dranakohr, seeking protection at the one place they thought safest from the coming storm.

Jeran thought them fools for thinking Dranakohr safe when it really served as a beacon to his enemies, announcing where best to strike at him, but he did not want to dissuade any from joining him. He would need workers to replace those who left, farmers to tend the fields, soldiers to swell his army, and craftsmen to supply his soldiers. If the illusion of safety brought him what he needed, he would do nothing to shatter it.

The courier had no other news of import, though he did bring letters from Wardel, Ehvan, and Alwen that Jeran intended to read immediately. He handed the man a stack of letters to take back and opened a Gate. The sight of full fields of wheat and vegetables, and even the start of orchards, the small trees arranged in precise squares, startled him. *I've been away too long. I must find some time to return soon.*

After the courier left, Jeran returned to his house and found Aemon waiting for him. He looked tired, but more a general weariness than the exhaustion Jeran endured. The thought of a MageWar renewed weighed upon him, as did the knowledge that despite all his efforts, the Assembly had divided again. Adding Salos to the mix—a rogue Mage with his own army and no respect for life—only worsened his guilt.

"I had hoped we might discuss—"

Jeran had no time to discuss Aemon's plans, or to coddle his conscience. The former High Wizard sought a way to reconcile the Assembly to their plans, but Jeran knew the Assembly's new leadership would never work with him. Devoting time and resources to such a fruitless endeavor was pointless.

"Why didn't the Assembly punish Yassik and Alwen?"

"What? Why would they—"

"No games, Tanar. I will ferret out the truth of matters. If I cannot get an answer from you, there are others I can ask."

Aemon drew a deep breath and heaved it out again. "There was a time no man would have spoken to me in such a tone, and a time when that fact frustrated me to no end. Be careful what you wish for, Jeran. If you get it, you might find yourself pining for the old days."

Jeran opened his mouth, but Aemon forestalled him. "I will answer your question, my boy. No need to browbeat me. The Assembly adopted a lenient policy toward those Magi who realized they had made a mistake and sought to rejoin us."

Jeran folded his arms across his chest. "Do you think me a fool?"

"What I tell you is the truth!"

"No doubt. But you're the one who taught Lorthas how to weave truth into a tapestry of misdirection. Yassik's philosophy was the driving ideology behind the MageWar. And Alwen did not return of her own volition. You made a special effort to redeem her. Would you have been so forgiving if Lorthas had sought forgiveness? Somehow, I doubt it. Every war needs a villain."

"I'm not quite sure I understand how this is relevant to the current situation."

"Your understanding is not required. I know the facts of the matter; I seek the rationale. You can give it to me now, or I will discover it through other methods."

Aemon drew in a breath and blew it out, his cheeks puffing out with exasperation. "You can be infuriatingly blunt."

"I'm sure you wish circumstances had not forced you to unleash me on the world so quickly. No doubt you intended to prepare me for a few more centuries."

A wry smile twisted Aemon's lips. "You're too clever, my boy. Yes. Tylor and Salos Durange forced my hand. I'm not disappointed with the results, though."

"Just with my pliability?"

"I would prefer it if you were a bit more susceptible to suggestion, yes."

"I might be more willing to listen when you speak if you'd speak when I ask, and on the matters I ask about."

"Very well." Aemon took a seat, settling back and staring Jeran straight in the eyes. "Yassik sought me out. I almost refused him an audience, but he begged my indulgence and implored me to listen to him on grounds that are not important to this conversation."

"He asked you to hear him out because he knew you were the one who had set him and Lorthas down the path they walked, only to abandon them at a crucial time for reasons you refused to reveal."

Jeran's interruption flustered Aemon, but he quickly regained his composure. "Yes, well, that's a bit of a simplification, but as I said, for the purposes of this story, the reasons behind my deciding to listen are inconsequential. In any case, he made a compelling argument and convinced me he was sincere in his desire to return to the Assembly."

"That doesn't explain why he was allowed to do so unpunished. Or why such great steps were taken to bring Alwen back."

"Gods, boy, have you grown impatient! I did not lie to you earlier when I said the Assembly offered forgiveness to any Mage who wanted to return. The Orog took their confessions, ferreting out any who thought to lie their way into our hierarchy, and even then they were kept separate from the other Magi, prevented from seeing anything sensitive.

"Add to that the fact that many of the old leadership, those who knew the details of the MageWar's start, were dead. As the war dragged on from seasons to centuries, the roles others had played was forgotten, and Lorthas became the focus for all that had occurred. It was easy to convince the Assembly that Yassik had returned as part of a grander scheme, and that the knowledge he held of Lorthas's operations made accepting him back a wise move on our part."

"And Alwen?"

"With her, I would not have been so forgiving, but rescuing her was Yassik's sole requirement for betraying his cause. In the end, I am forced to admit that he was right. I was biased against her, but she has proven herself a valuable ally."

Jeran mulled over Aemon's answers, but they created more questions than they answered. He needed more time to sort through the memories he held, the knowledge gleaned from his Readings. Then he needed to closet himself away with Aemon—Yassik and Alwen too, perhaps—and work his way straight to the truth.

He nodded. "Thank you, Tanar. That was helpful. But I still want to—"

The door to his house flew open, and the guard outside floated through it, bound by air and hovering several hands off the floor. The scarred Human followed him in, a wicked grin on his face, and Goshen followed, stooping to cross beneath the threshold.

"Time to fight," the Garun'ah said, a hunger in his eyes.

"We agreed to spar this evening," Jeran replied. "You must forgive me, but I have—"

"Not play," the Tsha'ma said. "Fight."

"What this giant is so eloquently saying," the Human Mage replied, "is that we've found one of the groups attempting to spy on us. It's time to put your training to the test."

Since the attack, all had felt the presences of other Gifted in the vicinity, oftentimes trying to observe. Even Jeran, who had little skill at detecting the presence of magic users, had felt them, so clumsy were their efforts. Yet despite the knowledge of their presence, the enemy had proved remarkably elusive. "I will gather the others," Jeran said, reaching for his sword belt.

Goshen and the Human Mage shared a quick, confused look. "Why need others?" Goshen asked. "You want them watch?"

Jeran paused in the act of buckling on his scabbard. "How many are there?"

The two Gifted shared another look. "Ten hands," Goshen stated.

"Sixty at the most," the Human agreed. "Only about half have the Gift."

"And you wonder why I think we should gather the others?"

"It's not much of a test of your abilities if you go in with an army," the Mage snorted. "If you'd prefer, I saw a litter of kittens down the street. Maybe you'd feel more comfortable practicing on them first."

Jeran weighed his options. It seemed foolish to rush into such overwhelming odds, something akin to what he had chided Dahr about on many occasions. But this is what he was here to learn; how many chances would he have to fight in a somewhat controlled environment, monitored by Magi who knew what they were doing and could take steps if things went awry?

"Let's go," he said, starting for the door.

Aemon followed, but the Human Mage shoved a hand against his chest, stopping him in his tracks. Aemon's eyes flashed with affront. "What's the meaning of this, J—"

"We don't need you slowing us down, old man. This is not the kind of fighting you're skilled at, and we need to be able to watch the boy, not coddle your squeamishness."

The former High Wizard looked to be on the verge of arguing, but he held his tongue. With the slightest of nods, the Mage signaled for Jeran to precede him outside, then he, Jeran, and Goshen crossed through a Gate into the forests outside of Shandar.

The *Tsha'ma* took the lead, and they crept through the underbrush, stalking their prey. Jeran kept a hand on the hilt of his Aelvin blade. The metal warmed to his touch, and he felt the hum of its power, of the magic used to forge it. The sword sang to him; if he did not know better, he would have said it yearned for the coming battle.

In his mind, the presences of his people grew muted, and yet more focused. It was as if they sensed the danger into which he had thrown himself, and had tensed until the situation was resolved. He wondered what it felt like on the other end of the bond, and determined that he should make inquiries of those he trusted most.

Goshen's hand shot up, and Jeran crouched. The *Tsha'ma* crept forward, parting the underbrush with a gentle touch that made no sound louder than the whisper of the wind. He signaled, and Jeran moved to join him.

Sheltered in a depression along the bank of a twisting stream, four dozen men lounged around a rough camp. Most were Human, and most of those simple soldiers in Tachan uniforms, but about a dozen wore the telling black outfits of ShadowMagi. A couple of Elves accompanied them, their pinched faces and imperious stares showing their distaste at the arrangement, especially whenever one of the hulking Tribesmen walked past.

The Gifted sat around the fire listening to the instructions of a narrow-faced Elf with high cheekbones and a flat expression. The others paid the Gifted no attention, nor did they interact much amongst themselves, preferring grim silence to sharing conversation between Races. The only sign of any camaraderie came when an Elf slipped on a loose stone, eliciting a comment from a Tribesman and muffled laughter from the Humans and Garun'ah. The Elves, however, did not seem amused, and for a moment, Jeran thought the followers of Kohr would save him the inconvenience of attacking them himself.

"I left," Goshen said. "Him right. You middle. Attack when ready."

"How long will you need?" Jeran whispered.

"Attack when ready," Goshen repeated as he slipped into the shadows. The Mage left too, moving silently through the trees.

Jeran surveyed the camp, plotting the best method of attack. The *Tsha'ma*'s plan left him closest to the Magi around the fire, but it also left him closest to the largest group of Tribesmen, all of whom looked to be waiting for three fools to leap into the camp. Ignoring one group to deal with the other would prove disastrous, no matter which of the two he focused on. He would have to fight both, balancing magic and blade and hoping he had learned enough control to keep from killing himself. No doubt that was what his teachers intended with this exercise.

He drew his blade slowly, feeling it creep from the scabbard without the familiar hum of singing steel. Once it was free, he set his grip, took a deep breath, and launched himself from concealment, opening himself to magic as he descended into the camp.

Magic rushed into him, and Jeran reached for the flows around the ShadowMagi, stripping their connections to magic. There were too many Gifted present for him to keep them from using magic, but the sudden loss would disorient them, buying him a few precious moments to start his attack.

The first Tribesman he caught by surprise, and his sword traced a bloody path across the Hunter's midriff. As he fell, another leapt to the attack, but Jeran unleashed his Gift, and a wall of hardened air engulfed the man, crushing him. The cracking of his ribs echoed through the still-silent camp, and his muffled scream brought it to life like the crow of a morning cock.

The transition from sword to Gift had been effortless, but Jeran knew it was not during attack he had to fear; it was during defense. With the Gifted restoring their hold on magic and the Tribesmen armed and closing for battle, defense would soon become a necessity.

Across the camp, a band of Human soldiers roused themselves, shouting for weapons and order. Without warning, Goshen appeared among them. The *Tsha'ma* towered over his opponents, a giant among children, and his spiked hammer knocked back any man too slow to flee outside its reach.

Jeran met a wild attack, dodging the Garun'ah's spear thrust and narrowly missing the *dolchek* in the Hunter's other hand. His return swing left a line of red on the man's forearm, but the Tribesman seemed not to notice. He pivoted for another attack, and a second Hunter joined him.

Around the fire, the ShadowMagi regained their wits. Three held enough magic to pose a threat, among them the Aelvin instructor. Jeran closed his eyes, seeking the harmony Jakal had described, and he wove the flows in a familiar pattern.

A dozen balls of colored light appeared around him. They began to move, circling him with increasing speed in a mesmerizing pattern. Their manifestation startled one of the Tribesmen, and Jeran seized the opportunity, jumping inside the man's reach and driving his sword deep into flesh. The Tribesman grabbed the blade as he fell, pulling it to the ground and leaving Jeran weaponless in the face of his other adversaries.

He increased the speed of the juggling balls, and added a new flow of energy to the mix, wrapping it around and through the existing forms until they burst into flame. Then he hurled the fireballs toward the Gifted, watching them trace a path through the air. Some were extinguished, but many found their mark, crackling as they met flesh and sending the ShadowMagi into flight toward the stream, where Jeran's other instructor waited.

With his perceptions wrapped around him, he sensed the threat behind him before he heard it, and he whirled about. The axe was already in motion, its broad steel head whistling as it arced toward his face. Jeran reached up to grab the blade, wondering at the sanity of his own action even as he unconsciously wove magic.

A cushion of air enveloped the axe head, and it stopped about a finger's width from his flesh. Jeran shared a look of surprise with the Tribesman who attacked him. Then his shock turned to amusement, and a grin spread across his face. He twisted his hand, and the blade twisted with it, wrenching free of the Tribesman's grip.

Jeran hurled it at the man, using his mind to direct its flight. The Hunter fell, his own axe buried deep in the center of his chest.

He retrieved his sword and raced toward the ShadowMagi. Two focused their Gifts on him, but he diverted their awkward attacks with his own precise use of magic. Then he was among them, and their powers offered little protection from the magic-wrought Aelvin steel of his sword.

They fell like leaves from a tree, their dark clothes billowing as they dropped to the forest floor. It all seemed to happen at half speed, and Jeran felt a strange sense of tranquility as he reaped his crop of death. That he had to kill disturbed him, but knowing that each man he sent to the Nothing here might save dozens of innocents—and more importantly, dozens of his people—outweighed his distaste for killing a hundredfold.

Soon, only the Elf remained of the Gifted. A handful of Human soldiers still lived, but most sought escape in the thick trees. Goshen hunted them; Jeran sensed the *Tsha'ma* stalking his prey, enjoying the hunt.

"You can never win, child," the Elf said. Despite the carnage around him, he seemed in no way unnerved, and his confidence bothered Jeran. The Elf shone with the power of the Gift, unfocused but ready to use in an instant.

"I appear to have accounted for myself quite well today," Jeran replied. He, too, readied magic, and he adjusted his grip on the sword.

"Against children and barbarians," the Elf replied. "In twenty winters, three of them might have made passable use of their Gift. And the Wildmen? Who among the Gifted cannot deal with a handful of savages?"

He's stalling for time. Why? Jeran cast out his perceptions, but felt nothing, only the fading presences of the men Goshen hunted. "You speak poorly of your allies," Jeran said. "Lorthas preaches unity among the Races. He would be displeased with your disloyalty."

"The *Kohrnodra* no longer serve that caged fool, if we ever did. The Father of Chaos has chosen a disciple. It is He we serve, and He cares only of destruction. Once this world has descended into the Nothing, He will exalt us above all others."

As Jeran bantered with the Elf, his perceptions whirled around the clearing, searching for any threats he might have missed. He saw nothing. Heard nothing. Nothing came to his senses in any way. And then the impression of nothing moved behind him, edging its way closer to him.

"Assassins!" Jeran yelled. He dove to the side, but too late to completely avoid the arrow that streaked from the shadows. It tore through his clothes, piercing his side along the ribs.

Another arrow launched toward his scarred Human ally, but Jeran's warning had come early enough. He blocked the shaft with his Gift, then started toward the trees at a run, clearing a path through the vegetation with magic even as his sword pulled back for an attack.

As soon as the *Noedra Synissti* attacked, the Aelvin Mage loosed his Gift. Off guard and in pain, Jeran barely deflected the magical assault. He rolled to his feet and ran forward, opening himself to magic, drawing it to him until he felt like it would burst out even as he tried not to use it.

Terror at the sheer volume of magic Jeran wielded entered the Elf's eyes, but his skill far exceeded Jeran's, and the finesse he used countered Jeran's power. They traded attacks for a time, some violent enough to char the clearing and lay waste to the trees around it. Other attacks showed no outward effects, but would have been just as destructive had they hit their mark.

In the end, it was steel that won the day. With every attack, Jeran edged his way closer to the Elf, who out of foolishness or stubborn arrogance refused to yield ground. Once within striking range, Jeran's sword flashed out. The Elf smiled when Jeran attacked, and he unleashed a violent torrent of magic.

Jeran countered it with a weave of his own magic, though the effort of wielding his Gift and his blade nearly felled him. The sword cut deep into the Elf, and the shock sent his magic wild. Flames and lightning crackled around him until the very air itself seemed on fire.

Jeran severed the Elf's connection to magic and watched as his body toppled to the ground. He followed it down, his knees hitting the hard-packed earth with enough force to send a jolt of pain up his spine. He gasped for air, and wondered if he would ever find his breath again.

"He didn't do bad," his Human instructor said.

"Too much talk," Goshen replied.

"It never hurts to get a little information from your enemies before you kill them."

"You think he hurt?"

"He's bleeding a bit, but if those two scratches are all the wounds he took today, then I think we've done a pretty good job."

"We help him up?"

Silence dominated for a moment. "No. He needs to reflect on what he's learned. He can find his own way back to camp. Let's go share a cup of *baqhat* while we wait for him."

Jeran sensed magic being used, and then he was alone.

CHAPTER 18

"What are they waiting for?" Martyn demanded, slamming his fist against the table and interrupting Lisandaer's report on the Tachan army. "Summer nears its end. New Kaper is in turmoil. They certainly know the condition of our garrison! It makes no sense!"

They sat around a broad rectangular table in a chamber once used to receive foreign dignitaries but which Aryn Odara had commandeered as his war room. Maps of Kaper in varying size and detail covered the ornate, hand-carved benches lining the walls; a detailed sketch of the river around the Great Bridge lay spread out on the table, with small colored markers showing troop strength and position: blue for Alrendrian, red for Tachan. Yesterday, Aryn had been forced to order another case of red markers.

"They fear to attack," Jaem said. Miriam's cousin sat straight-backed in his chair and looked upon the other members of the council as if he were King of Gilead, and not just kin. "We have repulsed every attack with ease, and with virtually no casualties. They hope to starve us out, no doubt, or cow us into surrender with their numbers."

Martyn despised the man, but his wife adored the insufferable lout, so he forced a smile. "They have not suffered much in the way of casualties either, just a few hundred boys and toothless men. They may seek to test our resolve, or frighten our people with reminders of their presence, but they have yet to make a serious attempt for Kaper."

"All the more reason for us to take the attack to them," Jaem stated. "A raid by river in the dead of night. Strike and run. Put the fear of the Gods into them."

"And risk what few troops we have?" Lisandaer snapped. As Guard Commander of the city, he had invested a great deal of time into recruiting and training the young Guardsmen protecting Kaper, not to mention the militias supporting the true soldiers. "I thought we stopped talk of such nonsense days ago!"

"It is always wise to keep your enemies off guard," Jaem retorted. "The last thing they expect is an attack. One strike will put them on the defensive."

"Perhaps Lord Douphan's idea deserves some consideration," Dayfid said. As usual, the Guardsman looked uncomfortable in the war room, surrounded as he was by his superiors, but as a veteran of the Corsan campaign and the battle of Vela, he shared with Martyn a unique insight into their enemy. "The Tachans can storm the city, or they can starve us out, but the result either way is the same, only the timing changes. If we take the fight to them—"

"Attack them how?" Bystral demanded. "The river poses as much a barrier to us as them. If we attempt to cross, their Magi can—"

"You'd rather wait for their Magi to cross the Celaan and do the work on land?" Jaem snapped. The Gilean nobleman stood, his chair grating against the floor as it slid back.

"No," the Guard Commander replied. "If we have any chance of winning, it's here in Kaper, behind the defenses we've spent seasons preparing, not—"

"Cower behind your walls, then!" Jaem glowered. "Once the Tachans have finished with my people, they'll turn their army west. What chance will Kaper have when it faces a foe with no river to cross?"

"Is that what this is about, Gilean?" Lisandaer snorted. "You want us to hurry up here so we can help your people in Gilead? We—"

"That is enough." Aryn spoke quietly, but his words carried unquestionable authority. "We will not be attacking across the river. The Tachans will be among us before long; there is no need to take battle to them."

"Lord Odara, if you would but listen to reason—"

"Our enemy has not attacked because they believe such a move pointless. Cut off from our allies, with their agents in the city, no doubt they hope to court rebellion and take the city without much loss of life. Their plan almost worked. The rioting lasted three days, and several vital stockpiles were destroyed in the process. Restoring the peace cost us dearly in men, supplies, and morale."

"If that's true, then what has changed?" Dayfid asked, shaking his head. "Why expect an attack now, when for two seasons we've done nothing but stare at each other across the river?"

"Because Harvest is approaching," Aryn said. "The Tachans may wish to save their troops to fight our more experienced forces in the eastern and western arenas, but they can't afford to quarter men around Kaper through the winter without taking the New City."

"Why bother with this place at all," Jaem muttered. "It serves them no purpose."

"The capture of Kaper would serve little strategic purpose," Aryn agreed, "but it would be a symbolic victory from which I suspect we would not recover. The seat of Alrendrian government, the focal point of our efforts at unity… If Kaper falls, then so does our alliance, and with it, our chances for victory."

"So what are our orders?" Bystral asked.

"Continue to bolster our defenses. Be ready to begin the withdrawal to Old Kaper as soon as the enemy breaches the bridge defenses. Keep an eye on their formations across the river, though. A raid might be foolish, but if they keep sending squads off to forage, it might be wise to put Jaem's plan into action. If we can—"

"Might I make a suggestion, Commander Odara?"

"Of course, Martyn."

"To this point, we have ignored one of our greatest military assets. The Aelvin embassy includes a fair number of *Ael Chatorra*. Their style of fighting is well suited to the defense of Kaper. Might I suggest that we incorporate the Aelvin warriors into our army? Perhaps work them in as irregular squads among the Guardsmen?"

Aryn frowned, and his eyes took on a distant glaze. "I doubt the Elves would be willing to follow the orders of a Human. We couldn't afford to have them acting on their own."

"The Elves realize that their lives are in jeopardy as well," Martyn replied. "I have brought up the matter with Prince Treloran. He says his troops will follow you, provided that an Elf is given a rank equal to your subcommanders."

"An Elf? Equal in rank to the City and Castle Commanders?" Dayfid exclaimed. "That's a—"

"Reasonable request," Aryn interrupted. "Does Prince Treloran have someone in mind?"

"No doubt he covets the position for himself," Dayfid muttered.

"He has suggested a warrior named Palatinae," Martyn replied, casting a warning glance at the outspoken Guardsman. "Treloran believes the man will be more amenable to taking orders from Humans than most *Ael Chatorra*, and the rest of the Aelvin warriors will take orders from him without question."

"I will consider the matter," Aryn said. "Would you have Prince Treloran arrange for me to meet with this Palatinae?" Aryn stood abruptly, and Martyn noticed that the Guard Commander clenched his hands on the edge of the table as if afraid of falling. "You have your orders. We will all meet here again in two days. If anything changes across the river, I expect to hear of it immediately."

The others filed from the room, until only Martyn remained with Aryn. "Is all well, Commander Odara?" he asked. He still worried over the man's sanity, though when talk of war abounded, Aryn offered little sign of instability.

Aryn shook himself as if waking from a dream. "Just a headache. They've been coming more frequently of late. I suspect it's lack of sleep."

"I could ask Mage Sheriza to attend you," Martyn said. "It would be ill advised for our Guard Commander to start this battle in compromised health."

"No!" Aryn stunned Martyn with the harshness of his tone. He calmed himself quickly, though. "My apologies, Prince Martyn. My time in Dranakohr gave me a healthy disinterest in the workings of magic. But I should have this problem looked into, and I would be grateful for your Mage's advice."

"I will send her to you," Martyn said. As the door closed behind him, he noted that Aryn had not yet released his death grip on the table.

The halls of Kaper bustled with activity, but there was a hushed urgency to every action. The servants sweeping dust from the halls pressed themselves against the walls as Martyn passed, resuming their work in his wake. The messengers shot past without seeming to notice his presence. The Guardsmen—many of whom he had known all his life—refused to return his warm greetings. Instead, they stood at rigid attention or saluted him fist-on-heart. *I am no longer their little prince. No longer their foster son. I am now Prince of Alrendria.* Part of him missed the easy camaraderie he had once shared with the soldiers.

He saw Kaeille in the distance, carrying a tray of steaming vegetables smothered in a spicy sauce that must be destined for Miriam's chambers. She smiled when she saw him, but he caught a sadness in her eyes.

"What's the matter?" he asked, hurrying to her.

"Nothing," she answered. "I must take this to the princess."

"Let a servant take it," Martyn said. "I haven't seen you in days. I must summon Sheriza, but then I have some time. We could share a meal, maybe—"

"Not today, my love," Kaeille interrupted. "I have other duties."

"Miriam? Surely she wouldn't begrudge you a single afternoon. I know she's come to rely on your—"

"It is not the princess to whom I am obligated today," Kaeille said. "I am meeting with Jaenaryn."

"Jaenaryn?" Martyn laughed. "Why would you want to meet with that old windbag?"

"I..." Kaeille stopped when she saw the laughter in Martyn's eyes. "It is of no consequence. I would not bore you with details."

She turned away, but Martyn caught her arm. His amusement fled. "Wait. Tell me what troubles you."

"It is nothing you can help with. Miriam's condition reminds me what I have given up to bond myself to you, and I seek solace in Valia's arms. I seek Jaenaryn in his role as priest, not ambassador."

"What you have given up?" Martyn repeated, confused. Understanding dawned, and he wrapped an arm around Kaeille's narrow hips. "You mean the child? We will have our own. I promise you! It's just a matter of time." A broad smile spread across the prince's face. "In fact, if you're so concerned, we could work at it some now."

The sadness returned to Kaeille's expression. "You do not understand, Martyn. The children of the Twins, Balan and Garun, are close enough in blood that offspring from their unions are common, but Valia did not get along well with her brothers, and the blood of her people does not so easily mesh with those of the other Gods. Elf and Human unions, which of themselves are few, rarely produce children, and those who are conceived often carry the weakest traits of both Races."

"That but means we must try harder," Martyn said, "and with greater enthusiasm!" His attempt at light-heartedness failed, and he pulled Kaeille into a side chamber, where he set aside her tray and enfolded her in his arms.

"Seeing Miriam's joy every time she touches the child growing in her belly reminds me of what I will be denied," Kaeille told him. "I seek the Goddess's wisdom, and her solace."

"I didn't know our union would cause you such pain." Martyn touched her cheek, wiping away the first tear to fall. "I will release you from your oath to me, if it will make you happier."

Kaeille shoved him away. "You don't understand anything! It is not that I will be denied children. I will be in the prime of life for centuries after you have left me. I will not be able to have *your* children, you fool! I will watch your children with Miriam grow, and their children after them, down through the generations, but without any direct bond of my own to you."

Action and consequence, and the consequences rarely to his liking. Despite their increasing frequency, situations like this one still frustrated him and left him at a loss for words.

"We'll figure something out," he said. "Perhaps the Goddess will bless our union, and we will be one of the few trusted with a child."

His words seemed to console Kaeille somewhat. She wiped the tears from her face and retrieved the tray. "I must take this to Miriam before it cools. I have no plans for the evening meal, if you wish to dine with me."

Martyn offered her a smile. "I look forward to it."

Kaeille left, but for some time Martyn remained in the antechamber, relishing the silence and sorting through his own thoughts. He had never considered the long term effects of his actions in Illendrylla, never thought much beyond his and Kaeille's immediate happiness. Now he wondered if he had done the Aelvin woman a grave disservice, saddling her to a foreign throne and forcing her to share his love with another woman, a woman who could bear his children and take his name.

He wondered if his short-sighted outlook had blinded him to other things, especially in regards to the situation in Kaper. The Tachans tightened their grip on Alrendria's throat with every passing day, yet up until now, Martyn had been content to sit and wait, watching while each day brought greater numbers to his enemies' army and thanking the Gods that they survived to see another sunset.

Perhaps Jaem is right. Maybe we should find a way to take the attack to them. But how?

In the end, he realized they had not done more because they could not. The very defenses protecting them from the Tachans also protected the Tachans from them. Attack over the river was suicide, and the last thing they needed was to throw away lives in a fruitless assault just to satisfy the misgivings of a fool.

But I will keep an open mind to the possibility. And look for ways to exploit our enemies' weaknesses.

Outside the chamber, servants and Guardsmen hustled through the halls. The first to spot him all but shoved him through the halls, leading Martyn to a dimly-lit chamber on the south side of the palace grounds. Bystral waited inside, and the impatience fled from his face when the prince was ushered inside.

"That took long enough," the Guard Commander said under his breath. "I've had half the garrison looking for you, and the servants besides."

"What's happened?" Martyn demanded. "Have the Tachans attacked? Why are we here—?"

"It's not that bad," Bystral said, unbolting the door on the southern wall, "but it could get worse if the wrong people happen upon him. He told me to be quick and discreet, and I get the impression that he no longer has the patience he once did. Come along if you don't mind, Prince Martyn."

"Who?"

"Lord Odara."

Martyn had to jog to keep up with the burly Guardsman's long strides. "Why would Aryn—"

"Not that Lord Odara," Bystral said, keeping his voice low.

Jeran. He's finally come. Elation and a wild sense of hope filled Martyn's chest, but it quickly subsided. *But if he's answering my summons, then why the secrecy. Something's not right.*

Bystral took him to a well house, an oft unused building on the back side of the palace, a relic from an era long past. Jeran had been fascinated with the place as a child. Martyn had never shared his friend's interest in watching chilled water flow from the fountain, or staring into the depths of the clear pool surrounding the fountain's feet, but he found this place fitting for a clandestine meeting with Jeran.

A Gate stood open on the far side of the fountain, offering a glimpse of a silent city. The buildings looked pristine and untouched, but no people hurried down the streets, and the only sound Martyn heard from the far side was the shrill shriek of a hunting bird.

Five men stood to one side of the Gate: a young Human with hard eyes and a thin beard Martyn suspected he wore to hide his cherubic face, and four stout, grey-skinned creatures he knew to be Orog only because he had met Jeran's friend Grendor. The tallest of the Orog barely reached Martyn's shoulder, but the shortest was half again as broad as the prince, and each carried a staff with a curved blade upon one end. All five wore black uniforms with an Odaran wolf stitched on the breast.

Jeran stood on the opposite side of the Gate. He did not wear the black uniform; his clothes looked decidedly more worn and far less conspicuous. A half-healed scar ran the length of his right arm, and a haunting sadness that Martyn had only ever seen in two others—Emperor Alwellyn and his father—filled his eyes. *What has happened to him?*

"Jeran! Thank the Gods you've come."

A fleeting smile perked the edges of Jeran's mouth. "It's good to see you too, Martyn. I examined the city while we were waiting. Your preparations have been thorough, though I suspect from the fortifications that you don't expect to hold the new city once the Tachans take the bridge."

"Your uncle is the architect of those changes," Martyn said with a dismissive wave. "But that doesn't matter anymore. With the aid you'll be bringing, we'll be able to—"

"I have no aid to send," Jeran interrupted. "At least not the kind you desire. By summer's end I can supply you with small stocks of arms and armor. If necessary, we will be able to supply grain shipments by midwinter. But the city... You will have to hold Kaper on your own for the time being."

"We've sent repeated requests for troops!" Martyn snapped. "You are duty-bound to provide them. You may not officially be First of Odara, but you hold the title in practice, if not in name, and I expect you to honor the obligations that go with the position."

Jeran's calm grin stood in stark contrast to Martyn's anger. "Your dispatches asked for soldiers and Magi; I have neither. If you had asked for children and trainees, I could provide an army."

"You know what we face and what we need. Your habit of interpreting words to suit your own purposes is best used on others."

"I understand your frustration," Jeran said, and his unflappable composure stirred Martyn's flaring emotions even more. "But I will not throw my people into the fire like twigs. When they might make a difference, they will come. So long as they will provide nothing more than additional targets for our enemies, they will not. I will not let Kaper fall."

Martyn spotted something in Jeran's eyes. "Unless?"

Jeran nodded as if conceding a point. "Unless it is in Alrendria's best interest for it to do so."

"You would let us all die...?"

"If it would preserve Alrendria and what it stands for, yes. Those obligations you mentioned a moment ago demand no less of me."

Martyn schooled his features and drew a calming breath. While such displays of temper rarely troubled him, for some reason he felt as if the simple act of getting angry somehow gave Jeran an edge in their discussion. "If you have no troops for me, then why are you here?"

"You have delegations from the other Houses," Jeran replied, "and, I presume, from the Mage Assembly. I thought it only prudent to send my own representatives to your court. That way, we can improve our communications and minimize any misunderstandings that may result from false information or bad assumptions."

Jeran gestured toward the bearded youth, who stepped forward and bowed. "This is Ehvan Myaklos, of Feldar, and formerly Commander of Dranakohr. He will now serve as my liaison to you."

Martyn studied the youth, whose impassive expression could not hide the disappointment in his eyes. "He does not appear to relish the assignment."

Jeran laughed, but it was a dry sound, lacking in humor. "He was not told to enjoy his post, just to serve where he was most needed. He has my complete trust, and he should have yours. Anything you tell him will reach me without embellishment."

Ehvan's features perked up at Jeran's praise, but only marginally. "And the Orog?" Martyn asked. "What purpose do they serve?"

"They are here as Ehvan's guard, but they may find their Truthsense a useful tool. I have advised them to assist you as they may." Jeran started toward the Gate. "I will send a few others to join Ehvan when they are ready. As for the troops you demand... I offer no timetable, but I promise that I will not stand idly by while Kaper falls."

"Jeran..."

"Mika is coming," Jeran told him. "And Konasi too. I do not wish to argue with the boy, and if he sees me, he will demand I take him with me. As for Konasi... No doubt he will demand that I submit myself to the Assembly for judgment. We both know how steadfast he is in his convictions. I don't wish to kill him, especially here, where it will do you more harm than it will do me. Best if I leave before he arrives." Jeran stepped through the Gate.

"Jeran," Martyn called out, taking a step forward. "Wait!"

Jeran turned around and faced the prince. "Yes?"

Martyn hesitated. *How do I ask him what I need to ask?* "How... How is Dahr?"

"The last I saw of him, he was furious. For Dahr, I suppose that means he was fine." Jeran stared at Martyn, his eyes, fueled by the power of the Gift, boring into the prince's soul. "What do you really want to ask me?"

"The uniforms... The disobedience to your King's orders... It has been suggested that you have your own agenda...."

"I see that you've spoken to Valkov. No doubt the High Wizard hopes to drive a wedge between us, so that when he offers the Assembly's aid, you will be more amenable to his one condition: that you denounce me as a Darklord."

He had more than one condition! The thought struck Martyn as an odd defense, despite the fact that it proved Jeran could still be wrong about some things. "Are you raising an army?" he asked, no longer trying to keep a rein on his emotions. "Do you intend to take Alrendria for yourself?"

Jeran laughed again. This time it was a heartfelt sound, one that rumbled up from deep within his gut. "I don't want the responsibilities I have. Why do you think I'd want yours too?"

With that, the Gate closed, leaving Martyn alone with Jeran's embassy.

CHAPTER 19

"They come," Frodel said, crouching beside Dahr. A hot wind blew from the north, sending ripples across the parched grass but offering no respite. "Greater numbers than expected. We should delay attack. Gather more warriors."

Dahr looked up, severing his connection to the Lesser Voices. They showed him what Frodel had seen with his own eyes, a force of *Kohr'adjin* nearly three times larger than anticipated and marching with the discipline of an organized army. He fixed the Tribesman with a scalding glare. "Those do not sound like the words of a Hunter."

Frodel grimaced, his jaw clenching under the weight of the insult. Yet it was Vyrina who grabbed Dahr's jaw and wrenched it around so that his eyes were on her. "They sound like the words of a soldier," she said through clenched teeth, "and a wise one at that. We should signal a retreat and call in more forces."

Dahr slapped her hand away. "I don't like your tone, Guardsman."

"You no longer have authority over me, and I couldn't care less about you being Garun's Chosen One. All I care about is running a successful campaign against our enemies. You seem more interested in personally leading them to the Nothing."

Her sharp tone dug at his control, but Dahr had weathered far worse from the Guardswoman over the last few ten-days. "They don't expect us," he said, his voice low. "They believe they're on the attack."

"Dahr speaks the truth, friend Vyrina," Grendor said. The Orog sat cross-legged in the grass, his *va'dasheran* balanced on his lap. The serenity expressed on the unblemished side of his face contrasted with the grotesque scars opposite. "No rabbit is more vulnerable than the one who thinks himself a lion."

Some of the Tribesmen chuckled at the Orog's words, a low rumble that barely carried beyond the clearing. "He claims he's no warrior," Grondellan said, elbowing a lanky Tribesman in the side, "but he speaks like one. And only men accustomed to battle wait for one so peacefully."

Vyrina turned her gaze, almost imploring, on Katya.

After a long pause, Katya said, "I say fight." She brushed dust onto her leather mail, dimming the sheen of the black armor with the soil of the land. "Dahr hasn't led us into a battle yet that we couldn't win."

"No, but he seeks longer odds with every attempt."

"I seek our enemy," Dahr growled. "They choose their numbers. I only choose where to build their funeral pyre."

"Enough!" Frodel snapped. "We fight. I speak... I spoke out of turn."

Dahr waved off the apology. "Speak your heart as you will. I want no fawning fools at my side. Just be sure to aim your spear where I say, and we will have no problems." He studied the landscape again through Shyrock's eyes. "Their path will bring them almost straight to us. When they crest that hill," Dahr pointed to a broad, grass-covered slope less than half a league distant, "the sun will fall in their faces. We should attack then."

Frodel barked hushed orders to a handful of Tribesmen at the periphery of their makeshift camp. The Hunters disappeared, moving as silently as shadows. Frodel and Vyrina went east to gather their own forces and get into position.

Dahr intended to meet his foe face to face, and he positioned himself at the center of the proposed battlefield. He made it no more than a dozen steps before a ring of Hunters formed around him. The Vahr Drekka had sworn themselves to the *Korahn* with a devotion that outshone even the commitment of the Channa, and their Hunters, under the supervision of Tarouk, had assumed the role of his personal protectors.

Their coddling presence infuriated Dahr, but a lifetime of battle against the other tribes made them unmatched fighters, and their unquestioning devotion to him made them useful tools, so he tolerated them despite the stirrings of gnawing anger they caused.

Grendor and Grondellan flanked him, but Katya raced ahead, leaving no trail as she picked a path through the waist-high grass. Fang remained at the tents, as did Jardelle, but Shyrock circled above, watching for unexpected movement and keeping Dahr apprised of his enemy's position. The other voices remained quiet, and Dahr urged them to stay away. This was a fight for men; he would not sacrifice them in so insignificant a battle.

They crouched at the top of the hill, and time crept along with the rapidity of a lame tortoise. Dahr had to restrain himself from charging forward, screaming a battlecry. *I am on the hunt. A good hunter waits for his prey.*

A sudden rustling drew his attention, and he shifted his gaze in time to see the grasses part and a Tribesman appear. From the surprise that flashed across his face, the gaunt and haggard scout had not expected to stumble across a raiding party. He opened his mouth to shout an alarm, but only a gurgle emerged as his body slumped forward.

Katya wiped her blade on the Tribesman's clothes, then signaled for them to ready themselves. Dahr drew his greatsword and crept upward until he saw the high point of the hill illuminated in the sun. A narrow game trail snaked between Dahr's Hunters and those under the command of Frodel. Here they waited again, until the column of *Kohr'adjin* topped the rise and started the descent into the neighboring depression.

"Now!" Dahr shouted as he exploded from concealment. His sword drove into the heart of a Tribesman before the enemy even acknowledged the attack. His troops were slower, but only by an instant, and their sudden appearance sent a ripple of confusion down the ranks of the enemy.

Shouts arose from the far side of hill, and Dahr knew that other squads of his forces were harassing the main body of the enemy, slowing their response until they dealt with the vanguard. The *Kohr'adjin* were disciplined, but Dahr had learned that their commanders preferred to travel at the head of their armies. Eliminating them left the mass of warriors without proper leadership, and under pressure they degenerated into a Blood Rage, where they became easier targets for his more regimented troops.

A *Kohr'adjin* lunged for him, but Grendor was there before Dahr could react, stabbing the Hunter in the gut and carving a deep cleft in his abdomen with the curved blade of his *va'dasheran*. Grondellan fought at the Orog's side, axe in one hand and short blade in the other. Sweat pooled on the Rachannan's face, slicking his hair and beard, but he fought as a man possessed, rivaling the Garun'ah in ferocity. Of Katya he saw nothing except the occasional shadow at the edge of his vision, the sudden flash of steel as her sword sliced through the air.

Surprise wore off quickly, but not before Dahr's forces decimated the enemy front. He topped the hill, and stood stunned when he saw the mass of enemy still arrayed against him. The estimates he had made through Shyrock were short by at least a third, the force arrayed against him still considerable. *Frodel was right*, he thought, though a dissenting voice within snarled at the admission. *I never should have engaged in this battle.*

"Plant it here," Dahr shouted, stabbing the point of his sword into the ground. An instant later, two Vahr Drekka raced forward and drove the shaft of his banner into the ground. The Alrendrian Sun rose to command the field, snapping in the brisk wind, and the razor-backed cat leapt into battle.

"I am *Cho Korahn Garun*," Dahr shouted, his voice booming over the din of battle. "I am salvation and destruction. Lay down your arms and I will bring you back to the Blood. Oppose me and I will lead you to the Nothing."

A roar arose from the *Kohr'adjin*, and their struggles grew more frenzied. Dahr had expected as much. They no longer served Garun; a new God held them in thrall. But the offer often stirred them to recklessness, and Dahr needed them as disorganized as possible if he hoped to win the field.

He ran down the hill and into the mass of screaming bodies. The *Vahr Drekka* followed at his heels like obedient beasts, and they engaged the enemy—many of whom were their kinsmen—with a ferocity unrivaled among Dahr's allies. Their charge drove deep into the *Kohr'adjin*, and Dahr instinctively sought the thickest battle. His sword flashed red in the fading light, and he reveled in the thrill of honest battle.

A spear thrust cut a line of fire across Dahr's shoulder. He pivoted, and his answering blow drove through his attacker. It took a massive pull to wrench the blade free, and the effort left him momentarily vulnerable. He braced to receive another attack, but his forces pushed past him in the interim, driving the *Kohr'adjin* before him and leaving Dahr in relative safety.

Howling at the indignity of being left behind, Dahr leapt forward, shoving aside his own men in his desperation to resume the battle. They accepted his manhandling with their customary stoicism—from another Tribesman, his actions would be taken as a grave insult; but Dahr was *Cho Korahn Garun*, and he had done worse upon occasion.

He sensed his enemies' resolve buckling, and Dahr pressed his assault, but more to enjoy every instant of battle than to hasten their surrender. Seeking out the stiffest resistance, he threw himself into the enemy, battering them to submission with the ferocity of his determination.

Dahr muttered a curse when the three *Kohr'adjin* in front of him threw down their spears and dropped to their knees in surrender, and cursed again when the others fled, routed by the combined might of the Tribes. He savored battle, but victory always brought the sour aftertaste of reality.

He had lost nearly a third of those who had followed him on this raid. Too many to make the outcome seem a win. His enemy's numbers seemed limitless, and his forces grew far too infrequently. *I must choose my battles more carefully.*

Still, they killed far more men than they lost, including most of the enemy's commanders, and defeated a force nearly four times their number. By any army's standards, this was a great triumph. *Then why does it feel so hollow? Why doesn't my heart sing now, as it did during the fight?*

Grondellan and Grendor approached. The Rachannan struggled to hide a limp, but blood soaked a cloth hastily tied around his thigh. He laughed off the pain and clapped Dahr on the shoulder. "Another success! And against even greater numbers. You never cease to surprise me."

"We didn't deserve this win," Dahr said. "The *Kohr'adjin* were sloppy. Where's Frodel? Gather my commanders."

As several Tribesmen ran off to carry out Dahr's orders, Tarouk appeared. "How handle prisoners?"

Dahr looked at the mass of Tribesmen on its knees, more than had been captured in his last five battles. "The same as always. Have each man vow to renounce Kohr and serve the *Korahn*. If their desire to return to the Blood is genuine, Grendor will know it; if not, then this place is as good as any for them to meet their God."

Tarouk frowned—slaughtering men did not sit well with him, even men who would immediately take up a spear against him again if set free—but he had fought against the *Kohr'adjin* long enough to know that the alternatives would lead to more death among his own. And he had fought with Dahr long enough to know not to argue about such matters. He led Grendor to the prisoners, so the Orog would take their confessions and judge them redeemed or condemned.

Dahr studied his troops while waiting for his commanders to trickle in from the field. More had fallen than he expected, and too many of the survivors nursed wounds, though one might not realize it if watching the Tribesmen. The Garun'ah refused to acknowledge pain in battle until they returned to the tents, and more than a few had died because they refused to admit to their injuries. *I need the Tsha'ma. They are no Healers, but their skill is considerable.*

"Where's Frodel?" he demanded, scanning the crowd for the Tribesman. "We need to get word to Rannarik. I—"

"Dahr."

Blood and grime smeared Katya's face, except beneath her eyes, where matching lines had been washed clean. *Has she been crying?* Dahr wondered, though he dismissed the thought as absurd. Regardless, a pain she sought to hide as desperately as the Tribesmen sought to hide their wounds, made him want to comfort her.

He extended a hand to cup her cheek, yearning to feel the soft touch of her skin, but when he realized what he was doing, he yanked it away. She did not react. "I have no time for you," Dahr said. "I am looking for Frodel."

"Then follow me." Her voice carried less heat than ice, which Dahr had long since realized meant she wanted to hide her feelings. He followed her, holding back his questions more because he knew she would not respond than because he already knew the answer.

Frodel lay in blood-stained grass among trampled wildflowers. The broken haft of a spear protruded from his chest, and his sightless eyes stared skyward. Five *Kohr'adjin* had fallen around him, one still clutching at the *dolchek* embedded in his throat. Vyrina huddled over his body, clutching at his shirt and occasionally reaching up to stroke his cheek.

When she saw Dahr, her tears receded, frozen no doubt by the iciness of her gaze. "You did this," she said, her voice as feral as any Tribesman's. "You killed him."

Somewhere deep inside, Dahr grieved. He could sense it, a sadness over the loss of an ally, but he could not access it, could not bring it to the surface to show the world that he shared the Guardswoman's pain. He felt numb, distant, detached from everything around him. Even the Lesser Voices were muted. "He died a Hunter's death," Dahr mumbled. "That's how he would have preferred to die."

"He would have preferred to live!" Vyrina shouted. She launched herself at Dahr, but Katya restrained her. They struggled for a moment, then Vyrina collapsed, sobbing in Katya's arms. "He would have preferred to live."

Dahr knew he should say something, that a good person would make an effort. "He was my friend, and I—"

"Your friend? You knew nothing about him! How many brothers did he have? What did he want from life? Do you even know what Tribe he was from? Your friend!"—she spat the word at Dahr. "To you he was a tool. An extra arm. An extra sword. The same as the rest of us. Do you even remember what friendship is, Dahr?"

"Hush," Katya said, leading Vyrina away. She glared at Dahr, warning him to keep a rein on his temper or he would have to deal with hers.

But Dahr felt no anger, which surprised him as much as it would have surprised Katya. The beast within slumbered, satiated with the feast of blood it had received. He yearned for a drink, for the numbing fire of *baqhat* to offer excuse for his lack of feeling. He turned to a group of young Hunters laughing at their victory. "Build a pyre," he said. "We have fallen to honor."

He stood in silence while his people built a funerary mound atop the hill and began to lay out the bodies of the fallen. They raised a separate mound some distance away for the *Kohr'adjin*, but constructed it with little of the reverence reserved for true Garun'ah.

Dahr waved away the Tribesmen who came to claim Frodel's body. He retrieved the Hunter's *dolchek* and returned it to its sheath, then carried the body to the pyre and set it atop the others. At his signal, the bodies were set aflame, and he watched as a column of smoke rose, carrying the souls of the fallen to the Twilight World.

He stepped back only as much as required to keep from charring his clothes and listened to the haunting dirge sung by the Tribesmen. He did not understand many of the words, but something in the song spoke to him about an end of suffering as reward for a life well lived, and about sorrow for those left behind to continue the struggle. He wondered who would sing to him when he lay upon the pyre, and what rewards the Twilight World might hold for a creature such as him.

Once the bodies were consumed, he gave the order to return to the tents. He did not speak during the travels, and ignored anyone who approached him.

Cheers greeted his arrival in the tents. Young girls ran out to hang circles of flowers around his head and the heads of his Hunters. Boys shouted his name, and hunched-over Tribesmen clinging to a thread of life poked their heads out of tents to welcome him home. He was praised as an *Uht'radar*—a Hunt leader—honored as *Kranach*, and revered as the *Korahn*.

Even the animosity shown to the Vahr Drekka was forgotten during Dahr's return. Generally, the simple presence of Vahr Drekka among the tents of the other Tribes forced the Garun'ah to stone-faced silence. A few times fights had broken out, and Dahr had been forced to order them subdued. But today, as with all of his homecomings, the Vahr Drekka were tolerated. They would continue to be until sunset, at which time the other Tribes would slowly force them back to their own section of camp, a collection of threadbare tents separated by several thousand hands from the main site.

The size of that camp astounded Dahr, and worried him. Every day saw a steady trickle of refugees—mostly women and youngsters, but with a handful of Hunters as well—flow to their tents. Now that word of a sanctuary was spreading, all those unwilling to swear themselves to Kohr the Destroyer sought out the *Korahn* and asked for a place among his people.

How can I refuse them? But what do I do with them? How long before the peace I have declared is broken?

He heard mocking laughter in his heart, and a voice he tried to ignore. *They are spears and axes, nothing more. Kill Kohr'adjin or kill each other, and there will still be blood.*

He paused at a pool of cool water and let the attendants sponge the dust and grime from his body with damp rags. The ministrations still made him feel awkward, the press of gentle hands—mostly girls approaching womanhood—brought a flush to his face, but he had accepted that this was no special treatment for the *Korahn*. All returning warriors had their bodies washed and wounds treated by the tribe.

"Another victory against long odds. You are to be honored, *Korahn*."

Yarchik's gravelly voice jarred Dahr from his musings, and his eyes snapped open. "This one was costly," he said.

"They usually are, especially when the fight is sought more than the victory," the ailing Tribesman said, drawing Dahr's gaze. Yarchik noted the look and smiled. "I have not seen such hate directed at me in a long time. Not even from my son."

Mention of Kraltir brought a surge of bile to Dahr's throat and set his heart to pounding, but he forced his features to smooth. "It is not hatred I feel for you, Yarchik. I just don't understand why you saddled me with this burden, when you know I long for nothing more than isolation."

Yarchik signaled, and his palanquin bearers lowered him to the ground. "You think I named you for your own sake, and that is the fount from which confusion springs. You are my friend, Dahr, dearer to me than my own son, but I am *Kranor* of the Channa before I am your friend. It is for my people that I named you *Kranach*. It is for the Blood that I acknowledged you as *Cho Korahn Garun*."

"And do you know what you have wreaked upon the Tribes? Does your *Prah'phetia* tell you what will become of us now?" Dahr could not hide the contempt from his voice. Garun's prophecy had tugged him from one end of Madryn to the other, but it only revealed itself after the fact. It never told him what to do until he had already committed to a course of action.

"The *Korahn* will save the Blood, or He will obliterate it," Yarchik said, as he had many times before. "But I will share a secret with you, Dahr. The path the Blood had chosen for itself led to destruction already, a wasting illness sucking the life from the Children of Garun, not unlike the way age wrings the life from my old bones. The *Prah'phetia* offers two fates: salvation or glorious destruction. Whichever path you lead us down, it is a better one than the one we walked before."

"That's a fine consolation," Dahr muttered, biting back the acid in his voice.

Yarchik laughed. "We can debate the finer points of the *Prah'phetia* tomorrow, if you would like, but I did not come here to lecture. I came to congratulate you on another victory, and to thank you for bringing the Orog to us."

"The Orog?"

"Yes, that boy carries a wealth of stories, and a wisdom beyond his winters. He and I have shared many discussions, and his insights have proven remarkable. He has eased the burdens of my final days, and you are the one who brought him to me." Yarchik stared at Dahr, his cloudy eyes piercing into the soul. "I will leave you to the celebration," he said at last, "but we will meet at sunrise. There is much I must teach my *Kranach*, and little time. So little time."

Yarchik waved, and his bearers raised the palanquin and trundled off into the crowd. As the sounds of music and singing rose around him, Dahr shrugged off the hands seeking to oil his flesh and sought his tent. He had no stomach for celebration. The victory tasted sour.

A jug of *baqhat* waited for him. He tugged out the cork and downed the liquid, savoring the warmth that flowed from throat to gut. The half-filled jug did not quench his thirst, but he had another unopened beside his pallet. He sat, taking long draughts from the new jug and staring at the canvas of his tent. The shadows of dancing Tribesmen moved on the walls, silhouetted in the evening sun, and Dahr sought to remember a time when he had felt such joy for life.

She entered without a sound, but her scent filled Dahr's nose, and her mere presence comforted him in a way that surprised him as much as it infuriated him. "Today's battle was a mistake," Katya said, letting the tent flap fall behind her. "The odds were too much against us. I should have sided with Frodel and cautioned against fighting."

"I am the only one here responsible for his death. For all their deaths. For this, your conscience is clean."

"I won't do it again," she said, more forcefully. "I won't let you lead men into battle just to satiate your own bloodlust. Next time, I'll stop you."

"Then you're a better leader than I. Perhaps you should be *Korahn*."

"Why are you doing this?" Anger flared in Katya's voice, the passionate temper that had drawn Dahr to her from the start. He stood, turning so he could see the color flush her cheeks, watch the pulse at her neck pound in time with her heart. "There are many—many whom you know—who suffered far worse than you. Why are you the one sprinting toward the Nothing?"

"What kindness has the world shown me?" Dahr demanded, his own temper flaring to match hers. "Slavery. Abandonment. Everything I cared for has been taken from me; everyone I loved has betrayed me. Martyn. You. Jeran… All that remains is responsibility, and that is heaped upon me like dirt on a grave. Why should I care?

"Why?" Katya stormed toward him, grabbing his shirt in her fists and shoving him backward despite the advantage in size he held over her. "Because you are a good man, Dahr. Because you deserve a happy life. Hate me, if you must. Gods know I earned it. Hate Jeran, too, for all I care. But don't hate life. There's always reason to live, even if we can't see it. I believe that, else I'd be long dead by now."

"Hate you?" Dahr said, intoxicated by more than *baqhat*. His own laughter mocked him. "Don't you realize that's my punishment? I want to hate you. I try to hate you! But you fill my thoughts and haunt my dreams. I can no more be rid of you than I can be rid of my heart."

"And that bothers you?" She tried to step away, but Dahr grabbed her hands and held her close.

"It torments me. But if my fate is to be saddled with duties I don't want, then yours will be to suffer at my side. I can't deny my heart, but I can make it share my misery."

As he pulled her to him, the hint of a smile cracked his stony face.

CHAPTER 20

Dahr woke to bright sunlight in a field of wildflowers, but the eerie silence of the Lesser Voices told him he awoke in the Twilight World. Squeezing his eyes shut, he felt around for his jug of *baqhat*, eager for that first sip to quiet his thoughts and ease the pounding in his head. When his hand met nothing but earth, he sought sleep, hoping slumber would return him to the waking world and save him from his headache.

The feel of eyes upon him kept sleep at bay, and he sat up, expecting Lorthas's icy presence. But instead of the Darklord, he found himself facing Frodel. The Tribesman's flesh was whole; his clothes showed no signs of the grisly wounds he had sustained. Dark eyes fastened on Dahr, but they held no accusation, no enmity. Dahr resented that. *I cost the man his life! Why doesn't he have the decency to hate me for it?*

"Since you can no longer hound me during the day, you seek to haunt me at night?" Dahr asked, stretching his arms high above his head, hoping his show of nonchalance was a convincing one.

"Did you expect my soul to go to the Nothing?" Frodel replied. "This is my home now. You are the intruder."

A frown pulled at Dahr's lips, and he studied the Tribesman. "I would leave if I could. I do not mean to disturb your rest."

Frodel's laughter was not mocking, but it dug at Dahr nonetheless. "You may not intend my rest to break, just as you did not intend me to die, but you are not a leaf tossed in the wind. It offends Garun that you believe yourself held beyond choice."

Dahr bristled at the comment. "What do you—?"

"The Hunter offers guidance. He expects respect. But He does not require obedience. You are free to stay, or go. You may save the Blood, or destroy it. Garun has given you the tools you need to restore the Balance, but He has left to you the method of that restoration."

Dahr paced before Frodel like a wild dog. "Guidance? I may not be a leaf in the wind, but I am no more than a worm to Garun, blind and lost, and expected to decide the fate of a Race on my own. That is not a fate I would curse my worst enemy with!"

"You are not alone, except that you refuse to listen. Garun—"

"What guides have the Gods offered me besides suffering and loss? Potent advice those two offer, but not generally in favor of saving anything, let alone an entire people."

The stirrings of anger flashed across Frodel's face, and he lunged forward. Despite his smaller frame and stature, he was able to restrain Dahr easily. "Self pity annoys Garun. It infuriates me. We are all given hardships to endure. How we deal with the aftermath is as important as how we deal with the obstacles themselves. Persevere or give up, but do not survive just so you can lament your survival."

He released Dahr and stepped back, but the power of his gaze held Dahr in thrall. "As to guides, you have them aplenty. Garun has given you the whole of nature to be your eyes and ears, and the Gods have provided for you in other ways as well. They gave you Katya to warm your heart, and Grendor to soothe your soul; Lord Grondellan to share your spirit, and Jeran's calculating dispassion to counter the fire in your blood. And now Garun sends me. But if the whole of the world stood behind you offering advice, I suspect you would swear you stood alone. You are a coward."

"A coward!" Frodel's accusation restored Dahr's ability to move, and he hurled himself toward the Tribesman. "How dare you say such a thing. We've fought side by side. You know I don't run from a fight."

"You seek to embrace death," Frodel said, easily sidestepping Dahr's mindless attack. "You seek release in the death of others, hoping all the time to find a noble death for yourself. But there is no nobility in battle unless you fight for a great purpose. Garun will not let you die a hero when you live like a craven."

"I will not listen to such—"

A roar echoed through the Twilight World. Dahr straightened and scanned the horizon, but saw nothing in the tall grasses. Another roar, closer than the last, shook the ground upon which he stood, and crashing footfalls moved closer.

"We must go," Dahr said. As the pounding drew nearer, he felt the life drain out of him, and a third roar, this one sounding of hunger, sent him scuttling backward.

But Frodel did not follow. The Hunter drew his *dolchek* and crouched, ready to pounce. "You cannot run from this, Dahr. If you want battle, then embrace your fear, for there is no greater opponent."

When the grasses to the north started to shudder and move, Dahr bolted, running as fast as his legs would carry him. His pounding heart drove out all other sounds, and the acrid taste of desperation poisoned his mouth. When his foot became tangled in the clinging grass, he thought himself captured, and he screamed as he tumbled toward the ground.

He bolted upright on his pallet, gasping for air and feeling the oily sweat clinging to his body in the cool morning air. Katya slumbered beside him, and he watched her, using the calm, steady rhythm of her breathing to still his racing heart. He found solace in the smoothness of her flesh, the spread of coppery curls arrayed about her head. *How can I still love her? How can she still love me? I keep her here only to torment her, to make her watch as I fall.*

He rose and dressed, taking only a single draught of *baqhat* before switching to cold water, leaving his greatsword in its sheath by the pallet. With only a *dolchek* to protect him from the hordes of Tribesmen who considered him a demigod, he strode into the camp.

Eyes followed him as he walked the gaps between the tents. He did not relish the attention, but he no longer discouraged it; all of his previous attempts had failed, and most had earned him more fervent worship from Tribesmen who thought him unconvinced by their devotion to the *Korahn*.

Fang joined him, loping at his side. The hound remained silent in his thoughts, but Dahr appreciated her presence. For some reason, the Tribesmen were more respectful—or at least more hesitant to bother him—when they remembered he was *Tier'sorahn* in addition to *Cho Korahn Garun*. Dahr reached down to scratch Fang's head, and she lolled out her tongue, panting a friendly welcome.

The smell of roasting meat filled the air, and of breakfast porridges and simmering stews. The day's hunting parties would already be long on the trail, as would the scouts Dahr demanded scour the countryside for signs of *Kohr'adjin*. Those they encountered thus far had been few and not well organized, but Dahr knew the bulk of the enemy still waited in the north, and that their military skill matched the most disciplined Guard squads. He needed to provide his own soldiers as much training as possible before the major battles began, and winnowing away at the enemy beat endless days parading around a practice field.

Today, most of his Hunters did practice in the fields, marching in formation, sparring in rings, or practicing techniques of meditation taught by Grendor. The Orog's training helped them control the Blood Rage, to harness the raw emotion that bubbled so close to the surface of the Blood. Dahr had expected little in the way of results—the Garun'ah prided themselves on their wild tempers—but once again the Orog surprised him. Though Dahr predicted that only a handful of Hunters would consent to the training, most of them prodded by *Tsha'ma*, Tribesmen by the score had flocked to Grendor from the start. When they reported success at controlling their tempers, hundreds more demanded his teaching.

He offered to show me his people's ways for seasons, and I have refused. Is it pride or ignorance that controls my soul? I should seek him out. What harm could come from it? At worst, I will be no different than I am now.

Another voice interrupted, though it sounded much like his own. *Mind games and breathing tricks will not make you Human. Stop running. Embrace your emotions and they will lead you where you need to go.*

Dahr wondered which commander had assumed Frodel's role and was surprised to see Vyrina at the head of the field, barking out orders in Garu, her voice cracking like a whip. Deep rings circled the Guardswoman's eyes, and her disheveled clothes and matted hair spoke of a restless slumber, but she stood straight-backed and imposing, and hid her pain behind a facade of command.

"Korahn?"

Dahr turned and found a robed figure behind him, head ducked low and hood drawn down to hide her features. She walked stooped to mask her height and hobbled slightly to mimic the movements of an aged one. If she carried a weapon, it was well hidden beneath the folds of her cloak. "Why do you come to me disguised, Meila?"

"It only way enter tents of tribes, *Korahn*, and you refuse come to mine."

"I do not refuse. I... I just don't have much time."

"However you see it, things must discuss. If you not come to Vahr Drekka, I come you. Risk attack in camp of brethren."

"I've told the *Kranora* that your people are not to be harmed."

"And *Kranora* not harm. But they not see everywhere, not control all. Two cubs taught yesterday price entering camps of... *real* Garun'ah. It take three *Tsha'ma* to guarantee they survive."

"I can't be everywhere either! So I'm not sure why you expect more of me than you do of them."

"I not." Anger tinged Meila's voice as well, but it did not enter her eyes. "That not reason I seek you out. Vahr Drekka know must earn respect other tribes. We have long walked in darkness."

"Then is it about food? I know you send out your own hunting parties, but I've told the others to share their supplies with your people."

"They share," Meila said, her lip quirking up in a wry smile. "They bring four rabbits and two squirrel before sundown."

"For all of you?" Frustration welled up in Dahr. *They claim I am their Korahn, but they only listen to what they want to hear!* "I will speak with them again—"

"I also not come discuss food."

"If this is another lecture about how I need to spend more time among your people—"

"I not come to discuss Vahr Drekka."

Dahr stopped walking and turned to face the priestess. He stared into her eyes, those dark, depthless pools that made him so uncomfortable. "Then why are you here?"

"It is said..." Meila hesitated, an uncommon show of uncertainty in the Tribeswoman. "It is said you speak with Fallen One in dreams. That he not turn your blood to ice. That you speak your mind to him and he not destroy you for it."

Does the whole world know I commune with the Darklord? The Garun'ah had some peculiar notions about Lorthas and his powers, and Dahr had not realized his meetings in the Twilight World had become common gossip. He wondered if that explained in part their strange behavior. "The Darklord speaks to me at times, when I can't avoid him."

"Then you must take him a message."

The hair on the back of Dahr's neck prickled, and his hand crept toward the *dolchek* at his side. Meila caught the motion, and stepped back. "I no Servant of the Fallen," she said, her voice resounding with conviction and affront. It was enough to stall Dahr's attack. "You must take him warning, the next time he seek you out."

Dahr folded his arms across his chest. "And what would you have me tell him?"

"That his hound off leash. Stories told by those from camps of *Kohr'adjin*. They sing the Fallen's song, but they dance to tune of *Sal'aqran*. Disciple of Kohr."

Sal'aqran. Scorpion. "You're sure of this?"

"I not ask you speak with Fallen One if I not. His path frightens me, but his vision pure. Dominion by *Kohr'adjin* leads only to Nothing."

Dahr said nothing for a time. He studied the camp, taking note of all the eyes on him. He wondered if they knew he spoke with a Vahr Drekka, or if their stares were just for the *Korahn*. "I will tell him, but I cannot seek him out. I will have to wait for him to find me."

A slight smile spread across Meila's face. "Since we here, maybe now time to ask again about joining council. Vahr Drekka deserve—"

Dahr laughed aloud, but it was a humorless sound. "You might as well ask a pack of wolves to share a meal with a *tigran*, or tell the sun to share the midday sky with the moon. So long as you are Drekka, the Blood will not welcome you back."

Anger flashed across Meila's face again, but it disappeared as quickly as it arrived. She squeezed his arm in a friendly manner. "*Danko, Korahn.*" Without a word of explanation, she turned and headed toward the tents of the Vahr Drekka, leaving Dahr staring after her in confusion.

Dahr visited the training grounds, stopping briefly to talk to Vyrina about Frodel's replacement. The Guardswoman kept her responses short and professional, but Dahr sensed seething emotion boiling beneath her outwardly calm surface. She recommended Olin, Kal's *chanda*, and Inesko, a Hunter from one of the smaller Tribes. Dahr wanted to say more, but did not know what would comfort her, and he doubted she wanted comfort from him in any case, so he left her to her duties.

He stopped by the tents housing the wounded, thanking them and bidding them to speed their recoveries so they could rejoin the fight. He circled the grain supplies and the smokehouses where stoop-shouldered Tribeswomen cured the game brought back from the hunts. He wandered without purpose, letting his body follow a path to match the turmoil in his mind, full of activity but lacking direction.

Quiet sobbing caught Dahr's ears, and against his will he was drawn to it. He found a cub, a boy no more than twelve winters, sitting in the shadow of a tent, a brown and grey striped cat curled in his lap.

When the boy saw Dahr, he choked back his tears and put on a mask of stoicism. "What's the matter?" Dahr asked, seeking to keep the edge from his voice.

At first, the child said nothing, and Dahr knelt, extending his hand toward the
cat. "There is something wrong with her, but no one believes me," the boy said as
Dahr ran a hand along the cat's flank. The child spoke with a hint of accent, an odd
but familiar sound Dahr could not quite place.

"I believe you," Dahr said, reaching out to the creature with his mind. He
sensed fear, and a strong bond to the child, but mostly he felt pain emanating from
the soft tissue below her shoulder.

"How old is your cat?" Dahr asked, lightly touching the mass growing beneath the flesh, feeling the heat as it grew to consume her body.

"I do not know," the boy answered. "I have had her all my life."

Dahr pressed his lips together. *You know?*

I know, came the reply, a silken sound that purred through his mind. *This is the
way of things. I have had my time.*

*Do I continue the lie his elders told to spare his feelings? Or do I spare him a greater
pain later and tell him the truth?*

"I know she is dying," the boy said suddenly. "My parents do not think I
know, but I do. But they did not believe me when I said Sieta had told me, and they
banished Naera back to her tents when she said Sieta spoke to her too. They called
her a witch, and a Child of Darkness. She does not deserve those names."

Sieta? Dahr wondered, and the cat sniffed.

I welcome you home, Cho Korahn Garun, the cat's voice whispered in his head.
She twisted her neck to look at Fang, who sat some distance back and made a show
of paying no attention. *Though I wonder at the company you choose to keep.*

Despite himself, Dahr laughed, but then the full weight of the child's words
dawned on him. "You said she told you? You spoke to her? You can hear her!"

"Yes," the boy said, nervous in the face of Dahr's growing excitement. "She
told me we had to find the First, the one who returned the gift of the Lesser Voices
to the Blood. She said she did not have much time, but that he was close, and she
could lead me to him. Are you *Tier'sorahn?*"

"I am." He no longer said it with reluctance. Of all the things he was, *Tier'sorahn*
was the only thing of which he could be proud. "But why seek me out?"

He needs to learn.

"And I am to teach him?" Dahr laughed again, but this time without amusement. "What knowledge I have could barely fill a cup."

*Yet that is an ocean compared to his understanding. All he knows is that he can speak
to his pet, a friend he has had his entire life. How many winters passed before you realized
the truth? How many before you gained a measure of control, even an unconscious one?
Your story is known to us, Korahn. The Hunter may leave the fate of his people in your
hands, but we demand that our voices be heard again, and that the Balance be maintained.*

More responsibility, now not just for the fate of a Race, but for the whole of
nature. Yet Dahr wondered how different his life might have been if he had known
what he was sooner, if he had been able to consciously commune with the Lesser
Voices during his youth. Even if he did not want the duty, he could not abandon
another to a lifetime of loneliness, of strangeness in a world of normalcy.

"I am *Tier'sorahn,*" he said again, fixing his gaze on the boy, "and so are you."

The child's eyes widened. "Me?" he said, but there was excitement where
Dahr had half expected dread. "You really think so?"

Dahr noted again the oddness in the way he spoke, an exaggeration in the way
his mouth formed the words. "I do. And you spoke of another? Where is she?"

"Naera? My parents banished her back to her tents. She is Vahr Drekka, and I am not to speak with her again. They say she is a monster, but she could hear Sieta too."

"I will find her," Dahr promised. "And anyone else who can hear the Lesser Voices. I will teach you what I can, little though it may be. Would you like that?"

"I would, *Korahn*. When can we begin?"

Dahr smiled. "I will need to speak with your parents first. Have them seek me out among the tents."

"Yes, *Korahn*. I will tell them now." The boy stood, cradling the ailing cat in his arms and starting toward the tents. "You were right, Sieta. He is not as scary as they say. And he knew right away where your pain—"

"What is your name, boy?" Dahr called after him.

"I am Tazahn, son of Keshik, of the Jalandi Tribe."

"You speak Human well for one so young, Tazahn."

The boy stopped and turned to face Dahr, his brow drawn down in confusion. "I do not speak Human, *Korahn*."

Dahr considered the strangeness of the boy's speech, and now realized that the voice he heard so clearly was in his mind, like the Lesser Voices'. *He speaks in Garu, but I hear in Human.* He directed a gaze on Sieta. *And you claim I understand what I am?*

You will learn. And you will teach. And our voices will be heard again.

After they left, Dahr noted the position of the sun and hurried toward the center of camp, where the *Kranora* gathered to discuss the fate of the Garun'ah. He found the meeting already underway, the speaking circle held by a grim-faced warrior from the Iahni Tribe. The others listened in silence—Arik, with his bear cloak strapped to his shoulder but the cowl down; Yarchik, reclining on his palanquin and working to hide his labored breathing; Crestan, of the Lhenapi, with hair as black as the eyes he directed at Dahr; Gresh, of the Charoke and Dag of the Turape, both expressionless and unreadable. Dozens of others surrounded the speaking circle, most of whom Dahr had never met, but three tribes Dahr desperately wanted to see were not represented.

Sadarak of the Afelda and Bysk of the Sahna were not present, and the absence of those large tribes was felt. Dahr had sent runners to both, with the hope of bringing them into his army, but he had yet to receive a response. Nor were the Vahr Drekka allowed to send a representative, in part because they had yet to choose a *Kranor*, and in part because they were not wanted. Dahr had pled for their inclusion, but in the speaking circle, he was a *Kranach*, and his demands carried little weight.

A handful of *Tsha'ma* advisors completed the assembly, hovering near their respective *Kranora* and occasionally whispering in their ears. Dahr noted the dark glares cast across the ring, the suspicious glances and calculating looks. Necessity had driven the tribes together, but centuries of blood feuds and mistrust could not be erased overnight.

Dahr listened for what seemed an eternity, waiting as one after another of the *Kranora* stepped into the circle to speak his piece, feeling his calm turn to impatience, and then to frustration. He welcomed Olin's appearance, and signaled for the Tribesman to join him.

"You stand like a *tigran* ready to pounce, *Korahn*," Olin smiled. He wore no shirt and only a modest covering around his loins, his well-muscled frame tanned and oiled. The man took pride in his body, and did not fear showing it off.

"I need a new second," Dahr whispered. "I would have it be you."

Olin nodded as if he had expected the request, but he said, "I thought you would name your Drekkan shadow your second."

"If I thought the other tribes would listen to him, I might. Tarouk will lead the Vahr Drekka, but I need someone to command the rest of our Hunters. Will you do it?"

Olin studied him as a man might study a wild horse he wanted to ride but was afraid might throw him. "Why me, *Korahn*?"

"You think me weak for living in captivity as long as I did, and you make no effort to hide it, even now that I have been named *Korahn*. Despite that, you've been willing to fight beside me for the good of the Blood. I know you to be a valiant warrior, and I know you will not shirk your duty. At the same time, you will not hesitate to tell me when you think me a fool. I need no sycophant as my second; I need men who will not hesitate to challenge me if they believe me wrong, but who fight to the last when commanded to."

"Do you know yet where you lead us, *Korahn*?"

"My second calls me Dahr."

Olin ran a hand along his angular chin. "I have no desire to lead my people to the Nothing. Is that where you intend to take us?"

"I have no destination planned," Dahr said. "I tread the path forced upon me, and if that trail leads me to the Nothing, then so be it. I seek neither destruction nor glory. I seek freedom for all."

Olin's gaze dug into Dahr's soul, and he struggled not to squirm under the Tribesman's intense gaze. "A blind hunt is a greater risk to the hunter than the prey, but I can accept your answer, Dahr. I will be your second."

"Our scouts should return tomorrow. If they have found more *Kohr'adjin*, then we must be ready—"

"What is that?" Olin interrupted, pointing toward the speaking circle.

The circle stood empty, recently abandoned by Dag *uvan* Dourak, but a mass of darkness appeared at its center, swirling in a tightening circle. As it coalesced, it exploded outward, and an all-too-familiar form stood before them.

"Salos..." Dahr growled, his hand reflexively going for his *dolchek*.

The Scorpion's eyes sought him out, and a cold smile spread on his lips, pulling the skin taut over the bones of his skull. "I cannot rid myself of you, or your friend. No matter where I go, no matter how far across Madryn I flee, there you are. One might begin to suspect the Gods test my patience."

Dahr snarled and started forward, but Rannarik appeared at his side, restraining him. "Save your anger for another time," the *Tsha'ma* said. "He is not here. It is a spirit picture he sends."

"He can do that?" Dahr asked. "Just appear at will wherever and whenever he wants?"

"No," Rannarik replied, a worried expression overtaking his face. "This is more a skill of *Tsha'ma* than Mage, and one must know well the location one projects to. There is at least one among us who serves this demon, and that is troublesome."

Troublesome? We have traitors among us, and Gifted ones at that. The Garun'ah have a knack for understatement. "Then what do we do?"

"We listen to what he says," Rannarik said, turning to face Salos.

Salos spun in a slow circle, taking in the assembly. Then he began to speak in Garu, the hard and guttural language sounding odd in his soft, sibilant voice. Dahr understood few of the words, and he turned to Olin for a translation.

"He says he is *Cho'na Kohr*, the Chosen One of Kohr, and that the Father has commanded him to reach out to the creations of his children, who have strayed from His will. He says this world has grown decadent, and the Father demands it be purified in fire and blood.

"He offers the tribes one chance to renounce Garun. If we swear ourselves to the Father and help him cleanse Madryn of the taint infecting it, we will be honored among His children."

Again Salos's dark eyes sought Dahr's. The Scorpion's gaze made him feel as if creatures crawled across his flesh, but Dahr refused to show his fear. He stiffened his back to hide the trembling, and a growl rose in his throat. He started forward again, and this time it took both Rannarik and Olin to hold him back.

"He says the time of decision is upon us," Olin continued in a low voice, his grip so tight Dahr had to grit his teeth together to endure it. "He says his children come, *Aqan Sal'aqran* from the north and *Synat Sal'aqran* from the south. When they arrive, he will close his fist"—with that, Salos closed his hand in a dramatic gesture—"and the Blood will flow to the earth."

"What are those names?" Dahr asked. He kept his eyes on Salos, but the Scorpion no longer seemed to notice him.

"*Aqan Sal'aqran*. The Claws of the Scorpion," Rannarik said. He had not yet released his grip on Dahr, but his eyes scanned the vicinity. "*Synat Sal'aqran*. The Scorpion's Sting."

Dahr opened his mouth to ask Rannarik about the names, but Salos concluded his speech with a dramatic flourish, and the skies erupted in flame. "Watch out!" Dahr yelled, knocking Rannarik to the ground as a fiery rock the size of a melon smashed into the ground where they stood.

Dozens of such stones fell to earth, setting alight whatever they touched. Screams arose from the tents, and Hunters raced to control the flames while panicked children sought their parents in a chaotic mass. Fire swept across the grain stores and concentrated in the most populous areas of the camp. Their placement was no accident.

The storm of stone only lasted a moment, but in the confusion, Salos vanished. Dahr took the opportunity to enter the ring of *Kranora*, though he was careful not to stand in the speaking circle. "Something must be done!" he shouted, drawing the eyes of the *Kranora*.

"And what you have us do, pup?" asked a scarred and aging Tribesman. "Strike at shadows? Fight ghosts and demons? I say leave. Scatter to winds."

"That will just delay your destruction," Dahr snapped. "If you want to defeat the *Kohr'adjin*, then we must strike now, before they mass their forces. No more waiting. No more debate. If the Sahna, Afelda and other tribes wish to join us, they can do so in the field."

"You speak out of place," the old *Kranor* growled. "While Yarchik breathes, he commands the Channa."

"In there," Dahr said, pointing toward the speaking circle, "I am *Kranach* of the Channa. But I speak now as *Cho Korahn Garun*, and I command you all. We have traitors in our midst, and enemies closing in from north and south. Are we now prey, waiting for the slaughter? We must take the fight to the *Kohr'adjin*, and teach them what it means to defy the will of the Hunter."

"And what if they number like stars in sky?" asked another *Kranor*. "What if we not able to win?"

"Then we will die," Dahr said, his voice calm. "But we will die restoring the Balance, and the Gods will honor us for our sacrifice." He wished he meant his words, but they sounded hollow even as he spoke them. He had no true faith remaining. Vengeance was what Dahr wanted, vengeance and an enemy upon which he could unleash the beast within.

"In a hail of fire shall He rise," Yarchik said, "and demand the Blood fulfill their purpose. And His enemies shall fall before Him like rain. And His allies shall be washed away like sands upon the shore. Praise unto the *Korahn*, for His coming spells our redemption. Praise unto the *Korahn*, though His coming spells our doom."

CHAPTER 21

Tendrils of steam rose from the river, coating Kaper in an oppressive blanket of moist air. Few clouds hovered overhead, but those that did were dark, foreboding in their intent. A stale breeze gusted irregularly from the north, bringing the stench of summerweed to the city.

Makan's Market remained silent despite the bright daylight. Most of the shopkeepers refused to open their doors or had closed up altogether, and the hawkers sought refuge closer to the old city, where their carts were not as often commandeered by soldiers seeking to bolster the defensive lines. Those few commoners who walked the streets moved with hurried steps, refusing to make eye contact with the militiamen standing watch at the intersections. A pall of desperation gripped the city, a tension at the prospect of battle, long expected and never realized.

"Something will happen today," Martyn said, his voice low, "I can feel it." The prince leaned against the wall at the end of an alley, his one bodyguard pacing at the junction with the main street. "Are your people ready?"

"As ready as we can be to face something without knowing what it might be," Lelani said. The former High Wizard wore a grey cloak and kept to the shadows. Though drawing the hood over her head would look suspicious in the late summer heat, she toyed with it anyway, as if considering the risks. "We will do what we can, but my primary goal is to protect my people, and that means keeping them hidden from the Assembly."

"And where do you propose to hide them once Kaper falls?" Martyn's tone grew sharp. "There's only one place I can think of. Have you swallowed enough pride to beg Jeran for his protection?"

Lelani's eyes flashed, but she held her tongue. Robbed of her title, she had also lost much of her spirit. The arrogance which had marked her last visit to Kaper swirled beneath the surface, but she no longer had the will to use it.

"We will do the best we can, Prince Martyn," Lelani said, sounding meek.

"That is all I ask. If the Tachans take the bridge, we do not intend to hold the new city. Lisandaer will signal the retreat and we'll move behind the protection of the Wall. I do not expect heroics from you, but you will need to offset whatever tricks the ShadowMagi use as we fall back."

In truth, a good portion of Kaper's residents had already evacuated to Old Kaper. Official policy had called for anyone with useable skills to move behind the Wall in advance of the enemy, but in recent days the rigorous strictures had been lifted and anyone seeking refuge had been granted entry. Old Kaper already seemed crowded; Martyn wondered how they would cram in everyone else when the time came.

"That is a wise precaution. The magical nature of the Wall will protect you from many of the... tricks... the Gifted can muster. You have our support. As much as we can provide."

"Good." Martyn walked toward the front of the alley, smoothing the wrinkles from his shirt.

"Is all well, my Prince?" asked the bodyguard, a dour Guardsman from the Family Habasi, in southern House Batai.

Martyn patted his breeches. "Just took a bit of time. Nerves, I suppose. What with the Tachans massing and all."

"I understand, Sir. You were just in there for a while, and I..."

"You didn't want to be the Guardsman who lost the prince on the day of the big battle," Martyn laughed. "It's a reasonable concern. My father would have been most displeased."

They returned to the main defensive line, a makeshift wall of brick and wood constructed around the square of Makan's Market. All of the roads out of the market save the southernmost had been blockaded, as had many of the streets throughout New Kaper. A clear path to the old city was available, but it required extensive familiarity with the city or one of a handful of maps drawn by Aryn Odara to navigate it properly.

Guardsmen formed the first line of defense, their polished armor and calmness in the face of a far greater enemy standing in stark contrast to the nervous, undisciplined movements of the militia, who surrounded the market as auxiliary troops but who would be instrumental in maintaining order if the retreat were signaled. High towers had been constructed atop buildings on either side of the market to offer views over the Celaan. It was to the western tower that Martyn went, dogged by his bodyguard, now returned to its normal strength of twenty able-bodied Guardsmen.

Atop the building, Treloran and a contingent of Aelvin archers waited alongside Ehvan and his Orog guards. Four Guardsmen stood in the watch tower, calling down movements across the river, but the bulk of the enemy line—made up of a mixture of Tachans, Corsans, and traitors from House Morrena—was visible from the edge of the roof and easily viewed through any of the dozen spyglasses resting on a rack beside the tower.

Aryn Odara stood off to one side, arguing with a man Martyn did not recognize until he turned and his hawk-like nose stood out in profile. The prince sucked in a breath, and High Wizard Valkov turned at the sound.

"Prince Martyn, I was just asking about you," the Mage said, his voice dispassionate, his eyes calculating. "I wondered if you intended to wait out the battle in the castle, and was asking your Guard Commander where I might find you."

"I do not hide from my enemies," Martyn answered, "nor would I choose to stand aside while an enemy as vile as the Tachans and their ShadowMagi tore Alrendria apart."

"Indeed?" The thinly-veiled insult had no effect on the Mage other than an amused quirking of the lips. "I had no idea you were such a valuable commodity. Another Prince Abele of House Calonia in the making, to force back the rising tide with nothing but a spade and bucket?"

"My people need to know their prince fights beside them." Martyn said. "It bolsters morale."

"I'm sure it does," Valkov sneered. "I wonder if you have any word of my missing Magi?" Martyn's breath caught, but he fought to show no outward reaction. "No? Odd. Reports have placed them in Kaper, and I would have thought

Lelani certain to seek you out, if for no other reason than to give her Assembly-in-Exile some legitimacy."

"I assure you, High Wizard, if I knew where your Magi were, I'd be sure to tell you."

One of Ehvan's Orog turned at that and stared at Martyn in a way that made his heart pound as if he had just run the length of Kaper in full battle gear. The *choupik* said nothing, though, and turned away again when Valkov fixed a harsh gaze in his direction.

"I also see that you have welcomed an embassy from Jeran. Does this mean I should recall Konasi and my other agents to Atol Domiar?"

Other agents? I should have expected as much, so why does it come as such a surprise? Martyn looked around in an exaggerated way. "I see no Gifted here, no armies. A delegation was sent from the north, and I deemed it wise to welcome it, if for no other reason than to keep from angering the man you claim is the gravest threat to the sanctity of Madryn. If you think it unwise to keep them here, under my eye, then I will tell them to go, and no doubt Jeran will place others in Kaper without my knowledge. What should I do, High Wizard? I beg your advice in this matter."

Valkov made no effort to hide his displeasure at seeing the Orog, but his thin grin grew in the face of Martyn's words. "By all means, keep them. We wouldn't want Odara's people running rampant through the city, sowing discord and inciting riots. Why, such a thing could put Kaper on the brink, and you might be forced to seek aid from just about anyone to restore order."

The implication was clear, but Martyn did not take the bait. "Are you here to offer the aid of the Assembly, High Wizard?"

"I am here to offer it again," Valkov said, his arms spread wide in disingenuous supplication. "I have hundreds of Magi ready to turn back the shadow threatening to engulf Kaper, to offer their lives in defense of Alrendria and freedom. All you have to do in return is a trifle in comparison."

"Jeran has committed no crime. If he does, my father will denounce him. Until he does, he remains a loyal citizen of Alrendria."

Valkov heaved an exaggerated sigh. "It grieves me to see such stubbornness. I hope, for your sake, that it does not cost Alrendria too dearly." A Gate opened beside him, and the High Wizard stepped through.

"An insufferable man," Aryn said once the High Wizard disappeared. "Another few moments with him, and I'd have started longing for the peaceful days in Tylor's Trophy Room."

"He wants me to—" Martyn lost his voice when he looked across the rooftop. "Is that my father?"

King Mathis strode across the roof, drawing the eyes of all who saw him. His hair and beard had been neatly trimmed, his armor polished until it gleamed. The sword at his hip bore the sigil of House Batai on a hilt beset with jewels. He walked oddly, like a sailor long from the sea who took to ship again, familiar with the movements of the deck and yet uncomfortable with them. His hand kept gliding to the hilt of his sword, then retracting, and he called out greetings, calling soldiers by name whenever he struck upon one he knew.

"What's he doing here?" Martyn exclaimed. "He should be back in the castle."

"His people need to know their King fights beside them," Aryn chuckled. "It boosts morale."

Martyn scowled. "Do not use my own words against me, Lord Odara."

"But one's own words are often the most effective ones," Aryn replied. "Excuse me, my Prince. I must see to the preparations."

Aryn left Martyn to join a group of subcommanders gathered in the shadow of the tower, and Martyn moved to join Ehvan at the building's edge. "Will he be coming today?" Martyn asked. It was his standard greeting to Ehvan.

The black-uniformed soldier gave his usual response. "Lord Odara will not let Kaper fall."

Martyn snorted. "I was hoping he wouldn't let any of it fall."

"The world is in chaos, Prince Martyn, and you want the impossible. Do you want an army to turn back the Tachans, or a herd of cattle to lead to slaughter?"

"I don't want my people to die."

"The men you so desperately want to come and die for you are your people. Perhaps if you remember that, it would make their absence less painful."

This was the standard rhythm of their dance; Martyn expressed disappointment, and Ehvan reminded him that Jeran's people were Alrendrian. *Except that they aren't, exactly. Not any more.*

"Why do you defend him so?" Martyn hoped the unanticipated question might trick Ehvan into revealing something. "How does he command such loyalty?"

"He makes us believe we are fighting for ourselves. You, and others like you, make men feel like they are fighting for you. The cause may be no less noble, but it is a lot more personal. That makes a difference."

The answer struck a chord, and Martyn fell into a grim silence, watching the distant horizon and the shifting mass of Tachan troops. For a time, he lost himself in their movements, the dance of soldiers and the twinkling of sunlight off arms and armor. It seemed not the prelude to battle, but a military parade without the music, a swirling mass of marching men, colorful banners, and superb horsemanship.

A violent explosion shook the building. Martyn whirled around and saw a great column of black smoke rising from a nearby warehouse. In rapid succession, several more tendrils of black rose to the sky, and the sounds of shouting men and clashing weaponry echoed down the streets.

The Guardsmen below stirred, but after quick reassurance from their commanders, they resumed their watch on the river. The militiamen showed less discipline, and as the sounds of battle grew fiercer behind them, as the black smoke rose to engulf Kaper in a blanket of choking night, they began to lose formation. Some individuals fell back to see what was taking place or to determine if the problem was near their homes; sometimes entire squads started marching out of the market, presumably to investigate the situation.

Aryn's booming voice echoed down to the streets. "Hold your posts! Hold your posts, or by the Five Gods, I'll come down there and throw the lot of you in the river. Asahn, get down there and make those fools stand their ground. Lonel, find out what's going on in the city. You, up there, get your eyes back on the Tachans!"

"It's coming," Martyn said. "That was the signal. The battle will begin now."

"How can you be sure?" Ehvan asked, but even as he asked it, the sound of a trumpet blasted over the Celaan, a single note, but ominous.

"Because that's how I would have done it," Martyn told him. "Find a way to draw as many troops away from the front as possible, and then launch an attack in the confusion. Lord Odara, 'ware the river!"

"Look at them all," said one young Guardsmen, a boy barely old enough to enlist. "How can we stop that?"

A sortie of soldiers started toward the bridge, moving forward in a tight cluster, shields interlocked and held high to ward off attacks by arrow. "They still have to cross the river, boy," Martyn heard a veteran say. "Half a hundred can hold that bridge for days."

To Martyn, the display was an unconvincing one, and his eyes were drawn to the men in clothes the color of darkest night that stepped out all along the enemy line. The very air around them danced with swirling shadows, and they made a slow progression to the edge of the river. "Commander!" he shouted, hurrying to Aryn's side.

The Guard Commander was listening to a breathless soldier. "—rioting all over the city. Small squads of fighters… Assassins shooting from rooftops… They kill anyone they find and set fire to any building of potential use to us. It's as if they know our every stockpile and cache."

"Lord Odara," Martyn said, grabbing Aryn's arm and hauling him away from the boy, "you must see this."

At Martyn's insistence, Aryn studied the ShadowMagi, his mouth drawn down in a frown that aged him a dozen winters. "I don't like this, Martyn."

"What do you—"

A frigid breeze blasted across the river, but it was fear, not the cold wind, that caused Martyn to shiver. "You don't think…" He found himself unable to voice his suspicions, and watched in awe as the ShadowMagi lifted their hands in unison and the late summer heat vanished. A numbing cold the like of which Kaper did not experience during the worst winter suffused the air, making men stamp their feet and watch in amazement as their breaths puffed out before them in small clouds.

Martyn turned his eyes on the thin sheet of ice that formed before the ShadowMagi and vanished again as the warm waters washed over it. Another layer formed and broke, and then a third, creeping across the Celaan. Great pieces broke off and drifted downriver, but more took their place, and the pace of its spread increased as the ShadowMagi robbed the heat from air and water.

Once wisps of ice reached the center of the river, another horn blast sent the soldiers arrayed along the bank marching forward. The river creaked and groaned under the weight of an army, but it held, and the Tachans began a slow, measured march into Kaper, the frozen river advancing before them like a demon's herald.

"Dear Gods…" Aryn whispered, his mask of composure slipping. For an instant, Martyn saw the face of a tortured man, a troubled and possibly insane man held captive by the Tachans for winters and subjected to only the Gods knew what punishments at the hands of ShadowMagi.

The mask came back quickly, and Aryn resumed command. "Signal the retreat!" he shouted. "Fire the docks and fall back to Old Kaper." He raced across the rooftop to where Mathis stared at the river slack-jawed, and after exchanging hurried words with the King, Aryn shoved him toward the stairs, trailed by a dozen or so Guardsmen.

The Guard Commander returned to Martyn's side. "There is no hope of holding the new city, my prince. You should join your father in leading the withdrawal. It would be unwise—"

Martyn bristled at the thought of abandoning his men. "I will not leave others to fight in my stead, Commander, and I thought you of all people—"

"I am the commander of this operation," Aryn snapped, his easy-going manner disappearing. His eyes grew bold and bright, his tone unswerving. Martyn had seen this transformation before, but had never been on the receiving end of Aryn's wrath. "By Alrendrian law, you are my subordinate in this matter and required to obey commands. I expect you to do so without question, or in our next operation you will be kept far from the front lines."

Martyn's jaw clenched to the point of pain, but he held his tongue. With a stiff salute, he turned, but Aryn's hand on his shoulder held him for a moment.

"There will be fighting aplenty during the retreat," Aryn told him. "From in front and behind. Duty requires me to stay here to ensure that nothing of use is left behind for the enemy, but I need someone reliable to secure the route to Old Kaper. There are few I trust anymore, but Jeran trusts you, and that is enough."

Though he said nothing in response, Martyn felt some of his anger dissipate. *Gods, he has a way of working a man's emotions. I wish I had half his skill at manipulation.* He shrugged off Aryn's hand, saluted again, and hurried toward the stairs, casting one last glance at the river, which had frozen nearly two-thirds of the way across.

His bodyguards followed him, as did Ehvan and the Orog. They emerged into Makan's Market amidst a mass of panicked shouting. Men, women, and children—those too stubborn to retreat toward the old city at Aryn's earlier request—fled from their homes or shops, lugging whatever valuables they could carry and casting terrified glances over their shoulders. The militia fared little better. Those at posts in view of the river watched the advance with horror, and those who could not see shouted for news, ignoring the cries of their commanding officers for quiet and order. Even the Guardsmen looked shaken by the display of magic, the near instantaneous negation of their primary defense.

Martyn was disappointed, but he could not blame them. With the exception of the handful of men who had served with him in Vela, none among his soldiers had fought in a battle against ShadowMagi before. And even though he had, the Gifted's ability to warp reality still unsettled him. *The only good to come of this is that such an effort must exhaust them. They plan on leaving the bulk of the battle to the fighting men, which might buy us some time.*

As if to belie his thoughts, balls of flame fell from the sky, exploding as they hit the ground, sending men and stone in all directions. The magical attack did not last long, but the militia broke under the first volley. Soon a steady stream forsook their posts and sprinted toward the assumed safety of Old Kaper. Their flight inspired others to acts of cowardice, and soon it appeared as if the Alrendrian line would break before the first Tachan set foot in Kaper.

"Guardsmen!" Martyn shouted to a squad of reserve pikemen stationed in an alley near the unblocked exit to the market. "Block the road. Any soldier abandoning his post before the appointed time is to be barred from leaving the square. Treat any soldier seeking to force a way past as the enemy. There is no room in Old Kaper for cowards and traitors!"

Martyn went with them, using his bodyguards and the odd mixture of fear and awe inspired by the Orog to convince the militiamen that possible death at the hands of the Tachans was preferable to certain death at the hands of their own countrymen. At first he thought they would be unable to stem the tide, that the swell of men fleeing the battle would overwhelm them, and a few sought to call his bluff, leaving Martyn no choice but to order them attacked. After that, the frightened men halted, and the hesitation gave them the time they needed to remember their training. And what was at stake.

One by one the civilian soldiers turned away. They looked as if they marched to their own funerals, but Martyn did not care if they were excited for the battle; he just wanted them in attendance.

"Women and children may pass," he told the Guardsman in charge of the squad defending the street. "Any able-bodied man is to be sent to the lines. When Lord Odara signals the full retreat, unbar this path and fall back to the second line. If we don't conduct this retreat in an orderly manner, then—"

"Prince Martyn!" A runner came up behind the line of soldiers. He was out of breath, and bleeding from several shallow cuts. "There is fighting across the city. Tachan spies and dissidents are pressing hard on our defenses. We've already lost two waystations, and nearly all the guardposts on the third line are under attack. Commander Inaerion asked me to request more men be sent back to bolster the defenses."

"As soon as the docks are fired, the entirety of our forces will be moving toward Old Kaper. Return to Bystral, and tell him we're coming. Advise the waystations to signal the retreat as well. Any man outside of Old Kaper by nightfall stays outside."

Martyn cast a final glance toward the river, where the ice had reached the near bank but was still too thin to support weight. The Tachans continued their slow advance, ignoring the arrows that showered down on them from the bridge and shore. When two small catapults were hastily drawn up and rocks were thrown onto the river to shatter the ice, they ignored them too, pausing only long enough for the ShadowMagi to reseal their path into Kaper.

Despite their discipline, there was a restlessness in their march, a hunger for battle. Martyn could sense it in the way they walked, in the way their gazes fixed upon Kaper as if upon some much-cherished treasure.

The first plume of heavy black smoke that rolled off the docks caused a reaction among the Tachans, and as more smoke poured from the docks, hastened by Guardsmen dumping barrels of pitch and setting them alight, the enemy's imperturbable calm broke, and an audible agitation swirled through their lines. They surged forward, stopping only when the ice began to creak and groan.

The unexplained winds Martyn expected to rise and push the flames back into the city never came, nor did the fires simply snuff out. *No doubt the ShadowMagi have their hands full keeping the river frozen. It's somehow comforting to know there are limits to their powers.*

A cheer rose among the Alrendrians, drawing Martyn's eyes in the direction of their excited pointing. A series of fireballs arced toward the river, slamming into the enemy and causing a panic their commanders quickly controlled. Gaping holes appeared in the river ice wherever the fireballs landed, and men whose bodies had been engulfed in flame threw themselves into the river only to be dragged under by the weight of their armor and the strength of the current.

No further magical attacks came to the Alrendrians' aid, and soon thick smoke obscured the river entirely. "That won't slow them long," Martyn said, signaling for his bodyguard to follow. "We need to secure the path to the second line."

They moved up the cobbled street, navigating a twisting path Martyn had long committed to memory, skipping broad avenues that appeared navigable in favor of a more indirect route. Traps and blockades waited down most of the larger thoroughfares, often out of sight from the intersections, and with militiamen stationed at each trap to pick off any Tachans foolish enough to take the easy route.

Martyn moved quickly, signaling for his men to keep quiet and watching the windows above for signs of movement. They had not gone far before a half dozen wild-eyed men carrying daggers and cudgels burst from a building, screaming for blood.

The Guardsmen enclosed Martyn behind a wall of steel before he had the chance to raise his sword. They met the undisciplined attack with seasons of training, and in a matter of moments, the enemy all lay dead, and the prince's allies had not a wound to show among them.

The first waystation they found overrun, the militiamen dead and the cache of arrows and bolts a smoldering heap. No enemy remained, but the sounds of clashing steel came from higher up the hill to the south, and it was toward that sound Martyn directed his men.

From below, Martyn heard the echoes of a powerful cry, and he knew that battle had been joined. Aryn would be leading the men into the city even now, slowing the Tachan advance as much as possible. As if on cue, a handful of civilians raced up behind them, soot-smeared faces registering terror at what they had seen. Martyn let them pass without comment, but he hoped that most of his people had already sought shelter in the old city. Flight now, in advance of the Tachans and with enemies secreted throughout New Kaper, would be perilous.

A thunderous jolt shook the ground, and a deafening crash followed an instant later. Martyn glanced back to see a tower of dust rising from below, but his position did not give him a proper view of Makan's Market. He offered a quick prayer to the Gods and hurried his men forward.

The fleeing commoners outpaced him, sprinting past his soldiers with no concern for what might lay ahead. Martyn grew accustomed to seeing them come, in packs of twos and tens, often carrying children or leading the elderly. Many darted down the wrong paths, but Martyn made no effort to stop them. His duty was to secure the way to Old Kaper, not to lead stragglers to safety. *Had they much concern for their lives, they'd have left days ago.*

They never found the source of the fighting, but the second waystation was also destroyed. Beyond that stood a more robust fortification, and the Guardsmen on duty reported no attack. Martyn warned them that Aryn had signaled the retreat and the Tachans had agents throughout the city before continuing toward the Wall.

They barely reached the next intersection before Ehvan and one of the Orog approached the prince. "Tell him," Ehvan commanded.

Then Orog frowned. "Your man back there did not tell the whole truth."

Martyn studied the *choupik*. "About what?"

"I do not know. But something... He misled us about some—"

A shout cut off behind them, and Martyn whirled around to see one of his bodyguards falling to the ground, blood gushing from his throat. One of the five soldiers from the guardpost stood behind him, his dagger red with blood. The others moved up quickly, swords drawn. Two more of Martyn's men were already down, their eyes fixed and lifeless.

Martyn shouted an alarm and dove to the attack. The Orog were faster, darting past him and holding the enemy back with lightning-fast jabs from their bladed staffs. His bodyguard recovered quickly, but Martyn had no intention of letting them keep him out of every fight. When the Orog provided an opening, he shot through it, swinging his sword in a wide arc.

The Tachan twisted so that Martyn's blade went wide, and used his momentum to level his own sweeping attack at the prince's flank. Martyn dodged, turned, and jabbed. He felt his blade dig into flesh, and the man jerked backward, blood running down his arm. His answering swing missed Martyn by a hand. The prince stepped inside the man's guard to deliver a fatal blow and turned to find another opponent, but the Orog had dispatched three and his bodyguard accounted for the final one.

A return to the guardpost found the real Guardsmen bound and slaughtered, stripped of their uniforms and shoved into an out-of-sight nook. "May the Mother protect them," one of the Orog muttered.

"You two stay here," Martyn said, pointing to two of his guards. "Trust no one you don't know by sight, but let anyone willing to throw down their weapons pass." The Guardsmen grudgingly obeyed, though they did not look pleased at the thought of leaving their prince even less protected.

Martyn resumed his march toward Old Kaper with greater haste. His guard now bordered on paranoid, lunging at every shifting shadow and watching every commoner—no matter how aged or helpless—as if expecting an attack. They encountered no more surprise attacks, but they found each waystation either overrun or under attack. Fast assaults from his men cut down the enemy units, biting into their rear before they knew they faced foes on both sides.

The reports he heard as he marched troubled him. The enemy knew where best to attack, and seemed little confused by the twisting paths required to reach Old Kaper. Fires flared up throughout the new city and spread quickly as hot winds from the south whipped them into a frenzy. One Guardsmen raced up from behind nursing a broken arm to report that the Tachans had taken Makan's Market and the Alrendrian forces were in full retreat.

As the Wall loomed ever nearer, Martyn worried about the thousands of his people still living in New Kaper. Not all would reach the protection of the Wall in time; not all would fit inside the old city if they did. *Would the Tachans be as merciful to them as I was with those we captured along the Corsan border? Somehow, I doubt it.*

They rounded a bend and stumbled across a full scale battle, dozens of Guardsmen facing a tenacious and more numerous foe. Only when Martyn saw the flash of his father's cloak, the Rising Sun of Alrendria glittering when it caught the light, did he understand the enemy's determination. A core of Guardsmen protected Mathis, but the bulk of his escort were militiamen, even more undisciplined than the men they faced.

"Protect the King!" Martyn shouted, moving forward at a run, not waiting to see how quickly his men responded. To his surprise, Ehvan and the two Orog reacted fastest, racing along beside him as he plowed into the side of the enemy troops.

The intersection became a mass of shifting bodies and swinging weapons. Martyn hacked and slashed, dodging the weak attempts at attack that his untrained opponents leveled at him. He cut through them like a scythe, opening a gap to his father, driving the enemy back with determination that far outweighed the superiority of numbers they held.

"Martyn," the King gasped when the prince appeared at his side. Blood coated his sword, but it also trickled down his arm and stained the side of his cloak. "I'm more out of practice than I thought. These boys never would have surprised me during the Tachan War."

"Open a path that way," Martyn told the Guardsmen, gesturing toward the avenue leading to the Wall with his chin even as he ducked the attack of a wild-eyed boy and responded with a stab of his own that cut deep into the gut. "Get the King to the Wall without delay."

The Guardsmen tightened their circle around King Mathis and edged away from the center of the plaza. Martyn and his men took up defensive positions and tried to draw off the enemy, but their numbers proved too few. Now that surprise had worn off, the Tachans pressed in, and his men fought desperately to hold them back. One by one he saw militiamen cut down, and when two of his bodyguard fell, he wondered if any of them would make it back to the castle.

Unexpected motion drew his eyes up to where a hooded form cloaked in shadow darted across the roof of a nearby building. The narrow figure leaned over the edge of the building for a moment, and then a bolt of lightning flashed down from above, crashing into the thickest part of the enemy line and scattering them like twigs.

The shockwave knocked Martyn to the ground, and by the time he regained his footing, the Mage was gone. In the ensuing panic, Martyn rallied his men and charged into the confused enemy. To his right he saw his father being hastened out of the intersection and toward the safety of the Wall.

Martyn soon lost count of the number of men he killed. He moved as if a machine, pushing the enemy back but maneuvering his men ever closer to the southern road up the hill and the imagined safety that lay beyond. When escape appeared all but certain, a single misstep sent him tripping over a body.

His head hit the stone-paved street hard enough to blur his vision. Before he could rise, three enemy soldiers loomed over him. One kicked him in the head, sending another wave of pain down his body and making the world whirl above him. Another stepped on his sword, pinning it down. All three moved in for the kill. *At least my father escaped.*

One of his attackers screamed, and a sword burst from his chest. The others turned at the sound, but were too slow to stop the black whirlwind that danced among them. Ehvan spun away from his first target, ripping his sword through the man's body as he lunged toward the second. His blade cut a long gash down the man's arm before his first opponent hit the ground.

The third man raised his weapon, but it did him little good. Ehvan drove him back with a relentless series of attack, his eyes hard, his face expressionless. His was the look of a man long used to battle, a man who had seen his fill of death. He looked as old as Aryn or the King, but the prince knew Ehvan to be a few winters his junior. *How much has he endured to be so familiar with death?*

When the third man hit the ground, blood gushing from a wound running from shoulder to groin, Ehvan turned and offered a hand. "Are you alright, Prince Martyn?"

Martyn could not find his voice. He took Ehvan's hand and stood, groaning at the pain and trying to ignore the way the world still spun every time he moved. "Thank... Thank you. I didn't expect—"

Ehvan laughed, urging Martyn to move. "You didn't think I'd save you? My orders are to see you safe until Lord Odara comes."

Around them, the Tachans fell back, vanishing into the narrow alleys between buildings. The few remaining men of his bodyguard formed up around him, adding to their ranks the remnants of the militia squad that had guarded the intersection. "It's nothing. I just wasn't—"

"You weren't sure how far you could trust me," Ehvan said, "because you are no longer sure how far you can trust him."

Embarrassed, Martyn could do nothing more than nod.

"Lord Odara does not play at politics. If he wanted you dead, he would not send me to kill you. If he wanted you dead, he would not wait for it to happen by chance." Ehvan grabbed Martyn's chin and twisted his head to the side. "You are bleeding heavily. We must get you to the old city so this wound can be tended. I have seen men die from lighter wounds to the head. We may not have much time."

Martyn glanced back to the north, where pillars of thick smoke obscured the sky and the sounds of distant battle echoed down the street. *We may not have any time at all.*

INTERIM

"For the Gods' sakes, Aryn, just sit! The Wall won't fall before sunset." Mathis gestured to the chair opposite his in the sparsely furnished antechamber of the King's apartments. He poured and offered Aryn a glass of wine, careful to keep his bandaged arm, out of the way. In the aftermath of battle, the King refused Healing, insisting that the Magi save their Gift for those with more dire injuries.

Aryn did as ordered, and as soon as he settled back in the seat, Mathis saw the tension flow from his body. He sipped at the wine, toying with the glass before setting it down upon the small, hand-carved table between them. "We lost too many men," Aryn said, his lips drawn down in a scowl.

"That you saved any is a testament to your abilities," Mathis told him. "Losses among the Guard were light, and—"

"Losses were unacceptable," Aryn cut him off. "Thousands of militia fled before the Tachans. Not to mention the civilians we abandoned to the mercy of the enemy."

"Stop brooding," Mathis snapped. "This is not the time for one of your bouts of melodrama! You did what you could. Had the militia squads held their posts, they wouldn't have been lost. And as for the commoners… They were given ample opportunity to seek shelter in Old Kaper. They chose to remain outside, and their fate rests in that decision."

Aryn heaved a heavy sigh. His hand hovered over the wineglass for a moment, but he did not take it. "It tortures me to see Kaper in flames, to hear the laughter of our enemy echoing down the streets we traveled in our youth. I'm sorry I failed you, Mathis."

Despite the images flashing through his mind—unchecked fires burning throughout the new city, the rubble of collapsed buildings, the sight of enemy soldiers patrolling—Mathis chuckled. "Always the poet," he said, shaking his head. "We never expected to hold New Kaper, remember? We just didn't expect the Tachans to stroll across the river. Without the bridge, there was no hope of victory."

Aryn nodded. "So many dead… I had forgotten what command felt like afterwards. They—"

"Are no longer your concern. Their souls are on my conscience. Your duty is to protect the living. To protect the rest of Kaper."

Aryn's eyes took on a distant, introspective look. "Have you marked the passages in the catacombs? They need to be ready."

"We will not be able to evacuate the whole city through the catacombs," Mathis said, his voice tart. When Aryn fixed him with a steady gaze, the gaze of the Guard Commander, unfazed by the criticism of a king, Mathis relented. "They are marked and ready, the exits clear. I will not use them until there are Tachans at my throat."

They sat in silence for a while, relishing the rare moment of peace. "Do you remember that time," Aryn asked, "when we went down to the docks, and you threw a fit because I refused to let you run off with those two sisters?"

Mathis hid his embarrassment by scratching at his beard. "I don't see what that—"

"You tried to leave anyway, and when the tavern owner came to see what the problem was, you told him that 'your prudish friend' wouldn't let you share the company of his paid harlots."

"Yes, I remember," Mathis said, clearing his throat, "But that really—"

"I thought the man's eyes were going to pop out of his head when he realized you were talking about his daughters!" A broad smile spread across Aryn's face, one of the few genuine smiles Mathis had seen since his friend's return.

Mathis laughed out loud. "I never thought we'd make it out of there alive."

"We wouldn't have," Aryn replied, his laughter mixing with the King's, "if Alic hadn't been there to summon the Guard. Your father was furious!" Abruptly, the laughter stopped, and Aryn stood, smoothing his uniform. "Those times are long gone, though. The docks are gone. New Kaper is gone. If we're not careful, we'll be gone too. If you'll excuse me, my King, I need to get back to my men."

"Of course." Mathis escorted Aryn to the door, eyeing the mountainous pile of dispatches awaiting him on his writing desk. It suddenly felt as if the weight of that mountain, and all the dire news it contained, sat upon his shoulders.

"Aryn?" he said before closing the door. The elder Odara turned to meet his gaze. "Come back tomorrow. We lost so much time. Let's not waste what little we might have left."

The hint of a smile touched Aryn's face, and he glanced at the portrait of the King and Queen, the portrait Aryn himself had painted what seemed an eternity ago. "As you command."

"You summoned me?"

Lorthas stopped swirling his wineglass and looked up from the dark red liquid. "Salos, how good of you to come."

"I did not intend to keep you waiting." The Scorpion showed no anxiety, no smugness; his was a perfect mask of impassivity. "Circumstances no longer allow me to immediately answer your summons. If you had delivered your message to me in the Twilight World instead of insisting we meet in person…"

Despite Salos's unreadable expression, Lorthas detected a change in the demeanor of his agent, a subtle shift in the way he held himself, the way he spoke. "The Twilight World, for all its convenience, lacks a certain nuance, especially once a person learns a measure of control there. You always were a quick student."

Salos inclined his head in acknowledgement of the compliment. Lorthas gestured toward the chair opposite him with a finger, but the Scorpion made no move to sit. Between them, the Boundary hovered like a nervous chaperone. Even after centuries Lorthas found it oppressive, like a down blanket doused in water.

"I have not had regular reports from you in some time," Lorthas said, drumming his fingers along the edge of the carved table beside his chair.

"Circumstances have not…"

"Do you take me for a fool?" No emotion entered Lorthas's voice, but it crackled with threat. "Yours are not the only eyes I have in Madryn."

Salos cocked his head to the side. "Then you have little need of daily accounts from me. Your other eyes can report, and I can be left to the other tasks assigned me."

Anger flared up white-hot inside Lorthas, but he refused to let it show. "More consistent meetings would provide us opportunity to adjust your assignments as needed. Your persecution of Madryn has grown somewhat... overzealous. In Feldar, thousands were slaughtered to convince a minor lordling to surrender his holdings, when a simple assassination would have had the same effect. Captured Gileans are used as pack mules for your army when beasts of burden are in ample supply. Your Drekka massacre every soul they happen across, man or woman, Human or Garun'ah. You seem to forget that to rule the world, one must have something left to rule."

Salos edged forward, the Gift making his emotionless eyes iridescent. "My instructions were to sow fear and disorder throughout Madryn while building my powerbase in the wreckage of my father's empire. Have I not achieved that goal?"

"Your methods are excessive and superfluous. We need the peoples of Madryn to doubt in the abilities of their leaders. We don't need them cowering under rocks, afraid to show themselves. Our goal is to have them see us as their saviors, an alternative to the poor choices they've been presented with for millennia."

Salos paced beside the Boundary, but his eyes never left Lorthas. "My brother told me many times that a great commander must learn to delegate responsibility, and that he must trust the decisions of his men in the field, even when those decisions are counter to his grand scheme. You do not have the knowledge I have of the situation in Madryn; consequently, you are not in the best position to dictate policy."

Lorthas stood slowly, his red eyes flaring. "I am your master."

The Scorpion paused opposite him, studying him as a kennel master might study a rabid hound, one with a good history but which had long outlived its usefulness. Lorthas saw the switch, watched Salos's feigned obeisance wash away. "You have always been a useful tool, Lorthas, but never my master. I serve the Father of Storms. He controls my fate, and it is His will I serve."

Anger surged through Lorthas. "I made you what you are."

"You taught me control of my Gift," the Scorpion corrected him. "A testament to your ability since you had to do so through description and false demonstration in the Twilight World. But I am Emperor of Ra Tachan by Jeran's hand. I am Kohr's Destroyer because the God deems it so."

Salos folded his hands together and bowed his head, an Aelvin expression of gratitude. "I thank you for the aid you've given me, but in truth, appeasing you has become an effort far more costly than the reward. You are a liability to me now, and the first lesson you taught me was to deal with liabilities before they drag you under."

With a lightning-fast motion, Lorthas snatched up the cane sitting unobtrusively beside his chair and hooked it around Salos's neck, drawing the Scorpion forward into the Boundary. Blue sparks danced around Salos as he contacted the magical barrier, and his face contorted in agony.

"Did you think I would call you here unaware of your treachery?" Lorthas asked, his voice cold. "Did you think my hand could not reach across the Boundary? Your brother was always a fool, but I expected more from you."

A crash resounded outside Lorthas's chambers, and he glanced over his shoulder. The door shook under another blow, and with the third, the head of an axe poked through. It took a moment before Lorthas realized the strange sound he heard was Salos's sibilant laughter beneath the crackle of the Boundary.

"Did you think me fool enough to walk into your clutches unaided? Or to have no agents in *Ael Shataq*? The Father wants chaos sowed throughout the world; your dominion is not to be spared. I intended to save you for last, so you could witness the folly of your ambition, watch as the world around you crumbled to ash. But I tire of theatrics, and question the wisdom of leaving foes as resourceful as you alive."

The door burst open, and two men raced in, axes raised. Lorthas released the cane and spun to face his attackers, weaving a complex combination of magic and ignoring the pain that accompanied its release. The men flew backward, dead well before Lorthas's attack slammed them into the wall.

"Did you think you were the only one to learn control of magic near the Boundary?" Lorthas asked, but when he turned, Salos was already gone.

Yarchik settled back in his palanquin, listening to the calming sounds of night. Sleep eluded him like a clever fox, ducking in and out of sight but never quite in reach. His bones ached with the ravages of a life outlived; his eyes clouded with age and hung heavy with exhaustion.

A gust of wind heralded the opening of his tent flap. Yarchik waited, but no one announced themselves. He drew a slow breath. "I have been expecting you, Kraltir. Have you come to fulfill your part of the *Prah'phetia*?"

"There are many I want to kill, father, but you are not one of them," Kraltir said, emerging from the shadows. His time in the north had not changed him, but it had accentuated the changes taking place before his departure. His face appeared carved of stone, his eyes set into a permanent glare. A scar graced his arm just beneath the shoulder, a scorpion, the edges still crusted with blood, its claws highlighted with dark ink. A scorpion tattoo wrapped around his throat and onto his face, the claws reaching out toward his eyes. Hatred cast a haze around him, a pall so strong Yarchik sensed it despite his weak connection to the Gift.

"Go back to where you came from. Your absence has proved… peaceful."

"I have been long in the north, but my time in the frozen wastes is finished. I have come to claim what is mine." Kraltir moved slowly around the palanquin. The candlelight played off his face, giving him the appearance of a *tigran* stalking through tall grass.

"I would have preferred it if you had stayed there," Yarchik told him. "You are not welcome among our people."

"I command my own Tribe now, a tribe which dwarfs the Channa in size and devotion to its God. I do not need *our* people."

"Is that why you have come? Do you seek a place among the *Kranora*? We would welcome the Drekka to our tents before we opened them to a servant of Kohr. You are no longer of the Blood."

Kraltir scowled, drawing the lines of his face even deeper. "I have risen high among the *Kohr'adjin*, high enough that I can offer the Channa a chance at salvation. I come to ask you to mark your final days with wisdom, to save your people from annihilation. The Hunter is weak. Kohr reasserts his right to rule upon the universe. Bind the Channa to me before it is too late, and I will make sure they survive what is to come."

Stabbing pain lanced down Yarchik's arm, but the old Tribesman ignored it. Breath wheezed from his lungs, but the gaze he fixed on his son held all that remained of the vibrancy of his youth. "I would sooner bind myself to a rock tumbling toward the sea," he said through clenched teeth. "The Channa do not need your help. Garun has sent our savior."

"Yes, I have heard." Kraltir's smug smile infuriated Yarchik, but prisoner as he was, betrayed by his own failing limbs, he could do nothing. "A Hunter with the thirst for blood and Garun's temper. A coward who picks off cubs and dawdlers, avoiding real fights with trained warriors. Who did you name this time?"

"Why should I tell you?"

"It does not matter," Kraltir answered, waving a hand dismissively. "He will die with all who oppose me. Like Norvik. Like the others you cursed by naming *Kranach*. In the end, he will beg for mercy like all the rest."

"In that you are wrong," Yarchik said. "Dahr would welcome death. He might even thank you for it." *And that is his only real failing. The only concern I have about leaving the Channa to him.*

Kraltir froze at the *Kranor*'s words. His jaw set so tight it trembled; his fingers clenched until blood began to drip from his palms. He stood unmoving for so long, Yarchik wondered if he still breathed. "You chose that Half-man as *Kranach*? You bestowed the tribe's greatest honor on an *Onatsal* raised by Humans?"

"I did not choose him; Garun did. And Half-man he may be, but still twice a man when compared to my own son. You—"

Kraltir lunged forward, wrapping his hands around Yarchik's throat. Yarchik struggled, but his son had youth and leverage to aid him, and he felt himself denied breath. His hand thrashed about and stumbled upon a pewter goblet, a prize taken ages ago in a battle Yarchik could not even remember. He gripped the heavy goblet and swung it, connecting with Kraltir's head. His son fell back, blood streaming down his face from the broad gash above his temple.

Yarchik slumped back, gasping for air. His laughter echoed through the tent. "What chance have you against Dahr Odara when you cannot even best a crippled old man?"

Kraltir regained his feet and wiped a hand across his forehead, smearing the blood across his flesh. His eyes clouded over with Blood Rage. He drew his *dolchek* and advanced. Yarchik made no move to fight. He could not flee, nor would he have even had it been an option.

Now begins your time, Dahr. Remember what I taught you and care well for our people.

Liseyl walked the empty back halls of Kaper castle, surveying long unused chambers and preparing a list of available space. An army of servants followed somewhere behind, removing dust and airing out rooms. Before the siege ended, the King would need every available space. The Elves had already taken over an empty wing of suites, cramming in eight to ten per room; and the extra Guardsmen—those who could not be billeted in the barracks outside—had been packed into other chambers. Hundreds more slept in tents or under tarps strung between trees, and thousands lodged in the old city, hoping for news of accommodation somewhere.

Her task of managing the palace had been difficult before the siege, now it was impossible. She used every trick learned administering her husband's estates in Rachannon and a few more besides, and still her list of work grew longer by the day. The storerooms in the catacombs overflowed, but she had been forced to station guards to prevent theft. She had nobles by the score demanding luxuries she could not provide and fuming at her whenever the King's orders forced them to move to smaller quarters, or worse, to share their quarters with another family. Her people were terrified, certain that the Tachans would storm the Wall any day and lay waste to the castle.

She threw open the door to a dust-covered anteroom and jumped when a voice shouted. "Why can't you just let me be?"

"My apologies," Liseyl said, bowing and stepping back. "I did not mean—" She paused when she saw the figure curled in the corner, sandy blonde hair disheveled, tear tracks prominent on his cheeks. He cringed away from the light pouring through the door, and the sound of his labored breathing reached across the room.

"Lord Odara?" Liseyl asked. "Is everything all right?"

"Did he send you to tempt me?" Aryn asked. Bitter laughter followed the question. "I am no saint, but I will not betray Alrendria for a pretty face or a shapely curve." The laughter turned to sobbing again, and Aryn buried his head in his arms, pushing himself even deeper into the corner.

This is the man to whom we have entrusted our safety? Liseyl thought, then chided herself for her callousness. *What did that monster do to him?*

She approached slowly, unsure how he would react to her presence. "Lord Odara, this is Kaper castle. You are no longer a prisoner of Tylor the Bull."

"My oath is all I have left!" Aryn shouted, and Liseyl jumped back. "You have taken everything from me, Tylor! Alic. Illendre. Jeran! He was a boy, Tylor! Just a boy. What crimes had he committed?"

Liseyl wanted to flee, but she could not. When Aryn resumed sobbing, his pain drew her to him. She knelt beside him and cradled his head in her arms. He resisted at first, then clung to her, sobbing into her dress, his mad muttering muffled by the cloth.

"Lady Liseyl, is all well? We thought we heard shouting." She heard voices in the hall, and the thunder of approaching footfalls.

"I am coming," she said, standing and moving away from Aryn. She did not want the guards assigned to her to find him in this state; it would be too much of a discourtesy to the uncle of the man who had saved her family.

The guards found her before she could exit the room. That she, castellan of the palace, needed soldiers assigned to watch her in the heart of her castle highlighted the direness of the situation in Kaper, but that situation would become far worse if they learned their commander was subject to bouts of madness.

"Lady Liseyl," said a short Guardsmen. He was new to her service, but she believed his name was Asahn. "We thought we heard shouting. Is everything— Commander Odara?"

Liseyl's heart sank. "He was here when I arrived, and—" She stopped when she saw Aryn behind her, his uniform unrumpled and his hair smoothed down.

"And Lady Liseyl was kind enough to explain how she intends to allocate this section of the palace." He looked into her eyes, piercing straight to her soul, the twin blue orbs that reminded her so much of Jeran's. "Thank you."

Aryn saluted the Guardsmen and then strode past them all into the hall. "If you will forgive me, other duties require my attention. Perhaps we will have a chance to speak again soon, Lady Liseyl."

CHAPTER 22

A chill wind howled from the north, rattling the windows, announcing the arrival of Harvest. Jeran sat at his desk, staring into the flames of the small fire crackling in the hearth. The wine he had opened remained untouched, as did the meal his guards brought at sunset. "You're certain?" he asked, breaking the blanketing silence.

"Would I have come here if I were not?" Alwen snapped. She glared at him as she stomped back and forth across the room, but Jeran detected concern in the bond they shared.

"No. I suppose not." He opened the dispatch clutched in his hand and read it again. "This is as good as any plan I devised. Advise Drogon and Wardel to begin training the soldiers, and tell Ehvan to proceed at his discretion. Nashime will command the apprentices. Work them hard. They should be ready to move on my command."

"Nashime?" Alwen cleared her throat. "I thought that I—"

"Nashime commands. You're needed at the Academy. You're more important to me there than dead on a battlefield."

Alwen rounded on him. "I was fighting battles centuries before Nashime wore swaddling." For emphasis, she jabbed her cane at Jeran's head every few words. "There's nothing he can teach them that I do not know."

"And when did you fight your last battle? Near the end of the MageWar, I believe. Since then, the only weapon you've used with any regularity is your tongue. As sharp as it may be, I suspect it won't be up to the task of killing Tachans."

A hint of a smile broke through Alwen's stormy facade, but she hid it. "Do you think me incapable? Unwilling to kill?"

"No. I think you're older than you realize, and slowed by infirmity. I think you will fight hard and kill many, perhaps to assuage your guilt over your role in the MageWar, perhaps because you miss the thrill of battle and want to recapture something of your youth. But I also believe that you will die, and that your loss would be a tragedy. We have great designs, Alwen, but you'll be of no help to me from your grave."

Alwen pursed her lips and studied him. "I liked it better when you were scared of me."

Despite himself, Jeran laughed. "You think I am not?"

Alwen grabbed the satchel of dispatches Jeran had prepared for Dranakohr. "I'll take these for you. Have you any other messages."

"No." Before Alwen could open a Gate, Jeran stood. "What made you betray Lorthas?"

The suddenness of the question caught Alwen off guard. Her cheeks reddened, though whether from anger or embarrassment, Jeran could not tell. For a moment, he thought she would not answer, or that he would have to endure one of her tirades.

"I did not have much of a choice. Yassik abducted me."

"You had no choice in the going, but you must have decided to ally yourself with the Assembly again, and you must have been convincing, else Aemon would not have taken you back. My understanding is that he thought you irredeemable."

"Yes, well, we have always had our differences of opinion." Alwen's eyes bored into him. "That I held a particular grudge against him no doubt did not help me in his eyes."

She's probably wondering whether it was Yassik or Aemon who gave her up to me. I don't envy whichever one she decides to blame. "Because he betrayed you, you mean?" Jeran asked. "Because he orchestrated the events leading up to the war and then abandoned you?"

Alwen's eyes narrowed. "How much do you know?"

"Not enough. Not near enough."

"If you're dredging all this up just to gauge my reaction, I'll tell you now, it won't be pleasant."

A slight smile played across Jeran's face. "I need no lessons in regards to your temper. I seek an understanding of my enemies… and my allies."

"Our cause was never supposed to be about killing," Alwen said. Her brow drew down as she spoke, highlighting the wrinkles about her face. "We didn't intend a war against fellow Magi, and never a more general conflict against Alrendria. The Assembly forced that on us when it declared Lorthas a Darklord. We wouldn't let him stand trial when we knew the verdict had already been decided, and they would never have left him free to lead a separate faction of Magi. The position of the Assembly has always been one of intolerance toward those who try to live outside its law." The last she said with a pointed look at Jeran, as if he needed reminding that he stood on the cusp of the Assembly's ire.

"Aemon's refusal to stand by us disappointed me," Alwen continued, "but it infuriated Lorthas. He felt betrayed and used, but it was Aemon's refusal to explain *why* he abandoned us that started the rift between them. The old man does things for his own reasons, and if he doesn't think there's anything to gain by explaining himself, he won't. Lorthas did not like being bandied about like a toy."

"I can empathize," Jeran said wryly. "But none of that explains why you turned against him."

"I didn't turn against him! And if you would find some of that patience your loyal supporters are always lauding, you'll get your answer." She paced the room, her cane slapping against the stones with regularity, her breaths coming out in hissing puffs.

"Even before Yassik abducted me, I began to question Lorthas's methods. As the winters dragged on, his obsession with victory grew worse. Both sides committed atrocities—don't think I'm unaware of the evils the Assembly supported in the name of freedom!—but after my capture, the things Lorthas did in my name…

"Eventually, I could no longer bear the perversion of our cause. Anything, even things the way they were before, was better than the world we were creating. And Lorthas… By embracing the title of Darklord, he changed more than the way the world viewed him; he changed how he viewed himself."

Jeran ran a hand along his chin, weighing Alwen's words. "But you believe there's something of the man he was still within him? The one who sought unity in Madryn?"

"You sound as if you seek to bargain with him," Alwen laughed. When Jeran did not share her mirth, her smile faded, and her voice cracked across the room like a whip. "You don't intend to deal with him, do you?"

"I expect that shortly, he will want to deal with me. I need to know how far I can trust him."

"Gods, boy, you do like to walk the narrows. You're worse than your father." Alwen bit down on her lip, and her gaze grew distant, introspective. "He's not the man I knew, but if he promises something, he'll keep his word. You must be wary, though. He learned to negotiate from Aemon himself, and only the old man can twist words better than him. Whatever he promises, he'll do, but if there's a gap a sweet ant can crawl through, he'll do as he pleases and tell you he did no wrong."

Jeran stood and walked around his desk. He put his arm on Alwen's shoulder, smirking at the suspicious way she watched him. "Thank you. I know that wasn't something you wanted to talk about. But it will be helpful to me."

He felt happiness through the bond they shared, pride at being useful again. "If you want my advice, which I'm sure you'll ignore: you're better off without him. Aemon, too, for that matter. Both have their own agendas, and neither can accept themselves as a pawn in anyone else's game."

Alwen hefted the satchel onto her shoulder. "I must go. They're waiting for me at the Academy." A gate opened, and with a final nod to Jeran, she disappeared.

Jeran pondered this new information, this added piece to the puzzle of the past he was trying to build. He thumbed half-heartedly through the dispatches, reading a few but setting most aside for later. With *The Forge of Faith* in hand, he settled back into a cushioned chair and opened it to his mark. He read for a time, then opened himself to the Readings hovering over the tome, following that pattern—with occasional bouts of sleep thrown in whenever exhaustion overwhelmed him—until the first hint of light hit the eastern horizon and his guards brought in a tray of bread and fruit.

He asked that a bath be drawn, and the guards obliged. He returned the favor by heeding their requests to eat, gnawing on a hard roll as he lounged in the hot water and contemplated his next move. He had hoped for more time to prepare but had expected less. News of the fall of New Kaper had not surprised him, but the ease with which the Tachans had taken the city did. The estimate of casualties had been staggering: thousands dead in the battle, tens of thousands more caught outside the Wall and subject to the enemy's whim.

For now, Old Kaper remained secure, and the Tachans seemed content to consolidate their holdings rather than force an attack. The magical construction of the Wall protected Kaper somewhat, and no doubt the sporadic reports of rogue Magi fighting on the King's side made the enemy more cautious.

Jeran wondered about that, too. Ehvan knew the Assembly had not cast its lot with Alrendria, so the identities and allegiance of these Magi remained a mystery. A fourth group of Gifted, hidden in shadow and free to pounce at any moment, was not something Jeran liked to think about.

I am running out of time. I am not yet ready, but I am running out of time. The irony of his fate did not escape him. A life of possibly millennia stretched out before him, yet time harried him with its quick passage, its indifference to his intentions.

What I plan will not go unchallenged, even by my friends. Even I have my doubts. But if I am to succeed, I must not miss a detail, I must plan for every contingency, and there are too many variables. Too many players in this game.

He dressed hurriedly, taking a few bites from an apple and throwing a few more rolls into the fire so his guards would believe him when he said he had eaten. The sun had not yet crested the horizon when he reached the plaza, but he knew something was wrong. The stone courtyard stood barren, and the Emperor was never late. The ancient Elf was the only soul in Shandar who slept less than Jeran.

As the moments dragged on, his apprehension grew. A thousand valid reasons for the Emperor's delay flickered through his mind, yet Jeran dismissed them all, and his vague uneasiness grew more potent with every breath. When he turned to call for his guards, he found two soldiers racing toward him, weapons drawn.

"What are you doing?" Jeran demanded.

The two men, one Human and one Orog, skidded to a stop. Owin, formerly a thatcher of the Family Duabay in House Odara gasped for breath and scanned the plaza as if expecting it to be filled with enemies. Serak, *choupik* of the Forna sept, demonstrated better control. He set the butt of his *va'dasheran* on the ground and studied Jeran with unreadable eyes.

"You... You needed us," Owin said between breaths.

He must have sprinted the entire distance to be so winded. I must find a way to mask my worries from them, or I will lead my people to their deaths.

"I believe something is wrong," Jeran told them. "Serak, find the Aelvin twins and bring them here immediately. Owin, gather everyone else in the main camp. Tell them I will join them presently."

Jeran ran back to his house and changed his simple, worn clothes for more stout garments. He belted on his sword and *dolchek* and grabbed the pack waiting by the door, stuffing what remained of his breakfast into the top compartment. By the time he returned to the training plaza, Nahrona and Nahrima waited there. Both Elves still wore night robes, and they looked puzzled by the haste with which Serak had ushered them into the brisk morning air.

"What is the matter, Jeran?" Nahrona asked.

"This fellow here would not even allow us time to dress," Nahrima said, pointing at Serak. "And yet we arrive to find nothing but cold stones and morning birds twittering on the building sills. Beautiful, but—"

"—hardly worth the disturbance."

"The Emperor was supposed to meet me here," Jeran said. "But I arrived to find him absent. Since he is not with you, I presume he is not in the house you share. I fear that something is wrong."

"No," Nahrima said, "He is not with us."

"He left yesterday to attend to some matters in Lynnaei. He said—"

"—he would be back by morning." The two twins shared a look, then Nahrima turned back to Jeran. "But I do not think it likely anything is amiss."

"He is very worried, brother," Nahrona said. "Look at his eyes."

"I see that," Nahrima answered, and the two Elves shared another questioning look. "You are not... He has not bonded you, has he?"

"I know little of how that aspect of my Gift works," Jeran scoffed, "but I don't think it's possible for a man who has ruled a nation for over five thousand winters to bond himself to a BattleMage. The bond requires a measure of submission. Not something an Emperor has in abundance."

"True," Nahrima admitted, "but then the question remains—"

"—as to why you are convinced there is danger."

"Because for days, everything has gone the way I expected, and I knew it could not last. He has never missed a lesson before, even when duty called him home. I need one of you to return to Lynnaei and find out what's happened."

"I will go," Nahrima said. "I would prefer to go in clothes, however."

"Just hurry. I'll prepare the others."

"Prepare them," Nahrona asked. "For what?"

"To leave. I have delayed here too long. I have learned what I needed to learn. One way or another, we are leaving Shandar today."

Nahrima hurried away. Nahrona followed with promises to meet Jeran in the main camp as soon as he, too, had dressed. Jeran seized magic and opened a Gate. The stark, mountainous walls of Dranakohr appeared on the other side. Snow swirled around the upper levels of the fortress but did not touch the lush green of the valley floor.

"Return to Dranakohr," he ordered Serak. "Tell them to stop sending shipments to Shandar."

"Should I advise them of your return, friend Jeran?" Serak asked.

"No. Not yet. Just tell them I will no longer be in Shandar."

Serak nodded and stepped through the Gate. Jeran let it close, watching until it vanished and the last vestiges of magic dissipated around him, then hurrying through the streets, oblivious to the sounds of the morning jays. Shandar no longer felt like a grave to him; it had taken on the feel of a refuge, a sanctuary not for men, but from them. Here, the cares of Madryn rarely penetrated, and beast and bird alike found solace in her empty trees and magically maintained gardens.

I violated that peace, Jeran thought, offering a silent apology to the city. *I added to this city's scars. But I needed a place few would dare go, a place scarcely remembered except in nightmares. I will return, but I will never again bring danger. You have my word.*

The others waited for him around a cook fire in the main camp, his guard assembled on one side of the plaza, standing in rank and looking ready for battle. Jes hovered over the fire tending a kettle, her hair and dress giving no impression of an abrupt awakening. Aemon, in contrast, appeared even more rumpled than normal and clung to consciousness with only the harshest of efforts.

Jakal and Goshen sat cross-legged before the flames. Jakal rose at Jeran's appearance, but the other *Tsha'ma* gave a slight shake of his head, and after a moment's reflection, Jakal sat again. Goshen remained stone still, bare-chested in the morning chill, his scarred and tattooed flesh displayed for all to see, a mural of his violent past. The scarred Human stood behind the *Tsha'ma*, his features cloaked in shadow. He said nothing, but his eyes followed Jeran across the square.

Nahrona arrived a few moments later, his nightclothes discarded in favor of the brown traveling robes favored by *Ael Maulle*. His late arrival, and without his brother, drew some stares, but Aemon approached Jeran, not the Aelvin Mage. "What is the reason for this, Jeran?"

"I am leaving Shandar today," Jeran announced. "To where, I will know shortly. Before I went, I wanted to thank you all for your efforts."

"Leaving?" Aemon stood. "There's still more for you to learn. I—"

"We could hide in Shandar for ten winters, and there would still be more for me to learn. I've learned to balance magic with battle. I've learned the skills required to keep me alive. The rest can be learned at leisure, or as the situation demands. I can no longer skulk in the shadows while the world burns."

Aemon bristled at the interruption. An imperious gaze fixed on his face, he strutted toward Jeran like a beast defending its lair. "I don't think you understand the full consequences of this decision. Any edge you can gain over your enemies—"

"I've made my decision," Jeran replied, the crisp calm of his voice contrasting with the rising emotion in Aemon's.

"Jeran, it's in your best interest to—"

"You are a teacher here, not High Wizard. Even if you had not abdicated that *hallowed* position in the Assembly to better manipulate events from the shadows, you would hold no authority over me." The scarred Human laughed at that, drawing Aemon's glare before Jeran continued. "I am a rogue Mage, little better than Lorthas in the Assembly's eyes and likely to be named a Darklord myself before this is finished. When I need your counsel, I will ask for it, but in this I am already certain: there is nothing more for me to learn in Shandar."

Jes's eyes shot up from the kettle. "What's wrong? What's happened?"

"I don't know yet," Jeran replied. "I may need your help, though, and I wanted everyone gathered together if I did." He looked to the fire, where steam poured from the mouth of the kettle. "I would welcome a cup while we waited."

"What aren't you telling me?" Jes demanded.

"Nothing of which I am certain. Should I get it myself, or will you be serving?"

Jes moved to the fire, her graceful, silent motion hiding the anxiety swirling beneath her unruffled surface. She produced cups from a small chest and poured tea for those who requested it. She even asked the subcommanders standing in front of their squads if they wanted some. When she handed Jeran his cup, she curtsied like a servant, but when he smiled at her feigned deference, anger bubbled closer to the surface, threatening to burst through the mask of calm she wore.

Silence pressed in on them, but no one dared break it with idle conversation. The moments dragged on, one after another, and Jeran shifted his gaze from one of his instructors to another, meeting their eyes and ducking his head in what he hoped would be taken as gratitude for the help they had given him.

When the air across the plaza wavered and Nahrima appeared, Jeran knew instantly that his fears had been justified. Something haunted the aged Elf's eyes, a pain long forgotten and just again realized, but it was the smear of soot across his face and the bloody tear along his sleeve that told of trouble.

Nahrona rushed forward. "What has happened, brother?"

"Luran has returned," Nahrima said, his voice a hollow rasp. "War has come to Lynnaei."

"Dear Gods," Aemon whispered. Jes jumped up, her cup shattering on the stones. "Where is the Emperor?" she demanded.

"He is in the palace," Nahrima told them. "He refuses to leave."

"Then my choice is made," Jeran said. "I go to Lynnaei. Any who wish to join me are welcome."

Aemon and Jes approached immediately, joining Jeran and the Aelvin twins. Yassik moved to join them as well, but the others hung back. Jakal and Goshen shared a long look, and finally the giant Sahna Hunter laughed.

"Kill *Aelva* who serve Kohr? Hard offer refuse."

The scarred Human Mage hefted a pack onto his shoulder, adjusted his sword in its sheath, and started forward. He stopped beside Jeran, taking a firm grip on his chin and turning his head from side to side, peering at him through narrowed eyes. "You'll do well enough. Good luck to you, Brother."

He walked away, his unhurried footfalls leading him from the plaza. "You're not coming?" Aemon demanded. Disbelief flooded his features, anger his voice, but the other Mage paid it no heed.

"I left this war centuries ago," the Mage said without looking back. "I only came here to keep a promise, and not one I made to you, no matter what you might think."

"People are dying," Jes snapped. "The Emperor may need—"

"He's made his choice," Jeran said, gripping Jes by the arm when she started forward to confront the Mage. "He has the right to go."

"Does he?" Jes rounded on Jeran. The power of the Gift made her eyes shine. "Does anyone have the right to turn his back on those in need?"

"Yes," Jeran said, his voice cold. He watched as the Mage disappeared into the ruins of Shandar. "Everyone does. That is the consequence of freedom. That is what you Magi and your precious Assembly consistently fail to understand. You cannot force a person down a path you choose and call it freedom, not even if your path is the better one."

"You bend people to your will all the time," Jes said. Jeran sensed her worry; he knew that, for once, he was not the cause of her anger, just the target of it.

"True, but I don't pretend they're free."

"You insufferable fool!" Color blossomed in Jes's cheeks, and if she had held a weapon or reached for magic, Jeran might have felt threatened. "You think in a handful of winters you've learned more wisdom than Magi with millennia of experience?"

"Wisdom? Perhaps not. But I've learned the meaning of hypocrisy. I—"

"Excuse me," Nahrona interrupted. "I love a good debate as much as anyone, but we must—"

"—return to Lynnaei even if you do not," Nahrima finished. "I fear we cannot long delay."

Jeran turned his gaze away from Jes. Her anxiety had transformed into anger, but he sensed a knot of fear lodged beneath the surface, so well hidden he wondered if she recognized it for what it was. Part of him wanted to comfort her, to reassure her that all would be well, but he knew such a move, particularly in the presence of others, would work against his designs. He needed Jes focused, drawn taut like a ready bow.

"Of course," he said to the Aelvin twins. "You have my apologies. Jakal, we will need to pool our Gifts. Explain to the others how to do it. Nahrima will direct the magic."

The *Tsha'ma* stiffened at Jeran's words. "Jeran, you know that—"

"Now is not the time to hold onto secrets," Jeran told him. "Aemon already knows. We both know that he'll keep his silence only until he believes sharing the knowledge will do more good than holding it." Aemon opened his mouth to protest, but Jeran cut him off with a gesture. "I don't have time to argue with all of you! Do as I ask or we can all make our own way to Lynnaei. I'm sure the Emperor will appreciate a scattering of sympathetic Gifted all over his city in the middle of a battle."

Jakal relented and quickly explained to the others how to hand control of their Gift over to another. When they were ready, Jeran offered Nahrima his magic first, and then one by one, the others did, until the old Elf glowed like the sun in the brightening sky.

"Where do we go?" he asked, gasping at the thrill of power dancing through his body.

"To the field where you celebrate *ael Chatel e Valia*," Jeran said. "We will gauge the situation from there and make our plans."

Nahrima nodded and focused his Gift. Around them, Shandar faded, growing colorless and less distinct. A new image superimposed itself over the ruined city: an open field of lush grass enveloped by trees that stretched to the heavens, their bases so broad twenty men with arms outstretched could not circle one completely. Twisting branches criss-crossed above them, the lower ones as wide as the streets in Shandar, and above the branches, a web of rope bridges connected the higher platforms, binding together the buildings of Lynnaei.

As the view grew more solid, the roar of wind caught their ears, gusting across the field with the hot breath of destruction. Ash swirled in the gusts like snow, obscuring visibility. Even with their vision impeded, they saw the roaring flames in the trees above. Dark, sticky sap leaked from the wounded trees, hissing wherever it contacted flames. Hundreds of silhouetted forms ran along the avenues above, cutting away burning branches and soaking untouched wood with buckets of water. Many more guarded intersections, watching for attack from all directions.

Someone saw them in the field and shouted. In an instant, a volley of arrows flew toward them. Jeran broke his connection to Nahrima and raised a shield of air upon which most of the arrows clattered harmlessly. The effort drained him more than it should have; no doubt from the strain of moving so many men halfway across Madryn. *I will have to marshal my strength. This fight will be one primarily of steel.*

"Lord Odara?" shouted a broad-shouldered soldier named Gerbin. "How do we tell friend from foe?"

Across the field, two dozen Elves and Tribesmen burst from the trees, running toward them with weapons drawn and a scream for blood on their lips. "Those are foes," Jeran told him, drawing his sword.

CHAPTER 23

Jeran signaled, and his men dropped to the ground or sought cover in the meticulously trimmed hedges spanning the distance between the trunks of the giant trees. He peered across the haze-filled expanse, searching the treeline for moving shadows. Moments passed with only the distant sounds of fighting echoing through the trees, but Jeran still did not give the order to move. He made another gesture. Jes and Aemon approached, crouched beside him, and extended their perceptions.

His own Gift gave him a clear sense of the vicinity, but he dared not reach too far in any one direction. Twice now, insistence on scouting himself had cost him men; the brief delay required to bring one's perceptions fully back into the body had given his enemies time enough to launch an ambush before he could ready a defense. The specters of pain still thrummed across his chest, back and throat, grim reminders of the fate which awaited all of his people if he did not take care. *Better to let the Magi be my eyes, and me, their sword.*

Moments passed, and impatience gnawed at his gut, but he dared not cross the open expanse until he knew the way was clear. They had found no way to announce their presence to the Emperor without warning Luran's followers, so their allegiance remained contested by every group they stumbled upon. Only Nahrona's presence—Nahrima and Yassik had slipped away to find Astalian—saved them from constant battle with troops loyal to the Emperor, but even the *Ael Maulle* could not protect them from arrows fired from concealment, or ambushes launched from the shadows, and Elves on both side of the conflict preferred such tactics to open combat. The day had turned into a series of blurry skirmishes.

"I wish this smoke would clear," one man said, his voice carrying through the stillness like a trumpet blast.

"This smoke is keeping you alive, soldier," another man replied, his voice a hissing whisper. "The enemy has to be close enough to see for us to kill them. But an Elf can shoot an arrow through a peach at three hundred hands and hit nothing but the pit."

"If we can't see them," the first soldier asked, his voice cracking through the air, "then how can we fight them?"

The conversation drew Jeran's stern gaze, and the second soldier smacked his companion on the shoulder. "Smoke doesn't obscure your voice, fool. My apologies, Lord Odara, I will keep the men silent."

"I see nothing, Jeran," Aemon said.

"Nor do I," Jes added. "But the branches above are a major intersection leading toward the palace. We should move quickly if we wish to cross this field undiscovered."

Jeran gave the order, and his men raced forward, moving in groups of two and three, crouched low. In the broad daylight, their black uniforms stood out in the open field even in the haze, but so long as they clung to the wood's edge they remained difficult to spot, blending in with the dancing shadows of branches playing in the wind.

Once across the field, Jeran gathered his men at the base of a Great Tree, under the cover of the broad staircase that wound around the towering monstrosity. "We must go up," he said after some reflection. "We'll be of little help down here. The battle for Lynnaei will be fought in the city above."

Nervous glances matched the spike of fear that suddenly impressed itself upon Jeran's consciousness. "We will keep to the lower levels," he promised. "The branches are as broad as city streets, and the height easy to forget if you refuse to look down. We will leave the treetop fighting to the Elves, but for our presence to be effective, we must move up."

He felt the steeling of resolve among his men. The terror remained, but suppressed. "As you command, Lord Odara," his subcommander, a former Guardsmen from House Aurelle named Dobrei, said. "Can't blame a bunch of tunnel rats for being afraid of heights, can ya, now? I'll tell you what, boys, them pretty Elves fall just as hard as we do."

Dobrei's words brought a quiet laugh to the men; even the stoic Orog seemed amused. "Let's go," Jeran said, and his men sprinted up the stairway two by two, crouched down but moving as fast as their legs could take them.

Jeran went in the fourth grouping, but before he made a single revolution around the massive trunk, arrows sprouted from it, quivering with the force of their impact. "Ambush!" someone shouted as more shafts struck the tree, sinking a hand deep in the hard wood.

"Climb!" Jeran said, urging the men in front of him for greater speed. He seized magic, readying the flows to harden the air around him into a shield, but he could not protect his men without his magic trapping them on the staircase. "To the platform above. Hurry now!"

He sprinted, winded by the steep climb and the weight of his gear, watching the trees across the way for signs of the enemy. He saw nothing; the thick foliage and interlocking branches offered perfect concealment. An army could lie in wait without being seen.

"Aemon, find them!" he shouted, clearing the last few steps and rolling onto the wooden platform of Lynnaei's lowest level. He unleashed his magic, weaving a dome two hundred hands across. His men dove behind whatever concealment offered itself. Two bore bleeding wounds; one still had the split shaft of an arrow protruding from his arm. From below, Jeran heard shouting and a single pained scream that quickly grew distant, then cut off with brutal finality. A phantom pain along Jeran's neck and back accompanied the cessation of sound, then disappeared as suddenly.

As more of his men reached the platform, Jeran began to circle it, eyes studying the meshwork of intersecting branch-roads. The red stone of the palace dominated the northeast, visible through every gap in the trees. Dozens of rope bridges crisscrossed the upper levels of the city; each one potentially harboring enemy archers. The broad sweeping branches sprouting from the Great Trees offered them cover on the lower levels, but the storehouses, shops, and barracks built onto the vast platforms could house far more enemies than those above. Dozens of fires burned, spotted here and there across the eerily quiet city, raining ash.

The green markers in the windows indicated that this was a market district, but Lynnaei was as large as Kaper, and it held dozens of such districts. A sign dominated the center of the platform, but a third of it had broken away under the crushing force of a fallen branch, and the gracefully curved Aelvin characters were incomprehensible to Jeran.

"Jes," he called as the Magi arrived on the platform. "I need to know where the nearest *Ael Chatorra* guardpost is. Aemon, find those archers!"

Jes moved to the sign, picking up the shattered fragments and arranging them. Aemon joined Jeran, breathing hard from the run up the stairs. "There's no one there," he insisted. "They've either gone or are wearing the amulets of the *Noedra Synissti.*"

"Hundreds of them?" Jeran frowned. "Has Luran equipped his entire army with such devices?"

"I hope not." Aemon did not sound hopeful, however, and Jeran called for Dobrei to gather the men.

"Elves," Goshen said, adjusting his grip on the long-handled hammer he carried. "I smell them. They want battle." If the heights or the threat of unseen assassins frightened him, the giant showed no sign of it. He strode outside Jeran's protection to the edge of the platform, where two parallel branches from neighboring trees had been bound and hewn into an avenue fifty hands across. "I here, Elves. Come! Come fight the Wildman!"

In response, a volley of arrows shot from concealment, but they shattered harmlessly on the air in front of the *Tsha'ma.* He laughed, a guttural chuckle that sent a chill through his own allies. "I not fear your splinters. You want fight, come fight like Hunter!"

"I found them," Aemon announced. The old man's gaze was blank; with his perceptions fully extended, he would be oblivious to everything around him. "Some are wearing masking amulets, but there are more behind them. Regular soldiers."

"Don't lose them," Jeran said. "Jurge. Samon. Protect Aemon." The *choupik* stationed themselves on either side of the Mage.

Jeran turned toward Dobrei. "Ready bows! Jakal, watch the other avenues. The Elves are not so foolish as to concentrate their attack when they can just as easily surround us."

"You will not come?" Goshen shouted. He tore at the hides he wore as a shirt, exposing flesh scarred from a thousand battles. "You lost, perhaps? I Goshen Shadowkiller, *Tsha'ma* of Sahna. I show you the way."

With startling speed, Goshen seized and released magic, a complex weave that sent sprays of fire and wind toward the nearest tree, blasting away the concealing foliage and rendering it into fine ash, revealing a few score Elves who scampered away from the burning branches. Deprived of their concealment, the Elves drew their swords and raced toward the avenue.

"Archers, fire!" Dobrei shouted, and a volley of Alrendrian shafts shot toward the enemy. Several fell, but the gusting crosswinds blew many of the arrows off target.

Jeran raced toward the enemy, his Aelvin sword at the ready, engraved sigils glimmering in the stray wisps of light filtering down from above. He made it only half way to Goshen before a startled cry and the shock of searing pain through his shoulder drew him around.

" 'Ware the rear!" shouted Nebekai, a shaft sprouting from his shoulder. Another dozen Elves—a mixture of archers and swordsmen—approached along a different path, hoping to take Jeran's men by surprise.

"Seven men to a Mage," Jeran shouted. "The Gifted will focus on defense. If the enemy falls back, let them flee."

He waited for his own team to form around him, then started forward again, offering protection to the soldiers assigned to Goshen until they reached the *Tsha'ma*'s side. The Tribesman stood in the thick of battle, his hammer swinging with an even, measured regularity, giving the impression that he worked at some mundane chore and was not caught in the middle of a battle. Occasional flare-ups from his aura highlighted the use of magic, usually followed by the sight of an Elf flung over the side of the railing or sent crashing into his allies.

Jeran ordered his men to plow into the rear of the Elves, and they did so with fervor. Two even ran along the railing, unmindful of the hundred hand fall to the forest floor, to put themselves in a better position to attack.

His own blade darted out, scoring a deep cut across the back of one Elf. The man screamed, turning to bring his weapon to bear against Jeran. He was too slow. Jeran's second swing sliced a gash along his throat, severing an artery. The soldier paled and dropped his sword. Pressing his hand against the wound, he fled, but the pallor had already entered his face, and Jeran spared him no other thought other than to wish him a speedy journey to the Nothing.

"I glad you come," Goshen laughed when Jeran appeared at his side. "I thought you want me fight them all."

"It didn't look like you needed our help," Jeran replied, parrying the blow of another Elf. He stepped in quick, but the Elf danced away. Jeran made two more attempts, but each caught nothing but air. "Gods, they move quick."

"Leap like gazelle," Goshen agreed. "Now you see why Tribes have such trouble winning battles with Aelva. They run too fast."

Three Elves darted forward in unison. Jeran accepted the attack of one, knocking his blade downward in the hopes of pinning it to the walkway, but a second attacker's sword sliced along his leg when he tried, and Jeran stepped away, leaving both men free to resume the attack.

Goshen had more luck. His attacker ducked beneath the Tribesman's swing and leapt in for the kill, but the *Tsha'ma* let go of his weapon with one hand and seized the Elf by the throat. His other hand slid up the haft until it rested at the base of the spiked hammer, then he slammed it into the head of the choking and sputtering Elf.

More Elves poured down the avenue, driving a wedge between Jeran and the Tribesman. A third Elf joined Jeran's two opponents, and the three of them spread out around him, keeping their distance and protecting each other. Unable to commit to an attack without exposing himself to the blades of the others, Jeran considered employing magic to even the odds, but when he attempted to gather more flows to him, the magic he already held rebelled. Keeping control of magic required a desperate struggle, and once he had the flows under control again, a numbing weariness suffused him.

He released his hold on magic entirely, preferring to risk his men to the threat of arrows over the possibility of wild magic. "Fall back to the platform," he said, grabbing at a soldier who attempted to push past him into the wall of Aelvin swords. "Gather our strength!"

They moved back slowly, giving ground with regret, and met at the center of the platform. Scores of Elves approached from every side, pressing them together. Jeran ordered the exhausted Magi to the center, reminding them to concentrate their Gift on defending the men. Only he and Goshen remained on the outer ring, and they stationed themselves opposite each other.

A line of pain lanced across his chest, and he heard a scream from Ansale, one of the youngest soldiers in his guard. Fear dominated the bond he shared with his men, fear and the certainty of death, but to a man he felt the conviction that each intended to die before they let him die. Their devotion brought a swell of unwelcome emotion.

"On my signal, shield your eyes," Jeran ordered, speaking as quietly as he dared. The Elves pressed in, but for the moment they were reluctant to commit to the attack. "Aemon, blind them. Perhaps in the confusion—"

Confused shouting interrupted Jeran, and he looked up to see his opponents turning. The song of flying arrows filled the air around them, and blurred streaks shot across the field from every direction. In moments, dying Elves littered the platform around them, and the few who yet lived sprinted for the concealment of the neighboring trees.

"You were not lying, Nahrima," Astalian, *Hohe Chatorra* of the Aelvin Empire said in disbelief from his perch on the rope bridge above. "He *is* in Lynnaei."

Dozens of *Ael Chatorra* lined the bridges and branches above. Even as Jeran watched, many faded back into the shadows, or resumed a lookout for the enemy. Astalian started toward them, and Jeran met him at the base of the stairway.

"We're here to rescue you!" Jeran said, earning a wan smile from the Elf. Char marks and ash marred Astalian's uniform, and blood stained it in several places. The *Hohe Chatorra* favored one leg, and when he stopped and gripped Jeran's arm in greeting, he leaned heavily on the stout Aelvin bow he carried.

"To offer yourselves up as bait to flush out our enemies..." With a flourish, he made a formal bow, the kind reserved for only the most honored of guests. "Such a noble act."

"We needed a way to flush *you* out," Jeran said. "I figured that shouting your name wouldn't work—" A violent tremor shook the platform and sent the rope bridges to swaying. A horrifying crack echoed through the forest, and in the distance a Great Tree, flames roaring in its heights, swayed and strained against its weakening trunk. With a final crack it split in a jagged diagonal near the base and crashed into its neighbors, spreading flames and debris across the city.

A murmur of awed terror rose up among the men, and Jeran sensed them reevaluating their own positions on this platform. "Quickly," Astalian said, gesturing for them to follow. No hint of the Elf's good humor remained; he resembled a statue, so taut and expressionless were his features.

Jeran followed Astalian through the labyrinthine streets of Lynnaei, up and down to various levels, past burnt corpses and smoldering trees. Thick smoke filled the city, obscuring all but the closest trees and choking the nostril with the acrid scent of death. The stench harassed them until Astalian led them into an encampment on the ground, a hastily-erected fortification in the shadow of the living wall of vines and trees protecting the city. Hundreds of soldiers labored to erect defenses, and dozens more patrolled the trees above. Refugees by the thousands from all castes of Aelvin society milled about outside. The familiar form of Elierian, *Hohe Namisa* and castellan of the palace, directed the refugees, assigning them tasks and issuing orders to the dozens of brown-robed *Ael Namisa* surrounding him.

In the center of the encampment, a solitary figure sat in the shadow of a broad tent, staring into the flames of a fire. Soldiers formed a protective ring around Princess Charylla, but the Aelvin woman paid them no heed. Her unfocused gaze gave the impression that she had extended her perceptions, but Jeran detected no swirl of magic around her.

"I do not like leaving her for this long," Astalian murmured.

"Is the Princess well?" Jeran asked. It seemed a ridiculous question before he finished asking it.

"As well as can be expected. Luran took us completely by surprise. I know not how he reached Lynnaei without our knowledge. I can only assume that there are traitors among my own people. But the gates were breached, and Luran's forces occupied half the city before I learned he was here. By the time I rallied our troops, he held the most defensible sites in the city, and the bulk of his forces were marching on the palace. The Princess wanted to meet him there, but the Emperor ordered an evacuation. He claimed that a principled suicide might make for a good story, but it would still leave Luran as Emperor."

"Then Emperor Alwellyn is with you?" Jeran asked. Again his question seemed foolish; if the Emperor were in the camp, there would be some sign of him, or the mood would not be quite as somber. He wondered what was prompting his tongue to outpace his reason.

"He refused to come, as did many of the older warriors. They are fighting in the palace even now." Guilt and regret painted the Aelvin warrior's face, aging him in a way the winters did not. "I should be there, directing the resistance, but the Emperor ordered me to take Charylla to safety."

Jeran studied the makeshift camp, the bedraggled army comprised mostly of servants and terrified families. "This is where you will make your stand?"

"No. I fear the only chance we have for survival is to flee the city. I sent runners to all of my men, advising them of my intentions and providing them with instructions on where to meet. But Charylla will not leave without the Emperor. I cannot force her to go, and by his order, I cannot go back. The men I have sent have not returned."

"I will find him for you," Jeran said, "if you will take my men into your protection."

"I could not ask you to—"

"I came here to find him, and because I suspected trouble. I will go."

Relief flooded Astalian's face. "You truly are sent by the Gods, *Teshou e Honoure*. Go quickly, my friend. If Luran overruns this camp, all is lost."

Jeran rejoined his small force. Now with the threat of battle temporarily gone, all of them—even the generally imperturbable Orog—gawked at the towering trees and slender Aelvin figures. When he told them what he planned, a general revolt broke out, as each man demanded that he take them along for protection. "I do not have the strength to take us all to the palace," Jeran told them. "And one man may move in secrecy when a dozen might draw attention. I will be well."

Jes was the hardest to convince. "You cannot stop me from going," she told him flatly.

"You are needed here," Jeran said with no hint of the camaraderie he had used on his troops. "You constantly talk of your duty to your people and your devotion to our cause. How will you serve either if we both die here today?"

She stared at him for a long time, her emotions masked even through the bond they shared. "You are infuriating," she said at last, but when Jeran tried to turn away, she grasped his arm so tightly he winced. "Bring him back to us." The command carried a note of plea in it.

Jeran opened a Gate and nearly collapsed from the effort. He hid his exhaustion and stepped through quickly, releasing magic as soon as he was on the other side. Before the Gate finished sliding shut, the pressure on his chest disappeared, and he could breathe easier.

He stood in the apartments he had occupied during the Alrendrian mission to Lynnaei. Everything was as he had left it; even the book he had been reading remained open, the passage marked with a scrap of parchment taken from a desk drawer. A layer of dust had claimed the room—this area of the palace was reserved for Human guests and was rarely visited when none were in attendance—but despite that, the first impression Jeran felt upon entering was one of homecoming. For a moment, memories of his time in Lynnaei flooded back to him, and a nostalgic grin tugged at his lips.

Reality returned like a hammer blow, and Jeran drew his sword, his smile fading, replaced with the stoic determination that kept him moving even when it seemed all the world had turned against him. He wanted to extend his perceptions, but he knew any further attempt to use magic posed an unacceptable risk. Until he rested, he would have to trust his wits and his blade.

He stepped into the hall, hurrying down the twisting labyrinth of corridors. He knew the path by rote; he had tread it so often he could have found his way in absolute dark. But the ancient magic of the palace aided him, lighting the way before him as he approached and then letting the light fade as he passed. Had he known how to extinguish those lights, beacons to any standing guard along the way, he would have.

From time to time he heard the frantic sounds of battle echoing through the red stone halls, the shouts of men and the pained screams of the dying. They faded as abruptly as they started, blocked by the odd acoustics of the ancient citadel. Twice Jeran ducked into shadowy alcoves certain the footfalls he heard approaching were around the next corner, but the only living soul he encountered was a cat, its soft white fur making it appear like a tiny specter drifting through the gloom.

He reached the door to the Vale without incident, and offered a quick prayer to the Gods for their aid. Remembering the loud creaking of its tortured hinges, Jeran drew open the door slowly, but the sound of running footsteps forced him to hasten through. He winced at the screech that preceded the crash of wood against stone, but he wasted no time throwing down the crossbeam and setting a second brace against the ground. Then he turned and faced the Vale.

The serenity of the vast garden complex belied the turmoil in the palace and the horrors of the burning city outside. Butterflies flitted between the flowering bushes and birdsong filled the air. Vibrant green foliage graced every tree, and even the leaves littering the forested floor seemed placed with exacting care. The bleached white stone of the Tower of the Five Gods rose above the trees, dominating the heights and disappearing into the clouds above. Stray wisps of sunlight filtered down through the opening in the rock above, but a dark haze ringed the plateau. Thin tendrils of oily smoke snaked down, grasping like hungry fingers at the Vale's magical vitality.

Jeran ran to the tower, no longer worried about pursuit. He found the Emperor sitting cross-legged in the grass, eyes closed and a sad smile pulling at his paper thin flesh. "You should not have come, dear boy," he said before Jeran even announced his presence, "but I am happy to see you again."

"The city is lost, Grandfather," Jeran said. He had no time to soften the words. "Luran's forces have breached the palace."

"I know," came the ancient Elf's reply.

A loud crash resounded in the distance; the sound of a ram battering against the door. Jeran glanced up to the entrance from the Emperor's throne room and saw tiny black figures racing down the stairs. "There is not much time. Astalian wants to evacuate the city."

"That is a wise decision. Luran's numbers far exceed our expectations. I had no idea that so much discontent fomented beneath the surface of Illendrylla."

"The promises made by men like Luran sound sweet to those dissatisfied with their lives, even when their problems are not caused by others. In the end, they will regret their decision to follow him, and they will need their Emperor to set things right."

"I am not going." The Emperor stood and handed Jeran a small satchel. "Take this to Charylla. Tell her she is ready... No. Tell her she is loved, and that I will watch her from the Heavens."

"She will not leave the city without you, Grandfather. Astalian says she is quite adamant." Another crash resounded in the distance, and then a third. More men poured through the door above, and the soldiers were more than halfway to the ground.

"She will have no reason to stay. I am too old to start anew." The Emperor chuckled, and a measure of life entered his cloudy green eyes. "And you... To you I fear I have done a grave disservice. I have charged you with a monumental task, a task which I have labored for millennia to achieve and have failed, and I ask you to carry on alone. Do not make my mistake, Jeran. Do not close yourself off to the world. There still remains beauty outside these walls. Promise me you will seek it. Do not build your own Vale to hide in."

The Emperor's guilt dug at Jeran, and he sought to reassure him. "You have done nothing wrong by me, Grandfather. I have chosen my path. I am the only one to blame for where it leads."

"Yes," the Emperor smiled. "That is what we all believe at first."

The crash that echoed through the Vale was different, louder and more prolonged. "The door has been breached," Jeran said. "You must come with me. Without their Emperor, the Elves will have no direction."

"Without their Emperor, the Elves will have to choose a new direction. For good or ill, I will no longer allow them to hide behind me. It is time for my people to find their own way." The Emperor's gaze shot past Jeran, and the swell of magic made his eyes burn a brilliant emerald. "You should not have returned, Luran. The Vale is no place for such as you."

The Aelvin warrior stood across the open field, flanked by two towering Tribesmen. His armor glittered in the weak light, but blood dulled the gleam of his blade. A narrow band encircled his head, finely wrought gold and platinum woven in the image of flowering vines.

"The Vale is *mine* now, Grandfather, as is all of Illendrylla." Luran's eyes flicked to Jeran, dropped longingly to the sword he held—a prize won from the Aelvin prince in combat—then returned to the Emperor. "I see you still welcome outsiders into your sanctuary. I am a compassionate man. Once I am installed as Emperor, you will be allowed whatever visitors you desire. With proper supervision, of course."

"I am not the only one to allow outsiders to walk the Vale." Command radiated through the Emperor's words, and something Jeran had never heard before from the old Elf. Rage.

Luran glanced at the Tribesmen behind him. "I have achieved what you always wanted, Grandfather. Unity. Once we have subdued Charylla and eliminated Astalian and the fools who follow him, we will turn the full might of Illendrylla on the Tribal Lands, and then the lands of Man. The Children of Kohr will soon control Madryn, and the Father will reward us for our sacrifice."

"You have betrayed the Goddess." The Emperor's words thundered across the Vale, stopping the dozens of soldiers pouring into the clearing in their tracks. They stared at him in awe; only the handful of scowling Tribesmen seemed able to move. "You defile Lynnaei with battle, and you bring your poison to the very heart of the city, to Valia's Garden itself. You do not deserve to be Emperor. Slinking through shadows and serving the Father of Chaos, you barely deserve to call yourself a man. Your army may have taken the city, but I will not allow you to have the Vale."

"Brave words," said a cold and sibilant voice. Salos stepped from the trees and crossed the distance to Luran with slow, measured steps. He held a purple flower streaked with yellow in one hand and admired the blossom as if it were a fine piece of art. He bowed his head to the Emperor, a slight obeisance, as if addressing an equal. "I would have expected no less from Alwellyn the Eternal." To Luran, he added, "I told you he would never hand over power without a struggle."

The Aelvin prince said nothing, but he refused to look in the Scorpion's direction. Salos's eyes moved to Jeran. "It seems I cannot escape you and your friend; like strays I once took pity on and fed, you are there whenever I turn around, begging for attention." He studied Jeran for a time, a slight smile twisting his lips in a mockery of pleasure. "It is kind of the Father to deliver you to me, though, and in such a state that you are unwilling even to seize magic for your protection."

The risks involved with using magic were foremost in Jeran's mind, but as more soldiers poured into the Vale, he doubted he had any other option. *Better to die in a torrent of magical energy than hand myself over to Salos again.* "Perhaps I do not fear you," Jeran said, stalling for time while he prepared himself.

"Perhaps. But you are not a fool." Salos turned to admire the Vale, his eyes rising up the sheer sides of the Tower of the Five Gods. "You have prepared a spectacular sanctuary for yourself, Alwellyn. Luran remains sentimental despite the Father's urgings to cut all ties with the past, and I have allowed him permission to let you remain here for the remainder of your days. But be warned; should you step even one hand from this Vale, your people will be the ones to suffer for it."

Jeran decided that further delay would serve no purpose, and he opened himself to magic, but the Emperor anticipated his actions, and the tiniest of gestures kept him from seizing his Gift. "This garden was never intended to be a prison," Alwellyn said. "It was designed to be a tomb. The Goddess willing, it will be all of ours."

The air chilled as the Emperor drew magic to him, flow upon flow diverted to his call, until the ancient Elf glowed like a beacon to anyone with the ability to see. Even Salos could not resist; the Emperor's call stripped magic from him, leaving him defenseless and registering surprise at the deprivation of his Gift.

"You may take Lynnaei, Luran, but you will never be Emperor of the Elves. You serve an evil far darker than Lorthas, an evil of intention, not merely of action. Valia will punish you for this blasphemy in Her own time. But with my last breath, I will deny you the peace of her Vale, and leave you a garden more suitable to your reign."

Flames engulfed the field around Jeran and the Emperor, moving outward in pulsing rings like ripples on a pond. Lightning flashed down from the sky, splitting tree trunks with violent explosions and adding new fires to the conflagration. The ground heaved and rolled, spilling men from their feet; huge jagged stones boiled up from below, some with such ferocity that they upended the men beneath them, snapping bones and slashing flesh.

The screams of man and beast reverberated through the Vale. To Jeran, it seemed as if nature itself wailed at its defilement. Only he and the Emperor—and across the way, Luran and Salos, who had regained a modicum of control over magic—remained untouched. The Scorpion studied the maelstrom with interest, but the Aelvin prince fumed. Flecks of spittle flew from his mouth as he demanded that his men attack the Emperor.

Those who found their feet obeyed with hesitation, but instead of directing their assault on the Emperor, to a man they focused on Jeran. Hot wind circled the Vale, feeding the flames and raising a haze of ash and smoldering leaves, obscuring the views of the archers. Dodging magic and leaping flames, Luran's forces raced forward, fear of facing the Emperor's wrath insufficient to risk the displeasure of their God's disciple.

Jeran raised his sword, steel meeting steel with a thunderous clang. A feinting stab sent one opponent dancing back into his companions, leaving an opening Jeran exploited. He pivoted, driving his blade deep into the gut of one Aelvin warrior, then stepped past, sliding the sword free and putting it in a ready position. He flowed from one stance to another, sowing death behind him, and he took grim pleasure in the realization of defeat he saw in each opponent's eyes even before their blades first met.

But even he, with his unnatural martial abilities and heightened awareness, could not win against such odds as were arrayed against him. One Elf scored a scratch on his arm; he twisted an ankle dodging the frantic swing of another. When Salos restored his connection with magic enough to unleash a violent attack, only the Emperor's swift intervention saved Jeran from annihilation.

"The time has come for you to leave," the Emperor said. A Gate opened behind him, a shimmering column of light that gave no hint of the destination. "May the blessing of the Goddess be on you, Child."

Jeran wanted to protest, but he knew the effort fruitless. Staying meant certain death; for every man he killed, five more entered the Vale. The Emperor would not leave, and Jeran had not the skill or the desire to force him. Moreover, a change had overtaken the Elf, a vibrant embracing of the moment Jeran had never before seen. Clothes smeared with ash, wispy hair blowing in the wind, eyes alight with the Gift, the Emperor seemed if not happy, then at least at peace.

A violent wind blew the attackers backward into the path of two falling trees, their burning upper branches giving them the appearance of giant torches. The thunder of their twin falls knocked everyone save the Emperor to the ground, and Jeran used the momentary lull to move to the column of light.

"Goodbye, Grandfather," he said, burning the image of the Vale—its flowerbeds trampled, its meticulous shrubs blackened and barren, its towering trees burnt or burning—into his mind.

The Emperor turned to him and smiled, the warm, grandfatherly smile Jeran had seen so often from the gentle man. But framed in the ashes of the Vale, with the scorched and blackened stones of the Tower of the Five Gods behind him, he looked a fearsome being, a testament to the legends of Alwellyn the Eternal still circulating throughout Alrendria.

The Gate closed, leaving Jeran's last sight that of the ancient Elf fending off a violent attack from Salos, with Luran's soldiers regaining their feet and closing in. When the light around him dimmed, he stood in a small bed of untouched flowers, with the massive red stone of the palace far to the north.

He began the long march back to Astalian's camp. Each step was an effort; it felt as if his legs dragged heavy stones behind them. He walked in a daze, oblivious to the echoes of battle above, the acrid stench of wood smoke and the sight of battered and broken bodies.

He found the camp with little difficultly, using his bond with Jes and the others as a beacon. No one challenged his approach; no one demanded he identify himself as he emerged from the haze. No one so much as called his name as he traversed the makeshift fortifications and hastily-erected tents.

Astalian appeared from the tent in the center of the camp, and behind him, the solemn form of Charylla watched Jeran's lonely approach. No words were necessary; one long look at Jeran and Astalian turned and dropped to one knee.

"Empress, what are your orders?"

CHAPTER 24

"No one passes this door without written permission from me, the King, or Lady Liseyl!"

The guard, a stable boy ripped from the streets and impressed into service in the aftermath of the battle, blanched under Martyn's tirade, but he raised his fist to his heart in a trembling salute. He resumed his post in front of the catacombs, careful to keep his eyes away from the prince.

Gods, I think he might start crying. The realization troubled Martyn, but he had no time to waste on bruised egos. With New Kaper firmly in the hands of the enemy and Old Kaper simmering like a cauldron on the verge of boiling over, coddling children ranked low on his priorities.

"If you think your duty tedious," Martyn said, starting down the hall, "if you think a few stolen apples or a missing bag of grain makes little difference, think again. Once the food held in the catacombs is gone, there will be no more. You and those guarding the other stores hold the key to our survival."

"Yes, my Lord!"

Treloran waited for him at the intersection of two halls. The Aelvin Prince's ageless face was expressionless, but Martyn sensed his disapproval. "What?"

"Do you not think your reaction a bit overdone? The boy is neither *Ael Namisa* nor *Ael Chatorra*. He understands nothing of what he has been asked to do. You thrust him into a position he is not trained for, and then seem concerned when he makes mistakes. The catacombs may hold your largest grain stores, but—"

"If the wrong people learn what—" Martyn cut off abruptly and visibly calmed himself. For all their shared experiences and strong friendship, the Elf's thinly-veiled air of superiority galled him. "We no longer have the luxury of time. That boy's a soldier now, whether he intended to be or not. I can't wait for people to be ready; they must serve when and how they're needed."

Treloran shrugged. "If you stick your hand in the fire, you should expect to be burned."

"You've been spending too much time with those Orog," Martyn scoffed. "Besides, why should I take advice from you? What do the Elves know of war? A few skirmishes with the Tribes on your border in the last hundred years in no way makes you masters of warfare. There's hardly an Elf alive who knows the terror of true battle, the certainty that no matter what you do, you are doomed."

"Hardly an Elf," Treloran agreed. "Only those who chose to come to Kaper."

The statement, calmly given, stopped Martyn in his tracks. "My apologies," he said, clasping his hands and bowing to Treloran in the Aelvin gesture of regret. "I spoke without thinking."

"When do you not?" Treloran replied, but Martyn caught the Aelvin Prince's amused grin.

"Arrogant Elf!"

"Foolish Human."

They resumed walking, and Martyn set a quick pace. Servants and refugees scurried through the halls, pressing themselves against the walls to give the princes room. The palace hummed with activity, the buzz of excitement merging with the oppressive pall of fear. Every chamber housed refugees: Elves and nobles and anyone important enough to buy their way out of the cramped confines of the old city. All but the most important had been impressed into one form of service or another, and those who refused to work were threatened with expulsion. Fear of being handed over to the Tachans made even the haughtiest noble eager to serve.

Though he could not see them, Martyn felt the presence of his guard. Even in the sanctity of the palace, he was no longer free of them. They dogged his steps, and the moment he set foot outside they would be at his side, ready for attack. That he had faced three attempts on his life in the last few ten-days made no difference. He did not question their necessity, he simply despised it.

The bustle of the grounds made the palace look desolate. Hundreds, from smooth-cheeked boys to grizzled old men, formed rank and worked the forms under the watchful eyes of grim Guardsmen. Dozens more patrolled the barriers erected around the farms, while an army of servants removed weeds and tended the growing shoots. The harvest would be small; the palace grounds did not have much land available to devote to growing food, but every bit would help. Every bit might prolong the siege another day.

Tents filled every gap. Ordered when possible, haphazard when not, the cream-colored canvas crackled in the stiff Harvest breeze, and the dying light of day played off the flapping material in a dance of light and shadow, giving the impression of movement, like the gentle swell of the sea. Small fires burned in the gaps between tents, with desperate hands reaching out toward the warming flames. Martyn should have ordered them extinguished—with wood and coal in dwindling supply, they would need what they had for the bitter cold of winter—but he could not find the heart to issue the command. One look at the hopelessness on his subjects' faces, and he thought a night of warmth worth the wasted resources.

"Prince Martyn!" cried a servant boy, running toward him. A Guardsmen leapt forward to intercept the child, half terrifying him. He shrieked and fell back, trembling and refusing to wrest his gaze from the scarred soldier until Martyn ordered the man away. Then he approached again, with caution. "Princess Miriam requests your attendance."

"Inform the princess I will join her presently."

"She says it is urgent, my Prince." The boy trembled again, but this time, at the memory of Miriam's temper.

"No doubt," Martyn said. The enforced bed rest imposed by Sheriza was driving Miriam mad, and the princess felt the need to distribute her misery to anyone fortunate enough to share her company. Kaeille endured it daily—his *advoutre* had set herself as Miriam's personal protector—but Martyn did not share the Aelvin woman's love of torture. Whenever duty called, he put the good of Alrendria above that of his wife. And sometimes when duty did not call, he went looking for it. "Everything is urgent in these desperate times. Tell the princess I will attend her as soon as I am able."

"Yes, Prince Martyn." The boy sprinted toward the palace. Martyn did not envy him the tirade he would endure when he returned without Miriam's quarry in tow.

"Do not rush into marriage," Martyn told Treloran. "And do not rush into love. Kaeille will chastise my absence nearly as much as Miriam. I get more rest along the ramparts than I do in my own chambers."

"What use are you to them?" the Aelvin Prince asked. "You are neither Healer nor midwife. What purpose can you serve?"

"Besides target?" Martyn quipped. "I have no idea. But if I am not there, I am reprimanded for it, and when I am there, I am punished for my presence."

"Such, they say, is the lot of a husband." Dayfid, his shining plate polished until it gleamed in the dying sunlight, strode forward and saluted Martyn fist-on-heart. "I bring you a report from the northern Wall, my Prince."

"Dayfid! It's good to see a friendly face. Have the Tachans made another assault?'

"Not today. We drove them back so easily yesterday I suspect they'll think twice before attacking again. They mill about beyond bowshot and taunt us with their atrocities in New Kaper, but they no longer appear in a hurry to attack."

"That's welcome news," Martyn said. "Commander Lisandaer commended your service in the recent series of battles."

Dayfid ducked his head in embarrassment, though Martyn knew it was just a show. The Guardsmen sought praise at every opportunity, basked in the admiration of his peers and superiors. That he deserved most of the attention lavished upon him was the most frustrating thing of all. Along with Brell Morrena and Aryn Odara, Dayfid had become one of the great heroes of the Siege of Kaper.

Even now, adoring eyes focused on the Guardsman, studying his rugged good looks. Martyn's ego screamed at the affront, but he sought to moderate his unreasonable anger. "The recruits need a role model, someone they can look to as an example. I would like you to take control of their training."

"Me, my Prince? I—" Dayfid looked startled, and perhaps a bit nervous. The anxiety he suddenly wore brought a slight smile to Martyn's face.

"—am the best choice for the duty. The men already look up to you. You've already proven yourself to them. If I have a thousand men with your courage when the final battle comes, then we cannot help but win."

"But my duties on the Wall—?"

"Are still yours. I cannot afford to reassign you, only to add to your burdens."

Indecision played across the Guardsman's face. "As you command, Prince Martyn," he said at last.

Martyn listened as Dayfid detailed troop strength and weapon stores, casualty lists and enemy positions. Three militia men had been cast beyond the wall for failing to man their posts, two more for attempting to incite riot. A sixth, suspected of being a Tachan traitor, awaited trial and a decision from the King regarding his fate. Enforced rationing had the men on edge, especially when they saw an abundance of vegetables and some grain growing in the makeshift gardens scattered about the Old City. Curious commoners kept approaching the Wall, hoping to watch a great battle, and some caused trouble when forced to leave. Lisandaer had requested permission to impress the curious into service, shoring up the defenses, relaying messages, or any of a dozen other tedious tasks he wanted to spare his men.

Martyn agreed. *Everyone inside Old Kaper needs to earn their safety; if someone cannot find a useful task, I have no qualms finding one for them.*

His report finished, Dayfid waited for dismissal then hurried back down the road to resume his post. Excited whispers and longing gazes marked his passage, and though Dayfid pretended ignorance of the attention, Martyn suspected that a broad smile was plastered across the man's face.

"Insufferable," Treloran whispered.

"He has his moments," Martyn said, "but he's no more arrogant than some others I know."

The Elf's eyes narrowed, but Martyn maintained such an even expression that Treloran could not properly tell if the jibe were directed at him. For a wonder, the Aelvin Prince chose to hold his acid tongue, and the two continued their inspection of the castle grounds.

No one spoke to them as they passed; the friendly camaraderie Martyn had once shared with the palace workers had fled since his return from Vela. Shadowed as they were by a score of Guardsmen, and no doubt with a handful of *Ael Chatorra* ghosting around them, the crowds parted for them. Proper respect was shown; not a man or woman failed to bow, and not a single person cheered his presence.

Have they changed, or have I? No doubt a little of both.

Tent rows staked into earth hard-packed by the passage of thousands of feet marked off the militia's billeting. Those few unlucky Guardsmen who earned the honor of commanding a squad of militiamen shared the tents with the common soldiers; the rest of the Guard packed themselves into the barracks on the other side of the palace grounds. Quarters were cramped with Guardsmen doubled-up in the bunks, but the solid roof and firepits were still a far improvement over the thick canvas of the tents.

Aryn's original plan had called for the construction of more barracks to replace the tents, but with the enemy outside the door, all non-defensive construction had been halted. As winter loomed, though, the differences in accommodation grew more acute. Martyn wondered how long the men would endure before rioting broke out.

Martyn caught sight of Aryn in the distance and altered his path to join the Guard Commander. He passed teams of workmen scouring the base of the palace wall, giving the fortifications a final inspection under the watchful eyes of architects and masons. The ivory stone glowed, seemingly of its own accord, and the copper ornamentation capping the parapets flashed in the sunlight. Martyn watched the preparations with a sense of foreboding.

"I'm not sure what bothers me more," he told Treloran. "That Aryn believes we will need the palace walls ready, or that no one realizes that if the enemy reaches them, we are already lost."

"There is always the chance for miracles," the Aelvin Prince replied. "This wall may be insignificant compared to the one guarding Old Kaper, but if it slows the enemy for even a day, that is one day more for the Gods to hear our prayers."

"You place far too much in the hands of the Gods."

"And you, far too little."

Aryn stood with Ehvan, talking in hushed voices. Jeran's ambassador, flanked as always by two Orog bodyguards, wore the black uniform of the Army of the Boundary, flaunting the near-treason of House Odara. Ehvan had saved his life and, in general, treated him the way one should treat his prince. Yet a hint of condescension lurked behind his eyes, and a powerful devotion to Jeran whenever anyone, even Martyn, so much as questioned his intentions. *Is he my subject, or a diplomat? If the latter, is he not... are they all not... traitors?*

"Will Jeran arrive today?" he asked, but the stricken look he received froze the jest he had prepared. "What has happened?"

"I don't know." Rings circled Ehvan's eyes, and his flesh had a pallor to it. His hand shot out with unconscious certainty, pointing northeast. "He's in that direction. Much farther away than before. He is hurt, somehow, though the impression is indistinct. In danger. More than that. It's more than just a danger to him; it's a danger to all Madryn."

"Wonderful," Martyn said wryly. "I thought the odds were stacking up a bit too much in our favor."

"This is not a joking matter, Prince Martyn." Ehvan's gaze carried a dark anger, a heat like the dull red glow of steel in a blacksmith's forge. "Our bond is lessened by distance. For me to receive such clear impressions, the situation must be dire."

"I do not doubt you," Martyn replied, hastily adopting a conciliatory tone. "But there's nothing we can do. We must trust that Jeran will endure whatever hardships he is given, and that our plan will not change because of it."

"There is some good news to be gleaned from this," Aryn said, and all eyes turned toward the Commander. "If he's to the northeast, we know the problem is not with the Boundary. The Darklord remains trapped, Portal and Dranakohr remain intact, and we need not fear another army marching on us from behind."

"Perhaps we should send someone to reconnoiter?" Treloran's proposition caught Martyn by surprise. Despite commanding the archers defending the walls, the Aelvin Prince rarely made suggestions in regards to conducting the campaign.

"How would we get them outside the walls?" Martyn asked, shaking his head. "Or past the Tachans?"

"When the next shipment of supplies arrives from Dranakohr," Ehvan suggested, "I can make arrangements. I do not like the delay, but we have no choice. I cannot station any Gifted here for fear they would be captured by the Assembly." He fixed a pointed gaze on the prince.

"We have discussed this before," Martyn said, his jaw tightening. "I will no more condemn them than I will you. I cannot risk the wrath of any potential allies, even those who might otherwise tear each other apart."

"Drive the Assembly from the city, and I can promise you a score of Gifted ready to protect Kaper. What does Mage Valkov offer?"

"You can offer a score of children, and a handful of rogue Magi. If Valkov can be convinced, I will have the might of the Assembly at my disposal, hundreds of experienced and well-trained Magi. I can't risk losing that over—"

"—over an army devoted to the defeat of your enemies and to the freedom of all souls in Madryn. The Assembly courts you like an equal, but Valkov sees you as a fool, a puppet he can use to restore power to—"

"—I am still your prince," Martyn snarled, "regardless of whether or not Jeran wants to pretend at kingship. Watch your tone with me."

"You are prince only because your people will it. Throw too many of them to the Tachans, all in the name of protecting House Batai, and you will find your people welcoming the Scorpion into Kaper."

"How dare you speak—"

"Martyn!"

Martyn turned at Kaeille's stern call. He had not seen her approach, but from her stance—arms crossed, foot tapping, mouth pressed into a narrow line—that had not been her first attempt to gain his attention.

His anger defused, he exhaled a heavy breath. "Yes?"

"The princess requires your attention."

"I sent word that I would be there as soon as duty permitted. Let Miriam know—"

"Your wife requires your attention." The Aelvin woman never blinked, and her cold green glare cowed Martyn.

"Very well," he said. "I will be along presently."

"You will be along now. I will accompany you."

Martyn seethed at being redressed before others, but he forced a smile, made a flourish as he bowed, and said, "Forgive me, my friends, but a threat to my life far more potent than the Tachans deserves my attention." He offered Kaeille his arm and let the Aelvin woman lead him to the palace.

Chapter 25

Dahr brushed aside the tent flap and hurried inside, pushing past the two sour-faced Hunters standing guard. His sprint across the camp had left him winded, but it was not the great heaving breaths he took that held his tongue, nor the chill morning breeze against his sweat-slicked flesh that made him shiver. The Channa's camp swirled with a whirlwind of rumors, but they had not prepared him.

The tent was a shambles, the sparse furnishings and trinkets collected over a lifetime scattered about. Ornate rugs captured in raids on Aelvin lands lay shredded as if clawed by a beast. A collection of fine Feldarian glasses bought long ago in Grenz stood shattered on their display table. The brazier had been upended, sending coals across the floor and leaving tiny chars on much of what might otherwise have been salvageable. Footprints, broken by scrapes and gouges that cut across the floor like scars, left imprints in the dirt.

Blood covered everything, more blood than Dahr thought could come from a single man. Streaks of it covered the canvas walls, flecks dotted the ceiling, and a broad pool spread over much of the floor, with tendrils reaching toward the flap as if it had tried to escape before time and temperature congealed it.

Set out on display in the center of the tent lay Yarchik. Dozens of small wounds covered his arms and legs, framing more grievous cuts on throat and torso. His face remained untouched, lifeless eyes staring toward the Heavens, the pallid expression carrying a mixture of agony and defiance.

Dahr knelt beside the body, mindless of the blood that stained his pants. A trembling hand touched the *Kranor*'s face. Hopelessness filled him, crashing against the bulwarks of ever present anger. It forced the anger to surface, hardening his expression, fixing his features in a snarl, and giving the impression of strength when all he truly felt was numbing despair.

"Who did this," he whispered.

"None know," answered the Tribesman who discovered the body. "None see enter tent. None see come out. No sounds."

"This was not done by the wind!" Dahr fumed. "The murderer did not tunnel away. How could he not be seen?"

Another Hunter, a warrior by the name of Akin, stepped forward. "Elves known to move like shadow. Kill without being seen."

Dahr rounded on the Tribesmen. "Use your eyes! And your wits, if you have any. These tracks are twice the size of the largest Elf, and no Elf would kill with such a lack of finesse. This was the work of a Tribesman."

"The Blood not kill old men in tents," Akin replied, looking as if Dahr's words had been a personal insult. "Children of Garun have more honor."

"I said this was done by a Tribesman. I did not say this was done by a Child of Garun."

Dahr stooped, pretending to examine the tracks. Once again responsibility had been thrust upon him; before long, the Channa would remember that he was now their *Kranor*, and they would start asking him for guidance. *Why did you have to die?* Dahr asked the lifeless Yarchik. *Why did you have to leave this burden to me?*

"Kraltir did this." The suddenness of the statement shocked Dahr as much as it did the others, but he could not doubt its certainty.

"*Kohr'adjin*? In tents?" Akin did not share Dahr's conviction. "Why he not seen? Why Yarchik not call help?"

"Blood has a way of obscuring loyalties and reason," Dahr said. "Yarchik would not call men to fight his son. He always harbored the hope of Kraltir's redemption."

The tent flap pulled aside and Katya entered. She had dressed hurriedly, forgoing armor in her haste, but wore both sword and dagger sheathed at her hip. The signs of sleep still marked her flesh, and stray curls framed her head with coppery locks. With a single step she saw the body, and the color drained from her face. Her eyes shifted from Dahr to Yarchik and back again, but she said nothing, and to her credit, she kept her distance.

"No," Akin set his face. "No! No *Kohr'adjin* enter tents."

"How can you be so certain?" Dahr asked, looking into the eyes of the Hunter.

Akin's eyes flicked toward the tent flap, and Dahr followed the gaze. Tarouk stood silhouetted in the morning sun, with two more Vahr Drekka Hunters flanking him. From outside he heard Lord Grondellan's booming voice demand to know what was happening. "He guard last night," Tarouk offered. "It dishonor him if enemy sneak past."

"Enemies not need sneak into tents when invited by Korahn," Akin growled.

Dahr leapt from the floor, catching Akin by the throat and slamming him to the ground. His other hand, balled into a fist, crashed against the Tribesman's jaw, sending a new spray of blood across the tent. Caught by surprise and stunned by the violence of the blow, the Hunter could do little as Dahr unleashed his pent up emotion.

A rough hand gripped his arm, pulling him away from Akin. "This not right," Tarouk told him. "*Cho Korahn Garun* must stand beyond grief."

"I will no longer allow this," Dahr snarled, wrenching his hand free and striking Akin again. "The Vahr Drekka are here by my choice. They will be treated with the respect given to any other tribe."

Tarouk grabbed at Dahr again, but Dahr shoved him away. Akin lay insensate, blood streaming from the corner of his mouth, face already swelling and distorted, but the Tribesman's appearance awakened little pity. Confronted by the grisly scene of Yarchik's death and spurred to action by the unfounded prejudice directed at the Vahr Drekka, Dahr surrendered to the beast within.

"Stop him!" Katya shouted as he lunged toward Akin, but only Tarouk had the courage to stand up to *Cho Korahn Garun*. This time when the Vahr Drekka approached, Dahr landed a quick blow in his midriff, then grabbed his arm and threw him to the ground. Akin stirred then, weakly struggling to flee, and Dahr returned the full focus of his wrath to the Tribesman pinned beneath him.

Vise-like hands clamped around Dahr's sweat-slicked shoulders, pulling him away. When he struggled, one of those hands let go long enough to cuff him across the head, then clamped back down with greater ferocity. "He's had enough, Hunter," Grondellan said as Katya pried Dahr's hands from Akin's throat. "More than enough, I'd say."

The sight of the unconscious Tribesman, and his own hands so firmly wrapped around the man's throat, returned Dahr to his senses. He released Akin and scrabbled backward, shamed by his display and desperate not to show it. He looked toward the tent flap, where the other guards watched with little expression. "The Vahr Drekka are not responsible for what happened here," he said. "Any who treat them as enemies will face my anger. Wait outside."

The guards nodded and stepped outside. As soon as they were gone, Dahr sat, hitting the ground with a thud. His breaths came in deep gasps; his heart pounded in his chest. But only when Dahr's head slumped forward did Grondellan release his grip.

"Gods," the Rachannan said. "Who could do such a thing? I've not seen such barbarism, even during the Tachan War."

"Kraltir did this," Dahr said, his voice as hollow as his heart.

"That makes no sense. What could the *Kohr'adjin* gain from—?"

Dahr heard the hiss of breath and felt Grondellan step away. He craned his neck around to see what had startled the Rachannan.

Grondellan's face had paled; the ruddy color highlighting his cheeks deserted him, leaching the vigor from his expression. He trembled; his mouth worked, but no sound emerged. In that moment, he showed every one of his advancing winters. Now pity did find Dahr, awakening a concern he had never expected to feel for his former Master.

Then he realized that the Rachannan's eyes were locked on his bare shoulder, staring at the scar highlighted golden in the flickering light of the tent's remaining lamps. The condor brand, sigil of the Grondellan holdings and the mark placed upon all its property, a shame he took great care to conceal except this one time, in the wake of Yarchik's death.

"All this time..." Grondellan whispered, his voice a shadow of its normal sound.

"Not now," Dahr said.

"Is it really you, *Nai'segare*? I thought... Why didn't you..."

"Not now!" Dahr roared, and Grondellan started at the sound like a rabbit hearing the bark of a fox. He stared at Dahr for a long moment, then turned and bolted from the tent. Dahr watched him go, his mouth drawn down in a cold grimace. Part of him was glad the truth was free, that Grondellan would now know he was in part responsible for what Dahr had become; part of him regretted the anguish he had seen on the man's face.

"Did you expect it to stay a secret forever?" Katya asked, approaching him.

"No."

"Then why that look? He should have known long ago. It would have eased both your burdens."

"I don't need lectures on compassion. Especially from a Durange."

Katya's mouth tightened, and anger flushed her cheeks crimson. "Of course not." She brushed past the Tribesmen at the tent flap and strode into the light.

Dahr sat staring at the ground, his mind a whirl of dark thoughts. He felt eyes on him, and turned to see the lifeless gaze of Yarchik boring into him. Accusing. Reminding. Pleading. *Even in death you scold me. Even in death, you continue to saddle me with responsibilities. Why would you leave the fate of the Blood to me, when I stand on the brink already, with one foot halfway to the Nothing?*

As if in answer, Dahr heard the old *Kranor*'s voice echo through his mind. "*The time has come for the Garun'ah to choose their fate. No man, not even the Korahn, can force us down a path. If we follow you to destruction, then it is because Garun, in His wisdom, decided it must be allowed. But perhaps, just perhaps, my friend, it is not you who will lead us to the Nothing, but we who will save you from it.*"

Yarchik had said as much to him on many occasions, and Dahr yearned to believe. But what redemption could he find now? Those eyes mocked him, asked him how he could have let such a thing happen, accused him of fighting against fate until the Gods had no choice but to force him to obey. He had delayed, and that delay cost the Channa their *Kranor*, and him another friend.

Light filled the tent, blinding him, and Dahr squinted to make out the form standing silhouetted in the tent flap. "Olin," he snarled. "Find them. There will be no more games, no more dancing about the fields picking off stragglers. Find the *Kohr'adjin* for me, wherever they hide. The Blood goes to war."

Excitement flashed across the Olin's face, but a caution rare to find in a Hunter battled with the thrill of a hunt. "Is that wise, Korahn? Are we ready? The *Kohr'adjin* fight like no Tribesmen before."

"We are either Hunters or prey," Dahr replied, his voice devoid of emotion. "I will not wait while our enemies whittle us down, until we have no one left to fight. I will no longer sit while the promises of the *Kohr'adjin* seduce our Hunters and spread doubt among the Blood. We will take the fight to them, and let our blades decide who is right."

Olin weighed the response, and the Tribesman's delay caused Dahr's temper to stir. "I will send out scouts," Olin said at last. "We will flush out our enemies."

"Send more runners to the Sahna and Afelda," Dahr added, climbing to his feet. "Tell them a time of reckoning is coming, and that we don't want to deny them a place at this feast of blood."

Dahr went to the body and closed Yarchik's eyes, then placed a hand on the old Hunter's cold brow and wished him a speedy journey to the Twilight World. "Tarouk, the Vahr Drekka now have the responsibility of guarding outside the tents. I do not want to hear of any more enemies slipping past our guards."

A protest rose among the other Tribesmen, and all eyes shot toward the slim warrior. "The Vahr Drekka will guard outside the tents," Dahr repeated. "Flushing out the enemies already inside falls to the rest of you. Use Grendor if you must, but I want no *Kohr'adjin* living among the Blood." An eager fervor swept through the Hunters arrayed around him, prompting Dahr to add. "Kill them only if forced. Any *Kohr'adjin* found must be brought to me for questioning."

Dahr draped a blanket over Yarchik's body, tucking the coarse fabric beneath him. "Eranda, request an assembly of the *Kranora*. Insist on haste. They must be told what has happened here so they can prepare for what is to come. Pran, Viska, prepare a pyre befitting one such as Yarchik, and tell the Blood that we will sing his soul to the Twilight World at sunset."

The Garun'ah hurried to carry out their orders, and Dahr, energized by the thought of action, burst from the tent into a morning of bright sunlight and clear skies. *Find the Kohr'adjin!* He sent out the thought, and all across camp birds took flight, spreading outward, their eyes scouring the countryside. They would find the enemy first and tell him what direction he should march; Olin's scouts would later provide a more accurate picture of what he faced. Relative strengths and troop formations were not matters that concerned the Lesser Voices.

Rannarik met him as he left the tents. The *Tsha'ma*, his long, white hair pulled back in a braid laced with feathers and beads, wore a grim expression. "It is true?"

Dahr nodded. "Murdered. I suspect Kraltir."

Rannarik closed his eyes, and his mouth moved in measured cadence as he communed silently with the Gods. "The Channa will want to name you *Kranor* quickly. You told them the ceremony will be held at sunset? Good. Have you given thought to who you might name *Kranach*?"

"I know few among the Channa well enough to—"

"You will need an advisor. Arik will welcome time free of my prattling, and the *Tsha'ma* belong to all tribes. I will aid you until Jakal can be summoned, or until you choose another from among the Channa to serve you."

"That would be welcome. I know little enough of your ways. I would prefer not to offend—"

"My first advice is that you abandon this foolish notion of hunting down *Kohr'adjin*. We know nothing of their numbers, but their devotion to the Father of Storms is absolute. They will slam against us like a tempest on the shores until the Blood is no more."

"As long as they exist," Dahr said, bile rising in his throat, "they will hunt us, courting those of the Blood whose faith is lacking and killing those whose faith is not. Better to stop them now, while our numbers are strong and our blood is hot."

"Better still to ensure that the Blood survives, that the teachings of Garun are not lost for all time because one man seeks revenge above reason."

"Is this what I can expect from you as my advisor?" Dahr's voice rose in volume, and he struggled to keep himself controlled.

Rannarik's laughter caught him off guard. "No doubt Arik will tell you to expect worse. I would be no help if I did not speak what I thought was in the Channa's best interest. In the Blood's best interest."

"We do not march today, but when I find the *Kohr'adjin*, there will be war."

Rannarik pressed his lips into a narrow line, debating whether or not to continue the discussion. He chose to move on. "The Vahr Drekka will cause much concern if allowed to patrol outside the tents."

"Word travels fast. Or *Tsha'ma* listen at tent flaps. The Vahr Drekka have their orders, as do the rest of the tribes. They are not our enemies."

"That I know, but others among the Blood are not as certain."

"Then educate them. That is what *Tsha'ma* do, isn't it? I will not have them treated like criminals. They fight and die for us the same as any other."

"I will do what I can," Rannarik replied, "but you risk battle amongst the Tribes if you give any Drekka authority over real Tribesmen."

"Real Tribesmen?" Meila stepped out from the tents, throwing back the cowl of her cloak. She made a respectful bow to Rannarik, holding her hands palm up, then faced Dahr and brushed a hand across his cheek, turning his face so their eyes met. The soft caress of her fingers made him flush. "I sorrow at your loss. Even we, poor shadows of true Tribesmen, knew of the great Yarchik, and I know you held special bond."

Dahr said nothing, but Rannarik bowed his head. "I did not mean disrespect, Priestess. I spoke—"

"As all Tribesmen do," she finished. "The crimes of our ancestors taint our blood. None know that better than Vahr Drekka."

Rannarik stared at her with the probing, piercing gaze so common among the Gifted. "You plan something."

"I plan nothing new. I seek to save my people, as you seek to save yours. Korahn, the Vahr Drekka wish to honor the great Yarchik. We wish to attend oration."

"I do not think that wise," Rannarik said, shaking his head. "The Tribes already suspect—"

"Then good for me it *Kranor* of the Channa I ask, not his *Tsha'ma*," Meila snapped. Her cheeks colored at the outburst, but she made no apology.

"Stop!" Dahr commanded, and both turned to face him. "The Vahr Drekka may attend the funeral."

"I also want speak *Kranora*," Meila told him. "I have—"

"The *Kranora* will never allow a—"

Dahr raised a hand, cutting of Rannarik. "I want the *Kranora* to hear what Meila has to say. If being *Cho Korahn Garun* gains me nothing else, it should gain me that."

"They will not approve," Rannarik warned.

"Then let them leave. But once they abandon the tents, advise them that they'll be enemies of the Blood."

Meila frowned over his words, but Rannarik looked aghast. "You mean to say you will turn your back on any Tribesman who will not fight with you?"

"I mean to say that any Tribesmen who thinks himself safer on his own is already dead. I will save him the trouble of wondering where death might find him."

"That is grief talking," Rannarik said. "Yarchik would never—"

"Yarchik is dead! If you think my decisions unbefitting a *Kranor*, then give the honor to another fool. I never pretended to want the titles you keep heaping upon me."

"You act as a spoiled cub," Rannarik said, bringing himself to full height. Though he could not see any change, Dahr suspected the *Tsha'ma* held magic, and was ready to use it if necessary. "Do you think the Channa would rather you lead them than Yarchik? Do you think you are the only one to grieve at his loss? The only one to suffer in these dark times?

"We endure much petulance from you because, though the blood of Garun flows in your veins, you are not *of* the Blood. I can see that we have indulged—"

"Korahn!" A young Hunter approached. Though obviously mortified to be interrupting the *Tsha'ma*, he inserted himself between Dahr and his advisor. "Olin send me. *Kohr'adjin* scouts flushed out to north. Word from south of Tribesmen approaching."

"Friend or foe?" Dahr asked.

"We not know," the young man said, shaking his head. "Olin only tell me—"

"Dahr, we must talk," Vyrina said, appearing on Dahr's right. The Guardswoman wore her uniform again, but her hair remained braided in the Garun'ah fashion. "My trainees are not ready for all out war. They do not have enough control yet. It's all they can do to hold formation in the heat of an exercise, let alone a—"

"Friend Dahr, I heard about honored Yarchik," Grendor said, limping forward on his *va'dasheran*. "The *Kranor* of the Channa and I had many talks and he wanted me to assure you—"

"There still matter I need discuss with you, Korahn," Meila said, her voice low. "You need know. The Vahr Drekka—"

"*Kranach! Gahst Treik uvan Marik nesast*—!"

Another voice, this one in his head. *Brother, there is danger. Are you ready to face it? Do you need our help?*

Others approached, demanding his attention, seeking his advice. They shouldered each other for position, skirting wide of only Rannarik and Meila, and them by only a hand's breadth. The cacophony of voices grated at Dahr's nerves; their overlapping words echoed in his ears like a discordant chorus, neither making sense nor deserving attention.

"Leave me be!" Dahr swept out his arms, clearing himself a path down which he stomped. The edge of the camp beckoned, and beyond that, a large swath of forest in which he could lose himself.

"Your bluster doesn't frighten me, Dahr!" Vyrina shouted. "What of my troops?"

"Train them fast. You have until I find the *Kohr'adjin* to make them ready."

A few Tribesmen started to follow—most were wise enough to catch his mood and keep their distance without additional warning. "Two more steps," Dahr snarled without looking back, "and they will be your last." In the moment of uncertainty that followed his threat, he fled.

CHAPTER 26

Dahr crawled forward, testing each movement before settling his weight so as to keep from warning his prey. The cool wetness of the leaf litter did little to chill his fiery blood, but the smell of fresh soil and the gentle rustling of the canopy overhead combined to calm the torrent raging within. Some.

He clutched his *dolchek* in one hand, the serrated blade dulled with mud to keep it from flashing in the stray wisps of light penetrating the branches. He stalked a giant beast with antlers half again as broad as he was, a powerful creature in whose death he hoped to satiate the hunger gnawing at his insides.

Yet it was not a hunger for food he fought; it was a hunger for action. Hiding among the tents, waiting for the *Kohr'adjin* to find them, brought him little peace. Watching as those who followed him disappeared one by one, killed in petty raids or lured away by the seductive promises of Kraltir, sickened him. He yearned for battle, yearned for a chance to settle this matter once and for all. Maybe then he could find the peace he wanted so desperately.

The silence surrounding him came as a blessed relief, a respite from the constant nagging he endured among the tents. His order to be left alone—and the threat he had delivered the orders with—guaranteed that no Tribesmen would follow him, and with some effort he had walled himself off from the Lesser Voices, freeing himself from the constant buzz of their conversation for a time.

Now he crept through a broad patch of forest paralleling a stream. The water ran low, barely more than a trickle at the bottom of the pebble-covered bank, emphasizing another reason he sought to hasten the Tribesmen to war. With water scarce and the Hunters forced to roam ever farther to find game, the time had come to move the tents, or they risked upsetting the Balance.

The Balance! Even here, in the midst of a hunt, the warnings of the Lesser Voices intruded upon him.

Yet this was a warning he could not dismiss. He had seen too many natural beauties to willingly be the cause of one's destruction. One way or another, the Tribes would pack their tents tomorrow.

A stick snapped, and Dahr froze. The sound had come from in front of him, but not from the direction he expected. Either his quarry had turned while he was lost in thought, or another creature moved with them through the trees.

He edged up the bank, moving with even greater care, keeping himself low to the ground. At the base of a broad tree, he stood and got his bearings, then slowly leaned around the trunk.

The massive stag had doubled back on his own trail and foraged in a patch of scrub and grass. Facing the creature's back, Dahr held the element of surprise, but it also gave the stag an opportunity for full flight should he become aware of the attack. Dahr tightened his grip on the *dolchek* and focused on the animal. He slowed his breathing, seeking the peace of the hunt, and felt his heartbeat match that of the stag's.

Then, with a casual air, as if aware he was being stalked and unconcerned by it, the stag turned its massive head to look into Dahr's eyes. *Danger, brother.*

Dahr jerked upright. *He shouldn't have known I was here! How...?* The words resonated in Dahr's head. *Danger? But not from me. For me?*

He had time to see a streak of black before a gauntleted fist caught him in the jaw and sent him sprawling to the ground. He sat up, spitting blood, to find Lord Grondellan standing over him. A look of fury contorted the Rachannan nobleman's face, a terrifying expression, the likes of which Dahr had never before seen on the older man, not even in the thick of battle.

A wave of dizziness staggered Dahr when he tried to stand, and he landed hard a second time. "Is this Rachannan honor?"

Grondellan spat on the ground. "It's Grondellan wisdom, boy. Any fool knows I'd never take you in duel. I figure that blow puts us on equal footing for a bit. So now's the time to air your grievances."

Careful not to move too fast, Dahr regained his feet. The world whirled around him, but he made an effort to hide how disoriented that single blow had left him. "What's to discuss? You were my Master. You'd be dead now, except I swore an oath to Jeran to leave you unharmed."

"I don't need protection, boy. Certainly not from a hot-headed pup so scared of making a decision he waits for events to make them for him. By the time you chose to fight me, I'd be ten winters in my grave."

Dahr lunged, but Grondellan was ready. The Rachannan dodged with surprising agility for one of his age and size, then landed another blow across Dahr's back that sent him speeding forward into a tree. "See," Grondellan laughed. "How long would you have stood there, debating whether or not to attack, if I hadn't goaded you to it?"

Baring his teeth, Dahr turned. This time he anticipated Grondellan's move and planned his attack accordingly, slipping around the Rachannan's guard and landing a solid blow into his gut. Grondellan grunted, but to Dahr it felt as if he had just hit a stone wall, and his balled fist thrummed as he drew it back for another blow.

"What happened, forget you had a blade in the other hand?" Grondellan asked, his returning blow hammering into Dahr's midriff with enough force to lift him off the ground. "You should have told me who you were!"

Dahr glanced at the *dolchek*, then tossed it to the ground. He hurled himself at Lord Grondellan, grabbing the Rachannan by the shoulders and pulling him down. "Why, so you could return me to my rightful place?" He rained down blows, but what had felled countless foes seemed to have little effect on his former Master. Lord Grondellan shrugged off Dahr's punches and returned his own, each one sending daggers of pain through Dahr's body.

"Why? Because I deserved that much, after all I did for you!" The words fueled Grondellan's attack. He rolled, pinning Dahr beneath his bulk and cuffing him across the jaw twice before Dahr was able to regain a semblance of control.

Dahr renewed his attack, and they rolled back and forth across the forest floor, exchanging blows. A half dozen times he knew he had lost, and then he'd draw upon some hidden reserve of strength and turn the tide. But even when he held the advantage, something deep within stayed his hand, prevented him from unleashing the full extent of his anger on the Rachannan. The beast within raged against that something, but Dahr no longer had control.

"All you did? You made me your property. You stole my soul."

Lord Grondellan laughed, spitting flecks of blood. "Stole your soul? You can use their words, you ungrateful whelp, but you'll never sound like them."

The words hit harder than any of Grondellan's blows. "Ungrateful?"

"Aye. I saved you from that slaver. I saved you from starvation! Without me, you'd have died. And you've not even the common decency to tell me you're still alive, even after we've been traveling together for so long. Even after you knew how much your *death* affected me."

With a savage kick, Grondellan took the advantage. Dahr landed on his back, and the Rachannan pounced upon him.

"I'd rather have died than be a slave," Dahr said, bracing for the blow.

Now Grondellan froze, fist drawn back to strike. "Do you really believe that?" He leaned in. "If you do, you're more a fool than I believed."

Dahr took the Rachannan's moment of indecision and used it to his advantage, grabbing him by the shoulders and pulling him down. He kicked his knees up at the same time, using the momentum to somersault Lord Grondellan over him. The Rachannan hit the ground with a thud that reverberated through the trees.

Dahr struggled to rise, desperate to hold the advantage now that he had taken it, but his body groaned with every movement, and the world spun around him. Yet, instead of the rustle of renewed attack, he heard a strange sound: the rumble of Grondellan's laughter.

"You find this funny?" Dahr demanded.

"I taught you how to do that," Lord Grondellan said between laughs. "Do you remember?"

Unbidden, a memory came to Dahr of a younger Lord Grondellan vaulting over him in an exaggerated way, landing in a bed of thick grass with a feigned grunt. The display had made the young Dahr howl with laughter; now it barely touched his lips with a grin, but it did extinguish the rage boiling within.

With a groan, Grondellan sat up and wiped blood from his lip. He hauled himself to his feet and hobbled toward Dahr, clutching at his gut. "Gods, you've the strength of a bear, lad." The humor left his eyes, and he regarded Dahr with severe seriousness. "No matter what grudge you may hold against me, we both know Salos and his servants pose a greater threat. We've proven that we fight well together, and if I taught you anything, I taught you to kill the lion before you kill the fox." He offered his hand, waited for Dahr to take it.

A voice within screamed at Dahr not to accept, to refuse an accord with the man who had once owned him, but another contested it, a calmer voice reminding him of the aid Lord Grondellan had lent in the past, and how many times he owed his life to the man. That both voices sounded like his own did little to reassure him.

In the end, it was Lord Iban's voice decided him, and the memory of a lecture where the grizzled Guardsman advised him to use whatever tools he had to deal with whatever threats he faced, and to reevaluate only as necessary.

Dahr grabbed Grondellan's hand and climbed to his feet. "I want this to be your decision, lad," the Rachannan said. "I don't want to stay because you made a promise to Jeran. You tell me to leave, I go. You want to fight, then we'll finish it here."

It was an effort for Dahr to summon up the politeness required. "I'll never forget that you were once my Master, but I cannot forget that my life would have been lost a dozen times over if not for your aid. I would welcome that aid against the *Kohr'adjin*."

Lord Grondellan smiled, but his gaze quickly hardened and he lunged forward, drawing a blade from concealment within his jerkin.

Betrayed! The voice screamed within Dahr's head, but it faded when the Rachannan lurched past him and threw, the blade smacking hilt first into a Garun'ah child. The boy fell, and the *dolchek* he held slipped from his grasp.

Grondellan leapt upon the boy before he could recover, binding him with vines ripped from a nearby tree. Once secure, the Rachannan hauled the child to a seated position, slamming him against a tree trunk to rouse him.

"Careful!" Dahr shouted. "He could be one of ours."

"Slinking through the trees with a blade drawn? Attempting to slip behind you when you all but promised murder to any Tribesman who followed you into the forest? Look at this?" He craned the boy's head around, showing an intricate tattoo wrapping around the back of the boy's neck. Among the Tribes, only the *Kohr'adjin* wore such markings.

"He's a child!" Dahr said, "No more than twelve winters." Anger resurfaced, but it met revulsion at what he knew he must do.

"Evil knows no age," Grondellan replied. "Nor foolishness."

Dahr leaned forward, grabbed the boy by the shoulders. "Who are you? What do you want?"

The boy's blank expression showed he did not understand, but his lips curled in a snarl of disgust. "*U'fasa Korahn!*" he spat at Dahr.

"He calls you a false savior," Lord Grondellan told him. "No doubt he seeks to earn honor among the *Kohr'adjin* by killing you. No doubt he's not the only one with such a plan."

The boy struggled, and Dahr cuffed him across the face hard enough to stun him to immobility. His eyes sought his own *dolchek*, lying in the leaf litter across the clearing, then they moved toward the boy's blade at his feet.

"Now's your chance, lad," Grondellan said, his voice hard.

Dahr looked at him in confusion.

"Show me what I should have done. Do you let him go to return in shame or seek death on his own? Do you kill him yourself and put the blood of a child—one far less innocent that you were, I might add—on your conscience? Or do you take him as a prisoner—as a *slave*—and hope that in time you can give him something better?" The hard glare from the Rachannan's dark eyes bored into Dahr. "Tell me, Garun's Chosen One, what will you do?"

With a swift motion, Dahr scooped up the blade at his feet and pressed it to the boy's throat. The child barely winced, and he showed no fear as the sharpened steel scratched a shallow cut across his flesh as it trembled in Dahr's grasp.

"He should die," Dahr said, his voice low.

"Yes, but you can't kill him, can you? So, could you kill one who intended no wrong? Could you leave one in the hands of a man such as the slaver who owned you before me? That was a sentence worse than death." The heat had come back to Grondellan's voice, even though he no longer looked ready to fight. "Look at me, and tell me again that what I did was wrong!"

"You two make more noise than herd of *bafal* in avalanche," a voice called behind them. Dahr turned and stepped away from the prisoner, scanning the shadows for threats. When Sadarak Cat's Claw, *Kranor* of the Afelda stepped into the light, he relaxed.

Dahr tossed the *dolchek* down and stepped toward the Tribesman, making the greeting gesture Yarchik said was appropriate for one as honored among the Tribes as Sadarak.

Sadarak studied Dahr for a moment, then returned the greeting in kind. "You honor me, Korahn, but with noise you make, I surprised only this one find you."

"Have you brought the Afelda to fight with us?" Dahr asked.

"What do you mean, only this one?" Grondellan asked. "There are others?"

The *Kranor* chose to answer Grondellan's question. "Dozens found slinking around tents like serpents. Most search for the Korahn, but some sought *Kranora* and *Kranacha*, or *Tsha'ma*. Cubs only, and none successful, but they fight like demons when cornered."

"We captured this one," Dahr said, though the words tasted foul as he spoke them. "Perhaps he'll tell us something useful."

"Not much with blade stuck in his chest," Sadarak said matter-of-factly.

"What—?" Horror overcame Dahr when he saw that the boy had wriggled free of his bonds and reclaimed his blade long enough to plunge it into his own heart. Blood drenched the child's hide shirt, and his eyes gleamed with fanatic ecstasy.

"No matter," Sadarak said. "He not speak. He not swear honor oath. This just save us from kill him."

Beneath his breath, Dahr heard Grondellan mutter, "Again fate takes the decision away from him." He was too numb, though, for the words to incite anger.

"Come," Sadarak said. "We must honor the death of Yarchik and name you *Kranor*. Then we will talk of battle, and what has driven me to join *Cho Korahn Garun*."

CHAPTER 27

In the flickering light of the bonfire, a tendril of smoke rose toward the Heavens, marking the passage of Yarchik *uvan* Greltar to the Twilight World. Dahr stared at the distant fire, listening as the dirge faded. More joyful songs would begin soon, ushering in a celebration of Yarchik's life, a fine counterpoint to the poignancy of his death.

Who will sing for me? Dahr wondered. He reached for the skin of *baqhat* at his foot but threw it away when he found it empty. *How much joy will memories of my life bring?*

He fled the funeral to stand a lonely vigil away from those who would name him their leader. Even the monster within slumbered, and the absence of his growing demands for battle left Dahr alone with somber thoughts and the distant chatter of the Lesser Voices. He considered blocking them as well, but the thought of total isolation kept him from it. Despite his pretense of strength, he could not bear the idea of enduring this night alone.

His own thoughts were no great comfort. He wondered if any part of Yarchik's death could be laid at his feet, if his insistence that they pursue the *Kohr'adjin* had brought about the old Tribesman's end. He wondered whether the Tribes were foolish to follow him, and if he were cruel for using their prophecies as a means to settle his own scores. He wondered how Jeran fared in Shandar, and what his old friend would think of all this. Mostly, he wondered why he still cared about such things.

"Friend Dahr?" Grendor hobbled toward him out of the shadows. The Orog had changed since Dahr first met him, and changed more so since coming to the tents of the Garun'ah. His scarred face showed none of the pain hovering behind his probing gaze; his once laughable naivety had given way to a subtle confidence and a growing, almost infuriating wisdom.

"Your presence is missed at the celebration," Grendor told him, but when the Orog stepped near to the small fire and caught sight of the dark bruises and blood-crusted cuts across Dahr's body, he sucked in a breath. "Dear Gods, what has happened?"

Dahr waved it off. "It's nothing. One of the assassins sent to the tents came upon me in the woods."

Grendor pursed his lips, and his eyes narrowed to slits. "If you do not want to tell me, I will respect your silence. There is no need to lie."

They faced each other for a time. Dahr remembered when the Orog could barely meet his gaze; now he was the one to turn away first, telling himself it was not guilt that made him do so. "How does Truthsense work?"

Grendor shook his head. "The same way our eyes work. Or our hearts. It just does. The Elders say that those who wonder at the glory of nature will find themselves humbled by their own insignificance." A grin spread across the Orog's face. "That is their way of saying they don't know, I think."

Dahr did not smile back. "And it allows you to see the truth of things?"

"It allows us to know if someone believes what they say."

"Isn't that the same thing?" Dahr asked, a bit more bitterly than he intended.

"No. Truth is perception, friend Dahr, not reality. It can be warped and twisted by experience." Grendor drummed his fingers along the haft of his *va'dasheran*. "When you were a child, had I asked you if you were Human, Truthsense would not have labeled you a liar when you said yes. Now, it would."

"So you will be able to help us find the *Kohr'adjin* spies among the tents."

"As long as they know they are spies, or believe themselves to be, I will know." Grendor frowned again; the expression contorted the serenity of his features. "What will you do with those I find?"

"They will be questioned and executed."

The harsh simplicity with which he gave the statement might have cowed a lesser man, but Grendor drew himself up. "You may kill them, and you may question them, but I will have your word that you will not torture them."

"If they will not talk—"

"I heard the screams of those the Durange 'questioned' in Dranakohr. I heard the lies such treatment brought to their lips, and I can tell you this: the few who returned believed those lies. They would have believed anything to make the pain stop. So I will have your word now, or you will not have my help."

Dahr rose to full height, towering over Grendor, but he could not find voice for any threat. For his part, Grendor faced him without flinching, until Dahr took a step back and ducked his head. "They will not be mistreated. You have my word."

Grendor nodded, as if the statement were bond enough to ease his conscience. "The *Kranora* are assembling. They sent me to find you."

"Grendor?" Something in Dahr's tone made the Orog turn back with concern in his eye. "What if I were to tell you that I have doubts?"

"I would tell you that only the blind walk with confidence, because they cannot see the dangers around them."

Dahr ran a hand across his jaw, forcing down the anxiety he felt. "What I intend… Many may die. They should die for something greater than my pride."

"Only a fool trusts himself without reservation when burdened with the lives of others. But the Garun'ah believe you are their salvation; turning them back will be harder than turning back the seasons. If you doubt what you intend, it is your motives you must change, not your followers."

Dahr's mouth dried, and he sought the comfort of a drink, but his *baqhat* skin lay empty in the grass. He found the courage within and fixed his gaze on Grendor. "I am a good man."

Grendor's lips tightened to a narrow line, but the grip he took on Dahr's arm was warm. "You *are* a good man, friend Dahr," he said, his voice quiet. "Come, the *Kranora* await."

They crossed the camp in silence, Dahr careful to avoid the larger congregations of Tribesmen. The revelry would last the night, and perhaps for Yarchik into the day beyond, but Dahr wanted no part of their happiness. After Yarchik's life had been properly honored, it would be time to avenge his death. That he would share in gladly.

In the center of the tents a second bonfire burned, and around it sat the *Kranora* of the gathered Tribes. Arik of the Tacha, clad in the bearskin cloak that made him look more monster than man, had taken Yarchik's place of honor, but Sadarak of the Afelda sat only a few hands off. The two *Kranora* eyed each other periodically, like wolves testing the air for dominance but not yet ready to fight.

With Dahr representing the Channa, three of the four major tribes were accounted for. Only the eccentric and elusive Sahna remained absent. Dahr hoped they came to his summons; their prowess in battle was legendary, and even if their Hunters had only a fraction of the skill the *Tsha'ma* Goshen had shown, they would make a fine addition to his army.

Dozens of smaller tribes had joined them over the past season, with more flocking to the safety of the tents every day. With the *Kohr'adjin* slaughtering any who opposed them—women and children as well as Hunters—the small tribes had nowhere else to turn. Their *Kranora* looked every bit as proud as Arik and Sadarak, but they knew their existence depended on the might of the larger tribes, and the positions they took around the fire reflected that hierarchy.

In the shadows cast by the bonfire, Dahr saw Meila hovering at the edge of the gathering. The *Kranora* ignored her, as if pretending they were invisible would make the Vahr Drekka truly vanish.

Dahr could not let them go, no matter how much the other tribes wanted it. The Vahr Drekka represented a sizable force, smaller only than the Tacha, Channa and Afelda, and they had been hardened by a lifetime of struggle. Their Hunters had never known peace, their faith had been tested daily, and they still refused to yield to the allure of Kohr's promises. Despised or not, Dahr needed that fervor and ferocity for the battles ahead.

Olin and Rannarik joined him as he approached the fire. The two would translate the *Kranora*'s words for him, and his for the other Tribesmen. This arrangement suited him well, eliminating the embarrassment of fumbled words and misunderstandings.

"The young Lord deems it wise to join us lowly Tribesmen," said Kodash *uvan* Pida, of the Turape.

Some chuckles rose from the gathered *Kranora*. "We should humble ourselves," added Burask *uvan* Meig, of the Dorasein, "and praise Garun for his wisdom."

Dahr's cheeks flushed at the poorly-veiled insults. "I mourn for the loss of Yarchik. I apologize if my remembrances took longer than yours."

Burask sniffed the air. "How many memories did you find at the bottom of that skin, Korahn?"

Dahr moved forward, but Olin's hand held him in check. "The Korahn deserves some respect—"

"Respect is earned, not given," Arik said. He stood to tower over the others, and even with the hood of his bear-cloak drawn back he made a menacing sight. He fixed a withering glare on Burask. "It can also be taken." After a moment, Burask turned away, leaving Arik in command of the circle.

At his signal, a stooped and wrinkled *Tsha'ma* appeared, taking a position so close to the fire Dahr wondered how he could not be burning. "It was the will of Yarchik *uvan* Greltar that Dahr Odara, He of No Tribe, *Cho Korahn Garun*, be taken as his son and made one with the Channa. It was the will of Yarchik *uvan* Greltar that upon his death, Dahr Odara be named *Kranor* and given responsibility for the tribe. Are there any who will dispute the wishes of the great Yarchik?"

Though he had expected no objections—this ceremony generally took place among one's own tribe and not with the leaders of others—Dahr noted several sets of glaring eyes boring into him, and others whose inscrutable expressions could mean dissatisfaction.

In the ensuing silence, the *Tsha'ma* moved forward. With a flick of the old man's wrist, hot liquid splashed across Dahr's face. He traced his fingers through it, then held them up to the light. Blood.

"You are the heart of the Channa," the *Tsha'ma* said, "and they are your blood. Without you they have no direction; without them you have no life. Guard well this honor, for your worthiness is now judged not through your own actions, but in the actions of the whole."

Dahr knelt before the old man, who anointed him with warm water and whispered a blessing to Garun. Then Arik hauled him to his feet, placed a bear-like grip on each of Dahr's shoulders, and said, "Welcome, Brother."

Dahr nodded a reply. He could not find words, though it was not Arik's great show of respect that stole his tongue. The revelry of the Tribesmen echoed through the night sky, and he really heard, perhaps for the first time, their heartfelt love for Yarchik. *What could I possibly do to match that love? All I have to offer them is blood and sacrifice.*

"I thank you all," he said, struggling to keep his voice humble. As *Cho Korahn Garun*, he had the right to command the *Kranora*, but tonight he stood here as *Kranor*, and it was as an equal, or perhaps less than equal, that he faced the others. "There is little I could do to rival the wisdom or bravery of Yarchik, but I will try to live by his example. He spoke only praise of his brothers among the Tribes; I will need your guidance and support for what is to come."

"Tonight he shows his throat," Kodash laughed, "but tomorrow I bet he bares his teeth again. Do you play at being a leper-fox, Brother, feigning injury to lure in your prey?"

Others laughed at that, too, and even Dahr managed a smile. "I seek to reassure you of my intentions because I have a request I know you'll find distasteful. Meila of the Vahr Drekka wishes to address this circle. I—"

"I will not hear the words of a Drekka!" Cahrat *uvan* Ties, of the Ciou Tribe snapped, spitting on the ground for emphasis.

"We do her people honor enough by letting them live," added Burask.

Other voices rose in protest, drowning out Dahr's calls for order. He looked to Arik for help, but the giant warrior said nothing; the stony look in his eyes showed where he stood on the issue.

"Enough!" Sadarak said, leaping to the center of the circle. Cat's Claw stalked around the fire, waiting as the cacophony of protests died under his fiery glare. "Has the Blood become so weak that we now fear the words of a priestess? Have we become so blind we cannot even see what Garun has placed in our hands? If these Vahr Drekka remain lost to the ways of Garun, then should we not listen to this Meila, if for no other reason than to ferret out her deception? And if they truly seek to rejoin the Blood, then by Garun's teachings should we not welcome them as our brothers?"

He turned to the shadows, where Meila stood stone-still and contemplative. "You may speak to me, Priestess. If others wish not to listen, there are other fires for them."

She approached slowly, walking with a calm assurance Dahr doubted she truly felt. When she reached the fire, she bowed deeply to Sadarak, then again to Dahr, and finally once to the other *Kranora*.

"When I was a girl," she began, circling the fire like a lioness guarding her cubs, "Garun visited my dreams. He told me the Drekka had gone astray long ago, but that, to him, none of his children were lost. In my dream, He promised to lead me to one who could restore us to the Balance, who could redeem us in the eyes of the Blood." Her gaze sought Dahr, and though she did not name him outright, the attention unsettled him even more than the eyes of the gathered *Kranora*.

"But the Great Hunter said to me something else, which until now I did not understand. He told me, 'To win back the trust of the Blood, you will have to destroy what you yearn to protect; to become a true Drekka, you must slaughter the Drekka.'"

A murmur went up among the *Kranora*, and some seemed eager to help Meila fulfill Garun's request, but Sadarak glared them to silence. "For many winters I thought His words instructed me to fight those lured away by the *Kohr'adjin*, but though they still call themselves Drekka, they are not of the Blood. Now I understand Garun's true meaning: there can be no forgiveness for the Drekka from the other tribes. For us to become part of the Blood again, the Drekka must cease to be."

A gasp went up among those gathered in the circle; even the *Tsha'ma* in attendance seemed shocked by the announcement. "You would give up your past, child?" Rannarik asked in hushed tones, with Olin whispering a hasty translation in Dahr's ear. "You would start anew, forsaking your heritage?"

"We would be as the first ones," Meila said, "who had no ancestors to bring them honor. On this day, we ask that the tribes acknowledge the disappearance of the Vahr Drekka and the birth of a new tribe, the Anada. Perhaps then the wounds of history can be mended, and we can stand united against our enemies."

"Your people?" Arik asked, rising to his feet. "They have no objection?"

"Those few who did have been asked to leave. None want the Drekka to fade to dust, but most know that without a chance at redemption, we will spend eternity in the Nothing."

"And who would you name *Kranor* of your 'tribe'?" sneered Quras *uvan* Tries, of the Pintuchae.

"We would name Dahr Odara," Meila said.

An excited murmur rose again among the *Kranora*, this time escalating into a full blown argument as they debated the legality of the decision. None were more surprised than Dahr, who stared at Meila with a mixture of shock and bitter resentment.

"I am already a *Kranor*," he said, to no one in particular.

"Argue though they might," Rannarik said, gesturing to the squabbling Garun'ah, "there is no rule against one serving as *Kranor* to two tribes."

"I don't want to be *Kranor* to the Channa, let alone to the Vahr Drekka!"

"To the Anada," Rannarik corrected. "And that is a different matter."

The debate lasted for some time, until Arik and Sadarak silenced it. They looked at each other, then Arik returned to Meila and grasped her by the arms. "Come, Sister. We welcome Meila, Mother of the Anada. May you always find peace in the tents of the Tacha." He touched his head to hers and gripped her shoulders in a respectful greeting.

Sadarak repeated the ritual, then one by one the other *Kranora* approached—though some did so reluctantly—and welcomed the Anada Tribe to the tents. "You witness history Dahr," Rannarik told him. "A new tribe has not been born in centuries."

"With luck," Olin added, "you will not also live to see it die."

"All things die," Dahr said sourly. "The Balance demands as much."

"Then hopefully you will not live long enough to kill it."

Dahr's head whipped around, the blood rushing to his face, but Olin appeared not to notice the threat. Any response he might have made was cut off by Meila asking, "And what of our *Kranor*?"

Another argument broke out among the Tribesmen, with many among the smaller tribes insisting on a voice in the selection, and many strongly opposed to Dahr. "Choosing a *Kranor* is not a matter to be debated among the Tribes," Rannarik said, his voice a rumble like low thunder, demanding silence. "Who among you wants your *Kranach* chosen by another?"

An unexpected panic rose up within Dahr as Rannarik gave Meila the *Tsha'ma's* blessing for the Anada to name whoever they wanted as *Kranor*. He sought in vain for a way out, and Olin gave him the escape he needed, whispering a few words to him that went a long way toward sparing the man from his earlier insult.

"The Anada need a wise hand to guide them," Dahr said, stepping into the circle. "They will need a *Kranor* who understands their unique standing among the Tribes. They will need a leader with the fire of passion and the strength to stand up to the fool Half-man who thinks himself *Cho Korahn Garun*."

The last brought a murmur of laughter from the *Kranora*. "Being Yarchik's successor binds me to the Garun'ah, and it makes personal my stake in this war. But it is an honor I should have refused. As *Cho Korahn Garun*, my duty is to all the Tribes, and to the Balance as well. Yarchik prepared the Channa; they know their needs will be placed second to the needs of all. I cannot ask the same of the Anada. I cannot demand their voice be muted, when it has just been heard.

"The Balance will not be served by heaping titles upon me. Binding me to each tribe will weigh me down, and only from the sky can the eagle see where he must fly." He walked to Meila, took her shoulders in his hands, and touched his head to hers. "There is only one among the Anada with the will to stand up to the Tribes. Only one with the courage to face the Korahn and tell him he is wrong. She is the one who should lead."

Meila flushed and started to protest. "No, that was not my intention. I am a priestess of Garun. I do not want to lead."

Dahr smirked at the irony, and the sight of the unflappable woman unsettled by the burden of responsibility. "Such is a sign that you deserve the honor," Rannarik said. "Those who covet power often use it unwisely."

Dahr stepped back and allowed the *Kranora* to continue their meeting. All eyes were on Meila, though the difference in attitude was palpable. For his part, Dahr was glad to no longer be the center of attention, but he did not understand it. *She's the same woman she was this morning. How does changing the name of her tribe make them any different?*

After a time, when the daily matters of the camp had been settled, Sadarak Cat's Claw called for silence. "We Afelda did not leave our ancestral lands merely to join the Korahn in his quest against the *Kohr'adjin*." The severity of his tone demanded immediate silence, drawing the eyes and attention of all in attendance. "An army sweeps north from Human lands, devouring all in its path like a plague of locusts. At its head stands a monster, the one-eyed demon who rebuilt the Dark Empire for *Sal'aqran*. Those who stand against him—Human and Tribesman alike—are slaughtered like cattle. He demands submission, and swears he will bathe in the blood of his enemies. He will not rest until the Children of Garun are ground to dust, that he will sow so much destruction that *Sal'aqran* will no longer doubt who is the greatest of his servants."

A cry of rage arose from the gathered *Kranora* over the desecration of their lands. "Who is this man?" asked Chyat *uvan* Kran, of the Eniou. He ground his fingers into his palms so hard that blood dripped from his flesh. "The Blood cannot allow such insult."

"Who is this man?" demanded others.

"I know little beyond what I have said," Sadarak told them. "He was a wanderer before, and knows the Tribal Lands well. And he marches under this sign." The Kranor of the Afelda scratched something into the dirt at his feet. Dahr moved closer to get a better look.

A Scorpion's tail, poised to strike.

Synat Sal'aqran.

As often happened at these meetings, the discussion quickly degenerated into a heated debate, with some *Kranora* demanding they finish their campaign against the *Kohr'adjin* and others believing that killing Humans should take precedence over killing other Garun'ah. Only a handful suggested caution, seeking protection for the women and children and letting their enemies come to them.

Their bloodlust suited Dahr fine, and he expected future reports of defilement of the Tribal Lands would bring more tribes under his control. Even still, part of him mourned for those caught in the Scorpion's path, and he, too, wondered which of his enemies he should face first: the one ahead or the one behind.

"You look lost, friend Dahr," Grendor said, pulling him around and gazing into his eyes.

Dahr started to dismiss the claim, but then remembered the Orog's accursed Truthsense and relented. "I wish... I wish Jeran were here. I need his counsel. Do you think if I sent a messenger to Shandar, he would come?"

"If he could, Jeran would come, but he is no longer..." Grendor cocked his head to the side. "You do not know? Of all people, I thought you... Jeran left Shandar some days ago. He is to the east, and he is terrified."

"Terrified?" That his bond to Jeran had grown so weak stunned him; that Grendor—among others—now held a similar bond, a stronger bond, reawakened the demon he tried so hard to control. "What does Jeran fear?"

Grendor's expression grew grim. "That we are losing."

Chapter 28

"What do you mean destroyed?"

Mathis spoke without emotion, but the room crackled with threat. The two noblemen—minor lords from Families Martyn had never before heard of—quaked under the King's unflinching gaze.

The bolder of the two, a wiry man by the name of Nathan, glanced at his companion then faced the King. "There... There was a fire. We did all we could—"

This was the third granary in as many nights lost to fire, a troubling occurrence in a city under siege. Even more troubling to Martyn was the knowledge that the locations of all food stores outside the palace grounds were known to only a handful of people. Martyn had insisted on the secrecy—though, in truth, the idea had been Miriam's—but the treachery in Kaper seemed to have reached the upper echelons of command.

"All you could?" Mathis's voice rumbled through the hall. "Where are the soot stains on your clothes? Where are the burns you earned ferrying the grain away from the flames? Do you think me—?"

Martyn raised a finger, catching the King's eye, then made a gesture toward the door. "Leave me," Mathis growled, and the two men all but leapt from the chamber. "Since your holdings have been destroyed, I expect to hear that you both nobly decided to join the militia to help defend Kaper."

Once they were gone, Mathis turned his gaze on Martyn. "Do you really think they will join the militia?" Martyn asked.

"Ha! I'd be less surprised to find out they'd smuggled themselves out of Kaper and were seeking passage to Roya."

Martyn's grin faded. "At worst, we have a traitor in our midst. At best, someone we trust has a loose tongue and poor judgment."

"And what do you propose we do?" Exasperation flared through the King's words. "Expel anyone we have doubts about from the old city? We'd be left with a few hundred men to defend the whole of Kaper."

"Miriam suggests a test. If we set up a handful of false granaries, then choose carefully who is told of each one, we can see which are attacked. Perhaps we can flush out some of the traitors that way."

Mathis's head perked up, and Martyn wished he would sometimes see such interest from his father at his own suggestions. "Such a ploy may yield no fruits," the King said.

"Then we have done little but waste some time and add a few false targets to our enemies' plans."

Mathis nodded, but then his expression grew somber. "And what if it is your betrothed who is our traitor? I do not mean to disrespect Miriam, but she—"

"—may have suggested this simply to aim us away from her?" Martyn waved a dismissive hand. "I don't believe it, but I considered it. We could devise a test for her as well. Provide her with the *real* list of new granaries."

The two shared a smile, then the King put his head in his hands and sighed. "What has become of us, Martyn? We see treason in every shadow, enemies among our allies."

"That is what the Durange want," Martyn reminded him. "To turn us against ourselves. To do their killing for them."

They spoke quietly for a time, deciding which of their most loyal advisors to test first and selecting locations for the dummy stockpiles on a map of Old Kaper the King kept on his desk. It was the longest time they had spent together in several ten-days, and the first time in recent memory that their conversation ended without one of them fighting to hide frustration.

The King rolled up the map and set it aside when a knock resounded on the door. "Come in." Martyn watched as his father smoothed his features for the new arrival, but caught sight of his hand slipping beneath the table to grasp his sword hilt. *Even here he does not feel safe. What has become of us?*

Mika entered, straight-backed and somber-faced. Gone was the boy Martyn had known, the exuberant youth devoted to Alrendria and enamored of Jeran. Now, harsh reality ringed his eyes, and the shortsword he wore settled against his side. He seemed as comfortable with the blade as with his own arms. Not long ago, such an observation would not have fazed Martyn; now, it troubled him.

After bowing his head in deference to his prince, Mika turned his full attention on the King. "It is time for your meeting with Brell Morrena, King Mathis. And then you wished to examine the defenses along the southern wall."

"Of course," Mathis said, pushing back his chair and standing. "I must have lost track of time. Would you inform my guards that I'll be leaving shortly?" Mika saluted and turned to leave.

"You'll be of age soon, won't you?" Martyn asked, forcing a jovial tone. "You've been looking forward to joining the Guard as long as I've known you."

"I will be of age," Mika told him, "but I will not be joining the Guard. Once Jeran returns and the siege is lifted, I intend to go to Dranakohr and put on the Black."

Martyn's expression hardened, and when his father signaled for him to stand down, Martyn ignored him, advancing instead on the boy. The King had developed a bond with Mika, a bond he and his father had never shared. Its existence galled him, but he would not allow Mika to hide behind it while courting treason.

"The Army of the Boundary only exists *because* of the siege," Martyn said. "Once this war is over, Jeran will be reminded of his oaths to Alrendria. He will disband his army and return overall governance of his House to Alrendria. Those who abandoned their posts in the Guard to serve under him will be lucky to receive clemency; those who joined him instead of the Guard will be labeled misguided fools, but they will never be trusted with the protection of Alrendria."

Martyn lashed out as if with a scourge, but the boy took the sharp words without flinching, and when the prince finally ended his tirade, he fastened an all-too-confident gaze on Martyn. "If you doubt Jeran's loyalty, then you are as foolish as the whispers in the streets claim. If you take offense at my wishing to serve in the Army of the Boundary, but not in my claim that you are waiting behind these walls for Jeran to come and save you, then you are as much a coward as the rumors claim.

"I see no fool here, my Prince, and I know you to be no coward. I see a man obsessed with preserving Alrendrian greatness, a man determined to keep things the way they have been. But like it or not, change is coming. One cannot walk the walls of this palace and not know that. The question is: whose change can benefit you most?"

Martyn's cheeks burned at being upbraided by a child. "And where did you learn to speak such treason?"

Mika said nothing, and his willful refusal drove Martyn into a furor. He lunged forward, but a hand clamped down on his arm, holding him steady, and his father's voice echoed in his ear. "From me."

"You?" Martyn asked, his anger defused by the revelation.

"In Alrendria's long history, those Kings who fought against the tide have all drowned. A good King must know how the wind is blowing and use it to his advantage. If you learn one thing from me, learn that."

"And why would you speak such gems of wisdom to Mika?"

"Who else do I have?" Mathis asked, and for an instance, Martyn saw weariness in his father's eyes, the heavy mantle of responsibility. "Who else beside the young bodyguard you set upon me to spare yourself the same burden? I thank you for his company, for he has proven to be a clever companion, but you should not chastise him for doing what you insisted he do."

Martyn was left speechless. He stared at the King, fighting the urge to glare at Mika, and fought down another surge of unwanted jealousy. "Come," Mathis said to Mika, leading the boy from the room. "We should not keep Brell waiting any longer."

How long Martyn stood alone in the chamber, he did not know, but the sunlight beaming through the opening on the eastern wall had dimmed considerably by the time he shook himself free of dark thoughts and entered the twisting halls of the palace. He skirted the busy sections of the castle, keeping to the lesser used halls and for once blissfully free of guards. Only in the deepest confines of the palace or in his own chambers could he exercise such independence, and in his rooms he was always subject to Miriam and her vacillating temper, so he relished what few moments like these he could steal.

As a child, vast sections of the palace had gone unused and silent, but now only a handful of chambers remained truly abandoned. In the wake of the evacuation of New Kaper, the Elves had been given quarters in an entire section of the palace, and even today a half dozen minor Lords had petitioned to bring their families into the perceived safety of the castle.

That a dozen more Elves had been murdered in Old Kaper in broad daylight contributed to the fear. Word of the murders had spread, and even though only Elves had been killed thus far, it had the Alrendrians panicky as well.

The sound of shuffling feet and what sounded like muffled screams caught Martyn's ear. Alert to the possible danger, but still hesitant to seek out Guardsmen, he followed the sound to a closed door at the end of a narrow corridor. Little light penetrated to the end of the hall, but the layer of dust covering the floor showed signs of recent visitors.

Drawing the short blade he kept at his side, Martyn threw open the door. No windows allowed sunlight in, but a solitary candle flickering in the corner warned of recent visitors. His eyes scanned the room but saw nothing save for a moving shadow tucked away in the farthest corner of the chamber. He moved forward cautiously, his eyes flicking from one edge of the room to the other, ready to dive backwards and call for help at the first sign of attack.

He moved toward the shadow, taking one careful step after another. When he drew close enough to see a slight figure bound in a chair, signs of a recent struggle on her simple, white dress, and a heavy cloth bag drawn down over her face, he hurried forward.

Untying the laces with as much haste as he could muster without releasing his grip on the dagger, Martyn pulled off the sack, and then stepped back in shock.

"Sheriza?"

The Healer looked up at him, a glare so fury-filled that Martyn wondered for a moment why he had not burst into flame the moment her eyes settled on him. "Are you alright?"

Sheriza struggled vainly against her bonds, and only the tiniest hint of muffled sound escaped her lips. Martyn could not sense it, but the sudden certainty that magic was in play chilled him to the core. He hid his fear and straightened, turning to place his back against the wall. "Show yourself!" he announced to the empty room. "Show yourself now or within a heartbeat I will have Magi scouring this room for you."

A familiar voice echoed out from the corner. "And whose Magi would you have searching for me? Konasi's or mine?"

A sphere of light flared up in the center of the room, chasing away the darkness. Lelani appeared as if from nowhere, walking toward him with that infuriating haughtiness she had, for a time, tried to hide behind a facade of humility.

"Lelani?" Martyn had not known what to expect, but he had not anticipated this. His surprise quickly faded, and he mustered as much of a commanding presence as he could. "Release her."

"She knows about me and my followers," Lelani replied in an icy voice. "She has not broken with the Assembly; she is not openly supporting Odara. I cannot trust that she—"

"Sheriza is a valued ally, and she is under my protection. If *you* wish to claim the same, you will release the bonds holding her this instant."

Lelani studied him for a moment, then ducked her head in acquiescence. In a flash, Sheriza leapt from her chair and lunged at the former High Wizard. Her slap staggered Lelani, but the blow had a more severe effect on the Healer, who as a consequence of their specialization suffered double whatever violence they meted out.

Martyn caught Sheriza as she doubled over and eased her back into the chair. The Healer's face paled, and her stomach convulsed. While she recovered, Lelani watched her with imperious superiority and an amused grin. "I hope that made you feel better," she said once Sheriza stopped retching.

Color blossomed in the Healer's cheeks, but Martyn laid a restraining hand on her shoulder. "What is going on here?" he demanded.

"I saw her snooping around the entrance to the catacombs," Sheriza gasped. "I did not realize you were foolish enough to offer succor to Magi being hunted by the Assembly, so I confronted her. She panicked at the thought of justice being served, and used her Gift on me."

"Valkov has no right to hold us to trial," Lelani replied, her voice sharp. "His coup is a sad grab for power and a dark day for the Assembly. Neither I nor any of my people did anything beyond the scope of our offices, and we—"

"If you are guiltless," Sheriza interrupted, "then there's no need to fear an inquiry."

"With Valkov controlling the Assembly and choosing the inquisitors?" Lelani scoffed. "I might as well condemn myself and save time."

"That still doesn't explain why you were skulking about the catacombs," Sheriza snapped, "or scuttling through the halls of the palace."

"We are here because Kaper needs us. Alrendria needs us. Even if we are at greater risk here than elsewhere, I would do what I can to honor our pledge to the Kings of Alrendria."

Martyn tried to interrupt, but he managed no more than a grunt before Sheriza said, "How noble. And I thought you came here because you know the King of Alrendria is the only one who might be able to offer you safety. After all, you do seem to be dancing quite readily to his whim, else I'd still be bound in the corner."

"How dare you! I made an arrangement with Prince Martyn, and I keep my word."

"Except for your word to the Assembly."

"The Assembly betrayed us! There comes a time when a person must stand up for ideals and stop clinging to outdated practices. The Assembly has become corrupt, and under Valkov it has taken a turn in a dark direction. We Magi must not isolate ourselves from the world."

"No longer High Wizard, but still a sheep I see," Sheriza laughed. "That's a convincing argument, but it sounds better coming from the Odara boy. If you truly hold to that belief, you should join him in Dranakohr... But I suspect that you remain unwilling to settle for second best."

"At least I'm willing to follow my heart. I haven't chained myself to the likes of Valkov. He—"

"There is an advantage to working within the system. My Healers are still in the good graces of the Assembly. My Healers need not scurry from shadow to shadow nor subjugate themselves to a royal House for protection. My Healers—"

"—refuse yet again to take a stand. As always, you sit the middle ground and do nothing but pick up the pieces."

"I do what I think is best for my people. For everyone concerned!"

"Of course you do! Everyone does what they *think* is best. I did. Odara does. I'm sure even Valkov thinks he's doing what's best for the Assembly. But—"

"Magi," Martyn interrupted, "Now is not the time for a philosophical debate—"

"This does not concern you," Lelani snapped, her eyes never leaving Sheriza. "Regardless of what you think is right, I cannot allow you to betray my people to Valkov."

"You cannot allow—?"

"I *will* not allow it. You Healers serve a vital function, but we will prove to be a greater asset to Kaper."

Martyn tried again. "That is really my decision, not—"

"You still talk like you're High Wizard, Lelani! I told Aemon he never should have recommended you. You feed too much on power."

"And you do not? You strut around like Queen of the Healers, dictating which people and what causes are worthy of your services. Times once were when Healers healed any who were in need, not just those who passed—"

"Enough!" Martyn yelled, but his words had no effect. The bickering continued, growing louder and more animated, until Martyn thought for sure that magic would be used again.

"I think this has gone on quite long enough," a new voice said from the doorway.

The yelling stopped immediately, and all eyes turned to the stooped form silhouetted in the doorway. Lelani gasped in a breath, and Sheriza bowed her head to the newcomer. "Lady Sionel," she said, a measure of awe in her voice.

As Martyn watched, the figure straightened and smoothed the stray strands from her hair. She entered the chamber with a bold, confident grace, her eyes flaring with the power of the Gift.

"Greatmother?" Martyn said, stunned.

"Oh please, child," Sionel said, a slight smile on her face. "How many winters did I have to live before someone began to suspect? You're not a stupid boy, nor is your father. But I will take it as a compliment of my performance."

"You're a Mage?" Martyn asked, mouth agape.

Sionel studied him for a moment. "You don't think this is the first time a Mage has been a member of a political family since that silly law was enacted, do you? No, of course you don't. You're not planning on having me hanged, are you? I'm not dressed for a hanging."

Martyn's mouth worked, but he could do nothing but stammer. "Hold on, dear," Sionel said to him. "We can discuss this more in a moment. I have something rather more frustrating to deal with now."

She turned toward the two women. "Lelani, might I remind you that you are a guest in this house, and there are certain protocols beyond your vows as a Mage that you must abide by. We do not tolerate snooping in the palace, nor do we like our guests to bind and manhandle other guests. You will learn to behave better while in our company, or I will move you and your followers to the kennels, where I suspect you might be able to learn some better manners."

Lelani blanched at the words, but the tirade Martyn expected to issue from the former High Wizard never came. Instead, she mumbled apologies and said nothing more. "And you," Sionel said, turning to Sheriza. "You like Valkov no more than the rest of us, and I suspect you like him far less than many. Climb down off your pedestal for a moment. Lelani's been unjustly accused and, if caught, will be tried on fictitious charges. Her only recourse is to submit herself to Jeran and beg his protection, or to hide here in Kaper and do what she can to help. Since pride has kept you from asking Jeran for help freeing your people from the Assembly, one should not expect any more from her."

"But Lady Sionel—"

"I am not here to entertain a debate," Sionel said, her voice cracking through the chamber. "When you leave this room, you will say nothing of Lelani to anyone. If you think yourself unable to hold your tongue, then I can arrange to wipe the memories from your mind. As it is not a pleasant experience, I would prefer to avoid it, but—"

Sionel broke off and turned to Martyn. "Marti, I need to have a word with the girls here in private. Would you please leave us for a time? I promise to seek you out later this evening, and we can discuss my lawbreaking to your heart's content. Thank you, dear."

Without waiting for an answer, she turned back toward the two Magi. They began to talk again, but Martyn heard no sound, and he had no recourse but to leave and hope that by morning some of his questions would be answered.

CHAPTER 29

Jeran slipped through tightly-packed trees and tangled vegetation, using his perceptions as much as his eyes to guide him. Even at midday little light penetrated the dense canopy, giving the Aelvin forest a sense of perpetual gloom. Exhaustion fought to draw his eyes closed and made his muscles ache, but sleep had become something virtually unknown to him, a fading memory of something he might have once enjoyed.

He considered opening himself to magic to create a light, but using his Gift for even the simplest task was a risk, not only because of his numbing fatigue but because of the scores of Elves loyal to Luran waiting for them. The least gifted of the Elves was attuned to magic in a way few Humans were, and to use magic anywhere except within Charylla's camp, which was concealed by some special trick of *Ael Maulle*, meant drawing enemies to him.

He walked alone, free for a short, blissful moment to submerge himself in his own thoughts. Since the flight from Illendrylla, his soldiers had clung to him as tightly as his shadow, partly out of concern, partly out of fear, and partly in response to the growing sense of hopelessness he struggled to hide.

Though he was never truly by himself anymore, he had made improvements in his ability to partition his mind, walling off his emotions from the thousands bonded to him. That most remained in Dranakohr, separated from him by the whole of Madryn, no doubt helped, but he had made strides with even those nearest him, and with those most eager to know the nuances of his every reaction.

He continued his circuit of the camp, stalking through the trees as if hunting game, though he knew that in this scenario, he was more prey than predator. His perceptions ranged out, seeking signs of the enemy, or even better, the site they had chosen from which to stage their next ambush. It had been nearly half a day; the next attack was sure to come soon.

He found nothing along his designated patrol and turned to return to camp. Goshen stood a hand behind him. The giant Tribesman held his bone-handled hammer as if expecting an attack. The ivory shaft seemed to have come from the leg of a creature that stood twice as tall as a man, and Jeran marveled at it as much as he fought to hide his surprise.

"You walk quiet," Goshen said. "But you breathe too much like Human. Elves have big ears. Will know difference." The toothy smile made Jeran suspect his words were in jest.

"They haven't found me yet," Jeran replied.

"That because they there." Goshen pointed southeast. "I think attack at sunset, when *Aelva* eyes best."

"Then you should warn the camp, not me."

"Camp knows. I had other business with you."

A sense of urgency filled Jeran. Goshen was the closest thing Jeran had found to a BattleMage. He had learned a lot from watching how the *Tsha'ma* balanced magic and battle. But more than that, his prowess in battle was virtually unmatched, and the thought that he might leave formed a cold knot in Jeran's gut.

"I know you Tribesmen have no love of Elves," Jeran said, "and you have no obligation to me, but—"

Goshen's chuckle cut him off. "Sahna not hate Elves like other Blood. Sahna not see Elves for centuries. Too many enemy here for me to leave." The Tribesman clapped his free hand to Jeran's shoulder. "We the blades of the brother Gods. Not many like us left. I not leave until Valia's children safe." Goshen paused, then shrugged. "Or until we dead."

Jeran frowned. "Then what—?"

"I not in your mind like others," Goshen said, tapping his forehead. "Yet even I can see your pain. You need rest. You need restore faith."

"I'm not sure—"

"You not fool. No need play dumb. You branch on which your people stand. If you break, all fall."

"So what should I do?"

"What you must. Today, we fight. Come."

Goshen did not speak at all while Jeran followed him back to the outskirts of the camp, a stretch of forest only different because when they approached it, a half dozen Elves slipped out of the shadows like ghosts and brought taut bows to bear on them. Jeran scanned the trees, wondering how many other *Ael Chatorra* watched from concealment.

"We found nothing," Jeran said. "Goshen believes the attack will come from the southeast."

The leader eyed them both, with his gaze lingering on the Tribesman. "Astalian wishes to see you, Lord Odara," he said, signaling his solders to return to cover. "And the Wildman is right; scouts reported movement south of here."

If Goshen took offense at the insult, he showed no sign of it, but in the camp, he let Jeran take the lead, following him through the hastily-raised collection of tents that still somehow managed to be arranged in precise rows, and with an almost comprehensible hierarchy. *Ael Chatorra* patrolled inside as well as out, and hundreds of *Ael Namisa* scurried about their chores, but just as many Elves slept in or around the tents, and others milled about, desperate to seek sleep themselves but kept from it by some impending duty.

The days since leaving Illendrylla had been a blur. At first their flight had been frantic but uneventful. With Luran's forces committed to securing the city, they had earned a few days without pursuit, their greatest challenge choosing in which direction to flee. Many had wanted to move straight for *Ael Shende Ruhl*, but Astalian and Jeran both believed Luran would have soldiers along the Path of Riches, and they prevailed upon the Empress to choose a route that would take them north through harsher but more friendly terrain.

Some worried that they were fleeing one threat into the arms of another, and as it became apparent that their meandering path led them inexorably toward the Tribal Lands, more and more voices were raised against the wisdom of the *Hohe Chatorra*. Several days past Charylla had ordered a halt, though the rationale behind it remained a mystery. The Empress offered no explanation, and in the days since had issued no additional orders.

Opposition to Astalian's leadership continued to grow, in large part as a response to the attacks. Small bands loyal to Luran had begun to circle their camp several days back, picking off scouts and raiding whenever circumstances permitted. Every day saw mounting casualties and larger concentrations of enemies, and more rumors that it was Astalian who had led them to this crucible.

At the Empress's tent they were confronted by another score of readied weapons. Astalian appeared, barking out a string of orders—and a few oaths—in Aelvin. "My apologies," he said to Goshen. "One would think my people would know their allies by now."

"I dishonored if they not think me dangerous," Goshen replied, flashing a toothy grin. "I go south. Not miss fight." He left without another word, but Jeran saw a half dozen Elves following him with their eyes, and a few seemed ready to use their weapons despite Astalian's upbraiding.

"Have you made any progress?" Jeran asked.

"I might as well be trying to convince a stone to float." Astalian smiled, but the expression held little humor. "She does not want to flee our homeland like a criminal, but she understands that Luran holds the strategic advantage. She realizes that we do not have the men or resources to retake Illendrylla, but she is hesitant to leave while anyone loyal to our cause remains under *Kohrnodran* oppression. She recognizes my obligation to see her to safety, but she will not leave so long as a single soul who risked their life to follow her remains behind."

The exhaustion Jeran had been holding at bay crashed down upon him with ferocity. "You must make her see reason."

"Make her see reason? I might have an easier time convincing Luran to abandon his ambition! If she were reasonable, we'd be running through the forest in small groups, not trumpeting our presence and sitting here while our enemies take their time encircling us. It is only a matter of time before these skirmishes escalate."

"She could go to Dranakohr with the others," Jeran said, perhaps for the hundredth time. "Once she's—"

"We have been over this. She refuses to leave until everyone else is safe. That is the only commitment I can get from her. Fool woman!" He hissed the last under his breath, careful that even the most trusted of his lieutenants did not hear him speak out against their Empress. "She refuses to make any decision except the one I know the right answer to." Astalian scrubbed a hand at eyes ringed with exhaustion. "Is there any more you can do?"

"We've been over that as well. I have every Mage capable of making a Gate ferrying Elves to safety. But there are limitations, and my people are already overexerting themselves. If some of your Gifted—"

"I have asked and asked and asked again," Astalian replied, cutting Jeran off. "They claim this Talent is something peculiar to Humans, and that only a handful of *Ael Maulle* have ever mastered it."

"Then there's nothing else to be done. We will evacuate as many as possible as quickly as possible. Hopefully, we can hold off Luran long enough to get the bulk of your people to safety."

"The bulk of our people..." Astalian sighed. "More arrive every day than you can evacuate. I start to suspect that Luran lets them through—maybe encourages it!—just to drive us that much closer to defeat."

Leaving Illendrylla, they had numbered almost two thousand, more than half *Ael Chatorra* ready for battle. But their party had swelled to nearly eight times that amount, increased by a tide of refugees, and by those with no particular love for Luran and his minions, and with far more civilians than soldiers. The influx of loyal Elves was one factor that had prompted Charylla's order to halt, but the Empress did not grasp the greater implications.

"If you can't convince her soon, then we are lost," Jeran said, no longer trying to hide his lack of confidence. Hopelessness permeated the bond, and he struggled to contain it lest it spread through his people like a plague.

"You sound no more optimistic than I do, my friend." Astalian laughed, but it was a weak sound, uncharacteristic in the boisterous Elf.

"Ambush!" Goshen's stark cry cut through the grim silence of the camp, and the *Tsha'ma* barreled through a cluster of Elves in his haste to cross from south to west, tossing them to the ground like a collection of straw dolls. The Tribesman never slowed, but he let out another bellow that drew the eyes of everyone present.

"Your friend has gone mad," Astalian grinned. "Luran's forces are south of here."

Jeran did not share the mirth, and his hand sought the blade at its hip, drawing it free of its scabbard. He started running after the Tribesman. "Goshen's sense of humor is odd, but I don't think—"

Screams erupted from the west, and a wave of Elves tumbled back into the heart of the camp, falling over themselves in their haste to flee. A roar followed, a sound like thunder in the heart of a storm and the primal scream of a great beast all at once. From the trees burst two dozen Tribesmen, and they plowed into the flank of the Aelvin camp, hacking with axe and club at any Elf within reach.

Goshen reached them first, driving two Tribesmen away from a cluster of cowering children. The *Tsha'ma* snarled something in Garu Jeran did not understand, but even with an utter lack of comprehension, he heard the contempt. The two *Kohr'adjin* lunged again, and Goshen unleashed his rage, using his hammer to shatter one assailant's club while crushing the life from the second with his Gift.

By the time the dead Tribesman hit the ground, Jeran joined the fray, with Astalian and a dozen Elves close behind. He heard distant cries announcing Luran's attack, but dismissed them. *That's someone else's battle for now.* He sensed his soldiers rallying, and some of the Magi from Dranakohr as well, but none were sure which enemy to attack.

A Tribesman tried to sweep around him, intent on the panicking Elves behind. "No true Garun'ah avoids a warrior to slaughter children," Jeran yelled, moving to intercept. "Is this what you are to become in the service of Kohr? Murderers and cowards?"

The Tribesman skidded to a stop, and Jeran saw his words had struck a chord. "Have you traded freedom to become lapdogs of some Elf?" Jeran forced a derisive laugh and watched as the Tribesman turned to face him, murder in his eyes. "No wonder Garun is unconcerned about losing you to his Father; your presence must have been an insult to all the Blood."

The Tribesmen bellowed and charged, and two others followed close behind. Jeran seized his Gift, but he remained unwilling to use it except as a last resort. Too many could be hurt if he lost control in the camp. But as the Tribesmen closed in on him, he wondered at the foolish audacity that had caused him to goad them to a crazed attack in the first place.

An arrow sprouted from the neck of one Tribesman, driving him to the ground. The second fell to a swing from Jeran's blade, a deep gash that caught in the Tribesman's thick hides and slowed Jeran just long enough for the third to close in on his unprotected flank.

Jeran dove aside, but pain exploded down his arm where the Tribesman's club bruised flesh and bone. Seeing his opponent down, the Tribesman pounced, and Jeran grunted as a wall of fighting muscle descended upon him, driving the breath from his lungs and forcing him to drop his blade. Hands closed around his throat. He fought, thrashing and struggling to break the vise-like grip, but the

Kohr'adjin held the advantage in size and leverage. As fire flared up within his lungs, the sounds of the battle faded, and darkness flitted around the edges of the wild Tribesman's eyes, his yellowed teeth bared in a victorious smile.

In the quiet that preceded total unconsciousness, an unexpected calm suffused Jeran, and something coalesced within. He felt a sudden clarity in his bond; he knew his soldiers were on their way to help. He knew, too, that they were unprepared to face the dozens of battle-frenzied Tribesman pouring into the camp. The tenuous grip he held on magic strengthened, and he unleashed it with focused intent.

The Tribesman's eyes widened the instant before he was hurled away, and his fingernails left burning scrapes on the flesh of Jeran's neck. He hit one of the great trees with enough force to shatter his spine and landed in a heap at its base.

Gasping in a breath, Jeran climbed to his feet, ignoring the pain in his throat and chest. His left arm felt as if someone had suspended a boulder from it. It hung uselessly at his side, throbbing in rhythm with his heart.

He retrieved his blade, dismissing the wave of nausea that clenched his gut when he bent over. Magic swirled within him, heightening his senses, making the clash of weapons ring in his ears. The scents of fertile forest and fresh blood clashed in his nose. *How dare these beasts desecrate this place with violence. How dare they threaten my people!*

"Enough!" The word cracked through the forest, aided by magic in a way Jeran had not intended. It drew eyes to him, pausing all but the most frenzied fighting. "You wish to see death? Come then," he called out, the Gift raging inside him. "Let us show them death."

Streaks of black and gray exploded from the trees, the *choupik* charging into the *Kohr'adjin* with a grim silence that matched the Tribesmen's berserker fervor. Black-uniformed Humans followed, discarding bows in favor of more personal weaponry. They raced forward, taunting the Tribesmen, drawing them away from the defenseless Aelvin refugees.

Their fury matched Jeran's, as did their thirst for justice. He knew this would be the last time he saw of some of them, maybe most of them, but he could not deny them this battle. Too much rested on the alliance with the Elves. If a few hundred of his people had to be sacrificed for that alliance, it was a price he had to accept.

The ready blades of Jeran's people slowed the Tribesmen's advance into the heart of the Aelvin encampment. As the fighting raged, Jeran felt phantom wounds tracing lines of fire across his body. A deep stab into his chest ended the *choupik* Aerak's life; a long gash across his midriff signaled Poul's fall. Dozens of other wounds, some fatal, some only incapacitating, drove thought from Jeran's mind. He became one with the battle, a whirlwind of destruction, carving a path through the forest, chasing down any enemy who fell into his field of vision.

He caught only glimpses of the fight outside his own focus. Astalian locked sword to axe with a hulking Tribesman. Goshen plunged into a knot of *Kohr'adjin*, his face drenched in the blood of his enemies. A Tribesman cleaved an Elf in two, then wrenched his blade free and looked for more prey. He fled when he saw Jeran approaching.

The sounds of battle faded to a distant din, as did the pain. He received a dozen more wounds in the fighting, all scratches compared to the throb in his arm, but he ignored them. He fell into a rhythm, moving between the trees, using his Gift to carve a path through the brush, using his blade to do the same to the *Kohr'adjin*.

When his enemies grew harder to find, frustration built, and when Astalian laid a cold hand on his wounded shoulder, Jeran spun to attack so fast he barely had time to stop the blade. Astalian never flinched, but fear flickered in his eyes when he saw the blood-stained Aelvin blade slashing toward him.

"It's done, my friend," he said, his voice a hoarse whisper.

Those words brought Jeran back to reality. Pain hobbled him, nearly crushed him, and Astalian threw down his blade so he could catch Jeran before he collapsed.

Atop his own pain, he felt more acutely the wounds of his people, and the gaping holes in his consciousness of those who had laid down their lives. More than a score of souls had departed for the Twilight World, and from his bond he knew at least four more men had not long to live.

"I have never seen anything like that," Astalian told him, helping Jeran sheath his sword then retrieving his own blade from the ground. "I almost think you didn't need our help. You fought like a— Dear Gods, I didn't realize you bore so many injuries. I will call for *Ael Maulle*!"

"Have them tend to my people. I will survive."

The loss of his own brought a deep grief to Jeran, one that he sought to temper. He needed his people to feel that loss, to understand what fate awaited them if they continued to follow him, but he did not want them to know how much each death affected him. They had their own pain to deal with; they did not need his as well.

"You must have a dozen wounds, and this arm—"

"Have them tend my people!" Jeran reined in his temper. "Just help me to my tent, Astalian. I'll be fine."

The Elf studied him for a moment. "If you insist."

They limped through the camp, Elf and man, and they drew eyes wherever they passed. Astalian reveled in the attention, trumpeting their great victory and attributing their success to Jeran and his followers. Jeran knew what the Elf was attempting; by uniting them in purpose, he hoped to forge stronger bonds between their peoples. Yet as they crossed the camp, Jeran felt new bonds form in the back of his mind. Though tenuous, he nonetheless knew them to be Elves who saw in him their best chance of survival. Though few, he knew that they would not be the last unless something was done, and done quickly, to quell the tide.

As Astalian laid him upon his pallet, he gripped the Elf's arm. "You must convince her to leave the forest."

"She is unwilling to make a decision," Astalian said, "and forcing us to wait here while we 'marshal our forces' gives her the perfect excuse to delay. This attack was bad, but once we have the fortifications complete—"

"You must convince her to abandon the Great Forest immediately," Jeran said again.

Astalian fell silent, his eyes probing for what Jeran had left unsaid. "Sleep, my friend. I will send *Ael Maulle* to you after they have tended to your people. And I will do what I can, but you must think I wield far more influence over the Empress than I do. Fear not; until we can convince her otherwise, we can keep her safe."

"If she stays," Jeran told the Elf, his voice grim, "she risks far more than her life. She risks her Empire."

CHAPTER 30

The light from the oil lantern flickered in the crisp night air, casting dim illumination through the tent but barely penetrating into the deep darkness beyond. Outside, Aelvin soldiers ghosted through the camp on patrol. Jeran felt their passage more than heard it; he held the Gift and kept his perceptions extended, partly to provide warning should another attack come, partly to dull the edge off his pain.

Harvest was full upon them. Soon snows would blanket the Great Forest, making travel more difficult and their path even harder to conceal. Not that such things mattered with Charylla's refusal to flee and Luran's army encircling them. Jeran slammed his fist into the small folding desk—a wonder of Aelvin craftsmanship, with near seamless construction and exquisite scrollwork—and immediately wished he had not as a lance of agony shot down his other arm.

He reached for his water, concentrating on stilling the trembling in his fingers, and took a long draught, then returned his attention to *The Forge of Faith*, alternating between the deep philosophical discussion in its text and the myriad of Readings dancing around it. He paused from time to time to examine different objects from a small chest he had brought from Shandar, comparing the information he learned from them to what he had gleaned from the book.

He had hoped his efforts would piece together the truth, perhaps provide some insight to aid him out of his own dilemma. Instead, his research left him more confused and wondering if such a thing as truth even existed.

"Lord Odara?"

"Enter."

Jeran drew a breath and shoved his pain to the deepest recesses of his mind. He silently began to repeat a child's rhyme, a trick he had learned that helped him hide his thoughts from those bonded to him.

Kahrva, *choupik* of the Inkiedou sept, entered and saluted. "We have a final count, Lord Odara." His voice remained controlled despite the deep sadness Jeran felt roiling within him.

"How many?"

"Seventeen, all told. Six of my brothers and eleven Humans. Five more have wounds severe enough that the Elves are unable to heal them completely, but they will survive until they can be returned to Dranakohr."

Seventeen. More than I had hoped. Less than I feared. "Ask the Elves for permission to return our fallen comrades to the ground."

"It is already done, Lord Odara. Astalian himself will preside over the ceremony." A heavy silence followed, but Jeran saw the question waiting in Kahrva's eyes. At his signal, the Orog spoke. "Should I request more men from Dranakohr?"

A frown creased Jeran's lips as he considered the request. "What would you do, *choupik*?" he asked, stalling for time more than anything.

"I do not wish to see the Elves suffer, but so long as they refuse to move, all we do is invite death to find us. We ask any man who joins us to face that fate as well."

Jeran was slow to respond. "Do the men tire of dying for Elves?"

"The men do not fear dying, Lord Odara. We will fall to a man if you tell us this is where we need to fight. But we do tire of burying our comrades. We trust in you"—Jeran noticed a hesitation, and he wondered how much his recent on-slaught of doubt had shaken that trust—"but none wish to see more men fall than necessary, or for any to fall in vain. If the Elves intend to doom themselves, then perhaps our forces would be better saved to fight another day."

"Thank you, Kahrva. Few are willing to speak their mind to me, and most who do strike a far more demanding tone."

"The Elders say that a man who does not mention his fear of water should not complain when asked to swim."

Jeran laughed, a genuine sound that brought warmth to the chill in his gut. "We will bring no more men from Dranakohr, not until the Elves have been made to see reason, at least. Our focus will be on protecting our Magi, and their focus will be on evacuating as many Elves as possible. Once her people are safe, perhaps the Empress will be easier to reason with."

"I will inform the men, Lord Odara."

Jeran moved to stand, but the pain in his arm and side hobbled him, and it took a great effort to keep it from his face. "Will the men disapprove if I do not at-tend the funeral? I have—"

"I will explain the situation, Lord Odara. They know your prayers are with our fallen."

"Again, thank you." He waited until the Orog closed the tent flap then exhaled sharply, cradling his arm against his body. For a moment, his vision swirled, and he thought he might collapse.

When the spell passed, he filled a tankard with wine scavenged from an aban-doned village. The dry wine burned his throat, but in short order it dispelled the worst of his pain. He considered pouring a second but switched back to water, then picked up *The Forge of Faith*, surprised again at how heavy the thin book felt, as if time itself had added its own burden to the ancient volume. The Readings suffusing it called to him, and he opened himself to them.

It proved a mistake worse than any he had made since returning to the Aelvin Lands. Weakened by pain and exhaustion, he found himself unhinged in time, trapped by the events so powerful, so wrought with emotion, that they had left impressions on the book itself. He danced through a whirlwind of sights and sounds, watched Lorthas metamorphose from a young idealist to a bitter warlord and back again, saw thousands of nameless strangers wrestle with the certainty of their own impending death. In that maelstrom dreams faded, hope died, and Jeran once again questioned the faith he held in his own vision. The crushing failure of well-laid plans, plans centuries in the making, made him reexamine his own hastily-cobbled goals; the perversion of what seemed to be pure ideals on both sides of the MageWar cast doubt on his own justifications. Despair circled, and the immensity of what he had taken on, what had been thrust upon him—

"Jeran?"

The voice drew him back to reality. He threw *The Forge of Faith* to the ground as if it were a viper, but his eyes moved to the tent flap, where Aemon stood. Con-cern mixed with curiosity in his gaze, and his eyes slipped to the book on the floor. "You did not answer," the old man said. "Is everything all right?"

Jeran had no bond with his grandfather; men such as Aemon did not blindly follow others. Nevertheless, he took a tight rein on his thoughts and walled himself off to his people, who no doubt felt at least a portion of the fear emanating from his tent. "I'm fine," he said, forcing a smile. "I must have fallen asleep."

"Not hard to do in conditions like these," Aemon sighed, sitting on the stool across the desk from Jeran. "I have not felt exhaustion like this in… I don't even remember when."

"The race to Shandar?" Jeran suggested.

"That was bad, my boy… But those days are all a blur to me. In some ways, this attrition is far worse than that wild run."

They stared at each other for a time, weighing, assessing, seeking a measure of advantage for the confrontation both knew was coming but neither wanted to initiate. Aemon broke the silence, heaving a sigh that shivered the bristles of his silver beard. "We cannot stay here."

"Agreed," Jeran said, forcing a grin. "I don't suppose you've attempted such convincing persuasion on the Elves?"

"Charylla is blinded by grief. She's a good girl, but in her condition, not a fit ruler. We both have worked too hard—sacrificed too much—to lose it all in the depths of the Aelvin Forest fighting between a handful of moss-covered trees."

"Charylla is frightened and overwhelmed by a responsibility she never truly believed would be thrust upon her. We all have our Dranakohrs. She will cross through the tunnel and emerge the stronger for it."

Aemon scrubbed a hand through his beard, then reached out to grab Jeran's arm, his fingers twitching, his grip tentative and gentle, as if he hoped to convey through touch a tenderness he dared not let enter his tone.

"We cannot risk the outcome of her ordeal. Too much happens, too quickly. Kaper stands at the edge of the abyss. The Tachans have reclaimed their empire and most of Gilead as well. The Black Fleet has cordoned off Roya, and our enemies advance on King Tobin's mountain fortress. All this happens while we defend a few thousand Elves intent on following their Empress to the Nothing."

Jeran settled back in his chair. "I did not know of Roya… But it doesn't matter. The Royans never factored into my plan."

"So you'll risk yourself for Elves, but not for Royans?"

"I know the Elves. The Royans are strangers. The losses they suffer will be regretful, but perhaps they will divert enough resources from elsewhere to make a difference."

Aemon turned away, his lips pursed with the taste of disgust. "You sound like Lorthas."

"No, Lorthas would find a way to benefit from the attack on Roya, to make their sacrifice aid his goal. I have neither the energy nor the ingenuity for such machinations. Nor do I have your gift of using such tragedies to galvanize support among my allies."

"You make me into some opportunistic monster," Aemon snapped, "and Lorthas into a gifted strategist."

"No, I make Lorthas into a man not wholly evil, and you into one not motivated solely by altruistic goals. You both strive toward the same ideal: a single, unified Madryn; you with the tools you learned from your teachers, and he with the tools he learned from his."

Aemon's head jerked around, a glare fastening on Jeran, cold like the icy ever-present daggers hanging from the covered walkways in Dranakohr. "Are you suggesting that I am somehow responsible for the evils Lorthas unleashed upon this world?"

"Lorthas makes his own decisions," Jeran replied, his voice calm despite the flare of magic he saw enter Aemon's eyes. For his own part, he dared not seize magic any more than the slender touch he now held. "You are no more responsible for him than I am for Dahr."

Jeran waited for Aemon to relax, to doubt his anger, and in that moment of indecision, he attacked. "But Lorthas strives toward the same thing as you, was taught by *you*, the only man I know more skilled at twisting men's hearts and minds."

Aemon's brow tightened, his face drawing down in a frown. "What are you implying?"

"I imply nothing. I simply wonder what prompted you to betray him."

"Betray... *him*?" The Gift surged in Aemon, his eyes flaring blue, seeming to shine enough to illumine the tent; his cheeks flushed deep red, the red of pure anger or unwilling embarrassment. "How dare you accuse—"

"I do not need a show of indignation," Jeran said, slamming his fist into the table as he rose to pace the five steps across the tent, ignoring the jolt of pain that flashed up from his other arm and through his chest. His voice betrayed none of the emotion of his actions, nor did those emotions truly influence his words. "Nor do I need another display of self-righteousness. You set up Lorthas as your heir presumptive, manipulated him to a position where he could take the reins and fulfill your dream; then you abandoned him, threw him to the Assembly and stood by while they labeled him an outlaw and villain, tearing down what you both had spent centuries to build. I wonder why, and I wonder if such a betrayal may await me in the future."

"What lies has he told you?" Aemon asked, his words rushed, his composure failing, the mask of righteousness slipping in the face of Jeran's onslaught. "Why would you believe him over me?"

"He never handed me willingly into the arms of my enemies, nor—"

"He *is* your enemy!"

"No, he is *your* enemy."

"I had no choice!"

"We always have a choice. You taught me that."

"It was for the good of Madryn!"

"Yes, that's Lorthas's excuse as well."

Aemon opened his mouth for yet another exclamation, but Jeran cut him off with a gesture so dismissive it left the old man sputtering for breath. "It doesn't matter. My knowledge does not come from Lorthas, but from a source with far fewer biases than either of you."

Mouth agape, stunned to silence by the stark dismissal, Aemon stared in unhidden confusion until Jeran's eyes flicked toward the floor. Only then did comprehension dawn.

"Your Readings?" he asked. "I have never seen that book before in my life."

"Maybe not, but it has seen you, and a great deal besides." Jeran stooped to retrieve the volume, letting his hand skim across the worn cover, giving the impression of reviewing a Reading when in truth he felt so exhausted that wading through the hundreds of vignettes the book held seemed a more daunting task than saving the Elves from Luran. "But Readings only tell me the what; from you, I need the why. Why did you betray Lorthas?"

Aemon swallowed his pride, regaining a measure of composure. "Betray is a very strong word, my—"

"Abandoned him, then, if you prefer, or another term of your choosing. But why did you do it?"

"Now see here! I have lived too long to be talked to in such a manner, let alone by a child—"

"Do not raise your voice to me," Jeran warned, his quiet voice cracking like a whip across the space between them. "And do not think to cow me with a show of temper. For a threat to be effective, you must be willing to commit to it. I have lived under the thumb of men with no compunction. Can you tell me you think yourself more of a threat to me than they?"

Aemon drew a breath, the war for control of his emotions evident on his face. "Of course. You're right. I didn't mean…"

"I know," Jeran said, allowing the hint of a smile to slip through the iron mask he wore. "But I still need to know: Why did you abandon him?"

"I did not abandon him," Aemon said, but his shoulders sagged as he said it, his features betraying an ages-old weariness. "I did it to save him. To save everything we worked for. I had a vision; in it I saw that if the plans Lorthas had concocted were allowed to come to fruition, then the Assembly would split and civil war would become inevitable. Alrendria would have been torn apart, and Lorthas would have ruled over a kingdom of ashes."

"So instead you had him labeled a Darklord and embroiled the whole of Madryn in a war far worse."

"I never named Lorthas Darklord until he embraced the title himself!" Aemon said, indignation replacing his earlier anger. "I worked relentlessly to heal the breach between us until *he* sent an assassin to me under a banner of truce. After that, I knew he could never be redeemed."

"Why didn't you just tell him?" Jeran asked. "If you had just explained—"

"I've told you before: Whenever I warn people about my visions, the results are always worse than if I just steer events in a different direction. If I had told Lorthas why he had to abandon his plan…"

He trailed off, perhaps caught by the absurdity of his own statement. "Good for us that you held your tongue," Jeran told him. "One might find it difficult to imagine an outcome worse than the MageWar."

Aemon's mouth clamped shut, and magic once again flared across his eyes, but instead of resuming his defense, he turned and stormed out of the tent. In the wake of his departure, Jeran fell to his chair, numbed by the pain radiating from his injuries and drained by the effort of battling against Aemon's will, one of the most enduring forces in Madryn. He cradled his head against the cool wood of the writing table, *The Forge of Faith* clutched in his fingers, tempting him with images of the past; the enormity of what yet stood before him weighing him down, eroding him like the waves against the shore of Atol Domiar.

He felt the tent flap pull aside again, the cool swish of air as it caressed his face, but he did not raise his head. "You did what you felt you had to do. I understand that. There's no need to—"

"I don't know what you said to him," Jes said, her unexpected voice quickening the pace of Jeran's heart, "but I've not seen him that mad in decades."

"He needed to understand that he no longer pulls the strings," Jeran replied, wiping the agony from his face and making sure he had full control over the bond they shared. "And I needed some answers."

As he stood, the grin Jes wore faded, replaced with an outward show of disapproval and an inward pang of concern, relayed to Jeran through their connection. "Dear Gods! Why didn't *Ael Maulle* heal you?"

"I told them not to."

"Of course you did," she sighed, her eyes darting toward the Heavens. "You wouldn't want your followers to think you're Human."

She moved toward him, brushing off his half-hearted attempts to keep her at bay. "Stand still. You'll be of no use to anyone if you don't let me do something about that. I'll bet the bone is broken."

"It's not broken," Jeran insisted, flinching at the icy touch of her fingertips. She opened herself to magic, probing his wounds with her perceptions, a gentle tingle that in no way prepared him for the stinging pain of the actual Healing. He fell to his knees, gasping for air as his flesh mended, his bone knitted, and his bruises faded to dim yellow.

When Jes released him, it was all Jeran could do to keep from collapsing. He staggered to his feet, leaning heavily on the desk for support. "Thank you," he managed.

"A measure of humility? From you, Lord Odara? You're quite welcome." She curtsied for emphasis.

"You should go..." Jeran said. "See about the others."

"They've all been tended to," she told him. "I'm more concerned about you. How long do you—"

"Like I told Aemon, I will stay here as long as it takes. We will not abandon our allies to Luran and Salos."

"If you'd hold your tongue for a moment, I was going to ask how long you planned on isolating yourself like this? For good or ill, this bond you forge with people... Your men are worried about you. I... The longer you stay in hiding like this, the more desperate they become. You must know that this canvas doesn't hide your feelings of failure, or fear, or hopelessness from us, no matter how well you've learned to control your gift."

"Gift." Jeran spat the word. It tasted foul, like spoiled meat doused in spices to fool the unwary into thinking it fresh. "You Magi claim that every ability bestowed upon us is a gift, when more oft than not I can think of no worse curse."

Jes stepped back, driven away by the venom in his voice, but Jeran again sensed that concern, concern she tried harder to hide from herself than she did from him. "Do you have any idea what it's like to share yourself with a thousand minds?" Jeran asked. "To feel their fears, their wounds, their deaths? To know that my actions, no matter how noble, no matter how well-intentioned or well-planned, will more likely than not see most of them to their graves?

"The world has given itself over to chaos. Millennia-old kingdoms topple, the Magi are at war, the Assembly in hiding, Alwellyn the Eternal dead. The foundations of our civilization crumble, and across Madryn people plead for something to believe in. My people, those in Dranakohr and House Odara, some in Kaper and Shandar—and even some among the Elves!—now turn to me to guide them, to give them faith, to protect them from a godless world in which the only surety is death. But how can I give them faith, Jes, when I have none myself? What am I left to believe in?"

Slowly, almost unconsciously, Jes reached out to him, but she stopped shy of actual contact. His all-but-defeated gaze, or perhaps the vulnerability he had shown her despite his fervent desire to keep his fears to himself, changed something in her. Jeran felt the change, a subtle adjustment in the bond they shared, but he did not understand it.

"How old are you?" Jes asked suddenly.

"What?" The question caught Jeran off-guard, by its suddenness as much as its strangeness.

Jes's cheeks flushed crimson. "The Emperor. He once told me to ask you how old you were."

A smile spread across Jeran's face. "He told you to ask me how many winters I had seen."

"That's the same..." She trailed off, and her face pinched, lips compressed to a thin line, eyes narrowed to near slits. "You were spying on us?"

"Who better to practice on than the person who advised me to improve the subtle use of my perceptions?"

"I do not appreciate being spied upon."

"I suppose few people do."

A breath hissed out like a snake, but she relented, and Jeran hoped this marked the beginning of a better relationship between them, one less punctuated with violent arguments and sarcastic jibes. "Fine, then. How many winters have you seen?"

"More than I can count," Jeran replied. He raised the book he still held in his hand. "This volume has survived a thousand winters, and holds hundreds of Readings. That crate over there contains hundreds more, all impressed upon items scavenged from Dranakohr and Shandar. Some last only moments, others days, but I can view each in an instant. And I have. I have studied each of those Readings relentlessly, viewed them from every angle. How many Winters have I seen? Far more than you have lived! Far more than I ever wanted to, countless lifetimes of death, betrayal, and atrocity, with the occasional glimpse of something more hopeful, just enough to make me think the world might not deserve utter destruction. That is the 'Gift' of being a Reader."

In that moment, she understood. He could tell by the shift in her posture, the nervous swallow she took, so unlike the confident, irrepressible Mage he had come to see her as; the unstoppable, willful force from which he drew strength. "All those other crates, those ridiculous baubles you were constantly playing with in Shandar?"

"All held Readings," Jeran nodded, "or were brought to me so I could see if they held them."

"But why? What is there to gain by torturing yourself with events so traumatic they left images on the objects around them?"

"Because maybe..." He faltered, not certain of his words, not certain he should share them, not sure she would truly understand, or worse, would come to find his path as flawed as the paths of those who had come before. "Maybe if I understand the mistakes, the misunderstandings, the motivations that led us to this place, then maybe I can change things. Maybe I can finally make things better."

"You would suffer all this anguish for the sake of those you do not even know?"

"Perhaps for them," Jeran answered, "but more for those I do know, or who I will know. They are the ones who will be asked to sacrifice. I only share a fraction of their pain."

Jes did reach out then, taking Jeran's cheeks in her hands and drawing his face toward hers. The warmth of her lips stood in stark contrast to the coolness of her fingertips, sending an electrifying jolt through his body, dispelling the weariness that plagued his bones and instilling in him a vigor he had not expected but sorely desired.

"Have faith in yourself, Jeran," Jes whispered, pulling back long enough to draw breath. Jeran saw the hunger in her eyes, a passion that matched his own, but one that she resisted even as she surrendered to it. "Believe in what you are doing, as I believe in you."

CHAPTER 31

A warm breeze played around the trunk of the massive oak, jostling the branches, teasing the broad green leaves, coaxing them to song, a melody as soothing as it was illusory. It danced through patches of wildflowers vibrant in color and pleasant in aroma; it swirled over the surface of a stream, picking up flecks of spray from the crystal waters, drawing those droplets upward where they caught the sun, spreading a rainbow curtain across the sky.

Jeran sat in a cushioned chair in the shadow of the great oak studying a game board, its hand-carved stone pieces sharp-edged and heavy, their color changing from black to white to black again, sometimes settling for a time on dark gray before resuming their constant transformations. His hand caressed one piece, started to move it, then reconsidered; he touched four others before returning his hand to the first, then removed his hand from the board completely, cradling his jaw instead and considering his options.

"A strange use of your time," said a familiar voice.

Jeran did not look up nor offer greetings to the man, a man who still refused to name himself anything other than 'a guide', a man whose insights had saved Jeran many times over but whose actual existence he still sometimes doubted. His presence was not wholly unexpected—the Guide often appeared when Jeran retreated to the Twilight World. Nor was it wholly undesired.

"Do you play?" Jeran asked, gesturing at the board.

"I have played similar games, but not in many winters." The Guide's shadow fell over him, and Jeran felt himself come under scrutiny. "Would this time not be better spent in real slumber? Exhaustion radiates from you like light from the sun."

"True sleep is over all too quickly, and no matter how deep is never enough. Here, at least, I have the luxury of silence, the illusion of time."

"That is the way of the world," the Guide said. "Centuries of quiet followed by an avalanche, one often triggered by the most inconsequential of events." The Guide lowered to one knee, his eyes shifting from Jeran to the game board. "None of that explains why you're sitting here playing a game by yourself."

"If you think I play alone," Jeran laughed, "then you are too long gone from the world." Jeran settled back in the chair, looking at the man for the first time, studying his angular features, his short dark hair, his sad blue eyes. "I seek not to Topple the Castle."

"When did I become the one asking questions, and you the one answering in riddles?" the Guide asked, a grin spreading across his face.

"In this game," Jeran explained, his hand sweeping across the board, "master players commonly place their pieces in jeopardy, into positions so weak their opponents feel they must go on the offensive. Once lured out, an unexpected move is made that shifts the balance of power. But mastering the strategy is almost impossible, and if a player misjudges his opponent even slightly, or if his position ends up weaker than he intended…"

"Then he loses the game."

"Such a failed stratagem is called Toppling the Castle." Jeran knocked over his pieces for emphasis.

"And do you feel that you've misjudged your enemies, or your allies?"

"Either... Both... What I truly fear is that I—"

A tortured scream pierced the serene landscape; a howl of pain and fear; a sound familiar to Jeran and yet utterly alien, desperate in its plea yet insistent in its independence. The sound itself would have been enough to draw him, but a twinge in his consciousness accompanied it, the slightest hint of a connection. He sought out the Twilight World specifically because it freed him of those bonds.

He leapt to his feet and hurried toward the sound, the Guide several steps behind and urging him to stop. Jeran paid him no heed; try though he might, he found it all but impossible to ignore the suffering of people, his people most of all.

In the distance he saw Dahr cowering in the grass, hands shielding his face, eyes clenched shut. Sweat slicked his skin, mixing with blood both fresh and old, his and not his; running in rivulets down his trembling body to stain the ground around him, around the pieces of a shattered *dolchek*, around the remnants of a battle sigil, a proud razor-backed cat barely discernible in the tattered cloth.

A shadow fell over Dahr, and Jeran felt a powerful presence. He moved to intercept, opening himself to magic, but the Guide grabbed his arm and held him still. "Dahr has his own guide," the man said, a hint of melancholy in his voice, "and he does not appreciate interference."

"Look at him!" Jeran cried. "He can't endure that."

"Dahr's guide favors an approach more... direct... than I do, but Dahr is the architect of his own suffering."

"What would you have me do? Just stand back and let him suffer?"

"We all have our Dranakohrs," the Guide said, and Jeran's eyes snapped around. "With luck, Dahr will survive his."

"Do you spy on me in the waking world, too?" Jeran asked, unable to keep the scorn from his voice.

The Guide fixed him with a blank gaze, leaving Jeran to wonder if he remained silent out of confusion or guilt. Before he could belabor the point, Dahr let out another howl and faded from sight. The presence disappeared with him.

"It is done," the Guide told him. "For a time."

"I lose my taste for the Twilight World," Jeran said, turning away. The Guide made no move to follow him. "I have one more place to visit, then I will return to my body."

Jeran stopped after a few paces and looked over his shoulder. "What? No warning? No advice urging caution?"

"Why advise the fox to fear the snake? I think Lorthas may now have more to fear from us than we from him. Just be sure the path you walk is the path you've chosen." With that, the Guide faded, a shimmering disappearance, similar to Dahr's and yet not as definite, not as complete.

Jeran drew a deep breath and let out his perceptions, a feeling far different in the Twilight World than the waking world; the scene faded, colors muting then turning to black, a black punctuated with pinpoint lights, bright and dim, white and colored, each representing the soul of a slumbering being. Jeran scanned the vastness, identified the sphere he sought almost immediately, and willed himself toward it.

As he came into contact with it, the world blurred, and he found himself in the chamber at Dranakohr where he had so often met with Lorthas. The stone walls were decorated as they had been during his incarceration: images of Tylor's triumphs hung prominently across half of the carved-out cave; more subtle reminders of Lorthas's dominion graced the other. The now ever-present Orog guards were nowhere to be seen. Even odder, there was no Boundary, no magical energy humming through the chamber, no sense of impending danger.

Lorthas sat in his chair, a glass of wine in one hand and his other placed on the cover of a thick book. "Isn't it an odd feeling?" he asked when Jeran appeared. "The world without a Boundary. I find it difficult to sit here sometimes, or at least to concentrate on anything else. But this is the way the world was, the way it is meant to be, the way it will be again in time. We cannot deny nature."

"I need to know what you're planning," Jeran said, his expression even, his tone masked. He conjured a chair opposite Lorthas and sat, moving neither with haste nor deliberate slowness. The Darklord had the ability to twist the most inconsequential things to his advantage, and Lorthas noticed everything, even the most subtle of details.

"No pleasantries?" Lorthas asked, settling back and sipping his wine. "No well wishes? Are circumstances so dire we must dispense with the niceties of life?"

"I stand in my enemies' palm, and they close the fist," Jeran said. "We have an arrangement, but this is an opportunity even the most honorable of opponents would have difficulty letting slip past. I need to know if you will honor our bargain."

Lorthas frowned, his lips narrowing to a thin, bloodless line; his eyes flared, but with umbrage and not the Gift; his fingers pressed against the wineglass with enough pressure to force out the blood, leaving them white even compared to the normal albino tones of his flesh. "I may do many things of which others disapprove, but I do not break my word. Even Aemon should be willing to admit that."

"Then I have your oath, given here in the Twilight World and spoken truly, that you do not intend to use this period of our mutual enemies' strength to force your way through the Boundary? My people in Portal and Dranakohr are safe?"

Lorthas cupped a hand to his chin, two fingers stroking the smooth skin of his cheek, his gaze turning calculating and cold, a man confronted with a puzzle and intent on solving it. "I do not desire to harm anyone under your protection."

"That is not the same thing. Will you withdraw your army from Portal, or is your plan to lull me to complacency and then resume your attack?"

"I have no desire to attack Portal."

"Another evasion! Do you think I have paid no attention to you during our discussions? You can attack my people without wanting to attack my people. You can capture Portal even while wishing I would throw open the gates and welcome your army in. I do not need to know what you want to do; I need to know what you will do."

A smile played across Lorthas's face, a grin he made no effort to control, a grin he made sure Jeran took note of. "At first I thought this display was out of concern for the thousands of souls under your care. After all, with your attention focused on the east and south, who knows what might happen to those poor, leaderless children along the Boundary. But now I see this is about something else, something greater. You have a plan, and my intentions might affect that plan. You are no longer concerned with your people or their well-being. You now understand that the destination is more important than the path."

"The path we walk determines our destination."

"You may debate the philosophy," Lorthas added, his tone smug, "but you have chosen your side."

"There is no side. No side worth taking, at least. Aemon concerns himself so much with the steps along the path that he keeps losing sight of his goal; you focus so hard on the destination that you veer too often from the path, trampling whatever gets in the way. It has turned him into a timid man, more comfortable forcing others to make decisions than making them himself, forcing change only when he feels he must, and then, without warning or explanation. It has turned you into a hated monster, willing to ally with the most vile creatures imaginable, to partner with your most hated enemies, to sacrifice your morals in the hopes of achieving a modicum of victory; a man abandoned by his friends, feared by his followers, too proud to admit his mistakes, too stubborn to seek a better way."

"Sometimes the quickest path is over! Sometimes, events must be forced. If I had waited—if you wait!—for the world to want to change, then it will all go to the Nothing. Sacrifices must be made!"

"A convenient attitude, when the sacrifice is never your own."

"You seek to goad me," Lorthas whispered. The tension in his jaw and in the fierce set of his eyes suggested that it was working.

"I seek nothing but reassurance. Do you wait until I am at my most vulnerable? Do you intend to force a path through the Portal?"

"Truth be told, I have no such designs." Lorthas sighed as he spoke, a sound full of defeat, and in part, of regret. "My interest in your world wanes. It is a poison, and it has spread into my realm. That creature's… Salos's corruption has spread into *Ael Shataq*." The air darkened, crackling with energy; the tapestries and banners adorning the chamber burst to flame, filling the room with acrid smoke; the portraits oozed, paint dripping like blood, running down the walls in ever-darkening streams.

"With blood and tears and the sweat of centuries I created my dream, mocking the prison Aemon built for me, designing a society free of the evils of your world, a place where no one group held dominion over another; and in a matter of seasons the Durange infected it with ambition, greed, and the notion of superiority I spent lifetimes winnowing out of my people. I face war now, war among my people, war among my own elite, those I trusted to govern in my stead while I prepared to bring salvation out of *Ael Shataq*.

"The masters of your world always claimed I was a threat, when in truth, it was your world that was the threat to mine. Your brand of reckless freedom breeds dissidence; your ridiculous faith in people opens you to constant betrayal."

"And to rule through fear is better?" Jeran asked. He cracked a smug smile, more to enrage Lorthas than out of true amusement. "Obedience obtained through threat, even unspoken threat, is no true obedience. This civil war you face is of your own design. You filled the tinderbox, you set the spark, and now you suffer the consequences."

"Consequences? I've spent my whole life suffering consequences. When the Assembly refused to act, I was the only one willing to do what the Gods demanded of the Gifted: to protect those who were not bestowed with Their blessing. When the Commons turned against us, I was once again among the few willing to protect the Gifted from persecution."

"You sulk like a spoiled child denied a treat," Jeran said, forcing a laugh, hoping it seemed spontaneous. "In your attempts to save the world, you nearly destroyed it. You used people like tools, sacrificing them at whim to—"

"Never at whim!"

"—sacrificing them as you saw fit, regardless of their desires, irrespective of their dreams, heedless of their fears. And when the world turned against you, when it labeled you a monster, when it judged your actions excessive and your morality lacking, you did not scorn the decision, you did not fight it. No, you embraced it."

"Madryn needed a shared enemy, a focal point to rally against! When the Assembly betrayed me, I used it to polarize the world. Win or lose, the Four Races could find something to fight for, to die for, to live for. But the MageWar did not make me a villain, losing it did."

"Losing allowed history to label you a monster, it may affect how you are remembered, but it did not change what you were, what you allowed yourself to become. You—"

"I did it for them!" Lorthas could no longer control his anger. He stood, the air around him crackling with energy. In the real world, Jeran might have been afraid; here, such a display did not concern him. "I did it to give everyone a better world, a more just world."

"You cannot send the herd to slaughter and claim to do it out of love for the cattle. That's not justice. You cannot impose tolerance; you must teach a better way, or you only drive the prejudice beneath the surface. You cannot force an idea on people and then dispose of any who claim to have a better one. That's hypocrisy, not justice."

"You did not live through it," Lorthas fumed. "You did not suffer through it. What gives you the right to lecture me, or Aemon, or any of us?"

"Because you left this for me—for those around me—to finish. Aemon did not have the courage to finish your war; he sealed you in *Ael Shataq* and hoped he'd be gone by the time you returned. You have unleashed another evil on Madryn—perhaps a greater evil!—and now you, too, turn your back and leave it for others to deal with. I do not fault either of you for your dreams; I fault you both for your cowardice."

Lorthas lunged at Jeran, hands clenched like claws and reaching for his throat. With a wave, Jeran lifted the Darklord into the air and held him a hand's length away. "I do not need to fear you here. You taught me that."

In a moment, control returned, and Lorthas leveled a cold glare at Jeran. "You are a dangerous man," he said. "I wonder if Aemon realizes what he's unleashed upon the world this time."

"Whatever I am," Jeran said as he released his hold on Lorthas and opened the pathway back to his real body, "you are both responsible."

The Twilight World faded and Jeran woke. He dressed with purpose but not with haste, smoothing his clothes and buckling on both sword and *dolchek*. By the time he left the tent, two dozen of his soldiers, men and Orog both, waited for him. All wore uniforms dusted and smoothed, and each had weapons sheathed or in hand. All looked as if they expected a fight.

Jeran looked around, to the bustle of the morning, the hurried motions of Elves to and fro. He listened to the distant shouts and trumpeting horn blasts. "There was another battle? You were under orders to wake me if there was more fighting."

"This was but a skirmish, Lord Odara," a young man named Nikos said. "No need to trouble you for it. We'd rather have you fresh for the real battles."

"Real battles?" echoed Drogon. "You think any of these have been real battles? Shael protect us, but I think the real battles are yet to come."

"True enough," Jeran told them. "We're about to fight one now. Maybe two."

He strode through the camp, aware of the eyes following his passage. In the days since those first tenuous bonds, hundreds more Elves had bonded to him, but he felt adoration from Human and Elf alike, and from many who had yet to forge their own connections to him.

He passed rows of tents where *Ael Namisa* huddled, waiting for the horn blast signaling the end of the fighting so they could return to their duties. Beside the tents a clearing had been made where a few dozen of his Gifted—all looking as exhausted as the soldiers protecting them—opened Gates to Dranakohr through which a line of women and children passed. Jeran caught hints of relief as they crossed through the Gate and into the comparative safety of his mountain fortress, but knowing that only a hundred or so of the tens of thousands waiting could escape before his Magi collapsed tempered his enjoyment of the feeling.

Aemon and Yassik both caught his eye as he passed. The former scowled and turned away when he saw Jeran; the latter started toward him, an expression on his face that meant a lecture on some remarkable observation. Jeran waved him away. He had no time for idle speculation this morning.

He burst into Jes's tent unannounced. She straightened as if startled, though their bond must have alerted her to his presence, and hastily pulled down her half-donned dress. "How dare you—!"

"Honestly, Jes, does there remain a need for modesty or pretense between us?"

"There remains a need for politeness."

A smile quirked Jeran's mouth. He offered a formal bow. "Of course. My apologies for the intrusion, Lady Jessandra. I need your presence. Please follow behind me, say nothing, and try to look like a Mage of the Assembly."

She smoothed her dress and then fixed him with an imperious glare, hands on her hips, chin held slightly lifted and turned aside, aloof and cold, superior and condescending. Jeran's smile broadened. "Yes, that will do nicely."

He felt Jes's anger follow him from the tent, but she followed as well, close behind, refusing to speak, refusing to acknowledge her compliance. He did not covet her ire, but if his comments had incensed her, then he hoped it would only add to the effect he wanted to achieve.

The Elves opened a path for him, hustling backward and offering deep bows, the kind of deference reserved for the highest of *Ael Alluya*. His entourage grew as well, bolstered by battle-weary and exhausted soldiers who slipped from the tents to join rank behind him. Goshen appeared, towering over Jes, spiked hammer held high on the haft and used as a walking stick, blood from the most recent skirmish conveniently left unwashed from his frightening visage. Another familiar figure, tall and slender, noble in bearing even without her chiseled features and exotic beauty, stepped out in front of Jeran.

"Lady Utari Hahna," he said, stopping to greet her. "I apologize for not seeking you out before now, but circumstances have not allowed it. I am glad you were able to escape Lynnaei unharmed."

He started to bow, but Utari stopped him, taking a firm grip on his shoulder and keeping him upright. "Firsts bow only to the King," she said, "and even to him with reluctance."

"I am not yet First of House Odara," he reminded her.

She studied him, her deep brown eyes probing and weighing. "You are a First," she announced, as if that settled a long standing argument. Her gaze slipped past him, to the cluster of soldiers behind him. "From the way you walk, it seemed you might want the weight of Alrendria behind you."

"Where I walk, I may make another enemy. I do not ask Alrendria to suffer for my indiscretions."

Utari pursed her lips. "Perhaps I was wrong," she said, gliding into place. "You may be more than a First."

Jeran said nothing, but he felt a renewed confidence, both from within and from those around him. From that point on, his passage through the camp went uncontested until he reached the Empress's tent, where a dozen Elves blocked entry and a few score more watched with bows drawn from concealment in the trees above.

"I would speak with the Empress," he announced to the Aelvin captain standing before the tent flap.

"The Empress does not wish to be disturbed," the soldier said. His hand hovered over his sword, afraid to draw it, afraid not to.

"I will speak with the Empress," Jeran said, and though neither his tone nor demeanor changed, the guards protecting the tent reacted as if he had threatened to attack. "I mean her no harm—if I did, I'd have left long ago, long before I lost so many of my own—but there are things which must be said, and I can no longer allow her the luxury of isolation."

"You... You must forgive me, *Teshou e Honoure*," the captain stuttered over the Human words, his eyes flicking from Jeran to his companions and back again. Around them a crowd formed, *Ael Namisa* mixed with *Ael Mireet* mixed with members of the Alrendrian Embassy, all irrespective of rank or Race. Only *Ael Chatorra* remained aloof, perhaps expecting a fight, perhaps fearing one.

"Let him pass, Iruvan," Astalian said, stepping up beside the tent and laying a gentle hand on his captain's shoulder. A smile spread across the *Hohe Chatorra*'s face. "It may be time for someone to treat our Empress as an Empress, and not as a petulant child."

The guards scowled at their commander's light-hearted insult, but they stepped aside, allowing Jeran entrance. Astalian led them in; Jes and Utari followed, silent but imposing, each radiating her own brand of power. The soldiers remained outside, visible through the pulled-back flaps but not daring to enter even without facing the unspoken challenge of *Ael Chatorra*.

Jeran moved quickly through the vast tent toward the high-backed chair at its center where Charylla sat. The Empress kept her back to the door and leaned heavily against one smoothed and polished arm. She made no motion, gave no indication that she was aware of the intrusion until Jeran stood no more than a hand's breadth behind her.

"I told you I did not want to be disturbed, Astalian."

"I did not give him a choice, Empress," Jeran replied.

Charylla jerked as if struck, then stood slowly, smoothing the wrinkles from her dress as she turned around to level a cold, green glare on Astalian. Her ministrations could not hide the exhaustion from her face, though, nor could it totally remove the burden she now carried, a weight which pressed upon her slender shoulders with crushing force.

"You have failed me again," she whispered. "I begin to believe the rumors whispered to me by *Ael Alluya*."

Astalian said nothing, his rigid features and blank expression doing well to hide the wound to his pride. Jeran, though, would not allow such an insult to his friend to go unanswered. "Do not lay blame for your decisions at the feet of those keeping you alive. You are not so naïve as to believe the scheming manipulations of the aristocracy as fact."

Charylla flinched again, and her glare shifted to Jeran. Not long ago, such a gaze would have terrified him; now it seemed a common expression, the kind he expected to receive. "Who are you to make demands of me?"

"I am one of those keeping you alive," Jeran replied.

"And for what do I owe the pleasure of this audience?"

"I come to warn you that you're in danger of losing your Empire."

"Ah... My thanks to you, Lord Odara. From the comforts of my palace here I had not noticed. Quick, Astalian, we must hasten back to Lynnaei or all is lost."

"It is not of Luran which I speak, nor of the loss of Illendrylla." Jeran remained firm, despite the knot of cold fear tucked deep down in his gut and growing with every step he took toward the imposing Aelvin woman. Charylla stood taller than him and held the advantage in dispassionate arrogance, yet Jeran felt as though he loomed over her, and he saw something—a hesitation, an uncertain fear—hiding deep within her gaze.

"The loss of the Emperor is a tragedy none of us expected to face," Jeran told her. "His loss lessens the world, but to stay here dishonors him; to hand over his Empire to Luran without a fight disgraces him and all he strove to accomplish. You have had time to mourn—that you need more I have no doubt!—but now, your people need you strong, and if you cannot be what they need, then they will find another."

"Brash Humans," Charylla sneered under her breath, then turned the full force of her presence on Jeran. "So you would have me fight? Take my army of servants and the pittance of soldiers Astalian has rallied and retake Lynnaei? Such heroics read well in your Human books, but they accomplish little in reality."

"I do not counsel attack," Jeran replied, striving to keep all emotion from his voice. He was tempted to seize magic, but to do so would show his fear to the Empress, and would no doubt convince the Elves he meant her harm.

"Then you agree with Astalian? That I should run to the Tribal Lands and beg the Garun'ah for help? That I should seek succor from my brother in the arms of our ages-old enemy?"

"I believe flight makes more sense, whether to Alrendria, the Tribal Lands, or another destination of your choosing. But if—"

"You may leave at any time, Lord Odara!" The panic in Charylla's gaze belied the offer. "Your aid has been invaluable, but We would not dream of keeping you against your wishes."

"But if you choose to fight, if you choose to risk all to reclaim your throne, then I will stand with you in that as well. You risk more with this indecision than with either other option. Your people need a leader, they need to know that what they have gained matches what they have lost. Staying here, you have allowed fear to take root, doubt to seep in."

"And so I should abandon my home or sacrifice myself—and my people!—in a vain attempt to reclaim it?"

"This forest is just a place," Jeran said, spinning slowly as if he could see the grand trees outside the dark green canvas. "This is not your Empire. Your Empire is here"—he tapped his chest—"in the hearts of your people, and the longer your delay, the smaller your Empire becomes."

"And how do you know such things?"

"Because some of those people now look to me for protection. I hold a bond with them as strong as the bonds I hold with my own, and the bond of a BattleMage cannot be shared; a man can offer complete loyalty to only one master. Each day sees more abandon you because they see greater hope of salvation in me, and if some see me as their best chance of survival, others no doubt are closer aligned to Luran."

Jeran bowed low, the formal greeting he had been taught in the days before his first journey to Illendrylla. "Fight or flee, I will stand beside you, but I will no longer wait for death to winnow us away. At first light tomorrow, my people march; if you have not chosen a direction for them, then I will do so. I wish you a long life, Empress."

With that, he left, ducking his head in parting to Astalian as he passed. Outside the tents, he called out to his men, making sure his orders were heard by everyone in earshot. Jes watched, a contemplative look on her face, and once his men had left to carry out their duties, she said, "That was a bit... abrasive... don't you think?"

Jeran offered her a cool smile. "If I waited for people to change on their own, then all would go to the Nothing. Sometimes events must be forced."

CHAPTER 32

Sweat clung to Martyn even in the burgeoning light of predawn, heralding another day of unseasonable heat and equally hot tempers. His horse plodded down the cobbled street, past slumbering estates and into the developed sections of Old Kaper, where militiamen stood silent vigil over the hawkers and merchants who worked to set up their stalls. The Wall loomed in the distance, a black shadow cutting across the horizon, visible only in the dim reflection of torchlight.

Aryn Odara rode to his right, at home on horseback. He sat straight-backed, eyes wide open but distant, as if they stared past the wall and into the enemies' camp beyond; uniform pressed and unstained despite constant use. He carried within him a need to work with his men no matter how onerous the duty, a trait uncommon among the nobility. A bow hung from his saddle horn, a quiver of arrows over his shoulder, and a sword clacked rhythmically against his hip. *Perhaps it's not the horse he's at home with*, Martyn mused, eyeing the weapons, *but something has changed in him. He has found a new center, something to ground him to the present.*

Aryn's persistent sanity still galled him at times—it would have been nice if *someone* else believed him about the man's unstable nature!—but the wound to Martyn's pride was small price to pay for the advantages gained. Despite his growing concerns about Jeran, Aryn Odara had proved a valuable resource, a Commander of the first order, and an unflinching supporter of the King. He regretted his initial resistance to the man, just as he regretted being the cause of the deep scowl Aryn now wore.

"My apologies again, Commander Odara," Martyn said, stifling a yawn. "I did not intend to delay us, but Miriam—"

"It is of no matter," Aryn replied, cutting him off. "I once knew a woman with a presence like your Princess's, and I remember what she was like when she neared her term. I had hoped to get this inspection underway before dawn, but—"

An orange glow appeared ahead, illuminating Old Kaper in a false dawn. It spread to the left and right with unnatural haste, racing along the top of the wall, billowing out toward them, expanding up toward the Heavens. "Dear Gods," Aryn said, "is that—" The rest of what he said drowned in a great roar as hot wind gusted down the street, bringing with it the acrid stench of smoke.

A bell resounded, weak at first then with greater urgency. More alarms rose, spreading through the old city with the urgency of terror. Around them, the city sprang to life. Militiamen, many only half dressed, poured from the buildings, girding weapons and hastening to their rallying points. The hawkers and shopkeepers started toward the palace, gathering what goods they could carry and abandoning what they could not, fighting the tide of soldiers heading toward the Wall and oft as not struggling against the families evacuating their homes.

"Prince Treloran," Martyn said to the rider on his left, "perhaps it would be best if you sought the protection of the castle."

The Aelvin Prince studied him for a moment, then fitted an arrow to his bow. "I, too, have soldiers along the Wall. If we fight, then we fight together."

"To me!" Aryn called, and the gathering militiamen rallied to him. The contingent of Guardsmen who had followed as bodyguards took the lead, and the procession resumed its journey, now with greater haste, first dodging around the growing throng of fleeing commoners, then forcing a path through them. Aryn rode at the point of the wedge, shouting for people to clear a path, threatening to use force if they did not. The press of bodies made the soldiers nervous, and Martyn spotted more than a few weapons raised in defense, though thankfully the threat of violence was enough to drive back even the most aggressive civilians.

Suddenly, the crowd disappeared, leaving them alone on the cobbled street. For a moment, there were no sounds other than the fleeing footfalls of the commoners behind them and the distant toll of bells before, no motion other than the wavering smoke. An eerie peace settled over them, a calm Martyn had experienced before, only then he had crouched in the tall grasses of the Alrendrian plains, laying in ambush, watching his unsuspecting targets mill about in the valley below.

"Scatter!" he shouted, and such was the command in his voice that the soldiers obeyed without hesitation. Aryn, too, seemed to suspect what was coming; he neither argued nor paused to spot their attackers, turning instead to force his mount through his own Guardsmen and tearing Martyn from his mount. The prince's choked protest cut off when a blinding flash tore open the street, rendering his horse a charred cinder and leaving the hairs on his arm charged with static. The lightning blast knocked many from their mounts and left more than a few clutching wounds.

"Head to the Wall! Defend Kaper!" Martyn shouted as they fled into an alley. His soldiers scattered, many of the militiamen fleeing in the direction of the castle. The Guardsmen showed better restraint, dodging down narrow streets and seeking shelter in the alcoves of Old Kaper's dark stone buildings. More lightning fell farther up the street, and the shrieks of the dying reached Martyn's ears until his flight took him far from the main avenue.

They halted in a dark courtyard, gasping for breath, and Martyn assessed their situation while Aryn fashioned torches from the materials he could scavenge. Treloran and his *Ael Chatorra* guards had followed to a man, but only a dozen or so of the Guardsmen and none of the militiamen joined them. Only Aryn and Treloran had kept their horses in the confusion, but for now the mounts were more liability than asset, stomping and rolling their eyes in terror, too large to easily negotiate the narrow alleys criss-crossing Old Kaper's broader avenues.

"You two," Aryn said, pointing to two Guardsmen, "Find out what's going on at the Wall." The men saluted and ran off.

Aryn next turned his gaze on Martyn, who bristled at the command he knew was coming. "If you think to suggest that I return to the palace, I—"

"I try not to waste orders," Aryn interrupted. "Men will only follow so many. It's best to make sure the ones you give will be obeyed. Besides, the enemy seeks control of the main avenues. Sending you back alone might be a greater risk than sending you forward." The elder Odara paused, a thoughtful frown pulling at his lips. "I wonder, though, if it might not be best to signal the general retreat."

"Once we lose the Wall, it's only a matter of time before we lose the siege," Martyn reminded him. "The palace fortifications are nothing compared to—"

"That would be true, if the Wall were lost by force." Aryn interrupted.

"What was that we just faced in the street?" Martyn demanded, his face flushed at the curt interruptions.

"Treachery," Aryn answered absently, his eyes distant. "No true assault could cross the Wall so quickly, or without an alarm being raised in advance. I wonder also about the timing. Why this of all mornings, except that we planned an inspection with both Princes and all three Guard Commanders."

"Few knew of our inspection," Martyn reminded him.

"Which only proves the traitor is someone we trust," Aryn replied. "Or someone we don't notice."

Gods! I just needed a little more time. A few more ten-days! Zarin Mahl had established several false granaries, but they had only been able to eliminate a handful of suspects. That Aryn Odara was one of the few proven innocent came as a small relief, but the failure of his plan to oust the traitor now might cost them all of Old Kaper.

"We should move toward the Wall," Aryn said, grabbing his horse's reins and leading the mount down one of the alleys. "There still may be a chance to close the breach. But I warn you, Martyn, as soon as we know that the situation is untenable—"

"I will signal the retreat myself," Martyn said. He had learned a great deal on the Corsan campaign. That running was not always a sign of cowardice was foremost among those lessons.

They moved fast and silently, following Aryn through the twisting alleyways, eyes scanning the buildings above and peering into the shadowy cut-throughs, searching for any sign of a possible ambush. The sounds of battle grew, a distant rumble rising in crescendo until the shouts of men and the clang of weapons almost drowned out the peal of alarm bells.

Something moved in the shadows, and a dozen *Ael Chatorra* nearly feathered the Guardsman with arrows before he identified himself. "What's the situation, Granbaer?" Aryn asked.

"Dire, Commander. But it's best if you see for yourself. This way." The Guardsman led them to a Guardpost overlooking the approach to the Wall. Concealed in the side of a building, worked into the stone during some ancient part of Kaper's violent past, the barracks could house a hundred. Through slits in the rock they observed the Wall, its northern gate, and the market square before it. All three were in the hands of the enemy: the massive doors stood unbarred and open; Tachans forced their way into Old Kaper like spawning salmon, struggling forward against the tide of their own numbers; and from within the Wall itself came the sounds of battle.

ShadowMagi clustered in the center of the market while the troops organized around them. As soon as a unit was ready they moved out, marching with speed and purpose, not with the reckless savagery of soldiers out to pillage but with the focused discipline of men determined to destroy a specific target. For every man who disappeared into the alleys of Old Kaper two more took his place, and still others clamored for a place with the old city. Atop the Wall, the first of the Alrendrian flags fell and was quickly replaced with the Tachan Bull.

A single knock resounded on the door, and then a voice announced Guardsman Granbaer's return. He ushered Commander Bystral inside, then hastily shut the door and took up watch at one of the slits.

"Commander Odara. Prince Martyn," Bystral greeted them with a half-hearted salute. Dust and blood caked his uniform, and his eyes already carried the weariness one only felt after fighting a losing battle. "We had heard that your party was attacked en route. Thank the Gods you escaped."

"If the Gods had anything to do with this," Martyn muttered, "they didn't help us."

"What's the situation, Commander?" Aryn said, directing a scathing look at Martyn. The prince had sense enough to feel ashamed for letting his anxiety show, and sense enough to keep his shame hidden, even as he tried to recover an air of confidence.

"Dire. The guards along the gate were murdered to a man before first light, and the gates thrown open from the inside. The Tachans were in the old city before we even knew to sound an alarm, and by the time we roused the troops, they controlled the square. Most of the Guardsmen are trapped within the Wall itself, fighting through its corridors or atop the battlements; a full third of the militia fled after the first charge. The enemy seems to know the location of all our safehouses, all our storerooms. Each of those squads you see out there already knows the location of its target."

"It seems our traitor is even more well-informed than we suspected," Martyn said.

"Perhaps," Aryn said. "Or perhaps their Magi have been studying this side of the Wall with their perceptions. They've had seasons to learn our defenses." He turned back to Bystral. "Commander Lisandaer?"

"Commanding the defense. The men are holding at the first fallback position, and for the moment, we have the Tachans contained within a few thousand hands of the Wall. Against those ShadowMagi though… I'm not sure how long we can hold out."

Aryn peered through the wall again, stroking his chin. When he turned back to face Bystral and Martyn, his expression was grim. "Do you think we can retake the Wall?"

Martyn expected confidence, grim resolve, or at the very least the quiet humor he had come to expect from the Guardsman. Instead, he faced a resignation so complete that it chilled him to the core. "No," Bystral told them. "Even if this attack was not repeated at the north gate, we'll never take back the ground we've lost."

Aryn sighed and nodded, closing his eyes for a moment, his lips moving in what Martyn assumed was a prayer. "Spread word among the Guard to fall back quickly. Once the bulk of our forces have passed the third fallback position, signal the general retreat."

"If we wait that long," Martyn said, "our people won't have time to flee before the Tachans overrun the city."

"The palace grounds cannot support the population of the entire city," Aryn reminded him. "We need to house as many soldiers as possible."

"And leave the rest to the mercy of the Tachans?" Strategically the plan made perfect sense, but it settled over Martyn like rancid oil.

"As Guard Commander," Aryn reminded him, "my duty is to ensure the success of the overall campaign."

"At what cost?" Martyn paced the chamber, his mind racing, searching desperately for an alternative. "As Prince of Alrendria, I could overrule your orders," he said, his voice sour.

"But you won't," Aryn told him. "You know as well as I that packing the palace grounds with people who can't contribute to the fight will only hasten our defeat."

The truth rankled, but Martyn could not dispute it. "Commander Odara is right," he said, making sure his voice carried enough that all present knew he stood with the Guard Commander. "We must think of what is best in the long term, not the short."

"The safety of the princes must be assured," Aryn said. "Whoever knows the backstreets and alleys of Old Kaper best must be found and tasked with returning them to the palace."

"Guardsman Cavon," Bystral said. "He's waiting outside."

"Then let's go." Aryn ushered the men toward the door. "I want you to take me to Lisandaer. We need to—"

Just as Aryn stepped outside, the rear of the safehouse exploded inward, showering the remaining Guardsmen and *Ael Chatorra* with debris. The blast tossed Martyn through the open door and across the alley, slamming him into the far wall. The breath fled his lungs on impact, and the hilt of his sword drove into his hip so hard he feared the bone had snapped.

Stunned, he struggled to regain his feet, and then to help Treloran stand. The Aelvin Prince nursed his arm and bled from a handful of shallow cuts, but otherwise seemed unscathed. The rest of their entourage had not fared as well. Though Aryn, Bystral and a handful of others escaped the blast entirely, most were incapacitated or fighting a desperate defense against the scores of Tachan soldiers pouring through the breach in the southern wall.

"Run!" Aryn shouted, shoving Martyn down the nearest alley. Martyn did, stumbling as another explosion rocked the building, and similar magical attacks rumbled across the old city. He dragged the still-disoriented Treloran with him, following Guardsman Cavon through the twisting alleys, climbing low fences, cutting through buildings, careful to keep from the broader roads and open market squares unless no other route existed. Their progress was torturously slow in the predawn gloom, relying on touch and faith in their guide as much as on what vague details their eyes presented. Yet the sounds of battle followed them, as did the shouts of the soldiers, leaving Martyn wondering what might happen once daylight betrayed them to their enemies. Never before had he so much appreciated the dark, or feared the sun.

"Martyn... a moment." Treloran's gasping plea brought Martyn to a stop, and Cavon glanced at them before peeking around a corner and disappearing. *He'll be back*, Martyn thought, though it felt too much like he was trying to convince himself. *He'll be back.*

The Aelvin Prince leaned against a wall, clutching his side and gasping for air. Dust caked Treloran's hair and clothes, and darkened his skin except for where sweat had washed it clean, exposing the pallor of his flesh. Martyn's eyes dropped to the Elf's hand, and noticed the red stain spreading from his abdomen, just below the ribcage.

"It is nothing," Treloran assured him. "A scratch and a bruise, but the bruise is making breathing difficult." Martyn did not argue, though he suspected the Aelvin Prince of downplaying his injuries; as things stood, there was little he could do to help at the moment.

Before Martyn could respond, a door near Treloran flew open, revealing two Tachan soldiers. A gleam entered one warrior's eye when he noticed the Aelvin Prince, unarmed and breathing hard. "Looks like we take the prize, Hassan," he said, aiming his sword.

Martyn reached for his blade, but a glare from one of the Tachans held his hand. He looked around but saw no sign of Cavon. He had few options, and none to his liking: surrender, and they were both lost to the Tachans; fight or flee, and Treloran was certainly lost.

"Bind them. We'll—" The soldier's command cut off in a gurgle, and he clutched at the blade protruding from his throat. The other Tachan reacted quickly, bringing his sword to bear, searching for the new threat, but he had no chance against the blur that shot past Martyn and savaged him with wicked blows that left him quivering on the ground, his life's blood pooling around him.

Kal retrieved his *dolchek* and wiped the blade clean before returning it to its sheath. "Fool Elf," he said, looking at Treloran, his expression unreadable. "Never turn your back on your enemy."

"Reckless savage," Treloran replied, the hint of a smile playing across his features. "It makes more sense to keep your blade until the end of the fight."

Kal turned his gaze on Martyn. "King asked me to find you when word of the battle reached the castle."

"We're fine, but we need to get out of here before the Tachans secure their holdings."

"This way," Cavon called, signaling from an intersection down the alley. "Hurry!"

Martyn moved toward the Guardsman, and Kal followed, putting Treloran's arm over his shoulder and half-carrying the Elf. This time, Cavon followed a straighter path, his pace quicker and his steps more certain. He stopped before another intersection, a break in the narrow alleys leading out to the main thoroughfare through Old Kaper.

Creeping to the corner, Martyn peeked out. To his left, no more than a hundred hands off, a line of Tachan soldiers supported by a half dozen ShadowMagi formed rank; farther away to his right stood the Alrendrian line, determined Guardsmen and terrified militiamen standing firm behind the imposing figure of Lisandaer and his Aelvin counterpart Palatinae.

Mouthing a curse, Martyn pressed himself against the wall, listening as the Tachans began to chant, a numbing sound punctuated by the drumming of weapons on shields that drove a chill to his very soul. He waited while the two forces faced off, seeking a way to cross the battlefield without exposing himself to certain death.

When the prince next glanced out, he saw Lisandaer looking at him, the Guardsman's gaze focused and determined. They shared a silent communication, and then Lisandaer turned away, but he saluted as he did so, and with a cry that carried over the Tachans' din, he led the Alrendrians into battle.

They rushed past Martyn in a blur, shouting their own battlecries as the ground around them exploded in fire and earth. The ShadowMagi showed little restraint, killing allies with impunity so long as such destruction took enemies as well. The sounds and smells of battle filled the air before the Alrendrian line fully passed the alleyway, yet it took not much longer before the fight turned against the Guardsmen. With ShadowMagi and a greater number of seasoned soldiers, the enemy held the advantage from the start; and when Lisandaer fell beneath a volley of feathered shafts, the resolve of the Guardsmen began to waver.

Martyn longed to join the fight, to lead his people in routing the Durange from his home, and his longing grew when he saw the standard of House Morrena among the enemy lines. But such a move was folly; Lisandaer's sacrifice would serve little purpose if Martyn followed the Guard Commander and his men to the Twilight World.

"Now," he said, leading the others from concealment. They sprinted down the avenue, moving toward the palace as fast as they could. Before them rose a wall of people hemmed in by the high walls of Old Kaper's estates, desperate commoners cramming the road, forcing their way up the hill to the presumed safety of the palace. Behind them, squads of Tachans separated themselves from the battle and began the pursuit. Pinned between the two, too few to force a path through or put up much resistance, Martyn prepared for his final battle.

In the end, salvation came from two unlikely sources. As the enemy approached, the ShadowMagi unleashed their Gift, and the crowd panicked. They fled in whatever direction they could, climbing the walls, crushing their neighbors, even rushing straight back to the waiting swords of the Tachan soldiers. In the chaos, Martyn and his small troupe, bolstered by a handful more Guardsmen who had seen their prince in flight and sought to protect him, started to make progress toward the castle again. But it was too little, and too slow; the Tachans continued to close on them, and when someone identified Martyn, the enemy hastened its approach.

A trumpet blast sounded from ahead, and Martyn turned with enough time to dodge the wedge of cavalry that galloped past. Dozens of horsemen rode by, brandishing short swords and other light arms, shrieking a high-pitched battlecry that seemed quite odd until Martyn realized the oldest of the riders was perhaps fifteen Winters; the youngest, no older than ten.

The Tachans faltered under the sudden attack, and in the confusion, the boys cut down as many as they could, then turned and broke contact to prepare for another charge. "Prince Martyn," Mika called to him. The boy led a handful of saddled but riderless horses. "We don't have much time, and I suspect my soldiers won't fare as well on the second charge. If you could mount, I'd like to signal the retreat."

Martyn took the reins and hauled himself into the saddle. "Your soldiers?" he asked, watching while Kal hefted Treloran onto the back of another horse and made sure he could keep a grip on the reins before he leapt onto the back of a third, massive warhorse. The *Kranach* looked immediately uncomfortable, but he turned the horse toward the palace and followed the Aelvin Prince. When Treloran urged his mount to a fast trot, Kal did so too, refusing to look afraid in the eyes of an Elf.

"Not quite Guardsmen, but better than most of the militia," Mika said, a note of pride in his voice. He raised a horn to his lips and blew a series of notes, then started to follow Treloran and Kal. The boys broke off their second charge and wheeled around to clear a path for them to the palace. "They've been training in some of the lesser used practice yards with the weapons we thought you could spare."

Martyn winced when a bolt of lightning fell among the boys, sending no less than six from the saddle and leaving a dozen others scattering and trying to regain control of their mounts. "You've been the one stealing from the armories?"

"Under the circumstances," Mika said, "I'm hoping you'll be lenient in your punishment."

"And the horses?"

A smile crept onto Mika's face. "Those we just borrowed. Most of my boys work in the stables, so when we heard there was trouble, I had them saddle whatever mounts were on hand.

Martyn studied the horse he was riding. "Is this Jaem's horse?"

"I thought you might appreciate a mount seasoned to battle."

And I'm sure Miriam's cousin will appreciate having his horse commandeered by a child to rescue me! Some of the tension knotting his shoulders dissipated in a wave of unexpected laughter, but his mirth cut off when he remembered the slaughter taking place in the city behind him. When the bells began to toll the full retreat, he winced again at the greater slaughter that was to come as the Durange ran uncontested through the streets of Old Kaper.

CHAPTER 33

A wind blew down from the north, cooling the sweat from Dahr's skin but raising dust in swirling bands that obscured much of the battlefield. His troops had once more dominated against aged Hunters and untried cubs; Kraltir had once again escaped with the bulk of his forces, biding time while Salos's second army, under the command of the creature known as *Synat Sal'aqran*, the Scorpion's Sting, marched north. Dahr hoped to eliminate Kraltir's forces before contending with *Synat Sal'aqran*, sparing his soldiers a war on two sides, but it seemed as if the Gods had other intentions.

"Can they see anything, Tazahn?" he asked, turning to the Garun'ah boy crouched beside him atop the hill.

Tazahn closed his eyes, then shook his head. "The Lesser Voices in the sky see little through the dust storm. The main body of *Kohr'adjin* move north beyond our forces. Our Hunters control the field and have surrounded the camp to the east. But we knew all that, Korahn. I am sorry."

Dahr studied the young *Tier'sorahn*, marveling again at their ability to communicate, the clear language he heard in his mind compared to the mostly incomprehensible Garu the boy spoke aloud. "You did far more than was asked of you," he said, trying to keep the disappointment from his voice. "Without your eyes we never would have found where the enemy hid, nor the ambush they planned."

The boy beamed with pride, then closed his eyes again to resume communion with the Lesser Voices. Dahr envied him his simple joy, the innocence that allowed him to serve his part with no doubts, with no hesitation, and with no poorly-hidden fury at being kept from battle. As for himself, he had doubts aplenty, about his motives, his goals, and even his reasons for using his students—if such a term could be applied to their strange relationship—to fight the *Kohr'adjin*.

It's to give them the practice they crave, and to allow me to focus on the battle without having to deal with the full cacophony of Lesser Voices. Such was the rationale he gave to those who voiced objections about the children, though he had not dared speak so around Grendor, lest the Orog's Truthsense prove the lie he at present only suspected.

Are you jealous of them? You curse the Gods for making you unique, then rail against Them when They provide you with brethren? You deserve whatever punishment They mete out.

"Assemble the others at sundown," Dahr told Tazahn, clapping the boy on the shoulder as he stood to leave. "We will discuss what we learned today." The boy smiled but said nothing; his distracted wave told Dahr he flew the skies as the eagles did, watching the world from their perspective.

Dahr descended through the remnants of the battle, past the bodies of the fallen, axes, clubs or *dolcheks* discarded in their death throes; through trampled grasses stained in blood, the dark red adding a macabre shade to the brown, brittle grass, as if the very earth itself bled. The wind whipped around scattered boulders, shrieking in pain, singing a howling dirge that made Dahr wonder if his war against the *Kohr'adjin* would preserve the balance of nature, or ultimately destroy it.

The bodies of the enemy far outnumbered those of his followers, but again his men had faced cripples and children, which made the victory bittersweet. The futility of it enraged Dahr, as did the knowledge that his forces were winnowed away with every battle while Kraltir lost only those who were a liability. Once the *Kohr'adjin* joined forces with the army in the south, Dahr suspected that the days of easy victories would be over.

Frustration dominated his heart when he gazed upon his fallen Hunters; sadness and regret came only when he saw the bodies of wolves, lions, bears, or any of the other Lesser Voices who had come to their aid. They would no longer stay away from the fighting, though he sometimes begged them to, and their deaths weighed heaviest upon him. This was not their fight—though they felt sworn to protect those among the Blood who could hear their words—and their souls were not burdened with the sins of man. *The innocent do not deserve to die, but who among mankind is innocent?*

He yearned for a drink, for the fiery wash of *baqhat* and the soothing dullness it brought, the respite from both the Lesser Voices and his own, internal beast. But now was not the time; he needed to hear both to survive the day ahead.

At the base of the valley, sheltered from the worst of the late Harvest winds, his Hunters built the funerary pyres, one to sing their own fallen to the Twilight World, another, less celebrated but far larger, for the enemy. They would labor despite their weariness from the day's fighting, stopping only if another attack began and resuming the grisly work as soon as it completed. Dahr admired their commitment to tradition, but as for himself, he would as soon find his pallet. The dead were a patient bunch.

Olin approached, a fresh scar weeping blood on his left arm, dirt and gore smearing his flesh, the fire of battle still in his eyes though tightly controlled. "Kraltir has escaped. If we pursue, we will lose the trail and waste time, or exhaust ourselves and open us to ambush." He braced himself, expecting an argument.

Dahr had neither the energy nor the desire for another fight, at least, not with his own commanders. "Send out trackers to mark their trail, and warn the troops that we move at sunrise. We'll need to march east; if Kraltir is allowed to join with *Synat Sal'aqran*, then we are lost."

"Yes, Korahn."

"How did we fight, Olin?"

"More like Humans than ever," came Olin's stoic reply. Dahr studied his second, looking for disappointment, rage, or resentment; but in Olin's eyes he saw only weariness, a soul-draining weariness of battle Dahr had never before noticed among the Tribesmen. *Is it because he, too, was raised among Humans? Or is my bloodlust more than even the Tribesmen can stomach?*

"We'll need to fight even smarter before this is done," Dahr said, his mind whirling around the prospect of the battles to come. "We did not lose many today, but we lost them to boys and toothless old men."

"Young and old they may have been, but they were all Hunters."

Olin slipped away, disappearing into the shoulder-high tufts of grass punctuating the valley's landscape and serving as trees to those few with time enough to seek a moment's rest. Dahr considered finding a spot of his own, a place to spare himself the brunt of the winds while he collected his thoughts, but days of sleeplessness hung over him like a millstone. He feared that if he stopped moving, he would sleep, and the Tribesmen might take offense if they found their savior napping.

Dahr moved along a path opposite Olin's, one that took him toward the enemy encampment, a collection of mismatched hide tents arranged in two sections:

an organized area that approximated a Guardsmen's camp and had housed the *Kohr'adjin* Hunters, and a more traditional arrangement which still held those who had not taken part in the battle.

Dahr studied the tents. Many in the warriors' section were packed prior to the start of the battle, leaving gaping holes in the regimented lines, the cookfires extinguished, the camp deprived of tools, weapons, and usable items despite the surprise of Dahr's attack. The other half of the *Kohr'adjin* camp had been a mass of confusion, with Garun'ah hurrying to flee before Dahr's troops sealed off the valley, hastily throwing down tents and gathering supplies; mothers scooping up children and what few small animals they could, leaving toys and tools scattered. Heirlooms and treasures were discarded in favor of food and water, breakfast left roasting over still-burning fires, no effort made to lessen the burden the camp had placed on nature, a tradition so deeply bred into Garun'ah that even those who served Kohr had not abandoned it.

"This was their ambush, not ours," Dahr muttered, catching a glimpse of the lines of prisoners forming in the far half of camp. "They burden me with more mouths, with enemy mouths, on the verge of winter. They gain mobility and another reason to fight to the last; I gain only vipers in my midst."

There is a solution. A simple one.

The thought flashed through Dahr's mind, but he dismissed it, banishing it to the recesses of his soul, burying it as deep as he could. It resurfaced quickly when he saw his own people crest the hill on the horizon, the thousands of Garun'ah depending on him for their survival. Only Grendor's soft-spoken voice drove the nagging thoughts away.

"Friend Dahr, Olin says we march east tomorrow."

Dahr turned to look at the Orog, whose face hung low with the heavy sadness it always carried in the wake of battle. "You sound eager," he said. "Are you developing a taste for blood?"

"A starving man may eat rotted flesh, but he need never grow fond of it." Grendor hobbled forward, favoring his right leg, where a blood-soaked bandage bound a serious wound earned in the fighting. "I am glad we are finally moving to help. I knew you could not ignore his plight forever."

Dahr stopped in his tracks. "What are you talking about?"

"We march east to help Jeran."

"We march east to stop the *Kohr'adjin*, to prevent them from joining with the army to our south. If they do, our struggle is lost." Grendor's disappointment hit Dahr like a condemnation, the restrained sadness of his features made him almost ashamed to face the Orog. "Why would Jeran need my help anyway?"

"I cannot believe you do not sense the danger he is in, or the desperation he feels," Grendor replied, his gaze taking on a more calculating feel, leaving Dahr wondering if he sought to gauge the truth of Dahr's response. "It is a stinging blade, clear despite the leagues that separate us, and you once were closer to him than any. But even if you can no longer sense him, you must hear the rumors trickling out of the Aelvin Forests. The servants of Kohr hold sway among the trees, and drive the Empress and her followers to extinction."

"Emperor," Dahr corrected. "The Elves have an Emperor. They always have."

"An evasion will not make me forget my question," Grendor said. "Why do you abandon Jeran in the time of his most dire need?"

"Abandon Jeran?" Dahr grasped the Orog by the shoulders with such force that his fingers ached. "Abandon Jeran! How can I abandon someone who has already forsaken me? He cast me out of Shandar. He sent me away, condemned me to wander the Tribal Lands alone. Now I am expected to run to his aid because he's running out of Elves to die for him?"

"I wonder which clouds your mind more," Grendor said softly, the unfrightened timbre of his voice leaving Dahr fighting the urge to squeeze until the Orog screamed, "the emotions you refuse to acknowledge or the drink you consume to quell them."

"Now who seeks evasion," Dahr growled. *Why doesn't he fear me!*

"I speak out of concern for you, not concern for myself," Grendor replied. "And as for Jeran: how could he have abandoned you, when he sent me to protect you?"

"No..." Dahr released his hold and stepped back, his mind whirling. "No! He sent me away, and when you offered to go with me, he argued with you."

"True, but not the truth. He told me that you had to leave—for your own good as well as for the good of all—and that you would accept no company if he forced it upon you. He asked me to volunteer, and warned me that he would feign resistance when I did."

Dahr staggered, unsure of his own feet, confused by the torrent of emotion rushing through him. An awareness sprang into his consciousness, both strangely new and wholly familiar; the certainty that Jeran stood somewhere to the southeast, and an equal certainty that danger surrounded him, an all-consuming danger that threatened to swallow him, and the hope of all Madryn with him.

"He... He sent you with me?"

"You see, friend Dahr? Jeran never abandoned you. He could not come himself, so he sent—"

"And Katya?" Dahr asked suddenly. The door to his reawakened awareness slammed shut, leaving a cold void in his soul, a bleak emptiness quickly filled by white-hot suspicion. "Lord Grondellan? Did he saddle me with their *help* as well?"

"For Katya I cannot speak," Grendor replied. "As for Harol Grondellan, he I know Jeran did not ask. Something in Harol's past weighed heavily upon him, and he saw in you a path to redemption."

"There are prisoners," Dahr said, dismissing Grendor. "You need to take their confessions and determine their fate."

Grendor stared at him for a long moment, but whatever sage advice he thought to offer, he had wisdom enough to keep to himself. "Of course, friend Dahr." He limped toward the stockade where the prisoners were being gathered, leaving Dahr in blissful solitude.

Dahr prowled through the camp of the *Kohr'adjin* Hunters, the mocking voice in his mind fueling his furor, the empty tents providing no outlets for it. His own soldiers all but ignored this portion of the camp, as much for its alien, human appearance as because it stood barren; but by twilight teams of Tribesmen would be forced inside to scavenge what items could be useful. For now only a handful of Hunters patrolled, searching for hidden Garun'ah, and occasionally a *Tsha'ma* walked past, or stooped among the ashes of a cook fire, or studied a trinket left behind in the trampled grass. Dahr did not ask them what they sought; if it was something of use, they would share it in their own time.

At the border between the Hunters' camp and that of their families, Dahr spotted Arik, Meila, and Sadarak embroiled in argument, their words unintelligible but their voices rumbling across the plains. All appeared ready to draw weapons, so heated was their exchange, so passionate their gesticulations.

Dahr changed directions, hoping to escape before he was spotted, but Sadarak's voice boomed toward him. "Korahn, come. We need fourth voice."

Setting his own features to calm took an effort, but he had found that the illusion of confident composure won him far more arguments with the *Kranora* than unrestrained rage. He approached slowly, ducking his head to each in turn. "I have only a moment," he advised them. "I am needed among the tents, and among the *Tier'sorahna*."

"This not take long, Korahn," Meila said. She had taken to her new position as *Kranor* of the Anada with fervor, if not with enthusiasm, and had already won much respect among her equals for wisdom and courage. In that, Dahr envied her; he fought daily with the *Kranora* of the smaller Tribes, and it was only with the support of Arik and Sadarak—and now Meila—that he was able to pursue his own ends.

"We dispute best course for Tribes," Arik said. Even without his bear cloak he struck an imposing figure, conveying anger and disappointment with ease, and satisfaction only under the rarest of circumstances.

"Arik want fight *Kohr'adjin*," Meila announced. "He think they run from fear. Be easy prey for us if catch."

"Arik fooled," Sadarak added, almost succeeding in hiding his scorn. "He fall into trap of Limping Wolf. Feign injury to lure in large prey, then whole pack pounce."

"*Kohr'adjin* are Tribes' true enemy," Arik growled. "Not band of Humans come from south."

"*Kohr'adjin* are Garun'ah," Sadarak countered. "They have claim to land. Once Humans come to Tribal Lands, they never go. Much lost to Humans already. Fight them first, then drive out *Kohr'adjin*."

"You motivated by good of Afelda, not good of Tribes. Humans overrun your lands."

"And *Kohr'adjin* overrun yours."

"And where do you stand in this debate?" Dahr asked Meila. His question earned glares from both Arik and Sadarak.

"She seek flight," Sadarak said.

"I thought her want fight *Kohr'adjin*, to avenge loss to her tribe," Arik said, his expression sour, "but fear grip her heart."

"Fear not drive my decision," Meila snapped, and if she could face the two *Kranora* with such a venomous glare, and unarmed, Dahr did not doubt her words. "It wisdom. *Kohr'adjin* lead and we follow, like rabbits to wolf den. Lions stalk us from south, and instead prepare, we ignore. We walk to jaws of Nothing, and you two blinded by vengeance."

"Is cowardice now the salvation of Tribes?" Arik growled. "The Blood not cower from fate; it face it."

"My people just become tribe again, just regain respect of Blood. I not sacrifice Anada to foolishness. If my caution saves other tribes, then better for all."

The three *Kranora* degenerated to hushed argument again, reverting for the most part to Garu and leaving Dahr confused about their words, if not about their sentiment. That they could debate so heatedly and with such passion and yet not harbor enmity toward each other amazed him; he had trouble thinking of Grendor at the moment without his jaw clenching, and their exchange had been casual compared to the argument before him.

"Enough!" Dahr said, his command driving the three combatants to instant silence. "We march east, to the ridge beyond the seven lakes. We will prepare our ambush there. Kraltir moves north now, but he will turn his Hunters south in a day or so in hopes of meeting up with the army marching north. Whichever group arrives first will face our might, and once they are vanquished, we will turn to face the other."

Sadarak and Arik shared a long look, and then both nodded, as if tacitly agreeing to the compromise in strategy. Meila did not appear satisfied. "And what if both arrive at once?"

An unwelcome excitement filled Dahr, as well as the understanding that he should not reveal that excitement. "Then we will face them both and let the Gods sort out the carnage."

"Do you take Tribes to precipice to atone for our sins, or yours?" Meila asked, her ire now directed solely at him.

"You were more polite when we first met," Dahr mumbled, "even when you held me as your slave."

"I had only my soul to watch then," Meila retorted, "before you force me be *Kranor*."

"The decision is made," Dahr told them. "We march at sunrise." He walked off, leaving the three staring after him. Their conversation resumed, equally passionate but without the anger. *No doubt they now discuss me. How best to handle me.*

From within bubbled up a voice hungry for the battle to come. *Let them talk. The longer they debate, the less time they have to try to stop me.*

Is this the legacy I want? Do I want to be remembered only as a bringer of death? Jeran and Martyn both create things to make amends for the destruction they cause, but I sow only ruin.

Do I want to be remembered at all? Feast upon the field of battle, fulfill the destiny the Gods have forced upon me, and then I can retreat from this world, in one way or another.

As usual, the debate with himself unnerved him. The two voices sounded like his, but each spoke with a different tone, a different motivation; each resounded with the weight of differing emotions. The conversations made him doubt his sanity at times. At other times they were the only anchor he had in the maelstrom of his life, the only constant amidst his relentlessly changing moods.

He stomped through the *Kohr'adjin* camp, so foul of feature that even the most fervent of his followers gave him the space he desired. The long lines of prisoners did nothing to improve his temperament. Their gaunt and travel-weary faces pained him as much as the unbridled hatred they lavished upon him. Crippled and infirm, heavy with child and hobbling with one foot in the Twilight World, the outcasts of a hundred tribes, they stared at him with a unifying hatred, a yearning for his death even greater than his own half-concealed desire. *An irony. As I am the bond that holds together the tribes against the* Kohr'adjin, *so too am I the abomination against which the followers of Kohr rally.*

A frantic howl burst through the block in his mind which held back the Lesser Voices; a cry of rage and pain, an incomprehensible jumble of sensation, overwhelming and all-encompassing, demanding action, fearing reprisal. Dahr winced at the sudden onslaught, and in the distance he caught sight of one of his pupils—a girl-child of the Inouk—on her knees, hands clasped against her temples, teeth bared and grinding together.

Dahr went to her, shoving back the Tribesmen who gathered around but refused to touch any of those blessed by Garun, lest they thwart the God's will. She collapsed into his arms, sobbing, and though the words she spoke aloud held little meaning to him, her request echoed loudly in his mind. "Help them, Korahn. Help them."

"Take her from here," Dahr said, and when no one moved to help, he screamed his command again. A few hesitant volunteers stepped forward and carried the child off.

Dahr moved through the camp at a run, knocking aside any who crossed his path, until he found himself before a pen of caged hounds. The beasts slavered, ramming into the iron bars of their too-small confines, barking and snapping at anything that crossed their path, whimpering when nothing presented itself for attack. Their thoughts mimicked their actions, an unpredictable vacillation between rage and melancholy, indignation and incomprehension.

Though he sought to comfort them, Dahr's efforts brought only increased agitation, as if the hounds sensed his presence and rebelled against it. As he neared, the beasts' howling increased, and they slammed their heads against the bars with greater need.

"Who did this?" Dahr asked. He scanned the lines of prisoners visible from his vantage point, but no one stepped forward. "Find them!" Disgust at the hounds' treatment gave extra fuel to his voice. "Find who did this and bring them here!"

The waiting nearly drove Dahr mad himself. The tortured thoughts of the dogs made a pitiable accompaniment to the mocking of his personal demons. Every attempt to comfort renewed their frenzy, but to ignore them made their suffering more insistent, until it drowned out all other thought and forced him to attempt consolation again.

By the time they tossed the *Kohr'adjin* at Dahr's feet, a boy of less than seventeen Winters, his clothes tattered to rags and his body bruised and bloodied, Dahr could barely control himself. The boy refused to meet his eyes no matter how much he demanded it; he refused to so much as glance at the hounds whose terror increased an order of magnitude at the first scent of their tormentor.

"Did you do this to them?" Dahr snarled, summoning all his restraint.

The boy nodded. He raised his eyes then, and Dahr saw in them a reflection of the terror he had induced, a haunted, hopeless gaze demanding punishment, desiring peace.

"You can hear them?" Dahr asked, a full realization dawning only now, when he could observe how the young Tribesman reacted, not to the yelps and howls audible to the crowd, but to the greater agony reserved for only a select few. "You can hear their thoughts?"

"Yes." He spoke without hesitation; with remorse, perhaps, but without the slightest delay and with not even a feeble attempt at justification or excuse.

"Why?"

"They made me. *He* made me. He said the Father demanded it."

Dahr's anger evaporated. He had sought a villain, yet was confronted with another victim. "Do you seek redemption?"

"There is no redemption. There is only the Nothing, and anguish by the side of the Father."

Dahr frowned, then nodded. "Do you wish to meet your God?"

"I earned the right to burn in the fires of Kohr's eternal mercy. Free me, Korahn. I did not desire the Hunter's Blessing, nor do I deserve it."

The *dolchek* came free of its scabbard with ease, and Dahr leapt the distance between them in a single bound. The blade slid home easily, without resistance, and the boy did not move save to open himself to the attack. Dahr made the death quick and as painless as possible, but he discarded the corpse as soon as life fled, loathe to touch it and unwilling to offer it the slightest reverence, the tiniest amount of dignity, as one ought to handle the bodies of the damned.

A few gasps followed his violent attack, but when he looked up he saw as many approving faces and far more impassive ones. "I hear the whispers through the camps," he said, standing to address the crowd gathered to watch him dispense justice. "Does he serve Kohr or Balan, Human or Garun'ah, the Channa or all the Blood? Doubt my motives all you want, question my allegiance to man or God as you will, but never doubt this: Above all, my loyalty is to the Lesser Voices. Cross them, and you have crossed me. Defile nature, abandon the Balance, and I will exact a retribution upon your souls."

A low murmur arose among the Tribes, but Dahr ignored the excited conversations and turned toward the hounds. He knelt, stretching his hand out to the nearest, using the full force of his will to reassure the maddened beast that he came to help. *Peace, little brother. I only want to bring you peace.*

The dog moved toward him, whining softly, head and tail tucked low. Dahr placed one hand upon its head, and as his other tightened upon the *dolchek*, hot tears began to fall across his cheek.

CHAPTER 34

"My, my… Look at all the blood."

Dahr jumped at the sound, whirling to face Lorthas, making one last feeble attempt to wipe off his hands and arms. He knelt in a field of trampled flowers, an ominous and slate-grey sky above, the constant growl of thunder barely audible in the distance. Blood stained the land around him, some fresh and red, still pungent with the scent of iron; some dried and dark, flaking off the brown vegetation and drifting away in the wind. It swirled around him, casting the world in a dim red haze. "Why are you here?"

"This is *my* realm you have entered," Lorthas replied, though the caustic tone he used never entered his appraising gaze, nor wiped the smug smile from his face. "This place is my escape from the prison your people enclosed me in. You are the intruder, despoiling this idyllic haven with your poisonous doubts, your troubled conscience."

"The Garun'ah claim the Twilight World is infinite," Dahr replied.

"And yet you continue to appear where I am. One might begin to suspect you desire my company."

"Why would I want anything to do with you?" Dahr scowled.

"Based on the scene you have drawn for yourself, I imagine that you plan a massacre, and you seek to console yourself by companioning with those you feel are even more lacking in morality than you." Lorthas glanced from left to right in an exaggerated way. "Was Salos unavailable? Perhaps he was too busy laying waste to every place you've ever called home."

"I do not need commiseration from a Darklord," Dahr growled. "Nor humor."

"Yet here you are. And here you stay. If my presence is so onerous, then wake yourself. Or walk over that way. Don't worry about the mess. The blood will go when you do."

"What do you want of me?" Dahr asked.

"Oh my, where to begin…" Lorthas trailed off, his gaze drifting skyward, a hand cupped to his chin. "I want you to stop bothering me with your petty problems. My world has turned itself upside down as well. My home is despoiled by war and suffering; the fruit of my labors, centuries of effort, are wasted, ground to dust in yet another war to determine the fate of Madryn. I come here to clear my thoughts, not to be saddled with the burdens of others, especially when those burdens are, in truth, blessings. 'Oh why do the Garun'ah worship me? Why have I been given the ability to bend nature to my whim? How dare the Alrendrians remember me as a hero, when I have done *such things*?' If you insist on forcing me to listen to your lamentations, at least complain about things horrid enough to make a child weep."

Dahr's cheeks reddened, and his face set in a dark scowl. "If you seek to anger me—"

"Please… Where is the challenge in forcing a bird to fly? You asked a question; I give an answer. Nothing more. But while the subject has been broached… There are other things I want from you. I want you to choose a side. It need not be mine, or Jeran's, or the Assembly's… or that of any established player. Play for yourself, if that's what you want. But what you do now, fighting for fighting's sake, seeking death or redemption, or whatever you think you're doing, helps nothing. It wastes lives and resources, and accomplishes nothing. War can be a useful means, but it must have an end, else it is just folly. What is your end, I wonder…"

"I want nothing but peace. Peace and the freedom to go my own way."

"Peace?" Lorthas chuckled, and the sound of such genuine mirth drove daggers into Dahr's gut. "An odd place to find it, at the head of an army that does naught but seek out battles of ever-worsening odds."

The Darklord tapped a bony finger to his chest. "But perhaps it is from the war within that you seek escape. If so, then you hunt in vain. That war will not end with death, little brother, not unless your sins have condemned your soul to the Nothing."

Dahr crashed to the ground like a tree brought down in a mighty storm. The air escaped his lungs in a forceful breath, deflating him, leaving him bereft, with no more will to fight. "Why do you care?"

"It is not out of love," Lorthas replied, circling Dahr like a raptor, his gaze burning into Dahr's flesh. "Nor out of concern for you. I pity our world, that one of such potential refuses to harness his talents to aid his brothers, that he rails against the fortunes bestowed upon him. I curse the God that saw a savior in you, who delivered unto Alrendria a cowardly hero, and unto the Garun'ah a petulant messiah. I condemn Jeran for wasting so much effort on your salvation, when you have all but sworn fealty to Salos and his God."

"I do not serve Salos!" Dahr screamed, surprised at the vehemence in his voice, but even more surprised by his lack of conviction.

"You fight without purpose, led by unrestricted emotion and without any thought to the future beyond finding your next kill. You lay waste to the Tribal Lands; you allow Kohr's Children dominion over the Aelvin Forests, and Salos's armies free reign over your former homeland. You've turned your back on all that you loved, all who loved you. Like it or not, you serve chaos, and by serving chaos, you serve Salos."

With some effort, Dahr regained his feet and made a show of bravery by squarely facing Lorthas and refusing to acknowledge the trembling in his hands. "And you, so loved by Madryn for the role you took in its salvation, what would you have me do?"

"You refuse to understand: It was never about being labeled hero or villain. What I did—what I do!—I did for the good of Madryn. Every choice I made was designed to bring our world to greater unity. And it worked! For a time, at least, and perhaps not as well as if I had emerged from the MageWar the victor. But it worked then as it is working now, and if the Four Races and the nations of man can unite in war, then there remains hope they can unite in peace.

"Perhaps my vision is flawed. Or Aemon's. Or the Assembly's. Or all of ours. Perhaps some of my methods were questionable, some of the results unfortunate. Certainly some of my decisions were… ill-conceived. But through it all I strove to make things better, to justify all the war, death, and destruction I had witnessed, that I had caused."

Lorthas gestured, and smoke billowed out of nothingness, blackening the stormy sky; the distant trees shriveled, adding swirling gray ash to the maelstrom. Corpses, thousands of corpses, of all Races, of all Lands, crowded a landscape now broken with exploded earth and charred grass. The bodies of the Lesser Voices filled the spaces between man and woman, their blasted bodies bringing an unwilling wail of despair from Dahr's lungs.

"Find something to fight for Dahr, or this will be the legacy you leave to Madryn."

When Dahr could wrest his eyes away from the carnage, Lorthas was gone, but a new voice addressed him. "A sad day, when the Fallen One gives good advice to Garun's Chosen."

Frodel stood before him, arms crossed before his chest, eyes forever appraising, forever disappointed. He wore the garb of a Tribesman on the hunt and had a *dolchek* sheathed at his hip. "Is it your turn to haunt my dreams?" Dahr asked, his voice choked with bitterness.

"Who did you expect? Yarchik?" Frodel's chiding laughter burned worse than the flames raging across the Twilight World. "What arrogance, to think you deserve one such as him as your guide."

"I have asked for no guides," Dahr said, turning his back on the Tribesman.

"You curse Garun for the responsibility he has given you, and lament that he has left you naked in the snow, with no idea of your location and no sense of your destination. Doubt fills your heart, wrath consumes your soul; you turn your back on all you were taught, all you loved. You avoid the Lesser Voices, ignore their advice even as you bring them forth to die in your name—"

"I told them to stay away!"

"You speak the words, but the Lesser Voices see into your heart. They come because you need them, because you want the comfort of their presence, because Garun commands them to help you find your way. Through it all you spurn their advice, as you have spurned all who have offered to help you. You will discount my words as well, and deny my role as guide, seeing in me only a ghost who haunts your conscience."

"You talk," Dahr muttered, "but you say little. I don't need confirmation of my doubt, reminders that I don't want the duties heaped upon me. I want someone to tell me what it is that I'm supposed to do!"

"Garun wants a leader for the Blood; he does not want a puppet!" Frodel bared his teeth in a snarl, and he lunged at Dahr, gripping him by the shoulders, forcing him to remain face to face, as if the rough contact would somehow make the words take better root. "But if it is premonition you want, then hear me: Garun says the time of reckoning comes, the time when you will decide the fate of the Blood. He is eager to see what you do, He accepts your choice, and He forgives you."

The landscape shifted again, the carnage of battle replaced with colorful wildflowers stretching across a lush green prairie. Bright sunlight beamed across the azure sky, broken only on the horizon, where the silhouette of a giant mound spewed dark smoke. The Tribesmen's dirge whispered in Dahr's ear, but it sounded different, more mournful, lacking the promise of rebirth and renewal.

"Forgives me?" Dahr asked, turning to face Frodel. "Forgives me for what?"

"Garun thinks you will choose poorly, but either way, the Balance will be restored, and above all, that is what He asked of you."

"And if I just walk away? If I left the Tribes and sought my own way?"

"Abandon the Blood?" Frodel laughed. "That choice has already been made. You cannot flee from it. The Scorpion's agents do not seek Garun's children; they seek you. Leave, and they will still find you. Alone and unprotected, you will fall to them with ease."

"First you claim I protect the Blood, and now that they protect me?"

"Protect the Blood? How well have you done that, Dahr Odara? How many Hunters burn behind you? How many of Garun's Children need not fear the cold this winter? Yours is not to protect the Blood; it is to decide its fate. Will you let some live, or will you send them all to the comfort of the Twilight World, the chaos of the Nothing?"

"But Yarchik—"

"—interprets the *Prah'phetia* as he wants, as do all when reciting prophecy."

Dahr raised himself to full height, his confidence bolstered by the rush of hot blood that lent color to his face, his courage strengthened by the belief that he could not be harmed in the Twilight World. "I do not want this! I want to be freed from the bonds Garun has tied to me, free to live my own life, to make my own choices; free to hunt and kill and die without the fate of others resting upon my every decision!"

Frodel's derisive laughter drove Dahr to the brink of madness. "None have that freedom, Dahr Odara. The choices we make are tied to the choices of others no matter how insignificant our lives may seem. But no doubt many among the Tribes wish the same, wish for a savior who saw them as more than weapons with which to kill, or cattle to lead to slaughter. No doubt many of them wish that Garun had chosen another, but His will is done, and woe unto the Blood."

Dahr swung at Frodel, unleashing all his pent up frustration, all the rage and hate and suffering he tried to control in the waking world. The Tribesman did not flinch as the blow drew near, and the hungry gleam in his eyes said he yearned for a fight, craved the chance to teach Dahr a lesson with the tools he had learned during his life, the tools of a warrior.

Before the blow landed, the Twilight World disappeared, and Dahr nearly pitched off Jardelle's back as he jerked awake. He caught himself before he fell, casting glances from side to side, wondering if any had noticed, then fumed when he saw that his caravan had once again stumbled to a halt.

He leapt from Jardelle's back and stormed down the trampled path, bellowing for an explanation, his feet crunching down into the two fingers-width of heavy snow that had fallen the night before. The last five days had been a march of fits and starts, of constant interruption, of raids upon their meager supplies and illness among his followers. They needed haste to reach the ambush site before Kraltir, and more haste to reach it before the Scorpion's two armies joined together; yet he was met with nothing but delay, pestered with trivialities, hounded by those who wanted to know where to hunt, where they would encamp the children and aged when the battle was joined, where they would go and what the Blood would do after they defeated the *Kohr'adjin*.

Dahr dismissed such concerns, or delegated them to his subordinates; he intended to worry about such things only if he lived. He saw no point in bothering with trivialities that only mattered if the Garun'ah survived beyond the fighting.

"Tarouk! What is the delay?"

The Anada Hunter, standing stone-faced with arms folded across his chest, turned from watching a group of young boys wrestling in the snow. "Wagon wheels choked by snow. Prisoners sick; unable to walk. Must make litters. Four boys found stealing from supply wagons. They take punishment."

Frustration ate at Dahr like vultures upon carrion, tearing at his insides. "How long?" he said through clenched teeth.

"Not long," Tarouk replied.

The Tribesman's blank expression never changed, but Dahr sensed a hesitation. "What aren't you telling me?"

Tarouk regarded him coolly. He had become one of Dahr's staunchest supporters, one of his greatest allies among the Anada Tribe, but he had no fear when confronting Dahr, no qualms about speaking his mind, even if he knew it would send Dahr into a rage. To him, the Korahn was a great leader, but only a man. Dahr wondered if he wished more Tribesmen felt as Tarouk did, or fewer.

"Storm come." Tarouk said, gesturing toward the thick grey clouds hovering over the northern horizon. "We not make ridge to east before snows, we forced camp."

"We can't lose another day," Dahr said. He stomped the ground like a restless horse, felt the pull of the bit in his mouth, holding him back. "Our enemies already have the advantage. Ready the Blood for a fast march."

"Our younglings have trouble make distance at speed required. The *Kohr'adjin* not able hold pace. Fatigue and hunger plague all, but them at door to Nothing."

Dahr exhaled a sharp breath. Grendor had yet to finish taking confession from the thousands of *Kohr'adjin* prisoners Kraltir had encumbered him with, and even though all but a handful had given heartfelt oaths and were not considered threats, they had proved a constant nuisance. Of ill-health and on the verge of starvation, they required a sizable proportion of the already meager provisions, leaving his own followers hungry and forced to scour ever farther afield for food. Their plodding steps dragged like an anchor, slowing Dahr's advance, costing him the time he needed to put his plan to action. Even if they did nothing to oppose him, they served his enemies.

"We must not be delayed," Dahr said, the knowledge of what he must do crystallizing. "Grendor does not believe them to be a threat?"

"The Orog think they misguided by teachings of Kohr, but he believe they keep their oaths."

"If they are not a threat, then they need not be our prisoners. Set them free."

For the first time, Tarouk's expression changed, his lip compressing into a thoughtful line as he turned his full attention on Dahr. "How much our food we leave?"

"None. We've already given them more than we can afford. They are Garun'ah; let them survive off the land."

"This land falls to dark of winter," Tarouk replied. "Our passage strip it; game felled or fled. Toss out to cold, with lion storm roar down from north, not many survive."

Dahr hardened his stance, readied himself for a fight. "They are not our people. They are not our concern. Let Kohr provide for them."

Tarouk faced him for a time, neither speaking, neither yielding. "I will tell your words to those who need to hear them," Tarouk said at last, turning and disappearing into the masses of Tribesmen.

Dahr paced in the snow, his manner so dark that only the most foolish dared approach him. Finally, he heard a bird's whistle in the west, and the sound was repeated up the line of Tribesmen: the signal that the Tribes were ready to resume the march. Head tucked low to shield his eyes from the gritty ice blown about by the wind, Dahr marched toward the front of the line, taking Jardelle's reins and continuing on foot, hoping the exercise would work away some of his frustration.

He looked back over the line of Tribesmen stretching toward the far horizon, women and craftsmen bunched close for warmth, young children riding in the wagons with the supplies, tribes separated by gaps that seemed less distinct than before the war, as if he had already begun his work of destroying the Blood. The Hunters ranged farther afield, scouring the land for the bands of raiders that had plagued their passage, scouting for signs of the enemy, and foraging for food. Among the tents, only around the *Kohr'adjin* did Hunters gather in any force, and even there they seemed indifferent, ignoring the prisoners except when one tried to pass into the realm of real Tribesmen.

Lines of young boys marched with spear and *dolchek* in hand, imagining the day when they would be allowed to join the battle. Tazahn and Shiena and the other *Tier'sorahna* gathered at the fringes of the camp, guarded by wolves, bears, and other beasts of the plains; shadowed by eagles, falcons, and the warriors of the sky. Vyrina, looking more Tribeswoman than Human, dressed in heavy hides and with her hair pulled back like the *dahrina*, loped before a regiment of Hunters who continued their training in warfare despite the nearness of battle. Dahr looked over it all and wondered how he had ended here, at the head of this army, leading men to their deaths, fighting a millennia old battle. *Does this show the Gods' blessing, or just Their cruel justice?*

He topped a hill and froze, his quick signal repeated in birdsong that sent runners moving down the line. "If you are waiting for me here, Olin, I expect bad news."

"Kraltir waits beyond the lakes," Olin said, his voice betraying none of the panic that Dahr felt race through his own veins. "*Synat Sal'aqran* moves north like snow rabbit. Armies will join before we are in position."

"Then it's finished," Dahr sighed, and the slow exhale took with it more tension than he expected, leaving him feeling unburdened. "Recall the Hunters. Find us a defensible position. We will make our foes come to us."

"Three days fast march will bring us to a ridge," Olin told him, sketching a hasty map in the packed snow. "From the heights we will hold our greatest advantage, but their numbers far exceed ours."

"Flight is not an option," Dahr reminded him. "The *Kohr'adjin* move unencumbered; they will overrun us if we flee, with results that will assuage even Kohr's thirst for blood."

"Burdened as we are, we will not reach the ridge fast enough." Olin's gaze slipped past Dahr.

"The prisoners have been dealt with. They will slow us no longer."

The slight widening of Olin's eyes was the only warning Dahr had before blinding pain exploded down Dahr's spine, knocking him forward into the snow. He rolled to his back, spitting blood and grit, and hastily drew his *dolchek*, though the blade fell from his grip when he saw Grendor standing over him, cheeks flushed dark grey, *va'dasheran* held butt-end toward Dahr, the thick oak hovering over his heart.

"What do you think—?"

"No!" Grendor shouted, his voice cracking like a branch succumbing to the weight of accumulated snow, a geyser held until it could no longer be contained, then bursting forth with the vigor of unbridled emotion. "You are to listen, not to talk. I have walked with you down this path, watched your descent into darkness, offered only counsel and withheld all judgment as you fulfilled the role the Gods carved for you, a role I know you want no part of.

"When you brought children to battle under the guise of teaching them control of the Lesser Voices, I held my tongue. When you turned a deaf ear to Jeran's call, a blind eye to the suffering of our brother Elves, I remained steadfast, certain of the integrity at the core of your being, the value of your desire to set right the Tribal Lands before turning to aid our comrades. At your behest, I took confessions from those we captured, used the blessings of my people to wrest information from our enemies, to test the oaths of our prisoners. For those who could not pass that test, I aided their journey to the final peace, sped their souls to judgment."

Dahr listened in stunned silence, struck dumb by the drastic change in the Orog's demeanor. Once he would have given much to see Grendor deprived of composure, slave to base emotion; now that he had been granted his wish, it offered no joy, just the bitter realization that the darkness in his soul could obscure even the light of the sun.

"For you, I have done all of this," Grendor continued. "Because Jeran needs you. Because he believes in you. As I believed. But now… Now you condemn to death women and children, people who have sworn vows not to betray you, people to whom I have offered my protection in your name."

"They are not condemned," Dahr managed, finding the strength to voice an objection. "They are free to go, to find their own way; free to serve Kohr or Garun or the Nothing, so long as they do not interfere with me."

"Free," Grendor spat the word back at him. "To send them out into this winter is worse than executing them, a death slower and far crueler."

"If you feel that way," Dahr mumbled, "the easier solution can be arranged."

Grendor's staff slammed against Dahr's jaw, knocking him back to the ground. Spots of light swirled before his eyes, and Grendor's response echoed hollowly in his ears.

"If you speak earnestly, friend Dahr, then you are more lost than I imagined; if your words were an attempt at humor, now is not the time for levity. You think you can utter the word 'free' and make the fate of your prisoners less your fault; you believe that if they are here, they are your concern, and if they are gone, they are not. But hear me! A slave is a being whose soul is held by another, whose fate is controlled by another. Cast out the *Kohr'adjin*, and you make them more your slaves than by keeping them. Cast them out, and you make yourself worse than those we fight, who sent them to us rather than let them die."

"You test the bounds of our friendship, Orog!" Dahr growled. His hand reached out, almost of its own accord, and gripped the hilt of his *dolchek*. He sat up, wiping blood from his lips, and glared at those who had gathered to watch the spectacle, but who dared not come to the assistance of their God's chosen savior. "Men have died for—"

"You have sought to goad me to fight since the day we met," Grendor said, the interruption galling Dahr. "Do not pretend otherwise. Throughout it all, I have held to the Mother's teachings and sought to battle ire with tranquility. But like the stones facing the wrath of the oceans, you have worn me away. The only language you hear is violence, and for the sake of our friendship, for the sake of my friendship with Jeran, I must make sure you hear." He stepped back, assuming a ready stance and adjusting his grip on the *va'dasheran*. "Fight me, Dahr. We will debate with steel and let the Gods determine which of us walks the path of right."

A voice inside his head screamed for Dahr to accept the challenge, to avenge the affront to his dignity, to show those who dared oppose him the consequences of such foolish action. The Lesser Voices remained strangely silent, their presence unmistakable but distant, a mirror to the throng of Tribesmen who gathered around the hilltop, or who waited for word to pass back down the caravan line in whispers so quiet that they could not be heard over the howl of the wind.

Dahr's hand tightened around the blade, and he cast it into the snow. "No. I will not fight you."

"I wonder if it is wisdom which holds you back, or cowardice." Grendor waited, but when the insult had no effect—the monster had fled, leaving Dahr with only shame to hold him upright—he shrugged. "Either way, I will be gone by morning. I can ignore Jeran's need no longer. I wish you peace, friend Dahr."

Grendor turned and walked away, leaning heavily upon his staff, as if the exchange had drained him of vital energy. A murmur arose from the Tribesmen, and then they began to disperse. The broad shadow of Harol Grondellan fell across

Dahr, and the Rachannan looked upon him with regret, with guilt that mirrored Dahr's own, as if he somehow were to blame for what had transpired.

"The Orog's right, lad. There's battle, and there's war, and then there's this Gods-forsaken mess we find ourselves caught in, but you have to hold yourself to something, or you wake one day and find out you've become worse than what you were fighting against. I can't do it anymore." Before he left, Lord Grondellan moved close enough to clap a hand to Dahr's shoulder, and he held it there for a moment before following Grendor.

Dahr sent word for the Tribes to make camp, then demanded solitude. The few Tribesmen who remained on the hilltop left at his command, and Dahr sat in the snow, staring west, stone still and unblinking until the setting sun forced him to avert his eyes.

He sensed her approach; her unmistakable scent brought fire to his blood. "You're leaving too?" It was not truly a question; the *Prah'phetia* had already told him of this day.

"I thought I could endure anything, so long as I endured it with you," Katya said, moving to stand behind him. "But I can't watch this. I can't let you…"

Dahr faced her, tortured by the pain worn so openly on her face. "You deserve better than me."

A slight smile twisted the corners of Katya's mouth. "I deserve exactly what I have."

She started to leave, but Dahr reached out and grabbed her arm. "Tell me something. Before we left Shandar, what did Jeran say to you?"

"He told me he understood why I wanted to go, but… He told me that if I ever thought you could not be redeemed, that I spare the world your suffering."

"And what will you tell him?" Dahr asked, his mouth dry. He longed for a drink, a single swallow of *baqhat* to warm the bleak chill spreading through him. "That you betrayed him again?"

"I don't have to," Katya whispered, pulling away and starting the lonely walk down the hill. "He already knows."

Chapter 35

Bitter winds blasted down from the north, carrying swirling wisps of snow that obscured visibility, a dancing white haze as distracting as it was protective. The winds carried icy grit too, driving it with enough force to leave pinpricks of pain on exposed flesh. Hunters huddled in small groups, backs to the wind, heads tucked low, voices muted and expressions somber.

Today is the last day many of them fight, Dahr thought. *And they know it.*

As he had done for most of the days since his companions abandoned him, Dahr sat alone, separated from the Hunters guarding their perimeter by a span of at least fifty hands. He refused company, discouraged the approach of any who did not bring news of the enemy; he sat as a statue, snow accumulating on his shoulders, staring west at the thousands of Tribesmen who had followed him here as much as he stared at the wall of dancing white to the east.

Somewhere out there, Kraltir's army approached, an invisible threat, free to fall upon them at will, an army unburdened with responsibility for the lives of women and children and not exhausted from a forced march to acquire even a modestly defensive position. The forces of *Synat Sal'aqran* raced north toward them too; the best reports had that army falling upon them within a day, though with them, Dahr welcomed the stormy weather. He had fought hard to convince the Tribesmen to clear concealing brush along the ridgeline and build a modest earthwork around the tents; arguing for more comprehensive defenses was futile, as was suggesting that the Hunters carry shields to protect against the arrows of the Human archers. If they had to die, his people refused to die trapped within walls or cowering behind a circle of wood and steel.

"You make terrible sentry," Olin said, appearing out of the blizzard. "Enemy could march past you before you call alarm." Tarouk stood behind Olin with two other Hunters Dahr did not recognize.

"I am not here to guard our camp," Dahr said. "I'm here to plan our defense. Do you have information for me?"

Olin turned to Tarouk and said something in Garu, and the Anada Hunter's lips twisted up in a smirk. "None you will like," Olin told him. "Runners have seen Humans to the south. Main body not yet found, but scouts already circling around lake. No sign Kraltir."

"None?" Dahr fumed. "I was certain the messages I sent to his camp would goad him to attack." He pounded his fist in the snow, shaking the accumulation off his shoulders in the process. "If we face both armies together, we have no chance."

"Scouts to north see tracks too," Tarouk added, his features once again somber.

"Tribesmen? To the north?" Dahr spat a curse, and cast his withering gaze to the Heavens. "Will they envelop us then? Attack from all sides? Has Garun finally abandoned us, or decided to back His Father in this war?"

Tarouk's back-handed blow jarred Dahr back to reality. He whirled around, but the Hunter's stoic expression never left his face. Whatever provoked the attack, it had not been anger. "Do you regret following me, Tarouk?"

"You still Korahn," Tarouk said. "But even Korahn not blaspheme."

Dahr returned his gaze to the east, intending to ignore the Hunters and return to his brooding silence. In the distance he caught sight of a snow leopard creeping through the powder, stalking a family of ground squirrels. The leopard made only a pretense of stealth; the squirrels already knew of its approach, but they had younglings huddled in a shallow den and would not abandon them.

Dahr opened his mind to them, wishing them a peaceful journey to the Twilight World, but the squirrels ignored his call. As one, the adults rushed the snow leopard, chittering and squeaking, gnashing teeth and flailing claws. The leopard fell back under the sudden onslaught, and though it tried to engage its prey-turned-predator, the tenacity of the attack drove it off. As it fled, the squirrels, wounded but alive, returned to the den and their mewling young.

Their victory brought Dahr a clarity of thought he had not experienced in seasons, an understanding of what he must do epiphanical in nature, divine in timing. "Ready the Hunters. Every man and woman who can hold a *dolchek*. Tarouk, gather the *Kranora*. Bring them to me. Run!"

As Olin and Tarouk hastened to carry out their orders, Dahr opened his mind to the Lesser Voices. *Rouse the Tier'sorahna. Send out word that the hunt begins.*

He waited with barely-restrained impatience, pacing the snowy hilltop until he had worn a path through to the rock beneath. Around him, the Garun'ah came alive; the sentries threw off their lethargy, leaping to their feet and sucking in deep breaths of the frigid air, stretching muscles stiff from a long night of silent vigil. Those among the tents formed rank at the barked orders of Olin and Vyrina, assembling with a discipline unknown among the tribes prior to this war. Despite their haste, the Tribesmen moved in relative silence, unconcerned with the icy snow blasting across the valley, unfazed by the women and children, whose eyes reflected the knowledge that few expected to be reunited at the day's end.

Tarouk ran among the tents of the *Kranora*, stopping only when he approached those of the Anada and Meila signaled for his presence. The two exchanged words, almost heated at times, but before he left to take his place before the Anada Hunters, Meila gripped Tarouk's shoulders in her hands and he ducked his head so she could place a gentle kiss on his brow.

The Anada showed even less discomfort in the harsh weather than the others; most wore sleeveless hides to display the tattoos etched into the flesh of their arms: prowling cats and soaring raptors, howling wolves and roaring bears. They pounded fists against their chests at Tarouk's approach, a show of solidarity Dahr welcomed, as it often goaded the other tribes to greater coherence.

Dahr watched the preparations through Shyrock's eyes, though the eagle had to fight swirling cross-currents to stay aloft. He broke his connection when the majority of the *Kranora*, many accompanied by their *Tsha'ma* advisors, joined him on the hilltop.

"You call us from fires to yell more?" asked Burask of the Dorasein, his voice tinged with the constrained anger Dahr faced from most of the *Kranora*. "Or just want to watch us freeze?"

"Korahn think it mercy let us sink slowly to death in the cold," added Hashan, *Kranor* of the Nourik. "Spare us agony of honest battle."

Though many among the Hunters understood and accepted his demand to learn the 'Human way of battle', his insistence that they prepare for a defense against the overwhelming odds arrayed against them, the leaders of the tribes, particularly those of the smaller tribes, resisted the changes he imposed upon tradition. "We must ready—"

"Perhaps the young Hunter run out of *baqhat*," laughed Kodash of the Turape. "We supposed to bring you more, Korahn?"

"Perhaps if you held your tongues the Korahn will tell you why he summoned us." Rannarik pushed past the other Tribesmen and placed a hand on Dahr's shoulder. The icy touch shocked him, drove away the desire to strangle Kodash for his insult.

"Perhaps if they do not," Sadarak said, shoving Hashan aside, "the Korahn will bless us all by silencing them for rest of us."

"I have counseled defense in the face of the odds arrayed against us," Dahr began, struggling to keep his tone even, his bearing bordering on deferential, "and I have faced resistance from those of you bound tightly to the traditions of the Blood."

"Not want to cower in tents, wait for enemy makes us slaves to tradition?" Kodash spat, turning his back on Dahr. Only Arik's hulking presence kept him from leaving.

"Defending the camp is our best chance against the combined armies of the Scorpion," Dahr said, ignoring the grumbling of the *Kranora*. "But our best chance remains no chance at all. At this desperate junction, I have come to ask—not to tell, but to ask!—that you follow me into battle. This may be the last battle the Blood ever fights, the last day we ever watch dawn; but if we fall, it will be defending the Balance from the *Kohr'adjin*, from all who would see chaos triumph over justice. If we fall, we will race to the Twilight World, trumpeting our defiance of Kohr and the chaos He brings."

The quiet murmuring grew in intensity, as the *Kranora* conferred with their *Tsha'ma* and each other in Garu. Dahr waited, though the show of patience wore at his stamina. He yearned to be on the hunt already; he knew that every moment's delay brought them that much closer to certain defeat.

When Arik approached, Dahr knew a decision had been reached, and when the *Kranor* of the Tacha drew the hood of his bear cloak over his head, a hungry grin spread across Dahr's face. "The Blood has long waited for this day," Arik said. "We will fight with you, Korahn."

"Ready the Hunters!" Hashan called, raising his spear over his head. "We go east to fight the *Kohr'adjin*!"

"No," Dahr told them, stunning the *Kranora* to silence and returning their full attention to him. "Kraltir expects an attack, and he will be ready for us. Our Hunters will be held fast, their backs exposed to the army of *Synat Sal'aqran*, and we will fall among a downpour of Human arrows. The Blood will cease to be, and our fall will be for nothing, for the Children of Kohr will reign over all the eastern lands, and none will remain to oppose them.

"But the army of *Synat Sal'aqran* is Human, fatigued from their race north to aid the *Kohr'adjin*, humbled by a winter unknown of in their soft lands, hobbled by winds that will render their arrows useless. We will run south to meet them." Dahr spread his arms, letting the icy snow beat against his outstretched palms. "This storm will be our shield, the *Tier'sorahna* our eyes. We will drive the Humans back before Kraltir learns what we do, and once they are gone, we can draw the *Kohr'adjin* out and defeat them on our own terms. We can restore the Balance and bring honor to Garun the Hunter."

The rousing response he received was far more than he had expected; even those who bore grudges against him shouted their support and raced off to ready for battle. As word spread through the camp, a new energy suffused the Garun'ah, more than just a hunger to fight. Dahr saw in them a reawakening pride, a renewed strength of purpose, a goal so pure it threatened to wipe out centuries of rivalries and unify the Blood. Dahr wished he could share in that vitalizing spirit, but if he could not experience it, he could at least use it.

He marched with the first of the Hunters, following only the scouts sent out ahead to seek their prey; his conscience would not permit him to send the Garun'ah to death without offering himself as an easy sacrifice. Fang loped at his side, teeth bared at the bitter cold; Shyrock soared above, buffeted by the winds but refusing to seek shelter no matter how many times Dahr requested it. As he walked, other animals joined him, and other *Tier'sorahna* as well, the eldest running beside their protectors, the youngest riding atop their backs.

"The call has been sent, Korahn," Tazahn said. Winded from a sprint across the camp, the boy took his place beside Dahr without complaint, a *dolchek* at his hip despite Dahr's insistence that the *Tier'sorahna* keep themselves as far from the fighting as their abilities permitted. A shaggy grey wolf, half again the size of Fang, ran beside him. "The Lesser Voices come to battle."

"The winged ones fight the skies," said Avah, a girl of twelve winters who rode proudly astride an elk. A long, slinky rodent wrapped around her neck like a shawl, watching Dahr with a sly gaze. "They fear their eyes will be little help."

"Tell them to watch the *Kohr'adjin*," Dahr said. "As soon as Kraltir learns what we are doing, his army will follow hoping to trap us. Foreknowledge of their approach will be of great benefit. Maugli! What are you doing here?"

The boy, an orphan of the Afelda and a child of barely six winters, sat astride a great brown bear. Dwarfed by the lumbering beast, nearly hidden within its shaggy fur, Maugli's cheeks turned crimson when caught in Dahr's angry glare. A family of chipmunks raced around him, barking and chittering in agitation; one even perched on his shoulder, standing sentry. "You summon *Tier'sorahna*," he said weakly.

"And I told you before that you were too young for battle!" A voice in his head asked why it mattered, why the child's death in the tents would be any better than his death on the battlefield, but Dahr drove it down, forced it to silence. Some lines he could not cross, no matter how far he fell.

"If you are not there, who will protect those in the tents?" he asked, schooling his features, forcing his voice to calm.

Maugli's eyes narrowed, and the bear's growl echoed the boy's misgivings. "This is not a trick?"

"I swear to you; if we are not victorious today, you will be the greatest defense the Blood has left."

Suspicion warred with duty, dancing across Maugli's expression in waves, but duty won. The bear turned, lumbering back toward the camp. Dahr saw a few more of the youngest *Tier'sorahna* following, and he heaved a sigh. *At least now I won't have to listen to Vyrina's lecturing again.*

He ran, covering ground quickly despite the dim light and pelting snow, and the might of the Blood fanned out behind him, moving in squads of fifty that somehow managed to retain the impression of hunting parties despite the formal, regimented movements drilled into them over the last few seasons. They moved with the precision of an army, responding to hand signals from their commanders with neither question nor delay, harnessing the fiery temper that surged so easily through the Children of Garun. Most had donned cloaks of white fur so they all but disappeared into the swirling snow, implacable ghosts racing toward an enemy, ready to mete out punishment to those who dared defile their home.

Dahr signaled a halt near the summit of a low rise, giving his Hunters a chance to regroup and catch their breath. Somewhere in the valley beyond, he sensed his prey; he knew the time was at hand. Opening himself to the Lesser Voices, he demanded that they protect the *Tier'sorahna* above all else, and insisted that if the tide of battle turned against them, they escort the children back to the tents and help them flee the *Kohr'adjin*. He issued more specific orders to the children, telling them how best to serve, demanding a promise from each to avoid the fighting at all costs, to limit themselves to directing the Lesser Voices.

To his commanders, orders were not necessary; each knew what must be done and knew as well as Dahr how best to do it. Instead, he honored them, and told them that at day's end, they would either share a drink in the tents or a feast in the Twilight World.

The moments stretched out until Dahr could think of no more reasons to delay. With only a final moment taken to wonder if this fight would be his last, he drew his greatsword and moved forward, followed by an army of ghosts, descending into the maelstrom, a violent world of howling winds and icy pain. The ferocity of the storm suited him well, matching his own fury; the beast he so often struggled to hide he now let roam free.

So intent was he on reaching the enemy that he ran past the first few soldiers without noticing, mistaking them for shadows in the gloom. Only when he heard the sound of fighting behind him did he realize his mistake, and by then he faced a wall of startled Humans, dark armored men marching in tight clusters, their movements made awkward by the cold.

One of the soldiers shouted a warning, but it was too late; Dahr thrust his sword through the man's gut, pivoting and wrenching the blade free only to plunge it into another soldier. The others fell back, fumbling with the bows slung over their shoulders, their primary weapons useless in the storm and the surprise attack.

Dahr shot past the frightened soldiers, leaving them to the Hunters who followed. Shock would last but a moment, lack of discipline an instant longer; he needed to wreak as much damage as possible through *Synat Sal'aqran's* army. He attacked every group of soldiers he encountered, darting off into the snow before they could react, pressing ever farther behind the enemy line. Of his allies he saw little, only glimpses of fighting going on behind him and dark shadows as the Lesser Voices rushed past. Their howls and growls filled the air around him, followed by the terrified screams of the enemy.

He heard the voice long before he saw the man, the unmistakable snarl impressed into Dahr since childhood. When the snows parted, revealing the scarred and tortured form of the slaver Gral, Dahr's heart froze; his vision clouded over, narrowing until all he could see was the slaver, until all he heard were the shouted commands and vile curses spewing forth as he tried to rally his army. His face had changed, the one half scarred and pitted, hardened by exposure to the elements, darkened by servitude to Salos, lips pressed thin and drawn down in a perpetual scowl; the other half bleached white and smooth, ravaged by the fire Dahr had left him to die in, the eye pure white and yet not sightless. The tattoo of a scorpion stretched across that taut canvas, tail curling up around the temple, stinger poised just above the too-white orb.

Dahr roared a challenge and raced toward the former slaver, ignoring the enemies along his path, killing only when they refused to flee or dared to attack. The blizzard closed around Gral again, and when it cleared he was gone, vanished into the storm, only the echo of his voice giving proof to his presence. Dahr fumed, reaping death on those around him, hacking and stabbing with great passion but little finesse, until he stood alone, heaving in breaths and staring down into the lifeless faces of his foes.

The Lesser Voices called to him, warning of danger, but Dahr ignored them; he ignored the calls of his men as well, the shouted commands to find the Korahn, the desperate calls to control their bloodlust and remain in formation. *I have taught them all I can. Vyrina and Grendor much more. Today we will see how they fare without me, and me without them.*

The Tachans fell back and Dahr pursued, his path crossing back and forth but drawing him ever farther from his own allies. Sporadic fighting erupted around him between Humans and Garun'ah, small bands of Hunters too eager for battle to stay with the slower advance of the army, or searching through the blizzard for their leader. Dahr aided his Hunters when they needed it, avoided them when they did not, and when confronted by any of his people he ordered them to rejoin their units and press the attack as they had been taught.

Though the Tribesmen rarely listened, the Lesser Voices utterly ignored him. Hundreds of beasts roamed the field of battle, darting and driving through the Tachan lines, dispatching wounded or isolated enemies, ambushing from the shadows and sowing confusion and terror among the supply wagons following the main army. At times the ground heaved and flowed as if alive, the hard-pack snow shaded black with the passage of thousands of rodents. Snow owls and hawks screeched defiance, though shifting winds kept them above the fighting. Other creatures called out to Dahr, vast herds and smaller packs, trumpeting their approach, demanding their place in the fight.

Gral appeared and disappeared before him, always out of reach, always close enough to spur him on. During his blind hunt he acquired followers; Hunters separated from their units fell in line behind him, knowing he would lead them to battle, seeing in him their greatest chance for survival. And before them the enemy fell to axe and spear and greatsword, or fled before an army who appeared out of the mists without so much as a sound to announce their presence, and who faded away once the killing was done.

The calls of the Lesser Voices buzzed in his head, growing in insistence. Dahr muted them, pushed them down into that part of his mind where he could wall them off for a time. He knew what he did was foolish; he knew he pushed too far, leaving himself exposed and his army to wonder about his safety; but he hungered to make someone pay for what he had become, and he saw in Gral the man who had set his life on its path. He plunged forward, driving the Humans before him.

"Korahn..."

The weak call robbed the thrill from the kill he had just made. Dahr let the body slide from his sword and turned to find the speaker. "Avah? What are you doing here?"

"The Lesser Voices did not understand why you could not hear," she said, swaying atop her elk mount. "They did not understand why you would not listen. Kraltir comes. His Hunters descend on our flanks, hidden by the wind and snow. Our Hunters will not see them until they feel the spears in their backs."

The ebullience Dahr felt at his wild advance faded, and he cast his eyes toward the north and west. Out there his people faced the organized might of the enemy, hoping to drive the intruders from the Tribal Lands, while he ran rampant behind the enemy, driving cowards and fools before him and seeking to come upon *Synat Sal'aqran* from behind. They trusted him to lead them, to protect them, and he had abandoned them to his own bloodlust.

Did Gral fall into my trap, or have I fallen into Salos's? The thought fled when Avah slumped forward and he saw the arrow protruding from her back.

He moved toward her, but the elk batted him away with a swing of its antlers, staring at him with what could only be described as disgust before turning and galloping back toward the tents, careful to keep the fallen *Tier'sorahn* atop its back. Dahr watched them disappear, felt the cold sting of snow on his cheeks where he should have felt tears, and listened to the beast within roar as he shoved it back into its cage.

"Kraltir is coming," he said to his men, turning his back on the Humans who fled at the sight of them. "We must warn the others."

He raced back the way he had come, begging the Lesser Voices to be his eyes. One Hunter beside him unslung a bone horn from his back and blew a series of notes, the pure tones tainted and twisted by the gusting winds. The others followed without question, knowing that wherever the Korahn led them, there would be more blood.

His spirit for the fight was gone though, banished with the part of him that relished battle, that taunted death. When the first of the fleeing Humans passed, Dahr barely noticed; when their numbers increased and he realized the enemy had been routed, that they fled before the might of his people and into his waiting maw, he could not bring himself to care. The Hunters who followed laid waste to them, carving a path of death, but Dahr moved on, fighting only when forced to, killing only when necessary. When he barely avoided an attack by one of his own, a young Hunter startled by the Korahn's sudden appearance, he had trouble telling whether the odd emptiness he felt was relief or disappointment.

"Hold!" he yelled. "The *Kohr'adjin* come! Turn and defend. Hold, I say!" At first none listened, and he had to find a *Tsha'ma* to give his voice power. Even then, forcing them to stop the advance drained what remained of Dahr's spirit, leaving him unable to convince his Hunters not to turn and race into a foolish charge. Chagrined, he took his place at the front of the advancing host and summoned the *Kranora*. They joined him on the march, each one covered in the gore of battle, many nursing wounds, and all with the fervor of victory in their eyes.

"Attack is suicide," Dahr told them, hoping that if they saw reason, they could bring the other Hunters in line. "We must set ourselves here. Kraltir will think us unaware of his approach. If we stand firm against their attack, we might be able to break them!"

"Fight like Human. Fight like Hunter," growled Kodash of the Turape. "Korahn live so long between worlds, he not know what he is any more. He change direction more often than kitten in field of grasshoppers."

He found more sympathy among the other *Kranora*, but not more support. Even Arik and Sadarak had been lured by the sweet taste of their victory over the Humans, the ease with which they had driven the enemy back. They urged a more cautious advance, but an advance nonetheless, and grated with impatience when Dahr made a second attempt to convince them. Of all he called to attend him, only Meila and Vyrina counseled defense, with Meila too new among the tribes for her voice to carry that much weight, and Vyrina remaining too Human in their eyes, her wisdom seen as reticence, a distaste to face the enemy in real battle.

Shyrock's call echoed in his mind, and he opened himself to the eagle's vision. He saw Gral astride a dark horse, waving his arms in broad sweeps and shouting out a string of commands while the warriors around him reformed rank and took to their own mounts, their panicked flight stopping as if it had never existed. A dozen ShadowMagi joined him, seeking positions among the army, their passage made easy by the gaps that opened around them wherever they moved. A hungry grin twisted Gral's face, and he called the order for his men to march.

We are done. Salos planned this from the start, and I led us straight to destruction. The realization drew a curtain of guilt over him, but it also killed his desire for caution. He opened himself to Shyrock again, giving the eagle a message to carry to Tazahn, then quickened his pace, resuming his position at the front of the advancing army of Garun'ah. He abandoned the path that would skirt the edge of his foe, aiming now toward the heart of the approaching *Kohr'adjin* host. He could no longer avert his fate, no longer avoid the consequences of his decisions.

The Blood Rage rose inside him, straining against the bonds Dahr held in place around it, but he refused to let the beast roam free again. His temper, his thirst for blood had led him to this place, and it seemed a fitting punishment for him to face this final fight alone, and a cruel retribution to force the part of him that relished combat, that yearned for blood and death, to watch the carnage but take no part.

So intent was he on this inner war that he nearly impaled himself on the first *Kohr'adjin* spear that poked through the thinning snows, dodging the thrust by only the narrowest of margins and praying the hulking warrior ran at least a few paces in front of his brethren. He tried to stop, shouting out a warning as he slid in the snow, moving his greatsword around to ward against any further attacks. By the time he regained his footing, the *Kohr'adjin* had been brought down by the Hunters who followed him, but a furious chant pealed out of the ice before him, heralding the beginning of a new conflict.

Dahr hastily drew his Hunters into formation, reminding them to hold to what they had been taught of Human warfare, knowing that little order would remain once the heat of battle was upon them, once the pent up animosity between Garun'ah and *Kohr'adjin* was allowed release. This was a fight simmering for centuries, a primal clash of ideologies with the fate of the Blood, and perhaps the whole of the Balance, at stake.

Out of the blizzard the enemy burst, sprinting toward them, axe and spear at the ready, howling defiance. A horn blast from behind trumpeted the return of Gral and his forces, close enough to cause a ripple of uncertainty among the Hunters.

"Ignore the horns! Focus on the enemy before you. Drive the *Kohr'adjin* back to the frozen wastes where they came from!"

"Humans already scatter like rabbits once!" Olin called, his voice rising beside Dahr's and instilling confidence among the warriors. Lower, so that only Dahr might hear, he added. "They come with ShadowMagi."

"I know. Let us hope Rannarik and the *Tsha'ma* can handle that threat. We have enough to deal with this day."

Dahr turned to face the oncoming army, but Olin grabbed his arm. "No matter your faults, Korahn, you are no Half-man. I am honored to die with you."

Whatever response Dahr might have summoned was lost as the *Kohr'adjin* army rolled across his waiting Hunters like an avalanche. The clash reverberated through the valley—the clang of steel, the shouts of men, and soon after, the cries of the wounded—a sound so terrible it drowned out the howling winds and made the distant horn blasts fade to memory.

Dahr lost himself in the rhythm of battle, the massive swings of his greatsword cleaving deep into his foes, forcing many to keep their distance or rush in to stab with short spear or *dolchek*. He hacked and stabbed, stepped and parried, moving in a relentless pattern, never predictable, always with an eye toward dispatching his foe with the least amount of effort, as he had been taught by his commanders in the Alrendrian Guard.

Those around him fought for their lives, for the lives of their families, for their way of life, and such stakes inspired them to great acts of courage. But it was not enough. Dahr had hoped to drive the *Kohr'adjin* back up the hill, where they could hold the high ground against their foes, but the enemy pushed them back, step after precious step, ever closer to the riders approaching from behind. Once pinned between those two armies, Dahr knew it would take a miracle for any to survive unscathed.

Down the line Dahr saw Kraltir drive a wedge of Hunters into his soldiers. The *Kohr'adjin* leader wielded twin *dolcheks* soaked in blood; he fought shirtless despite the bitter cold, his body painted with black and red markings. He had been marked like Gral: a scorpion climbed his throat, its legs clinging to neck and chin, its open claws stretching over taut cheeks and poised to pluck out his eyes. He saw Dahr and laughed, and then turned his back, dismissing him.

Dahr closed the distance between them, but while Kraltir no doubt thought to goad his temper by showing indifference, Dahr stood above emotion. The needs of his people motivated his attack: eliminate Kraltir, and the spirit of the *Kohr'adjin* would be broken, leaving his Hunters to face two dispirited foes.

But for every step he took, Kraltir moved two, staying always just beyond Dahr's reach, taunting him with his nearness, provoking him to hasten his assault. The chase drew Dahr far from his original position, past combat so chaotic it became near impossible to tell friend from foe. All the while Dahr heard the thunder of approaching hooves echoing in his mind, the death knell of trumpet blasts growing ever closer.

We are ready, Korahn! Tazahn called out within his mind, his words carried to Dahr by the Lesser Voices.

Not yet! Not until it seems that all is lost, or we risk everything. Until then, protect the young ones.

A flash of fire rose behind him, and moments later the concussion of falling debris. In the weakening storm, Dahr saw Gral's army descending upon his flank, the ShadowMagi wreaking havoc with fire and lightning, and sometimes with more subtle means of execution. A few bolts fell among the enemy as well—the *Tsha'ma* doing what they could—but by and large the Gifted of all Races did not train themselves for war; they styled themselves as being above such things. Now more than ever before, Dahr resented them for their fickle morality.

"Hold!" Dahr called. "Form twin lines, back to back! Let the reserves hold off the Humans, while the rest of us—"

He felt the blow coming well before he saw the blade out of the corner of his eye, and he threw himself aside. Fire burned across his back where the *dolchek* scored a shallow gash, but he rolled to his feet unmindful of the pain.

"Yarchik dishonored all the Blood by naming you to follow him," Kraltir said, slipping again into the throng. "Come, Korahn!"—he spat the title like a curse— "Let us find a place to end our hatred."

Dahr hastened after him, but Kraltir disappeared into the crowd. Screaming his frustration, Dahr followed, hacking at any *Kohr'adjin* who crossed his path, driving ever farther from the safety of his own warriors, pushing to the fringes of the battle. Thinking he meant to lead an assault, his Hunters followed, driving the enemy before them and leaving those behind to pay the price for their valor; for once the line separating Garun'ah from *Kohr'adjin* became distinct, the ShadowMagi were free to unleash the full might of their magic on the Blood.

The slaughter added to Dahr's guilt, but death was an end he had expected, one that all the Hunters who followed him knew to expect. Validation of his choices rested in the death of Kraltir, in leaving the *Kohr'adjin* leaderless, so that any who survived the day might have a chance to escape. Yet Kraltir seemed to sense his purpose, and taunted him by keeping just in sight, darting in to attack when Dahr's attention was diverted, slipping away before he could recover and pursue.

Fatigue wore at him, but when he saw Kraltir running toward the hilltop, he pursued nonetheless, heedless of the distance he put between himself and his allies.

Yet it was not Kraltir who awaited him atop the hill, but Gral. The slaver stood beside a lathered horse, sword at the ready, his face drawn down in a scowl.

"The Master promised me my revenge," Gral said, making Dahr dance back with a series of lightning blows. "I thought it an empty promise. Yet here you are."

Winded and bleeding from a dozen shallow wounds received during his pursuit of Kraltir, Dahr could do little but move away. He sensed more than saw the *Kohr'adjin* encircling him; they did not attack, but Dahr knew they would never let him leave alive.

Knowing defense would serve him little, Dahr pressed the attack, and for a time was able to hold Gral at bay. But the slaver was determined, and his skill with a blade exceeded Dahr's; it did not take long for him to halt Dahr's advance, and not much longer before it was all Dahr could do to keep the slaver's attacks from hitting home.

"I have waited for this day a long time," Gral told him, stabbing at Dahr's gut as he raced forward, then launching another attack as he passed. Dahr avoided both blows, but only barely. The shock of their blades clashing numbed his arm, and the slaver easily dodged his return swing.

Now, Korahn? Tazahn's voice came to him again, and he saw a vision of Gral's horsemen pressing deep into the Garun'ah line and then pulling back for another charge, the Hunters back to back, bracing spears to ground and leveling them at the throats of the oncoming horses.

Now! But flee to the tents as soon as you're done. There's nothing more you can do here, and the Blood will need someone to guide them.

The distraction was all Gral needed. He stepped in close, slipping around the great arc of Dahr's greatsword, his own blade stopped only because it hit against the *dolchek* sheathed at Dahr's hip. Dahr howled as the blade dug into his leg, and again when Gral hooked a foot behind his and flipped him to his back. As the air exploded from Dahr's lungs, the slaver kicked the greatsword from his hand and pressed the tip of his own blade to Dahr's throat.

"I should thank you," he said. "If I had killed you winters ago, I wouldn't be the man I am today. And soon, I will be one of the most powerful men in the Tachan Empire. Why—No!"

Gral's eyes lifted to the horizon, and though Dahr could not see as the slaver did, he knew what drew his gaze. A cluster of *Tier'sorahna* raced across the battlefield atop their odd mounts, using their combined abilities to panic the enemy. Horses bucked and reared, casting riders to the ground and trampling them underfoot; others turned to flee, colliding with their neighbors, terrorized by the onslaught of the voices screaming in their heads.

From behind the Human army came the Lesser Voices, those who survived the first part of the battle and those who had arrived too late to join the fighting. Tazahn and the others had directed them to wait, and now they unleashed them upon the flank of Gral's army. Packs of wolves and solitary *tigrans*, vast herds of elk and other creatures the likes of which Dahr had never seen slammed into the rear of the enemy, sowing as much fear among the Humans as the *Tier'sorahna* did among their mounts.

"You may kill me," Dahr chuckled, surprised by his own lack of fear, "But will Salos reward you for returning with a broken army? If any survive this battle, they will be haunted by memories of this day. Live or die, I served my purpose; can you claim the same?"

Hatred burned across Gral's face, and Dahr braced himself for the blow. The sound of clanging steel drew the slaver's eyes to a band of wild Tribesmen on the northern slope. Though bare-chested and painted much in the same manner as Kraltir, these Hunters slaughtered the *Kohr'adjin* with a viciousness greater than that of Dahr's own people. Only when he saw the wild eyes of Bysk *uvan* Tohrpa, *Kranor* of the Sahna, did he understand from where salvation had come.

A hulking form dashed by, driving Gral away. Dahr grasped at his throat where the slaver's blade drew blood and scrambled to retrieve his greatsword, eager to resume his part in the battle.

The sight of Harol Grondellan wielding his battleaxe, shouting for Gral to stand still while he pursued the slaver around the hilltop, shocked Dahr to stillness. He moved only when a *Kohr'adjin* Hunter dove at him, dodging the attack and then cutting off the Hunter's battlecry with a slice of the sword. After that, he lost himself in the fighting, the calming rhythm of combat, delivering death to those who dared attack him and then seeking out more, traversing the hilltop in ever widening circles until he stood unopposed and gasping for breath.

Through Shyrock's eyes, he inspected the carnage. Hunters lay dead and dying everywhere, and interspersed among them Humans and the bodies of the Lesser Voices. And still the battle raged. Small packs of warriors fought among the dead, pursued the fleeing Humans, or gathered for yet another charge. Even those still yearning for blood moved as if dragging heavy stones, clutching gaping wounds, struggling to ignore their pain.

Dahr marveled at the outcome, even as the sight of all those sacrificed to his whim left him numb. *Never in the history of Madryn has a victory felt so empty, a triumph so tragic.*

Bysk approached, blood freezing around a gash that ran from shoulder to hip across his chest. "You try kill all *Kohr'adjin* self. Sahna not like that, Korahn." He showed a toothy grin, but before Dahr could thank him for his help, the *Kranor* darted down the hill toward a cluster of *Kohr'adjin.*

A boy appeared with Dahr's sigil and planted the flag atop the hill, proclaiming to all that the Korahn had won the day. Dahr waited beside it while his Hunters cleared the remaining pockets of enemy from the field. The sounds of battle still rang out from all around him, growing more sporadic with every passing moment, but it no longer had the power to lure him.

Grondellan returned, axe broken at the haft and a sour scowl on his face. "The bastard got away," he fumed. "Ran like a girl."

"What are you doing here?" Dahr demanded, and though he tried, he could not make himself sound angry.

"Well, as to that," Grondellan explained, ducking his head in what Dahr assumed was some sort of embarrassment. "You don't abandon your family, lad. Not even when they're behaving like a fool. We agreed that one of us should stay behind to keep an eye on you, and I won the draw. Lucky I did, too. The Sahna were planning on attacking the *Kohr'adjin* two days back. Probably would have been slaughtered, too. I convinced them to wait and see what you were planning. Your mad dash this morning caught us completely off—"

Lord Grondellan fell to his knees, a spear bursting through his chest in a spray of blood. Eyes wide, he grasped at the three-finger thick shaft of wood, trying to pull it free.

Dahr started toward the Rachannan, then saw the snarling face of Kraltir across the hill, surrounded by a few dozen fanatic *Kohr'adjin* and hefting a second throwing spear. He changed course immediately, skirting past Lord Grondellan, neither calling for help nor waiting for his allies to rush to his aid. His greatsword he discarded, drawing instead the serrated *dolchek* that rested at his hip, oblivious to the pain as it slid across the raw wound on his leg.

Kraltir loosed the spear, but Dahr dodged it easily, barely slowing as he closed the distance between him and his foes. A handful of Sahna beat him to the *Kohr'adjin*, diverting their attention, leaving Dahr free to plunge through the mass and straight at Kraltir.

They grappled, exchanging blows, the blades of their *dolcheks* sparking with every contact. The fatigue that held him evaporated, replaced by a river of emotion so strong Dahr thought it would carry him away. He fed off the energy, driving Kraltir back with a series of violent attacks, ignoring the hammer-like punches the *Kohr'adjin* leader pounded into him.

The struggle took them over the steepest slope of the hill. Focused only on each other, they fought as they fell, tumbling end over end. A boulder loomed out of the spinning horizon. Dahr slammed against it with enough force to knock himself senseless, leaving him prone while Kraltir continued down unimpeded.

His muscles burned as he tried to rise, his stomach heaved as the world shifted around him, but Dahr forced himself to his feet, strained to keep a grip on his *dolchek*, and staggered forward. Kraltir was gone, swallowed in the chaos of the valley below. Frustrated and unsated, Dahr climbed back to the hilltop.

He did not want to seek out Lord Grondellan, but he could not stay away. The Rachannan lay on his side, blood flecking his lips and freezing in pools around him, but he still clung to life with a passion Dahr had come to respect, even envy.

"There's nothing to be done," Dahr said. Such simple words; something within told him Grondellan deserved better.

"Death finds us all," Lord Grondellan rasped. "Better this way than withered and feeble, no longer able to feed myself. The cold… With the cold, there's hardly any pain."

"I should thank you. If you had not brought the Sahna, all would have been lost."

"Having the Sahna wouldn't have mattered if you hadn't drawn the enemy here. You've a fine eye for war, lad."

Dahr turned away, uncomfortable with the conflicting emotions playing across his face. Lord Grondellan mistook his movement and gripped Dahr's arm tightly, making it impossible to leave. "Wait… I have to tell you… For whatever part my actions played in causing the torment you suffer…"

"No!" Dahr brushed aside Grondellan's weakening grip. But instead of fleeing as he wanted, he took the Rachannan's hand in his own. "My life has followed a dark path, but you caused none of that suffering. You are a good man, Harol Grondellan. You deserve better than my hatred; you deserve far better than my friendship."

He received no response, and when he looked down, he saw the blank specter of death staring at him from Lord Grondellan's eyes. A torrent of emotions rushed through him; of them all, bitter resentment and humbling guilt dominated.

He sat in the shadow of his great banner, the razor-backed cat framed by the Rising Sun of Alrendria bathing him in disappointment. His gaze shifted from north, where Kraltir led the *Kohr'adjin* retreat, to the south, where Gral led his Human army back toward the lands of man. Kraltir would regroup and nurse his wounds, and then return to harass the Blood; Gral would turn his attention on Alrendria and unleash upon it the destruction he had already wreaked upon the Tribal Lands.

"Which way do I go?" Dahr whispered, wishing Grondellan had lived long enough to answer that question for him. *Aqan Sal'aqran*, the Claws of the Scorpion, or *Synat Sal'aqran*, the Scorpion's Sting; each instilled in him a measure of fear, the former for his future, the latter from his past; yet each deserved to meet death at his hands. His instinct was to pursue Kraltir, to drive the *Kohr'adjin* from the face of Madryn, to make the Tribal Lands safe for the Garun'ah again, to avenge the deaths of Yarchik and Grondellan. Yet a voice within told him both might disapprove of such petty vengeance, and that his duty was to lead the Blood to safer lands, to protect those he had once called friends and the place he had once called home.

He sat in solitude until the storm passed and the setting sun beamed the slightest hint of warmth onto his flesh. In the dying light, he summoned Vyrina, and when the Guardswoman took a seat across from him without comment, he laughed.

"No criticisms?" he asked. "No condemnations?"

Vyrina's eyes studied Dahr's face, then dropped to the body of Lord Grondellan, still cradled in Dahr's lap. "It seems you've suffered enough today."

"You taught the Garun'ah well," Dahr told her. "If not for that training, the Blood would have ceased to be. On behalf of the Tribes, I thank you."

Vyrina ducked her head in acknowledgement. "But there is nothing more they can learn from you," Dahr added, earning a glare from the Guardswomen who had devoted herself to a Tribesman. "There's nothing more I can learn from you. By sunrise, you will leave the tents."

Vyrina stood, her momentary calm shattered by Dahr's harsh proclamation. "You have no right! You cannot—"

"Enough!" The crackle of his command silenced even the obdurate Guardswoman. He signaled a Hunter, bidding him bring a skin of *baqhat*. "Tonight, drink with me to those who have fallen, to those who will yet fall. Tomorrow, when you ride south, then you can hate me again. To Frodel!" Dahr tilted back his head and drank a long swallow of the fiery liquid, then offered the skin to Vyrina. She hesitated an instant before snatching the hide from his hand.

Chapter 36

A chill hung in the afternoon air, a damp cold that numbed flesh and robbed men of their will; a cold that rendered the sun impotent, its brilliant rays mocking with the promise of warmth never realized. Men and women clad in the same soiled clothes they had worn during the assault on Old Kaper huddled in tight clusters, the puffs of their breathing mingling and rising like the smoke of fires. But few cookfires burned among the refugees; little enough fuel remained, and all lived in fear of an inferno raised by the ShadowMagi camped beyond the palace wall.

More Guardsmen stood watch around the granaries and larders than patrolled the walls. Militiamen circled the barren gardens and orchards like hawks, with orders to arrest any who tried to camp upon the open fields or scavenge for food in the frozen soil. Their presence did little good; fights had become a daily occurrence, looters and thieves skulked through the shadows each night, and dissent bordering on insurrection, fueled by the whispers of the Tachan agents who had infiltrated the grounds during the panic, left the interior of the palace walls nearly as dangerous as the exterior.

Servants from the palace accompanied by a contingent of Guardsmen circled among the masses, dolling out portions of watered-down broth in strictly rationed amounts. The refugees watched the servants with envy and glared at the well-fed Guardsmen with outright enmity; all knew that food stocks remained full despite the raids in the dead of night, and rumors held that the catacombs beneath the castle held chamber after chamber of supplies in anticipation of a long siege. But the King had decreed that only those engaged in the defense of the castle could enjoy the privilege of food, and while the order may have driven a few men and women to enlist, it had done more to sour morale than to inspire loyalty.

Martyn knew the truth of the matter, that while food reserves did exist, they were not as abundant as believed, especially in light of the thousands who had sought refuge at the palace when the Tachans took the old city. And though Ehvan continued to promise grain from Dranakohr once their own needs had been met, Martyn suspected that even magic would not be able to supply enough to feed all of the mouths packed inside the walls.

Two full squads of Guardsmen followed him down the paved path, and a third preceded him, clearing commoners from the road and scanning the masses for assassins. Everywhere he looked he saw fear, fear and hunger and a growing resentment which made him regret the starvation forced on his people, even though it had been his own suggestion. Weakened from hunger and cold, the grumblings of the masses would likely not flare into uprising, not even with the whispers of the Tachans inspiring treason.

We let too many in. It seemed the right thing to do, but we would have been better without them, marshalling our strength, ensuring our protection. Here they are a drain on morale, a viper in our midst, a constant reminder of our failures.

No one spoke during their march. The only sounds were the howling of the winds and the distant sounds of drilling troops. Aryn and another contingent of Guardsmen surveyed the western walls, Bystral the east, and Dayfid the south, leaving Martyn to inspect the defenses on the north side of the city. The inspections had become a daily routine, their goal as much to maintain morale as to seek out weaknesses.

Martyn caught sight of a hooded figure mirroring his path, walking beyond the crowd lining the road with head tucked low. He wondered how Lelani's Magi had managed to stay hidden for so long when such conspicuous stealth was the best most could manage. Nevertheless, he welcomed the Mage's company, especially with ShadowMagi camped just beyond the walls, inspiring terror with their very presence, sowing chaos with unpredictable storms of fire and lighting, of darkness at midday or waves of heat that melted snow and then allowed it to quickly refreeze. Knowing he had something to counter the threat of magic lessened Martyn's burden, even if the need for secrecy meant his people had to think they faced the ShadowMagi unprotected.

The gates to Old Kaper stood barred and barricaded, then braced with heavy timbers scavenged from the city in the days before the attack. Ordered rows of barracks ran along the curve of the wall, simple structures of wood and thatch housing a score of Guardsmen each, intended to keep the bulk of the defenders visible and within a moment's run from the defenses. Three squads guarded the gate, and more soldiers patrolled atop the fortification and along the base, protecting against assault from without and treason from within.

So far, no attack had come. The days following the assault on Old Kaper had been ones of relative quiet, of sudden magical attacks and occasional sorties, of agony as they watched the old city pillaged, its inhabitants brutalized. The Tachans knew no mercy, and worse, delighted in showing off their handiwork to those who still lived free within the palace walls.

At the gate, Martyn sought out the subcommander in charge and listened while the young man reported on the day's events. As usual, the report was tedious, but Martyn feigned interest and complimented the Guardsman on his thoroughness. "The attack is coming, men," he announced to the soldiers standing around him. "Never doubt it. But as long as the Guard is here to defend the city, I know I have nothing to fear."

When Martyn started toward the stairs, the subcommander nearly shouted in his haste to stop him. "My Prince! It's not safe for you up there."

Martyn brushed off the man's concerns. "It is not safe for me anywhere. I want to see my city."

He climbed slowly, followed by his bodyguard, wondering when their presence stopped annoying him. Now, he barely noticed the Guardsmen. In fact, he welcomed them, and it bothered him more when their numbers were reduced by necessity than when they insisted on increasing their size.

The tension atop the fortification was a palpable thing. A heavy curtain closed around him instantly, tearing away the mask of confidence he had determined to wear. He did not need to see the haggard faces of the Guardsmen, the way they moved as if dragging boulders, the dull look in their eyes; these were people who expected defeat, going through the motions solely by virtue of their training. Never as much as now did he approve of Aryn's decision to keep the militiamen off the walls until the attack came. To allow them to face this kind of desperation would be to invite uprising.

He moved down the wall, stopping to offer encouragement to each Guardsman he passed, hoping he managed at least a modicum of sincerity. For the most part the Guard responded well to his presence, and he knew these daily visits had done something to maintain their morale. He doubted it was enough.

He settled between two crenellations in the ivory stone, leaning against the cold rock while he readied himself. With a deep breath, he leaned around the corner and peeked out into Old Kaper.

Fires smoldered throughout the old city, sending tendrils of oily smoke rising into the cloudless sky, where they mingled with the whiter smoke from hearths and cookfires. With so much of the city destroyed, finding fuel to keep warm posed no problem to the Tachans, and they flaunted the luxuries of their occupation, building bonfires just outside of bowshot, feasting on the spoils of war while the defenders looked on from atop the frigid walls.

The manor houses and great estates around the palace had been commandeered, their fields and gardens trampled, their treasures looted. The buildings farther down the hill—those still standing—housed the bulk of the Tachan army or were used as pens to corral those people deemed too dangerous to let roam free yet too valuable to slaughter. Screams rose from the city at all times of day and night, never stopping, hardly lessening in all the days since the attack. The tortured cries pierced the soul, every shriek a plea left unanswered, every cut-off prayer a cruel rebuke. The Tachans displayed the dead in haphazard piles before the walls, taunting the defenders, showing what awaited them when the palace walls came down.

We should have let them in. It was wrong to leave them to such a fate, to such cruel treatment. How many hundreds out there have died who might have joined us, who might even now be ready to defend the palace against the horde?

A short look was all Martyn could stand. "You need not fear the ShadowMagi," Treloran said, misinterpreting the reason the prince ducked behind the stone again. "They never attack anyone admiring their handiwork."

The Aelvin Prince spent more time on the wall than Martyn, circling the fortification and monitoring the preparations of *Ael Chatorra*. The Aelvin archers had been divided into small groups and sprinkled among the Guardsmen. Their keen eyes and deadly aim had been vital in keeping the enemy at bay, but separation from their comrades wore at them, as did thoughts of death far from home and the rumors of troubles back in Illendrylla. Martyn knew more about those troubles than most—sporadic reports from Ehvan about the Empress' desperate flight, pursued and driven north by Luran's forces—and though he had shared his knowledge with Treloran and Jaenaryn, all agreed that common knowledge of the fall of Lynnaei should be suppressed.

Kal accompanied Treloran in his travels, claiming he preferred the open air to the cramped confines of the palace, the threat of battle to the ogling eyes of those who had never seen a Garun'ah. Martyn suspected something else: that the *Kranach* had discovered a kindred soul in the Aelvin Prince, that their shared isolation in Kaper had forged a bond akin to friendship between the two mortal enemies.

"It is not the ShadowMagi I fear," Martyn told them. "I fear that if I look too long upon the carnage, I may lose heart. Or worse, I may demand an attack."

"Battle will come soon," Kal said. "I can smell the blood in the air, the hunger on both sides. You will not wait long."

Martyn blew out a sharp breath, half laugh, half sigh. "Part of me yearns for that day, though the rest of me suspects it will be my last."

"If you fear death, Prince Martyn, I can help. You need but give the word and I will have a thousand Magi on these walls, ready to use their Gift to drive the Tachans out of Kaper."

Martyn whirled around, hand darting to the sword at his side, relieved to see fear akin to his own dance across the faces of Kal and Treloran as they reacted in surprise to the unexpected voice.

Valkov watched from a few hands off, cold eyes staring down his hooked beak of a nose, amusement plastered on his face, the smug confidence in his smile enough to make Martyn want to drive his blade forward instead of return it to its sheath. The High Wizard held the brown-robed Mage who had dogged Martyn's steps by the arm, her cowl thrown back to reveal a thin, dirt-smudged face and terrified eyes. She refused to look at anyone; her gaze kept shifting from the ground to the scene beyond the wall.

"You brought a companion this time?" Martyn asked, hoping his act of ignorance proved convincing enough.

"Ah. Then you don't know who she is?" Valkov shook his head, and his cold gaze fell upon the woman. "I had hoped she was here by your command. Perhaps one of Lelani's rogue Magi seeking succor at the palace?"

"I've never seen that woman before," Martyn said, glad to have the strength of truth behind the statement to cover the lie it hid.

"No? A pity. If she is not with Lelani, then I won't be able to be as gentle in her treatment, as lenient in her punishment." The woman began to tremble, but she held her tongue, and her eyes moved even farther from Martyn. "It should serve as a warning to you though, Prince Martyn. With ShadowMagi on the loose, no defenses are strong enough to protect you. They could have their army inside this palace in an instant, moving with impunity, attacking without warning."

"Beware Magi bearing Gifts, Martyn," Ehvan said, approaching from opposite Valkov and eyeing the High Wizard with a distaste generally reserved for something found living beneath a rock. "The glimmer of gold on the outside often hides a lead core."

"Has he arrived, Ehvan?" Martyn called out.

"Events hold him in the north," Ehvan replied. "Lord Odara will not abandon those who need him. But he will not allow Kaper to fall."

"A convenient promise," Valkov sneered. "One only proven false when it is too late. Odara is not the loyal subject you believe him to be, Prince Martyn. He plays his own game, makes his own rules. He promises help some day; I promise help immediately. He offers you an army of children, Gifted barely old enough to harness their powers; I offer an army of Magi, many of whom have honed their Gift over centuries. He—"

"—will leave you free to rule Alrendria," Ehvan interrupted, "while the High Wizard will make you a slave to the Assembly. How much has he demanded for his aid? How much more will he demand once you are dependent upon him?"

"Better to make an accord with the Assembly now than to wait until your very existence hangs in the balance," Valkov insisted. "When you are desperate, what leverage will you wield over Odara then? In the meantime, who will protect you when the ShadowMagi open Gateways beyond your defenses and flood the palace with soldiers?"

Such a possibility had occurred to Martyn, but his attempts to broach the subject with others—Treloran, Aryn, Lelani, even his greatmother—had all proved fruitless. Treloran and Aryn knew little about the workings of magic; Lelani and Sionel remained surprisingly tight-lipped despite their promises of support. His hesitation did not go unnoticed by Valkov, whose smug smile grew in the face of Martyn's discomfiture.

It was Ehvan who spoke though, hollowing the Mage's victory. "High Wizard, surely you do not attempt to frighten the prince with half truths. Anyone with even a basic understanding of magic knows that to open a Gate with any sort of accuracy, an intimate familiarity with the destination must exist. And that even the most powerful Gifted can only send through a dozen or so soldiers before exhausting himself, which would leave the Mage unable to contribute to the battle in any other way. Or even that the mere fact of crossing through a Gate leaves the traveler disoriented and easily overwhelmed—a fact I can attest to from personal experience."

Martyn, too, remembered the dizziness and uncertainty that had accompanied his sudden return to Kaper from Vela. He could see the truth of Ehvan's other assertions reflected in the sour glare from Valkov. "But how—?"

Ehvan turned toward the prince. "Jeran's Academy welcomes all into its halls, Gifted and Common alike, to foster a better understanding of magic and reduce the tensions that have developed over the centuries. Those who serve him are required to gain an understanding of magic's workings, its strengths and limitations, so that it can be properly employed."

"A prudent move—" Martyn started, but Valkov, his face flushed with a rare display of emotion, cut him off.

"Is that all magic is to Odara, a tool to be wielded, a resource to be harnessed? Has he no respect for the gift of the Gods, no reverence for the majesty of our power?"

"He has no delusions," Ehvan countered, facing the Mage without fear, a feat Martyn believed few alive, man or Mage, could accomplish. "He knows the ability to use magic is a skill, little different than the ability to forge a blade or sail a ship, and that there's nothing inherent in it that makes the Gifted better than any other. Whether it is used to create works of great magnificence or to wreak destruction lies solely within the hearts of its practitioners, men and women no less susceptible to temptations and vices than common men."

Valkov bristled at the implied accusation, glaring with such restrained malevolence that Martyn half expected to see Ehvan burst into flame on the spot. "Odara blasphemes against the very concept of the Gift! We have been entrusted by the Gods—"

"I would not presume to speak for Lord Odara," Ehvan countered, "but perhaps he feels it wiser to blaspheme against the Assembly's hypocrisy than to claim a divine responsibility to protect life and then dangle the promise of magical aid before others in an attempt to maneuver for political gain."

"How dare you speak—!"

"Do you honestly believe that after enduring the manipulations of Lorthas, the brutal passions of Tylor Durange, and the pure malice of Salos the Scorpion that any who come from Dranakohr would show fear before the likes of you? You are the rumble of distant thunder, Mage Valkov, trumpeting danger yet offering no true threat."

Martyn hid a smile, hoping that Valkov mistook his tight-lipped, fixed expression for controlled anger at Ehvan's affront, while wishing he had the political leverage to speak out against the Mage Assembly without risking the safety of Kaper. The High Wizard purpled, struggling to maintain the composure so essential to his performance. Ehvan gave him no chance to speak.

"Also, might I ask why you are manhandling my Mage?"

"*Your* Mage?" Valkov and Martyn said simultaneously.

"Did you think my reports were flown in on the backs of birds, or whispered to me on the wind? My people have been assured of safe passage in Kaper by the King; his assurances have come from the Assembly. Will you release her to me, High Wizard, or should I instruct my Orog to begin detaining any Assembly Magi we stumble across?"

Valkov bit down on his lip, and with a flick of his wrist shoved the Mage toward Ehvan. The young woman trembled, her eyes flicking between Ehvan and Valkov and finally settling on Martyn. "You tread along the razor's edge, Prince Martyn. Marginalize the Assembly at your own risk. Those who have associated with rogue Magi in the past have often regretted it." A Gate opened and the High Wizard vanished.

"A lovable sort, that one," Ehvan said, breaking the silence that filled Valkov's disappearance.

"Why are your Magi wandering the palace grounds?" Martyn demanded. "I thought we agreed they should remain out of sight, to prevent situations just like this one."

Ehvan's face screwed up in confusion. "My Magi...? Oh, her! Never seen her before. Just figured no one wanted the Assembly to have her, least of all her." He turned toward the Mage, who had recovered a measure of decorum and a mountain of indignity. "You and your companions sneak around about as well as fish can sing. It might be best if you confined yourself to the halls of the place. Less conspicuous, at least. And let your mistress know that there's a place for her at our Academy. Lord Odara would not turn away a Mage of her convictions."

The woman said nothing, turning away and hurrying toward the nearest staircase. "You're welcome," Ehvan said to her retreating back.

"Do you intend to infuriate Valkov," Martyn asked, "or is it just a natural ability?"

"I deal with enough condescension from the Magi who've chosen to serve Lord Odara. To the Magi of the Assembly, I get to say much of what I wish I could say to those who claim to be my allies."

In the wake of the Magi's departure, silence fell upon the four, and they turned their attention back to the tortured sights of Old Kaper, the fields of dead displayed for the defenders' pleasure, the regiments drilling just beyond bow range.

"I hope we can survive this," Martyn whispered.

"Hope," Kal spat the word. "What a Human thing to say."

Martyn turned toward the Tribesman and was surprised to find Treloran nodding in agreement. His glare must have demanded an explanation, for the Aelvin Prince addressed him. "Hope is nothing more than faith without conviction. You cannot wish and have something be; to make it true you must believe it."

"The Gods do not grant wishes to the faithless," Kal added. "To receive Their blessings, you must expect Their blessings."

"And if I expect Their blessings and we still lose...?"

"Then you did not have enough faith," Kal replied, "or the faith of your enemies was greater."

"So if good fortune shines upon you, you thank the Gods; and if bad fortune falls, you blame yourself?" Martyn smirked, and shook his head in exasperation. "It sounds like a wonderful ideology... If you're one of the Gods."

Kal bristled, but Treloran laid a restraining hand on the Tribesman's arm. "You must forgive his insult. Remember, their God abandoned them millennia ago. They know no better."

"Every day is a test of faith," Ehvan said, drawing the eyes of the other three, "every experience a hammer blow upon one's character. Upon the forge of life, we are molded by suffering, tempered by tragedy. It is there, when only faith remains, that we will be our strongest. It is there, when life is at its bleakest, that we will understand love." He smiled then, a cautious grin contrary to the mask of stern decorum he generally wore. "I have been to the *lientou*. I have listened to the words of the Mother. Not all Humans are godless."

"Wonderful. That one has lost sight of his soul," Kal said, jutting his chin out toward Martyn, "and that one rambles on like a Gray-skin. I will know no peace among humanity."

"Not everyone can be as cultured as you Wildmen," Treloran said.

Kal looked at the Aelvin Prince silently for a moment, studying his serious demeanor. Then he began to laugh, a roaring sound that filled the air and by its very warmth brought a measure of cheer to all who heard it.

"Come," he told them. "Staring at our death will do us no good. Let us find some *baqhat*, or some of that water you call ale, and drink to those already gone to meet the Gods!"

CHAPTER 37

"That's folly. You don't have the forces to make a strike into the Tachan Empire, not even in diversion. Pull men from any of the areas you seek to control and you risk losing a far more strategic site than any you might claim."

The markers on the map moved, shifting back to their original positions, concentrated clusters spread about the whole of Madryn. Jeran frowned as he studied the pieces, frowned deeper when he considered the deployment of the enemy, separating his armies, hemming them in, slowly tightening the noose around Alrendria. "But a feint at the heart of the Empire might draw—"

"Such a tactic would have worked against Tylor," Lorthas said, settling back in his cushioned seat and drinking deeply from the dark wine he perpetually carried during these meetings. "But Salos sees the bigger picture more clearly and cares nothing about the souls of those under his care. His goal is to sow chaos for his God, to break the bonds that hold societies together until the whole of civilization crumbles. Then he will bask in the glory of anarchy and reap a harvest of blood."

"I don't need the benefit of your imagery."

"My apologies, Lord Odara," Lorthas said with a dip of his head. "I spent many centuries as an orator. One does not shut off the gift of rhetoric so easily."

"You counsel against offense," Jeran said, watching as he shifted the pieces around into a new set of positions, "and you claim I cannot maintain our defense. So what do you propose?"

"I never claimed to have a better plan. I was just pointing out the flaws in yours." Lorthas's finger tapped against his wine glass with rhythmic precision. "Of course, you could redraw your lines, give up on places significant only because you act as if they are. Concentrate your forces and strike back once you've secured your new positions."

Jeran followed the Darklord's gaze across the map. "Kaper? You want me to abandon Kaper?"

"Gilead as well," Lorthas said, as if the addition made the suggestion more palatable. "Kaper is a city significant only because of its role in history and because of the control it exerts on trade up the Celaan. Gilead is lost; there will be no more trade with it, or with the Elves, or with the Garun'ah. Evacuate your people across the river and you have a natural fortification across half of your lands."

"Kaper is a symbol. Its fall would be a death knell for Alrendria."

"Alrendria as it was should fall! It is the shell of a great ideal, propped up by hypocrisy and controlled by a class that fears those with a skill beyond theirs and abuses those born without the privileges of rank. A few decades of oppression might do it some good."

"I made a promise," Jeran snapped. "I will not abandon Kaper on your whim."

"If you intend to succeed, you must learn when to set sentimentality aside, when to abandon casual promises made out of friendship and embrace the choices which will lead you more quickly to your ultimate goal."

"As you did, when you sent assassins to the Assembly under a flag of truce?"

Lorthas's face tightened, his condescending smile stretching until his lips formed a thin, bloodless line. "I am willing to make the decisions that others refuse to make, but I have never lied to my own, nor sent agents under the guise of friendship to harm any Mage, not even those for whom I thought death would benefit all the world."

"Yet Aemon claims—"

"Aemon has claimed many things to further his own ends. If I intended to assassinate him, would I really have sent a child, a boy barely out of his apprenticeship? Kalsbad went to seek accord, to negotiate peace with the Assembly, and after a single day, after a single closeted meeting with the High Wizard, he was denounced and executed without trial! He begged me for the chance to attempt reconciliation, and his devotion to the Assembly was repaid in blood. Tell me, Jeran; who does that make the monster?"

Jeran leaned back in his chair, considering this new insight into the events of the past, and knowing that to press Lorthas too hard would cost him whatever else he might glean from him. "How best to defeat Salos, then?"

"The Scorpion is loyal to nothing, has feelings for no one. You can not threaten him by attacking his lands nor trouble him by massacring his people. To lure him out, the lure must be personal. If he believes he's won, he'll come to watch his victory; if you sufficiently disrupt his designs, he'll come to set matters right. In both cases, you must strike swiftly. Once he knows he is lost, he'll abandon all and start again. He realizes that time matters little to the Gifted, and he would rather hide for a century than risk immediate defeat."

"It's nearly morning," Jeran said, rising from his chair and preparing to leave the Twilight World, "and Jes will give me no peace if I don't get at least a little true sleep. The forced march has us at the limits of our endurance, and her temper balances on a razor's edge."

Jeran moved, and Lorthas's hand shot forward, gripping his arm and holding him tight. "You should not let her get too close," he warned, his voice carrying the power of desperate certitude.

"You don't even know her," Jeran said, pulling his arm free. "She was a child when you were imprisoned."

"It's not that." Lorthas warred with himself, a battle displayed plainly across his generally unreadable expression. "It is when I lost Alwen that I... That I began to make mistakes. For the good of the world, you cannot allow yourself that kind of weakness."

"I cannot wall myself off from the world in order to save it," Jeran said, his voice a match for Lorthas's in conviction. "I cannot accomplish what I hope to accomplish if I do not share the burden with others."

Lorthas's grin turned mocking. "Can you see the future now, too? Do your powers know no bounds?"

"The future, no. But I have seen the past, yours and Aemon's in particular. I have seen how well withholding motives serves one's cause."

With that, Jeran left Lorthas fuming in the Twilight World, but instead of seeking sleep he woke himself. He lay within his tent instead of beneath the night sky only because of the misting rain which had started the evening before, a mist which had cooled overnight and now blanketed the forest in snow and ice. Snow would mark their passage clearly, eliminating any hope of avoiding followers, but only the foolish believed their movements were not closely watched by Luran, even when days passed between attacks; and no one doubted that among those who had sought shelter with Charylla were some loyal to her brother, reporting to their master, biding their time, waiting like tree vipers for the right moment to strike from the shadows.

The Empress's decision to lead her people into exile had provided them with a goal, and even if many feared the thought of abandoning the safety of their ages-old forest, it also instilled in them a sense of purpose, a hope for the future. More importantly, it had restored their faith in the Empress, and for her to survive the trials before her, she would need the trust and devotion of her people, even more, perhaps, than they needed someone like the Empress to believe in.

Jeran dressed and left his tent, walking into the mist, enjoying the feel of the frigid air as it hit his lungs. Sunrise was yet some time off, but already the camp stirred. *Ael Namisa* had begun the arduous chore of preparing provisions for the thousands who had joined them, and of packing the camp away for another day of hard marching. Terror drove their actions, terror and the certainty that an attack was imminent, that it would arrive all the faster if they remained, and that their only chance for survival lay in following the Empress out of Illendrylla.

With his perceptions enhanced by magic, Jeran had no trouble navigating the maze of tents and Elves huddled beneath blankets on the snow-covered ground, but he often wondered how the Elves managed so well. Even with the barest fraction of illumination, they moved with the confidence of midday; on the coldest of nights, they shivered without complaint. Their stoic resolve left his soldiers, with their flickering torches and demand for warming fires, as easy targets for Luran's assassins, beacons to the scouts dogging their trail. Their calm acceptance of the risk, their eager desire to draw Luran out even if it meant they would be the ones to face the brunt of an attack, only compounded Jeran's frustration.

"You stir early, my friend." The *Hohe Chatorra* patrolled with a handful of his soldiers. The ordeal weighed heavily upon Astalian, dragging down his once-proud shoulders and turning the grin he once wore so casually into a mockery of its former mirth.

"And I begin to wonder if you ever sleep," Jeran replied.

"I have slept," Astalian told him, though it sounded like a reminiscence more than a statement.

"The Empress is well?"

"As well as can be expected. She fumes about our direction, but every time we turn west, Luran is waiting. He funnels us north."

"If they push us north, it's because they expect us to find our deaths there."

"No doubt, but we cannot force our way through their lines, not with so many civilians among us."

"My Magi move them as fast as possible. They can't—"

"It is not an accusation, my friend. It is merely the truth. In the end, it will be a comfort to know that some among us have escaped, that Treloran will be left with something to rule."

"We are not dead yet," Jeran reminded him.

"Nor are we safe yet. Luran toys with us now, herding us like cattle. We live only at his whim, while he marshals his forces. When he drops the hammer...." The Aelvin warrior gripped Jeran's arm, and the gesture felt like a parting. "Perhaps it is time for you to leave, my friend. Your empire may yet be saved, though not if you throw away your life here."

"What of the other *Ael Chatorra* you have been in contact with?"

Astalian shook his head. "We can slip scouts through undetected, but gathering them to us remains impossible. Move more than a handful, and Luran falls upon them. All have been told of our destination and have orders to lead as many of our people there as possible. But our faith is faltering, and if we do not trust in the wisdom of Valia, then how can we expect the Goddess to protect us? Without the Gods, there is only the Nothing. I do not jest when I say the end may be coming, Jeran. You would be wise to lead your people from here."

"If success hinges upon the intervention of the Gods, then we *are* lost," Jeran said. "Have faith instead in yourself, in the training and loyalty of your people, and in the support of your allies. United, we can determine our own fates; separated we will fall one by one to our enemies."

"You speak as one of deep conviction, yet you know no God. From where do you draw your strength?"

"If the Gods have the powers you claim, I wonder how they could let such things as I have seen occur. At best they must be constrained by rules of which we do not know; at worst... I do not mean to belittle your faith, but it does not come as easily to me."

"You must believe in the wisdom of the Gods, Jeran." Astalian's features had tightened, his expression a mixture of fanatical devotion and pity, and beneath that, a hidden mirror of shared understanding. "To question their motives is to invite the Nothing into your heart."

"If I believe that the trees will come alive to save us, if I truly believe it, it will not make it so. I do not discount the roles of the Gods, nor do I deny Them; but I will not trust my faith to Them. If one or all of Them covets my devotion, They will have to earn it."

The *Hohe Chatorra* laughed, a genuine laugh that Jeran had thought long banished by the ordeals through which they suffered. "No Elf would dare demand the Gods fight to win their favor. Are all Humans as bold, or do you hold a special place among them?"

"In truth, most Humans devote little time to the contemplation of such matters, even those who still claim a bond to the Gods." Jeran turned his head to where a shifting of the shadows indicated motion, Elves sprinting silently through the darkness to take up positions around the edge of the camp. "Tell your archers to hold their fire, and not to sound the alarm."

Astalian studied him for a moment, then signaled his guards. Two disappeared into the gloom, moving to intercept the sentries. "Is someone coming?"

"Yes." Jeran altered his direction to intercept the new arrivals. "And it is no one we need fear."

On the outskirts of the camp, a boundary visible only to the Elves who guarded it, Jeran waited. When the first glow of light began to filter between the trees, two figures emerged from the mist, huddled in their cloaks, one walking with a limp and leaning heavily on a bladed staff, the other moving with graceful strides, a snow leopard stalking prey through the thick forest.

"Friend Jeran," Grendor called, throwing back his hood and hurrying forward to draw Jeran into an embrace. "I had worried we'd never find you."

"Your return has been greatly anticipated," Jeran warned him. "We suffer under the onslaughts we have endured. Our people demand faith and direction, and I can only offer the latter. I need someone of greater conviction to heal their spirits, someone less calloused to the cruelty of our world, less cynical about the motives of our Gods. No doubt you felt my need through our bond."

Grendor's cheeks flushed dark gray, an embarrassment that flowed from the Orog into Jeran's consciousness. "You heap responsibilities upon me, friend Jeran," he whispered, "and make my own faith a greater thing than it is."

"Only because I must. Only because compared to mine, your faith is a mountain, a bulwark against the suffering I know we must endure." He turned his eyes to Katya, who watched their exchange with a tight smile, but with eyes that showed a hurt so deeply concealed it barely reached him. "I had hoped you'd bring an army. Or, at least, that you wouldn't come alone."

"He would not come, nor would you have wanted him. And I..."

"It was wrong of me to ask you. If it needs to be done, I will do it myself. But I will not give up on him until he has given himself completely to Kohr."

"Dahr serves no God—"

"It doesn't matter what he believes. The path he treads leads to chaos, and chaos serves the disciples of Kohr."

Jeran introduced his companions to Astalian, and the group started back to the heart of the camp. Katya studied their defenses in the growing light, her eyes darting from tree to tree, to the archers positioned among the branches, to the smaller groups of Humans and Orog concealed within thick brush. She saw then the vast array of tents spread before them, the thousands of servants, merchants, and tradesmen seeking protection from Luran's forces, and her expression grew grim.

"You need more men along the periphery," she told him. "There are Tribesmen massing north of here. Your defenders could never stop them all, and one well timed strike would end in slaughter."

"Man a post," Jeran said. "You're all the extra swords we have at the moment."

"You have an entire army training in Dranakohr. Bring them—"

"I have forbidden it," Astalian announced. "And the Empress agrees with me. If our survival had not depended so often on Jeran's presence, we would have sent him and the rest of his people away as well. There is no gain in sacrificing two for the chance to save one, whether you speak of men or nations."

"I see…" Katya saw beyond Astalian's statement, to the truth Jeran concealed from all: even had the Empress demanded every sword at his disposal, or begged for them, he would have refused. She sensed the conflict within him, the desire to protect a friend, the need to preserve an ally balanced against the welfare of Alrendria and the goals of the greater war.

Their arrival at the camp was greeted with cheers from Jeran's followers and curious, half-hidden staring from the Elves. The Alrendrians from the embassy, Utari primarily, eyed Katya with suspicion, but when Jeran treated her as a friend, the noblewoman hid whatever animosity she harbored for the Durange and with quietly-issued commands demanded that her entourage do the same.

The Gifted, however, barely paused in their task, stopping only long enough to make sure the noise they heard did not signal the start of another attack before resuming their duty. Fatigue tethered them to the ground. Like ships moored in harbor they shifted back and forth but could not find the strength to move from their berths. When exhaustion overwhelmed them, they collapsed where they stood and were nursed by *Ael Namisa* until strong enough to open another Gate.

"It seems you fare worse than the Tribes," Katya said, though she spoke low enough that only Jeran could hear.

"The retreat has been difficult," Jeran admitted. "Luran swells our numbers with refugees, knowing that the Empress will not abandon them, and then harasses us from the shadows."

"You should be evacuating the soldiers first," Katya told him, "and then those with serviceable skills. An army of servants and merchants—"

"Means that the Aelvin culture will not die out, even if all we struggle for here is gone." Jeran regretted his curt tone, and he moved to soothe what he knew without his strange abilities would have flared Katya's temper. "Your suggestion makes practical sense, but one cannot always follow logic, even in war. What army could function knowing it had abandoned those who depended on it?"

"Only my father's," came Katya's terse response.

The attack came with little warning, a strangled, cut-off horn blast followed by a hail of arrows. The camp burst to life, with warriors discarding breakfast bowls and taking up weapons, running—sometimes half-clothed—in the direction of clashing swords. *Ael Maulle* directed their Gifts into the trees, using their magic to spot the enemy and direct the soldiers. Some of Jeran's forces drew a protective ring around their Magi, and other squads advanced through the trees, systematically sweeping the camp for the assassins that often accompanied these raids.

The battle ended as quickly as it began, with another trumpet blast signaling the retreat of Luran's forces. The day's march began soon after, a swift pace made more arduous by the wet snow and tangled underbrush through which they had to navigate. Their path led northwest—not by choice, scouts reported enemy archers massing to the south and west—driving them farther away from their goal, closer to the Tribal Lands, where even those who did not serve Kohr the Destroyer would be likely to treat an army of Elves as enemies.

The jubilation of Katya and Grendor's arrival soon faded, and they, too, were drawn into the pattern of march and fight, fight and march. The days that followed blended together, merging into a single, convoluted memory, a nightmare maelstrom of lightning attacks, hurried flights, and restless slumber. Even in the aftermath of successful skirmishes, the morale of the army deteriorated; the more costly battles made it all but impossible to resume the hopeless, plodding march north, away from the lands of men, a direction which meant death in any case, just not by the hands of Elves.

One such day dawned cold and clear, a crisp wind keening through the trees, an elegy for those gone before, a dirge for those yet to die. Ice clung to the branches, glittering in the morning sunlight, sparkling and dancing like daytime stars. Jeran wondered at the thick snow on the ground, wondered how it accumulated so fully despite the dense, interwoven limbs, wondered how it could look so beautiful, so pure, even when death hovered so closely over it.

His subcommanders gathered around him, waiting for orders. "Today... Today is the day." Jeran caught the curiosity in the eyes of his men. "No, I have no magical insight, no premonition; today just feels different. I can see in your eyes that many of you feel it too. We have been driven to the slaughterhouse. Now the butchers come."

A murmur of consent arose from his men, but it died down quickly when Jeran stood. "Advise the Magi to rest. If the battle is lost, they are to take those of us who remain to safety, and as many Elves as they can carry besides. Should it come to that, the Empress should be taken to Dranakohr, Astalian as well. By request if possible, by coercion if necessary. Both will serve us better alive than dead, even if they would prefer the Twilight World to ours."

"Why did we stay, Lord Odara?" asked a man Jeran barely knew, a former prisoner of Tylor's, a stranger who had devoted himself to Jeran and the cause he fought for. "If we plan to abandon them now rather than fight to the last; if our efforts still leave the Aelvin army dead on the roots of these Gods-forsaken trees, then what good have we done?"

"What good? We have brought thousands to safety and given thousands more who would otherwise already be dead a chance to live. We have ensured that, even if this day sees us all dead upon these 'Gods-forsaken trees', that some measure of the Aelvin Empire, of all that was built by Alwellyn the Eternal, will survive. If that is not enough to justify our sacrifice, then consider that the Elves here are our allies, and to many of us, our friends, and that should be answer enough."

"Then why forsake them now?"

Jeran's slight smile carried more sadness than mirth. "We have not forsaken them yet, nor do I hope it comes to that. But we fight a larger war. If throwing our lives away here on a principle leaves even thousands more to die, if it leaves Madryn to the mercy of Salos and the servants of Kohr, then our deaths serve no purpose. In the end, though, you have all served with distinction; it is I who must make the tough choices, and it is I who history will hate if I choose poorly."

"Now go," he told them. "You know where you're needed. You know what must be done." He watched as his men receded into the trees, wondering how many of them he would see again at twilight. The mere thought of their deaths started an ache in his gut, played a symphony of sorrow across the bonds that held him to his people.

Dressed for battle and looking eager for a fight, Astalian appeared a moment later. "You know?" he asked, studying Jeran's garb and the way he had made little effort to pack up his belongings.

"Do they come from the north, or the south?" Jeran asked.

"Both. We will be squeezed in the vise."

The imagery evoked by the Elf's statement did not instill confidence, and Jeran banished such thoughts from his mind. He sought the meditative peace of the Orog, the calm nothingness that gave them their poise, their unflappable composure. He had only marginal success.

"It will be a hard day to win."

"That is why I am here. Charylla... The Empress requires a promise from you. If the battle turns against us, you will take your men and leave, and you will take this to Treloran." He handed Jeran an envelope sealed with the Imperial Signet. "Your service to the Empire has been noted—and appreciated—but the Empress fears that your presence in the Twilight World will torment her for eternity."

"I did not realize my company was so onerous," Jeran replied, and when Astalian blanched, he smirked. "The day is not lost yet, my friend. But if the battle turns against us, you have my word that I will leave the forest with as many as my Magi can carry."

"We should go," Astalian told him, offering a hand and pulling Jeran into a swift embrace when he stood. "Our scouts report that the enemy will be here before full light."

Jeran circled the camp once before the battle, studying the clusters of archers perched in the trees, the knots of foot soldiers bunched behind broad trunks. Human, Orog, and Elf working together toward a common goal, sharing their lives and deaths as brothers. Some had worked for millennia to achieve such a sight, and if not for the knowledge that this newfound unity could easily lie dead on the floor of the Great Forest by nightfall, Jeran would have felt pride at his accomplishment.

The Aelvin commoners clustered in the center of the camp, huddled together for protection. When the battle started, the youngest would be hidden beneath thick blankets and protected by a wall of thin shields. Every Elf, from the lowliest *Ael Namisa* to the most arrogant *Ael Alluya* shared in the defense of the children. Each had been issued weapons that they held like vipers, and all stood shoulder to shoulder, ready to defend their people to the last. They would fight until the end to defend their Empress, but should Charylla signal flight, they would scatter, scatter and hope that at least a fraction might escape the wrath of Luran.

Jeran's Gifted formed a second circle not far from the Elves, but even closer to the well-guarded tents of the Empress. A ring of soldiers stood around them, and a ring of archers around them. Losing the Elves would hurt his cause, but the loss of so many Gifted would cripple him in the greater war. *I never should have allowed so many to come. Lorthas is right. I allowed sentimentality to cloud my judgment. Let's hope I don't pay for it in the days to come.*

He had little time to mull over his mistakes. A shrill note signaled the start of the attack, and a moment later the hum of arrows filled the air, the dark streaks of their passage like the fall of deadly rain. Shouts and screams echoed through the trees; the clang of steel beat the cadence of battle. From the north came the howls of the *Kohr'adjin*, answered by the roar of the soldiers following Goshen.

Jeran opened himself to magic, extending his perceptions, making himself aware of the battle around him even as he focused on the area of fiercest fighting. He tried to ignore the shadow pain dancing across the body, the sudden ache as bonds were severed by death, the emptiness he felt after each such loss; but every wounded soldier, every fallen comrade increased his anger, heightened his desire for vengeance. That too traversed the bonds, inspiring those who yet lived to acts of boldness.

His own sword thirsted for blood, and Jeran let it gorge upon his enemies. He raced among the trees, running ahead of most of the defenders, cutting down any enemy who dared to cross his path. With his Gift he hauled archers down from the trees, where they made easier targets for his own men. Walls of air slammed against massed attackers, the concussive blasts deafening those around them, driving many to the ground with such force that they made no attempt to rise again. Steel and magic worked in unison, a perfect balance, as beautiful in symmetry as it was abhorrent in destruction.

His soldiers followed behind, cutting down those who remained standing, slaughtering the insensate and the wounded. The barbarity of it struck at Jeran, even as he understood the necessity, even as he used his Gift to topple a tree into a massed line of enemy and watched as it crushed the life from their bodies.

His morning became a constant race, a rush to where the fighting was direst, to where the defense was weakest. His efforts consistently drove the enemy back, but they always found another path, pushed ever closer to the center of camp, until the shrieks of children sliced across the forest, a terrified wail that hurt Jeran more than all the deaths he had shared during the fighting.

Jeran sprinted toward the camp and found a knot of Tribesmen and Elves engaged in a massacre unlike anything he had ever before seen. *Ael Namisa* stood bravely against the horde but were swept aside by the broad axes of the Tribesmen or cut down by the finer swords of the Elves. Hundreds upon hundreds lay dead or dying, and the Elves guarding the Empress watched in horror from the distance, unwilling to forsake their posts to protect their people. Even farther off, the soldiers he had left to protect the Magi hovered on the verge of a charge, and the Magi themselves fought to restrain themselves, saving their Gift for the evacuation they knew was coming.

Why do they choose now to obey my orders, rather than do 'what they think is right'? Not waiting for his men to catch up, Jeran dove into the fray, relieved to see Grendor lead a force of Orog and Elves out of the trees opposite him. Unable to use magic for fear of harming his allies, Jeran relied on his blade. He came upon his enemy from the side, carving a path through them, bolstered with a perverse joy as he watched the child-killers fall to his sword.

He met Grendor in the middle of the field, noting the anger in the Orog's gaze, the lack of remorse that usually hovered about him whenever he was forced to kill. "This savagery is beyond even what the Gods could imagine," Grendor said. "I have never been so glad the Mother no longer walks among us."

The decision Jeran knew he had to make burdened him, made him feel a coward and a traitor all at once, but he could no longer stare at the odds arrayed against them and pretend they had a chance of survival. "Signal the retreat." A hasty series of horn blasts cut off with abrupt finality, justifying Jeran's decision. "It seems the Elves agree. Grendor, come with me."

The Orog eyed him curiously as they hastened toward the Empress's tents. "Charylla will not want to leave," Jeran said. "I may need you to quiet her Gift long enough to get her away."

"We are going to kidnap the Empress?"

"If it comes to that."

Across the clearing hundreds of Gates appeared, glimmering jewels twinkling in the distance, tantalizing with images of safety, with lush fields and tranquil greenery backed by the thick, snow-covered mountains beyond the protection of Dranakohr. In this last flight from Illendrylla, his Gifted would push themselves to the edge of death to get as many away as possible. After the last Gate closed, all who remained would be left to find their own fate.

From the north Jeran heard the distant sound of renewed fighting, and he wondered how Goshen still had the strength. His own arms felt like lead, his legs burned with the effort, and his heart ached at the thought of more death. To the south, the sounds of battle were more sporadic, but far nearer and drawing closer.

The Aelvin guards blocked his passage. "The Empress commanded that no one is to pass," announced a hard-eyed veteran, his gaunt face drawn in a cold frown.

"I intend to take the Empress to safety, regardless of her wishes." The Elves tensed, but Jeran stayed them with a gesture. "I do not want to fight you, but I will not be dissuaded. I will not let the Empress die here, or be held by Luran as a trophy of his victory. As long as she lives, so does the Empire."

The war on the Aelvin warrior's face was plain, but it was a short one. "I have served the Empire my entire life. I will not disobey my final command, not even if it is a foolish one. I will take comfort knowing that once I am dead, you—"

A new roar came toward them from the north, a thundering chant growing nearer by the moment, and driving before it not Jeran's allies, but the scattered remains of the Tribesmen who fought them.

Jeran readied for a renewed fight, but the *Kohr'adjin* darted around them, seeking the quickest path back to the trees and disappearing again as quickly as they arrived. Before anyone had a chance to discuss their incredulity, more Tribesmen burst from the trees, led by Goshen and a woman on horseback, a woman carrying Alrendrian weaponry but dressed like a Tribesman. Free of the trees, the chant of the Tribesmen became clear. "*Korahn! Korahn! Korahn!*"

Vyrina spotted Jeran and turned her horse toward him, skidding to a stop a few hands distant. "Your timing is remarkable, Guardsman," Jeran said, a slight smile tugging at his lips.

"As to that," Vyrina replied, leaping from her horse and gripping Jeran's arm in greeting, "we may have provoked this attack. The *Kohr'adjin* discovered our approach and rushed to assault you before we could arrive."

"This attack was planned regardless," Jeran told her, noting how her eyes riveted on the field of dead not far behind them, the twisted bodies of men, women and children and those still alive who had nowhere to go to escape the grisly sight. "If you were what started it, you are also what may have altered its conclusion."

A measure of relief entered the Guardswoman's expression, and Jeran turned his eyes to the Garun'ah. Many pursued the *Kohr'adjin*, or drove south toward Luran's army, joined by *Ael Chatorra* who ran beside them to prove that they were allies. A few milled about the edge of the clearing, shifting uncomfortably beneath the stares of so many Elves.

"He is not here," Vyrina said, answering Jeran's unspoken question. "Dahr said his path took him in another direction, to a battle he must face alone, but he could not abandon his family. He said he's sorry for taking so long to realize that, and for other things as well. And he wishes you well."

Jeran drew a slow breath and nodded. "And Frodel? I can't believe he'd let you—" He regretted the question immediately, even before he saw the color drain from Vyrina's face, the mantle of suffering settle so firmly on her shoulders. "Gods... He was a good man."

"He was the—" The rest of what Vyrina intended was cut off by motion within the Aelvin tents. Charylla approached, dressed in the finest garb she had in her sparse, travel-worn collection, and studied both the Guardswoman and the Garun'ah who encircled her camp.

Vyrina dropped to one knee. "Empress, I bear tidings from Dahr Odara, *Cho Korahn Garun* and *Kranor* of the Channa. 'There has been much strife between Elf and Garun'ah. There remains much difference. But our peoples fear chaos more than each other. We each struggle against servants of Kohr, monsters determined to destroy what those before us have built. I will not suffer any people—not even if they are called my blood enemies—to live enslaved. My Hunters are yours to command until you reclaim your old throne or reach your new one.' "

For a time, Charylla said nothing; the only sound was the battle, moving steadily south, fading for the first time since the clash started. The Empress's gaze shifted between Vyrina and Jeran, and it seemed as if moisture glistened behind those probing green eyes.

"For too long have we let the differences in belief drive wedges between us. The intervention of Garun's Chosen One may have very well saved my Empire this day, and that is a sacrifice not easily forgotten. May Valia bless him for all of his days, and when next you see him, tell him wherever I rule, he and his people will be well come."

A ripple of conversation spread out from the Empress, a moving wave spoken low, a fresh wind blowing in with the dawn. Jeran stepped forward. "Empress, I should rejoin the fight, and if Luran truly has been forced back—"

"You have already stayed too long, Lord Odara," Charylla said, though her stern expression carried both gratitude and humor. "I know other battles call you; other nations need your help. But do not think your plan to take me from my people would have gone as smoothly as you wanted. You are not undefeatable."

"Do you know where—?"

"We have discussed it endlessly. I know our destination. I have the documents you prepared. I do not need a child to hold my hand through the remainder of the journey." She turned once more to study Vyrina. "Especially not with my own honor guard of Garun'ah."

Jeran bowed his head. "Then, with your permission..."

"Go, Lord Odara. And if you think they will aid your cause, take as many of my archers as you can stuff through your Gates. I suspect our victory today will stall Luran long enough for us to escape unharassed."

Jeran moved south to seek out the battle, but it advanced ahead of him, always out of reach, moving steadily away from the camp. The only enemies he encountered were dead or dying; the only allies he found limped toward the camp or had already departed for the Twilight World. He returned after a time, relieved to have been spared more fighting.

In his absence, Grendor and Katya gathered those of his men who were not still pursuing the enemy. They waited in two groups: the injured and the uninjured. *Ael Namisa* tended the former, the latter, exhausted and covered in the gore of battle, stood ready to follow Jeran. A group comprised of a few dozen *Ael Chatorra* joined them, and the Gifted approached as well, waiting for Jeran's orders.

"You served me well today," Jeran told his people, feeling his pride reflected back at him through the bonds they shared, a synergistic loop that renewed the strength of all. "You deserve a rest. You deserve to live out the rest of your days in blissful peace, but for us, the battles may just be beginning. We can tarry here no longer. It is time to go."

A hand grabbed his shoulder, pulling him around. Panic suffused Aemon's gaze, a wild terror Jeran had never before seen in the old Mage's knowing eyes. "Where are you going?"

They had spoken little in the past season. Aemon had avoided his company as much as possible, sharing words with him only when forced.

"Home."

"You can't go there!" It sounded as much a plea as a command.

"The Empress believes she's safe. Safe enough to escape Luran—"

"This is not about the Empress. Or the Elves! You cannot go!"

"Why?"

Aemon hesitated, but in the end refused to offer an explanation. "You just can't."

"For days you've demanded that I leave." Jeran said, anger tingeing his voice. "Now that I plan to, you want me to stay?" He turned to the Gifted. "Prepare to link your Gift to me. I will open the Gate."

Aemon's grip became more desperate. "If you go now, Lorthas will walk free of the Boundary." He spoke low, his words a hushed whisper. "If you go now, he will laugh amidst the ruins of the Assembly Hall. I have seen it!"

"Another Foretelling?" Jeran pulled free of Aemon's grip. "I have seen the salvation wrought by listening to your Gift in the past. I will not ignore the threats of today for the possibilities of tomorrow."

"I will not let you go," Aemon snarled, opening himself to magic. "I will not let that monster roam free in Madryn again. Not after what—"

"Do not make me humble you," Jeran snapped. He whispered now, but his words carried the direst of threats. "It would serve no one here—the great Aemon least of all—for you to be publicly defeated by a child barely old enough to harness his Gift. And we both know who will arise the victor in a duel of magic, don't we?"

Louder, so that his words carried over the assemblage, Jeran said, "I appreciate your advice, Aemon, and I agree. You should remain here to speed the evacuation and warn us if Luran's forces return."

Jeran left Aemon red-cheeked and struggling to hold his temper in check, to save face before those who saw him as more a legend than a man. He had even less desire to coddle the old man's pride than he did to change his plans based on a snippet of vision caught in a moment of panic.

Once among the Gifted, Jeran assumed control of magic. The rush of power invigorated him, and the focusing of so much energy would allow him to move far more men, but it came with its own cost: everyone involved would arrive too tired to wield magic for some time, and he would be lucky not to collapse on the spot, as the one who focused the Gift bore the brunt of the efforts.

A Gate spun open before him, leading to a dark, torch-lit cavern. At his signal, men began marching through—Humans and Orog without hesitation, Elves staring at the darkness as if they approached the Nothing. More than a hundred Human soldiers and half again as many Orog and Elves crossed through the Gate before Jeran began to feel the strain, at which point he signaled the soldiers to stop and the Gifted to cross.

Two by two the Gifted passed through, clearing the opening and then dropping to the stone floor, heaving deep breaths with the effort of maintaining the link. By the time Katya and Grendor crossed, Jeran could barely draw breath. He gave a parting wave to Astalian, who wore a smile that spoke of renewed hope as he saluted back.

The darkness hid the hammer blow that staggered him as he entered the cavern. Jeran closed the Gate and released his hold on magic, hoping for a moment of respite. Instead of relief, it felt as if the mountain fell upon him, crushing the air from his lungs, with an iron vise squeezing the life from his muscles and a mire of thick mud beneath, slowing his movements and threatening to suck him under. He looked for a wall to lean on, or any sort of crutch. When none were available, he swallowed the pain, hid his exhaustion, and forced himself to move.

"Who's in charge here?" he called out, gasping for air. A flurry of movement exploded in the distance.

"I am, Lord Odara," said a man of middle age, a soldier with whom Jeran had no bond, nor any recollection.

"Find our people food and pallets. I'm going topside."

"Will you need an escort?"

"No. I remember the way."

Jeran moved through the twisting caverns, the cold halls chiseled into the stone. He passed chambers filled with provisions or packed with soldiers wearing the black uniforms of The Army of the Boundary. Dozens of young Gifted meditated under the supervision of Orog *choupik*, or practiced wielding magic before groups of stern-eyed Magi. He heard the echoes of sparring and the distant murmur of conversation, caught and carried by the twisting caves.

When he reached the bolted door, Grendor grabbed his arm. "Friend Jeran, where are we? These are our people, but not the caves of Dranakohr."

"There was no time to visit Dranakohr," Jeran answered. He unbolted the door and swung it open, startling the young Guardsman who stood outside.

"I am Lord Odara," he told the boy, who struggled to pull the sword he carried free of its scabbard. "Take me to Prince Martyn."

"I told you he was here," Ehvan said, turning a corner, the prince walking at his side. A few dozen Guardsmen followed behind, and they were not so slow to draw their blades when they saw Jeran, armed and filthy from the battle in the Aelvin forests.

"So you did," Martyn said, signaling the Guardsmen to lower their weapons. His gaze slipped past Jeran, and the momentary joy that had flashed across his features was replaced with a caustic animosity.

"I promised I wouldn't let Kaper fall," Jeran said, moving forward and gripping Martyn's arms fondly at the shoulders. In a low voice meant for the prince alone, he said, "She is under my protection. No harm will come to her. Do you understand me, Martyn?"

"You waited until there wasn't much left standing, though." Martyn's smile remained fixed, his tone jovial, but under his voice he added, "Is this the price of your service? Must I suffer the enemy on my very threshold? Wonder at which step she will thrust the knife into my back again?"

"My service has no price," Jeran replied. Down the hall, he saw the Mage Konasi poke his head around a corner. Seeing Jeran, he disappeared again, his hasty footfalls fading quickly out of earshot. "But my patience has its limits. Trust her or not, however you see fit. But I tell you she is no traitor and poses no threat to Kaper. There was once a time when my word would have been enough."

"There was once a time when the whole of Kaper wouldn't be in flames before you found the time to come to its aid, or when an army loyal only to you camped in the catacombs beneath my castle."

The bile in Martyn's voice fled as he waved a Guardsman forward. "Find them quarters. And bring food. I will inform the King of their arrival." He turned his eyes on the bodyguard arrayed behind him. "And hold your tongues about what you've seen. Victory may depend on your silence."

Martyn turned toward Jeran. "When do we attack?"

"This was Ehvan's plan," Jeran said, turning toward his subcommander. "I know nothing of the numbers waiting in the catacombs below, nor of the readiness of the forces topside."

"Two days," Ehvan answered. "Haste is essential, but you're on the verge of collapse. No doubt the men you brought are just as exhausted."

"Two days," Martyn agreed. "Two days will decide our fate."

CHAPTER 38

"It's time." Dahr prodded the blanket-wrapped form with a foot. A groggy groan issued from beneath, but Dahr sensed the instant change in consciousness, saw the hidden movement of a hand clutching a dagger and then releasing it.

"It's as black a night as I've ever seen," Lord Fayrd said, throwing off his blanket as he sat up, frustration and fatigue reflected in the flickering of distant torchlight. The Keeper of Grenz disliked leaving his city to pursue the Tachan army; he liked relying on Dahr and his Hunters for information about the enemy far less. "You Garun'ah may be able to run in the dark, but Humans require at least a hint of light."

"Sunrise will come before long. We need to be ready to move when it does."

"It won't do us any good to come upon the enemy if we're too exhausted to fight," Fayrd snapped, but he rose and began folding his bedroll. Guardsman's leather armor—well-cared-for but showing obvious disuse—lay atop Fayrd's gear, and the old warrior began donning it as soon as he secured his blankets to the loops on his saddlebags.

"It won't do our allies any good if we come too late," Dahr replied. "Or would you want the fate of Eastern Grenz visited on Aurach… or Kaper?"

Fayrd grimaced, but made no additional complaints while rousing his sub-commanders. Dahr had not expected much of a fight from the old Guard Commander; images of Grenz haunted his own dreams, and he had thought himself long calloused to such sights. For one like Lord Fayrd, a Guardsman committed to the ideals of Alrendria, a man troubled by the choices he had made long ago, reminders of Gral's destruction were a tool highly effective and easily used.

In the wake of the Battle of the Ten Hills, Dahr had debated which army to pursue, which vengeance to seek first. The weather decided him; a violent storm from the north obscured Kraltir's tracks, bringing with it numbing cold and driving what game remained into hiding. Faced with an entire winter of snow and ice pushed by winds powerful enough to scour flesh from bone, saddled with tens of thousands of mouths, women and children and those who could not fight, duty compelled him south.

The *Kranora* resisted his decision. Abandoning the Tribal Lands to the *Kohr'adjin* smelled too much like defeat. But the Blood's losses at Ten Hills had been staggering, and with so many Hunters fallen, with so many already suffering from hunger and exposure, and with the *Tsha'ma* siding with Dahr, reminding all that the Korahn had come to save the Blood, not the Tribal Lands, the *Kranora* had little choice but to relent. They complained bitterly, and many glared at him as if he were their true enemy, but they followed.

Tracking Gral proved simple even with the weather working against them. The Tachan army ravaged the earth wherever they passed, leaving a bare and blasted scar the worst of hunters could follow. And Dahr had the best, both in his Tribesmen and in the thousands of eyes that roved the skies for him.

A countryside devoid of life, stripped of vegetation, with game slaughtered even when it was not used to feed the passing warhost justified Dahr's decision. Gral represented a threat to nature itself, and his casual destruction showed a scorn for life that Kraltir by nature of his upbringing would never be able to match. Yet the carnage seen whenever the Tachan army encountered civilization made the blasted landscape vibrant in comparison. Fields poisoned so nothing would grow, livestock massacred and left to rot; whole villages razed, the inhabitants slaughtered and set out in macabre display; the blackened husks of buildings, the ashes of entire lives, all for Dahr's benefit. Gral taunted him, tested him, tried to draw the monster forth, to goad him into a suicidal attack.

"A bit early for that," Lord Fayrd said, gesturing at the flask of *baqhat* Dahr raised to his mouth. Dahr glared at him but held his tongue. His temper had no effect on the old Guardsman, who claimed to have companioned with Tribesman far more volatile. The few tirades he had witnessed brought more mirth to Fayrd's face than fear, and the mocking smiles did little to assuage Dahr's temper.

The fiery liquid dulled the ache; it dimmed the memories of Grenz, the blasted shell of a once-great city, the eerie silence of its debris-filled streets, the taunting accusation that, once again, he had arrived too late to matter.

"I understand, though," Fayrd told him. "I've sought solace in a bottle. Once it's gone, the demons return. There's only two ways to make them die. Forget them, or avenge them."

Dahr looked at the Guardsman, a man besieged by his own monsters, with eyes haunted by dark memories, and tossed the skin to the ground. Fayrd was a mirror of what Dahr feared he might become. "Is that why you agreed to come with me?"

Fayrd held his tongue for a time, as if debating how much he wanted to admit. "Duty compelled me south, but the chance at redemption made it an easier choice." He looked to the east, where the faintest light dusted the horizon. "I thought you were in a hurry."

Dahr mounted Jardelle and gave the signal to march. All around him shadows came alive with moving Tribesmen, wraith-like hunters on the prowl, rank after silent rank moving south, first at a walk and then a jog, fast enough to keep pace with the Humans' horses. Behind them marched Guardsmen, more professional but far louder. The clatter of their armor, the stomping and snorting horses, and snippets of idle conversations drowned out whatever whisper-like noises the Hunters made. Dahr prided himself on his troops, and from the way Fayrd and his subcommanders studied the Tribesmen, they shared in his admiration. And yet Dahr wondered if by teaching the Garun'ah how to control their tempers and fight as an army, he had lessened them in some way.

Dahr rode in silence, lost in the memories of Grenz, harassed by visions of the Tribal Lands, anxious over the fate of those he had sent east with Vyrina, and of the tens of thousands who had crossed the Celaan, seeking safety from the *Kohr'adjin* on Alrendrian soil. Lord Fayrd rode beside him, eyes fixed on the horizon, mouth set in an unreadable line, humming what sounded like a dirge.

The Keeper of Grenz had not liked the idea of letting Dahr's people into Alrendria, even if his *army* had consisted mostly of children and toothless Tribesmen. Dahr understood his reluctance—the last time Fayrd let an army cross the Celaan it precipitated the Tachan War—and he appreciated the compassion which eventually compelled the Guardsman to relent.

"It is said that *Synat Sal'aqran*'s army only razed Grenz after you refused to let them cross into Alrendria," Dahr said, breaking the silence. Fayrd's humming stopped, his head shifting ever so slightly in Dahr's direction. "Which troubles you more: your decision to let Tylor the Bull cross unchallenged, or your refusal to let Gral do the same?"

"It is said that Garun's Chosen likes to find the blade in a man's heart and twist it until he screams," Fayrd answered. He showed no outward reaction, but his tone held all the fury of an avalanche about to fall. "One might wonder at the wisdom of goading one's allies on the eve of battle."

Something stirred within Dahr, a seething tide seeking release, but he held it down. "My words were chosen poorly. For once I sought wisdom, not battle. I wish to know what haunts a man more: a tragedy visited upon his own people, or a horror visited upon another's."

Fayrd studied him for some time, his profile silhouetted in the gray light of morning. "Both haunt me, and will until the end of my life, perhaps into the Twilight World beyond. Yet even if the consequences of my choices drive me toward madness, the belief that I made the right decisions, the best decisions given the circumstances, allows me to cling to sanity. I wonder though, who you consider your own people..."

"Korahn!" Tarouk appeared, dragging a bloodied and unconscious human, tossing the Tachan to the ground at the feet of their horses. A handful of trackers followed behind, two clutching wounds severe enough to have felled lesser men.

"Have the *Tsha'ma* tend their wounds before they die before me, swearing they feel no pain," Dahr snarled, and the injured Tribesmen walked away after Tarouk repeated the orders in Garu. "Where is he from?"

"*Synat Sal'aqran* half day ahead. We catch by morning. Hunters find man foraging. Think you might want talk."

Fayrd looked at the battered man splayed out before them and shook his head. "By the time we got anything useful out of him—if he knows anything useful—we'll have let the Tachans grow their lead. Better to kill him here and be on our way. There's a steep bend in the river not too far south. If we push hard, we may be able to trap—"

The Tachan's groan cut off the rest of Fayrd's words. As his eyes fluttered open and he made a move to stand, a half dozen *dolchek*s slipped from their sheaths, but Dahr drew no weapon as he leapt from Jardelle's back. Landing beside the Tachan, he pinned the man to the ground by clamping a hand around his throat. "If you value your life," he said, his voice cracking like thin ice on a frozen river, with the current rushing past beneath, "you will tell us all you know."

"Men do not obey dogs," the Tachan spat back, "not even well trained ones. I can tell you nothing you don't already know, and I will not tell you even that much."

Dahr squeezed until the man had trouble drawing breath. The veneer of control he maintained strained; something pounded against the ice from below, striving to hasten its breaking. "Do you know who I am?"

"We all know who you are, Dahr Odara, traitor of Alrendria, murderer of Tribesmen, beloved disciple of Kohr the Father. You are revered among the priests, honored by our warriors, and feared less than only the Scorpion himself. But you are still a Tribesman, and men do not take orders from beasts."

Dahr's control fell away, and he unleashed a series of blows upon the Tachan. It took both Tarouk and Lord Fayrd to pry him off, and still the Tachan smiled at him through bloody teeth and laughed. "You are fearsome, but there is nothing you can do worse than what *Sal'aqran* will do if I betray him."

"In that, you are wrong, for I have tools that even the Scorpion does not have."

Tarouk gripped Dahr's hand and pried it away from the Tachan's throat. He showed no fear at the venomous gaze his actions drew from Dahr. "Garun teach that those captured in battle need be treated with same respect as Lesser Voices captured on hunt, and that those who mistreat their prey spend eternity in the Nothing."

"This man is no Hunter," Dahr growled.

"Crow not eagle, nor rat lion, yet Garun teach that all equal in His eyes."

Dahr looked to Lord Fayrd for support, but the Guardsman shook his head. "Like as not he knows as little as he claims. Do what you must, but don't pretend it's for anyone but yourself."

Dahr drew a deep breath, then backed away from the Tachan. "You need not fear for my soul, Tarouk. I will abide by the Hunter's teachings, and leave his fate to nature." He opened himself to the Lesser Voices, calling for those bearing a grudge against man, those angered by the desecration of nature.

Relief flashed across the Tachan's face, but only for a moment. Suspicion replaced it when the first judge appeared, a fox with the shaft of an arrow still protruding from its side. It circled him slowly, teeth bared and the foam of madness bubbling from its maw. Others soon followed, rats and wolves and vultures, and a multitude of others, some just to watch, some eager to mete out justice.

Dahr was the last to leave, and even he fled before the sentence was complete. His cleverness won him only a few tidbits of knowledge and the oily feel of self-revulsion. He prodded Jardelle for greater speed, but it did no good; he could escape his own actions no easier than he could escape Lord Fayrd, who clung to him like a shadow, his anguished eyes boring into Dahr's back, unwavering in their disgust and yet refusing to condemn. He sensed no fear from the man, nor adulation, nor enmity, none of the reactions he had come to expect. In Fayrd, he sensed a man who saw the path ahead and felt only pity for the man who must tread it.

He signaled the halt with the sun still high in the west, then sent runners out to scout the enemy's position. While the others readied the camp, Dahr sought solitude, a quiet glen left undisturbed by the Tachans' passage, a hidden retreat where he could escape the devils of the world and confront the ones within.

Sleep brought him to the Twilight World, but not to the grassland he was accustomed to. He found himself back in the twisted remains of Eastern Grenz, surrounded by death and with the scent of ash and blood mingling in the frigid wind. Nothing moved, not even sound dared enter the blighted land, and the light itself wavered, dimmed by columns of inky smoke.

The roar shook the buildings, echoing off the shattered walls so its direction could not be determined. It came from everywhere and nowhere, a feral cry that spoke of rage and hunger, driven by the need to destroy, the yearning to share the agony it felt with the world that had caused its torment.

A terror worse than any he ever before endured overwhelmed Dahr, but this time he refused to run. He now understood what stalked him in his dreams, what made him the Half-Man most of the world thought him to be. Fate had cornered him, forced him down one of two paths; to survive, he would need to face the thing he feared most of all.

He crept forward as if hunting, though in truth he was as much prey as hunter, testing each step with a tentative foot, moving through the rubble with slow, steady movements. But stalking served no purpose; the creature he sought remained hidden though it thundered its presence across the Twilight World. He could not surprise it; he could never escape it.

"I know what you are!" Dahr shouted into the emptiness. The roaring stopped immediately. The deadly quiet that followed was just as terrifying in its own way. "Show yourself!"

The creature exploded from the shadows, a blur too fast to follow, driving Dahr to the ground with a numbing blow. Dahr hit with a thud, the breath driven from his lungs, and he fought the urge to scramble backward. Staying there, staring into the face of the beast, was the hardest thing he had ever done, harder even than walking the fields of dead Hunters or staring at the bodies of the innocents who had died because they followed him.

The face he stared at was his own, but tortured and twisted, eyes yellowed and narrow, devoid of compassion; lips drawn back in a permanent snarl, the exposed teeth sharpened to fangs. It circled Dahr, studying him, disgusted by the fear it sensed, perplexed by the confrontation. And hungry. Always hungry.

"A battle is coming," Dahr said, gasping for breath, rubbing a hand across the bruised flesh on his chest. The creature sniffed the air, testing it for blood, and a grin spread across its face. "A chance for vengeance. A feast of death. Perhaps even enough to satiate you."

The creature unsheathed its greatsword free and ran two fingers along its length. Its grin widened at the thought of combat. "But you will fail," Dahr told him, and the insult drove home. The smile vanished, and the blade leveled at Dahr's chest. Rage and pain and unbearable isolation warred for dominance, but as rage fed on the other two, it once again emerged the victor.

"I will fall too," Dahr said, surprised at his sudden lack of fear, at the calm which suffused him. *Is it because I know this a dream, or because I now know the truth?* "I am too weak, too consumed by doubt and guilt to do what must be done; you are careless with lives and unconcerned with strategy so long as you are in the thick of battle. Either one of us will find defeat... should have found defeat long ago! Me driven into a corner, afraid to choose a direction; you racing headlong into battle, blinded by your desires and heedless of the dangers you face."

Dahr levered himself up, half-surprised when the movement did not provoke an attack. "Alone, we find death one way or another. Together, we might just be able to find the things we both seek."

He approached slowly, the way he would approach a skittish colt, and grasped the creature's arm, shocked when it was the one to jerk away. "I don't want to fight you anymore. I'm no longer afraid of what I might become. If my path leads to our destruction, then let Kohr and His children decide which one of Them deserves the guilt."

"I could kill you here," the creature snarled. "You are weak. Nothing like a real Garun'ah."

"You could," Dahr agreed. "And you'll die soon after, deprived of all the blood that flows through our future. I lack your passion, but you lack compassion, and without that, you are nothing more than a tool for our enemies. You saw what havoc we wreaked on the Tribal Lands. Is that the fate we want for all of Madryn?"

The creature stared at him for a long time, and Dahr wondered what would happen if his gamble failed and the monster fought for dominance. Would he wake a different man, with his own consciousness trapped in the Twilight World, struggling for attention in the back of his mind, or would the changes be more subtle? Would the outcome here make no difference to those around him, since he was in truth already both man and monster?

He was spared his reflections by the creature, who snorted his derision and sheathed his blade. "I will never give you the peace you crave," he said, disappearing again into the shadows of the buildings, "the silence of a contented soul. But if you forget your promise of blood, I will return. And I will never let you go."

With the creature gone, Dahr felt eyes on his back, and he turned to find three Tribesmen in the distance, watching in the way one watched a cub out on his first hunt, judging him in a way reserved for those whose failures might spell doom for many. Frodel stood proud and tall, a Hunter's spear in hand, the scars from a life-time of battles displayed proudly, his expression unreadable but his gaze lacking the disappointment Dahr had often seen within it. Beside him stood Yarchik, but not the Yarchik Dahr knew, the withered Tribesman trapped in his body, confined to a palanquin; this was Yarchik as he remembered himself, young and powerful, guardian of the Channa, leading his people toward a better future and searching, always searching, for the one chosen by Garun to carry on his work.

The third Tribesmen towered over them both, a stranger to Dahr and yet eerily familiar. His presence overpowered the others, but his thoughts were even less discernible than Frodel's. His face remained expressionless, his stance neutral; he studied Dahr with curiosity, perhaps with interest, but Dahr sensed neither approval nor dissatisfaction.

No sooner had he caught sight of the trio then they vanished, leaving Dahr to wonder if they had really been there, or if he just wanted them to be. He troubled himself over it little—far stranger things had happened in the Twilight World, things created by his own mind and by the minds of others—and settled back against a wall, cradling his head in his hands and watching the clouds pass overhead until the call of the real world pulled him from his slumber.

CHAPTER 39

Two Guardsmen pulled open the doors of the palace amidst the fanfare of trumpets, clearing the way for Jeran and his army. His soldiers filed out of the palace in ranks five abreast, each Gifted flanked by a pair of Orog and a pair of Human soldiers. Days spent in the gloom of the catacombs, moved from Dranakohr a handful at a time at Ehvan's command, left few ready for the assault of daylight and the crisp crackle of the wind, but the sight of the Army of the Boundary appearing out of the confines of the palace brought a murmur of hopeful excitement to the crowd gathered to watch the spectacle.

Jeran preceded them all, dressed in a leather cuirass dyed deep black to match the uniforms of his soldiers, the snarling maw of a wolf emblazoned across the chest. Grendor followed at his left shoulder, his expression a mask of grim focus that frightened any who did not know his good heart. Katya walked on Jeran's right, unfazed by the venomous stares she received by any who knew her to be a Durange.

"Stay close to me," Jeran murmured to her. "I don't think many will remember you're an ally if you stray."

King Mathis watched their approach from across the courtyard, his presence diminished by the exhaustion dragging down his shoulders, betrayed by the doubt evident in his gaze. Martyn and Brell Morrena stood to either side of the King, and each stared at Jeran with a frown seemingly meant to outdo the other's.

"It is customary for a Guardsman defending Alrendria to wear the grey uniform," Martyn chided when Jeran stopped before them and saluted the King fist-on-heart.

"It is also customary for the First of a House to hold back from the forefront of battle," Brell added, "since his concerns should transcend the demands of combat."

"Then it is fortunate I am neither Guardsman nor First," Jeran said, unable to keep the smirk from his lips. "And as you both know this display is for a purpose, I'm not sure why you choose to take issue over it."

"What purpose," Brell snorted, "save to stoke your already inflated ego? Parading about the palace does naught but warn our enemies of your presence. A surprise assault would have served us far better."

"Our presence was known the moment I stepped out of the catacombs." Jeran's voice remained even, unruffled despite Brell's accusing tone, and the lack of emotion brought a renewed wave of red to the nobleman's face. "If you believe otherwise, then you're more a fool than I ever imagined. If you can't take your quarry by surprise, you dangle a lure in front of it and hope to draw it out. Except in this case, we attempt to lure an ally, not an enemy."

"I see no allies here, Odara."

"If my presence offends, I can always return to Dranakohr. Some have already counseled that as the wiser move. I did not come here out of strategy; I came out of loyalty."

"Enough bickering," Mathis said, and if his bearing showed the weakness of his position, his voice still carried the command of a king. "Brell, I thought we had put these petty jealousies behind us. Jeran, you need not flaunt the strength of your position so much. All here know your presence is a deciding factor in the struggle. To rub our faces in it does nothing but show your youth."

"My apologies, King Mathis," Jeran said, chagrined. "I am not always able to maintain the detachment you encouraged."

Mathis laughed aloud. "You affect it well, even if you do not feel it. Your uncle guards the north wall. Shall we proceed there?"

Jeran looked past the King. "I don't think we need to. Have you come to participate in the battle for Kaper, High Wizard, or just to capitalize on the aftermath?"

All eyes followed Jeran's gaze to an open area where over a dozen gates appeared, and through which hundreds of Magi in the garb of the Assembly passed. Valkov stood before them all, black eyes glaring at Jeran down his hooked nose. One by one the Gates began to close, usually preceded by the collapse of a Mage on the other side. Jeran waited, but no more appeared. "It seems few of your Gifted remember the way to Kaper."

Martyn sought to interject himself between Jeran and the Magi. "High Wizard Valkov, how—"

"Spare me your platitudes, Prince Martyn," Valkov brushed past the prince, leaving him red-faced and fuming. "It's clear you've chosen your side in my conflict. No doubt you still expect me to side with you in yours."

The High Wizard barely spared a glance at the King, ignored everyone else in attendance, and stopped a few hands from Jeran. "You threaten everything the Assembly of Magi is."

"But not everything it was," Jeran replied, "nor everything it was meant to be."

"I cannot allow you to run unchecked. I will not turn my back forever."

"But for today?"

"For today, there is a worse menace which must be dealt with. You, for all your faults, think you are saving the world; Salos covets nothing more than its destruction. But if even a single one of my—"

"Your Magi have nothing to fear from me," Jeran interrupted. "I have not sent spies to live among you, nor do I seek to incite dissent and rebellion among your Assembly. I simply offer a different way of engaging the world, and I want only those who choose to share my vision."

Valkov stiffened, a wolf whose hackles have risen in response to a challenge of dominance. "And yet Oto kidnapped our apprentices and whisked them off to your fortress. Yet my Magi do not announce their departures, but slip away in the dead of night. These are not the actions of... Lelani! Yes, I suspected I'd find you here as well."

Jeran shifted his gaze marginally, never fully taking them away from Valkov. The former High Wizard had changed, diminished by her fall from power. Yet an ember of Lelani's former self remained, and it flared to life in the face of Valkov's unspoken accusations.

"My loyalty has always been to Alrendria," she said, her voice crackling like a cold wind coming off the Anvil. "I urged support for House Batai in this conflict while the bulk of the Assembly debated bringing the subject up for debate. Do you think I'd turn my back at this pivotal moment out of fear of you? I have done no wrong. I need not fear your justice!"

"Then you've come to face the Assembly?" Valkov asked. "Your flight from Atoll Domiar will not bear well in the proceedings, but should you deliver yourself and your followers to me, and aid the Assembly in its role during the battle, I imagine that clemency can be offered."

Lelani turned her icy gaze on Jeran. "And do you offer anything better than leniency for my support, Lord Odara?"

"I offer nothing, Mage Lelani. I will not woo you with false promises or cajole you with polite threats. You and your people must join me on the same terms as any other. But I have an Academy in sore need of teachers, and it is rumored that before the lure of power drew you to politics, you were a coveted instructor. There is a place for you in Dranakohr, should you desire it."

"That is an interesting proposition, and—"

A clearing throat silenced the former High Wizard, and drew all eyes to Sionel, who stood before them no longer as a doddering old woman, but proud and strong, with a glare that spoke of great frustration. "Perhaps you could save the negotiations until after the battle? Besides, once you reach the part where you start dividing up my grandson's lands, he might take offense at being excluded."

The realization that Sionel was not just a senile old woman hit Jeran like a thunderbolt and left him wondering how many other spies Aemon had placed around him during his youth. Embarrassment that he had never before made the connection warred with frustration that he had once again been aimed, though in this case very subtly, in a direction of Aemon's choosing.

Sionel noticed his war of emotion despite his efforts to conceal it, and her lips quirked up as she offered him a sly wink. Jeran returned his attention to the Magi. "Then we are all agreed?"

The High Wizard glanced at Jeran's outstretched hand and turned away, ushering his Magi toward the south. "Allies it is. Until the city is safe."

"Allies," Lelani echoed, signaling her Magi to leave. "My followers are most familiar with the northern sections of the palace grounds. We will defend there unless needed elsewhere."

"Wonderful," Martyn muttered, low enough that Lelani could not hear. "That's exactly where you're needed. Thank you for consulting with those in charge of the defense."

Jeran laughed at the prince's wry remark, though the mirth brought with it bittersweet nostalgia for a time forever past. "My Prince," Jeran said with a formal salute. "Where might my people be of the most use?"

Martyn's caustic glare dissipated in the face of Jeran's exaggerated deference, and he, too, began to laugh.

"Isn't this nice," Sionel mused. "Everyone getting along so well. Makes you almost wish the Nothing wasn't hovering outside the door. Anyone else interested in dispensing with the posturing and maybe driving these monsters from my home?"

"They're close," Dahr said, staring at the twisted corpses arrayed about the clearing, caught in the wisps of dawn sunlight that filtered through the breaks in the clouds. Man and beast slaughtered indiscriminately and displayed prominently, the carcasses of deer, wolves, and even simple creatures such as rabbits left unbutchered, killed for the sole purpose of goading Dahr, of driving him to another act of rashness. Gral's ploy almost worked; Dahr held control by a finger's grip, and a tenuous one at that. The Lesser Voices had been whipped to a frenzy by the massacre, and even the Guardsmen from Grenz spoke out against the desecration.

"They wait over next rise. Hold high ground. No surprise." Tarouk ignored the wounds he received in the skirmishing overnight and described the enemy's formation to Dahr. There was no need; as soon as Tarouk acknowledged their presence, Dahr turned to Shyrock to show him the Tachan army firsthand. They numbered in the thousands, bolstered by troops moving up from the south and by a large contingent from the army penning Joam and the Gilean army in Aurach. Word had also come of other soldiers moving toward them from Rachannon, but they were of little concern. They could not arrive in time for this battle, and after today, their appearance would matter little.

"Have we word from the runners sent to Aurach?" Lord Fayrd asked.

"None," Olin replied. "We do not know if they survived to reach the Alrendrians or if our allies were able to respond."

"It doesn't matter," Dahr said. He opened his thoughts to the *Tier'sorahna*, told them the time had come, that they should summon the Lesser Voices and prepare. "Their presence would be helpful, but it isn't required. We cannot allow this opportunity to pass. If we fail to kill the Tachans here, the towns of southern Gilead will share the fate of the villages up north, and the route to Alrendria will stand open, beckoning them toward Kaper."

Fayrd did not look convinced. "They outnumber us three to one, and—"

"You forget to count the animals in your tally," Dahr reminded him.

"Wolves and bears I count as allies. But squirrels? Oxen? Our enemy holds the high ground, and we will fight the morning with the sun in our eyes and then have it at our backs again if we need to retreat."

"Lucky for us then that retreat is not an option," Dahr said. "And while it's true that few of the Lesser Voices can kill alone, it is their numbers and unity that inspire fear. It's the same for us. Our enemy may hold more swords, they may pretend at alliance, but we share a bond far stronger, a purpose more noble, and a future far more intertwined. When they see our resolve, the Tachans will wish for five times their numbers and an easy route of flight."

"You find faith?" Tarouk asked suspiciously, eyeing Dahr as if he saw a stranger. "Has the word of Garun finally grasped you?"

"I have found myself," Dahr countered, "and have remembered how to trust. And I know that when the only alternative to victory is the Nothing, there is no motivator more powerful. Not even faith in the Gods."

Dahr drew his greatsword and ran his fingers down the length of the blade, seeking the calm he knew he needed before the maelstrom. "Sound the advance, Lord Fayrd. Kohr may have come to bless his troops today. Let's honor Him with the destruction he so covets."

The Army of the Boundary poured through the open gates of Kaper castle, driven forward by the press of eager men and the desire to protect Jeran, who insisted on being the first into the fray. His decision had been as much political as personal, but no one else had pressed hard for the 'honor'. Aelvin and Alrendrian archers lined the parapets above, raining death upon the massed formations of the enemy. Magi of the Assembly were more selective in the use of their Gift than his own people, using it primarily for defense or to thwart the efforts of the ShadowMagi; yet fire and lightning and other instruments of destruction did fall, and Salos's troops seemed far less impressed by the majesty of magic when it was used against them.

Battle was joined under a slate sky further darkened by a hail of arrows, and the Tachans proved themselves unflappable despite the implacable advance of men and Orog. Jeran's Gifted blasted through the barricades and obstructions assembled by the enemy, and his men pressed forward until they hit the Tachans' main line, where stiff resistance stalled their advance. Behind them, Guardsmen and militia raced out from the castle grounds, spreading to the flanks and forcing the enemy to guard an ever larger area. Jaem and the remaining Gilean horsemen galloped past the foot soldiers and turned west, driving through the Tachans and disappearing into the city. A group of elite Alrendrian cavalry raced east along a similar path. Everywhere men sought weakness, looked for gaps to press through. Aryn's plan called for rapid deployment and the creation of chaos; if they could not take back the city, their goal became to sow destruction and disrupt life for the enemy, to make living in Kaper city as difficult as living penned in the castle.

It was a clever plan, though Jeran saw it as flawed. The siege could not be survived indefinitely, and the odds of a force large enough to lift it arriving was slim. If they could not retake the city, today or in the days to come, then the Battle of Kaper would be lost, and with it the war against Salos.

A scarred soldier drove forward, swinging his blade in a broad arc which Jeran easily dodged and then answered by plunging his own blade into the man's gut. The man fell, exposing a tight cluster of enemy behind him. "Dominic!" Jeran shouted to one of the Gifted fighting beside him. The young man barely glanced at him before grasping Jeran's intention. With the crash of a small avalanche, the wall of an inn split outward from its foundation, crushing the enemy in rubble.

"You couldn't do that?" Katya asked. Sweat slicked her hair despite the chill wind of morning, but she danced from one enemy to the next effortlessly, an artist painting death across the battlefield.

"I have my reasons." Jeran held magic, was ready to draw as much as he could hold, but he dare not use it. He hoped to draw Salos to the fray, and if a confrontation did occur, he would need to face the Scorpion with the full extent of his Gift.

"Press forward!" he shouted, sprinting into the midst of the enemy, knowing that his jeopardy would inspire those bonded to him to greater acts of heroism. The gambit worked; the enemy crumbled under a sudden onslaught of berserker attacks as desperate men and women struggled to rejoin him. Jeran's mind exploded with the pain of his people, the phantom echoes of their sacrifices. On the morrow, he would regret this decision, and the deaths of his people would haunt him for the remainder of his days. But for now he had made his choice, and the price must be paid.

He moved forward, keeping just far enough ahead to concern his followers, forcing them to carve a path through the enemy, to push the Scorpion's army back step after bloody step. Only when he stood at the intersection of two broad avenues with the narrower streets of old Kaper and the majority of the nobles' estates behind did he stop to catch his breath. Katya and Grendor were the first to reach him.

"You're as foolhardy as Dahr!" Katya laughed, her eyes alight with the thrill of battle.

In the moment of calm that followed while the enemy regrouped, Jeran let his perceptions roam over the battle. Martyn drove a contingent of Guardsmen forward, breaking through a fortification and sending the enemy scurrying over a low stone fence and into one of the large estates that graced the upper sections of Old Kaper. Instead of pursuing, the prince turned west, leading his men to assault the flank of a second barricade where Dayfid and his squads faced heavy resistance from a pair of ShadowMagi. All around him the defenders of Kaper, from the most seasoned Guardsman to the rawest recruit, dove at the enemy with a vigor most had thought lost, exacting vengeance for a city destroyed, a nation torn asunder.

A trumpet sounded, and the gates to the castle opened again to allow more militia access to the fray, men who would take up garrison duty at the strategic positions captured. Several hundred *Ael Chatorra*, with Prince Treloran at the head of the column, passed under the arch. Joined by Aryn and ten squads of Guardsmen, they hastened north; Bystral and Drogon led a similar force south, with both contingents hoping to retake control of the Wall and seal off the enemy from access to the old city.

Katya gasped, "Is that—?"

Jeran did not hear the rest, as an icy shock drove through his body. The sudden loss of the Gift stunned him, confused him too, until he felt the grip of Grendor's hand on his arm. "Friend Jeran," the Orog said, his voice as close to a whisper as possible in the middle of the battle. "Look up there."

Jeran saw a slender form silhouetted on the roof of a distant building. He shook off Grendor's grip and re-seized magic, extending his perceptions. The angular profile and dark eyes of the Scorpion were unmistakable. As if sensing Jeran's eyes on him, Salos smiled, a cruel grin that screamed victory despite the mounting losses his forces endured.

"Katya—?" Jeran cut off his command when he realized the Guardswoman was no longer with him.

"Where did she go?" Grendor asked.

"We don't have time to find her," Jeran said, running in the direction of the Scorpion.

"Korahn!"

The battlecry of the Garun'ah drowned out the charge of the Alrendrians as they raced to be the first to hit the Tachan formation through a hail of arrows and sporadic magical attacks. Fayrd's horsemen held a slight advantage in speed, and they plowed into the enemy's line in a tight wedge, breaking a hole in the defense and leaving the Tachans disoriented for the massed assault of Hunters who followed.

Lord Fayrd withdrew for another charge, but Dahr ordered his men to press in, to use the enemy as a shield against the archers and ShadowMagi. It did little good; Gral cared little for the lives of his troops. Shafts continued to fall among the Tribesmen, and if anything, the ShadowMagi increased their efforts as Dahr's army drew nearer.

The battle degenerated to chaos, with the ordered formations of Tribesmen breaking apart to offer greater protection from ranged assault. Thousands of raptors circled above, their shadows dancing across the ground in a disorienting pattern of light and dark. Nearly as many smaller birds darted about the fray, flying in to harass the enemy and then disappearing again into the melee. Howls and roars reverberated over the cries of men, coming from everywhere, and the presence of such great beasts had a noticeable effect.

Dahr smiled at the enemy's discomfort. He hated forcing the *Tier'sorahna* into another battle, but he doubted he could win without them. Alone, he could not direct the Lesser Voices with any sort of strategy, not over the extent of the battlefield. But the *Tier'sorahna* could hold the Lesser Voices to their tasks, and with the children on the fringes of the battle, the beasts were far more likely to obey than to surrender to their baser instincts.

Perhaps the same is true of the Hunters. Perhaps the same is true of me.

Death surrounded him, death and the metallic stench of fresh blood. He dismissed his anxieties and focused on the task at hand. This was the hunt he had dreamed of, a game of Seeker through a field of flowing blood. The Lesser Voices were to harass the prey, to keep the enemy from regrouping; the Hunters and Guardsmen were to carve at the body, whittling it away; but his task was to find the head of this serpent. Find it, and sever it.

"Where's Dayfid?" Martyn demanded, shoving a body out of his way so he could lean against the low wall surrounding the manor of a minor nobleman, taking shelter from the arrows that assaulted anyone foolish enough to stand too long in the open. His men worked to clear the fortification guarding the intersection while they waited for militiamen to arrive and assume garrison duty. Even now an Alrendria flag was hoisted over the guardpost, signaling yet another small step in the reclamation of Kaper.

Will even a hundred such steps make a difference? How much of what we gain today will be lost again once the Tachans regroup? Even if we succeed, what price will we pay for our victory?

"Where's Dayfid?!" Martyn repeated, his temper slipping through despite the air of calm confidence he hoped to present.

"I don't know, my Prince," a Guardsman stammered. "After we took this guardpost, he saw some of our enemies taking flight and took a handful of men in pursuit. He has not yet returned."

"That Gods-damned fool," Martyn muttered. Aryn had impressed upon them all how much victory depended on re-taking ground and seizing strategic stockpiles, not on slaughtering every enemy soldier that walked into view. Dayfid's reckless bravado was fast becoming a liability; even if his exploits made him popular among the people, he would have to be rebuked.

But after the battle. "What's your name, Guardsman?"

"Viko. Of Family Ronasti, of House Aurelle."

"You are in command until Dayfid returns. Do you know your objectives?"

"Yes, Prince Martyn!"

"My men will hold the guardpost until reinforcements arrive. Continue the advance at your discretion."

The Guardsman saluted and started shouting out orders. His men quickly gathered and began moving north. Martyn sighed when he saw them racing down the middle of the avenue, and the scream as a soldier fell to an arrow shot from concealment justified his concerns.

"Eye out for archers!" Martyn shouted after them. "Clear the buildings behind you after you take the next guardpost!"

Whatever response was shouted back got lost in the chorus of battle, and Martyn settled against the wall while he surveyed the city. With the approach to the castle still a dominant feature to the south, the battle could not be long underway, but already his arms felt like lead and sweat slicked his head and arms; already he saw more dead and dying than he could stomach, with his men showing little mercy to the Morrenan traitors and Tachans who had desecrated Kaper. Their bodies lay everywhere, abandoned in the initial flight, and those who showed signs of life were given the sword's mercy by any who happened upon them.

Despite the advance, the battle was proving costly for the Alrendrians. Dozens in his own squads had fallen in the initial assault, and hundreds more lay dead on the streets around the palace. The militia suffered the brunt of the casualties, but they fought as madmen nevertheless, driving into the enemy with the fanaticism of a people on the verge of annihilation, exacting a vengeance of blood from those who had stolen their lives and homes.

Casualties were even higher among Jeran's soldiers, who at times seemed fanatical in their assaults, willing to throw themselves against entrenched foes for little gain or race beyond the protection of the archers and Assembly Magi in pursuit of Jeran, who himself appeared to have forgotten that he had an army to fight beside him. Martyn wondered about their utter devotion to Jeran, and whether if it would save Alrendria or eventually destroy it.

His eyes moved from the soldiers to the city itself. Kaper had turned into a hellscape, the once-lush gardens of the manors blackened, the buildings cracked and broken by misuse and magic, the winding avenues a twisting maze of rubble with the threat of ambush at every blockade. But the sights did not torture him so much as the realization that the screams of the dying, rumble of collapsing walls, and acrid stench of smoke no longer seemed out of place. A macabre memorial to those who had fought within its walls, Kaper had become a monument to destruction.

Will we have enough men left to defend the city if we retake it? Will we have a city left to defend?

Martyn's eyes skirted back toward the castle gate. "For the Gods' sakes, somebody guard those Healers! Move! Move!" Despite his orders, Sheriza and the other practitioners of her arts moved outside the protection of the castle and raced among the fallen, seeking to restore those within their power and bring peace to any they could not save.

Every extra sword will be a blessing, but the Healers' Gift is invaluable. Each of them is worth more than a full squad of soldiers. Just once, I wish they'd heed my command and wait for the wounded to be brought to them.

Guardsmen hastened to protect the Magi, passing the militiamen en route to hold the guardpost. "Ready yourselves," Martyn called. "It's time for us to—"

He broke off, his eyes drawn to a lithe, leather-clad form moving toward the castle at a run. *Where is she going?*

"Guardsmen Pio, do you know our objectives?"

"Yes, my Prince."

"You are in command. I will rejoin you when I can."

"Yes, Prince Martyn. For Alrendria! For House Batai!"

Martyn returned the Guardsman's salute and then started toward the castle at a flat run.

The battle raged around him, and yet it seemed somewhere else altogether, a distant distraction, ephemeral like a Reading and with the detached otherworldliness of the Twilight World. Jeran wove through the narrow avenues of a merchant's district, perceptions expanded, probing the buildings for signs of the Scorpion. Grendor limped beside him, *va'dasheran* at the ready, eyes darting from one shadow to the next. The rest of Jeran's forces remained far behind, delayed by a fierce counterassault launched when the enemy realized control of Old Kaper was in jeopardy.

"Friend Jeran, I do not believe this is wise. We should rejoin our brothers."

"This war will not be won by retaking Kaper," Jeran replied. He could sense the Orog's trepidation, but also his resolve to die in Jeran's defense. "Eliminating Salos is the key to victory. None of the ShadowMagi truly share his vision of destruction; none of the Commons under his command can rule the Tachans for centuries. Without him, their cause withers. I must stop him."

At the fringe of his awareness Jeran felt a presence, a dark swirl of consciousness taunting him, flickering into being and then disappearing again. He focused on the impression, narrowing his awareness, trying to determine its precise location.

"Watch out!"

Grendor shoved him aside and the arrow slipped past with an audible whoosh, drawing blood on the Orog's arm. Jeran rolled to his feet and brought his attention fully on the attackers: a group of five Tachans half-concealed at the intersection ahead. Grendor raced ahead, bladed staff poised to strike.

Jeran unleashed his Gift. A blue-white ball of fire shot past Grendor, leaving two of the soldiers lying on the ground, smoke rising from their ashy remains. Two more died when the wall behind them exploded outward, showering them with jagged bits of rock. The fifth tried to flee, and Jeran grabbed him in a vise of air, crushing the life from him and then lowering him to the ground to lay beside his comrades.

Grendor slid to a stop on the rubble strewn across the paved streets and turned toward Jeran. When their eyes met, the Orog sensed something, realized Jeran's intentions, and his eyes grew saucer-wide. "Friend Jeran! You—"

With his Gift still held at the ready, Jeran pulled down the walls between him and Grendor, creating a barricade difficult to climb. Similar bursts of magic felled walls all around the Orog, enclosing him in the intersection.

"Friend Jeran, you cannot face him alone!"

"The Scorpion would decimate an army or slip through a Gate and evade it. The only way to approach him is in small numbers, and there are only a few who I would make share such a burden with me." Jeran could sense Grendor's frustration through their bond, and also a growing concern among the rest of his people, so he started toward the alley down which he had sensed Salos's presence.

"For all the hatred she harbors toward him, I could not ask Katya to help kill her father. And you... All will be well, friend Grendor."

"It is you who counsels that only together can we defeat our foes! That our unity makes us stronger than the Scorpion."

"Yes, but as the Elders' say, 'Follow a fool to his death and be scorned; lead a man to a foolish death and be damned.' I will sacrifice all of my people if that is what's required, but I will not waste a single life. Taking you to battle the Scorpion is asking to watch you die."

Jeran hastened his pace, ignoring Grendor's demands to be freed. *Salos already took half of you, my friend; I would never forgive myself if I gave him the rest.*

The battle had long since lost any semblance of order, the precise formations of both combatants giving way to the chaos of combat. Humans and Garun'ah fought in tight clusters, Guardsmen and Hunters side by side, protecting one another, fighting for the destruction of their mutual enemy. The land lay blasted and scarred, twisted by the attacks of ShadowMagi, and while their assaults lessened as the battle dragged on, they never ceased. Wild beasts roamed the field at will, ravaging the wounded and attacking as they could; enthralled by bloodlust, held by only a tenuous link, they bordered on becoming a liability. Dahr doubted he could banish them from the field, even with the combined will of the *Tier'sorahna*. In many ways, Madryn had not seen a battle like this since the time of the MageWar.

And yet no one could gain an advantage. Fortune ebbed and flowed like a tide, first favoring one side and then the other. With the sun now high overhead, the battle showed no sign of slowing, no chance of ending.

Dahr noted these things only absently. He fought more like one of the beasts than one of the soldiers, prowling the field, killing when an opportunity appeared, always on the hunt for Gral. Only by killing Gral could he bring an end to this battle. Only by killing Gral could he bring an end to the battle within himself.

The enemy learned to give him a wide berth, that by keeping in numbers and ignoring his presence they could spare themselves his wrath. Those who sought to stop him inevitably fell, as did those unfortunate enough to cross his path unawares. He offered no mercy, no pity. If his attacks did not kill, he left his enemies writhing on the ground behind him, unless he thought they might rise again to challenge his presence. In those rare instances when a whole squad approached, the Lesser Voices joined him, falling on the Tachans from air and ground, rending with tooth and talon, marking his passage with the bodies of their enemies.

He had spent so long searching for Gral, that when he found himself suddenly face to face with the slaver, staring at his perverted visage and into the depths of the solid white orb of his one eye, Dahr thought himself dreaming. A rush of blood clouded his vision, banishing all other thoughts; his greatsword rose to meet the lightning-fast strike from the slaver, pushing it aside and away.

Gral stepped back, but not in fear. He circled Dahr slowly, testing him with a few feints and gauging his reactions. "Our lives seem to be linked, Half-man. We share an odd path. I start to believe the Scorpion's ramblings."

"We share nothing," Dahr snapped. "Our only link is that history will cite me as the one who killed you."

Gral darted in, and Dahr dodged, but not fast enough to avoid a slice along his arm. His answering attack was met with steel and then they faced off as before. "You must wonder about it... Had I not stumbled across those farmers in the mountains, you would still be there now. What kind of life would you have had? If we had not crossed paths in Grenz... Would the Aelvin Empire still stand? Would your friend have ever fallen into my master's hands? Would the Durange whose bed you share still be whispering secrets to the enemy?"

Dahr lunged again, hammering three successive blows into Gral's sword, never striking flesh but forcing the slaver to back farther away. "It seems I struck a nerve," Gral laughed as he maneuvered around the embers of a cook fire. "You never could control that temper. Not even as a cub."

Dahr feinted then leapt over the fire, bringing his sword around in a broad arc. The move caught Gral off guard, and the slaver stumbled, but Dahr landed on the edge of a log, and the shifting of the wood caused him to drop to one knee. Gral moved in, pounding him with a series of attacks. Dahr blocked the assault and regained his footing, but as he turned to confront the slaver, Gral stooped and threw a handful of ash and embers at him.

The fine powder blinded Dahr and filled his mouth with an acrid taste. He backed away, waving his sword wildly while he sought to clear his vision. Gral swept around behind and slammed the pommel of his sword into the back of Dahr's knee. As he fell, the blow of a fist cracked across Dahr's jaw, leaving the taste of blood in his mouth.

Gral kicked Dahr's sword away, and he felt a multitude of hands pounding upon him. A half dozen men pinned him down, taking his slightest movement as justification for another round of blows.

"Even now you don't dare kill me unaided?" he growled.

"I've been denied that pleasure," Gral lamented. "Salos made it clear that I could humble you, that I could take you to the edge of death, but that you were to leave here alive. To do otherwise would cost me my own life... And thanks to you, I like where my life has taken me."

Dahr struggled, but his captors held him tight. As he watched, Gral bent over the coals of the fire and removed a brand, the end glowing bright red. "The Scorpion also had other instructions for me," he said, pointing the iron at Dahr.

The palace seemed eerily quiet, especially when compared to the turmoil outside. A few lonesome Guardsmen protected key storerooms, and Martyn passed a handful of servants tiptoeing through the corridors, but by and large the castle halls remained empty and silent. Any who could hold a weapon or tend the wounded waited outside where they could put up a last-ditch defense if things went awry; those too young or infirm had been confined to their chambers until sundown, and against all odds it seemed as if everyone had obeyed.

Katya paused at an intersection, poking her head around the corner before darting down the hall and out of sight. Martyn hurried after her, cursing the sounds his footfalls made as he ran down the corridor. *How does she move so silently? Why is it the one time I need the constant noise of these halls they stand silent?*

He reached the intersection only to find it empty, with no indication of where Katya had gone. Martyn walked down the hall, testing doors as he passed, peering into the chambers in hopes of stumbling across his quarry. "What could a traitor hope to accomplish here, the one day the whole of our defenses is…"

Dear Gods! Martyn ran, no longer mindful of announcing his presence, and burst into his chambers. "Miriam!" The princess was not there, nor were there any signs of struggle. The bed stood unruffled, a half-eaten meal laid out on the table in the sitting room. Martyn searched the apartments anyway, shoving aside dresses in the closets and checking within every hidden nook.

Then he remembered: Miriam told him she intended to watch the battle from the tower with the King. Martyn ran again, sprinting down the halls and up the long winding stairs, drawing his sword as he neared the top. Gasping for breath, he threw open the door and raced into the blinding light. Squinting while his eyes adjusted, he sought his bearings, spotted his father and Jaenaryn to one side, shadowed by Mika and a handful of his child-Guardsmen; to the other side, Miriam leaned heavily on the arm of Zarin Mahl, the swell of her abdomen pronounced in profile against the wall. Kaeille stood beside them, sword drawn, green eyes narrowed to near slits.

"Don't move, Durange," Martyn growled, readying his sword. Katya stood not two steps away, crossbow raised and aimed not at Miriam, but at Dayfid and the half-dozen Guardsmen who stood with him in the center of the tower.

"What are you doing here, Guardsman?" Martyn demanded, taking his eyes off of Katya for an instant. "Your men need you."

"I saw that traitor moving toward the castle," Dayfid replied, "and I sought to protect the princess."

"Don't believe him," Katya said. Her gaze never moved from Dayfid, even when Martyn edged closer and brought his sword back to strike. "*He* is the traitor. The son of Tylor Durange. One of those, like me, sent to infiltrate your world."

Zarin frowned at Katya's words, but Miriam shouted out her displeasure, demanding that Martyn silence the Scorpion's traitor daughter and invoking a string of epithets coarse enough that under other circumstances they might have brought a flush to his own cheeks.

"It seems he has done a far better job than I ever did," Katya mused, "to have your wife so convinced of his innocence."

"Be silent!" Martyn demanded. His eyes flicked back and forth between Dayfid and Katya, noting the similarities in their features, the differences. "And drop your weapon. The only reason you are not already dead is a promise I made to Jeran."

"Must he exact a promise from everyone we meet, or just from those he holds most dear? Kill me if you must, but I am the only thing keeping your princess alive. Your father and mistress too, perhaps, though they can fight for themselves."

Dayfid edged toward Miriam, and Katya tensed. "Stand still, Guardsman," Martyn shouted. "Don't provoke an attack."

"Answer this, Martyn," Katya snapped. "What do I have to gain? Jeran is a far greater threat to my father's designs. As is Dahr. Both have slept defenseless while I guarded them. So has Aemon. Even the Empress of the Elves has stood within range of my sword. Why bide my time, waiting in the shadows for the perfect opportunity to strike at your wife or father, when so many better targets have offered their throats to me? Because I don't like you? I've never liked you, and that's not likely to change, but I'd not risk my own life just to goad you. I stand to gain nothing but death by this assassination. But Dayfid... Had I not followed him, had he been able to kill the King and princess, and then claim he attempted to save them, naming whomever he chose as their murderers, would he not stand even higher in your esteem? Would he not have been able to sow the sort of chaos and doubt that Salos craves?"

"Martyn, don't listen to her!" Dayfid shrieked, his confidence shattered by the accusations. "Have I not served you faithfully? Kill the traitor. Kill her now! Or let me do it for you!"

"Be silent!" Doubt crept into Martyn, and his sword fell marginally as he considered the facts.

"Do you recognize even one of the soldiers with him?" Katya asked. "A single Guardsman?"

While Martyn struggled to reconcile his feelings with the facts, Zarin pulled a dagger from concealment and ran toward Dayfid. "It fits," he shouted. "It explains every—"

Dayfid whirled around and plunged his sword through Zarin's chest, and before the man hit the ground, Dayfid had spun again and threw, his dagger flashing in an errant ray of sunlight before plunging into Katya's shoulder. His men reacted as well, drawing weapons and fanning out, only to find themselves faced by equal numbers of stern-faced children and an Aelvin woman, who rushed to guard Miriam and the child.

"Now you've betrayed me twice, *cousin*," Dayfid snarled. "The Nothing is not a good enough punishment for you. Once I deal with the prince, I'll find a way to make you suffer."

Jeran darted across the intersection and pressed himself into the shadows of the next building. Around him, the streets remained deserted, but sounds of fierce battle reverberated from the Wall, which stretched across the northern skyline, its grey stones a shade darker than the slate sky. To the south, the palace dominated the heights, pristine and peaceful in appearance, the Rising Sun of Alrendria snapping in the brisk wind. Tendrils of smoke rose throughout the old city, gnarled fingers of oily black reaching up into a murky sky.

The fate of those bonded to him was a mystery. To protect them, he had walled off his consciousness, muting their bonds until he could sense only a general presence, knowing they felt even less about him, and knowing as well that he must move fast, for he could not maintain the level of concentration needed to hide himself for long.

Magic, too, he held with the most tentative grasp; to hold more would make him a beacon to the Gifted. To surprise Salos, he must move unprotected, but to defeat the Scorpion, he would need every bit of magic he could hold.

His perceptions extended, he moved toward a muted presence in a nearby building. He focused on the tricks Jes had taught him, the ways to minimize his own impression, to make it more difficult for another Gifted to sense *his* presence.

The door to the inn creaked open, and Jeran hastened inside, ducking into the shadow cast by a large wine rack. He waited in tense silence, listening for unnatural sounds, testing the area with the barest trickle of magic. Creeping toward and then up the stairs, he cast his perceptions down the hall, pulling back at the first hint of the dark presence. With measured steps he approached the door, took several slow, deep breaths, and then burst inside, seizing as much magic as he could hold and unleashing it upon...

Nothing.

He stepped inside, drawing his sword as he swept his gaze from left to right. The empty chamber boasted little furniture, few places of concealment. Confused, he lessened his grip on magic, and in that instant the presence appeared behind him, a caustic and cruel soul feeding off the destruction, unconcerned that control of the city was the price of the devastation.

Jeran attempted to regain the magic he had released, but the flows were pulled away from him. He locked wills with the Scorpion, a battle of minds no less exhausting or deadly despite the lack of motion; a struggle of primal forces, intricate weaves of magic intertwining and bludgeoning, feinting and parrying, with each combatant testing his opponent for weakness.

They fought in this manner for some time, motionless, not even facing each other, with neither gaining the upper hand and each drawing upon more magic than half a dozen average Gifted could wield. Sweat slicked Jeran's back, his heart pounded as if it sought to burst from his chest, and spots of color began to dance before his wavering vision.

Salos began a new weave, a minor blend of magic in which Jeran could discern no threat. It coalesced into a flash of light that left him blind and momentarily disoriented. In that moment of distraction, the Scorpion attacked, ripping magic away from Jeran, leaving him heaving for breath and struggling to stand.

"It is always the simple things which fell the mighty," Salos said, stepping fully into the room. "Your arrogance has grown to match your abilities. Did you truly think you were the only one to exploit the Boundary's... gift? I had far more winters in Dranakohr to hone my talents, though I must admit to never using a collar to speed my training... Though to be fair, my brother deserves far more credit for that than you, doesn't he?"

Magic bound Jeran with invisible cords, driving him toward the wall and turning him so he faced the Scorpion. Pale and near-skeletal, Salos's chest rose and fell with rapidity, and sweat drenched his brow as it did Jeran's, but the Scorpion showed no hint of exhaustion. In his delving gaze Jeran saw only victory, victory and a perverse joy.

"Did you think you could best me after a few seasons of training?" Salos asked, pinching Jeran's chin with thumb and forefinger, turning his head from side to side as if examining a prized trophy. "Did you believe you could approach me undetected, using the same tricks favored by the Assembly?"

The bonds holding Jeran drew tighter, pressing against his flesh until he had to struggle for breath. A fiery pain began in his extremities, spreading through his limbs, a nagging irritation which soon transformed into an agony. He endured it, refusing to give Salos the satisfaction of his screams.

"It's all right," Salos said, patting his cheek. "I know it hurts. Consider it a penance. Though you've helped me more than you can imagine, you've done it for the wrong reasons. You've done it to thwart the will of the Father, and His will should never be thwarted. Such blasphemy cannot go unpunished."

"Help... you...?" Jeran gasped. "You have lost... Kaper. You failed... to capture the Empress... You—"

"Do you think any of that is important?" Salos laughed, a dry rasping sound that chilled Jeran despite the torturous pain. "The Father cares only for destruction. I covet only pain. This city is a point on a map, important only because people believe it to be. Hold it, and I hold the hearts of Alrendrians; lose it, and I lose nothing, but you gain a city in ruins, a people brutalized and demoralized. Everything I hoped to accomplished in Kaper is done, or will be before sundown. Your victory here will cause as much suffering as your defeat.

"Even better, you have sown for me the seeds of greater chaos. Your ascendency will distract the Mage Assembly, and it will plant doubt in the mind of your prince. To maintain its power, Alrendria will be forced to go on the offensive, and war serves my purposes far more than yours."

The fire spread across the whole of his body, leaving Jeran choking for breath. Tears streamed down his face, in part from the agony of his torture, in part for the ease in which he had played into Salos's hands.

"As for the Elves," Salos continued, "had Luran succeeded in defeating his sister, he would have attempted to reassert his independence. But with her free, with an Aelvin Empire in exile, he remains bound to me."

"Enough!" Jeran yelled through gritted teeth. "Kill me... Exact your revenge."

"Kill you?" Salos laughed again. "Rid Madryn of my most useful ally? You have been a blessing to me, Jeran. A gift from the Father Himself. You should be rewarded, not killed in an act of senseless vengeance."

The Scorpion cupped a hand to Jeran's cheek, and pain far worse than anything Jeran had yet endured seared his face. Now he did scream, a cry of agony that shook the building but was lost in the chorus of screams in the city beyond. Salos stepped back but the pain did not lessen, it merged into his flesh, moving of its own accord, crawling up the left side of his face from jaw to temple.

A shadow coalesced behind the Scorpion, a Gate to a destination Jeran had never before seen. "We will meet again," the Scorpion promised, "though I doubt it will be any time soon. In the meantime, continue to do the work of the Father. There is a special place reserved in the Twilight World for—"

"There!" The door crashed open and Grendor dashed inside, throwing his *va'dasheran* like a spear. Salos seized magic to weave a shield, but Valkov followed the Orog, and his magic countered the Scorpion's, leaving him unprotected as the blade pierced his gut and pushed him through the Gate. As the Scorpion lost his hold on magic, the Gate disappeared in a puff of dark smoke, snapping the shaft of the *va'dasheran* in half.

Along with the Gate went the bonds binding Jeran. He fell to the floor, unable to find his breath, struggling to regain his composure and the ability to seize magic. Valkov approached, circling like a predator sizing up his prey. Jeran made it to his knees, pulling heavily on the windowsill to stand, but he could not yet grasp magic. He saw another defeat staring at him in the High Wizard's eyes, and this one he thought he might like even less than the Scorpion's.

Grendor grasped Valkov by the arm, and Jeran saw the shudder as magic was ripped away from the Mage. "Thank you for your assistance, High Wizard," Grendor said. "I would not have been able to stop the Scorpion alone."

Valkov's lips compressed into a thin line, and for a moment, he said nothing. With great effort, Jeran seized magic, only a trickle, but it was enough. He straightened and released his grip on the wall, then faced his saviors and thanked them for their rescue.

"As I said earlier," Valkov replied. "Today the Assembly faced bigger threats than you." He turned and walked from the room.

As soon as he was gone, Jeran fell back to the floor, leaning against the wall as he struggled for air. Grendor studied him. "Are you all right, friend Jeran?"

"I will survive," Jeran answered.

Grendor limped across the room, stooping to retrieve the haft of his weapon. He examined it for a moment, and then said, "Never before have I hoped my actions killed another of the Gods' creations. Do you think he is dead?"

"I doubt the Gods would show us such mercy," Jeran replied.

Using the broken haft as a cane, Grendor hobbled toward Jeran. "Do you know why the bear will never defeat the wolf, friend Jeran? Despite its great size and strength, the bear has one fatal flaw: It thinks it can survive on its own. A wolf never abandons the pack, and that is why it can never truly be defeated."

Despite himself, Jeran chuckled. "I am humbled by your teachings, Elder."

"Then perhaps you should start to heed them." Grendor beckoned toward the door. "The others will sense that you live, but after what we felt through the bond, they will want to see you for themselves."

Dahr clung to pain as a man cast overboard clings to a bit of jetsam, focusing on it rather than the stench of burning flesh, the raucous laughter of Gral and his followers. The Tachans held him fast, pummeling him with fist and foot if he so much as twitched, while the slaver pressed the iron against the flesh of his cheek, searing the right half of his face. When he stepped back, it was only to admire his handiwork, and then to draw a curved blade with barbed, serrated teeth from a sheath at his hip, a wicked mockery of a *dolchek*.

"That was for the Master, pup," he snarled. "This one will be for me."

We come, Brother. Tazahn's voice called to him, echoed by a chorus of the Lesser Voices. He sensed them racing toward him, harried by the Tachan soldiers; the air above darkened with a mass of birds held at bay by the powers of the ShadowMagi.

No! If the Tachans defeat us here, then who will protect the Blood? Do not rescue me at the cost of the Balance!

Reluctantly, the Lesser Voices obeyed, attacking the Tachans with renewed vigor. Dahr laughed then despite the blade lowering slowly toward his eye, and Gral jumped back as if struck.

"Has the pain driven you mad, cub? I assure you, you have not felt the half of it yet. Once I've destroyed your pitiful army, I will hunt down everyone you ever cared about and exact from them the retribution I am denied with you. I will pay a bounty on the head of every Wildman, for the skin of every slaughtered beast. Your prince and King will dare not leave their castle for fear of assassins. Any who so much as whisper the name Dahr Odara will risk torture and death. And for those closest to you... I will handle their punishments personally. Especially that red-headed traitor you call your wife!"

Something changed within Dahr, but it was not the violent, blinding Bloodrage he expected. A calm suffused him, a certainty of purpose, an acceptance of his fate. The hunger for blood remained, the need to kill, but paired with a clarity he rarely experienced, and certainly never experienced in the heat of battle.

"You are a fool if you believe that any one man can destroy the Balance," he said, earning a sneer from the slaver, "and doubly a fool to think that Salos will let you off your leash enough to seek your own pleasures. But your gravest mistake was believing that a mere six men would be enough to keep me from your throat."

Dahr heaved with legs and arms, casting two men off of him and slamming two more together, leaving them disoriented enough for him to shove them away and into Gral, who lunged toward him with his blade. Another twisting roll found him free and on his feet, with his hand around a Tachan's throat. He squeezed, satisfied by the crunch that left the man wheezing for breath as he collapsed.

His greatsword lay a dozen paces away, too far to be retrieved. Yet the blade seemed unnecessary, a crude implement that would make the work he had to do too impersonal. He turned toward his next opponent, driving a fist into his gut with enough force to lift the man off the ground, then pivoting and hitting him again, chopping with the edge of his hand like a woodsmen chopping a tree, and felling the Tachan with about the same effect.

The other four men and Gral had by now recovered, and they faced Dahr as a group, some bearing weapons, some more skittishly with fists at the ready. A few more soldiers ran up to the aid of their commander. Dahr looked at them all and laughed, then launched himself into the attack.

Figures darted past him on either side, plunging *dolcheks* into the chests of two Tachans in synchrony, then turning to find new targets. Dozens of minor wounds covered Olin's and Tarouk's arms and chests, but they looked as if they had fought for only moments and not half a day, and seemed eager for more.

"Korahn want help?" Tarouk asked. "Or prefer hunt alone?"

"I am what I am," Dahr said, advancing toward the Tachans. "I have nothing more to prove. To myself or to anyone else. Let's drive these monsters back to the Nothing they sprang from."

He leapt forward without waiting for reply, deflecting an awkward thrust with the flat of his arm and driving a fist at full force into the soldier's nose. The man fell back, his twisted face already soaked in blood, and dropped to the ground when Dahr's second blow caught him square in the gut.

Dahr hurtled past a second Tachan, leaving the rest of the common soldiers to Olin and Tarouk, and focused on Gral, who once again began to circle with the calm confidence of a seasoned swordsman.

"Do you not yet understand?" Gral snarled. "I am blessed by the Father, the chosen disciple of Salos the Scorpion. This is my world to destroy. Who are you to deny me what is mine?"

Gral's blade darted forward, and Dahr dodged. The slaver lashed out again and again, but Dahr circled wide, keeping out of reach, never dropping his guard, ignoring the constant string of epithets, refusing to surrender to the relentless desire to rush in for the kill.

"I am *Cho Korahn Garun*," Dahr said, a feral smile overcoming his features. "I am the preserver of the Balance, the guardian of the Lesser Voices. As Garun defied His father, so too do I defy Kohr's servants. But if your God craves destruction, I will appease him with yours."

"The only way this fight ends is with you spitted on my blade," Gral spat.

"Then so be it."

Dahr sprinted toward the slaver's readied blade, shifting sideways at the last possible instant. The dagger cut into the flesh of his abdomen, slicing through muscle and scraping against his lowest rib. The pain barely registered after the beating he had endured. Only when he twisted, wrenching his body around to pull the weapon free of Gral's hand, did he cry out, and that scream was as much in triumph as agony.

Deprived of his weapon, Gral fled, but Dahr fell upon him like a beast, pounding with fists, scraping with clawed hands, taking blows without acknowledging them and returning the punishment ten-fold. Never before had he allowed himself to so fully enjoy a fight, and the exhilaration he felt, the sweet freedom of release as he unleashed a lifetime of rage upon the slaver was an experience unmatched in his life.

In time the slaver's struggles slowed, then ceased, but it was not until rough hands dragged him away, slammed him into the ground and forced him to look at the mangled mass of flesh and bone that he regained control of himself.

"It over, Korahn," Tarouk said, hesitant to release him even now, perhaps worried about facing his wrath.

"You should have the *Tsha'ma* look at that," Olin added. "Removing that blade without their help…"

Dahr grabbed the hilt of the dagger and pulled sideways, wincing as the blade sliced through the finger's width of flesh holding it captive. He ripped the shirt off a fallen Tachan and bound the wound, then retrieved his greatsword.

"The *Tsha'ma* can tend my wounds when the battle is over. For the time being, there are more Tachans to kill."

Martyn fell back under Dayfid's assault, using the sum of his skills to block the traitor's relentless assaults. His own attacks clanged harmlessly off Dayfid's prized silvered mail. His opponent advanced recklessly, showing the wild confidence that had made him such a liability, and that had made him so beloved of the people. He barely bothered to defend himself, making half-hearted attempts to knock away Martyn's sword, but always with an eye on the next attack.

Katya joined Martyn, one arm hanging limp at her side, the other clutching her own sword, though it proved no more effective on the former Guardsman. "His armor is Mage-crafted," she warned. "Only the seams are vulnerable. He is without his helmet; focus your attacks on his head and neck."

Understanding dawned. A great deal of Dayfid's odd behavior was suddenly explained. "A gift from Master Albion," Dayfid told him. "Somewhat more encumbering than yours, cousin, but perhaps the only good thing ever to come from magic." He launched into a violent series of attacks, driving both Martyn and Katya back against the walls.

"You should not have followed her," Dayfid said, admonishing the prince. "I would have made their deaths quick. Painless. A courtesy to you for all the honors you bestowed upon me."

Across the tower, Dayfid's men drove the boys back, and at least two lay unmoving. Kaeille and the King fought side by side with the children, protecting Jaenaryn and Miriam, but they remained outnumbered and outskilled. "Help them," Martyn ordered, dodging another of Dayfid's blows.

"You can't defeat him alone," Katya warned.

"You claim to be loyal. You claimed to be a Guardsman. Do as you're commanded!"

He felt her eyes land on him, the fiery stare he hated so much, but she obeyed, slipping outside Dayfid's guard and running to aid King Mathis.

"You just hastened your own death," Dayfid said.

"Anything that shortens the time I must endure your ranting," Martyn replied.

They traded blows, but Martyn remained on the defensive, driven further back with each of Dayfid's attacks. Before long his arm ached with the effort of parrying, and blood flowed from a dozen wounds he had been too slow to avoid.

He needed total concentration simply to avoid death; defeating Dayfid ceased to be an option, as did so much as thinking about aiding the others.

"Under different circumstances..." Dayfid cut off his words and laughed. "No. I could never follow a Batai, especially not one as blind as you."

Dayfid lunged, his sword sweeping down in an arc, missing Martyn by a finger's breadth and striking sparks as it hit the parapet. The prince dashed toward Dayfid, pivoting when they stood side by side, throwing out a leg and catching the Durange behind the knee, knocking him off balance and to the ground.

Such a move would have disabled most fighters in heavy armor, but Dayfid rolled away as if the mail he wore bore no weight at all, and he rose to his knees holding Katya's discarded crossbow.

Martyn froze, but Dayfid cast his eyes across the tower and took aim.

"Father!" Martyn shouted, and the King turned in time to see the threat, diving sideways and knocking Jaenaryn to the ground beneath him. The bolt sailed harmlessly over their heads, clattering against the stones behind them.

In the moment of calm that followed, Martyn saw that his allies had dealt with all but two of Dayfid's companions. Most of the young men lay dead or gravely wounded, but Mika stood beside Miriam, spoiling to rejoin the fight but concern for the princess forcing him to stand as her guard.

King Mathis regained his feet and offered his hand to the Aelvin Ambassador. Jaenaryn took it, and as he rose drew a dagger from his robes and plunged it into the King's side. "A gift from Emperor Luran," he said, tucking a black rose into the King's collar.

"NO!" Mika's cry echoed Martyn's. Dayfid's renewed assault prevented the prince from going to his father's side, but Mika abandoned the princess and leapt upon Jaenaryn, stabbing his sword into the Elf's chest and then savaging him, clawing at his eyes, pounding him with fist and foot.

Martyn lost sight of them as he refocused his attention on his own attacker. The traitor drove him back, unleashing a string of overhand blows that left Martyn staggering and gasping for breath. He retreated until he felt the press of the parapet against his back, and he knew then that his fight was over.

Dayfid's next blow knocked the sword from Martyn's hand and left his whole arm numb from the jarring impact. He braced himself, readied himself for death, and wondered whether the Gods might forgive him for a lack of faith that persisted even as Dayfid's sword began its descent.

Suddenly, the sword was gone, and Katya leapt into Martyn's vision, diving at her cousin and carrying him toward the rampart. They grappled against the stones for a moment, but when Dayfid seemed to be getting the upper hand, Katya jumped, throwing her legs out over the wall and dragging Dayfid with her.

Martyn ran toward them, catching one of Katya's arms just as Dayfid's weight shifted to the outside of the tower. Martyn grunted as Katya slammed him against the wall, but he held fast, listening with morbid delight as Dayfid's scream faded and cut off abruptly.

He reached over the wall with his other hand and secured his grip. With Kaeille's help, he managed to haul Katya back onto the tower. Face pale and sucking in quick breaths, she stammered thanks.

"And to you," Martyn said. "If not for you... That is... I...." He struggled to find the right words. "I still don't like you."

"Dahr would prefer to find you alive when he returns to Kaper. Don't worry about me. See to the King."

Katya's words brought reality slamming home like the strike of a blacksmith's hammer.

AFTERTHOUGHTS

The opening door brought with it a grim pall, the cruel sting of hope bred from denial. Dahr looked at the sweat-soaked sheets covering King Mathis, wincing at the tortured movements beneath the soiled linens, at the rasping breaths and nearly inaudible groans hissing through the chamber. Aryn and Liseyl stood on one side of the bed, Aryn holding down the King's thrashing arms while Liseyl mopped his brow. Sheriza stood across from them, appearing as near to death as the King, skin wan, eyes sunken and half-closed, body hunched under its own weight. Martyn paced at the foot the bed, unmindful of Dahr's arrival, lost in a bleak future of responsibility and duty.

Jeran smiled when their eyes met, but the expression carried little warmth. "I'm glad my people found you. I'm glad you came. I—What is it?"

Dahr's eyes were drawn to Jeran's left cheek, where the figure of a glossy black Scorpion tattooed his flesh, its barbed tail poised to strike at the eye. His own hand moved to the still-aching scar upon his own cheek, the raw and raised wound a stark contrast to the masterful artistry of Jeran's brand.

"Something Yarchik said to me. 'So will they be marked, *Sabiya Sal'aqran*, Children of the Scorpion, brothers but of different blood, saviors but of different Gods. By their will the world will be sundered, the old ways cast like carrion unto the winds; by their might will bonds be shattered, and the world reforged anew; by their grace alone might the Blood be spared the Nothing, and the children of the Gods survive the coming storm.'" Dahr could not contain the sigh that escaped his lips. "Even in death I can't escape his Gods-damned prophecies."

Jeran clapped a hand to his arm. "Come. We've shattered enough of the world for a little while."

"The King?"

"Sheriza doesn't expect him to survive another ten-day."

"I thought those Healers could do all but raise the dead." Sheriza's head snapped around at Dahr's sour words, and she fixed him with a glare so venomous that he withdrew to the side of the chamber.

"The poisons of the *Noedra Synissti* have a magic of their own," Jeran told him, "and the Healers exhausted themselves in the wake of the battle. Salos planned this assassination well."

Jeran's expression grew thoughtful, his eyes distant. "The Gift has limitations; it is a tool like any other. And just like a blacksmith's hammer, it is far easier to destroy with it than to restore. That is one of the things I hope to teach with my Academy."

"So what do we do?"

"We...?" Jeran repeated. "It's nice to hear you're part of the world again. We will do our best to make this tragedy benefit us more than it benefits our enemies."

"Is that all you see now?" Martyn hissed as he joined them. "Move and counter-move, plotting and politics? Have you forgotten where you would be if not for my father?"

Jeran's expression never faltered, nor did he rise to Martyn's goading. "If you think to question my love of the King—"

"No…" Martyn cut him off, clapping a hand to Jeran's shoulder in apology. "No. I speak from grief, not from truth. And you…." He turned toward Dahr, gripping his shoulders in greeting. "Alrendria owes you a great debt. Your victory along the Celaan has driven the Tachans back, reconnecting us with our armies in Gilead. Even now, Brell and Jaem plot a counterattack. With the might of the Army of the Boundary beside us"—Martyn managed to say the last without a note of derision—"we will drive our enemies into the Eastern Sea."

"My forces are not yet ready for prolonged battle," Jeran replied. "They are young. Inexperienced. Spreading them out to fight campaigns is folly, especially when Lorthas's true intentions remain a mystery."

"Your Gifted are the best counter we have against Salos's ShadowMagi, especially now that I earned the Mage Assembly's ire by defending you. Without them, how do you expect us to reclaim and hold Gilead, or gain any foothold within the Tachan Empire?"

Jeran's silence was answer enough. "You expect me to let it fall to the Tachans?" Martyn exclaimed. "You expect me to tell my wife that her lands do not deserve to be saved? That we have abandoned her people to the mercy of the Scorpion?"

"I expect you to realize that you can't win this war fighting to east and west, with the Black Fleet controlling the sea lanes between and the threat of Lorthas's armies climbing over the Boundary hovering over all else." Jeran rose up to full height and faced off against Martyn as if they were equals, or perhaps as if he were the superior. "I expect you to understand that with the *Kohr'adjin* and the *Kohrno-dra* allied with the Tachan Empire, Gilead is lost regardless. I expect you to open the borders to the Gileans, and the Rachannan, and even to any Tachans who hope to escape the Scorpion's tyranny, and then to use them to bolster defenses along the borderlands."

"You counsel defense? You counsel cowardice?"

"I counsel survival. You gamble with the lives of your people, and moreso with the lives of mine, since your grand strategy involves throwing them into the jaws of the enemy so that your Guardsman need not face the brunt of the attack."

"How dare you speak to me in such a tone," Martyn snapped, his voice rising. "I am your—"

"I will speak to you this way until you start acting like a King, until you look beyond the glory of the next few ten-days and plan for a distant future, until you show a hint of concern for those whose lives you control. And if you do not care for my words, you will like far less some of the other things you'll have to endure if you want the Army of the Boundary to fight your battles for you."

Fury darkened Martyn's face, an anger so pure that Dahr stepped closer in case he needed to keep the two from coming to blows. "Valkov was right! You said you were loyal to me—"

"I said I would never let Kaper fall, and that I was loyal to the King. Kaper stands, and I stand at my King's side. But your father would never drive Alrendria to the cusp of the Nothing for glory, and then walk home crying out victory over the corpses of his people. Listen to my counsel, and then do as you want. I will not force you down any path." Jeran smiled that emotionless and calculating smile he wore so often of late. "I think you'll even approve of most of what I have to say."

"You know nothing of what we endured here, or what I intend to—"

"I know who you were before I was taken to Dranakohr, and I know what you must become if we are to survive this war, but you are right: I know nothing of who you are. That is why I fear for our future."

"And what of you?" Martyn asked, turning his venomous gaze on Dahr. "Does the hero of countless battles also counsel flight? Surely I can convince you to take up arms against Alrendria's enemies."

The thought of more battle did not sicken Dahr, but neither did it sing to him, calling him like the lure of a snake charmer's flute. "We broke the Tachan's spirit, but not their will. So too with the *Kohr'adjin*. Our enemies will return, in greater numbers and with more determination. Drive recklessly into Ra Tachan now, and you may be cut off from your army again, or lose it entirely."

"I thought for sure that you, of all my friends, would not cower from the Tachans like a rabbit before a fox." Martyn made a show of disappointment, a tactic that had once worked so well on him, but now just made Dahr take firm hold of his own temper.

"It says something of your leadership," Jeran murmured, "that you cannot even convince a fish to swim."

"There are some among the Assembly of Houses who want you named traitor," Martyn snarled. He tried to look imperious, but forced to look up into Jeran's ice blue eyes, eyes that showed no fear, no apprehension at condemning the wishes of a man who would soon be one of Madryn's most influential powers, he appeared little more than a petulant child. "Those who want your Family stripped of its honors and your lands divided among others. Do you court such a future?"

"The future holds far worse for me than black marks on a piece of paper. As for my holdings… Try to take them, and we will see where they land."

"That is enough!" Aryn barked, prying their eyes off each other and driving all three back with the air of command bred from winters as a Guard Commander. "Might I remind you that this is neither a council hall nor a tavern. If you feel the need to debate Alrendria's future or list each other's failings, I suggest you find one. But if you wish to see your King, then now is the time; your bickering woke him."

They crowded around the bed, their dispute forgotten, and took turns gripping Mathis's ice cold hands, ignoring the frailty in the once firm grip. His eyes focused slowly, but when he recognized who stood beside him, a smile flitted across his face.

"My… boys… I never thought to see you three together again." He studied them, and his face contorted in agony, not from his wounds, but from a more internal pain, a deeper one. "I fear… I fear I misused you, placed too many burdens, too soon. And now… And now the evils I leave for you to fight in my absence… Your suffering will haunt me in the Twilight World."

They protested as one, seeking to reassure the King, to bring him peace in his final moments. Tears flowed freely down Martyn's cheeks, and moisture caressed Dahr's own flesh; Jeran's expression remained impassive, his demeanor controlled, but Dahr could sense through the tenuous bond they again shared a hurt as deep as his own, perhaps one that ran even deeper.

"You are wise to feign hostility," Mathis said, taking one each of Jeran's and Martyn's hands. "You both will have many enemies within Alrendria, and they can use your friendship to rally support for their own agendas. In public, make a show of restrained tolerance, but in private remember the friendship you have, the brotherhood you've shared. United, I suspect that none alive will be able to stand against you.

"And you...." Mathis turned his eyes on Dahr. "The wounds you suffered run far deeper than the scars you show, and I am the one who sent you down that path, who took a gentle soul and scourged him until all the world looks black and cold. Your anguish pains me more than any other. Forgive me... Forgive me...."

Dahr fought to find words, looked within to find the strength he needed, but the monster fled at the sight of the King; this was not the kind of battle it was inclined to fight.

"Aryn...? Aryn...?" The King began to thrash, and though Aryn was at his side immediately, Mathis did not notice. "I had my time with them, Aryn; now it's up to you. I hope I did... Cerril? Cerril, where have you gone?"

The King's words turned to rambling, and Sheriza ushered them away from the bed. "He needs to rest," the Healer said, but she took a firm hold on Martyn's arm and pulled him around to face her. "I do not have the strength to purge the poison from his body, but there is no need for him to suffer."

The Healer's words, laden with implication, did not take Martyn entirely by surprise. The prince looked at the writhing form of his father, then at his two friends. Dahr gave an almost imperceptible nod; when death was assured, only one kindness remained. Again Jeran said nothing, but the look he gave the prince spoke volumes.

"No..." Martyn whispered, though it seemed as if the word had to be ripped from his throat. "My ascension will be difficult enough without rumors of regicide. Do what you can for his pain, but do not speed his death. And make sure I am never alone in his presence."

Sheriza frowned, but whatever else she might have wished to say went unspoken when Jeran and Dahr closed ranks around Martyn and led him from the room.

"You make an interesting proposal, High Wizard, but Roya and Alrendria have long been allies."

"I do not ask you to abandon that friendship, King Tobin," Valkov replied. "In the coming conflict, the Assembly will still choose Alrendria over the Tachan Empire. However, Mathis's son has already shown his ambition, and we expect more innocents to suffer for it. Has the Prince of Alrendria not already demanded a delegation from Roya be transported to Kaper by followers of the rogue Mage Odara?"

"Prince Martyn requested a delegation," Tobin said after a pronounced pause, "and I obliged him. There was no coercion. No threat."

"I must have been misinformed, your Majesty. Though I wonder what might have happened had you refused. In the end, it matters little. The Assembly does not ask you to turn your back on your alliance with Alrendria; the Assembly asks only that you ally yourself with us as well. Salos's fleet wreaked havoc along your coasts. They are gone for now, but wouldn't you prefer to have us here to counter them when they return?"

"As I said, High Wizard, you make an interesting proposal. I will have to think on it."

"Very well. But don't think too long, King Tobin." Valkov focused his Gift and opened a Gate. "In these troubled times, a day's delay can spell destruction."

"I understand your frustration, Miriam, but I see no alternatives—"

"My frustration!" Miriam hurled a vase, and Martyn winced as the fine crystal shattered on the wall behind him. "Why would I be frustrated that you've decided to condemn my people to slavery under the Tachans. We should have abandoned Gilead as soon as we finished gutting it of useful resources!"

"Your homeland is indefensible." Martyn clung to his patience by the narrowest of threads. For days he had known no peace, could not share a room with his wife without reigniting this debate. Today, he sought to use flattery and reason to win her over. "You understand strategy as well as any I've ever known. To hold Gilead, or even just Aurach, is to court defeat in the great conflict. What we do, we do for the greater good."

"That is easy to say when it's not your home you're abandoning."

"Your father—"

"My father has lost his will to rule! He's a shadow of the man I knew, a gutless worm unwilling to defend his people. He—"

"He understands that a kingdom in exile is better than no kingdom at all. We are abandoning Gilead, but not the Gileans. Our plan calls for—"

"Our plan? *His* plan, you mean."

"Jeran and I worked out the details together. We will draw back—"

"Perhaps he's as great a Mage as they claim," Miriam mused. "He's at least powerful enough to convince my husband he's still a King."

"What would you have me do?!" Martyn shouted, his composure failing. "What alternative do you see? Show me a different path and I will take it. But I will no longer—"

This time, he caught the bottle before it hit him. He stared at the green glass for a moment, his hand tightening around the neck, and Miriam winced when he drew it back to throw.

The bottle shattered on the floorstones, surrounding Miriam in a circle of glittering daggers. "I will hear no more of this," Martyn growled before storming from the room. He ignored Miriam's outstretched hand, the way her acid tongue miraculously turned sweet when faced with another evening alone.

In the hall, he encountered a servant refilling the oil lanterns. "Have you seen Lady Kaeille?"

"She left the palace yesterday, my Lord," the girl stammered. "I don't know when she plans on returning."

Martyn remembered Kaeille's insistence that she be taken to the Empress to report on Jaenaryn's treachery, and the eagerness with which Jeran spirited her away. He looked again at the girl before him, young and firm, fair of hair and complexion, with an appealing swell at chest and hip. Moreover, she looked at him with awe, and maybe even a hint of fear, not with the disappointment he so often endured from the women he loved. *A King stands before her, and she knows it.*

A playful smile quirked Martyn's lips. "Come with me. I have need of you."

"I am honored, uncle."

"Don't be," Salos said, reclining against the cool wood of his throne. Bandages wrapped his gut, the wound raw and red, throbbing from the 'healing' he had received at the hands of his Gifted. "You are my choice because I have no one else available. You have too much of your father's temperament, prone to mood swings and fits of passion, acts of revenge and outdated notions of honor. Even that fool of a slaver had a better idea of when to fight, and when flight was the wiser option."

Keldon's expression hardened, the pride he had worn frozen in a mockery of self-importance. "Still, to be named commander of all our forces, to earn the right to lead those forces against the Alrendrians... I consider it a great honor. If you require greater discipline from me, then you will have it. I will not fail you. And to prove my worth, my first task will be to resume the assault on Kaper, and bring you the heads of the Batai."

"This is what I talk of, Keldon," Salos sighed, feigning greater disappointment than he felt, enjoying the confusion and doubt that played across his nephew's face. "You have no concept of strategy, no understanding of our greater purpose. Our foes think they have won a victory, but they do not have the will to follow up on it. Instead of bringing the battle to us, they will consolidate their holdings, strengthen their borders, and redraw their maps; the nations of the west will scramble to make new alliances, and in the process they will unwittingly become our allies. All the while we can tighten our grip on the lands we control, from the Eastern Ocean to the border of Alrendria, from the most barren stretches of the Tachan Land to the depths of the Aelvin Empire. We can find and train an army of Gifted, and use our subtle touch to tighten our fist around the throats of any who oppose us. When Alrendria thinks itself ready for war, it will face an Empire unlike anything Madryn has seen, and it will have at its back a thousand vipers, a thousand enemies it thinks are friends, a thousand hounds to nip at its heels while we scourge it. And then, when the world is consumed in flame, when the rivers are stained red with blood, then will the Father reward us with His greatest honor."

Keldon stared at his uncle for a time. "So, I am not to resume the war against Alrendria. Then how is my army to be employed?"

"Crush Gilead, and bring its resources under our control. Secure our border with Alrendria. Then bring order to Rachannon. Remind them that they are Tachans. Be forceful if you must, but remember that they may be more useful alive. After that... We will have to see, but I may need to broker a peace between the Elves and Garun'ah. An army may make such a thing simpler."

"And the war with Alrendria?"

"We will let them think they've cowed us for now. A break in hostilities benefits us far more than it benefits them, no matter what they think."

Guardsmen lined the walls of the Great Hall, expressions hidden in flickering shadow, eyes locked forward, trained on the massed dignitaries. Crossbowmen trained bolts on the floor from concealment above, and a full squad of heavily-armed men waited in a hidden chamber behind the dais. *Choupik* paced the chamber, their short and solid frames moving without so much as a whisper of sound. The Orog carried no weapons; should they be needed, it was their touch, not their military prowess that would be required.

Representatives from the six Great Houses dominated the front rows, though only three Firsts sat in attendance: Jessandra Vela, in a dress of muted blue, studied the theatrics with the seasoned eye of an experienced politician and the casual disinterest of a Mage; Ivor Menglor, barrel-chested and hale despite his advancing winters, kept his eyes on the soldiers, a thoughtful hand cupped over the sweeping expanse of his full, white beard; and Naveen Aurelle, stern and forbidding in countenance, held both her own advisors and the wasting illness leaching the strength from her body at bay with the sheer force of her will. From House Morrena only Brell, Alynna and a few lesser nobles stood in attendance; Lord and Lady Talbot, Gated to the proceedings by Jeran's Magi, represented the interests of House Odara; and the onerous Rafel and his retinue carried the honor of House Batai. Representatives from hundreds of Families packed the hall, and interspersed among them sat representatives from Gilead, Rachannan, Roya, and New Arkam, all brought at Martyn's insistence, all studying each other, competing to look the least uncomfortable at this Alrendrian show of might.

On one side of the Hall sat a delegation from the exiled Aelvin Empire, a cluster of aged, robed Elves who would have occasioned great comment if not for the presence of the Empress before them. Charylla sat aloof, slightly separated from her people, appearing to radiate her own soft, green light. *Ael Chatorra* and *Ael Maulle* surrounded her, none of them armed but all looking as if they were springs wound to the point of breaking.

Across from the Aelvin embassy sat a delegation from the tribes: bear-cloaked Arik and his *Kranach* Kal sat beside Sadarak Cat's Claw, Meila and grim-faced Tarouk of the Anada; Rannarik, Goshen, and Jakal presided over a dozen other *Tsha'ma*. The presence of so many Tribesmen unnerved the nobility, though not so much as the presence of so many Humans, and the dark confines of the Great Hall, unnerved the Tribesmen. If the Elves sat like coiled springs, the Tribesmen twitched like caged animals expecting the lash.

From the Mage Assembly only Aemon stood in attendance, though it was widely known that he had been ousted from any role of responsibility and had no authority among them, and that only millennia as their High Wizard prevented him from severing ties to the Assembly altogether. The old Mage sat alone in a section reserved for the Gifted, but his isolation did little to lessen the aura radiating from him, the air of command that had made whole nations jump when he whispered.

Shadows cloaked the front of the hall, hiding it from view as surely as if a curtain had been drawn across, leaving everyone to believe the new King of Alrendria had yet to pull himself away from the distractions of his morning. As the assemblage grew frustrated, their murmured grumblings rising in a swelling crescendo not unlike the crash of surf upon the shore, he watched, observing every movement, noting every shared glance, every nervous laugh. When he thought them sufficiently roused, Martyn signaled, and Jeran released the magic surrounding them.

The lamps lining the chamber flickered and dimmed, plunging the chamber into an eerie semi-darkness. At the same time, the weave of magic blocking the round quartz above the main entrance dissipated, allowing the sun's rays to focus on the dais, surrounding it in a golden glow, drawing all eyes to the new King of Alrendria.

Martyn sat the throne with ease, not yet burdened by the weight of the crown nor hunched under the mantle of the king's cloak, the Golden Sun of Alrendrian emblazoned across its pristine white material. An unsheathed blade leaned against the throne beside him, glinting in the light of the focused sun, a reminder that his reign began in violence, and that violence would never be far from it. Miriam sat beside him, alabaster skin even paler than normal, the swell of her abdomen unhidden despite the folds of the gown she wore. Rigid and of fixed expression, but regal in both demeanor and bearing, she was as much a prop as the sword, honor-bound to silence even though she had decried nearly every move Martyn had decided to make.

To the left of the throne, Aryn Odara wore the uniform of the Alrendrian Guard, decorated with the symbols of his rank and the honors from his many victories. Beside him stood Dahr, hands lightly gripping the hilt of his greatsword, its point resting on the floor. Shyrock rested upon his shoulder, studying the crowd, spreading out the broad sweep of his wings indignantly whenever he found eyes upon him; Fang pressed against Dahr's side, teeth drawn back, looking as if she intended to launch herself into the crowd at the slightest provocation.

To Martyn's right, Jeran took a position only slightly behind the King, dressed in the black uniform of the Army of the Boundary but with the Odaran wolf embroidered onto the chest. His magic-wrought Aelvin blade rested on one hip opposite a *dolchek*. But the halo of flickering flame around him elicited more comment than the presence of the Garun'ah, and drew more fearful gazes than the wild beasts at Dahr's side.

Few remain ignorant of my Gift, Jeran mused, *but it is one thing to know something, and another to see it flaunted before you.*

Grendor and Katya flanked Jeran, the scarred Orog occasioning as much comment as the presence of a Durange. Behind them stood a dozen more men wearing the Black, and should anyone doubt who they were, each held enough magic to make their eyes shine with the power of the Gift. The Guardsman—even Aryn—had rankled that the Army of the Boundary would guard the stage, that the Guard's presence would be confined to the walls and shadows. But Martyn agreed with Jeran that the threat of magic would prove a far better motivator than the threat of steel.

"Alrendria has won great victories." Martyn spoke low, but Jeran's Gift carried his words throughout the chamber, so that no matter how distant one sat, the words were as clear as if spoken face to face. "Kaper is ours again. The Boundary is secure. Portal and Tylor Durange's fortress of Dranakohr are under the control of House Odara. The Tachans have been driven from our borders, and our victories along the Celaan have taught them not to stare too long at the Rising Sun.

"We have won great victories," Martyn repeated, "but they have cost us greatly. This city lies in ruins, as does Portal... and Vela... and far too much of Alrendria. We have seen our brothers and fathers, our mothers and daughters cut down in a macabre harvest, until scholars wonder if the dead now outnumber the living. We have learned to fear, to doubt the motives of strangers and the intentions of our neighbors. The murder of my father proves that not even Kings are spared the Scorpion's machinations. His death spread distrust among us all, for we no longer know which of our friends may be in league with the enemy.

"The Scorpion's allies have won control of Illendrylla and the Tribal Lands, forcing two great nations into exile, while our own allies fight a losing struggle against the Durange in Rachannon and Gilead. If victorious there, Salos will control the whole of Eastern Madryn, and he will draw down a curtain through which none shall see... and through which none shall pass. Even our own great nation is not without treachery: Jysin Morrena has betrayed his oaths to Alrendria, splintering this land in a way not seen since the days of Peitr Arkam.

"Perhaps worst of all, this war has brought to glaring light our own failings, Alrendria's mistakes compiled over millennia. Long ago, we turned our back on the Gifted, driving them from their homes and their Academies, ousting them from public life, treating them as different and thus forcing them to see themselves as different. Now, when we need them to defend us from the wrath of Salos's ShadowMagi, they have turned their backs on us, demanding unconscionable concessions for their aid, forcing us to break our age-old alliance and seek help from others.

"This war taught us that Alrendria has outgrown its ability to protect itself. The Alrendrian Guard, spread to protect our borders from threats without, failed to protect our people from threats within, and the ravaged landscape, the blighted farms, the abandoned villages will for winters remind me of that failure. The Great Houses once numbered in the hundreds, but over time have consolidated until only six remain, and those too big to serve the needs of the people within them."

Martyn paused to let his words sink in, to let the enormity of the problems facing Alrendria descend upon all the nobility, upon all the dignitaries from other lands invited to this audience. "This war has shown us that Alrendria as it was is no more. It died with my father. To survive, Alrendria must change. To survive those who serve the God of Chaos, we all must change! To survive, We will demand great sacrifices of you; but in exchange, We will offer great opportunities."

The gentle rumble of conversation sprang up among the assembly until a sharp crash reverberated throughout the chamber, a thunderclap emanating from everywhere and yet nowhere, a stark reminder of the powers held in check throughout the chamber.

"Alrendria cannot win in the east," Martyn continued, cutting off all discussion. "Our allies cannot hope to hold out against the might of the Tachan Empire. We have issued orders to our Guard Commanders to withdraw from Aurach, to fall back as far as necessary to ensure that our positions cannot be overrun. Word has been sent throughout Gilead and Rachannan that their lands are lost, but that their lives need not be. We will welcome all who wish to come, establish new Families within the borders of Alrendria, and spread slowly back into the lands controlled by the Tachans, annexing only what we know we can hold, using the Celaan and the border forts to contain the Tachan threat."

Another ripple of comment crossed the room, with reactions ranging from confusion to resentment, the loudest voices coming from Lord Jaem and his Gilean horsemen. Miriam sat statue still, her face a mask of decorum, but Jeran knew that of all his demands, the sacrifice of Gilead had rankled her the most, and perhaps had earned him her lifelong enmity. *It is of no comfort to her that I would have sacrificed House Odara the same way were our positions reversed. She sees only a power-hungry Mage demanding the destruction of her home, even though Alrendria is her home now and she is wise enough to realize Gilead is lost. But I can live with her hatred, though it will drive another wedge between me and Martyn, if it earns us the time we need.*

"In the north, Lord Fayrd will spearhead the reconstruction of Grenz, holding the port as a staging area for future efforts against the Tachans and controlling access to the Celaan. Volunteers will be needed to swell his ranks, to rebuild the city, to restore trade. Lands and titles will be given to any who resettle Eastern Grenz, and with our Rakers patrolling the Celaan, harassing and destroying any settlements along the Tachan side, much wealth can be earned."

Lord Fayrd's past haunts him; he will be fanatic in his defense of Grenz. At least this does not have to plague my conscience—Martyn is the one who saw the value in holding Eastern Grenz, in denying the Tachans access to the river. It is a good reminder that his expertise complements mine, not opposes it.

"We may have to abandon the lands of our allies, but We will not abandon them." Martyn made a broad sweep of his hand to encompass the dignitaries from Gilead and Rachannan. "All who flee to Alrendria will be cared for and protected, established with holdings and given the first opportunity to resettle lands reclaimed from the Tachans.

"We have granted our Aelvin allies asylum within Alrendria until they reclaim their ancestral home, and they will turn the impassable tangle of the Forest of Shadows into a wonder to rival the fabled beauty of Lynnaei. So, too, will our allies among the Tribes be given a home in House Odara, settling the empty expanses of the north in the shadow of the Boundary, where few men dare live. Their willingness to set aside centuries of hostilities and embrace each other as friends and allies will serve as a bold example to us all."

The impassive stares cast between Elf and Garun'ah carried all the warmth of a glacier on the verge of avalanche, but the mere fact they sat in the same room without coming to blows was miracle enough.

The exodus of Tribesmen is something I never planned on, but I cannot turn them away. I wonder if Dahr has served our cause with this act of kindness, or condemned it. In the end, it doesn't matter. The die is cast.

"We cannot yet conquer the Tachan Empire," Martyn continued, his sharp tone demanding silence, "but We can and will restore the Alrendria of old. Our battle will start with the traitors in Morrena, ousting Jysin and handing power to Brell Morrena, who forsook the bonds of family to keep those made to Alrendria. After We regain control of Morrena, We will take our war to our old enemies in Corsa and our new ones in Midlyn, restoring lands lost to Alrendria since the time of the Secession.

"We will not stop until our flank is secure and we can focus on efforts in the east. We will conquer what We must and unite what We can. To that end I announce the reincorporation of New Arkam into Alrendria, the restoration of a Great House long thought lost. Chovra Arkam will assume the duties of First, and with the single stroke of the diplomat's pen we have surrounded our enemies in the west. A similar offer has been sent to King Tobin of Roya; with his acceptance We will unite the world against Salos and his minions!

"But the restoration of Alrendria cannot be done without sacrifice. As the maps are redrawn, all Houses will be forced to cede lands, and new Great Houses will be forged from the pieces. Conquered lands will be divided into new Houses, with titles distributed to those who sacrifice the most for Our cause. In the end, We will have an Alrendria able to protect itself, an Alrendria able to protect its people, an Alrendria where power is no longer concentrated into the hands of a privileged few, and where the Houses again wield enough influence to sway the voice of even a King."

A great tumult rose among the chamber, especially among the elite of Alrendrian nobility. "This remains Alrendria," Martyn said, waiting for the hall to still. "We will hear your petitions, and We will take into consideration your concerns. But We expect all to bow to the will of the Houses, and three of the six have already agreed to support Our wishes. Since House Morrena has no vote until Jysin is dead and his lands are returned to Alrendrian control..."

The rumble began again, and Martyn raised a hand for silence. "We also announce today the merging of two Great Houses, Velan and Odara. The union will be sealed with the marriage of Jeran Odara to Jessandra Vela, with the city of Vela and all lands north of the River Alren coming under Odaran control, and lands south of the Alren divided into new Houses. The wedding will—"

The hall exploded in an uproar, a hundred voices from a hundred Families raised in indignant protest, each demanding to know why their lands were being confiscated while Odara's grew. Martyn let them rail for a time, then raised a hand and shouted, "Silence!"

At that word, Jeran unleashed his Gift, silencing the chamber. Flames of red and orange rose around the dais, radiating heat but not burning; sparks of blue lightning flickered around the Gifted, crackling with the menace of a dam about to burst. As one, the Guardsmen around the chamber readied their weapons, the swords and halberds glowing with their own faint, flickering light. And atop

Dahr's shoulders Shyrock spread his wings and shrieked, a dire sound that Jeran allowed through his cloak of silence, a haunting sound which drove more fear into the hearts of those assembled than the weaponry.

King Martyn's gaze shifted to the side, taking in Jeran and his flickering aura of magic. His expression tightened as their eyes met, lips turning down in a slight frown, eyes glaring daggers, the furrow across his brow hardening like clay in the fire. And then he turned away, and his features resumed the calm display he had shown the assembled nobility thus far.

That was perfect. Just enough to make them expect coercion, not enough for it to look rehearsed. I only wonder how much of it was faked.

"Some might suggest it unfair to ask Lord Odara to incorporate two exiled nations onto his lands, and then confiscate his holdings." Martyn's voice cracked like a whip, but no hint of anger touched his face. He spoke with the authority of a King, with all the subtle tricks of power learned from watching his father. "Some might deem it wise to let the man charged with defending the Boundary defend its entire length.

"In the end, it will be so because I am King of Alrendria, and I have decreed it. Those who think Our decisions misguided may bring them up in council, or you may declare your secession and test Our resolve with steel. Either way, We will end with your… support."

Martyn stood, and he bowed to the assembled Families as did the Kings of old. "We have much to plan, and much more to do. We will meet with all of you in the days to come, to discuss your particular roles in building our new Alrendria. For now, I must plan the withdrawal of our forces from Gilead, as well as our strategy for retaking House Morrena. May Balan's wisdom guide you."

Linked to the Gifted behind him, Jeran opened a Gate, a broad expanse that obscured the entire dais. They all stepped through, leaving the stage barren save for the flames which continued to burn around the platform. As Jeran let go the weave and the Gate began to close, he heard the tumult in the hall resume with more passion than even before. *Alrendria has been frozen for so long, this thaw may cause it to fracture. Martyn was wise to insist that we not burden them with everything at once. He will make a good King, if I can help him step out from his father's shadow.*

"You did well in there," he told Martyn.

Miriam shoved herself between them, facing Jeran with an air of petulant haughtiness that could rival Martyn's most exaggerated condescension. "I'm so glad you feel His Royal Puppet danced properly to your pull of the strings, Lord Odara. I, for one, think it was rude of him to wear the crown himself."

Martyn placed a restraining hand on the Queen's arm. "Enough, Miriam."

"With Odara controlling everything north of the Alren, a House four times the size of the next largest; and with him in command of an army to rival the Guard but spared its loyalty to Alrendria, what is there to stop him should he ever decide to take the throne for himself?"

"If I wanted the crown," Jeran said, "I would be wearing it. All I want is to make sure there's an Alrendria left for Martyn to rule, an Alrendria left for your son to rule."

"Is that supposed to comfort me?" Miriam shrieked. "That my husband remains King of Alrendria at your whim? That my children will rule at your discretion? That my homeland will be overrun by Tachans because saving it does not fit into your grand plan? You claim you don't covet power, yet you wield it easily enough, manipulating lives with skill enough to rival the Scorpion."

"Miriam, be silent!" Martyn's voice snapped with command. "Jeran remains our friend and ally. He has convinced me that what he proposes offers Alrendria its best chance. You will not dishonor him, not to his face and not from the shadows. I will not stand for it!"

Miriam pursed her lips. "It's nice to know you still have enough King in you to lord it over me." She turned on her heel and stomped into their quarters.

Martyn looked at Jeran, a shame and anger to rival his Queen's hidden deep within his eyes. Then he, too, stepped into the royal chambers and shut the door.

"Enter!"

Dahr opened the door, and paused only a moment when he saw the crossbow leveled at his chest. "Expecting someone?"

"Kaper's not as welcoming as it once was," Katya said, setting aside her weapon and gesturing for Dahr to sit. "I never thought to hear myself say this, but I'll be glad to see Dranakohr."

"Jeran would have sent you back at any time."

"And let Martyn know he's won?" A smile pulled up the corners of Katya's mouth. "I'd never be able to live with myself. Do you want a drink?"

Dahr glanced at the wine bottle sitting upon the windowsill and cleared his throat. "It's a bit early in the day for—"

"And yet somehow I doubt it would be your first. The walls of Kaper don't fit you as well as they once did either." Green eyes studied him, delved into him, understood him in a way Dahr doubted anyone save perhaps Jeran ever would. "Why are you here?"

"After Tylor captured Jeran…" He broke off, his eyes drawn back to the bottle until he forced them away. "I… I watched the world crumble around me, and for a long time, I was unwilling to see how much of it was of my own doing. I blamed you, hated you, and once you were back, once you insisted on following me, I hoped to see you share my anguish."

Dahr fell silent, lost in a maelstrom of emotion, and wondered where his darker half hid when he needed to draw on its strength. "Harol Grondellan died thinking he had wronged me, and now he'll never know that without him, I'd have condemned myself and all the Tribes to the Nothing. I can't let you… I…"

Katya went to him, silencing him with a brush of her lips. Then she shoved a travel pack into his gut. "Get your things. Jeran says we leave in the morning."

The Gate closed, sealing off the path to Dranakohr and leaving them in the shadowy confines of the Darkwood. Silence greeted them, the branches above quivering with the nervous excitement of forest denizens surprised by the appearance of so many strangers. A narrow game trail snaked off into the distance, the thick brush and interwoven branches making passage of anything more than a single file column impossible.

Charylla, Treloran, and Astalian spun in slow circles, the Empress with her arms outstretched, as if testing the very air. *Ael Chatorra* disappeared into the forest, their footfalls making no sound as they glided through the trees.

"The Forest of Shadows has a long history of monsters," Jeran told them, "and recent events have reinforced the legends of old. You should have the peace and solitude you require here, though I hope you won't sever all ties with the outside world."

"I think the time of our isolation must end," Charylla said, turning her prob-ing gaze onto Jeran. "If it does not, I fear we will never see the Great Forest again. You will have your teachers, Jeran, and your students. As many as wish to go."

"Will any wish it?" Jeran asked. "Elves do not have a reputation for having much curiosity about the world outside your forest."

Charylla and Astalian shared a look. "I suspect much of that reputation is due to the isolation *Ael Alluya* forced on our people," Treloran told him. "*Ael Pieroci* have desired renewed trade for decades, as have our craftsmen."

"Entire squads of *Ael Chatorra* have requested permission to visit the fortress of Portal," Astalian added, "and to see the mighty stronghold of Dranakohr. I my-self would like to see these places of legend."

Jeran clapped him on the shoulder. "Then you will see them, my friend. I hope to see you restored to the Great Forest quickly, but I also hope to see much of you in the seasons to come, especially while you reside within House Odara."

Another Gate opened, this one to the palace in Kaper. "I will leave you to in-spect your home, and prepare the way for the rest of your people. My Gifted will begin transporting them shortly. Keiton here will bring your messages to me." He signaled, and the young Gifted behind him stepped forward, trembling in the presence of the Empress. "Whatever your needs, do not hesitate to ask."

Before Jeran could go, Charylla took him by the shoulders and placed a gentle kiss upon his brow. "What you have accomplished... What you hope to accom-plish... Your vision remains so clear, your enthusiasm infectious. One cannot help but hope you achieve it. Grandfather would be proud."

"It is his dream I hope to realize, Empress. With your support, perhaps we will even succeed."

Martyn looked out over those assembled with a broad smile. "In the days since my father's death, few events have given me reason for joy. To preside over the union of these two people, whose loyalty to Alrendria is unquestioned and whose service has earned them hallowed spots in the Twilight World, will forever reside among my fondest of memories."

At his side, Miriam cradled their newborn son, Prince Justyn, in her arms, the wide-eyed infant gurgling and cooing, a shock of hair framing his head in curls. The Queen offered her blessing as well, bending to place a kiss upon the forehead of those who knelt before her.

"This union that We have witnessed," Martyn intoned, "now may only the Gods sunder. Rise, Aryn Odara. Rise Lady Odara."

Aryn stood, taking Liseyl into a tight embrace before turning to present his new wife to the world. As they descended the dais, they were greeted by those they held most dear—Jeran and Dahr; Liseyl's children Mika, Ryanda, and Eilean; Lord and Lady Talbot—who followed them down the aisle and into the crowd beyond. Amidst cheers loud enough to shake the stones of the hall, the couple was raised upon shoulders and hauled from the castle, to be carried about the palace on display.

"You are certain of this, Mika?" Jeran asked as they followed the procession. "Your valor during the siege has earned you much respect. If you stay here and join the Guard, you could be a subcommander in a winter or two. Our future in Dranakohr is... unsure at best."

"The halls of Kaper hold only reminders of my failure," Mika replied, his too-somber expression a mirror of Jeran's. "He should not have died."

"You protected the King better than a thousand Guardsmen," Jeran told him. "And my uncle told me how much joy you brought to him during his final seasons. We are men, Mika. Just men. We cannot prevent the sun from rising, nor turn back the passing of time. We can only have faith that Mathis's death will serve a greater purpose, and we must strive to make sure that it does."

They walked in silence for a time, two implacable islands amidst a sea of revelry. "They claim you deal with the Darklord," Mika said at last. "They whisper that you serve him, that you will renew the MageWar and bring destruction to all Madryn."

Jeran smiled at that. "Speak with Lorthas, and you may in fact serve him, however unwittingly. There are few alive who can twist words and motives as well as he. As for the rest... The MageWar may resume, and I may be painted as much the villain as Lorthas, but I will not be the first to strike. If the Assembly wishes a war, they will have to start one."

Mika opened his mouth again, but Jeran forestalled him with a wave. "Such talk is too morose for this day. We will have winters to debate such matters. Today, let us celebrate the union of our Families, and do our best to take what joy we can from this world."

"As you say, Lord Jeran." Mika smiled then, an imitation of Jeran's own expression, but the mirth refused to spread across his face.

"Don't you think you're making a mistake?"

Jeran looked down at the black uniform he had donned. "You think Odaran blue instead?"

Jes sighed as she set aside her cup of tea, turning away from the balcony overlooking the valley of Dranakohr. Framed in the light of a clear sky, with the snow-capped peaks of the Boundary behind her, she made a radiant sight, and Jeran admired her beauty almost as much as he enjoyed the frustration that played across her face.

"Must we do this every time?" she asked.

"I'm sure I don't know what you mean," he laughed, smoothing his shirt. He left his Aelvin sword hanging on the wall, but slipped his *dolchek* into its sheath on his belt before reconsidering and returning it to the table. Fragmenting the Velani lands had been tough on Jes, as had the decision to relocate to Dranakohr, dismantling one of Alrendria's Great Houses in the process. These word games they played amused her, distracted her from the deep melancholy he sensed building within her, and he would sacrifice anything, his pride included, to keep her happy.

"This meeting with the Assembly is a waste of time."

"No doubt. But Martyn wishes it. He hopes to broker a peace."

"And you do not sense a trap?"

"I am not a fool. But Valkov will tread softly in Kaper."

"Only if he works alone."

Jeran's smile slipped. Martyn joining league with the Mage Assembly was a possibility he had given no serious thought until Jes suggested it. "Martyn will not hand me over to the Assembly."

"Don't be blind. There is friendship, and there is politics. The two have little overlap. Even the staunchest of allies would rankle under the conditions you've imposed."

"Martyn chafes under the terms of our arrangement, but he needs the Army of the Boundary to fight his wars. Until the Mage Assembly is willing to field an army of Gifted able to counter Salos's ShadowMagi, I have little to fear from Kaper."

"Some husbands heed the advice of their wives. Queen Miriam harbors no love for you."

"Miriam is nearly as shrewd as my own wife," Jeran countered, though his flattery earned him little more than a roll of the eyes. "She may be seeking a time to strike, but she will not do so openly."

"No retinue? No weapons? If this is a trap..."

"To refuse now would make me look the coward, and play into Valkov's contention that I am no true ally of Alrendria."

"And to go under these conditions makes you look arrogant and foolhardy."

"The world already thinks me the former," Jeran laughed, "and all the better if they think me the latter. But perhaps... Alrendrian law grants me the right to take an advisor. Who better than my wife? You'll want to criticize my handling of the affair anyway. Best if you are there to witness it yourself."

"Both Valkov and Martyn know what I am."

"But they're the only ones. If they cry 'Mage' when they see you, we can reveal the identities of hundreds of Assembly Magi. No doubt Valkov would prefer to avoid that."

Jes stood and glided toward him. That she already wore a dress suitable for a state meeting meant she had anticipated the outcome of this conversation long before it started. "You think you have everything figured out, don't you?"

"I don't need to," Jeran replied, offering his arm as a Gate to Kaper opened before them. "Not so long as I have you to do my thinking for me."

"Why are we here?" Dahr asked, staring at the decaying remains of the Odara farm. Weeds had overgrown the porch, and brush choked the fields beyond. Little remained of the farm as Dahr had known it, but even still, returning brought a sense of peace to him, a simple contentment he rarely experienced but often longed for.

"Why wouldn't you come home?" Jeran asked, sharing a smile with Katya.

Dahr looked up toward the plateau, then toward the remains of the barn. "Once, perhaps, but now—Is somebody in there?"

"Once, and again," Jeran replied. "The Elves control the Darkwood and the Tribes roam the empty plains to the north and west. Both sides have promised no bloodshed, but I need someone to mediate any disputes. Who better than Garun's Chosen One, the man whose army saved the Aelvin Empire from destruction?"

"I... I can't. This is the Odara farm."

"Lucky for me then that I give it to an Odara. This, and the surrounding lands as well, from the Red Hills to the edge of the Darkwood. You are no mere farmer, Dahr Odara, but a Lord in your own right."

"No... This is Aryn's home. I couldn't—"

"Aryn will be in Dranakohr with his wife... Or in Portal... Or on campaign. He has no need of this place, but you do."

Suspicion edged Dahr's voice. Suspicion and anger. "Because Aryn is needed in Dranakohr and I am not?"

"The confines of Dranakohr were not meant to hold a Garun'ah. Not even a tame one like you. I hope to see you there often, and one of my Gifted will be at your disposal at all times, to take you wherever you wish, but I could not condemn you to a life there. Nor could I insist that your *bahlova* dwell within those dark halls. She claims it does not bother her, but she can hide little from me."

Emotion welled up within Dahr. "I don't know how to thank you."

"Keep the Tribes and the Elves from killing each other," Jeran replied, stepping back through the Gate. "And don't thank me yet. I'll return before sunset tonight, and we can feast to your new home."

The Gate slid closed, and Dahr stood in silence for a time, arm around Katya's shoulder, staring at the shuttered farmhouse, watching the shifting shadows play across the greyed wood in the summer breeze.

"There *is* someone in there!" Dahr shouted when he saw the hint of color pass behind the cracked doorway. He raced forward, drawing his sword from the sheath over his shoulder, and burst through the front door. A half dozen young women went screaming from the room at his arrival, darting through the swinging door to the kitchen, their shrieks fading behind them.

Dahr followed, confused by their presence, and by the fact that they had been setting out carpets and furnishing, not ransacking the remains of Aryn's farm. In the kitchen he found a cauldron bubbling over the fireplace, half its contents spilled across the floor, the spoon only a few hands from escaping out the door.

At the rear entrance to the house stood a woman, a broad and buxom woman with hair of chestnut brown and eyes the color of molasses. "Who do you think you are to burst into this house?" she demanded, thumping a hand against his chest. "We don't condone that kind of behavior here, not even from a Wildman."

Scores of people gathered outside, pouring out of the barn, climbing out of a row of tents half-hidden behind the tangled orchard, or peering down from the pasture above. A dozen or so were armed soldiers, but most wore the clothes of common folk, with a handful—like the woman before him—dressed in finer garb.

"I am Dahr Odara," Dahr answered slowly. "And this is my land."

The woman's gaze drifted past him, to where a familiar voice said, "He is who he says he is, Sasha."

Dahr whirled around, as annoyed by the amused and knowing smile on Katya's face as he was surprised to see Lord Grondellan's steward sheathing the curved dagger he held within striking distance of Dahr's back. "Yurs? What are you doing here."

"It's him, is it?" the woman said, grabbing Dahr by the chin and turning him around, examining him like a young girl might examine her newest bauble. "Grown a bit since the last I saw you. Father intended to marry us, you know, to insure your inheritance. Too late for that, though," she said with a sidelong glance at Katya. "I'm no Gilean wh— I lack the tolerance of certain Gilean ladies to share her husband. You'll just have to find me someone else, someone suitable to my station."

Memories of Grondellan's manor came back, to the eldest of three daughters, a girl a few Winters his senior, a brown-haired wild child who could do no wrong in her father's eyes. "Lady Sasha...? Why are you here? Why are you in my house?"

"Lord of the Manor already, are we? Where else do you expect us to stay? Those timid villagers about fainted dead away when we rode through town. Started screaming that the Tachans had returned. Tachans! You don't expect me to stay anyplace where they think *I* am a Tachan, do you?"

"But why are you *here*?" Dahr asked. "In Alrendria!"

"Lord Grondellan sent me to Rachannon with strict instructions regarding his succession," Yurs explained. "He sensed the way the wind was blowing, and knew that even if he returned, he was too close in line to the throne to survive the occupation. He named you his heir, and by Rachannan law, adopted you as his rightful son. We brought with us the balance of his holdings, the amassed wealth of Grondellan, and all the privileges and duties that go with the title of Lord of Grondellan."

"No..." All he desired was freedom and isolation, and yet now he was saddled with duties to four different nations, and considered a noble in two different Houses. "No! Go away! All of you leave! Now!"

His words made a few of those outside cringe, but a single gesture from Lady Sasha had the maids brushing past him into the house and renewing their duties. A few words had the others dispersing and resuming their various tasks, all but ignoring Dahr's continued attempts to make them flee.

"An irony, that," Yurs said, his low chuckle grating against Dahr's composure. "Were they still slaves, they'd be required to obey you; but at your insistence, Lord Grondellan freed us before he died. Now we can go where we choose, serve whomever we choose. And we choose to serve you, Lord Odara."

In the recesses of his mind, Dahr heard the monster laughing.

The chamber was cold and almost barren, the dark stone walls rough from the pain-staking labor required to carve it out of the mountain. Candles flickered in sconces of wrought iron, the dancing shadows adding to the room's eerie gloom. Few decorations adorned the hall: a broad map of Madryn, another of Alrendria, and a smaller diagram of House Odara, the cartographer's ink still damp from the additions of new lands. A broad, elliptical table dominated the center of the room, its finely-polished surface a masterwork of craftsmanship. A score of matching chairs surrounded the table, all identical except one placed at the vertex of the table farthest from the chamber's door. That chair had a slightly higher back, a slightly broader beam, its arms decorated with just a hint more scrollwork, giving it the slightest impression of prominence in a room that screamed equality.

"Why are we here?" Aemon asked with an air of command that hid a growing unease. He sat at the center of the table, but his eyes kept drifting away from Jeran, to the place on the table where three empty chairs remained, where the invisible pull of the Boundary held his attention.

"It was your idea for representatives of the Four Races to meet regularly," Jeran reminded him. "You proposed a formal council at the end of the MageWar, though all nations soundly rejected the notion. Some have hinted that you held such meetings in secret anyway, prodding events in the direction you deemed best. By adding structure and an air of formality to such proceedings, we—"

"I understand the purpose of these meetings, my boy," Aemon exclaimed. "Why are we meeting *here*!"

"And why not hold these meetings in Kaper," Jes added, "or at least with members of the other Houses, the other nations?"

"Alrendria is in turmoil, as is the rest of Madryn," Jeran replied. "You've been to the Assembly of Houses, Jes! You've seen how little is accomplished, how much time is wasted with frivolities, how much suspicion and revulsion they cast toward me, for being Gifted and for the political necessities that demanded our ascension. Alrendria is not yet ready to add the other Races to their vision, to cast aside more prejudices as old or older than their fear of the Gifted. As for why we meet here, in this place…"

Jeran looked around the room, studying the faces of his allies. Aemon sat between Jes and Oto, here to represent the Gifted, and Yassik and Alwen, here to advocate for the students of the Academy. Of the five, only Aemon exhibited any signs of apprehension, though he had had less time to accustom himself to Dranakohr.

The Elves, however, mirrored Aemon's disquiet, even exaggerated it. Treloran's gaze rested firmly on the three empty chairs, while the Aelvin twins, Nahrona and Nahrima, pointedly looked away from them. The Empress hid her discomfort behind a mask of propriety, a stern wall of control. Only Astalian showed no hint of anxiety, but of all the Elves he was the least attuned to the magic around them.

Dahr sat among the representatives of the Tribes, calm and controlled, looking decidedly like a leader of men. His casual comfort made the other Garun'ah view him in a new way, as a different man, perhaps in truth as Garun's chosen savior. Where Dahr showed no fear, the others all but cowered, their eyes drawn to the dark stone above, their shoulders hunched under the press of mountain, their savage strength sapped by the walk through narrow tunnels. Rannarik and Jakal lost the illusion of self-assurance common to the Gifted of every Race, and Arik and Meila, among the strongest of the *Kranora*, fixed their gaze on the table, or on the maps, as if dreaming themselves back in the world outside.

Beside the Tribesmen, Ehvan sat beside the Elder Lorana. Neither had a sense of what made the others afraid, and both called the caverns of Dranakohr home. Their confusion at the discomfiture evident throughout the room was almost enough to make Jeran laugh.

"We meet here for two reasons," Jeran said. "The Assembly of Houses is in turmoil, and I have seen firsthand the tide of passions that ripple through those proceedings. Yet they are all of the same nation; here, we will negotiate the fate of four nations, of man and Mage, of Elf and Orog, of Human and Garun'ah. No doubt our discussions will be spirited, our convictions heartfelt. We agreed to enter this chamber unarmed, and the Gift is a weapon as dangerous as any other. By sitting this close to the Boundary"—Jeran held his arm out toward Lorana, and at the extent of his reach blue sparks began to jump toward his fingers—"we are not only reminded of the mistakes of the past, we are all rendered equal, in truth as well as in spirit."

"And what is it, exactly, that you hope to accomplish?" Charylla asked. It was the first the Empress had spoken since arriving, and her words drew the eyes of all in attendance. "Do you expect to change the world overnight?"

"Change is rarely slow, Empress. Throughout Madryn's history, the greatest transformations occur over the course of a few frantic winters, with the consequences rippling across the centuries. In a handful of seasons, Salos has taken control of half of Madryn and caused turmoil and revolution in all the rest. Unless we can unite all the west against him, then the world may, in fact, be returned to the Nothing."

Aemon cleared his throat. "You said four nations, my boy. Elves and Garun'ah, and Alrendria… Have you already forgotten that House Odara is part of Alrendria, as the rest of the nobility claim?"

"No…" Jeran said, his eyes drifting toward the empty end of the hall, toward the Boundary. "But I did say we had to unite *all* the west against Salos."

"I apologize for the delay," Lorthas said, stepping into the chamber from the small door concealed in a twist of stone. "Salos's minions have infiltrated *Ael Shataq*, and our war is already well underway."

The Darklord moved forward, flanked by Grendor and Drogon, who escorted him toward the table, careful to keep a grip on Lorthas despite his proximity to the Boundary. The mood in the chamber changed instantly, switching from tense apprehension to outright revulsion. A chorus of voices rose in protest, Aemon's loudest among them, demanding that Lorthas be executed for his crimes, demanding that Jeran explain himself. Lorthas himself joined the fray, countering the threats made against him in his characteristic smug tone.

"Silence!" Jeran shouted, bringing the great leaders of Madryn to heel with a single word. "I've seen enough of the past to know the stories we tell are never as true as we would like them to be. History is a poor reflection of reality, twisted by time. There are none of us here guiltless, none of us who have not taken lives—or sacrificed them!—for what we believed a greater purpose. Those who've heard nothing but the perversion of truth should be forgiven their misbeliefs, but many of you who sit with me today witnessed the truth, and have deluded yourself into believing your truth rather than real truth.

"I do not condone all of Lorthas's actions, even though I understand many of them. Neither do I condone all of Aemon's, or the Aelvin Empire's, or even, in retrospect, my own. But we, despite our great powers, cannot change what has happened. We can change what will.

"We face a threat greater than Lorthas's imposed order, or Aemon's fanciful dream of universal nobility and un-coerced sacrifice. Salos does not want power or wealth, he wants only to cause destruction and watch as Madryn writhes in agony. He does not need to plan for the future, because his future is the Nothing. If we cannot shed the specters of our own blighted past, then we will speed him toward his goal."

Lorthas sat, flanked by his two Orog guards, placed his elbows on the table, and rested his chin atop his folded hands. "So, my friends, where do we begin?"

Publisher's Notes

Tyrannosaurus Press was founded in 2001 with two primary missions: to find, publish, and promote promising works of speculative fiction, and to encourage reading and literacy, not just of our books or of speculative fiction, but of all books in every genre. Since our founding we've released several novels, sponsored two anthology projects, and produced *The Illuminata*, a free ezine focused on speculative fiction and writing.

Tyrannosaurus Press does not believe in the draconian restrictions of digital rights management (DRM), or in the exclusive, anti-sharing policies promoted by some other companies. DRM and other efforts to restrict the easy flow of content does not help us realize either of our goals. We want our books read, and we would prefer it if our readers recycle our books rather than throw them away. So we encourage readers to share our titles however they see fit, from suggesting other readers check out a copy of our books from the local library, to lending a personal copy to a friend who might appreciate it. Though we rely on book sales to stay in business, we believe the more people who have read our books, the more people who will want to read our books in the future.

However, without the support of their readers, it is impossible for publishers and authors to produce books. We value your feedback, and we hope you enjoy our titles, but we also need your help. If you were loaned this book, discovered it at your library, or otherwise came upon it without purchasing it, we request that you help sponsor this and future projects. A donation page has been set up at our website, or you may contact us for other options. We suggest a donation equal to the cost of the title's ebook (typically $5-$10), but we leave the final donation amount to the individual. If you feel a work deserves more and want to show your support, we welcome it; if you only have a dollar to spare, we understand and appreciate your donation just as much.

Patronage is about more than dollar amount. It is about recognizing the effort an author puts into producing a work, and about showing appreciation for the risk he or she takes in releasing that work to the criticisms of the reading public. If you enjoy what you read, please take the time to acknowledge that enjoyment, even if only with a simple thank-you note to the author or a positive online review.

Thank you for taking the time to read our book. We hope you enjoy it.